"AN IRRESISTIBLE TALE

with surprising twists right up to the last sentence . . .
Peter Straub is a master at keeping secrets. . . . He lures his
reader into a complex plot, replete with dark undercurrents
[and] sinister ghostly figures."
—*St. Louis Post-Dispatch*

"*Mr. X* marks Straub's triumphant return to the tale of the
paranormal and the supernatural. . . . The plot is challenging,
the characters are intriguing in their complexity, and the
language is a delight."
—STEPHEN KING

"There's no shortage of memorable players in [Straub's]
latest effort, *Mr. X*. . . . A classic doppelgänger tale with
supernatural elements, passages of H. P. Lovecraft parody,
and an unexpected stable of wickedly droll oddball characters."
—*Entertainment Weekly*

A Main Selection of the Book-of-the-Month Club

*Please turn the page
for more reviews. . . .*

"PETER STRAUB IS A FINE STORYTELLER."
—*The Washington Post*

"One of the most invigorating horror reads of the year . . . Straub has specialized in macabre mysteries dense with the details of small-town life and cast with ordinary people who find that the extraordinary crimes they investigate raise doubts about their own moral integrity. In this bravura new outing, he returns to his horror roots, lacing an ingenious whodunit with an intoxicating shot of the supernatural. . . . Discerning readers will recognize this surprise-filled tale of tortuous family relationships as a modern variation on Lovecraft's classic shocker *The Dunwich Horror*. But Straub turns his pulp model inside out, transforming its vast cosmic mystery into an ingrown odyssey of self-discovery and a probing study of human nature."

—*Publishers Weekly* (starred review)

"[An] impressive new novel . . . As crafty as it is well-crafted, *Mr. X* soars."

—*LOCUS*

"Compelling . . . Straub is worthy of his reputation as a master of horror."

—*Library Journal*

Also by Peter Straub:

Novels
Marriages
Under Venus
Julia
If You Could See Me Now*
Ghost Story
Shadowland
Floating Dragon
The Talisman (with Stephen King)
Koko
Mystery
Mrs. God
The Throat
The Hellfire Club*

Poetry
Open Air
Leeson Park & Belsize Square

Collections
Wild Animals
Houses Without Doors
Peter Straub's Ghosts (editor)
Magic Terror

*Published by Ballantine Books

MR. X

Peter Straub

BALLANTINE BOOKS • NEW YORK

A Ballantine Book
Published by The Ballantine Publishing Group
Copyright ©1999 by Seafront Corporation

All rights reserved under International and Pan-American Copyright Conventions. Published in the United States by The Ballantine Publishing Group, a division of Random House, Inc., New York, and simultaneously in Canada by Random House of Canada Limited, Toronto.

www.randomhouse.com/BB/

Library of Congress Catalog Card Number: 00-190731

ISBN 0-449-14990-0

This edition published by arrangement with Random House, Inc.

Manufactured in the United States of America

First Ballantine Books Edition: July 2000

10 9 8 7 6 5 4 3 2 1

For my brothers, John and Gordon Straub

I could not weigh myself—Myself—
My size felt small—to me—I read your Chapter in the Atlantic—and experienced honor for you—I was sure you would not reject a confiding question—
Is this—Sir—what you asked me to tell you?
    E— Dickinson

    —Emily Dickinson,
      letter to Thomas Wentworth Higginson, April 25, 1862

■ CONTENTS

MR. X

1 HOW I CAME HOME, AND WHY

■ Stupid me—I fell right into the old pattern and spent a week pretending I was a moving target. All along, a part of me knew that I was hitching toward southern Illinois because my mother was passing. When your mother's checking out, you get yourself back home.

She had been living in East Cicero with two elderly brothers above their club, the Panorama. On weekends she sang two nightly sets with the house trio. She was doing what she had always done, living without worrying about consequences, which tends to make the consequences come harder and faster than they do for other people. When she could no longer ignore her sense of fatality, my mother kissed the old brothers goodbye and went back to the only place I'd be able to find her.

Star had been eighteen when I was born, a generous, large-souled girl with no more notion of a settled life than a one-eyed cat, and after I turned four I bounced back and forth between Edgerton and a parade of foster homes. My mother was one of those people who are artists without a specific art. She apprenticed herself sequentially and many times over to painting, writing, pottery, and other crafts as well as to the men she thought embodied these skills. She cared least about the one thing she was best at, so when she stood up and sang she communicated a laid-back, good-humored ease her audiences found charming. Until the last few years of her life she had a soft, melting prettiness that was girlish and knowing, feline and earthy, all at once.

I lived with six different couples in four different towns, but it wasn't as bad as it sounds. The best of my six couples, Phil and Laura Grant, the Ozzie and Harriet of Naperville, Illinois, were almost saintly in their straightforward goodness. One other couple would have given them a run for their money if they hadn't taken in so many kids they wore themselves out, and two others were nice enough, in a this-is-our-house-and-these-are-the-rules way.

Before I went to Naperville, now and then I did go back to Cherry Street, where the Dunstans lived in their various old houses. Aunt Nettie and Uncle Clark took me in as though I were an extra piece of luggage Star had brought along. For a month, maybe six weeks, I shared a room with my mother, holding my breath and waiting for the next earthquake. After I moved in with the Grants, this pattern changed, and Star visited me in Naperville. She and I had come to an agreement: one of those deep agreements people don't need words to strike.

The core of our agreement, around which everything else wrapped itself, was that my mother loved me and I loved her. But no matter how much she loved me, Star didn't have it in her to stay in one place longer than a year or two. She was *my* mother, but she couldn't be *a* mother. Which meant that she couldn't help me deal with the besetting problem that frightened, distressed, or angered the foster parents I had before the Grants. The Grants accompanied me on a procession through doctors' offices, radiology departments, blood tests, urine tests, brain tests, I can't even remember them all.

Boiled down to essentials, it comes out this way: even though Star loved me, she could not care for me as well as the Grants could. On those days when Star came to Naperville, we put our arms around each other and we cried, but we both knew the deal. She usually showed up just after Christmas and almost always right at the start of summer, after I got out of school. But she never came on my birthdays, and she never sent me anything more than a card. Birthdays were when my problem came down on me, and my problem made her feel so rotten she didn't want to think about it.

I think I always understood this, but it didn't make conscious sense, a sense I could *use*, until two days after my fifteenth birthday. I came home from school to find waiting on the hall table an envelope addressed in my mother's back-slanted handwriting. It had been mailed from Peoria on my birthday, June 25. I took the envelope into my room, dropped it on my desk, put Gene Ammons's *Groove Blues* on the turntable, and, once the music began flowing into the air, opened the envelope and looked at the card my mother had sent me.

Balloons, streamers, and lighted candles floated above an idealized suburban house. Inside, beneath the printed *Happy*

Birthday!, she had written the only message she ever put on one of her cards:

> *My beautiful boy—*
> *I hope . . .*
> *I hope . . .*
> *Lots o love,*
> *Star*

I knew that her wishes weren't for a happy birthday but an untroubled one, which would have been happiness enough. A half second after this insight opened the door, the first adult recognition of my life slammed into me, and I saw that my mother slighted my birthdays because she blamed herself for what befell me then. She thought I got it from her; she could not bear to think about my birthdays because they made her feel guilty, and guilt was the emotion free spirits like Star could least handle.

The sound of Gene Ammons playing "It Might as Well Be Spring" soared out of the speakers and passed straight into the center of my body.

In khaki shorts and polo shirts, the Grants were monitoring the progress of herbs and vegetables in their garden. In the moment before they noticed me, I experienced the first in about a month of those *What's wrong with this picture?* moments, an animal awareness of my incongruity in this sweet suburban landscape. Danger; shame; isolation: exposure. Me and my shadow, there we were. Laura turned her head, and the bad feeling vanished even before her face warmed and somehow deepened, as if she knew everything going on inside me.

"Action Jackson," Phil said.

Laura glanced at the card, then back into my eyes. "Star could never forget your birthday. Can I see it?"

Both Grants liked my mother, though they liked her in different ways. When Star came to Naperville, Phil turned on an old-fashioned courtliness he thought was suave but Laura and I found hilarious, and Laura made room to talk by going out with her for an hour's shopping. I think she usually slipped her fifty or sixty bucks, too.

Laura smiled at the elegant white house and birthday-party froufrou on the front of the card and looked up at me. The second grown-up recognition of my life flew between us like a spark. Star had chosen this card for a reason. Laura did not evade the issue. "Wouldn't it be nice if we had dormer windows and a wraparound porch? If I lived in a place like that, I'd impress my*self*."

Phil moved closer, and she opened the card. Her eyebrows contracted as she read the message. " '*I hope . . .*' "

"I hope for that, too," I said.

"Of course you do," she said, getting it.

Phil squeezed my shoulder, getting into executive mode. He was a products manager at 3M. "I don't care what these clowns say, it's a physical problem. Once we find the right doctor, we're going to lick that thing."

"These clowns" were my pediatrician, the Grants' GP, and the half dozen specialists who had failed to diagnose my condition. The specialists had concluded that my problem was "not of organic origin," another way of saying that it was all in my head.

"Do you think I got it from her?" I asked Laura.

"I don't think you got it from anybody," Laura said. "But if you're asking me does she feel terrible about it, sure she does."

"Star?" Phil said. "Star would have to be nuts to blame herself."

Laura was watching to see how much I understood. "Mothers want to take on anything that could hurt their kids, even the things they can't do anything about. What happens to you makes me feel terrible, and I can't even imagine what it does to Star. At least I get to see you every day. If I were your real mother, and my only chance to end world hunger for the next thousand years meant I had to go out of town on your birthday, I'd still feel awful about letting you down. I'd feel awful anyway, real mother or not."

"Like you weren't doing the right thing," I said.

"Your mother loves you so much that sometimes she can't stand not being Betty Crocker."

The idea of Star Dunstan being anything like Betty Crocker made me laugh out loud.

Laura said, "Doing the right thing doesn't always make you feel good, no matter what anybody says. Doing the right thing can hurt like the dickens! If you want my opinion, you have a great mom."

I would have laughed again, this time at her Girl Scout's notion of cursing, but my eyes stung and a thick obstruction filled my throat. A little while ago, I said that two days after my fifteenth birthday I came to understand my mother's feelings in a way I could *use*, and this is what I meant. I learned to ask questions about the things that scare you; that doing right could make you hurt too bad to think straight; that once you are you that's who you are, and you have to pay the price.

2 ■ Mr. X

■ O Great Old Ones, read these words inscribed within this stout Journal by the hand of Your Devoted Servant and rejoice!

I always liked walking late at night. In a comfortable city like Edgerton, the enormous blanket of darkness cushions even the sound of your footsteps on the pavement. I walk down the avenues, past the empty department stores and movie theaters. I drift down Hatchtown's narrow lanes and look up at shuttered windows I could pass through in a second, but do not: part of my happiness is in the weighing and measuring of the lives about me. And like anyone else, I enjoy getting out of the house, escaping the captivity of that sty to which I am self-condemned. During my rambles I avoid street lamps, though regardless of the season I am dressed in a black coat and hat—a moving shadow, invisible in the darkness.

Or: nearly invisible. Invisible to all but a deeply unfortunate few, many of whom I admit to killing less from the need to protect myself than out of . . . pique, maybe, or whimsy. There was one exception.

I subtracted from the world the gangly hooker in stacked, high-heel sandals and a skirt the size of a washcloth who launched herself toward me from a Chester Street doorway, so high on whatever girls were doing for fun that year that she grabbed my elbow to keep from swaying. I looked at the pinpoint dots of her pupils and let her pull me toward the doorway, opened her up like a can of sardines, and broke her neck before she remembered to scream.

I gave more or less the same treatment to the kid wearing a

black sweatshirt and fatigue pants who saw me because he thought he was looking for someone like me, surprise, surprise, and the young woman with a black eye and swollen lips who wavered out of a parked car at the sound of my footsteps and tried to get back into the car once she saw me, but it was too late, poor baby. And let us not forget the actual baby I found abandoned atop a Dumpster and assisted in its departure from an inhospitable world by detaching its darling little hands and excising its little outraged eyes.

The baby had not seen me, true. I believe that requires an especially heightened degree of sorrow or misery, loss so irreparable as to make the rest of life an eternal wound, and the baby was merely cold and hungry. But long ago, an untimely arrest and imprisonment kept me from doing the same to another newborn, and anger got the better of me. I never claimed to be perfect.

The noisome, Night Train–reeking dwarf I killed to protect myself had pulled himself upright between the garbage cans in the alley alongside Merchants Hotel and gaped at my approach. All but a few of his ilk fail to see me even when they are looking directly at me, and those few have the sense to back away. This fellow was still too foggy for sense. A ragged shaft of star-shine caught his eye. "Root-toot-toot, fuckin' Dracula," he said. He giggled and leaned shakily over the garbage cans to inspect the grubby cement. "Hey, where'd Piney go to? You seen Piney, Drac?" He referred to a more functional version of himself, a shabby outcast of whose existence I had long been vaguely aware.

"Rooty-tooty," said the wretch, who would have gone on destroying himself without my assistance had he not followed his mantra by suddenly peering at me with a hideous mixture of delight and confusion and saying, "Hey, man, talk about long time no see. I thought I heard . . . I thought you was . . . aah . . ."

He was one Erwin "Pipey" Leake, some thirty years previous a hard-drinking young English instructor at Albertus University and a hanger-on of my bohemian period.

"Is Star . . . Star Dunstan, isn't she . . ."

I gripped his throat and slammed his head against the bricks. He tugged at my wrist, and I clamped my free hand over his face and twice more drove his head against the wall. The eyes of the former acolyte floated upward, and a stench of dead fish came from his mouth. When I let go, he crumpled between the garbage cans. I smashed my boot onto his head, heard his skull crack, and kept stamping until the side of his head turned soft.

These idiots should know enough to keep their mouths shut.

■ Great Beings, You who in aeons to come shall linger over these words penned by Your Devoted Servant, You alone comprehend my certainty that a great change is in the air. The culmination of that Sacred Mission entrusted to me and so teasingly adumbrated by the Providence Master has begun to declare its appearance upon the earthly stage. As I walk unseen through the city, the flow of information sharpens and intensifies, bringing with it the promise of that destiny for which I have waited since I was a boy taking lessons from the foxes and owls in Johnson's Woods.

Here, in a room stacked with microwave ovens and laptop computers, a professional thief and occasional arsonist named Anton "Frenchy" La Chapelle lies unconscious in sleeping embrace with one Cassandra "Cassie" Little, a hard-bitten little scrubber. Hello, Frenchy, you delightfully nasty piece of work! You don't know it, but I imagine that your pointless life is going to serve some purpose after all.

Here, on the second floor of a rooming house, Otto Bremen, a grade-school crossing guard, slumbers before his television screen with a not quite empty bottle of bourbon nestled in his crotch. The last half inch of a cigarette burns inexorably toward the first two fingers of his right hand. The conjunction of the cigarette and Frenchy's secondary occupation suggests a possibility, but many things are possible, Otto, and whether or not you are to die in a fire—as I rather think you are—I wish, with the puppet-master's fondness for his insensate and pliable creatures, that you might know a minute portion of the triumph rushing toward me.

For in my city's secret corners I already see runners of the blue fire. It hovers over Frenchy and his partner, it travels down the crossing guard's arm, and it gathers itself for an electrifying moment along the rain gutters on Cherry Street, where the surviving Dunstans eke out their blasted lives. Enormous forces have begun to come into play. Around our tiny illuminated platform suspended in the cosmic darkness, the ancient Gods, my true ancestors, congregate with rustlings of leathery wings and rattlings of filthy claws to witness what their great-grandson shall accomplish.

A most marvelous event has taken place. Star Dunstan has come home to die.

Can you hear me, slug-spittle?

Listen to me, you exhausted bag of skin—

My dearest hope is that your flesh should blister, that you should have to labor for the smallest gulps of air and feel individual organs explode within you, so on and so forth, your eyes to burst, that kind of thing, but though I shall not be able to manage these matters on your behalf, my old sweetheart, I shall do my best to arrange them for our son.

■ 3

■ Right from the beginning, I had the sense that something crucially significant, something without which I could never be whole, was *missing*. When I was seven, my mother told me that as soon as I'd learned to sit up by myself, I used to do this funny thing where I turned around and tried to look behind me. Boom, down I'd go, but the second I hit the ground I'd turn my head to check that same spot. According to Star, Aunt Nettie said, "That boy must think the doctor cut off his tail when he was born." Uncle Clark chimed in with, "He appears to think someone's sneakin' up on him."

"They meant you had something wrong with you," Star told me, "which was to be expected, me being your mother. I said, 'My boy Neddie's smart as a whip, and he's seeing if his shadow followed him inside the house.' They shut up, because that was exactly how you looked—like you were trying to find your shadow."

I can scarcely describe the combination of relief and uncertainty this caused in me. Star had given me proof that my sense of loss was real, for it had been a part of me long before I could have made it up. Even before I could walk, back when my thoughts could have been little more than the recognition of states like hunger, fear, comfort, warmth, I had been aware that it had been missing, whatever it was, and when I tried to look behind me, I was trying to find it. And if at the age of six months I was looking for the absent thing, didn't that mean that at one time it had not been absent?

A few days later, I resolved to ask her about the difference between me and other children. A couple of things made me hesitate, as I had before. Did everyone else's claim to a father mean that I had to have one? Or could someone like Uncle Clark or Uncle James have stepped in to sign the papers, or whatever men did to make them fathers? Uncle Clark and Uncle James displayed so little paternal feeling that they had to make an effort merely to tolerate my existence. From the start, I felt welcome in their houses only by virtue of my best behavior. A child knows these things. You know when you have to earn acceptance. On top of that, I already had the caretaker child's sense of emotional obligation, and my mother was as unpredictable as the weather.

In the summer of my seventh year, Star was comfortable and relaxed with her family. She moved at about half her normal speed. For the first time in my life, I heard stories about her childhood and what I had been like as a baby. She helped Aunt Nettie in the kitchen and let Uncle Clark expound without telling him he was a bigoted ignoramus. Being Star Dunstan, she had signed up for a poetry workshop and a night class in watercolor painting at Albertus, which Uncle Clark called "Albino U."

Three days a week, she clerked at the pawnshop owned by her stepfather, Toby Kraft, who in spite of universal Dunstan disapproval years before had married Star's mother. Toby Kraft had reinforced the family's distrust by moving his bride into the apartment above his shop instead of submitting to Cherry Street. Despite their general dislike, he had participated in family gatherings for the rest of Queenie's life and continued to do so after her death, the occasion for Star's most recent return to Edgerton and my release from the latest set of foster parents. It did not occur to me until much later that the death of her mother was behind Star's new ease. She must have experienced an elemental relief at the lifting of Queenie's everlasting scorn. Her second job involved what she described as "modeling" a couple of nights each week at Albertus. I did not grasp at the time that this meant posing nude for students in a life-drawing class.

Our orderly existence permitted me to ask my question. I waited until we were alone in Aunt Nettie's kitchen, me drying the dishes she washed while Nettie gabbed on the porch rocker with Aunt May, and Uncle Clark and Uncle James watched a cop show on television. Star handed me a dish, and I rubbed the cloth over its glistening surface while she described a jazz concert she had seen in the Albertus auditorium a month after my conception.

"At first, I wasn't even sure I liked that group. It was a quartet from the West Coast, and I was never all that crazy about West Coast jazz. Then this alto player who looked like a stork pushed himself off the curve of the piano and stuck his horn in his mouth and started playing 'These Foolish Things.' " The memory still had the power to make her gasp. "And, oh, Neddie, it was like going to some new place you'd never heard about, but where you felt at home right away. He just touched that melody for a second before he lifted off and began climbing and climbing, and everything he played linked up, one step after another, like a story. Neddie! It was like hearing the whole world open up in front of me. It was like going to heaven. If I could sing the way that man played alto, Neddie, I'd stop time forever and just keep on singing."

She was trying to communicate the importance of music in her life, but at the time I had no idea of the impact these words would have on me. It would certainly never have occurred to me that one day I would find it possible to witness the rapture she was describing. All of that was far ahead of me, and I thought she was trying to keep me from asking my question.

When she stopped talking, I said, "I really want to know something."

She turned her head to smile at me, warmed by the memory of the music and expecting a question about it. Then the smile clicked off, and her hands stopped moving in the water. She already knew that my question had nothing to do with an alto saxophone solo on "These Foolish Things."

"Ask away." She plucked a dish out of the foam with self-conscious gravity.

I knew that whatever she was going to tell me would be a lie, and that I would believe it for as long as I could. "Who's my dad? He isn't Uncle Clark, is he?"

She glanced over her shoulder, shook her head, and smiled

down at me. "No, honey, he sure isn't. If Uncle Clark was your daddy, Aunt Nettie would be your mommy, and wouldn't you be in a pickle?"

"But who is he? What happened to him?"

She seemed to concentrate on scrubbing the plate in her hands. I know now that she sat next to my father during the concert she had been talking about. "Your father went into the army after we got married. Because he was so smart and so strong, it wasn't long before they made him an officer."

"He was an army man?"

"One of the best army men ever," she said, locking into place both my disbelief and the need to deny it. "They sent him places ordinary soldiers couldn't go. He wasn't allowed to tell me about them. When you're on a Top Secret mission, you can't talk about it." She passed the plate beneath a stream of water and handed it to me. "That's what your father was doing when he died. He was out on a secret mission. All they could tell me was that he died like a hero. And he's buried in a special hero's grave, way up on a mountainside on the other side of the world, overlooking the sea."

I could see an American flag on a mountainous promontory far above silvery water and endless waves, marking the grave of that without which I would forever be incomplete.

"I wasn't supposed to tell you, but now you're old enough to keep it to yourself. Nobody else knows what I just told you, except his superior officers."

We washed and dried the remaining dishes in a charged but companionable silence. I knew that she was in a rush to change clothes and drive to her modeling job, but she stopped and turned around on her way to the kitchen door. "I want you to know something else, too, Neddie. Your father isn't the only thing you have to be proud of. Our family used to be important people here in Edgerton. They took most of it away, but folks here remember, and that's why we're different from everyone else. You come from a special family."

I sat on the living room rug and tried to see what was special in my aunts and uncles. The detectives had solved the weekly murder, and the aunts had come inside to sit on the green davenport and enjoy their favorite program. From my low, sidelong perspective, Nettie and May resembled monuments of Egyptian statuary. Their massive bodies in shapeless print dresses reared up side by side above four hugely stationary legs. In a sleeveless mesh T-shirt, his suspenders clipped to the waistband of tan gabardine trousers, Uncle Clark was canted back in his easy chair, his wide mouth twisted into a sneer. Eyes closed, arms folded over his chest, Uncle James filled the high-backed rocker. A man with wavy blond hair and an aristocratic profile was sawing away at a violin.

"Mr. Florian Zabach has a gift which comes straight from God," said Aunt Nettie. "I never heard prettier sounds in all my life."

"Remember the time we went up to Chicago and saw Eddie South?" said Uncle Clark.

"Eddie South brought a beautiful tone out of his fiddle," said Aunt May. "I have wondered if he might have been one of our category. A number of musicians are, I believe."

"Little pitchers," Nettie said. "Mind what you say."

Uncle James snorted and stirred, and the other three looked at him until his chin dropped as far as his redwood neck would permit.

"That tone was why they called Eddie South 'The Dark Angel of the Violin,' " Uncle Clark said. "But if Stuff Smith got up there, he'd gobble your Florsheim Swayback down in one bite."

"Nettie," said Aunt May, "I believe Mr. Welk is putting on some weight."

My eyelids sagged, and I pushed myself upright before I fell asleep in the living room, like Uncle James.

My mother woke me up when she let herself into our room. I waited while she took off her clothes, put on her nightshirt, and found her way to bed. I heard her yank up the sheet and wrestle her pillow into shape. She had carried into the room an odor of smoke and beer mingled with fresh air and summer rainfall, and I tried to sort out these traces of her evening's history as she relaxed into sleep. Her breathing stretched out and slowed down. When I heard it catch in her throat and release itself in what was almost a snore, I crept across and crawled in beside her. Star seemed enormous, a huge female animal still wrapped in the atmosphere of the adventures through which she had passed on her way home. I nestled my back against hers. My body instantly doubled in weight and began to slip toward the center of the earth, where my hero father lay buried. Star shuddered and spoke a single word I trapped in my hands as I plummeted out of consciousness. *Rinehart*.

■ **4**

■ At the whispery pop of a seam I looked over my shoulder, saw a shadow fleeing down sunny Cherry Street, and fell bang on my bottom in surprise. At least once a week during my childhood and adolescence, this happened the moment my head hit the pillow. My shadow elongated over the white sidewalk and bent sideways to slip around the corner. The terror of an irredeemable loss immobilized me on the warm pavement. I got up, ran to the corner, and saw my shadow floating like a solid substance above the sidewalk ahead. When I pounded forward, the sidewalk tilted like a slide, and the familiar houses and dark porches softened in the heat.

Edgerton was gone.

I ran down a beaten track leading to a narrow river and an arched wooden bridge. The upright shadow scampered on. On the far side of the bridge, a line of stunted trees marked the beginning of a forest. I glimpsed the peaked roof and broken upper windows of an abandoned house above the treetops. My shadow moved up the arch of the bridge, leaned on the curved iron railing, and crossed one foot over the other. It faced me without having turned around.

Like an optical illusion, the mocking shadow receded with every stride I took. When finally I stood on the bridge, the shadow regarded me from fifty feet away and a point well above my head.

"You seem to be trying to catch me," my shadow said.

"I need you," I said.

"Then you'd better come along." The shadow did its trick of switching front and back and moved on.

By the time I reached the top of the arch, the shadow was far down the descending slope. The iron handrails had become slim and delicate, and the planks bent beneath my weight.

The shadow patted the railing. "The longer it gets, the thinner it becomes. Like toffee. In the end, it disappears."

"Can I get to the other end?"

"Maybe, if you get into some fancy sliding, use your momentum."

"We need each other," I said. "We're the same thing."

"You are me, and I am you, yes," said the shadow. "But only in the sense that we each have qualities the other lacks. Unfortunately, your qualities are boring."

"Boring?"

"Dear me, am I doing the right thing? What do other people think of me? Why don't they like me?" The shadow flicked its hands in the air, as if to scatter a cloud of gnats. "I don't give a damn what people think of me."

"You're a shadow," I said. "People don't think about you at all."

"Then why care about getting me back?"

I had no answer for that.

"You won't even be able to go out by yourself at night for another six or seven years. When do we have our first cigarette? Our first drink? When do we get to have actual sex?" He shook his head in disgust. "I want *darkness*, I want *night*. I want to see a big steak in front of me and a glass of whiskey beside the plate. I want cards in my hand and a cigar in my mouth and a little grown-up fun, and, kid, with you, it's going to be too much work to get them."

"Without me, you can't get them at all," I said.

"On the contrary. Without you, I can do whatever I like. If you catch me, I have to come back, but I won't be easy to catch, and you'll be in considerable danger during the pursuit."

"What kind of danger?" I asked.

"That kind, for one." He swept his arm toward the forest. Imaginary blue fire flickered from branch to branch. My heart went cold and my mind became a stone.

■ Four years before the dream I just described started wrecking my sleep two or three nights every month, my aunts and uncles had seen conclusive proof of their doubts that Star could produce an undamaged child. I hope they were gratified. I was not. I had been looking forward to my third birthday.

I can remember the balloons bobbing on the clotheslines and the big ladder between the house and the picnic table, and I know what I was wearing. Among the few of my mother's possessions I retain is a photograph of me in the striped T-shirt and new dungarees given me by Queenie. I have to tell the truth: I was an angelic child. If I saw a kid like that, I'd tuck a dollar into his hand for sheer good luck. Mine, I mean, not his. But when I look at his cherub face I have to wonder what this little smiling boy is concealing.

That is:

I wonder if he has begun to feel a mild, increasing tingle like an electric current pass up his arms and into his chest. I wonder if his mouth feels dry, if the colors striped across his shirt and the vibrant reds and yellows of the balloons have begun to glow. That angelic boy in his birthday-boy clothes may have felt the tightening of the screws at the heart of the world, but he has no idea of the misery speeding toward him. He has not yet seen the first sly tongues of the blue fire.

The aunts and uncles, my grandmother, and my mother must have spent much of the morning preparing the scene. Someone had blown up the balloons and used the ladder to fasten them to the clotheslines. A paper tablecloth printed with birthday cakes and candles had been stretched out across the picnic table and arrayed with paper plates, plastic cups, and cutlery. (Now that I know how they managed to get all this stuff, I pity the owner of the local five-and-dime.) Jugs of fresh lemonade and cherry Kool-Aid and the containers of food held down the tablecloth.

Aunt Nettie had made a tuna casserole, Aunt May brought over a tray of fried chicken, and Queenie had baked her legendary sweet-potato pie. Reclusive Uncle Clarence and Aunt Joy had consented to emerge from their house across the street, a building so forbidding and funny smelling I dreaded entering it. Clarence brought along his banjo. Joy contributed a loaf of her black-olive bread. Star made lime Jell-O and the birthday cake, angel food with chocolate frosting. I can remember Toby Kraft, his face so white he reminded me of Casper the Friendly Ghost, strutting around the table and patting people on the back.

They must have gossiped, they must have told stories and teased one another as they dug into the fried chicken. I can't remember that any more than I can remember the actual disaster itself. What I can remember—the most commanding mental photograph I retain from my third birthday—is an image so dissonant that it sank indelibly into me.

It begins with a sudden awareness of the warmth and color of the light, as if I had never before really noticed how this rich, vibrant substance streamed from above to coat the world like a liquid. I saw the brightness gather in a shining skin on the backs of my mother's hands. Then the earth opened beneath me, and I plummeted downward and away from the picnic table, too startled to be frightened. I came to rest and found myself in a large, untidy room. Books covered a table and stood in piles on the floor. In the distance, an embittered voice ranted about smoke and gold. My eyes fastened on the mantel, where a fern drooped beside a fox stepping delicately toward the edge of a glass dome. The weights of a brass clock swung this way–that way on the other side of the fox's confinement. I had been *pushed back*: I was in the museum of the past.

It ended so quickly that I did not have time to react. In the space between two halves of a second I had traveled at enormous speed back to my chair at the picnic table, restored to the present. A fraction of a beat ahead of the moment when I had seen the sunlight glowing on my mother's hands, Uncle James was still telling the same joke to Uncle Clark, Aunt May still smiling at compliments to her fried chicken—I'm inventing these details to suggest the normality of the scene, but all I remember is what I just described. By then, the sensations in my body would have built to an almost unbearable pitch.

"You scrambled off the picnic bench," Star told me, not once but many times, retelling this story to help herself deal with it. "I asked if anything was wrong, but you just put your hands over your eyes and started running. Toby tried to grab you, but you scooted past him and ran right into that ladder. Down it went, I don't know how a little thing like you had the strength, the ladder fell smash into the table, right next to my mother. Food went flying straight up in the air. Clarence was pouring Kool-Aid into his cup, and the jug got away from him and landed in the cake.

"After you got past the top of the table, you fell down flat and stiffened up like a board. The spasms hit you so hard you bounced off the ground. Foam was coming out of your mouth. I heard Uncle Clark say something about rabies, and I clouted him on the side of his head without even breaking stride. Some of those people were so busy mopping at themselves and taking care of Momma, they didn't know what was happening to you! I swear, I was so scared I thought I was going to faint. When I got my arms around you, I couldn't even hold you still.

"Then you went limp. I picked you up and put you to bed. After a while, Nettie and May came in to feel your forehead and tell me about everybody they ever knew who had fits. I put up with it as long as I could, and then I shooed them out.

"The doctor said it could have been anything. Too much excitement. Dehydration. He picked you up and put you on his lap and said, 'Neddie, your mommy says you put your hands over your eyes before all the trouble started. Was that because you saw something you didn't like?' "

What age was I, when she slipped that in? Eight?

"Now, that struck me, because I was wondering the same thing. You were too young to answer him, and besides, I don't think you remembered anything that happened. But, honey, you covered your eyes the next year, too, and you did it again on your fifth birthday. Did you see something that made you unhappy?"

I never told Star what happened during my "attacks." For a long time, I would not have known how to describe those visions, and later on I was afraid of sounding crazy. It was bad enough that other people saw me thrashing on the ground—it would have been worse if they had known what was going on inside.

Even now, writing about this is like trying to reconstruct a half-destroyed mosaic. Many patterns and images seem possible, and even after you think you have identified the design, you cannot be certain that you have not merely imposed it. From the border, men and women attend or not to what is represented in the missing section. Some smile, some appear to be frozen in wonderment or shock. Others look away: have they chosen to ignore the enigmatic event or not yet noticed it?

■ 6

■ The internal story of my third birthday cannot ever be reconstructed. The people arranged around its borders, my aunts and uncles, my grandmother, Toby Kraft, are staring at a blankness. My mother holds me in her arms, but she has averted her head.

The path to wisdom leads downward, and anyone who decides to take it had better buckle on armor, remember to bring a sword, and get used to the idea that when and if he gets back everyone he talks to is going to think he's a phony.

■ 7

■ It would have looked like this:

Through walls of blue fire I follow a being into the ordinary world, and we are standing before a house with a basketball hoop hung over the garage door and a bicycle canted over its kickstand at the edge of the driveway. The lighted windows glow a luminous turquoise, and the dark windows shine blue-black. There is a number on the front door and I can see a street sign, but since I am three and cannot read, these things are symbols without meanings. At once completely unknown and deeply familiar, the being beside me frightens me like Aunt Nettie's stories of the Bogeyman. The brim of his black hat shades his face. His coat nearly touches the ground.

In my terror I turn away and see the dark shapes of mountains rising like animals into the sky. Blue starlight defines the jagged ridges and gleams from vertical snowfields. The air smells like Christmas trees.

The being moves forward, and a pressure like a tide urges me along in his wake. He turns to the front door and moves onto a welcome mat. Gleeful flames swarm around him. He reaches into his coat with one hand and pushes the doorbell with the other. He doesn't have to use the bell, he could melt through the door if he felt like it, but ringing the bell amuses him. Then, as if because of my insight, I am within the being and looking horrified through his eyes. I see a blue-white hand pull a knife from the depths of the black coat. Flame moves along the blade. The unopened door is a blue tissue.

On the other side of the shimmering tissue a heavyset man in jeans and a sweatshirt approaches. His pulled-down mouth tells me that he is annoyed. He engulfs the doorknob in his free hand, and as he turns it steps forward to block the doorway. This takes place in seconds. When the man opens the door and thrusts himself forward, I try to wrench free of the being. A force clamps down to hold me still. Before me, the man's eyes flare and darken. I try to scream, but my mouth is not mine and will not obey. We follow the man through the door, and the blue fire surges in with us. For a second that is like a dance the man's right leg glides back and our left leg glides forward and we move together in unison. He bends to get away, and we bend with him. His teeth shine milky blue.

The knife slides into the band of flesh between the bottom of his sweatshirt and the waist of his jeans. The man breaks the dance by going still. We lean into him so closely that our chin rubs his cheek. He makes a sound and puts his hands on our shoulders and straightens up, and then we are back in the dance. We move behind him and pull up on the knife. His knees dip. Black in the trembling blue light, a sheet of blood cascades over his jeans. A silver rope emerges. Another rope slides out. I feel a relaxation around me and break free.

Then I am standing behind the being, and I can do nothing but witness what I cannot understand.

The man lowers his hands to the ropes and holds them as if making an offering. Slowly, he tries to move the ropes back inside his body.

The being says, "Mr. Anscombe, I presume?" His voice tells me that this, too, amuses him.

Down the side of the room, blue flames swarm across the wall and form a glowing transparency through which I can see a woman in a nightdress sitting on a bed with a little girl on her lap. She holds a book but has stopped reading to look at the place in the wall where the door must be.

She can't see how the man is trying to stay on his feet, stepping a little bit forward, then a little bit back, or how his knees sag until he sinks all the way to the floor, all the time staring at the fat loops falling out of his hands. The being leans down, sets the knife hard against the side of the man's neck and jerks it across. Black fluid streams over the sweatshirt, and in the center of the stream a bump rises and falls, bump bump bump. The man tilts over his knees and keeps on tilting with the same amazing slowness until his forehead meets the carpet. The being steps back. Beneath the shadow of his hat, a blank pane of darkness ends in a strip of jaw.

I understand: He is Mr. X.

Luxuriantly, Mr. X turns to gaze through the blue veils at the woman and the little girl on the side of the bed.

The dying man makes an airy sound. The woman pats her little girl's head.

In delight, the being moves forward, and the veils reshape themselves into a bright tunnel. Without warning, the wind presses me forward in his wake. A mild, almost weightless resistance like that of a spiderweb yields instantly as I pass through the invisible wall. On all sides, the blue tunnel hums like electricity. Mr. X strides ahead, and he, too, hums with his own electricity, which is joy. His next stride carries him into the bedroom, and although his body conceals the woman and child from me I hear a woman's gasp. The child begins whimpering. They have seen a man in a black coat and hat walk straight through the bedroom wall. The woman scrambles across the bed, and I see bare legs flashing blue-white.

Clamping the little girl to her chest, the woman spins off the far side of the bed and hits the dresser. They have shiny, dark brown, just-washed hair and immense dark eyes. I step back, and the little girl's eyes glance in my direction, more as if looking for than at me. When I try to retreat into the tunnel, the pressure slides against my back.

The girl buries her face in her mother's chest, and the mother hoists her up. She is as pretty as a movie star. "I want you to get out of here right now, whoever you are," she says.

Concealing the knife in the folds of his coat, he moves along the bottom of the bed. She backs against the wall and shouts, "Mike!"

"No help from that quarter, Mrs. Anscombe," he says. "Tell me, don't you find it awfully dull out here in the sticks?"

"My name isn't Anscombe," she says. "I don't know anyone named Anscombe. You're making a terrible mistake."

He comes toward her. "Someone did, anyhow."

She springs onto the bed. Her legs churn. Mr. X wraps a hand around her ankle. The nightdress slides up over her hips when he pulls her toward him. She releases the little girl and shouts, "Run, baby! Run outside and hide!"

He yanks the woman off the bed and kicks her in the stomach.

The little girl stares at him. He flicks a hand at her, and she shuffles an inch forward on her knees. "Too cold outside for a nice baby," he says. "Dangerous. Baby might meet a big, bad bear."

The woman struggles to her feet and stands with her hands pressed against her stomach. Her eyes are like water. "Run, Lisa!" she hisses. "Run away!"

He waves the knife at the woman, playfully. His teeth glint. "Baby Lisa doesn't like bears," he says. "Does she, Lisa?"

Baby Lisa shakes her head.

"Do anything you like to me," the woman says. "Just don't hurt my baby. No matter who you are, she doesn't have anything to do with why you're here. Please."

"Oh," he says with what sounds like real curiosity, "why am I here?"

She leaps toward him, and he whirls out of her path and knocks her to the floor. He bends down, grabs her hair, hauls her to her feet, and throws her back against the wall. "Was there an answer to that question?" he asks.

Then the terrible thing happens again. A giant hand seizes me and rips me from my body. I am nothing but a shadow-space that looks out through his eyes. In panic and terror I fight to escape but cannot. This always happened. The clamps knew me, they held me in a knowing accommodation. Through his eyes I see more than I can through my own—it's true, she is almost as pretty as a movie star, but her face, chipped by too much experience, would look bitter on the screen. An unhappy knowledge moves into her eyes.

She says, "So I guess this is what happened to the Bookers."

I gather and flex myself, and the restraints drop away. With no transition, I am back in my body, looking across the bed where the baby named Lisa kneels on the covers.

"Should I know that name?" asks Mr. X. "By the way, isn't there a little boy in the Anscombe family?"

"He's gone," she says.

He says nothing.

"I don't know where," she says. "You don't have to hurt my baby."

"I wouldn't hurt an innocent child." He summons the girl. She creeps across the blanket, and he scoops her up. "But I often wonder why the very people who should know better think that this is a benign universe." He anchors the child in the crook of his elbow, grips the top of her head, and twists. There is an audible snap, and the child sags.

I don't want to go on, it's all wrong anyhow, I kept mixing up the details because the actual memory was too painful. That time, the name wasn't Anscombe. Anscombe came in later.

■ It took me an absurdly long time to understand who and what I was. You, my Masters, had it easy by comparison, and I beg You to understand the nature of my struggle.

Until I reached that cataclysm known as adolescence, my impersonation of an ordinary child met with passable success. That in the course of a schoolyard brawl I was sufficiently provoked by a fellow second-grader named Lenny Beech as to batter his blond head against the cement was put down to his remark that I was a piece of dog poo-poo. That I was obliged to repeat the third grade was explained by what the administration described as my "daydreaming," my "inability to pay attention during class," and the like, a reference to my habit of completing assignments any old way I felt like, so that when asked to write about My Favorite Christmas I might hand in a page filled with question marks, or in answer to a sheet of subtraction problems, submit a drawing of a monster eating a dog. The word *creative* came in handy, although it failed to appease the parents of Maureen Orth, a scrawny nonentity with overlapping front teeth whom I talked into letting me strip naked and tie to a birch tree in Johnson's Woods when we were in the eighth grade. Maureen had been grateful for my attentions until I reminded her that wild Indians, one of which I was pretending to be, customarily tortured their captives, one of which she was pretending to be. The pathetic screams induced by the sight of my penknife led me to untie her, and she would not listen to my avowals that I never intended to cause her any actual harm.

In the end, my father wrote Mr. Orth a check for a thousand dollars, and that was that, apart from the grumbling.

My father cut my allowance in half, "for," as he put it, "encouraging that creature's attentions," and my mother wiped her eyes and forbade me ever again to go into Johnson's Woods.

Of course I had no intention of obeying. Thirty acres so thick with pines, birches, maples, and hickory that sunlight pierced their canopy only in shimmering, coin-shaped spangles and containing, like an emerald hidden in a bowl of pennies, the mysterious ruins into which I would have dragged Maureen Orth had she been up to snuff, Johnson's Woods was sacred ground to me.

All that was left of property which otherwise had been transformed into streets lined with houses for the people my father called "the rising scum," the woods were mine not because they belonged to my family, but because they had spoken to me the first time I really looked at them.

I must have been transported past Johnson's Woods hundreds of times before I looked through the rear window of the bus delivering Edgerton Academy's sixth grade to Pioneer Village and felt a fishhook strike my heart as a voice out there or inside my head boomed *Come to me*. Words of that order. *You need me, You are mine, Be with me,* whatever. The fishhook tried to pull me through the window, and I turned around and pushed against the glass. My heart pounded, my face blazed. The driver yelled an order to sit down. In justifiable expectation of fireworks, my classmates snickered, but fell silent as soon as I obeyed. The astonished teacher thanked me for my cooperation. I wasn't being cooperative. I wasn't strong enough to push out the window.

Pioneer Village was two streets lined with log cabins and the Meeting House, the Place of Worship, the Trading Post, and the Smithy. Women in frilly caps cooked in big pots hung over fireplaces, and men in coonskin caps and gunnysack shirts shot rabbits with muskets. These people grew vegetables and made their own soap. Their hair was stiff with grease, and nobody looked too clean. I believe they were adepts of some punitive faith.

Rendering unto Caesar what was Caesar's, I stumbled through the day and got back on the bus ahead of everybody else. When we passed the woods on the way home, I twisted sideways on my seat and waited for that tug at my inmost being and the booming voice I alone would hear. Instead, I felt only a warm, powerful pulsation—it was enough.

Blessedly, the next day was Saturday. I arose with the sun and idled around the house until my mother appeared to make breakfast. My father took off on a business errand, which was what he did on Saturdays. With premature cunning, I told my mother that I thought I'd ride my bike for a while. On my usual Saturdays, I wandered down Manor Street in a black, bored rage, scratching the sides of our neighbors' cars and crouching under a bush to shoot passing dogs with my BB gun. That I wanted to do something as conventional as ride my bike filled my mother with a pleasure tainted only mildly with suspicion. I promised not to get into trouble. Because I had no choice, I also promised to come home for lunch. I could see her consider giving me a hug, and, to our mutual relief, veto the notion. I pedaled down the driveway in a flawless impersonation of a kid with nothing special on his mind. The second I got out of sight, I stood up on the pedals and made that clunker fly.

At the place in the road where I had felt the tug and heard the wondrous voice, I dragged the bike behind a tree and stood up straight, *knowing* I was in the right place, the place I was *supposed* to be. I stepped forward, trembling with anticipation. Nothing happened. In a manner of speaking. Nothing happened except for the subtly intensifying awareness of having arrived within that space in the world most connected to the secret sources of all that made my life a furious misery, therefore the space most necessary to me and for the same reasons the most terrifying.

At that moment, I realized that I had already chosen knowledge over ignorance, whatever the consequences. My heart calmed, and I began to take in what was around me.

The trunks of many trees filled my vision, brown, gray, silver, some almost black, their hides varied from wrinkled corrugations to perfect shining smoothness. Trembling pools of light lay across the gray-green floor. The air was a floating, silvery gray. Far off loomed the wooden mountain of a deadfall. Overhead, leafy crowns knitted together, and squirrels' nests sat on upper branches like ragged bolls.

Then, as if they had come into being all at once, I could see the squirrels everywhere, leaping from branches, landing on twiggy shoots, and swaying downward to rocket up again in an endless chase. Birds of all descriptions crisscrossed the gauzy air. A fox materialized within a cube of empty air, pricked up its ears, and stopped moving with one paw still raised.

■ On the last Sunday before summer vacation, when coincidentally or not Canon Reed had spent the morning vainly attempting to take the sting out of Luke 12:49, *I came to cast fire upon the earth, and would have it that it were already kindled!*, I saw the first faint traces of the blue fire and knew that the summer would be a time of wonders.

Intermittent, vertical strips of pale green appeared and coalesced between the more distant trees. When I came nearer, I saw that I was approaching a clearing. I reached the last of the trees. Before me was a grassy oval, unnervingly quiet. Unobstructed sun beat down upon a pad of yellow-green grasses.

As soon as I moved out from beneath the canopy, the temperature heated up but good. I could hardly see, in all that brightness. At the center of the clearing, I sat down with my eyes just above the top of the grass. A flattened trail arrowed toward me. I wiped my forehead and blinked against the dazzle of the sun. When I breathed in, the clearing breathed with me. An electric current ran up my arms and into my chest.

I knew awe and pleasure. I knew more was to come. Within the me within the clearing sat a me who needed time to get used to his surroundings. We sat together in our different realms and adjusted to our new conditions. There would be more, but the nature of the more could not as yet be imagined.

A bluebird ventured out of the woods, and I tracked its arrogant, overhead loop.

Within, my newborn self spoke, and I sent a thought flying to the bluebird. As quick as anything, that bluebird crumpled its wings and fell, lifeless as an anvil.

On the way home, I tried to do the same to a crow sneering at me from a telephone wire, but the blasted thing refused to drop dead. So did a holstein ruminating behind a fence at the edge of the road, and I had no better luck with Sarge, an elderly police dog twitching in sleep on his owner's front lawn. I had been given a tool that had come without an instruction manual. Thinking as a child, I assumed that installments of the instruction manual were to be steadily delivered over a reasonable time.

Little did I know.

■ Because my board scores were surprisingly good, I wound up being accepted by all four of the colleges I applied to. As a product of foster care whose only legal parent made so little money she had never even filed with the IRS, I was offered full-tuition scholarships, free housing, and a variety of jobs at each school, so I did not have to count on Phil Grant to lay out the customary fortune. He would have refinanced his house and taken out loans to keep him in debt until retirement, if that was what I needed. That I would not be costing Phil a lot of money made me happy, but most of my happiness was relief.

In the end, I decided on Middlemount, disappointing Phil, who had all but assumed since my acceptance at Princeton, his alma mater, that I would wind up there. I couldn't see myself at such a high-pressure school, and I didn't like the idea of being surrounded by a lot of rich kids. Also, although I never mentioned it during our talks over the kitchen table, I knew that in spite of all the financial aid, Princeton would take more money out of Phil's pocket than Middlemount. On the sensible grounds that we were talking about my decision, not his, Laura took my side in these discussions, which helped him come around. So I went to Middlemount College in Middlemount, Vermont, and my life began to unravel.

When my jock roommate followed his instantaneous loathing of everything I represented by crowding great numbers of his prep-school chums into our room night after night to yell about fags, niggers, kikes, car wrecks, sailing catastrophes, broken backs, broken necks, instances of total paralysis, kikes, fags, spics, and niggers, I complained loudly enough to get reassigned to a single room.

Once I got a single room I hardly saw anyone at all outside of classes. In spite of my SAT scores, my math and science courses seemed to be conducted in a foreign language. I had to struggle up to and past exhaustion just to lag behind. Sometimes I looked up from my desk at a string of gibberish Professor Flagship, the calculus teacher, was scrolling across the blackboard and felt myself fall through a hole in the earth's crust. I spent whole weeks doing nothing but shuttling between the dorm, classrooms, my meal job, and the library. Then it started to get cold.

Winter hit Vermont right after Thanksgiving. The temperature sank to twenty degrees, and the cold gripped my skin like a claw. When it went down to ten degrees, the wind rolling down out of the mountains threatened to tear off my face. In the overheated classrooms, I could feel the cold moving into the marrow of my bones. For two months, the sun retreated behind a lead-lined curtain the color of gray flannel. Before long, starless night clamped down abruptly at 5:00. The worst cold of my life brought on perpetual sneezing and coughing and sent aches to every part of my body. I trudged to classes, but the supervisor at my meal job declared me a health hazard and granted sick leave. After forcing down whatever I could of the cafeteria's starchy dinners, too tired to face another Nanook-style trek across the tundra to the library, I fell asleep at my desk while trying to cram Introductory Calculus into my stupefied head. Daily, second by second, I was being erased into a shadow.

The one thing that kept me from feeling as though I already had become a shadow was my guitar and what happened when I played it. For my twelfth birthday, which had not failed to be marked by the usual horror show, the Grants had given me a nice old Gibson, along with what turned out to be years of lessons from a sympathetic teacher. I brought my guitar with me to Middlemount, and now and then when my room closed in around me, I went to a corner of the dorm's lounge and played there.

Mostly, I added voicings to harmonies in my dogged, step-by-step way, but sometimes other students came in and sat close enough to listen. When I found that I had an audience, I played things like a Bach fugue my teacher had transcribed, a blues line I learned off a Gene Ammons record, and a version of "Things Ain't What They Used to Be" cribbed from Jim Hall. If anyone was still listening, I threw in a few songs whose chord changes I could remember. "My Romance" was one, and "Easy Living," "Moonlight in Vermont," and a jazz tune called "Whisper Not." I made mistakes and got lost, but none of my fellow dormies knew anything was wrong unless I stopped and went back to where I'd been before my fingers turned into Popsicle sticks. Half of them never listened to anything but the Rolling Stones, Eric Clapton, and Tina Turner, and the other half never listened to anything but the Carpenters, the Bee Gees, and Elton John. (The ones that always wore black and listened to Bob Dylan and Leonard Cohen avoided the lounge like the plague.) What I played sounded like classical music to most of them, but they liked it anyhow. And I liked playing for them, because it reminded me that I had not always been a hermit. The other happy result of my playing was the renovation of my public identity from That Weird Ned Guy Who Never Comes Out of His Room to That Freaky Ned Who Can Play Really Good Guitar Once He Gets Out of His Room.

■ At Christmas break, I went back to Naperville and acted as though everything was fine, apart from some trouble with calculus. Without telling any actual lies, I described a challenging routine of work and occasional pleasures, and put down my unhappiness to homesickness. As soon as I said the word, I realized that I had been more homesick for Naperville and the Grants than I had been willing to admit. As my cold lessened and I alternated between writing a paper for English, reviewing notes for my final exams, and settling back into my old place in the household, the version of college life I had invented began to seem less fictional and more like the reality I would have known had I not felt so lost.

The day after Christmas, I heard a car turn into the driveway and went to the living room window to watch Star wheel up to the garage in a handsome old Lincoln. She emerged wearing high heels, an elaborate hat, and a black coat too light for the cold. Star was living in Cleveland that year, exchanging work at a lithography studio for lessons from an artist she had met while he was in residence at Albertus. On weekends, she was singing in a club called Inside the Outside. Laura Grant called out from the kitchen, "Ned, your mother's here!" Buttoning his blazer and sucking in his tummy, Phil came out of the alcove off the living room, where he watched television. "Don't make her freeze out there, kiddo," he said. Star was hurrying up the flagstone path, and when I opened the door she sailed in like a swan, hiding her nervousness behind a brilliant smile. She put her arms around me, and the Grants both started talking at once, and I could feel her begin to calm down.

The rest of the day was comfortable and relaxed. Star gave me a cashmere sweater, I gave her a boxed set of Billie Holiday reissues, and what she got from the Grants nicely balanced the few little things she had brought for them. Laura prepared two lavish meals, and I continued to develop my sanitized version of life at Middlemount. Phil and Laura left us alone after dinner, and Star asked, "Are you thinking about being a musician? I sure liked hearing about you playing for your friends at that school."

I told her that I'd never be good enough to satisfy myself.

"You could be better than you are now," she said, "and you'd be able to work, so you could leave college, if you wanted to. If any of the musicians I know have college degrees, they keep it a secret."

Surprised, I asked her why I would want to leave college.

"Know how you sound when you talk about Middlemount?" she asked. "Like you're describing a movie."

"It's a good college."

"You don't have to tell *me* it's a good college. I just wonder if it's a good college for Ned Dunstan. Look at you. You lost about fifteen, twenty pounds, and you've been missing way too much sleep. The only reason you're halfway healthy is Laura's been giving you plenty of her good food."

"I had a rotten cold," I said.

"Your cold wasn't all that was rotten, if you ask me. Maybe you want to make college sound better than it is."

"After I get through the finals, everything'll be fine," I said. Phil and Laura came in offering coffee and nightcaps, and before everybody went to bed we listened to the eighteen-year-old Billie Holiday singing "When You're Smiling" and "Ooh Ooh Ooh, What a Little Moonlight Can Do."

The next morning Laura and Star went out shopping, and Star came home with a new coat from Biegelman's purchased at 60 percent off because Mr. Biegelman thought it would never look as good on anyone else. As Laura told the story, she gave me a sideways look that was half question, half accusation. Star seemed to be avoiding looking at me altogether. Laura finished talking and my mother left to hang up the coat. She gave me a murky glance on her way out of the room. Phil noticed nothing, for which I was grateful. Laura said, "Did you boys stay home all the time we were out?"

"You bet," Phil said. "We had a hell of a time kicking out the dancing girls before you got back."

My mother drifted into the living room, smiled more in my direction than at me, and glanced at the couch like a cat deciding where to settle down. Phil cleared his throat and challenged her to their annual Christmas chess championship. She grinned at him with what looked to me like relief.

Before the start of this tradition, I would have said that given two tries at telling a pawn from a rook, my mother would have been right at least once, but she was good enough to beat Phil about one game in four. This time, he was frowning at the board and muttering, "Hold on, I don't get it," ten minutes after they started. (It turned out that the lithographer in Cleveland was a demon chess player.)

I followed Laura into the kitchen, expecting her to share my amusement at her husband's consternation. "Either she got a lot better since last year, or Phil forgot how to play," I said.

Laura moved across the kitchen, leaned against the sink, and permitted my remark to shrivel in the air between us. The look she gave me had nothing to do with amusement. "I thought I knew you pretty well, but now I'm beginning to wonder." She crossed her arms across her chest.

"About what?"

"Did you leave the house while we were gone?"

I shook my head.

"You didn't go downtown. Or to Biegelman's."

"What's all this about? You and Star have been acting weird ever since you got back."

"That's not an answer." She was staring fiercely into my eyes.

"No," I said, beginning to get irritated. "I didn't go to Biegelman's. Biegelman's is a women's clothing store. I don't think I've ever been inside it in my whole life." I made myself calm down. "What's going on?"

"A mistake, I guess," Laura said.

In the other room, my mother laughed and cried out, "Phil, don't you know anything about Capablanca?"

"He's dead, and so am I," Phil said.

"Star's worried about you." Laura was still searching my face.

"There's nothing to worry about."

"Are you getting enough sleep? Do you walk around feeling exhausted all the time?"

Most of the time, I walked around feeling half-dead. "I'm tired sometimes, but it's no big deal."

"Are you happy at Middlemount? If it's getting to be too much for you, you can always take a semester off."

I began to get angry all over again. "First everybody is pushing me into college, and now everybody wants to push me out. I wish you'd make up your minds."

She looked stricken. "Ned, did we push you into college? Is that how it feels to you?"

I already regretted my words.

"Think of how much those colleges wanted you. It's a great opportunity. Besides that, not having a college degree would be a tremendous disadvantage later in life." She lifted her chin and looked away. "Boy oh boy. Maybe we did push you. But all we wanted was what we thought would be best for you." She looked back at me. "You're the only person who can tell me what's best for you, and you better be honest about it. Don't worry about Phil, either. He feels the same way."

She meant that she would be able to explain a leave of absence to him, if that was what I wanted. The thought of Phil's disappointment made me feel like a traitor. "I guess I'll have to get straight As and be elected president of my class before you and Star stop worrying," I said.

"Hey, Ned!" Phil shouted from the other room. "Your mother and Bobby Fischer, separated at birth, is that the deal?"

"Okay," Laura said. "We'll see how you feel at semester break. In the meantime, please remember that Alexander Graham Bell invented the telephone, all right?"

Over lunch, the astonished Phil explained the Machiavellian stratagems by which my mother had sandbagged him. Star ate half of what was on her plate, looked at her watch, and stood up from the table. She had a long drive ahead of her, time to go, thanks so much, goodbye.

By the time I carried her bag downstairs, she was giving Laura a hug from the depths of her new winter coat. I walked her down the path to the Lincoln, wondering if she thought she could get in and drive away without speaking to me. We came up to the car door, and I said, "Mom." She wrapped me in her arms.

"Come with me," she said. "Throw a few things into a suitcase and tell those nice people you're going to stay with me while you think things over."

"What?" I pulled back and looked at her. She was serious.

"I have enough room to put you up. You can wait tables at Inside the Outside until we find something better."

If she had sandbagged Phil, what she was doing to me felt like a mugging. "What's going on? Laura's after me about transferring or dropping out for a semester, you can't even look at me, both of you act like I turned into some person you don't even like. . . . I'm not where I'm supposed to be, I'm too skinny, I'm a liar. . . . All of a sudden, come to Cleveland . . ." I raised my arms and shook my head in bafflement. "If you can, explain it to me, how about that?"

"I want to protect you," she said.

I couldn't help it—I laughed at her. "Middlemount's a lot safer than a nightclub in the middle of Cleveland."

Some thought, an explanation or rebuttal, surged across her face. She visibly thrust it away. "Maybe I never had a chance to go to college. But you know what? Working at Inside the Outside isn't such a bad deal."

I had offended her. Even worse, I had insulted her. "Hey, Mom, I never wanted to go to Middlemount, it just happened."

"Then get in the car."

"I can't." In the face of her huge, silent challenge, I said, "I did have a lot of problems, but I can work them out."

"Uh-huh," she said. "The things you don't know, they'd fill a football stadium."

"Like what?" I said, remembering the refusal I had just seen.

"You and me, honey, we don't know anything at all." The warmth of the new coat enveloped me once more, and when I felt her arms and shoulders tremble as she kissed my cheek, I almost decided to climb into the old Lincoln and drive away. Star patted the back of my head twice, three times, waited a beat, then once more. "Get back inside before you freeze to death."

I spent most of the next few days studying.

The Grants kept up a cheerful patter during the drive to O'Hare, though I could tell that Laura was still unhappy. Phil marveled at my mother's progress in the year since their last championship. In the past, he had been able to predict her decisions three or four moves ahead. "I knew her game better than she knew mine. I could surprise her, whereas she always had to take chances to surprise me."

"Whereas?" Laura said.

"Yes. The point is, once you get to that stage, the situation never changes. But this year, Star figured out my strategies before I knew what they were. I thought she was just messing around until she started taking my pieces off the board. The level of her game went way past mine, which means that her ability is out of sight."

"Whereas yours is merely above average," Laura said from the backseat.

"Why are you picking on me? Ned, she's picking on me, isn't she?"

"Sounds like it," I said.

"You in a bad mood, honey?"

"I'm afraid of losing Ned."

Phil looked at her in the rearview mirror. "We can't get rid of the guy. He's coming back in a couple of weeks."

"I hope he does," Laura said.

Phil glanced at me, then back up at the mirror. "After you two got back from downtown, Star seemed sort of antsy, like she was upset. Did she seem upset, Ned, when you were saying goodbye?"

"More like worried," I said. "She wanted me to drive back to Cleveland with her."

"Oh, no," Laura said.

"Just get in the car and drive away?"

"After telling you I was leaving."

Laura said, "I knew it," and Phil said, "I'll be damned." He checked the mirror again. "What did you say?"

"It's not important."

"I don't know," Phil said. "Ned, one thing about your mother, and I've always thought she was great—"

"No kidding," Laura supplied.

"You do, too, Laura, come on, one thing about Star, she's full of surprises."

I tried to say goodbye to the Grants at the security check, but they talked their way past the guards and walked me to the departure gate. We were about half an hour early. Phil wandered off to inspect a gift shop. Laura slumped against a square column and smiled at me from a face filled with complicated feeling. I remember thinking that she had never looked so beautiful, and that I had rarely been so conscious of how much I loved her. "At least you didn't run away to Cleveland."

"I thought about it for a second or two," I said. "You knew what she was going to say?"

She nodded, and her warm eyes again met mine. "Star and I have *some* things in common, anyhow. We both want our Ned to be safe and happy."

I looked down the corridor, where Phil was peering at a rack of baseball caps. "What was all that about Biegelman's? When you and Star got back, you were mad at me, and she was in outer space."

"Forget about it, Ned, please. I made a mistake."

"You thought you saw me in Biegelman's?"

Laura rammed her hands into the pockets of her down coat and bent her blue-jeaned right leg to plant the sole of a pretty black boot on the flank of the column. The back of her head fell against its flat surface. She turned her head toward the people moving up and down the corridor and smiled reflexively at a small boy encased in a snowsuit waddling ahead of his stroller.

"There was a little more to it."

A long stretch of corridor opened up in front of the boy, and he broke into a lumbering run until sheer momentum got the better of him. He flopped down onto the tiles, his arms and legs spread-eagled like a starfish. Without breaking stride, his mother leaned over, scooped him up, and dumped him into the stroller.

"Eventually, I got tired of trailing after Star." Laura was watching the boy's mother move efficiently down the corridor. "I love her a lot, Ned, but sometimes she can make it hard to give her what she needs." She turned her head and smiled at me again. "We got to Biegelman's, she found exactly the right coat, it was on sale, we hadn't seen anything else all morning, so it should have been simple. All right, it was a little expensive, but not much. I would have bought it for her in a second."

I was thinking: *The story always hides some other, secret story, the story you are not supposed to know.*

"But Star didn't like my spending so much on her, so she had to play this game. The coat wasn't the right color. Could the clerk see if they had one in a lighter color? It was obvious they only had that one, and the only woman in Naperville likely to buy it already had it on. Mr. Biegelman came up to help, and I walked away. When I looked back, your mother was gone. Then I looked through the window, and there she was, out on the sidewalk in that coat. She was talking to you."

"Me?"

"That's how it looked," she said. "Star seemed so unhappy . . .
so *disturbed* . . . I don't know what. You, the person I thought
was you, turned his back on her and walked away. I started to go
toward the door, but Star came back in and gave me this *look*, so
I didn't say anything. Mr. Biegelman gave us the extra discount,
and I pulled out my credit card. But I did ask her about it on the
way home."

"What did she say about the guy?"

Laura pushed herself off the pillar. "First she said there wasn't
any guy. Then she said, oh, she forgot, a stranger came up and
asked for directions. Then she cried. She didn't want me to notice, and to tell you the truth, I was a lot more interested in what
you'd have to say, because Star wasn't about to tell me anything
at all. But it wasn't you, so I made a mistake. Obviously."

"I guess so," I said.

My flight was announced, and Phil pulled me into an embrace
and told me he was proud of me. Laura's hug was longer and
tighter than Phil's. I told her I loved her, and she said the same to
me. I surrendered my ticket, stepped into the mouth of the
jetway, and looked back. Phil was smiling and Laura was staring
at me as though memorizing my face. I waved goodbye. Identi-
cally, like witnesses being sworn in at a trial, they raised their
right hands. Other passengers swept forward in a confusion of
ski jackets and carry-on bags and urged me down the jetway.

■ 10

■ Middlemount closed around me like a fist. In the week before
finals, I sank deeper into the old pattern, rushing under metal
skies between classes, the meal job, and the library, often falling
asleep with my churning head on an open book. Sometimes it
seemed as though I had passed from one frozen night into another without the intervention of daylight; sometimes I looked at
my watch, saw the hands pointing to four o'clock, and could not

tell if I had missed some badly needed sleep or a couple of classes and an appearance before the pots and pans.

On the first day of finals I had the English and French exams, history on the second day, then a day off, chemistry on the next, and calculus on the final day. Through Monday and Tuesday I can remember coming into the bright classrooms, taking my seat, getting the blue books and the exam sheets, and thinking myself so far behind that I was incapable even of understanding the questions. Then the words began to sink in, the darkness to lift, and soon, as if more by radio transmission than by thought, coherent sentences declared themselves in my mind. I took dictation until the blue books were filled, and then I stopped.

On Wednesday night I fell asleep at my desk. Raps at the door jolted me awake. When I opened it, I was startled to see Simone Feigenbaum, a girl from my French class, standing in front of me, dressed, as always, in black. Simone was from Scarsdale. She smoked Gitanes and was in the Bob Dylan–Leonard Cohen crowd. The thought that she probably wanted to borrow a textbook evaporated as she flowed in and put her arms around me. In the midst of a lengthy kiss, she pulled down my zipper and reached, with a sly, comic bravado, within.

My clothes windmilled away, and hers flew off over her head. We toppled into my narrow bed.

Instantly, Simone Feigenbaum was zooming over, under, alongside my body, her breasts in my face, then her stomach, then her buttocks, then her face was in my face and both of us were working away like pistons until I seemed suddenly to turn inside out. Her breasts nudged my face and I got hard without ever actually getting soft and we did everything all over again, only slower. And so on, repeatedly, until my thighs ached and my penis was waving a limp white flag. I was eighteen, and a virgin besides, technically speaking.

Around six in the morning, Simone slipped out of bed and into her clothes. She asked if I had an exam that day. "Chemistry," I said. She produced a vial of pills, shook one into her hand, and dropped it on my desk. "Take that fifteen minutes before you go in. It's magic. You'll amaze yourself."

"Simone," I said, "why did you come here?"

"I had to make sure I screwed you at least once before you flunked out." She opened the window of my ground-floor room and jumped down into the crest of snow between the dormitory and the path. I closed the window and slept for a couple of hours.

I swallowed the pill on my way to the exam. Another bright classroom, another menacing desk. During the distribution of the blue books and question sheets, I felt as if I had taken nothing stronger than a cup of coffee. I opened the blue book, read the first question, and discovered that not only did I understand it perfectly, I could visualize every detail of the relevant pages in the textbook as if they were displayed before me. At the end of the hour I had filled three blue books and completed all but one of the extra-credit questions. I floated out of the classroom and gulped a quart of cold water from the nearest fountain.

The calculus exam was twenty-two hours away. I took my guitar into the lounge and spent the afternoon playing better than I had thought possible for me. I skipped dinner and forgot about my meal job. Instead, I remembered the bridge to "Skylark" and the verse to "But Not for Me." I knew who my mother had met on the sidewalk outside Biegelman's—me, the real me, this one. After six or seven hours I said, "I have to memorize the math book," and returned to my room on a wave of applause.

When I opened the calculus textbook, I found that I had already memorized every page, including footnotes. I stretched out on the bed and observed that the cracks in the ceiling described mathematical symbols. Someone yelled, "Dunstan, phone call!" I floated to the telephone and heard Simone Feigenbaum asking me how I felt. Great, I said. Had the pill done any good? I think it did, I said. Did I want another one? No, I said, but maybe you could come back to my room.

"Are you kidding?" Simone laughed. "I'm still sore. Besides, I have to study for my last exam. I'm going home afterward, but I'll see you after the break."

I levitated back to my room and stretched out. Sleep refused to come until seven in the morning, when absolute darkness swarmed from every wall and corner and escorted me into unconsciousness.

Someone who may or may not have been me had possessed the foresight to set my alarm clock for an hour before the exam. The same someone had shifted the clock to my desk, forcing me to get up when it yowled. Once I was on my feet, I reeled to the showers and stood beneath alternating blasts of hot and cold water, realizing that I had slept through both breakfast and lunch, in the process missing two tours of duty before the pots and pans, and would have to survive the math exam before satisfying my hunger. I rummaged through my desk drawers, discovered half a packet of M&M's, an entire Reese's peanut butter cup, and the greenish, salt-flecked remains clinging to the bottom of a potato chip bag. I rammed this gunk into my mouth on the way to the exam. Professor Flagship strolled from chair to chair, handing out thick wads of paper covered with mathematical formulae. He said, "This is a multiple-choice examination. Check off the answers and use the blue books for calculations." To me, he added, "I wish you luck, Mr. Dunstan."

I believe that I had a dim grasp of the first few problems. All the rest were in a mixture of Old Icelandic and Basque. I kept falling asleep for two-second, three-second naps. Occasionally I covered a page with doodles or scrawled the random words that limped across my mind's surface. At the end of the hour I tossed the question sheets and blue books into the heap on the table and went off-campus to guzzle beer at a student bar until the return of unconsciousness.

My recurring dream descended once again.

All the next day I lay in bed listening to the slamming of car doors and shouts of farewell. Because I didn't remember going to the bar, I did not understand that I had a monstrous hangover. How could I be hungover? I almost never drank alcohol. To the extent I was capable of thinking anything at all, I thought that I had come down with some spectacular new variety of flu.

Memory returned in dreamlike, photographic flashes. I watched my hand add a caricature of Professor Flagship's face to the body of a lion with stubby wings, protruding breasts, and a bloated penis. For a second, Simone Feigenbaum revolved her lush little body above me, and I thought: *Hey, that happened!* I opened a blue book to a fresh page and in neat block letters wrote, THE MAIN CAUSE OF PROBLEMS IS SOLUTIONS. I remembered tossing my test papers on the professor's desk and watching, many hours later, a stiff, disapproving bartender swiping a cloth over five inches of polished mahogany and setting down a glass crowned with foam. I realized where I was and what I had done. It was the Saturday after final exams, and the campus was filled with parents picking up their sons and daughters. Other students, myself supposedly among them, were taking the bus to the airport.

The universe in which people could pack bags and climb into their fathers' cars seemed unbridgeably distant from mine. I huddled in bed until the window was dark and the last car had driven away.

By tradition, our instructors posted exam grades in a glass-encased bulletin board on the quad before the college mailed them out. After the break, the board would be surrounded by students looking up other people's grades. I expected to see my English and French results on the coming Monday, history no later than Tuesday, chemistry on Tuesday or Wednesday. I had extravagant hopes for chemistry. Calculus, the one that terrified me, probably would not show up until Wednesday.

The Grants expected me to come into O'Hare on Sunday afternoon. I was to call them Saturday to confirm, and my ticket was already waiting at the airport. When I felt capable of rational speech, I put in a collect call to Naperville and spoke an escalating series of whoppers about an invitation to join a friend in Barbados, and if they didn't mind. . . . My friend's sister had backed out, so I'd be taking her place, the tickets were already paid for, and the family didn't mind because I'd bunk with my friend and save them the price of a room . . .

The Grants said they'd be sorry not to see me, but spring vacation wasn't far away. Phil asked if my friend might happen to be of the female variety. I said, no, he was Clark Darkmund, the name of a cherubic, porn-obsessed Minnesotan who had been rotated into the single next to mine after disagreeing about the merits of the philosophy expressed in *Mein Kampf* with his former roommate, Steven Glucksman of Great Neck, Long Island. Yes, I said, Clark was an interesting character. Great conversationalist, too.

"How did the finals go?" Phil asked.

"We'll see."

"I know my Ned," Phil told me. "You're going to surprise yourself."

After dinner in a student bar, I walked back to the campus. When I turned onto the path to my dorm, a German exchange student named Horst who looked like an *Esquire* model hastened up out of nowhere and appeared beside me. Had he been cherubic, Horst would have resembled Clark Darkmund, but there was nothing cherubic about him. He smiled at me. "Here we are again, alone in this desolate place. Now that you are sober, let us go to my room and undress each other very, very slowly."

His proposition deepened my gloom, and my response surprised me even more than it did Horst. "I have a knife in my pocket," I said. "Unless you disappear right away, your guts will freeze before you know you're cut."

"Ned." He looked stricken. "Didn't we have an understanding?"

"All right," I said. "I'll count to three. Here goes. One."

He summoned a charming smile. "That object in your trousers is undoubtedly far more magnificent than a knife."

"Two."

"You do not remember our conversation of last night?"

I shoved my hand into my pocket and closed it around the remnant of a roll of Life Savers.

Horst slid into the darkness with a regretful moue.

The next morning, transparent sunlight streamed down from a sky of clear, hard azure. The crisp shadows of leafless poplars stretched out across the bright snow.

Accompanied by my own crisp shadow, I walked into Middlemount and wandered around, sipping at a container of coffee and biting into an apple danish. Church bells announced the beginnings or endings of services, I didn't know which. I inspected shop windows and otherwise goofed off. The church bells broke again into speech. Through down-sluicing light, I walked back to the college and at a crucial junction experimentally turned left instead of right and soon found myself at the edge of what appeared to be an extensive forest. Weather-beaten letters on a wooden sign nailed to the trunk of an oak read JONES'S WOODS.

At the time, all I understood was that if I walked into the woods I would feel better, so I left the road and walked into the woods.

■ I felt better, instantly. I seemed to be magically at home, or if not precisely at home at least in *the right place.* Across crunching snow packed so hard it scarcely registered my footprints, I wound through trees until I reached a ring of maples and sat down in the center of their circle, more at peace with myself than I had been since my arrival in Vermont. My anxieties dwindled, and my life was going to be all right. If I had to leave college, that was all right, too. I could always wait on tables at Inside the Outside. I could marry Simone Feigenbaum and be a kept man. Squirrels with fat winter coats raced down the trunks of oak trees and skidded across glassy snow. Eventually the light began to die, and the trees crowded closer together. I stood up and walked out.

Monday morning I went into town and bought a long salami, a square of cheddar cheese, a jar of peanut butter, a loaf of bread, a bag of Cape Cod potato chips and two smaller bags of peanut M&M's, a quart of milk, and a six-pack of Coca-Cola. Back in my room, I wrapped slices of salami and cheese in bread and washed down spoonfuls of peanut butter with Coke. Then I put on my coat and hurried to the quad to find three of my grades posted on the board. In English, I got a B+ on the exam and a B+ for the semester; in French, B and B, disappointing but not entirely unexpected. History, in which I thought I had done well, was a disaster. My C on the exam lowered my semester grade to B−. One of the conditions of my scholarship was that I had to maintain a certain average, and I'd been counting on a B in history to balance Ds or even a potential failure in my other two courses.

I stepped back from the bulletin board and noticed something move off to my left. Horst was watching me from beside a pillar at the top of the library steps. His attitude, of an almost regal patience, suggested that he had been there for some time. He drew a gloved hand from the pocket of his duffle coat and gave a slow, ironic wave. I lowered my head and took the nearest path in the opposite direction, on my way back to *the right place*.

Once I had entered the clearing, worries about examinations and grade-point averages floated off into the transparent air. For a disembodied time, I became a recording eye. Squirrels repeated their comic turns. A fox stepped out between the maples, froze, and rewound itself as if on film. When the air began to darken, I reluctantly got to my feet.

Tuesday morning, I cowered starving in bed until 11:00 A.M., got up to gulp milk from the carton and gnaw at cheese and bread, climbed back in bed for another hour of deep-breathing exercises, and finally managed to propel myself into the shower. There was the slightest possibility that our chemistry grades might be announced that afternoon. Most professors posted their grades before 3:00 P.M., and shortly before that hour I hurried into the quad and inspected the board. My section's chemistry results had not been posted. I rammed junk food into my pockets and on the way to my sanctuary went into the brick cubicle of the dormitory post office to check my mailbox.

Wedged like a letter bomb behind the glass door of my box was an unstamped, cream-colored envelope addressed to "Mr. Ned Dunstar." It bore the return address of the dean of student affairs.

Dear Mr. Dunstar,

I regret the necessity of informing you of a troubling matter recently brought to my attention by Mr. Roman Polk, the Manager of Food Service Personnel at Middlemount College, in which capacity Mr. Polk supervises our full-time kitchen staff and those members of the student body for whom Food Services Placements have been awarded in accordance with the conditions of their Middlemount Student Support Scholarships.

Mr. Polk informs me that you have failed to meet seven out of ten of your last Food Service Placement appointments, furthermore that you were absent on sick leave upon nine previous occasions. This is a matter of concern to us all.

We will meet in my office at 7:30 A.M. on the first academic day of the coming term, January 20, for a discussion of Mr. Polk's charges. You remain a valued member of the Middlemount community, and if for some reason Food Services was an inappropriate placement, another might be found. In the meantime, I wish you success in your examinations.

Sincerely yours,
Clive Macanudo
Dean of Student Affairs

When I emerged from the little cell block housing our mailboxes, who stood in the cold athwart the cement path, resplendent in a long, forest-green loden coat, fresh comb tracks dividing his thick hair? Horst might as well have been wearing a Tyrolean hat with a feather jutting from the band. He glanced at the letter protruding from my coat pocket. "Are you all right?"

"Stop following me, you creep." I tried to walk around him.

"Please, forget about the other night." Horst moved in front of me. "I made a silly mistake and misinterpreted our brief conversation of the day before."

Evidently I had spoken to him in the student bar that Friday and forgotten about it later. That was fine with me. I had succeeded in forgetting most of Friday's events as they were happening, and I certainly did not want to remember anything I might have said to Horst. "Fine," I said. "But if you don't stop following me, I'm still going to cut you."

"Please, Ned, really!" He stepped back and raised his gloved hands in surrender. "Only, you do not look well. I ask as a friend, are you all right? Is anything wrong?"

"Here we go," I said. "Count of three, remember? One."

"Ned, please, you don't own a knife. In fact, you are about as dangerous as a bunny rabbit." Smiling, he lowered his hands. "Let me buy you a cup of coffee. You could tell your problems to me, after which I will explain how to fix them, after which I will bore you with mine, after which we will drink a beer and decide our problems are not so serious after all."

"After which we will go back to your room and fix your boring problems by taking off our clothes."

"I'm not talking about that," Horst said. "Honestly. I am simply offering to be of help."

"Then simply get out of my way." I walked straight toward him, and he got out of my way.

Later that afternoon, I sat frozen at the base of a giant oak and attended to the deep, nearly inaudible sound, as of powerful machinery at work, filtering up through the snowpack. Snatches of high-pitched music resounded either from the air itself or from the movement of the air through the branches. The music-laden air filled with grains of darkness, the grains coalesced, and the darkness blotted out the light.

Wednesday morning, I saw my guitar case propped beside the door. The sight immediately suggested the inspiration of adding to the music of Jones's Woods. I jumped out of bed.

Having breakfasted on sour milk and Cape Cod potato chips, I edged into the quad, keeping a weather eye out for Horst. He did not show himself. Neither did my chemistry results, although Professor Medley's conclusions had been posted on the board. While the names of everyone else in my section were followed by letters indicating their grades, after "Dunstan, Ned" appeared only the nongrade "Inc," abbreviation-speak for "Incomplete." I stumbled back to my room and rammed the day's nourishment into my coat pockets, remembering as I did so the summons from On High. Once again I entered the glum post office and found an official envelope pressed against the glass window of my box. Clive Macanudo: The Sequel. This time, he spelled my name right.

Dear Mr. Dunstan,

I apologize for the secretarial error which resulted in the misspelling of your name throughout my letter of yesterday.

This morning, Professor Arnold Medley of our Chemistry Department spoke to me concerning your performance in his Chemistry 1 course. Professor Medley greeted your results on his final examination with a great deal of surprise. As you submitted the only perfect examination of the Professor's long experience and went on to solve several extra-credit questions, your numerical grade on the examination was 127 out of 100, or A++.

Professor Medley is of the opinion that no student with grades consistently at or below the C level could have so greatly improved his grasp of the material as to earn an A++ on the final examination without unlawful assistance. I spoke on your behalf. Professor Medley agreed that at no time had he observed you cheating in any way and could offer no proof that you had not earned your result honestly. However, he found the result so anomalous as to justify his suspicions.

We have reached the following accommodation. You shall retake the Chemistry 1 final examination under conditions of the strictest security and at your earliest convenience. I suggest 7:45 A.M. on this coming Friday, should you be present on campus, and if not, at 6:30 A.M. on January 20, immediately prior to our meeting concerning Mr. Polk's allegations. The retesting shall take place in my office, with Professor Medley and myself present. I take the liberty of recommending that you spend the intervening days in preparation.

Sincerely yours,
Clive Macanudo
Dean of Student Affairs

The usual sense of being *home* settled my nerves as soon as I entered the woods. The rushing in my ears yielded to the creaking of laden branches, the territorial chatter of birds, the clicks and taps made by squirrels in the course of their missions. Eventually I began to hear the trebles chiming from glittering icicles and soon after, the deep bass humming beneath the ice-pack. I opened the guitar case, took out my instrument, and reverently settled it into the hollow between my hunched shoulders and the tops of my thighs.

Shortly before noon the next day, I awoke with no memory of having returned to the campus. I stumbled out of bed, sneezed thunderously, and thrust myself into the most convenient clothing. By force of habit I stopped into the mail-jail on the way out of the dormitory complex. Another official envelope had been jammed against the rectangular glass window. "Clive, baby," I said and tugged out the enclosed letter with great curiosity.

Mr. Dunstan,

Once again the morning has been disrupted by a visit from one of your Professors. Your position here at Middlemount is in grave peril.

Professor Roger Flagship demanded that I inspect the three blue books which you submitted to him upon conclusion of the final examination in Introductory Calculus. Professor Flagship informed me the examination was of the multiple-choice variety and that blue books were to be used for computation. He further informed me that he intended to take the steps necessary to effect your expulsion from Middlemount College. Not only had you failed the exam by correctly answering only twelve out of one hundred questions, you had subjected both his course and himself to mockery. Professor Flagship drew my attention to several obscene caricatures of himself contained within the blue books.

Furthermore, Professor Flagship states that on the evening of the examination you appeared in his office to beg for the return of your blue books, a grade of Incomplete in Introductory Calculus, and an opportunity to repeat the course. Following his refusal of these extraordinary requests, you responded to his efforts to secure the blue books, which he had as yet not read, by pushing him back into his chair and then fleeing. He attributed your behavior to hysterical panic and chose not to bring it to my attention. The contents of the blue books decided him otherwise.

After thoughtful consideration, also after factoring in the other matters before us, I ask you to report to our January 20 meeting at the originally designated time of 7:30 A.M. with any records, along with evidence of previous psychiatric treatment, which might assist me in protecting your position here at Middlemount College.

To facilitate the search for your records, I am sending a copy of this letter to your guardians, Mr. and Mrs. Philip Grant of Naperville, Illinois.

Sincerely yours,
Clive Macanudo
Dean of Student Affairs

I blew my nose on Clive's letter and pitched it into the waste-basket, more disturbed by his sending it to the Grants than by my imminent expulsion. Phil and Laura would understand that what I was doing was vastly more important than the pablum dished out in my classes.

On my way back to the center of the universe I thought I caught a glimpse of a green loden coat and a flash of bright hair in the midst of the row of trees bordering the western end of the campus. The lovesick stalker vanished the instant I looked again, and I put him out of my mind.

After an hour's silent meditation had permitted me to hear the music in the air, after another hour of adding my part to it, a gathering sense of being as yet not absolutely in *the right place* caused me to get back on my feet and move deeper into the woods until I came upon the ruins of a cottage. I creaked open the door and beheld the rotted wooden walls, the single broken window, the litter of feathers, tiny skeletons, and dried animal feces on the dirty floor, and knew that here it was at last, *the right place*. It, too, was an instrument. Steady music flowed through the cottage, produced by the wind hissing through the gaps in the timbers and the patter of squirrels in the crawl space overhead. I enjoyed a blissful hour of adding a modest accompaniment and, just before dark, ran to my room for blankets and provisions and hurried back while I still had light enough to see.

The cottage emerged from the surrounding darkness like a tall shadow in the sacred woods. Faint strains of the music within called to me, and I rushed over the snow and opened the creaking door. When I entered, I seemed instantly to plummet through the rotting floor. I fell; I saw nothing; I did not fear. A long, shabby, once-handsome room took shape before me. Out of my range of vision, a man spoke of smoke and gold and corpses on a battlefield. My head pounded, and my stomach was afflicted. On the mantel over the fireplace stood a dying Boston fern, a stuffed fox advancing within a glass bell, and a brass clock with weights revolving left-right, right-left, left-right. This was *backward*, it was *past*, and I had been here before. I fell to my knees on the worn Oriental carpet. Before I vomited, the world melted and restored itself, and the contents of my stomach drizzled onto the ruined floor. *Home,* I thought.

■ 11

■ While still presentable enough to go into town, I stocked up on canned food and camping equipment. I got a sleeping bag and a battery-powered lamp. After I realized that I could make use of the fireplace, I bought bags of charcoal briquettes, a hatchet, lots of fire starter, a grate, and packages of frozen meat I buried in the snow and thawed out over flames coaxed from lumps of charcoal and chopped-up deadwood. Some nights, raccoons climbed through gaps in the flooring and fell asleep like dogs in front of the dwindling fire. Toward the end of my forty-five days in the cottage, when going into town would have invited arrest or hospitalization, I dropped into my old meal-job kitchen late at night and stole whatever I couldn't gobble on the spot. Forest-music, nature-music, planet-music took up the rest of my time. My cold turned into pneumonia, and I took the fevers, sweats, and exhaustion for signs of grace.

Everyone else feared that the loss of my scholarship had driven me to suicide. Phil and Laura flew to Middlemount and participated in the search for my hypothetical remains. A livid Clark Darkmund declared that not only had he not invited me on a family vacation to Barbados, his winter break had been spent entirely in Hibbing, Minnesota. The police searched the college grounds, with no result. The town of Middlemount was canvassed, with next to no result. The winsome senior photo in my high school yearbook reminded one Main Street shop owner of a recent customer, but he had no idea of where the customer might have gone after leaving the store. After stapling posters all over town and campus, the Grants returned to Naperville.

Horst never bothered to look at the posters. He assumed that I had been ducking him. When he did finally happen to notice the resemblance between the photograph and myself, he reported to Dean Macanudo. Within the hour, he was leading a deputation of local police and emergency medical technicians into Jones's Woods. They found me slumped over my warped guitar and picking at its two remaining strings, and unceremoniously rolled me onto a stretcher.

Seeing a dream-Horst peering down at me from within the upturned collar of his loden coat, I asked, "Why do I think you're following me, Horst?"

"You told me to watch out for you," said the figment.

I looked around at the crumbling walls and the mess of blankets on the floor in an unwelcome return of sanity. It had all been a gigantic error. Horst was real after all, and I had been wrong. This had never been the right place for which I had mistaken it.

The first person to visit me in Middlemount's Tri-Community Hospital was Dean Clive Macanudo, a glossy diplomat whose pencil mustache and Sen-Sen breath could not entirely conceal his terror of any actions I or my guardians might see fit to take against the college. It never occurred to me to sue Middlemount, nor did it occur to Laura, who walked into my room on the second day of my hospitalization. Phil had been denied permission to leave work, or so she said, and although his absence meant that we could speak more freely, the weight of my guilt made her stricken presence a torment. Two days later, Laura went back to the Middlemount Inn for a nap, and I checked out of the hospital, went into the middle of town, passed the inn, turned into the bus station, and vamoosed.

From then on, I kept moving. I had jobs in grocery stores, in bars and shoe stores, jobs where I strapped on headsets and tried to persuade strangers to buy things they didn't need. I lived in

Chapel Hill, Gainesville, Boulder, Madison, Beaverton, Sequim, Evanston, and little towns you wouldn't know unless you were from Wisconsin or Ohio. (Rice Lake, anyone? Azure?) I spent about a year in Chicago, but never went to either Edgerton or Naperville. After I'd been living at the same address long enough to get a telephone listing, Star surprised me a couple of times by phoning me or sending a card. Three or four times a year, I called the Grants and tried to convince them that my life had not dwindled into failure. In 1984, Phil, a lifelong non-smoker, died of lung cancer. I went to his funeral and spent a couple of days in my old room, staying up late and talking with Laura. She seemed more beautiful than ever before. Sometimes we clung together and wept for everything that could not be undone. Two years later, Laura told me that she was remarrying and moving to Hawaii. Her new husband was a retired lawyer with a lot of land on Maui.

■ Every now and again, a stranger would approach me and back away in embarrassment or annoyance at my failure to give acknowledgment; some version of this happens to almost everybody. In the Omaha Greyhound bus terminal, a woman of about thirty recoiled from the sight of me, grabbed the arm of the man next to her, and pulled him through a departure gate. Two years later, an older woman in a fur coat strode up to me in the Denver airport and slapped my face hard enough to raise a welt that showed the stitching on her glove. On a street corner in Chicago's Loop, someone gripped my collar and jerked me out of the path of a hurtling taxicab, and when I looked around, a kid in a stocking cap said, "Man, your brother, he took *off*." Fine. Another time in another year, a guy next to me in a bar, I don't even remember where, told me that my name was George Peters and that I had been his history T.A. at Tulane.

Sometimes I think that everyone I've ever known has had the feeling of missing a mysterious but essential quality, that they all wanted to find an unfindable place that would be *the right place*, and that since Adam in the Garden human life has been made of these aches and bruises. Just before I turned twenty-six, I got a job in telephone sales for an infant software company in Durham, North Carolina, and did well enough to get promoted into a job where I more or less had to enroll in a programming course at UNC. Not long after, the company made me a full-time programmer.

In all of my wandering I stayed clear of New York. I thought the Apple would slam me to the pavement and squash me flat. Three years after I took the programming job, the software company relocated to New Brunswick, New Jersey. For the first time in my life I had a little money in the bank, and once I got to New Brunswick, New York started flashing and gleaming in the distance, beckoning me to the party. Two or three nights every month, I took the train to the city and stopped in at restaurants and jazz clubs. I went to a Beethoven piano recital by Alfred Brendel at Avery Fisher Hall and Robert Shaw's *Missa Solemnis* at Carnegie Hall. I heard B. B. King and Phil Woods and one of Ella Fitzgerald's last concerts. Eventually I started calling a few software outfits in New York, and two years after moving to New Jersey I got a better job, packed up, and went to the party.

I had an apartment across from St. Mark's Church on East Tenth Street and a decent job, and I was happier than ever before in my life. The right place turned out to be the one I'd been most afraid of all along, which sounded about right. On my birthdays, I called in sick and stayed in bed. And then, in the midst of my orderly life, I started getting this feeling about my mother.

■ 12

■ It began as a kind of foreboding. A few months after moving to New York, I telephoned Aunt Nettie to ask if she had heard anything from Star. No, she said, how about you? I told her I'd been worried and gave her my number. "That girl, she's made out of iron," Nettie said. "Instead of fretting about your mother, you ought to worry about yourself for a change."

I told myself that Nettie would call me if anything serious happened. Nettie loved disaster, she would sound any necessary alarm. But what if Star had not alerted her? I called Aunt Nettie again. She told me that my mother was in East Cicero, "whoopin' it up," she said, "with two old rascals." I asked her for Star's telephone number, but Nettie had lost it and could not remember the names of the two old rascals. They owned a nightclub, but she couldn't remember its name, either.

"It's no difference," she said. "Star is going to let us know if she needs help, and if anything happens to us, she won't have to be told to get here as fast as she can. She'll just know. A streak of second sight runs through the Dunstans, and Star has her share. You do, too, I think."

"Second sight?" I asked. "That's news to me."

"You don't know beans about your own family, that's why. They say no one would play cards with my father because he could see what they had in their hands."

"You don't really believe that," I said.

She gave a soft, knowing laugh. "You'd be surprised at some of the things I believe."

One night I dreamed that I crawled into my mother's bed on Cherry Street and heard her mutter a name or word that sounded like "Rinehart." Part of the dream's experience was the awareness that I was dreaming, and part of my awareness was of replaying a moment from childhood. My worries subsided again, though the underlying anxiety surfaced when I was alone in my apartment, especially if I was doing something that reminded me of her, like washing the dishes or listening to Billie Holiday on WBGO. At the start of the third week in May, I asked for all my accumulated sick leave on the grounds of a family emergency. My boss told me to take as much time as I needed and keep in touch. I started shoving things into my duffel bag as soon as I got home.

I didn't think I was going anywhere in particular. It never occurred to me that under the pressure of anxiety, I was reverting to my old, self-protective pattern. At the same time, as I said before, I knew exactly where I was going and why. At the moment Star was boarding the Greyhound, I was in the cab of a Nationwide Paper sixteen-wheeler bound for Flagstaff, enjoyably discussing the condition of African Americans in the United States with its driver, Mr. Bob Mims, and my defenses collapsed and the truth rushed in. Star had used the last of her strength to get herself home, and I was going there to be with her when she died. Once Bob Mims found out why I wanted to get to Edgerton, he veered from his normal route to take me to the Motel Comfort south of Chicago on the interstate.

After an hour of waving my thumb at the side of the highway, I checked in to the motel. All the car-rental agencies were closed for the night. I went to the bar and started talking to a young assistant D.A. from Louisville named Ashleigh Ashton who was on maybe her second sea breeze. When she spelled her name and asked if I thought it was (a) pretentious and (b) too cute for a prosecutor, the drink in front of her seemed more likely to have been her third. If she didn't like the way defendants grinned when they heard her name, I said, she should grin back and put 'em away. That was a pretty good idea, she said, would I like to hear another one?

Whoops, I thought, three for sure, and said, "I have to get out of here pretty early."

"I do, too. Let's leave. If I stay here any longer, one of these guys is going to jump me."

Sitting at the bar were two heavyweights with graying beards and biker jackets, a kid in a T-shirt reading MO' BEER HERE, a couple of guys with chains around their necks and tattoos peeping out from under their short-sleeved sport shirts, and a specter in a cheap gray suit who looked like a serial killer taking a break from his life's work. All of them were eyeing her like starving dogs.

I walked her through what seemed a half mile of empty corridors. She gave me a quizzical, questioning look when she unlocked her door, and I followed her in. She said, "What's your story anyhow, Ned Dunstan? I hate to bring it up, but your clothes look like you've been hitchhiking."

I gave her a short-form answer that implied that I had learned of my mother's illness while hitchhiking for pleasure on a whim. "It was something I used to do when I was a kid," I said. "I should have known better. If I had a car, I could get to Edgerton tonight."

"Edgerton? That's where I'm going!" Suspicion rose into her eyes for a moment, and then she realized that I could not have known of her destination until she announced it. "If we're still speaking to each other tomorrow morning, I could give you a ride."

"Why wouldn't we be speaking to each other?"

"*I* don't know." She raised her arms and looked wildly from side to side in only half a parody of extremity. "Don't guys hate the idea of waking up beside someone they don't know? Or get disgusted with themselves, because they think the woman's cheap? It's a mystery to me. I haven't had sex in a year. Thirteen months, to be exact."

Ashleigh Ashton was a small, athletic-looking woman with short, shiny-blond hair and the face of a model for Windfoil parkas in an Eddie Bauer catalog. She had spent years proving to the men who took her for a cupcake that she was capable, smart, and tough.

"Why is that?" I asked.

"The charming process of getting divorced from my husband, I suppose. I found out he was screwing half his female clients." An ironic light shone in her eye. "Guess what kind of practice he had."

"Divorce law."

She pressed her palm to her forehead. "Ashleigh, you're a cliché! Anyhow, I asked you those questions because I'm thinking about going back to my maiden name. Turner. Ashleigh Turner."

"Good idea," I said. Her divorce was probably no more than a week old. "The bad boys won't smirk at you. But if you weren't looking to get picked up, why did you go to the bar?"

"I thought I was waiting for you." She glanced away, and the corner of her mouth curled up. "Sal and Jimmy asked me on a tour of their favorite Sinatra bars. The kid in the beer shirt, Ray, invited me into his room to do coke. He has a *lot* of coke with him, and he's on his way to Florida. Isn't that the wrong way around? Don't people go to Florida to get the stuff and bring it back here? Those bikers, Ernie and Choke, wanted. . . . Forget what they wanted, but it sure would have been adventurous."

"If Ray wants to make it to Florida, he better not hustle Ernie and Choke," I said.

She snickered, then looked chagrined. "I'm in this stupid mood."

"Did your divorce just come through?"

This time, she pressed both hands over her eyes. "Okay, you're perceptive." She lowered her arms and turned in a complete circle. "I knew that, I really did."

She sat on the edge of the bed and took off her nice lady-lawyer shoes. "The other reason I'm in a funny mood is that I can see my case going down the drain. Now that I'm being indiscreet, you've probably heard of the guy we're after. He's one of Edgerton's leading citizens."

"Probably not," I said. "I left when I was a kid."

"His name is Stewart Hatch. Tons of money. His family sort of runs Edgerton, from what I hear."

"We didn't move in those circles."

"You should be grateful, but I'll never understand why a guy with so much going for him would decide to turn into a crook." She efficiently buttoned herself out of her pin-striped suit.

About a quarter to six in the morning, I jumped out of bed before I was fully awake. Nettie's sixth sense was operating at full strength. The only thought in my head was that whatever was going to happen to my mother was rushing toward her, it was *already on the way*, and I had to get to Edgerton in a hurry. Still foggy, I fumbled around for my clothes and saw a naked woman on the disarranged sheets. One of her legs was drawn up, as if in midstride. Her name came back to me, and I put a hand on her shoulder. "Ashleigh, wake up, it's time to go."

She opened an eye. "Huh?"

"It's almost six. Something's happening, and I have to get to Edgerton, fast."

"Oh, yeah. Edgerton." She opened the other eye. "Goo' morning."

"I'm going to take the world's fastest shower, change clothes, and check out. Should I come back here to get you?"

"Get me?" She smiled.

"You're still willing to give me a ride?"

She rolled onto her back and stretched her arms. "Meet me outside. I'm sorry you had bad news."

A speedy shower and shave; a scramble into clean khakis, a blue button-down shirt, a lightweight blue blazer, loafers. I was going to see all my relatives, and for Star's sake as well as my own, I wanted to look respectable.

Hoping she would not make me wait more than twenty minutes, I carried my duffel and knapsack through the revolving door into the cool morning light and heard a female voice call my name. Across the parking lot, Ashleigh stood beside the open trunk of a blaze-red little car. She was wearing a trim navy blue suit that showed off her legs, and she looked as if she'd had maybe twice the time most people need to look the way she did.

"Slowpoke," she said.

She sailed down the nearly empty highway at a comfortable sixty-five, fiddling with the radio and letting the occasional trucker blast on by. Neither one of us knew quite what to say to each other. She found a university FM station playing a mixture of hard bop and Chicago blues and let the digital counter stay where it was. "Did you call the hospital before you woke me up?"

I said that I had not.

"But you told me something happened to your mother. You didn't get a call in my room, did you? I mean, I don't really care, but . . ."

But if you didn't tell them you were in my room, how did they find you?

"I guess I had a premonition." She shot me a sidelong look. "Maybe it was just anxiety. I don't know. I wish I could explain it better."

She glanced at me again. "I hope she'll be all right."

"I'm just glad you were there."

"Well, I am, too," she said. "I think you should probably go around the country giving hope to depressed women. And you were so tactful, you never made anything seem prearranged."

"Prearranged?"

"Maybe not prearranged, but you know, from Chicago, with my law school friend, Mandy."

A sign announcing the approach of a highway restaurant and gas station floated toward us. I said, "Why don't we pull in there and get something to eat?"

The story emerged over breakfast. In the bar of a Chicago hotel, Mandy, the law school friend, had sent me a drink. When I left my chair to thank them, Mandy invited me to sit down. The conversation led to our various reasons for being in that hotel lobby on that particular evening, and I had mentioned that I was going to the southern part of the state late the next day and would probably spend the following night in another hotel. To Mandy's chagrin, I had seemed more interested in Ashleigh Ashton than herself. Mandy knew that after working into the evening of the following day, Ashleigh would be driving south. She whisked her off to the bathroom and imparted worldly advice. Not long after, Ashleigh had inserted the Motel Comfort into our conversation, and I had expressed the hope of returning the favor and buying her a drink in whatever passed for a bar in the place if I wound up there, too.

"I told Mandy you'd never show up, but she said, Go to the bar an hour or two after you check in, and he'll find you. I wasn't even sure it was you! In Chicago, you were wearing a suit, and here you had on jeans, but the more I looked at you, it *was* you. And you were so tactful, it was like you would have come anyhow, not just to meet me."

"I didn't think you needed any more pressure," I said.

Apparently someone who looked a lot like me, a former Tulane teaching assistant named George Peters or the man for whom the woman in the old Denver airport had mistaken me, had been cruising the lobby of a Chicago hotel. No other rational explanation seemed possible. At the same time, the sheer unlikeliness of the coincidence prickled the hairs at the nape of my neck. If George Peters, or whatever his name was, had succeeded in setting up an assignation with Ashleigh, what had kept him from it?

For the rest of the drive, a caffeine-enhanced Ashleigh maintained a steady sixty-five miles per hour while describing the misdeeds of her scoundrel millionaire. I made accommodating noises and pretended to listen.

The sign at the first of the Edgerton exits read EDGERTON ELLENDALE. "Is this it?" she asked.

"The next one," I said.

At the next sign, EDGERTON CENTER, she spun the little car off the highway. For a time we drove past hilly fields on a divided four-lane road and then, without transition, found ourselves in the wasteland of fast-food outlets, gas stations, motels, and strip malls at the fringes of most American cities. At the moment we passed a billboard welcoming us to EDGERTON, THE CITY WITH A HEART OF GOLD, the mild, sunlit air shimmered into a wavering veil like a heat mirage, then cleared again.

"I have time to take you to the hospital, if that's where you want to go," she said.

A stoplight turned red at an intersection bordered by two three-story red brick office buildings, a vacant lot, and a bar called The Nowhere Lounge. Below the street sign, a rectangular

green placard pointed the way to St. Ann's Community Hospital. "I think that's the place," I said.

Four blocks later, she pulled up before the hospital entrance. I said, "Ashleigh . . ."

"Don't. You won't have time to see me. I hope your mother gets better. If you were going to ask where I'm staying, it's Merchants Hotel, wherever that is."

She stayed in the car while I took my bags from the trunk. I came up to kiss her goodbye.

At the information desk, a woman told me that there was no patient named Star Dunstan, but that Valerie Dunstan was in intensive care. She gave me a green plastic visitor's card and told me to make a right past the coffee shop, take the elevator to the third floor, and follow the signs.

Numb with dread, I wandered through dingy hospital corridors until a nurse led me to a set of swinging doors and a plaque reading INTENSIVE CARE UNIT. I obeyed a sign hung over a basin and washed my hands, then pushed open another swinging door and carried my bags into a long, dimly lighted chamber lined with curtained-off cubicles around a brighter central station. From the counter in front of me, a nurse gave me the once-over a store detective aims at a potential shoplifter. Far down the length of the room Aunt Nettie and Aunt May were standing in front of one of the cubicles. They were heavier than I remembered them, and their hair had turned a pure, ethereal white.

The nurse rolled her chair a half inch nearer the counter and asked, "May I help you?" An instantaneous, nonverbal exchange made it clear that I was not going to take another step until her authority had been acknowledged. The name tag pinned to her loose green staff shirt read L. ZWICK, R.N.

"Dunstan," I said. "Star Dunstan. Sorry, Valerie."

The nurse bent her head to examine a clipboard. "Fifteen."

Nettie was already surging toward me.

■ O Great Beings and Inhuman Ancestors!

Only days before the prison walls of the academy's eighth grade were to close around me, I came to a break in the woods and an overgrown field extending toward a road I did not know. On both sides of the field, the woods swept toward the road. Between the top of the field and the curve of the woods was a three-fourths-crumbled building of brick and stone. In a rubble of stone blocks at its center, the monolith of a fireplace reared into the air. At its far end, another chimney and a fire-blackened wall supported the remnants of a shingled roof extending over the remaining portion of the house. Beyond, bare joists dangled above empty space. The instant I beheld these remains, the hook in my entrails nearly yanked me off my feet, and a voice from within or without boomed, *Come at last!* Something like that. It might've been, *You are here!* Anyhow, the mighty voice informed me that we were getting down to brass tacks.

I knew it was my duty to take a survey of my property, so to speak, before rushing in to stake claim, and I processed around the perimeter of the ruin, observing how weeds had thrust themselves up between the stones, how the fire had charred the scattered bricks to the shade of overdone toast, how swales in the earth marked the former cellars. I saw destruction continuing in the pull of gravity on rotting beams and the erosion of roof tiles. At the front of the building, roof-high courses of joined stone extended some twenty feet from the fireplace wall. Rectangular casings with deep sills marked the third- and second-story windows. Beneath them, at roughly the level of my chin, smooth, arched casements speckled with bird dung gazed out from what had been the parlor. I placed my trembling hands on a gritty sill and looked within.

Light streamed into a two-sided enclosure three stories high. Dusty particles filtered down to a cement floor littered with plaster, broken pipes, and charred timbers. Here and there, grass struggled up through cracks in the cement. Paw prints dotted the thick, feather-strewn dust. On the other side stood the forest. I jumped, grabbed the far side of the sill with both hands, and squirmed forward until I could get my legs onto the flat stone. Then I lowered myself to the floor and entered my inheritance for the first time.

■ Or: my inheritance entered me.

■ You who read the words I here inscribe upon the pages of a Boorum & Pease record book or journal with the same dependable Mont Blanc fountain pen used in former days to draft my instructional missives to the world already know the significance of the ruined house to Your Great Race. It was within its sacred enclosure that the Great Old Ones imbued my early torments and humiliations with the salvific Splendor of Preparation. An Elder God spoke, and I learned All. His Voice was low, husky, confiding, weary with age-old authority, yet powerful, commanding. I heard some pleasure in there, too, for my Unearthly Father, whose True Identity I still knew not, was giving me the lowdown on the Mighty Task for which I had been placed upon this Earth. My Role came clear, my Nature given Explanation. Half-human, half-God, I was the Opener of the Way, and my Task was Annihilation. After me, the Apocalypse, the entry through a riven sky of my leathery, winged, beclawed, ravenous Ancestors the Elder Gods, the Destruction of mankind, Your long-awaited repossession of the earthly realm. I advanced through the rubble, added my rump's outline to the footprints of passing animals and was *spoken to.* By reason of my own frailty I should be cursed in time with a traitorous shadow *it was my responsibility to eliminate.* (In the surprisingly congenial surroundings of the Fortress Military Academy, Owlsburg, PA, I was to hear more of this.) You Great Ones, my Fathers, *depended upon my efforts.* The mighty Voice said, *We are the smoke from the cannon's mouth.* I loved that phrase, it spoke to me of that inexorable devastation Given as my Sacred Task. I repeat it to myself, talismanically: *We are the smoke from the cannon's mouth.* These words sustain me. I was told that my only significant pleasures should be found *in the accomplishment of my Task.* On the other hand, insignificant pleasures, precisely those of a sort most appealing to a lad like myself, would not be denied. In the midst of the *endless sorrow*, a great deal of fun was in the offing.

I could certainly have gotten away scot-free if I had killed Maureen Orth, which was what I had in mind for her once I got the sex part out of the way. The only reason I ran into trouble was that she got home. Her sense of humor went south about a minute after I tied her up. I wasn't going to kill her in the *woods*, I was going to kill her in the *ruins*.

I wanted to see Maureen's close-set eyes fly open when I looked at some visiting pigeon, stopped its heart, and tumbled it stone-cold dead from its perch. I wished to add to the effect by announcing my intention of floating eight inches off the ground and lingering there for a count of, say, ten, even though the effort would have brought sweat cascading from every pore of my body. I depended on the lassie to declare, That's a fib, nobody can do that. Then I wanted to see the expression on her homely mug when I proved her wrong. I looked forward to dazzling my pathetic sweetie with a few other tricks, too, before I killed her.

In the meantime, I couldn't help myself, I was impulsive, I know, a number of insecure maidens had accompanied me into the woods to end their pointless lives on the floor of my classroom. I did go to the trouble of interring most of the bodies, but I might as well have let them rot. The search parties never came near the ruins. In any case, I had outgrown this sort of exhibitionism by the time I was thrown out of the academy.

14 ■ Mr.X

■ In essence, boarding schools are all the same, especially to those who are as smoke from the cannon's mouth and wind up getting expelled from one tweedy snakepit after another. Actual military school, in my case good old Fortress, of Owlsburg, Pennsylvania, to which my father sent me in a last convulsion of disgust, suited me far better than its civilian imitations. My father had informed me that failure at this last resort would derail the gravy train—no more monthly deposits into my account, no inheritance, no trust fund, finis—thereby compelling me to work at least hard enough to pass the courses. I rather liked my uniform's chill, fascist pomp. Because I entered in the senior, or Cavalry, year, one of my duties was to bully the students beneath me, those in Artillery, Quartermaster, and especially Infantry, which was packed like sardines with doe-eyed fourteen-year-olds in a desperate sweat to please their overlords. We were *supposed to* reduce these children to whimpering blobs of panic, and they had to take it without protest or complaint.

I spent one of the happiest years of my young life in that place. As soon as I understood the deal, I drove out my roommate, a prep-school expellee like myself named Squiers whose babble had exhausted my patience before the end of our first day together. Thereafter, in my palatial single I was free to do as I wished. I did not at all mind the necessity, due to my parents' refusal to have me come home, of spending the Thanksgiving vacation and Christmas break at school.

The only sign of impending difficulty occurred early in March, when my calculus instructor and unit commander, Captain Todd Squadron, drew me aside to announce that he would be visiting my quarters at 2100 hours that evening. I found this news alarming. Captain Squadron, a by-the-book regular army type whom I had bluffed into admiration from the day of my arrival, lately had grown cooler, almost dismissive. I feared that he had seen through my performance. I hoped that he had not discussed my "case" with an all-seeing dreadnought named Major Audrey Arndt, whom I had taken considerable pains to avoid. One other possibility was an even greater worry. After his arrival in my room, I discovered that both of these matters, the not so serious and the positively grave, were on his mind.

I saluted and stood at attention. Captain Squadron growled, "At ease," and gestured me to my cot. His oddly wary, knowing attitude was laced with the dismissiveness I had lately sensed in him. When I had perched on the cot, Squadron leaned against my dresser and gazed down at me for a long moment transparently intended to unnerve.

"What is it with you, anyhow, Pledge?"

I asked what he meant.

"You're different, aren't you?"

"I hope I might take that as a compliment, sir."

"There's an example of what I mean, right there. After the Infantry intake, most transfers are foul balls." He pulled at his uniform jacket, automatically aligning it with his trousers. "They got bounced out of so many schools their parents just want to keep them in line. Even though most of them aren't too swift, they all think they're smarter than we are. Every last one has a big, big problem with authority."

"Not me, sir," I said. "I respect authority."

He gave me a sullen glare. "I cordially suggest that you stop jukin' with me, Pledge."

We were all pledges, no matter what class we were in. I considered saying "Sir, the pledge is not familiar with the term 'jukin' with,' sir," but kept my mouth shut.

"It falls to us to straighten up these sorry-ass rebels as best we can. As a general rule, we have about a sixty-forty chance if we get them in their second year. If they come into Artillery, it's less than fifty-fifty we can pound some sense into their heads. By Cavalry, it's a lost cause. All we do is, we concentrate on teaching them to stand up straight and how to tell their right foot from the left one so they can manage the drills, and we push them through the course work until they graduate and get the hell out." He folded at the waist like a puppet, tightened his shoelaces, and snapped upright again. "If it was up to me, we'd refuse to transfer students into Cavalry. Eighteen is too old to adapt to our way of life."

He turned to face the mirror over my dresser and gave the jacket another series of precise tugs. He lifted his chin and examined the effect. "The little clowns come in laughing, and I have to waste a hellacious amount of time convincing them with all the means at my disposal, which are many, that we are not to be sneered at." He caught my eyes in the mirror. "I believe I can claim a one hundred percent success rate at carrying out that particular mission. Maybe those feebs were a long way from being soldiers when they walked through the gate for the last time, but I guarantee you this much, they were believers." He was still holding my eyes.

"I became a believer as soon as I got here," I said. "Sir."

Squadron turned around and leaned against the dresser without bending. His wide, blunt face was distorted by a broken nose that would have made him look like a fighter had it not been the size of the nose on a shrunken head. "I'll give you this much, you had me fooled."

"Sir?"

"You had me thinking, this pledge is going to change your mind about admissions policy, Captain. In a couple of days, he snaps off a salute could shatter a brick. Trims his uniform like a West Point grad. In a week, memorized the Reg Book and *Lore and Traditions*. Respectful and well prepared in class. Okay, he had a little problem with his roommate, but these things happen. Fact is, Pledge Squiers is an unrelenting motormouth who should have been paired with a deaf-mute. This new pledge fit in from the moment his shoe leather hit Pershing Quad and is a fine asset to his class. Look at the way he braces those squirts in Infantry! He's a goddamned natural! You know what that young man is?" He pushed himself off the dresser, raised his arms at his sides and gazed upward. "That young man is officer material!"

"I do my best," I said.

Captain Squadron canted backward against the dresser and pushed his hands into his pockets. In the mirror, the clean line of a fresh haircut curved above the starched collar of his tan shirt. The dark stubble on his head and his tiny, dented nose made him look like a gas station attendant. "You're a real piece of work, aren't you?" He smiled exactly as if he had just decided to punch someone in the face.

"I don't follow you, sir," I said.

"How many friends have you made here? Who are your pals, your asshole buddies?"

I named three or four dullards in my class.

"When was the last time you and one or more of your buddies took the bus into town, caught a movie, had a few burgers, that kind of thing?"

The question meant that he already knew the answer. When we left the grounds we had to sign out in groups. I had taken the bus into Owlsburg once, looked around at the dreary streets, and returned immediately. "I tend to devote my weekends to study."

He rocked back and smiled again. "I'm inclined to think that you have no friends and zero interest in making any. Didn't go home for Thanksgiving, did we? Or over Christmas break."

"You know I didn't, sir," I said, beginning to get irritated with the captain's theatrics.

"Christmas is a major, major holiday. It's a rare pledge who doesn't get home for Christmas."

"I explained that," I said. "My folks invited me to go to Barbados with them, but I wanted to spend the vacation studying for the finals."

He grinned like a wolf. "Should we go down the hall and call your parents, ask them a few questions?"

Again, he already knew the truth. Squadron had checked on my story. "Okay," I said, cursing myself for having succumbed to the temptation of a colorful lie. "If I got along with my family, would I be here in the first place? It isn't easy to say that your parents hate you so much they won't even let you come for Christmas!"

"Why would they hate their own kid like that?"

"We had misunderstandings," I said.

He looked up at the ceiling. "I was so impressed by your conduct that I started to wonder why a young man like yourself had been asked to leave all those boarding schools. Five of them, to be exact. Didn't mesh with what I was seeing. So I looked into your files." He smiled at me with his smug challenge. "Damned if I could find anything there but smoke."

"Smoke, sir?"

"Evasions. 'Bad influence on the school.' 'Antagonistic behavior.' 'Considered threatening.' None of these dildos was willing to get down to the nitty-gritty. You know what that told me?"

"I'm sorry to admit it, but I probably acted like a bully," I said.

He pretended not to have heard. "Two things. Put on record, your infractions would bar you from admission anywhere except the state pen. But they couldn't pin anything on you, so they took the easy way out and passed you along."

"I don't think—"

He held up a hand like a stop sign. "So far this year, six pledges in Infantry have washed out voluntarily. Normally, it'd be two at most. Over at the infirmary? A rash of broken bones. Once or twice in a normal year, a pledge breaks an arm. Now, they're coming in once a week with broken fingers, broken wrists, broken arms. Concussion. One boy turned out to have internal bleeding from a ruptured spleen. How'd he get it? 'I twisted my ankle and fell down the stairs.' And then there's the case of Artillery Pledge Fletcher. You knew him, didn't you?"

"After a fashion," I said, meaning that I had known Artillery Pledge Fletcher in a most specific fashion. This was the serious matter I had hoped Captain Squadron would not bring up. An unassuming, scholarly-looking boy with round, horn-rimmed glasses and a rosebud face, Fletcher had forever enriched my life through an ultimately fatal act of courtesy.

■ On the Thursday of the week given over to the examinations before the Christmas break, I had seen him immersed in a book at a long table in the library. The pledges on both sides were also reading books from stacks piled in front of them, and it was not until the second time I looked at them that I noticed what was different about Fletcher. The others were taking notes on the contents of volumes of military history, but Fletcher was perusing, apparently for his own entertainment, a brightly jacketed work of fiction. Moved by an instinct I did not as yet comprehend, I walked past the table and saw that the title of the book was *The Dunwich Horror.* The combination of the title and the lurid cover illustration instantly struck me with a lesser version of that force which had first drawn me into Johnson's Woods. I had to have that book. That book was *mine.* For an hour, I twitched in my seat, taking desultory notes and keeping an eye on Fletcher.

When he stood up, I collected my things and rushed alongside him. Yes, he said, he would be happy to loan me the book after he had finished reading it. He surrendered it for inspection with the comment that it was "really spooky." Fletcher had no idea of the accuracy of his description. Emitting a series of pulsations, the little tract shivered in my hands. It was like gripping a hummingbird.

During the following day, roughly half the pledges, those finished with exams, left campus in wave upon wave of family cars. Fletcher's last final, chemistry, took place on Saturday at the same hour as mine, military philosophy. However, Fletcher assumed that I had already left school, and at five-thirty on Friday afternoon, while on his way to Mess Hall, entered my room without pausing to knock. He found me in, so to speak.

Until my delivery into Fortress Military Academy, the struggles to continue my real education had been largely unrewarded. I needed privacy, and even when I managed to secure a safely uninterrupted hour or two, my efforts had advanced me little beyond what I had already attained. Now I see that weary lull largely as a matter of physical maturation. A developmental spurt had added two inches and twenty pounds to my frame before my admission to the world of close-order drills, and by the time Pledge Fletcher charged in with the sacred book, I was making my first baby steps toward Moveless Movement, whatever it's called, disappearing from one place and turning up in another.

As ever, a paradox is involved, namely that until it becomes second nature the muscular capacity demanded by this stunt gets in the way of doing it. By Christmas break of that year I had succeeded in shifting myself across the four feet from the edge of my cot to my desk chair by means of a sweaty interlude during which I was neither in one place or the other but in both, imperfectly. Whatever that looked like while it was happening is what Fletcher saw when he barged into my room. I can't even guess. My bowels churned, and someone was driving a railroad spike into my head. What I was able to see in the midst of the clamor increased my distress. Two uniformed pledges charged in through two different doors. A swarm of glittering light and my considerable physical distress rendered the invader or invaders visible only in silhouette form as he or they abruptly ceased to move.

From the cot, I saw one of them freeze in front of the open door. From the slightly clearer, closer perspective of the chair, I saw a uniformed torso and waist come to rest beside the door's dark green panel. From both positions I observed the bright dust jacket of the book in my visitor's hand, and both the me on the cot and the me in the chair experienced a surge of demand. Our attempt at an order commanding the pledge to stay put produced the sibilant hiss of a needle striking the grooves of a 78-rpm record. The pledge couldn't have moved if he had wanted to—the kid was glued to the floor.

An endless second later, I was seated beside the immobilized Artillery Pledge Fletcher as glowing sparks fell and died in the air, especially around the end of the cot. I was stark naked and, despite the red-hot agony in my head and the tumult in my guts, brandished the sort of obdurate erection known at Fortress as "blue steel." Artillery Pledge Fletcher's mouth hung open, and his eyes were glazed. He stared at me, then at the place where I had been. A smell like that of burning circuitry hung in the room. I bent forward and closed the door with my fingertips.

Artillery Pledge Fletcher moved his vacant gaze to me, to the cot, then back to me. "Uhhh . . ." He recalled why he had come to my room. His trembling hand proffered the book. "I thought . . . I wanted to . . ." Pledge Fletcher's eyes landed on my erection.

I slid the book from his fingers. My groin expanded into what from the standpoint of envious old age I must call remarkable dimensions.

Fletcher kept his eyes on the prize. "Well. I don't. . . . That is, I didn't . . ." His gaze snapped up to meet mine. "Aaah, when I came in I couldn't really see what was going on. Probably I got dizzy. It's sort of hot in here." He looked down again. "Hey, keep the book. I have to get to mess."

"No, you don't," I said.

He backed toward the door. I put the book on my desk, stood up, grasped his upper arms, and moved him sideways.

"Oh, Christ," he said. "Look, I'll get a late-for-mess tick, but if you want a Mary, I'll give you one."

A "tick" was a demerit, and "Mary" meant a "five-finger Mary," school slang for masturbation. He was trying to bargain his way down from whatever else I might have had in mind. I had no idea of what I intended to do, apart from ensuring that he never leave the room alive. My frenum slid up the coarse fabric of his tunic, leaving a transparent glister like the track of a snail.

"Don't cream all over my uniform." He stepped to one side, settled his hand midshaft, and, not untenderly, moved it up and down as if he were milking a cow. I clamped my left arm around his waist, my right hand on his shoulder.

"What was that with the sparks?"

"I'll explain later," I said.

"Nuts to the tick. Do me afterwards."

"Anything you want," I said. Oh, the lies told by randy boys! Oh, the foolish young things who believe them!

My knees locked and my spine straightened. Ivory gouts flew across ten feet of floor and splatted against the window. Artillery Pledge Fletcher hooted, playfully aimed me at the ceiling and pumped on. A ribbon of melted ice cream hurtled up and struck the plaster. In almost scientific curiosity, he watched gruel stream over his knuckles and plop to the floor. "Amazing."

I released my grip on him, he his on me. A flush mottled his face. He fumbled with his zipper and groped into his trousers.

"Thanks for the book," I said, knowing for the first time since my experiments in the ruined house that I could freeze a human heart, and sent an icicle into his. Hand in his fly, Fletcher tumbled dead to the floor.

Whatever I decided to do with his body would have to wait until after curfew. I shoved him under the bed and dressed in my uniform, then used a towel to wipe the mess off the floor and the window. I stood on a chair and swabbed the ceiling. Then I settled down to read.

I might as well say: to experience an ecstasy more profound than sexual release. To witness the most hidden aspects of what I knew to be true about the world and myself laid bare in lines of type running across the receptive page. More than that, to learn that this sage, this prophet (a resident of Providence, Rhode Island, according to the infuriatingly cursory paragraph on the flap) had penetrated the Mystery far more deeply than I. Certain allowances had to be made due to the sage's decision to present his knowledge in fictional form, but he confirmed the origins of my Mission and the nature of my Ancestors. He uttered their mighty names: Nyarlathotep, Yog-Sothoth, Shub-Niggurath, great Cthulhu.

The Dunwich Horror became my Genesis, my Gospels, my gnosis. In wonder and joy, I read through it twice, interrupted only by Artillery Pledge Fletcher's roommates, pop-eyed future Rotarians named Woodlett and Bartland who burst in without bothering to knock and burst out again ten seconds later to go baying around the courtyard. Before beginning to devour the book a third time, I looked up and noticed the darkness beyond the window. The time was 3:00 A.M. I reluctantly closed the book, dragged the corpse from beneath my cot, transported it to a colonnade overlooking the dormitory courtyard, and dumped it over the side. It was a four-story drop onto the concrete, good enough, I thought. In my haste, I neglected to remove Fletcher's hand from his fly.

This was the matter I had hoped the captain would leave unmentioned.

■ "After a fashion," Squadron said. "He wasn't a friend of yours."

"I don't have friends, remember?"

"You and he never passed the time of day, chewed the fat, anything like that."

"Not that I recall," I said.

"Artillery Pledge Fletcher brought us a great deal of unwelcome attention."

The apparent suicide of a Fortress pledge had attracted national attention, and, although what appeared to be its autoerotic aspect was never officially announced, that Fletcher's right hand had been in the "Mary" position at the time of death had spread rapidly through the school and its surrounding community, arousing a mixture of shock, distaste, and ribaldry. He had jumped to his death doing *that*?

The autopsy deepened the mystery. Fletcher had died as the result of a massive heart attack, not the fractures sustained by his fall from the colonnade. Not only had he been dead before his body struck the ground, the death had taken place between six and twelve hours before one or more people had dropped him onto the courtyard. Once again, police and reporters invaded the school. Everyone who had been present on the Friday evening before Christmas break, myself included, was questioned and requestioned in an attempt to determine where Fletcher had been at the time of his death, where his body had been hidden during the missing hours, and who had pitched it into the courtyard. A trace of semen belatedly discovered on his tunic led to the widely reported theory that the cadet had died in the midst of a "sex party," and that his guilty partners had secreted the body until it could be disposed of in a manner they hoped to be taken for suicide.

The Fortress administration thundered that sexual misconduct was specifically forbidden by the Reg Book's honor code. The administration's final attempt at dampening the scandal was to announce that a depraved outsider had accosted Artillery Pledge Fletcher on the way to mess hall and had forced him into a remote area of the campus, where the fiend's immoral advances had induced a heart attack, whereupon the fiend had lain in wait until he could so deal with the body as to place suspicion on the innocent. Artillery Pledge Fletcher had submitted to death rather than dishonor, and the school would inaugurate a Valor Cup in his name to be presented at each year's awards convocation to the Artillery Pledge Who Most Typifies the Values Expressed in the Honor Code. I found it hardly unwelcome when this bilge carried the day. The story had long ago dropped out of the papers, and we had not seen a cop or reporter for at least a month. The only significant result of the investigations had been the expulsion of a notorious, much-missed Cavalry femme who, as if measuring fish he had caught, separated his hands by varying distances when other cadets' names were mentioned.

"It's interesting that you might have been the last person to see the pledge before he died," Squadron said.

I shook my head in a display of wondering disbelief.

"The pledge tells his roommates he's going to mess, and oh, on the way he might as well go up to your room to drop off this book you wanted to borrow, otherwise he might forget, he'll see them at dinner, goodbye. He waltzes into your room, finds out you're still here, and gives you the book. Right?"

"It was thoughtful of him," I said. "He wanted to be sure I'd have it when I got back." I smoothed my blanket with the palm of my hand.

"You couldn't get this book from the library?"

All the times I had been questioned, no one had ever thought to ask about the book. The notion of showing it to Captain Squadron seemed filled with danger. "We don't have it in the library. It was a collection of stories."

"Like short stories?"

I smoothed another nonexistent wrinkle.

"What kind of stories?"

"I don't know what you'd call them."

"Let me have a look at it."

I went to my desk and opened the top drawer. The hideous image of Squadron's fingerprints contaminating the sacred text filled my mind. I held it up and gave him a look at the cover. He narrowed his eyes. "I never heard of the guy."

"Me neither." I put the book on my desk, relief at escaping what seemed like both pollution and danger making my heart thump. When I looked back at Squadron, he was frowning and holding out his hand.

"I thought you wanted . . ."

He waggled his fingers.

I surrendered the treasure to his waiting paw.

"You kids think these stupid tricks bamboozle everybody, but we've seen it all before." He opened the book and flipped forward. When he failed to find pictures of naked women, he riffled the pages with his thumb. He folded back the cover and looked at the front binding. "You're too jumpy. Something's funny here."

Holding both covers, he upended the book and shook it. Nothing fell out of the pages.

Squadron tossed the book onto the dresser and leaned back again. "You didn't go to the mess that night."

"I wasn't hungry."

"Kids your age are hungry all the time, but let that pass. What do you think happened to Artillery Pledge Fletcher?"

"The commandant hit the nail on the head, sir. Some outsider jumped him between here and mess hall, and the pledge got so scared he dropped dead. I wish I'd gone with Pledge Fletcher. He wouldn't have attacked the two of us." I made the mistake of glancing at the treasure. Squadron saw my eyes move. Grinning, he slid the book to the edge of the dresser.

"No outsider has ever, and I mean ever, managed to sneak in here without being seen. It's almost impossible to get in or out without passing a guard station. Breaking into the dorms, you have to set that up in advance, don't you? Get a buddy to crack a window for you, talk him into hanging around a fire door?"

Once or twice a month, a reckless cadet who had escaped into town regained entry to the dorms by precisely those means. "I don't know anything about that."

He folded his arms over his chest and tilted his head to one side, still smirking at me. "But since this is between you and I, we both know the commandant's story is horse puckey, don't we?"

I did my best to look puzzled. "Sir, I don't understand."

"I probably don't, either. But here's what I know." He unfolded his arms and used the index finger of his left hand to tick off points on the fingers of his right, as he did in our calculus class. "Point one. Only two other cadets with fourth-floor rooms were still around on the night in question. Cavalry Pledges Holbrook and Joys reported to the mess by 1800 hours and returned to their quarters before 1900 hours to study for the same final in military philosophy you had to take. They observed lights-out at 2330 hours.

"Two. Artillery Pledge Fletcher's roommates, Artillery Pledges Woodlett and Bartland, witness to his intention of dropping off in your quarters a book you wanted to borrow, thereafter to proceed to the evening meal in time to arrive approximately when they would do so, then report back to the third floor and prepare for his chem final until lights-out.

"Three. When their roommate failed to appear at mess, Artillery Pledges Woodlett and Bartland assumed that he had chosen to forgo dinner in favor of study in the library. Shortly before lights-out, they went downstairs into the courtyard for the purpose of greeting the pledge on his return from his solitary labors. He did not return, guess why, the poor kid was already dead. Artillery Pledges Woodlett and Bartland remained down there until 2330 hours, at which time a single window on the north side of the fourth floor remained alight. That was the window of your room, Pledge."

"I apologize for the infraction, sir," I said.

He focused on the wall above my cot. "They came up here, thinking that the pledge might have been in your room all that time. During their short conversation with you, they were informed that he had loaned you the book and gone on his merry way. They returned to quarters in the hopes that the pledge would appear before the night was out. Unfortunately, the pledge did not. Instead, a deal of trouble was visited upon us, and the name of this fine institution was dragged through the mud."

He fixed me with a blunt stare. "At which time, and I think we have come to point number four, you came into my mind. I suppose you had been in my mind all along. I was already starting to wonder if you had put all those pledges into the infirmary."

"Sir," I said, "accidents happen. Did any of them blame me for their injuries?"

"Right. Point five. Accidents happen. After careful consideration, I have surprised myself by concluding that you are one of those accidents." He was staring directly into my eyes. "I think you're something new. I don't even know what to call it. You spooked those kids so bad they're afraid to open their mouths. Know what I think? I think our setup here was exactly what you were looking for."

"Sir, excuse me, but this is incredible," I said. "A bunch of kids fall down and break some bones, and you blame it on me."

"Point six." Captain Squadron was still holding my eyes. "Let's get back to that light in your window. Artillery Pledges Woodlett and Bartland were surprised to see that it was turned on. There were a number of reasons why that could be. You might have forgotten to turn it off before leaving. Or Artillery Pledge Fletcher forgot to turn it off. Or, what they were hoping, he hadn't switched off your light because he was still in the room. So up they come and, surprise, surprise, you're here after all."

He gave me an odd, twisted smile and tilted his head against his raised fist in a charged, deliberate pause. I was surprised to feel a chill of fear in my stomach, and I hated him for causing it. "Did they knock before they came in?"

"I think they did," I said. He was getting too close. "Everybody does. Section three, paragraph six of chapter two in the Reg Book, 'Pledge Deportment.' "

He looked as if he was figuring out how to get a nasty stain off the wall. "But you don't knock on the door of an empty room. The pledges, whose memories seem to be better than yours, say they just barged in."

"It's possible," I said.

Squadron held his pose for another beat. He lowered his hand and gave me a slow, subzero smile. "Artillery Pledge Fletcher did the same thing, didn't he?"

Humiliating fear sparkled in my viscera. "I believe he followed regs and knocked first."

"I believe he did not." Squadron gazed around the room for a moment, then shot me a speculative glance. "Where are we, point eight?"

"Seven," I said. "Sir."

"Okay, seven. Point seven. After a *tremendous* amount of thought, I have come to believe that Artillery Pledge Fletcher came across something he shouldn't have seen. He surprised you. All of a sudden he was a threat. Boy, I really wonder what that kid stumbled into. And I wonder how you managed to scare him so bad his heart actually stopped, but I don't suppose you'll tell me. You did it, though. And you knew what you were doing."

"That's crazy," I said. I felt as if a truck had run into me. "You can't actually be telling me that you think I killed Fletcher."

"I'm not saying you planned on doing it, and I'm not even saying that you did it directly. Otherwise, Pledge, that's an affirmative. I think he put you in a position where you had to get rid of him, and somehow you managed to do that. Hell, I don't think you killed him, I know you did. That kid walked in here and never walked out."

I stared at him with what I hoped looked like rubber-faced shock. "Sir," I said, "on my honor as a pledge, he came in, gave me the book, and left. That's all."

Squadron moved to the door and slouched against it. His demeanor had changed from hard-edged aggression to a weary certainty shot through with sadness. That this uncomplicated ramrod of a man had risen to something like emotional subtlety heightened my fear.

"I suppose you hid the body under your cot until you could move it without being seen."

"How can you say these things? Because I'm new? Because you decided you didn't like me?" My anger floated dangerously close to the surface. "I should have gone out for football. Then I'd still be your fair-haired boy, and you wouldn't be blaming me every time one of your prize dumbbells gets a broken bone." Before I went any further over the line, I managed to get myself under control. "Excuse me, please, sir, that remark was uncalled for. I apologize. But I repeat, I swear on my honor as a pledge—"

"Halt," he said. "Stop right there."

"But sir, I—"

"Halt, I said." His eyes had darkened with disgust. "I have only one more thing to say to you, and I don't want you fouling the air before I do." Captain Squadron gave his jacket a yank and then gripped the flaps of his pockets and yanked again, savagely, as if he were trying to rip them off. "I don't want to hear any more bullshit about your honor as a pledge, because as ridiculous as it must seem to you, I happen to take our code very, very seriously. It takes some transfers a little while to figure out that the code isn't just empty words, but most of them get it in the end. You never will. You're like a species of one. You're a disease."

I stopped pretending to be shocked and sat on the edge of my cot, watching and listening. The inside of my body, everything from the back of my throat down to below my waist, had become a block of ice.

"Are we done now, sir?"

"Affirmative. This conversation is concluded." He locked my eyes with his. "I'll be watching you, Pledge. If I catch you stepping an inch out of line, I'll come down on you like a ton of bricks, and you'll be out of uniform before you know what happened. Is that understood?"

"Affirmative," I said. "Sir."

"I wish to God your parents had put you into some other military school." He gave me a withering glare. "I'll take Artillery

Pledge Fletcher's book with me. I want to see what's so god-awful important in those stories."

My heart nearly stopped, like Fletcher's. "Please don't, sir. I haven't read it yet."

He tucked the book under his elbow. "Report to my office one week from today, and I'll give it back. Unless Mr. and Mrs. Fletcher want it returned to them. That will be all."

I watched him strut to the door of my room.

What happened next can only be explained by the combination of loathing, terror, and desperation blasting through me. If I had any thoughts, they had to do with the necessity of reclaiming the sacred book, but it would be more truthful to say that I was incapable of anything like thought. Without having moved, I was standing next to Captain Squadron, who was beginning to register the first traces of alarm. I seemed to be twice my actual size, though I believe this to have been an illusion produced by the condition that enables mothers to lift up the fronts of cars posing threats to their infants.

I had no idea of what I was going to do. I certainly had no idea of what I was going to do to Captain Squadron. In fact, I still don't really know how I did it, since duplication of the feat has resisted me ever since. I don't suppose any of those mothers ever picked up a car a second time, either. I touched the book and, as if I had done this kind of thing a hundred times before, felt myself flow into his mind and voicelessly command its surrender. With the book safely returned to my hands, I used the same instinctive power to impel him toward the center of the room. The interior of Squadron's mind reported a sensation akin to that of being blown backward by a great wind.

Captain Squadron remained incapable of speech as I withdrew from his mind. An enormous battery deep within me thrummed into life. At that moment, a certain crucial revelation that was to shape all the rest of my life came to me. I say "came to me," meaning that it entered me like a clear, silver stream and gave momentary form to the uproar. Once again I had heard the voice from Johnson's Woods.

Captain Squadron stood in the center of my room, perhaps two yards away from me. I glided toward him as if across an icy pond on a pair of figure skates. I don't think I touched him. I recall that almost impersonal sensation of *emptying* that accompanies evacuation. My joints suffered the bone-deep ache associated with arthritis. My head seemed to have been split by an axe. Maybe the mommies who hoist those automobiles off their babies feel the same way, I don't know. What I do know is that Captain Squadron had vanished from the room. A greenish puddle about four inches in diameter lay on the floor, and a wet, deathly stink hung in the air.

I overcame my agonies long enough to wipe up the captain's remains with a towel, washed it off in the sink, and fell on the cot to dwell on my revelation.

This was what I had been told a fraction of a second before I reduced Captain Todd Squadron to a half-pint of bile: one day, a day long distant, there would appear in the earthly realm an enemy more serious, more consequential, than Captain Squadron. My enemy would be like a shadow-self or a hidden double self, for when grown to adulthood he would possess the power to inhibit the coming of the Last Days, as certain protagonists in the tales of the Providence Master had frustrated the designs of my true ancestors. This Anti-Christ would be most vulnerable when still a child, yet evil forces would conspire to protect him from destruction at my hands. As my enemy grew to adulthood, he would partake of a portion of my own talents, thereby increasing the difficulty of my task, and for this damnable complication there was an excellent reason. My enemy was also the smoke from the cannon's mouth—he was going to be a member of the family. In fact, he was going to be my son.

15 ■ Mr. X

■ Only a little remains to be told before I lay down my pen for the night. The disappearance of Captain Squadron from the academy excited a brief flurry of renewed attention centered upon the possibility of a connection between the captain's flight and the death of Artillery Pledge Fletcher. When a rigorous check of his background revealed that the captain had retired from the regular army under suspicion of having molested a small boy in the town of Lawton, Oklahoma, the possibility hardened into a certainty. The subsequent manhunt went on, I believe, for several years, with no more result than the temporary detention of a surprising number of fellows bearing a resemblance to its target. I kept an amused eye on the proceedings throughout the remainder of my career as a pledge and was rewarded for my good behavior by the gift of a summer abroad.

I idled away the happy hours in the fleshpots of Cannes, Nice, and Monte Carlo. My parents may not have wanted me to come home, but my father, as ever good as his word, engineered by means of a hefty donation my acceptance to his alma mater, Yale University. An arrest and imprisonment for the petty crime of breaking and entering soon put an end to that, and after release from prison, I embarked upon my wandering career. I found a convenient way in which to persuade the family of my demise, no doubt a great relief. As a source of funds I turned instinctively to what is known as racketeering. Crime is a form of study akin to calculus or military philosophy, and like them yields itself to the superior intellect. It was not long before my understanding of every variety of criminal endeavor, including the care, feeding, and intimidation of one's staff, placed me in a position of leadership. Carefully timed use of my powers didn't hurt, either, especially when it came to intimidation. Your average thug's carapace of hoodlum detachment covers a deep well of superstition. Before I was thirty, I had become a Lord of Crime and done so, it should be noted, without any of the customary family connections.

Yet I grew weary of the constant obligations attendant upon being a Lord of Crime and began to feel, as do ordinary mortals, the tug of home. Call it a midlife crisis, I could care less, but the truth is that I considered myself an artist as well as a criminal. (If only I had known then what I know now!) Only a handful of writers, none of them worthy, had taken up the challenge of the author of *The Dunwich Horror*, the Providence Master, and I wanted to prove myself his only true inheritor.

So in my middle years I renounced worldly success and returned to Edgerton, there to pursue my writing while dabbling in whatever I found of interest. The local criminal element welcomed me precisely to the extent I wished, meaning that before long I was running whatever I wanted to run from behind the scenes. Less successfully, I wrote my tales—wrote them superbly, thereby inviting the rejection and contumely known to all who will not merely grind out commercial pap. I did my part. I gave mankind the opportunity to discover the truth, and mankind dropped the ball. Anyone with an ounce of empathy will understand my bitterness.

During this period, I moved through the entertaining demi-monde of would-be artists and hangers-on to be found in the vicinity of any college or university. Many were the nights when my abode was the scene of lively discussion nearly overwhelmed by the music from the record player, the fumes of wine and cigarettes legal and illicit, the sexual tension broadcast by bearded boys in turtlenecks and splendid young women wearing what at times appeared to be merely paint. Many were the pneumatic girls whose bodies I rode into eye-rolling spasms of bliss at the ends of these nights. After all, if one of my essential tasks was the murder of my son, I first had to create the little darling.

And if all of my ewes produced lambie-kins, I was prepared to slaughter every last one, but I assumed that I would recognize the Anti-Christ when I saw the little turd. I took for granted that when little Mr. Sweet of Face but Nasty of Purpose tumbled from Heather's, Moongirl's, Sarah's, Rachel's, Nanette's, Mei-Liu's, Skunk's, Avis's, Subindra's, Pang's, Low Rider's, Arquetta's, Sujit's, Tammy's, Georgy-Porgy's, Akiko's, Conchita's, Suki's, Sammie's, Big Indian's, or Zelda's womb, the brat would arrive all but surrounded by flashing arrows and neon signs. Despite my inspired exertions, none of these ardent maidens bore fruit. Of all the art-infatuated, experiment-minded dumbbells I bedded during this enchanted period of my life, only Star Dunstan managed to get pregnant.

The voice of revelation was not kidding around when it informed me that my adversary would prove elusive. Foolish me, I thought I had it all sewn up. After Star discovered that she was pregnant, I countered the usual whines about "commitment" even an airy-fairy type like Star could not keep from uttering by suggesting the next best thing, that she move in with me. Star was so grateful I didn't order her to an abortionist that almost anything I proposed would have made her happy. She could not have known that the whole point of rogering her had been to get her pregnant. I wanted a good, healthy birth. A few days after Mommy and Cherub returned from the maternity ward, I would press Cherub's face into his pillow until he went limp. It was a flawless plan, but as the voice had promised, it blew up in my face, not through any fault of my own.

I forced myself to utter the nauseating endearments expected by a female with an expanding belly. For a couple of months, I made cutesy-poo faces and uttered lies about the golden future. Yet there came a night when I went out on a ramble and returned to an empty house. Empty, that is, of my bloated companion and her possessions. She had scarpered—taken flight. I suspected a new boyfriend. I still think I was right, but because I could not find her in spite of looking under every rock within a fifty-mile radius, I had no proof. In desperation, I sought the help of Johnson's Woods and learned that, having spoken, the Voice was now eternally silent. A month later, I heard from Erwin "Pipey" Leake, at the time still clinging to his position at Albertus, that my beloved had turned up back in Edgerton and given birth. Wearing a cheap wedding band, she was presently ensconced in one of her aunts' houses on Cherry Street.

Fine, I thought: a few tentative visits accompanied by bouquets of flowers and boxes of chocolate, a statement of total forgiveness, a show of infant adoration, and she'd be back in an eye blink, the precious lad clamped to a handsome mammary. *Then* I could suffocate my only-begotten darling. A few hours later, the arrival on my doorstep of two blueboys instructed me that someone had "dropped," as they say, "the dime" on my participation in a number of illegal activities. A speedy trial led to a second imprisonment, this one in the state facility known as Greenhaven.

I brought with me a reputation guaranteed to ensure respect, obedience, power, and the considerable degree of comfort to be obtained in such quarters. Whatever I desired, but for the opportunity to rid the world of Star's spawn, was provided on the double.

I took this deprivation with a lighter heart than I would have those of an adequate suite with a private bathroom and telephone line, decent meals, sexual encounters with female visitors, the various books and magazines important to my researches, including those relevant to the life and works of the Providence Master (then experiencing something of a revival), and enlightening conversation with amusing companions, all of which I had in spades. The little darling was still advancing from diapers to the potty, from baby-babble to his first lisping excursions into English, and could not for decades pose a threat to my destiny as Herald of the Apocalypse. That I had been told my task would be arduous reinforced my faith in the wisdom of my inhuman ancestors. I could kill the little beast when I got out, and I positively looked forward to the hunt. In the meantime, a good deal of my research dealt with the shape and direction of the coming pursuit.

Just at the time I grew tired of pampered confinement, a prison riot enabled me simultaneously to exit Greenhaven and guarantee my anonymity, never mind how. Let us say, a mild exercise of my powers enabled me to inter my official identity in the safest of repositories and walk free. I returned to my hometown, there to live in seclusion as I carried out the search that continues to this day.

The years have been long and frustrating. The adversary proved as slippery as promised, and there were times when he escaped my grasp just as it seemed to be closing around his miserable little neck. However, the year I escaped from prison I found that I had been granted one final, annually bestowed, ancestral boon, and this gift, which each year thereafter I anticipate with a savage, ferociously tender eagerness still capable of quickening my step and heartbeat alike, has sustained and nourished me throughout the bleak decades. By the indulgence of the Ancient Gods, a shadow's shadow who was Star Dunstan's son became present to me each year on his birthday.

He has one more birthday left to him, his last. And wherever he is now, whether he slinks and skulks through the hospital corridors, the old houses on Cherry Street, or the Hatchtown taverns, whether he hides himself or walks unknowing through Edgerton's avenues, streets, and hidden lanes, that day arrives in exactly one week.

2
HOW I LEARNED ABOUT RIVER-BOTTOM

16

■ Nettie's running shoes slapped against the hard red tiles, and a carpet-weave bag the size of a suitcase bounced against her hip. Most of the nurses and technicians inside the oval of the central station raised their heads. They wore loose green scrub suits like pajamas, and my state of mind gave them ash-blond hair and Nordic eyes. The combination suggested science fiction and alien abductions, an effect heightened by the space-station glow of their realm.

Far down the room, Aunt May turned to the nearest crew member and announced, "That's my niece's son, Ned. He has fits."

Nettie pulled me into an embrace. Through the fabric of her bag I felt the hard shapes of bottles and jars. "When I called your place this morning, the phone rang and rang, and I said to May, 'The boy's on his way home,' didn't I, May?" She looked over her shoulder without releasing me, and the bag knocked into my ribs.

"The Lord is my witness," May said.

"Please," said Nurse Zwick. "I shouldn't have to remind you people that this is an intensive care unit."

Nettie dropped her arms and stepped back. "Zwick, when you call us 'you people,' what does that mean?"

For a moment Nurse Zwick savored the pleasures to be had from explaining the meaning of the term "you people." Then she swung her chair toward the counter. "I was merely asking you to speak more softly."

The nurses and technicians had returned to their desks and private conversations. One of the men inside the station was an Indian or a Pakistani and one of the women was black, but to me, they still all looked alike. "Nettie, what happened?" I asked. "How bad is it?"

Her broad face was nearly unlined, but the misleading air of serenity given Nettie by smooth cheeks and a youthful forehead had been eroded by worry. "It's bad," she said.

Aunt May came toward us, supporting herself on a shiny metal cane. "It does me good to see this boy back in Edgerton." Both sisters wore the loose print dresses they had always favored, but where Nettie filled out hers with a columnar massivity, Aunt May's hung like a sack. The cords of her neck stood out beside a deep hollow. When I got close enough for a hug, she lifted the cane, and I took all of her weight.

"Oof," she said. I held her up until she could get the cane back into position. "I'm not as bad off as I look, so don't go feeling sorry for me." Her whisper could have been heard across the room. "Ever since I got sick last year, I can't walk like I used to. If I could put on some weight I'd be fine, only it seems like I have to force myself to eat."

We moved toward cubicle 15.

"Is the doctor with her?"

"We were waiting for him to come out when I saw you," Nettie said. "A mighty weight went off my shoulders."

I looked at the curtain in front of the cubicle. "What happened to her?"

May leaned toward me. "It was this morning! Dropped down and hit the floor! Clark jumped up and called 911."

Nettie said, "Young as she is, your mother had a stroke."

Aunt May brushed the backs of her fingers against my blazer. "I bet this coat came from a fine New York store, like that Saks on Fifth Avenue." She raised her eyes to mine, and her voice grew thinner and sharper. "When did you get back home?"

"About a minute ago," I said. "I hitchhiked. I'm still carrying my bags." I pointed at the knapsack and the duffel on the floor beside the entrance.

Aunt Nettie was regarding me in frowning consideration. She might as well have been wearing a black robe. "Maybe you should have saved up your money for travel, instead of throwing it all over Fifth Avenue. I guess you were lucky, to get here so fast."

A trim little man in a white jacket bustled out through the curtain. His blond hair receded from a bulging head accentuated by oversized, black-framed glasses. The doctor shot me a noncommittal glance, and my aunts braced themselves for whatever he had to say.

"You're . . ." He looked at his clipboard. "Ned, Valerie Dunstan's son?"

I said, "Yes, I am."

"Dr. Barnhill," he said, and pursed his lips. His head seemed to bulge because it was out of proportion to his body and his vanishing fair hair exposed so much scalp. Short bald men are balder than tall ones. He gave me a brief, dry handshake. "Earlier this morning, your mother suffered an extensive stroke. Her condition remains grave. I wish I could give you better news." Dr. Barnhill held his clipboard to his chest as if he feared we would try to read his secrets. "Do you know what is involved in a stroke?"

"I'm not sure," I said.

"A blood clot entered her brain and cut off the flow of oxygen. If oxygen cannot reach a certain area of the brain, that area experiences tissue damage. In your mother's case, the area involved represents a portion of the left hemisphere." He touched the left side of his head. "Soon after admission to the ICU, her heart developed arrhythmia, due to the general shock to her system. I've given her medication for that condition, but we observe a general weakening of heart functions. Is your mother a heavy smoker?"

"She doesn't smoke," I said.

"Star worked in a lot of smoky nightclubs," Aunt May said. "She has a lovely singing voice."

"To your knowledge, has she ever taken drugs of any kind?"

"She smoked her share of pot," May said. "Some of those people she hung out with, you could smell it on them."

"Secondhand cigarette smoke and a history of marijuana use could be contributing factors," the doctor said. "Your mother is . . ." He looked at the clipboard and did an almost invisible double take. "Fifty-three. Ordinarily, that would give us a good prognosis. We are hoping that the Coumadin will break up the clot. If your mother survives the next twelve hours, we are looking at a long recovery involving extensive therapy. That's the best news I can give you."

"Twelve hours," I said.

His face smoothed out like a mask. "Everything depends upon the state of the individual patient."

"Will she recognize me?"

"You shouldn't expect much more than that." He looked at his clipboard again. "Do you in fact have any siblings?"

"No," I said, and Aunt Nettie immediately put in, "I told you that. Star only had the one boy, this one here."

Dr. Barnhill nodded and left. May had disappeared somewhere behind me.

"Siblings?"

"Zwick went to town on whatever your mother was babbling when we got here, and you know, if someone sets it down on paper, someone else is going to believe it."

I looked over my shoulder. Aunt May was leaning on her cane and talking to a burly young man with a short blond beard and a lot of hair pulled back into a blunt ponytail. He stepped back and said, "Hey, it doesn't mean anything to me."

I pushed aside the curtain and went in. The stranger at the focus of all the blinking machines instantly resolved into a frail but still recognizable version of Star Dunstan. Her cheeks looked distended and waxen. Clear fluid in suspended bags ran through lines that entered beneath the bandages low on her forearms. A glowing red light had been taped to her right index finger. I took her hand and kissed her forehead.

Both of her eyes opened wide. *"Uunnd."* The right side of her mouth tugged down and stalled like wax softening and rehardening. She fought to raise herself from the pillow, and her hand tightened on mine. *"Aaah . . . vvv . . . ooo."*

"I love you, too," I said. She nodded and sank back onto the pillow.

Little sounds and signals kept on announcing themselves with a discreet stridency that seemed on the verge of falling into a melodic pattern. The light on the blanket, the rises and falls of the moving graph, the descending curves of the tubes were more present to me than my own feelings. It was as though I, too, were in a sort of coma, moving and walking on autopilot.

My hand rose from the guardrail and touched my mother's cheek. It was yielding and slightly chill. Star opened her eyes and smiled up with the working half of her face.

"Do you know where you are?"

"Eee spitl."

"Right. I'm going to stay here until you get better."

Her right eye clamped shut, and the left side of her mouth opened and closed. She tried again. *"Whaa . . . mmmdd . . . kkk . . . kkmm . . . rrr?"*

"I thought you were in trouble," I said.

A tear spilled from her right eye and trailed down her cheek. *"Pur Unnd."*

"Don't worry about me," I said, but she was asleep again.

17

■ A white-haired Irish politician introduced himself as Dr. Muldoon, the heart specialist assigned to my mother's case, and described Star's condition as "touch and go." His confidential whiskey baritone made it sound like an invitation to a cruise. Shortly after Muldoon's campaign stop, the muscular guy with the ponytail who had been talking to May went into the cubicle, and I followed him.

He was taking notes on the readouts of a machine that would have looked at home in the cockpit of a 747. When he saw me, he stood up, nearly filling the entire space between the equipment and the side of the bed. The tag on his chest said his name was Vincent Hardtke, and he looked like an old high school football player who put away a lot of beer on the weekends.

I asked him how long he had been working at St. Ann's.

"Six years. This is a great staff, in case you have any doubts. Lawndale gets the fancy Ellendale clientele, but if I got sick, this is where I'd come. Straight up. Hey, if it was my mom, I'd want to know she was getting good care, too."

"You've seen other patients like my mother. How did they do?"

"I've seen people worse off come through fine. Your mom's pretty steady right now." Hardtke stepped back. "That old lady with the cane, she's a piece of work." He pushed the curtain aside and grinned at Aunt May. She snubbed him with the authority of a duchess.

By late morning, visitors had gathered in the passages between the nurses' station and the two rows of cubicles. Stretching my legs, I walked all the way around the nurses' station a couple of times and remembered something Nettie had said.

Nurse Zwick ignored me until I had come to a full stop directly in front of her. "Nurse," I said, indicating my duffel bag and knapsack against the wall, "if you think my bags are in the way, I'd be happy to move them anywhere you might suggest."

She had forgotten all about them. "Well, this isn't a luggage car." She momentarily considered ordering me to take them to the basement or somewhere else equally distant. "Your things don't seem to be in anyone's way. Leave them there for the time being."

"Thank you." I moved away, then approached her again.

"Yes?"

"Dr. Barnhill told me that you spoke to my mother this morning."

She began looking prickly, and a trace of pink came into her cheeks. "Your mother came in while we were having the first patient summaries."

I nodded.

"She was confused, which is normal for a stroke person, but when she saw my uniform, she got hold of my arm and tried to say something."

"Could you make it out?"

Anger heightened the color in her cheeks. "*I* didn't make her say anything, Mr. Dunstan, she wanted to talk to *me*. Afterwards, I came up here and made a note. If my report to Dr. Barnhill displeased your aunts, I'm sorry, but I was just doing my job. Stroke victims are often disordered in their cognition."

"She must have been grateful for your attention," I said.

Most of her anger went into temporary hiding. "It's nice to deal with a gentleman."

"My mother used to say, No point in not being friendly." This was not strictly truthful. Now and again my mother had used to say, *You have to give some to get some.* "Could you tell me what you reported to the doctor?"

Zwick frowned at a stack of papers. "At first I couldn't make out her words. Then we transferred her to the bed, and she pulled me in close and said, '*They stole my babies.*'"

18

■ As regal as a pair of queens in a poker hand, Nettie and May surveyed their realm from chairs brazenly appropriated from the nurses' station. Somehow they had managed to learn the names, occupations, and conditions of almost everyone else in the ICU.

Number 3 was a combination gunshot wound and heart attack named Clyde Prentiss, a trashy lowlife who had broken his mother's heart. 5, Mr. Temple, had been handsome as a movie star until his horrible industrial accident. Mrs. Helen Loome, the cleaning woman in 9, had been operated on for colon cancer. Four feet of intestine had been removed from Mr. Bargeron in number 8, a professional accordionist in a polka band. Mr. Bargeron drank so much that he saw ghosts flitting through his cubicle.

"It's the alcohol leaving his system," said Nettie. "Those ghosts are named Jim Beam and Johnnie Walker."

May said, "Mr. Temple will look like a jigsaw puzzle all the rest of his life."

Their real subject, my mother, floated beneath the surface of the gossip. What they saw as her heedlessness had brought them pain and disappointment. Nettie and May loved her, but they could not help feeling that she had more in common with the drunken accordionist and Clyde Prentiss than with Mr. Temple.

Technically, Nettie and May had ceased to be Dunstans when they got married, but their husbands had been absorbed into the self-protective world of Cherry Street as if born to it. Queenie's marriage to Toby Kraft and her desertion to his pawnshop had taken place late in her life and only minimally separated her from her sisters.

"Is Toby Kraft still around?" I asked.

"Last I heard, dogs still have fleas," Nettie fired back.

Aunt May levered herself to her feet like a rusty derrick. Her eyes glittered. "Pearl Gates turned up in her second-best dress.

Pearlie's in that Mount Hebron congregation with Helen Loome, you know, she went there from Galilee Holiness."

Nettie craned her neck. "The dress she dyed pea-soup green, that makes her look like a turtle?"

Aunt May stumped up to a hunchbacked woman outside cubicle 9. I turned to Nettie. "Pearlie Gates?"

"She was Pearl Hooper until she married Mr. Gates. In a case like that, the man should take the woman's name, instead of making a fool out of her. Considering the pride your Uncle Clark takes in our family, it's a wonder he didn't call himself Clark Dunstan, instead of me becoming Mrs. Annette Rutledge."

"Uncle Clark is all right, I hope?"

"An expert on everything under the sun, same as ever. What time is it?"

"Not quite twelve-thirty."

"He's driving around the parking lot to find a good enough place. Unless Clark has empty spaces on both sides, he's afraid someone'll put a scratch on his car." She looked up at me. "James passed away last year. Fell asleep in front of the television and never woke up. Didn't I give you that news?"

"I wish you had."

"Probably I got mixed up if I called you or not."

For the first time, I was seeing my relatives from an adult perspective. Nettie had not considered telling me about James's death for as long as a heartbeat.

"Here comes your Uncle Clark, right on schedule."

The old man in the loose yellow shirt coming around the desk bore only a generic resemblance to the man I remembered. His ears protruded at right angles, like Dumbo's, from the walnut of his skull. Above the raw pink of his drooping lower lids, the whites of his eyes shone the ivory of old piano keys.

Uncle Clark drew up in front of his wife like a vintage automobile coming to rest before a public monument. "How are we doing at the moment?"

"The same," said Nettie.

He lifted his head to inspect me. "If you're little Ned, I'm the man who saved your mother's life."

"Hello, Uncle Clark," I said. "Thanks for calling the ambulance."

He waved me aside and moved through the curtain. I followed him inside.

Clark went to the side of the bed. "Your boy is here. That should help you pull through." He examined the lights and monitors. "Hadn't been for me, you'd still be on the kitchen floor." He raised a bent finger to a screen. "This is her heart, you know. You get a picture of how it beats."

I nodded.

"Up, down, up, then that big one—see? That's a strong heart."

I wrapped my hand around my mother's. Her breathing changed, and her eyelids flickered.

Clark looked at me with a familiar combination of provisional acceptance and lasting suspicion. "About lunchtime, isn't it?"

My mother's suddenly open eyes fastened on me.

He patted Star's flank. "Get yourself back on your feet now, honey." The curtain swung shut behind him.

Star clutched my hand, lifted her head a few inches off the pillow, and uttered my name with absolute clarity. *"Hvv . . . tkk tt ooo."*

The machines emitted squawks of alarm. "You have to get some rest, Mom."

She propelled herself upright. Her fingers fastened around my bicep like a handcuff. She dragged in an enormous breath and on the exhalation breathed, "Your father."

A nurse brushed me aside to place one hand on my mother's chest, the other on her forehead. "Valerie, you have to relax. That's an order." She hitched up the bedclothes, introduced herself as June Cook, the head nurse in the ICU, and clasped my mother's hand. "We're going to go out now, Valerie, so you get some rest."

"She's called Star," I said.

My mother licked her lips and said, *"Rob. Ert."* Her eyes closed, and she was instantly asleep.

Outside the cubicle, Uncle Clark was tottering up the row of curtains in black-and-white spectator shoes, like Cab Calloway's.

"Where's he going?" I asked.

"Late for lunch," Nettie said. "Lunch is late for him, more like."

On the way out, I took off my blazer, folded it into my duffel, and zipped the bag shut again.

■ Nettie lowered her bag onto a table in the visitors' lounge and pulled out sandwiches wrapped in cling film and a Tupperware container filled with potato salad. "No sense spending good money on cafeteria food."

Clark dumped potato salad onto his plate, sectioned off a portion the size of a gnat, and raised it to his mouth. "When did you blow in, Neddie, a couple days ago?"

"This morning," I said.

He cocked his head. "Is that right? I heard something about a big-money poker game."

May gave me a look of bright approval.

"I don't play poker." I bit into a roast beef sandwich.

"Where did you happen to hear a thing like that?" Nettie asked him.

"Checking my traps."

"Uh-huh." Nettie rolled her eyes at me. "The old fool can hardly walk upstairs anymore, but he has no trouble getting to his favorite bars. If he missed a day they'd think he dropped dead."

"Neddie, did you win a lot of money?" Aunt May asked.

"I didn't win any money," I said.

"Where was the game?"

Clark took a minuscule bite of his sandwich. "Upstairs in the Speedway Lounge. My friends there treat me like royalty. Like a king."

"Friends like that common tramp Piney Woods, I suppose."

Clark coaxed another pebble of potato salad onto his fork. "There's no harm in Piney. Son, I hope to have the pleasure of introducing you to Piney Woods one of these days. I consider Piney a man of the world." He brought the speck of potato salad to his mouth. "Matter of fact, it was Piney who told me about you winning that money."

"How much?" May asked. "A whole lot, like a thousand, or a little lot, like a hundred?"

"I didn't win any money," I said. "I got into town this morning, and I came straight to the hospital."

May said, "Joy told me—"

"You heard him," Clark said. "Joy doesn't see too good these days."

"How are Aunt Joy and Uncle Clarence?" I asked.

"Clarence and Joy don't get out much," May said.

Clark nibbled at his sandwich. "It could be put that way. My advice is, die young, while you can still enjoy it." He examined the contents of my plate. "A boy like that could eat you out of house and home."

"I'd be happy to help out with the shopping and cooking, things like that."

"Is that what you do now, son? You a short-order cook?"

"I'm a programmer for a software company in New York," I said. His expression told me that he had never before heard the words *programmer* or *software*. "We make things that tell computers what to do."

"Factory work keeps a man out of trouble, anyhow." He bit off a tiny wedge of sandwich and put the rest on his plate, getting into stride. "The problem today is that young men do nothing but hang out on the street. I blame the parents. Too selfish to give their children the necessary discipline. Our people are the worst of all, sad to say."

He could have gone on for hours. "Tell me about this morning, Uncle Clark. I still don't know what happened."

He leaned back in his chair and aimed his best sneer at me. "Carl Lewis wouldn't have been out of his chair by the time I was dialing the second 1 in 911. Saved the girl's life."

"The bell rang about six in the morning," Nettie said. "I'm up at that hour because I have trouble sleeping. *That's Star,* I said to myself, *and the poor girl needs her family's loving care.* I could feel my insides start to worry."

"The Dunstan blood," Clark said, nodding at me.

"As soon as I opened the door, Neddie, your mother fell right into my arms. I never in my life thought I'd see her look so bad. Your mother was always a pretty, pretty woman, and she still would have been, in spite of how she let herself go."

"Extra body weight never hurt a woman's looks," Clark said.

"It wasn't the pounds she put on, and it wasn't the gray in her hair. She was scared. 'You're worried about something, plain as day,' I said. The poor thing said she had to get some sleep before she could talk. 'Okay, honey,' I said, 'rest up on the davenport, and I'll make up your old bed and get breakfast ready for when you want it.' She told me to take her address book from her bag and call you in New York. Of course, I had your number right in my kitchen.

"I had a feeling you were already on the way, Neddie, but I didn't know how close you were! After that, I did the coffee and went up to put clean sheets on the bed. When I came back down, she wasn't on the davenport. I went into the kitchen. No Star. All of a sudden, I heard the front door open and close, and I rushed out, and there she was, walking back to the davenport. Told me she was feeling dizzy and thought fresh air would help."

She turned her head from side to side in emphatic contradiction. "I didn't believe it at the time, and I don't believe it now, though I'm sorry to say it to her own son. She was looking for someone. Or she saw someone walk up."

May said, "According to Joy—"

Nettie glanced at her sister before looking back at me. "I asked her, 'What's happening, sweetheart? You can tell me,' and she said, 'Aunt Nettie, I'm afraid something bad is going to happen.' Then she asked if I called you. 'Your boy's on the way,' I said, and she closed her eyes and let herself go to sleep. I sat with her a while, and then I went back into the kitchen."

Sensing an opening, Clark leaned forward again. "I come downstairs and see a woman holed up on my davenport! What in tarnation is this, I wonder, and come up slow and easy and bend over to get a good look. 'Hello, Clark,' she said, and just like that she was out again."

"May came over, and I made all of us a nice breakfast. After a while, in she comes, putting on a nice smile. She told Clark, 'I thought I saw your handsome face, Uncle Clark, but I thought I was dreaming.' She sat at the table, but wouldn't take any nourishment."

"Those two took it for her," Clark said. "Eat like a couple of tobacco farmers."

"Not me," May said. "It's all I can do to eat enough to stay alive."

"She looked better, but she didn't look *right*. Her skin had a gray cast, and there wasn't any shine to her eyes. The worst thing was, I could see she was so *fearful*."

"That girl was never afraid of anything," Clark announced. "She knew she was sick, that's what you saw."

"She knew she was sick, but she was afraid for Neddie."

"For me?" I said.

"That's right," May put in.

"Clark heard her, too, but he paid no attention because it wasn't about his handsome face."

"What did she say?" I thought my mother had already given me a clue.

" 'A terrible thing could happen to my son, and I have to stop it.' That's what she said."

"I ain't deaf," Clark said.

■ **20**

■ A few minutes later, I jumped into a brief, uncharacteristic lull to ask if my mother had said anything more about the terrible thing from which she wanted to protect me.

"It wasn't much," Nettie said. "I don't suppose she could have explained."

May said, "She asked how I was getting on without James. Star was here for his funeral, you know." A dark glance reminded me that I had been absent. "She didn't seem lively and full of fun, the way she used to be. I remember she asked Nettie to get in touch with some of her old friends. Then she started toward the counter and made this funny *surprised* sound. That's when she fell smack down on the floor. I swear, I thought she had left us. Lickety-split, Clark was on the phone."

"Superman never moved faster," Clark said.

I drew in a large breath and let it out. "This is going to sound funny, but did she mention anything about my father?"

May and Nettie stared at me, and Clark's mouth dropped open, momentarily making him look witless.

"I think she wants me to know who he was." An irresistible

idea soared into my mind, and I hitched forward in my chair. "She wanted me to get here before it was too late. She didn't want me to spend the rest of my life wondering about him."

Clark seemed baffled. "Why in heaven would you wonder about that?"

"Star never said a word about your father from the day you were born," Nettie said.

"Probably she kept putting it off and putting it off until she realized that time was running out."

The aunts exchanged a glance I could not interpret. "You must have felt that my mother brought shame on your family. You took her in, and you gave me a home. Aunt Nettie and Aunt May, I'm grateful for everything you did. But I'm not ashamed that Star wasn't married when I was born."

"What the dickens are you talking about?" Clark said.

Nettie said, "Star never brought shame on our family."

"At the time, you must have thought you had to conceal . . ." The sentence trailed off before their absolute incomprehension.

May seemed to try to get me into better focus. "Neddie, Star was married when she had you."

"No, she wasn't," I said. "This is exactly what I'm talking about."

"She most certainly was," Nettie insisted. "She took off, the way she did, and when she came back she was a married woman about a week before delivery. Her husband had left her, but I saw the papers."

All three regarded me with varying degrees of disapproval, even indignation.

"How come she never told me?"

"Women don't have to tell their children they were born on the right side of the blanket."

A myriad of odd sensations, like the flares of tiny fireworks, sparkled through my chest. "Why did she give me her name instead of his?"

"You were more a Dunstan than whatever he was. *His* name didn't count for anything."

"Do you still have the papers?"

"They'd be long gone, by now."

I silently agreed. With the exception of her driver's license, my mother's attitude toward official documents tended toward a relaxation well past the point of carelessness.

"Let me see if I have this right," I said. "She left home with a man you didn't know, married him, and became pregnant. Her husband abandoned her shortly before I was born."

"It was something like that," Nettie said.

"What did I get wrong?"

Nettie pursed her lips and folded her hands in her lap. Either she was trying to remember, or she was editing the story into acceptable form. "I recall her telling me that the fellow took off a couple months after she learned she was carrying. She could have come back here, but she bought a ticket somewhere. . . . I can't remember, but she had a girlfriend in school there. At the time she left town, Star wasn't living with me. She was in with a crowd from Albertus, doing God knows what."

The women got to their feet. A second later, I joined them. "Didn't Star want us to call her friends?"

Nettie rammed the pickle jar into her bag. "Most of those people didn't know how to conduct themselves in a decent home. Besides, they probably moved out a long time ago."

"She must have had someone in mind."

"If you want to waste your time, here's her address book." She groped through the contents of her bag and brought out a worn, black leather book like a pocket diary.

From the door of the lounge, Clark was casting irritated glances at May's efforts to unhook her cane from a chair. Nettie moved grandly away. I knelt down to free the cane and placed it in May's outstretched hand.

"Aunt May," I asked, "what did Joy say to you this morning?"

"Oh. We straightened that out. Joy made a mistake."

"About what?"

"I said to her, 'Joy, you'll never guess, Star's over at Nettie's.' 'I know,' she said, 'I saw her with my own eyes, standing out front and talking to her boy. He's an extremely handsome young man!' "

"I guess that proves it wasn't me," I said.

"No, it doesn't," she said, "but I know what does. If Star met you outside the house, she wouldn't ask Nettie to call you on the telephone."

■ Star's address book was a palimpsest of the comings and go-ings of herself and her acquaintances over what looked like a great many years. I stood beside the bank of telephones on the ground floor and leafed through the chaos, looking for the Edgerton area code. I came up with three names, one of them that of a person in deep disfavor with Nettie and May.

I dialed his number first. A sandpaper voice said, "Pawn-shop." When I spoke his name, he said, "Who were you ex-pecting, Harry Truman?" The impression that Nettie and May were right to despise their late sister's husband vanished as soon as I had explained myself. "Ned, that's terrible news. How is she doing?"

I told him what I could.

"Look," Toby Kraft said, "I got some people in from out of town on a big estate deal, and I'm trying to expand my business, understand? I'll be there quick as I can. Hey, I want to get a look at you, too, kid, it's been a long time."

Before he could hang up, I said, "Toby, Star wanted us to call her old friends, and I wondered if you knew two people who were in her book."

"Make it fast," he said.

I turned to the first of the Edgerton names. "Rachel Milton?"

"Forget it. Way back when, she used to be Rachel Newborn. Used to go to Albertus. Nice knockers. Rachel was okay until she married this prick, Grennie Milton, and moved out to Ellen-dale." He put his hand over the mouthpiece and said something I could not hear. "Kid, I have to go."

"One more. Suki Teeter."

"Yeah, call Suki. Talk about jugs, she was the champ. She and your mom, they liked each other. Bye."

The former jug champ's telephone rang six times, then twice more without the intervention of an answering machine. I was about to hang up when she answered on the tenth ring. Suki

Teeter was no more given to conventional greetings than Toby Kraft.

"Sweetheart, if you're looking for money, too bad, this is the wrong number." The underlying buoyancy in her voice made a little self-contained comedy of the time she had taken to answer, the unknown caller, her financial condition, and anyone strait-laced enough to take offense.

I told her who I was.

"Ned Dunstan? I can't believe it. Where are you, in town? Did Star give you my number?"

"In a way," I said. "I'm calling from St. Ann's Community."

"Star's in the hospital."

I described what had happened that morning. "Before the stroke, she said to call her friends and let them know if there was an emergency. Maybe you'd like to come here. It might do her some good." Without warning, sorrow blasted through my de-fenses and clutched my chest. "Sorry," I said. "I didn't mean to do this to you."

"I don't mind if you cry," she said. "Is she conscious?"

The question helped me climb back into control. "When she isn't asleep."

"I'll be there as soon as I put myself together. Who else did you call?"

"Toby Kraft. And I have one other name. Rachel Milton."

"Really? I'm surprised. Maybe they stayed friends, I don't know. Rachel sure as hell dropped everybody else. Ned? I hope we can spend some time together."

In a voice made of honey and molasses, the woman who an-swered the Miltons' telephone told me that she would inform Mrs. Rachel she had a call, and who was it from? I gave her my name and added that I was the son of an old friend. The line went dead for a couple of minutes. When Rachel Milton finally picked up, she sounded nervous, impatient, and bored.

"*Please* let me apologize for the time you've been waiting. Lulu went wandering all around the house trying to find me when all she had to do was use the intercom."

I was almost certain that she had spent two minutes deciding whether or not to take my call.

"Is there something I should know?"

After I explained, Rachel Milton clicked her tongue against her teeth. I could practically see the wheels going around in her head. "I hope you won't think I'm terrible, but I won't be able to get there today. I'm due at the Sesquicentennial Committee in about five minutes, but please give your mother my love. Tell her I'll see her just as soon as I can." The wish not to be unnecessarily brusque led her to say, "Thank you for calling, and I hope Star has a speedy recovery. The way I'm going, I'll probably wind up in the hospital, too!"

"I could reserve you a room at St. Ann's," I said.

"Grenville, my husband, would kill me. He's on the board of Lawndale. You ought to hear him get going on the federal funds pouring into St. Ann's Community. They should be able to raise King Tut from his tomb, is all I can say."

After Rachel Milton hung up, I shoved my hands in my pockets and followed the corridor past the glass wall of the gift shop. A few men and women in bathrobes sat on the padded benches on the side of the immense, gray lobby, and half a dozen people stood in a line before the reception desk.

A small, fair-haired boy with gleeful blue eyes took in my approach from a stroller. His T-shirt bore the image of a pink dinosaur. Babies and small children charm me right out of my socks. I can't help it, I love that moment when they look inside you and spot a fellow spirit. I waggled my fingers and pulled an idiotic face that had been a big hit with the toddler set on previous occasions. The little boy whooped with delight. The tall, sturdy-looking woman beside him glanced down, looked up at me, then back to the child, who was crying "Bill! Bill!" and trying to propel himself out of the stroller. "Honey," she said, "this isn't Bill."

My first impression, that she looked like the female half of a local anchor team, vanished before the acknowledgment of the intelligence that irradiated her striking, even strikingly beautiful, presence. Her beauty and her intelligence were inextricable, and my second impression, standing before her lithe, tawny gaze and smiling at the efforts of her son to escape the stroller and hurl himself at me, was that if she resembled anything at all, it was a blond, particularly conscious female panther. Some quick recognition flashed in her eyes, and I thought she had seen everything that had just passed through my mind.

I would probably have blushed—my admiration was that naked—if she had not almost deliberately released me by attending to her son, allowing me the psychic space to register the

perfection with which her dark blond hair had been cut to fall
like a veil across her face and the expensive simplicity of her
blue silk blouse and white linen skirt. Lined up before the information desk with a dozen shapeless Edgertonians in T-shirts and
shorts, she seemed unreasonably exotic. She smiled up at me,
and again I saw that at least half of her smooth, shieldlike beauty
was the intelligence that flowed through it.

"He's a beautiful boy," I said, unable to avoid the word.

The beautiful boy was struggling to pull his feet through the
straps of the stroller, in the process levering off a blue sneaker
with a Velcro strap. "Thanks," she said. "This man is very nice,
Cobbie, but he isn't Bill."

I put my hands on my knees, and the boy swiveled and stared
at my face. His eyes darkened in confusion, then cleared again.
He chortled.

She said, "Good, this line is finally starting to move."

I straightened up and waved goodbye. Cobbie ecstatically
waved back, and she met my eyes with a glance that warmed me
all across the lobby and outside into the sunlight. Beyond the
low stone wall at the far end of the parking lot, the land dropped
away to the bank of the slow, brown-gray Mississippi. It struck
me that the river crawled along the city's western flank like an
unhappy secret. I wondered if the aunts had old stories from the
days when Edgerton had been a river town. Then, foolishly, I
started to wonder if I would see the woman I had met in the
lobby ever again. What was supposed to happen if I did? She had
a child, therefore a husband, and what she represented to me was
no more than a convenient distraction from my fears for my
mother. It was enough to have been reminded that such people
actually existed.

■ **22**

■ Thinking of the nights ahead, I ducked into the gift shop and
picked up a couple of paperback mystery novels and some
candy. The white-haired volunteer behind the cash register

searched the books' covers for the prices and dowsed a finger over the keys.

Behind me, a childish voice said, "You're—not—Bill," and burst into giggles. I turned around to see a familiar pair of dancing blue eyes. He was holding a sneaker in one hand and a new teddy bear in the other.

"I'm not?" I smiled at his mother. Her attractiveness seemed more than ever like a shield behind which she could come to her private conclusions about the responses it evoked.

"We meet again," she said.

"The way this hospital is designed, sooner or later you see everybody twice."

"Do you know how to find the intensive care unit? I've never been here before."

"Third floor," I said. "Follow me."

The woman behind the counter counted out my change and slid the paperbacks and the candy into a bag. I moved aside, and the boy's mother came up to the counter. "How much are the teddy bears?"

The woman peered at the child. In high hilarity, the child peered back. "Our ICU patients can't receive gifts or flowers."

"It's for him." She groped into her bag. "A reward for behaving himself. Or maybe a bribe, I don't know. Our otherwise completely adorable baby-sitter abandoned us this afternoon."

The boy pointed at me and said, "You're—not—not—not—Bill!"

"I am too," I said.

The boy clapped the sneaker and the teddy bear to his chest and roared with laughter. Ah, appreciation. I tried to remember his name but could not. He fixed his eyes on mine and said, "Bill rides a *lawn mower*!"

"No, you ride a lawn mower," I said, contradiction being the first principle of four-year-old humor. We left the shop and turned toward the elevators.

"Your new best friend is my son Cobbie, and I'm Laurie Hatch," she said. "My cleaning woman had an operation yesterday, and I wanted to say hello. You're seeing someone in intensive care, too?"

"My mother." We came to the rank of closed doors, and I pushed the button. "Ned Dunstan. Hello."

"Hello, Ned Dunstan," she said with a feathery brush of irony, and then looked at me more thoughtfully, almost impersonally. "I've heard that name before. Do you live here in town?"

"No, I'm from New York." I looked up at the illuminated numbers above the doors.

"I hope your mother is doing all right."

Cobbie glanced back and forth between us.

"She had a stroke," I said. For a moment both of us regarded the yellow glow of the UP button. "Your cleaning woman must be Mrs. Loome."

She gave me an astonished smile. "Do you know her?"

"No, but my aunts do," I said.

People had been trickling in from the lobby as we talked. Everybody watched the number above the elevator on the left change from 3 to 2. When it flashed to 1, the crowd pushed to the left. The doors opened on a dense, compressed mob, which began pouring out as the waiting crowd pushed forward. Laurie Hatch moved back, pulling the stroller with her.

Cobbie said, "What's your *name*?"

"Ned." I watched the light above the elevator on our right flash 2 and change to 1.

The doors of the laden car closed. A second or two later, the others opened to release a cart pushed by a workman. He stared at Laurie, glanced at Cobbie, and gave me a meaningful smirk as I followed them in. I said, "Don't jump to conclusions."

"I ain't concluded, and so far I ain't jumped," he said. We both laughed.

Cobbie brandished the teddy bear. "His name is Ned. He's a bear named Ned."

"Oh, Cobbie." Laurie knelt down to wriggle the sneaker onto his foot.

Cobbie leaned over the strap of the stroller and in his deepest voice intoned, *"I ain't concluded, and so faw I ain't jumped."*

The car came to a stop, and the doors slid open. Embarrassed, Laurie glanced at me. "I don't know where he gets it from." She pushed the stroller into the corridor and turned in the wrong direction. I gestured toward the ICU. "He just picks things up and repeats them."

I looked down at Cobbie. He fixed me with an expression of comically adult gravity and growled, *"And SOO FAW, I ain't JUMPED."*

"He must be part tape recorder," Laurie said.

"He has great ears," I replied, still grinning. "If he doesn't make it as a comedian, he could always be a musician."

"His father would have a heart attack." She startled me with a look so charged with resentment it felt like the touch of a branding iron. "We're separated."

Both of us looked down. Cobbie was holding the teddy bear's ear to his mouth and whispering that so far he hadn't jumped. "He'd even hate my bringing Cobbie to St. Ann's."

"Doesn't your husband approve of St. Ann's?"

"Stewart's on the board at Lawndale. He thinks you can contract a virus just by looking at this place."

"He must know Grenville Milton," I said.

She stopped moving and looked at me in dubious surprise. "Don't tell me *you* know Grennie Milton!" Chagrin instantly softened her face. "There's no reason you shouldn't, except that he never goes anywhere except the University Club and Le Madrigal."

"It's okay," I said. "His wife used to be a friend of my mother's. About five minutes ago, I called to tell her what was going on, and she mentioned that her husband was on the Lawndale board."

"Rachel Milton and your mother were friends? Am I likely to run into her in the next five minutes?"

"You're in the clear," I said.

"Good. Anyhow, there's the ICU, dead ahead."

I swung open one of the big doors to let her pass through. Zwick glanced up from her post and prepared for battle. Beneath the window, a notice I had previously overlooked told me why. "Uh-oh," I said. "Slight change of plans." I pointed to the notice. CHILDREN ARE NOT PERMITTED ENTRY.

"Oh, no," she said. "Darn it. They don't let kids in there, Cobbie. You'll have to wait for me. I won't be more than a couple of minutes, I promise."

He looked up at her with the beginnings of alarm.

"I can put you in front of the window, and you'll be able to see me the whole time."

"I'll stay with Cobbie," I said. "It's no problem."

"I can't let you do that."

"I want to stay with Ned and Ned," Cobbie announced. "With this Ned and with that Ned."

"First you're my guide, then you put up with my complaints, and now you're my baby-sitter."

Aunt Nettie surged out and came to a halt with her hand still on the door. "Did I pick a bad time to go to the washroom?"

"Don't be silly, Aunt Nettie. This is Mrs. Hatch. She's visiting Mrs. Loome. We met downstairs, and I offered to stay with her son while she goes in. Laurie, my aunt, Mrs. Rutledge." I could not keep from grinning at the absurdity of having to explain myself.

"Hello, Mrs. Rutledge." Laurie contained her sense of the ridiculous better than I. "If your nephew hadn't led me up here, I would never have found the way."

Cobbie chose this moment to come out with *"I ain't con-cluded, and SOO faw I ain't JUMPED!"* He sounded a little like Kingfish on the old *Amos 'n' Andy* programs.

Laurie Hatch moaned something that might have been "Oh, Cobbie." Nettie transferred her indignation to the boy and almost immediately relented. "Out of the mouths of babes. Honey, what's your name?"

"COBDEN CARPENTER HATCH!" Cobbie shouted. He fell back into the stroller, giggling.

"That's a mighty important name." She turned magisterially to Laurie. "I'm sure Mrs. Loome will appreciate your visit."

Smiling at her cue, Laurie patted her son's head and left us.

"Mrs. Hatch must be a good-hearted person." It was her way of apologizing. With a smile at Cobbie, Nettie sailed off.

Through the window, I could see Laurie Hatch approaching Mrs. Loome's cubicle and Aunt May stumping toward the nurses' station. I hunkered beside the stroller. Dinosaurs were Cobbie's favorite animals, and his favorite was *Tyrannosaurus rex*. Aunt Nettie reappeared and went back into the ICU. Aunt May gave the nurses' station a close inspection, leaned over the counter, and snatched a stapler off a desk. She shoved the stapler into her bag.

"Oh, my God," I said, realizing what Vince Hardtke had witnessed.

"Oh, my *GAHD*!" Cobbie chanted. "Oh, my *GAHD*, my mommy is coming."

Aunt May moved down the counter and took a pad of paper and a pencil from another desk.

Laurie came through the doors. "Did you two have a nice time while I was gone?"

"How is Mrs. Loome?"

"She's recovering well, but very groggy. I'll come back when they put her in a regular room." Her eyes sparkled, and she gave a little laugh. "Did your aunt make you feel like you were back in high school?"

Whatever I was going to say disappeared into a sudden whirl-wind of physical sensation. A woman's body was swarming over mine. Hair slid across my face, and teeth nipped the base of my neck. An odor of sweat and perfume swam into my nostrils. Laurie's smile faded. The hands hanging at my sides kneaded the buttocks of the woman on top of me. A breast offered its nipple to my mouth. My tongue lapped the nipple. The woman above me tilted her hips, and I began moving in and out of her.

"Ned, are you all right?"

I tried to speak. "I'm not . . ." I clapped my hands to my face, and the woman entwined around me turned to smoke. I lowered my hands.

"I'm sorry." I cleared my throat. "Yes, I'm all right." I wiped my handkerchief across my forehead and gave Laurie what I hoped was a reassuring look. "I guess I didn't get enough sleep last night."

"I don't want to leave if you're ill."

I wanted overwhelmingly to be left alone. "I'm restored," I said. "Honest." I went to the outer door and opened it for her. Still puzzled, Laurie got behind the stroller, and tendrils of con-sciousness seemed to extend toward me. I remembered thinking that she looked like a great glowing golden panther.

"The look on your face—it was like you were eating the most delicious ice cream in the world, but it gave you that ache in the middle of your forehead. Pleasure and pain."

"No wonder you thought I was sick," I said.

■ Okay, I was stressed out, I told myself. At a time when think-ing about anything but Star's plight made me feel guilty, a good-looking stranger named Laurie Hatch had unknowingly pushed my buttons and induced a ten-second meltdown. On the other hand, maybe I was heading for another bizarre crack-up. Dr. Barnhill's perfunctory update faded in and out of focus. Over the top of his Martian head I glimpsed the entry into the ICU of a woman who would have been perfectly at home on the corner of Tenth Street and Second Avenue, and the sight of her reddish brown hair bushed out around the kindly, roguish moon-face floating above an opalescent tunic buttoned from waist to neck over loose black trousers made me feel better even before I real-ized who she was. Suki Teeter looked like a visiting maharanee. Dr. Barnhill scurried up the aisle, and the maharanee rustled for-ward in a manner that suggested the chiming accompaniment of many little bells.

Nettie and May swung around with the stateliness of ocean liners and moved toward the curtain.

"You have to be Suki Teeter." I held out my hand.

"Honey-baby, please." She engulfed me in a hug. Her hair gave off the faint, pleasant odors of peppermint and sandalwood. "I would have been here earlier, but I practically had to recite the 'Gettysburg Address' to get my car out of the shop!" She stepped back. "I'm so glad you called me. And you're sort of . . . sort of incredibly. . . . My God! You're a marvel, that's what you are."

"You're a marvel, too." The glow of Suki's benevolent face in-tensified. Her wide-set, literally sparkling eyes were of two dif-ferent colors, the right one a transparent aquamarine and the left as green as jade.

"Tell me everything."

I had nearly finished when Nettie swept the curtain aside and billowed out, May a step behind her. "Aunt Nettie," I said, "have you ever met Star's old friend Suki Teeter?"

"We met. You flicked cigarette ashes all over my porch."

Suki said, "I'm very sorry about Star, Aunt Nettie," and went into the cubicle.

Minutes later, Nettie's head snapped forward, and she seemed to turn to stone. "Now I have seen it all."

"What?"

Nettie scorched me with a look of the sort usually described as "baleful." "You called Toby Kraft."

"I thought he should know," I said.

Coming toward us in an ugly plaid jacket too heavy for the weather was a man with a gray, pockmarked face, Coke-bottle glasses, and a body like a cigar butt. His white hair swept back to a few inches above his shoulders, George Washington–style. Beneath the sweaty, savagely tiny knot of a defeated necktie curled the collar points of a shirt that appeared to have been worn for a week straight.

"Who's next?" Nettie asked. "Mr. John Dillinger?"

"Why, that's Toby Kraft," May said. "He must talk to the Devil himself."

Suki Teeter parted the curtain, and my aunts moved sideways in unison. Sorrow had erased Suki's normal radiance. She wrapped her arms around me. "Call me tonight, will you? Call me before that, if anything changes." She wiped her eyes without taking them from mine. The peculiarity of their coloring suggested that I was looking at two people contained in the same body.

Suki broke away and began moving up the aisle. Toby's eyes, the size of eggs behind his thick glasses, focused on the front of her tunic.

May said, "Push those manhole covers off his nose, he looked any harder."

Close up, Toby's face looked like cottage cheese. "A good sport, that girl. Loyal as the day is long. Hiya, kid. Great to see you. Thanks for calling."

He held out a fat white paw liberally covered with silver fur. "Isn't it great to see this kid?" The aunts did not respond. He released my tingling hand. "I wish I could look like the kid here for twenty-four hours. That's all I ask—twenty-four hours. Hell, at least I got all my hair. How's Star doing?"

I gave him a brief description.

"What a lousy deal." He smoothed his hand over his hair. "I'll let her know I'm here."

May said, "I'll come with you." She took his arm, and the two of them disappeared through the curtain.

"Aunt Nettie," I whispered, "you must know that your sister is taking things from the nurses' desks. What's going on?"

She gave me a glance more aggrieved than angry and pulled me toward the end of the room. "Let me tell you some things you ought to know. What your Aunt May does is none of your business. She's a magpie. That doesn't hurt anybody. What did you see her take?"

"A stapler," I said. "Some pencils and paper. But it doesn't—"

"These people, if they want writing supplies, they go to the storeroom and get for free what would cost us ten dollars at the store. May helps level out the balance. And you're a Dunstan. You have to stand by your own people."

I couldn't think of a single thing to say.

Nettie's force-field lost most of its intensity. "Now let me set your mind at ease. My sister might be slow on her feet, but she still has fast hands. May's the best magpie in the world. Has been ever since Queenie passed away."

"Queenie?"

"Queen of the magpies. How do you think she got that name? Your grandmother could leave a store, a color television set under one arm, pulling a dishwasher on a handcart with the other, and the manager would hold the door and wish her good morning."

We returned to cubicle 15 in what must have appeared to be harmony. Nettie radiated the satisfaction of one who had accomplished a difficult task, and I was managing to hold myself upright.

Toby came out rubbing his fingers over a quilted cheek with what in him passed for melancholy. "Keep in touch, you hear? I want to know everything that happens. Your momma worked for me when you were just a squirt, did you know that?"

"I remember," I said. "How did the estate deal go?" His eyes hardened, and I added, "The one you were telling me about."

"Oh, yeah. We're moving, definitely." He gave me a sidelong look and strolled to the counter. "You staying at Nettie's?"

I nodded.

"If it gets tight over there, I can find you a room in a good clean place, no problem. And if you could use a couple extra bucks, maybe I'll want some help in the shop. On account of you remind me of your momma."

"I'll keep it in mind," I said.

He nodded, and I nodded back, as if we had agreed on a business deal. Toby put a hand on my shoulder and pulled me down into a miasma of smoke and hair gel. "Between you and I, you spot May doing something which it might seem out of character for an old lady like her? Turn a blind eye. Word to the wise."

"She already swiped everything that wasn't nailed down," I said.

Toby batted the side of my head and chuckled.

"Nettie said it runs in the family."

"Queenie, the woman was a virtuoso." He raised his furry hand to his mouth and kissed the tips of his fingers.

■ **24**

■ Dinner consisted of the same sandwiches, pickles, and potato salad as lunch. Clark negotiated a white pebble onto his fork and said, "Heard about you, boy."

I waited.

"Remember my mention of Piney Woods? I ran into Piney this afternoon. Six hundred dollars, he said."

"Is that right?"

"A fellow named Joe Staggers and three of his friends are looking to get it back." Clark sent me another yellow glance. "These are Mountry boys. You don't want to mess with boys from Mountry."

"Uncle Clark," I said, "the next time you run into Piney Woods, do me a favor. Tell him I didn't take six hundred dollars off someone named Joe Staggers. I never met anyone named Joe Staggers. I don't play cards, and I'm tired of hearing about it."

Clark dipped his fork into the potato salad. "I did tell him some of that. Piney said he'd give out the same story himself, if it was him."

Before the change of shift, I wandered up to the counter and noticed that the duffel had been partially unzipped. On one of her predatory rambles through the unit, May had opened the bag and nabbed whatever caught her magpie eye—she didn't know it was mine. I knelt down and took out the blazer, which had been shoved back in by someone even less worried about wrinkles than me, and sorted through my clothes. Nothing seemed to be missing, including the Discman and the CDs. I went to the desk.

"Nurse Zwick," I said, "did you see anyone touch my bag? Or open it up?"

"Only you," she said.

After 7:00 P.M., a nurse said that Mrs. Grenville Milton had sent a bouquet, but since flowers were not permitted in the ICU, it was being held downstairs. I told her to give it to the children's ward.

Clark dropped into a chair and fell sonorously asleep.

Star kept rising toward clarity and fading back. My aunts told her she needed sleep. I thought my mother needed to talk to me, and that was why she never let go of my hand.

Around 9:00 P.M., Nettie poked her head around the curtain and whispered, "May, Clyde Prentiss has two visitors. You have to see them to believe them."

"Maybe it's his *gang*," May said, and hustled out.

The arrival of two uniformed policemen and a plainclothes detective at cubicle 3 that afternoon had roused them into an investigative flurry. Prentiss's history of wrongdoing ranged from petty larceny, in my aunts' book merely a technique of economic redistribution, through assault with a deadly weapon and conspiracy to distribute illegal substances, to the big-time villainy of armed robbery, assault with intent to kill, and one accusation of rape. That he had been acquitted of most of these charges in no way implied his innocence. Hadn't he been shot by a night watchman while attempting to flee through a warehouse window? Hadn't his accomplices made their getaway in a pickup truck laden with microwave ovens? Added to his transgressions was that world-class felony, the breaking of his mother's heart. Nettie and May would have hammered a stake through Clyde Prentiss's own heart in an instant, and they were not about to pass up an opportunity to inspect his partners in crime.

Star clutched my hand. "Do you want to tell me about my father?" I asked.

Her eyes bore into mine. She opened her mouth and uttered a succession of vowels. She gasped with frustration.

"Was his name Robert?"

"Nnnn!"

"I thought that's what you were telling me before."

She summoned her powers. "Not *Rrrr. Bert.*" She spent a few seconds concentrating on her breathing. "Edwuh. *Edward.*"

"What was his last name?"

She sipped air and met my eyes with a glance that nearly lifted me off the floor. *"Rnnn. T!"*

"Rinnt?"

Star jerked herself up from the pillow. *"Rhine."* A machine clamored. *"Hrrrt."*

A name came to me from the furthest reaches of my childhood. "Rinehart?"

The night nurse erupted through the curtain and threw me out, but not before I saw her nod.

Ten feet up the aisle, the aunts were poised at the counter like bird dogs.

Clark issued a thunderclap snore that jerked him to his feet. He staggered, recovered himself, and joined us. "What're you gawping at?"

Nettie said, "The Clyde Prentiss gang is over there. The ones that got away when he almost met his Maker."

A scrawny little weasel with a goatee and a black leather jacket twitched out through the curtain, followed by a sturdy blonde wearing a lot of mascara, a brief black leather skirt, and a denim jacket buttoned to her bra. Clark chuckled.

The blonde looked across the station and said, "Hey, Clark."

"You're lookin' mighty fine, Cassie," Clark said. "Sorry about your friend." The weasel glanced at him and pulled the blonde through the doors.

The aunts turned to Clark in astonishment. "How do you know trash like that?"

"Cassie Little isn't trash. She tends bar down at the Speedway. The shrimpy fellow, Frenchy, I don't know him but to greet. Seems to me Cassie ought to be able to find a better man than that."

I went back inside and said goodbye to Star. Her hands lay at her sides, and her chest rose and fell. I told her I would see her in the morning, said that I loved her, and kissed her cheek.

Alongside May in the backseat of the Buick, I said that I wanted to talk about something before everybody went to bed.

■ Nettie placed herself on the old davenport, thumped her bag on the floor, peeked inside, and folded it shut again. Clark gave me a wary glance from the easy chair. May sat beside Nettie with a deep sigh. I dropped my bags next to the staircase and took the rocking chair. I knit my hands together and leaned forward. The rocker creaked. Multiple doubts, doubts arranged into layers, whirled through my head and stalled my tongue.

"I saw you wave to Joy," Nettie said. "If you don't stop off and see her after escorting May home, her feelings will be wounded. Now I guess you had better tell us what's on your mind."

"I'm trying to figure out how to begin," I said. "When you were waiting to see Clyde Prentiss's visitors, my mother wouldn't let go of my hand. She wanted to give me a name."

A beat ahead of the others, Nettie fixed me with a warning glare.

"I don't know what we're talking about," May said. "Shouldn't we divide up what's in Nettie's bag, so I can go home?"

"Does Edward Rinehart mean anything to you?"

My aunts exchanged a glance almost too brief to be seen. May said, "Do you know that name, Nettie?"

"I do not," Nettie said.

"Star moved out of here to live with this man. She and her friends used to visit you, and they scattered cigarette ash all over the porch. Probably Edward Rinehart came with them."

"It was just Suki and a couple other mixed-up girls, all jabbering away about Al-Bear Cam-oo," said Nettie, proving that her memory hadn't lost any ground.

"If you can remember Albert Camus, you can hardly have forgotten the name of the man who took my mother away from Cherry Street."

"You'd be surprised what you forget when you get to be my age."

"What you got in that bag?" Clark asked.

The seat cushion between my aunts disappeared beneath a mound of pens and pencils, pads of paper, scissors, paperclips, tubes of lip balm and skin moisturizer, cigarette lighters, paperweights, envelopes, desk calendars, coffee mugs, wrapped coils of plastic tubing, light bulbs, antihistamines and nasal steroids in sample packets, cotton balls, a stack of gauze bandages and rolls of tape, stamps, and toilet paper. After a while, my dismay surrendered to amazement, and I had to force myself not to laugh. It was like going to the circus and watching the clowns pile out of the little car.

The sisters began dividing the plunder into two equal piles, now and then adding things to a third, smaller share.

I could no longer keep from laughing. "No alligator shoes for Uncle Clark? I could use some new underwear and socks."

"Medical gentlemen seldom wear alligator," May said, "and as for the other, you'll have to wait until the next time I go to Lyall's."

Nettie floated into the kitchen and returned with two grocery bags, one to hold May's spoils and the other for the smaller pile. "After you see May home, you can drop this off at Joy's. I'll leave some lights on."

I helped May down the steps. On the other side of the street, Joy's dark figure peered through a slit in her curtain. The lamps cast circles of thick yellow light onto the pavement and threw the trees into stark relief. The moist night air hovered like fog. May and I stepped down from the curb. "Don't you ever worry about getting caught?" I asked.

May shook her head. "Neddie, I'm too good to get caught. Now hush up, because talking brings bad luck."

I got her up onto the opposite sidewalk, and we moved into the light of the street lamp. Our shadows blotted the cement. "Hush up about that other thing, too, if you know what's good for you."

"I don't get it," I said. "We're talking about a man who disappeared thirty-five years ago."

"I'll have to hush up for both of us, then." She did not say another word until she thanked me for accompanying her home.

Next door, a bent, osteoporotic Joy accepted her bag of goodies and, in a voice age or unhappiness had ground to semitransparency, so hesitantly asked me in that my refusal came as a relief to us both. The most infirm of the three surviving sisters seemed to exude the same musty, faintly corrupt atmosphere as the barrenness dimly visible behind her. I promised to visit the following afternoon. Inside Nettie's house, I carried my bags upstairs.

A lamp burned on a table beside a metal-spring bed opposite a sink with an overhanging mirror and medicine chest. Through the open window at the front of the room, I saw Joy's house go dark. I put my bags on the linoleum, unzipped the duffel, and took out my blazer, the CD equipment, and my Dopp Kit. The next day's clothing went on the seat of a rush chair, the blazer over its back.

The bedsprings yelped when I stretched out. I pulled up the sheet and the thin blanket. A disc of Emma Kirkby singing Monteverdi went into the player, the headphones over my ears. Before I pressed the PLAY button, I noticed my blazer splayed askew over the back of the chair and got up to hang it in the closet. When I lifted it from the chair, the blazer drooped to one side, weighted by something in its right pocket.

I reached into the pocket and pulled out a thick wad of bills. I fanned the money over the blanket. Three fifties, lots of tens and twenties, a lot more fives and ones—it added up to five hundred and seventy-six dollars. I separated two fives glued together with beer and counted it again. Five hundred and eighty-one dollars. I stared at the money, feeling as though I ought to lock the door. Then I thought I should tear the bills into confetti and flush them down the toilet. In the end, I pushed the money into a front pocket of my knapsack. I went to the mirror and looked at my face without seeing anything all that familiar or all that new. I pushed the knapsack under the bed, switched off the light, and buried my head in the pillow.

■ 25

■ For the first time in years, unconsciousness pulled me into my recurring nightmare. Despite its long absence, each of its details remained as fresh as the images on a reel of film.

In my earlier years, the dream began with the shadow ripping the seams that connected us and ended with the shadow's gesture toward the forest. Later, I pursued my shadow through the trees. Monstrous beings launched themselves from overhanging rocks, dug claws into my shoulders, and fastened their jaws around my neck. Years after I ran away from Vermont, a hitherto unexpected dream-capacity kept me from jolting out of sleep. Until that point, my fear, above all the sense that I *recognized the monsters*, blasted the dream apart. The unexpected capacity I mentioned was the ability to defeat the monsters. When the dream-self had finally come to trust its capacity for survival, the dream went away.

But, hundreds of times before I seemed free of my nightmare, the shadow appeared before me, leaning against a tree trunk or perching on a low-hanging branch. Sometimes it sprawled in midair, head propped on one hand.

"You keep on coming, don't you?" it said. "Haven't you ever wondered where this is going to end?"

"I'm going to catch you," I said.

"What did I ask: where this will end, or how?"

"It'll end here." Even as I indicated the forest, I doubted what I had said.

"Is that the best you can do?"

"I don't give a damn where it happens."

"Ding-dong," the shadow said. "Would you give a damn if our conclusion were to take place in Jones's Woods, just outside the town of Middlemount, in Vermont?"

"No." A chill radiated upward from the pit of my stomach.

"Ding-dong. We'd think twice about going back to Jones's Woods, wouldn't we?"

"This isn't Jones's Woods."

"Ding. A half-lie. Remember what is going on. You are *dreaming*. For all you know, we could be smack-dab in the middle of that forest where you nearly shuffled off the old mortal coil." The invisible smile lengthened on the invisible face, another impossibility, but there you are.

"Jones's Woods didn't look anything like this." The cold threading up from my stomach brushed my lungs.

"Ding." He sighed. "Isn't it your impression that dreams turn one thing into another and exaggerate like crazy? That they display a tendency toward the surreal?"

"What's your point?"

"We are getting closer to something you used to be able to see."

"I don't know what—"

"Ding-dong. You do too."

I remembered peaks and gables rising above the trees.

"Not very fond of old houses in the woods, are we?"

"You're not scaring me."

"*Ding*-dong, *ding*-dong! The last time, you were looking in the wrong place. If ever you come upon the right one, you'll be in danger of finding out who you are."

I fell back on an old conviction. "There is no right place."

"The right place is where you least want to go. When you get there, it's where you least want to be. If you answer a question of mine, I'll answer one of yours."

"Go ahead."

"All your life, you have felt the loss of something extraordinarily important. If you found it, could you live with the consequences?"

No one with half a brain would answer a question like that. Cracker-barrel mottoes about wooden nickels and pigs in pokes suggested themselves. Yet what came out was "Yes," and it was too late to say, *Ask me another.*

"Now it's my turn," I said.

"I changed my mind," the shadow said. "You don't get a turn, sorry." It flew on ahead.

■ As if I were twenty again, I followed the shadow through a deep wood. The insolent shadow floated above the ground, and we had the ding-dongs, the bit about surrealism, the allusions to houses in wooded areas, the paradoxes about real right places, the question, the shadow's flight. Like a dope, I wondered: *So is that all? There isn't any more?*

I took two or three steps deeper into the forest and froze in my tracks, stunned by vivid sensory reality.

Sunlight filtered through the canopy swishing in a mild breeze and printed glowing coins on the spongy floor. Spicy, process-laden fragrances sifted in the warm air. I could not be asleep, because I was not dreaming. The air darkened to silver-gray. I glimpsed muddy clouds sliding across the open spaces between treetops.

A sparse rain patted onto the leaves overhead, and I took shelter beneath a big maple. Twenty or thirty yards away, the woods ended in a wall of thick oaks marking the boundary of a meadow. A thunderclap boomed, then another, and the air filled with the sound of wingbeats. Half the distance to the edge of the forest stood an enormous oak. Vertical sheets of water hurtled out of the sky. I took off and scrambled into the shelter of the oak. A drift of wind precise as an atomizer coated me with a film of mist.

A jagged branch of lightning tore through the sky and illuminated the landscape. In the few seconds of brightness, I saw that I had come nearer the border of the woods than I had imagined.

Twenty feet of woodland and half as many trees stood between me and a broad field ending at a road. Something tucked into a bend in the woods registered in the corner of my eye, then disappeared back into streaming darkness. The road on the other side of the field would get me back to Edgerton, but I was worried about Star, and the storm was going to delay my return to the hospital. I wondered if what I had seen was a house. A house was exactly what I needed. If its owners let me in, I could telephone Clark and ask him to pick me up before he drove Nettie and May to St. Ann's.

Another lightning bolt shattered the sky and divided into sections that turned the air white as they sizzled toward the woods. I leaned forward and made out a tall portico and a stone facade with shuttered windows. About a hundred feet behind me, a glowing electric arrow shot into the forest. I heard a series of loud cracks, like the breaking of giant bones.

Then another sizzle, another stupendous crack. Rays of lightning darted across the sky, cutting off from a central bolt that executed a left-face over the meadow, stretched out, and angled for the woods. I smelled ozone even before the shaft came slicing down over the top of the oak and hammered into my old friend the maple. It split apart and burst into flame.

A vertical column of lightning erased the darkness. It sped in the direction of the house, executed a right-hand turn, and began working back toward my part of the woods. For lightning, it moved slowly, almost deliberately, and the entire fork remained in place as its business end winged down, carving Z-shapes in the air. I jumped away from the oak and tore through the tail end of the woods. A missile the size of a freight train brushed close enough to heat up my back. All the oxygen was sucked out of the air. I charged onto open ground, and a wall of water sent me stumbling for balance as the missile exploded against the oak tree. I kept running until I reached the stone slab beneath the portico.

Rainwater streamed from my ruined clothes and puddled on the stone. I wrapped my hand around the metal knocker and slammed it down. I waited; I raised the knocker for another blow.

A lock clicked; a bolt slid into a casing. Soft light spilled out.

"I'm sorry to bother you," I said to the person invisible behind the door. "I was caught in the rain, and I wondered . . ."

Behind the figure who held one hand against the door lay a gallery lined with glowing porcelain vases on delicate side tables.

In the middle distance, a chandelier like a great ship made of light cast brilliant illumination that turned the man in front of me into a silhouette. A white cuff fastened with a golden link protruded from the sleeve of his gray suit. His fingernails gleamed.

". . . if I could use your telephone."

He leaned into the darkness to hold the door, and I stepped across the threshold. As soon as I entered, I experienced a recurrence of the sense of familiarity that had always shocked me out of my nightmares. The door slammed shut. A lock resoundingly clicked.

My host's almost entirely familiar eyes shone in triumph; his almost entirely familiar mouth opened in a smile. He offered an ironic bow. Although the utterly striking handsomeness of the man before me in no way resembled the way I looked, his individual features, taken one by one, mysteriously replicated my own. In combination, all resemblance vanished. His forehead, eyebrows, eyes, nose, and mouth fused with the modeling of his jaw and cheekbones to create an extraordinary physical beauty. It was like seeing what I might have looked like if I had hit the genetic jackpot. But more than his good fortune separated this man from me—thousands of miles of experience lay between us. He had gone further, survived more, risked more, won more— simply, nakedly, taken more, and done so with an instinctive, passionate rage beyond any emotion I had ever known.

Surrounded by the vulgar splendor of his domain, odious to the core, the shadow stood before me and laughed at my helplessness. I cried out and shuddered awake.

26 ■ Mr. X

■ Listen to me, You Star-Flung Entities, this isn't easy. It never has been, if You want to know the truth.

No one not born into my condition, in other words no one, except He of whom it now occurs to me You may have never heard, can understand the agonies of uncertainty I have endured. Great

Ones, should You exist at all, I hereby request a degree of Recognition commensurate to my Service. Unless my life has been wasted, I deserve an honored Immortality. This Account of my Travails should be displayed in a Great Museum of the Elder Gods. Call it, say, the Patriot's Museum, or the Museum of Triumphs. I ought to have, if I may make a suggestion, a diorama reconstructing these humble chambers. The present Journal would be installed upon a replica of my desk. I also see a model of myself, animated if possible, now deep in thought over the page, now standing in a contemplative pose by the sink. A descriptive plaque or framed text of not less than eight hundred words would fill the bill. I am being modest. Remember, if You will, that the Nazarene has been represented in works of art all over the world, and his Image hangs in every Christian house of worship.

Do You in Your Otherness even *know* about The Other Guy? I mean, providing that You do exist, is it possible that You chose Him before me and watched everything go down the tubes? Attend—

Even the Jesus brainlessly sentimentalized in Canon Reed's Sunday school exercises had his moments of frustration, doubt, and despair. After all, He was half human too! I bet He stormed around in a black, blinding rage a lot more often than the Gospels let on. What I want to know is, didn't Jesus sometimes wonder if that Messiah stuff was a delusion? And this: did He have dreams?

A being in possession of supernatural powers and a world-altering Mission ofttimes finds Himself down in the dumps for weeks on end. More often than any mortal, He endures periods of psychic sludge when the emotional landscape looks like a river-bank at low tide on an overcast day. A few old tires, broken bits of wood, and a couple of beer bottles lay scattered across the mud. All the best sources agree that these bleak periods are necessary to spiritual evolution. It isn't depression, it's the Dark Night of the Soul. I'd give you a hundred to one that whoever came up with that convenient equation was figuring out a way to turn his doubts into aspects of belief.

And if Jesus got it wrong, what about me? I *know*, but how can I be sure that I *really* know?

Until I was well into my twenties, the egotism and arrogance attendant upon the human condition prevented me from being distracted by those aspects of the Master's work not directly applicable. God knows there was enough to keep me happy. Doubt tiptoed in when I admitted that a number of the Master's tales did not quite come up to the mark. Some of them refused to get down to business altogether.

I told myself that sometimes His antennae had garbled the message, that He had kept trying even when He wasn't on the right wavelength. I told myself that He may have been incapable of distinguishing between truth and fiction in His own work.

Ah, before me rises the possibility that what I had taken as Sacred Text was all along merely pulp fiction. Night after night of Dark Night, I whisper to myself: *Your life is a grotesque error, and you are far, far smaller than you think.*

Misery-laden dreams pollute my sleep. I enter a shabby room where a man toils at a desk. The lantern jaw and cheap suit familiar from a dozen photographs identify the Providence Master, and I move forward. At last I stand before Him. I ask, *Who am I?* He smiles to Himself, and the pen drifts across the page. He has not seen or heard me—I am not there—I do not exist.

Only days ago, confident energy sent me loping through the night streets, abuzz with pleasure. The Grand Design swept toward its conclusion, and Star's wretched brat was to meet an excruciating death. Now . . . now it's all I can do to get out of bed. *I think I was mistaken. I think I got it wrong.*

If You do not exist—if the Elder Gods did not place me on earth to prepare its destruction—what am I doing here? Who *was* my true father?

▪ **27**

▪ Faint, oyster-colored light washed through the window, making the chair and the dresser look two-dimensional. The hands on the sheet in front of me also seemed two-dimensional. From the blurry face of my two-dimensional watch I managed to make out that it was a few minutes past five-thirty.

I didn't have a prayer of getting back to sleep, so I brushed my teeth, washed, and shaved, telling myself that the money in my jacket pocket had been a part of the nightmare. It had the same unreal quality—it seemed real in the same unreal way—besides,

I *knew* I had not won that money, therefore I had dreamed about finding it. Then I dried my face and looked in the closet.

The blazer hung evenly, displaying no signs of dream-boodle. I poked my hand into the side pockets and found only Ashleigh Ashton's business card. Male vanity suggested that she had slipped it into my pocket when I wasn't looking. Showing off, I even checked the inside pockets.

See? I told myself. *You knew it all along.*

When I pulled a pair of jeans out of the duffel, I caught sight of my knapsack under the bed. Everything inside me stopped moving. I put on my socks and regarded the knapsack. An ominously dreamlike quality suffused my old companion. I got into my shorts, pulled a polo shirt over my head, thrust my legs into the jeans, and yanked the thing onto the bed. Dream-memory singled out one of the buckled pouches. I worked the buckle, raised the flap, and drew the zipper across the top of the pouch. When I reached inside, I touched what felt like currency. My hand came back into view gripping a fat wad of bills.

Five hundred and eighty-one dollars. Two fives had been plastered together with beer.

I rammed the money back into the pouch, zipped it shut, and shoved the knapsack under the bed.

■ 28

■ A purple shirt hung from Uncle Clark's shoulders, and a turquoise bracelet swam on one of his wrists. He looked like a conga player awaiting the summons onstage, but what he was waiting for was breakfast. I got coffee going and started opening cabinet doors.

"Cereal is down at the end, bowls are right in front of you. I take Bran Buds and Grape-Nuts, fifty-fifty, with a spoonful of honey and some milk. It could be you're too young to handle Bran Buds."

He monitored the buckshot rattle of the cereal into the bowl and nodded when it was half filled. "Don't go light on the honey, and level the milk right up so I can give it a good stir. Keep your eye on that coffee."

I covered everything with milk and placed the bowl on the table. He dumped in three scoops of sugar. After I joined him at the table, he slid his ivory eyes toward me. "From all that racket you made last night, I'd guess you had a grade-A nightmare. Some will tell you that's a sign of a bad conscience."

"I'm sorry if I woke you up."

He ate down to the bottom of the bowl and pushed his spoon around, roping in stray pellets. "What was your nightmare about?"

"I was in a big storm."

"They say a dream of heavy rainfall indicates unexpected money."

"What about almost being struck by lightning?"

"That's supposed to mean a change of fortune. Could be a whole lot of money coming your way. Better hold your umbrella upside down and steer clear of Mr. Toby Kraft. Money has a way of winding up in that man's pocket."

I had an uneasy vision of the bills folded into my knapsack.

"Rainstorms, now," he said. "We used to get us some doozies in the old days. The river rolled right into town. Picked up anything it could get along the way. Cars. Livestock. Full-grown men. In the water a corpse will turn *blue*. It will swell up with gas and float on the current. The hands will look like catcher's mitts. I've lived next to the Mississippi all my life. People think rivers are pretty things, but those with common sense won't trust one any wider than you can jump across."

I told him that until yesterday, when I had seen the river from St. Ann's, I had nearly forgotten that Edgerton was built along the Mississippi. He gave me a frown-sneer and then perked up again. "You didn't remember about the river?"

"Not until I saw it yesterday afternoon."

"Best part of a river is when it lets you forget it. Way back, we needed the river, and history tells you towns like this got built because of it. And a river town is a different kind of place."

"Different how?"

"A river town is *irregular*," Clark said. "You get your gamblers and your sharpies before you get your preachers, and it might be some considerable time before any of 'em find an advantage in turning respectable. There's a different *mentality*, you understand me?"

What he was describing sounded more like the Barbary Coast than southern Illinois, but I nodded anyhow.

"And maybe you go twenty years without a flood. If one comes, you build everything back up afterwards. The river needs the town, and the town needs the river. A month or two later, even the smell is gone."

"The smell?"

Clark gave me a prolonged smirk-sneer. "I have pondered the question of why a river will smell fresh and clean when it runs between its banks and will leave behind such a stink after it floods. I believe the answer is that a flood will turn a river upside down and bring the bottom to the top. When it runs off, you will have river-bottom everywhere you look. Not mud—mud is just dirt that got too wet for its own good. River-bottom is what is supposed to be kept out of sight. River-bottom is the ugly part of nature, where everything gets broken down and turned into something else. It has a lot of death in it, and death carries a powerful charge of smell. Death is a lively business, when you think about it."

"Must be hard to clean up."

"That stuff will *cling*. I figure Edgerton rebuilt itself three times between the 1870s and the start of the century. Every time they built it up, it got bigger. There was a full-time circus in a full-time fairground, you could find two saloons and two gambling houses on every block. It had that same old mentality, you know what I'm saying?"

"Wide open," I said.

"But you had your banks and your businesses, and you had your fine ladies along with your fancy ladies." He sneered at me with what looked like pride. "It was at that time your people arrived in Edgerton, you know. The famous Dunstan brothers, Omar and Sylvan. 1874."

"Omar and Sylvan?" I said. "I never heard of them before."

"The Dunstan brothers rode into town on the back of a hay wagon and jumped off with a couple of valises and two hundred dollars in gold coins. Don't let that hay wagon give you the wrong idea. The Dunstans had a big-city style about them. Smart, good-looking gentlemen who spoke the King's English, knew the best manners, and dressed in the latest fashions. After they found temporary lodgings, Omar and Sylvan walked into a gambling establishment and tripled their grubstake in a single afternoon."

"They were gamblers?"

"Their livelihoods were in commerce and finance. Nobody ever found out what they did before they came to Edgerton, though there was considerable talk. Some said they'd been bounty hunters. One or both of them was rumored to have been in prison."

"What did they do when they got here?"

"Everything they touched prospered. When the floods came along, Omar and Sylvan wound up better off than before. Bought properties cheap off those who left town. Bought land where they figured the town would grow. Fifteen, twenty years later, they held the leases on a lot of important buildings. Naturally, they were as catnip to the ladies."

Clark loved the story of the Dunstan brothers. The arc from the hay wagon to wealth thrilled his imagination. By now, he all but considered Omar and Sylvan blood relatives whose achievements added to his own merit.

"I bet they were," I said.

"Handsome as the Devil, they say." The glorious sneer declared that despite the ravages of age, Clark Rutledge knew himself to be no less handsome. "You couldn't tell 'em apart. They say, from time to time their high spirits led them to give the ladies the impression that they were having a good time with someone other than they thought, if you catch my drift. You can put your money on one thing, they were let into a lot of nice houses when the Mister wasn't at home." He hesitated for a moment. "Howard fell pretty close to the same tree, from what I hear. And so did a couple of the other sons, but they either passed away early in life or ran off."

"There must have been a lot of resentment."

Clark hesitated again. "You know how it goes. Get too high, they slap you down. Omar married a woman from New Orleans name of Ethel Bridges and settled down a bit. Still and all, one morning he left the house we're sitting in right now, and someone shot him dead while he was walking to his carriage. Sylvan heard the shot and got outside just in time to see a man on horseback galloping down the street. That man was never brought to justice. Don't you think he could have been identified? If it was supposed to go that way?"

I nodded.

"Sylvan married his brother's widow, built a house outside of town, and moved in. He and Ethel had some kids, three, four, nobody knows for sure."

"There must be records."

"You're forgetting the *time*, and you're forgetting the *place*. Those babies were all born at home, and the Dunstans didn't care to use midwives or medical men."

"Why not?"

Clark momentarily lost his sneer, but his natural garrulousness won out over discretion. "A long time ago, an old-timer told me the Dunstan brothers never knew if their babies were going to come out deformed in some way medicine never heard about. Like with a huge big head and a body no bigger than a pin. Or a thing with gills under its ears and no arms and legs. Or worse than that. Nearly all those babies died, he told me, but the few that lived were kept in the attic."

He glanced at me. "If you ask me, one or two of Ethel's babies took a wrong turn in the oven, and Howard, the oldest child in the family, overheard more than was good for a little boy. Which could explain why the man became so wild and squandered his money. Howard did considerable damage, all in all. Toward the end, I believe he was plumb out of his head. You'd have to say he was in a kind of dream world."

I thought all of it had come from the dream world, specifically the dream world invented in the rumor mills of a small town. "Which brother was my great-great-grandfather? If Howard was the oldest child of the next generation, I guess it was Omar."

"What I heard was, the brothers shared everything. I don't think they knew which one was Howard's father."

I said something, but I couldn't tell you what it was.

Clark displayed a sneer of magnificent worldliness. "I'd pick Sylvan. Omar was the steadier of the two. Sylvan kept on romancing the ladies even when he was living in that house with Ethel and their kids. When Howard came of age, he acted the same way, except more so. Which counted against him, because by that time Edgerton wasn't the way it used to be."

"It got respectable," I said.

"What happened was, Howard needed an Omar of his own, and because he didn't have one, he ran to seed. The Hatches and the Miltons took advantage of his weakness."

The stairs creaked, and Clark straightened up in his chair. "Best not go into this around Nettie."

■ **29**

■ Registering suspicion at a change in the daily pattern, Nettie lowered her eyebrows at Clark. "Surprised to see you up so soon." She turned her attention to me. "How was your night's sleep?"

"Good enough."

"From what I heard, you thought the Devil was after you. All of us are so worried, it's a wonder we can sleep at all." Nettie billowed to the stove and turned on the gas flame beneath a cast-iron skillet. She took a carton of eggs and a package of bacon out of the refrigerator, slapped the bacon into the skillet, and, like a chef, neatly broke five eggs into a glass bowl with her right hand. "My feeling is that we are going to see some improvement in your mother."

"I hope so," I said.

Nettie whisked the eggs, turned the bacon over in the pan, and took a transparent bag filled with okra from the refrigerator. Soon, about a third of the okra was simmering in another skillet. When the bacon turned brown and crisp, she arrayed the strips on a thick length of paper toweling. She poured the eggs into the skillet and gave them another whisk. The toast had been slathered with butter, sliced diagonally in half, and set at the edges of the plates. She sprinkled pepper and dried parsley into the skillet, gave the eggs another stir, and divided the okra between the plates.

"Do you eat this kind of breakfast every day?"

"Sometimes we add home-fried potatoes, and sometimes we have chicken livers, but today I don't want to take the time. Is the coffee still hot?"

"I'll warm it up," I said, and turned on the flame under the percolator.

The doorbell chimed. "There's May," Nettie said. "Would you let her in, son?"

A UPS driver in a summer uniform stood on the porch,

holding a box wrapped in butcher paper. "Delivery for . . ." He looked at the name above the address. "Ms. Star Dunstan?"

I saw an East Cicero return address in the top left-hand corner of the box. After I signed the pad, I carried the package into the kitchen. "UPS," I said. "Star must have sent some of her things before she came here."

Nettie flapped her hand at the package. "Put that on the floor." I placed it against the wainscoting. Nettie divided the scrambled eggs with a spatula and slid them out onto the plates. The doorbell rang again.

I went back through the living room and opened the door. Resplendent in a flowered hat, Aunt May extended a gnarled paw. "Help me over the doorstep, Neddie. I'm on the late side, but I thought I'd say good morning to Joy. Any chicken livers today?"

"Aunt Nettie thought they would take too much time."

"Chicken livers take only a little bitty time."

May clung to me on the way to the kitchen. I held her arm as she lowered herself into her chair. She made a show of admiring the overflowing plate before her. "Truthfully, chicken livers would have been too much for me today." She handed me her cane.

I sat down between May and Nettie under Clark's ripe gaze. The sisters pitched into their breakfasts. The telephone rang. May dabbed her mouth with a napkin and said, "Perhaps Joy has had another vision."

Shaking her head, Nettie got up from the table and lifted the receiver. "All right," she said. She put her hand over the mouthpiece. "It's that doctor with the big head and the little red mouth."

Within my skull I felt a lightness like a reduction of gravity. I leaned against the counter and said, "Dr. Barnhill? This is Ned Dunstan."

Dr. Barnhill informed me that my mother had experienced another stroke thirty minutes earlier and that the efforts to revive her had been unsuccessful. He also said a lot of other things. It sounded as though he were reading them off a sheet of paper.

I hung up and saw their faces staring at me, suspended between hope and what they already knew to be the truth.

3 HOW I NEARLY WAS KILLED

■ Neither Nettie nor Clark had seemed heartbroken when I told them not to expect me for dinner. Clark had spent the afternoon sulking over having been kept from checking his traps, and Nettie had not forgiven me for the crime of squandering far too much money on a coffin. After the sales pitch in the display room of Mr. Spaulding's Heavenly Rest Funeral Home, she drew me into a corner for a lecture on the subject of sensible behavior. Still under the illusion that my decision had to be sensible because it was mine, I reminded Nettie that I was spending my own money on my mother's burial. She couldn't argue with that, could she? I should have known better.

Mr. Spaulding's ambassadorial presence filtered in and out of view, and Clark shifted his shoulders in his conga-player's shirt and sneered at the velvety carpet. When I took the leather chair before Mr. Spaulding's desk and made out the check, Nettie muttered in complaint. It occurred to me that my selection of the third-least expensive coffin over the bottom of the line had violated the principle that there was no sense spending money on the dead when you could give it to the living. Any illusions that Nettie did not have designs on my checkbook died when Clark nudged the Buick through the brick pillars at the end of Mr. Spaulding's drive, turned toward the Commercial Street office of Little Ridge Cemetery, and said, "Sometimes, boy, you have to think of other people, not just yourself."

My hour and a half with Aunt Joy and Uncle Clarence had been even worse. I went over with the idea that I was performing an act of charity for two old people. I hoped for some information about the interesting figure of Howard Dunstan, and I wanted to see what would happen when I brought up Edward Rinehart. Clarence, remembered as a chipper old party, might still be lively enough to brighten my visit, I thought.

Mindless as an infant, and like an infant oblivious to the stench of his own excrement, Clarence slumped over the leather strap pinning him to his wheelchair. Splotches of dried and drying baby food adorned his shirt. Joy told me that every night at 7:00 she pushed him down the hall to the tub and cleaned him off, although she didn't know where she found the strength. Clarence was getting along just fine. Joy wished that she could say the same for herself.

We sat in the two chairs that were their living room furniture. As Joy escorted me into her maze and my pity yielded to empty-headed horror, the older, drier fetor I had noticed the previous night gradually overwhelmed Clarence's atmosphere. Established, ingrained, it seemed as much an aspect of the house as the floorboards and beams. Everything absorbed it, including Joy, who virtually swam in its sea.

The youngest and most diminished of Howard Dunstan's daughters perched on the edge of her chair and spoke as if she had been saving up the words for decades. There was no point in trying to interrupt her: Joy's bitterness claimed all the conversational space. Her transparent voice grabbed the oars and rowed straight toward the horizon of the known world. When she had reached it, she kept on rowing. Joy was talking about herself, our family, and Howard Dunstan. She plied her oars, and the dry, in-human stink of her father's house carried her forward. Clark's river-bottom had poured into Joy's house and coated everything with what he called "the ugly part of nature." If that was nature, I wanted no part of it.

A flashing crimson hand halted me at an intersection. When my feet stopped moving, my mind filled with the image of Joy perched on a filthy cushion with one bony arm extended toward her husband. I saw what happened next. Blindly, I turned to the left and kept walking. Two blocks down on Pine Street, the next traffic light burned green, enabling me to cross what I half-registered was Cordwainer Avenue.

I barreled along on Pine Street, seeing nothing until a gray-haired giant with the face of a warrior and wearing a red and green dashiki slowed down and stared at me as the distance between us decreased. His expression combined anger and sorrow. I waited for him to speak. At the moment we drew abreast, the giant turned his head but said nothing. The current of tension passing between us snapped almost audibly when we drew apart.

I moved on for another two or three paces, then stopped

walking and looked over my shoulder. The man in the dashiki immediately wheeled around.

"Son, you look like shit and sound like a steam engine. Please tell me you're not about to have a coronary."

"My mother died this morning."

"If you don't start paying more attention to what's going on around you, you'll see your momma a lot sooner than you think. Take care of yourself, boy."

"Okay," I said, and watched him walk off.

I blotted my face with a handkerchief, leaned against a NO PARKING sign, and closed my eyes. Grief flooded upward from the center of my body like a physical presence. I pressed the handkerchief to my eyes. Grief is an industrial-strength emotion, that's all I can say. Grief takes care of business, it tells you where you are.

When the onslaught subsided, I took in my surroundings. Parking lots and chain-link fences bordered auto-parts suppliers, die stampers, storage facilities, and other, less identifiable, concerns. Most of the buildings on Pine Street were one-story and none higher than two. With their grimy brick facades and pebble-glass windows, they looked like reductions of larger, more accommodating structures.

Three blocks later, the chain-link fences and empty lots disappeared, and the brick buildings grew closer and taller. Traffic lights sprouted from every corner. I turned left and walked past windows displaying videotapes and liquor bottles. My shirt began to dry out. A street sign told me that I was on Cobden Avenue. I started feeling hungry.

Cars occupied by young couples and groups of teenagers flowed by. After two more traffic lights, Cobden came to an end at a four-lane boulevard and a small, triangular park. I had reached Commercial Avenue, the center of town. I turned right and moved toward what looked like the action. Ahead of me, two couples with the uncomplicated, affable assurance of Midwestern wealth spun out of a revolving door under the attention of an impassive doorman in epaulets and brass buttons. A flushed, fiftyish man said, "Does he know what's going on? I mean, can you believe that?"

The taller, thinner man he was addressing placed a hand on his shoulder. Gold-rimmed glasses caught the fading sunlight. His rim of white hair had been cropped to a stubble. "You bet I do." Vertical wrinkles creased his face, and yellow teeth filled his carnivorous smile. "In about five minutes, he'll believe it, too."

The dark-haired woman with him said, "Honey, are you going to tell him?" Twenty years younger than the man she called "honey," she had the aerobicized, face-lifted look of a second wife fighting to stay in the game. She sent me an irritated glare that almost immediately turned into something else, something I could not quite identify but that combined surprise, dismay, and embarrassment.

Her husband's chesty *har har har* ridiculed the suggestion of "telling." "I don't have to, because, as everybody knows, our friend . . ." He noticed the look on his wife's face, glanced at me, and abruptly pulled himself upright. He was at least six foot six, another giant, in a grass-green linen jacket and sharply creased pink trousers. A lot of vibrant colors zigzagged across his bow tie. He was in his early seventies and still an unrepentant bully who thought of himself as a powerhouse.

"Do you require some form of assistance?"

I liked the "require." It had a nasty edge you couldn't get from "need." "Require" put you in your place. "Form" was a nice touch, too.

"I'm looking for a good restaurant. What would you recommend?"

Managing his surprise better than I had expected, he swept his hand toward the building beside us. A bronze plate beside the revolving door read MERCHANTS HOTEL. "Le Madrigal. Right off the lobby. We just had dinner there." He noticed something about me that stopped him cold, and his smile faded. "It's pricey, though—pricey. Try Loretta's, three blocks north. They can fix you up a good steak, ribs, anything you want."

"The Madrigal sounds perfect."

"*Lllluuuh* Madrigal, not *The* Madrigal. Around here, it's where the good people get together."

The other man said, "I love it when you talk dirty, G-Man."

"Word of advice, buddy." The G-Man slammed a big hand down on my shoulder. A silken wing of the bow tie slid across my temple. "You can show off, sure, throw your money around, fine, but stop off at the boys' room first and make yourself presentable. A polite little fellow like you wants to fit in, am I right?"

I tilted my face toward his leathery ear. "I don't need your advice, you overbearing small-town shithead."

Recoiling like a compressed spring, he grabbed his wife's arm and yanked her into the street. The other couple flapped their mouths and scurried after them. My friend forced himself to go around the front of a dark green Town Car to open his wife's door while the other couple climbed into the backseat.

For a second or two, the doorman permitted himself to smile at me.

An elderly bellboy directed me up a marble staircase to the men's room. I washed my hands and face under the regard of the black-suited attendant. I trained the hand dryer's flow of warm air onto my shirt, reknotted my necktie, and patted my hair. I used the mouthwash and a splash of designer cologne. The attendant remarked an improvement in my appearance, and I contributed two dollars to his porcelain saucer.

On the other side of the lobby, I went up a smaller, carpeted flight of stairs. An illuminated podium and a headwaiter whose name tag identified him as Vincent stood guard before tables with candles and white tablecloths. Vincent brushed his lips with a forefinger to indicate contemplation and conducted me to a table near the bar. He produced a parchment menu and a leather-bound wine list. My waiter's name would be Julian. A girl who looked like a Norwegian high school student poured ice water into a glass, and a Malaysian sourpuss came by with biscuits and bread sticks. I opened the menu and heard someone speak my name.

Ashleigh Ashton was moving across the room. From the other side of their window table, Laurie Hatch raised her eyebrows and gave me a look that weakened my knees.

■ **31**

■ I ordered salad frisée, a hanger steak, and a glass of cabernet from Julian, a roguish pixie. As for the cabernet, he had a special little something he wanted me to try. If Laurie Hatch saw anything unlikely in Ashleigh's story of giving me a ride to Edgerton, she kept her reservations to herself. Ashleigh had invited Laurie to dinner by reason of her connection to the legal case, but the connection went unexplained. Julian delivered his special little something and awaited the verdict. I expressed my wonder at the majesty of the little something. Julian asked if the ladies would care for their coffee now, or would they like something else? Now, Ashleigh said, she had to go upstairs to make some calls. Laurie requested a glass of the little something.

"How is your mother doing?" she asked.

"Oh, God," Ashleigh said. "I promise you, I've been thinking about your mother ever since you got out of my car. What was it, anyhow?"

"A stroke," Laurie said. "What do the doctors say?"

"They say she died this morning. They better be right, because I just bought a coffin and a cemetery plot." They stared at me in shock. "I'm sorry. I shouldn't have put it like that. It's been a weird day."

Ashleigh said, "At least you were able to spend a whole day with her. Could she talk to you?"

"She was able to say a few things." For a brief time, I found myself unable to speak. The Malaysian sourpuss removed their plates, and the Norwegian girl refilled our water glasses. Julian scurried up with the coffee and the wine.

Laurie asked, "Are you going to stay around after the funeral?"

"I might. I'd like to see more of the town."

"Let me be your tour guide. After all, I'm in your debt."

"Sounds like a great idea," I said, and made myself stop looking at her. "Ashleigh, what's happening with your project?" Her reasons for coming to Edgerton had entirely escaped me.

"If I don't get anywhere in the next day or two, I'll throw in the towel. The guy lives behind too many walls."

"That's Stewart," Laurie said, explaining everything. "I wish I could have been more helpful."

Ashleigh gave me a rueful smile. "We spent most of dinner trading dreadful husband tales."

She had intended to pump her target's estranged wife, and the estranged wife was more than willing to talk. The next exchange between the women brought another clarification.

"Laurie, you won't be in any trouble, will you?"

Laurie shrugged. "I don't care if Stewart knows we had dinner together. Grennie can't hurt me."

"Grenville Milton?"

"The one and only Groin Vile," Laurie said. "And his wife, your mother's old friend. Plus two other people who think I'm a terrible person. They left about five minutes before you got here."

"Is Groin Vile a big old bald-headed character in a bow tie and a green linen jacket who thinks he owns the world?"

"You encountered our Grennie," Laurie said. "I hope he didn't *say* anything to you."

"He told me that I probably wanted to act like a big shot and tip waiters with hundred-dollar bills. Then he advised me to visit the men's room and spruce up."

Laurie groaned. "Grenville felt *good* about it. His state of mind improved no end."

"It took a turn for the worse when I called him an overbearing small-town shithead." Laurie laughed, and Ashleigh opened her mouth in a disbelieving half smile. Julian, whom I had not seen approaching, placed my salad before me with only a trace of his former vivacity and retreated. "I must be on a roll," I said.

"Julian has high moral standards," Laurie said. "Everyone in Edgerton has high moral standards, except me. If I'd heard you call Grennie a shithead, I would have brightened up immediately. I gather he's getting ready to dump Rachel. She's been leaving sad little messages on my answering machine."

She gave me an apologetic look. "When I married Stewart, Rachel Milton took me under her wing and helped me with the kinds of things she cares about, like finding a good hairdresser and the right caterer. She looked at me and saw herself."

"Herself?" I said. "Oh, I get it. A younger woman, an outsider . . ."

Laurie Hatch's dazzling face opened into beautifully ironic assent. "Rachel was too busy identifying to see that ambition had nothing to do with my marrying Stewart."

"Ned, let me put your dinner on my bill, will you?" Ashleigh said. "It's on the state of Kentucky. Laurie, thanks for a nice evening. I'll call you soon."

She signed the check. Julian asked if I would like a second

glass of wine. Laurie Hatch asked for another, too. Ashleigh pushed her chair away from the table.

I said, "I'll walk you to the elevator."

The other patrons watched us wind through the tables.

"I wish Laurie had suggested another restaurant."

"Didn't you get what you wanted?"

She smiled. "I called Laurie to see if she could confirm some details. I thought we'd do the whole thing on the telephone, but she said she was free for the evening. Basically, we spent the entire time complaining about our husbands."

"Better than being alone."

She tucked in her chin with a sharp little nod and pushed the elevator button. "It must be nice, having a woman like Laurie Hatch waiting for you."

"I don't think Laurie has any special plans for me."

"Don't be so sure."

"Ashleigh, when dinner is over, I'm going to walk around for a while. That's it."

"You could come back here. I'm in room 554."

I put my arms around her. "I need some time alone."

Ashleigh bumped her head against my chest and pulled away. "I'm sorry about your mother."

The elevator opened onto mahogany and dark mirrors. Through the half inch of space before the doors closed, I saw her sag against the rear of the car.

■ 32

■ Vinnie glided a hand toward the far side of the room. I didn't fool him for a second, but he had to admit I had good moves.

Laurie Hatch looked at me with a relaxed, self-possessed amusement imbued with the innate consciousness that seemed to radiate from her. Julian snapped the cover from my plate and executed an about-face and a formal departure.

"Remember the old Julian? Remember the pixie?"

Laurie's flickering glance informed me that I had missed the point. "Julian has to wait on Grennie and Rachel at least once a week. He puts up with more innuendos about masculinity than you'll hear if you live to be a thousand."

It was like having my windows cleaned, like putting on new eyeglasses. I said, "Ah. Uh-huh," and cut into the steak.

Her smile changed. "I wish I'd been able to do more for Ashleigh. She's so smart and dedicated. You two get on very well together." *For a hitchhiker and the person who gave him a ride.*

"Ashleigh's easy to get on with. She wanted to hear more about my mother."

"I know how it feels to lose your mother. How is your father doing?"

"I wonder." I smiled at her chagrin. "I never knew my father."

"Do you know where he is?"

"I didn't even know his name until yesterday, when my mother told it to me. I thought I might see what I can find out about him. My family isn't too happy about that."

"They don't understand it? Or are they afraid of what you could find out?"

The question startled me. "They act like I'm being outrageous. They won't talk about things I know they remember."

"What could they be afraid of?"

"God knows. My family is . . . let's say, eccentric."

I had a memory-flash of Aunt Joy leaning forward and aiming a scrawny forefinger across the room to send Clarence's wheelchair rolling a yard forward, a yard back. She squinted. The wheelchair floated four feet off the ground and swung from side to side while Clarence pushed his tongue in and out of his mouth in babyish pleasure.

That's all I can do, now most of my strength is gone. At least I can get him in and out of the bath, because how else is an old lady like me supposed to handle a full-grown man? Wasn't supposed to end up like this, Neddie. We used to be like royalty in this town.

"I loved Aunt Nettie," Laurie said, delivering me from the river-bottom and back to Le Madrigal.

"You can have her. Aunt May, too. Once you have May in your family, you never have to pay for anything again. May just picks it up for you. She's a kind of magician."

"What do you mean? She's a kleptomaniac?"

"May's beyond kleptomania. It's like Zen, like a mystical kleptomania."

Laurie appeared to contemplate the existence of a mystical kleptomania. "But you still want to do it, don't you? You're not afraid."

A tingle of fear threaded my spine. "I want to find out whatever I can."

I heard Joy saying, *Sylvan moved the family out of town, and he and Ethel had a batch of kids, but some of those children, my daddy said, they didn't look human at all. The word for that in French is "épouvante." I was always superior to my sisters in my command of the French language.*

"What was your father's name?"

Speaking his name in public seemed a violation of my privacy, or of some ancient code. I said it anyhow. "Edward Rinehart." It brought back the other name my mother had spoken, Robert. Who was *Robert*?

"What a great name. Swirling fog. A mansion on a rocky cliff above the coastline. A devastatingly handsome man in a trench coat and evening clothes. He never talks about his past. Ladies and gentlemen, I give you . . . Mr. Edward Rinehart."

Feeling even more uncomfortable than before, I said, "I don't think he was much like Maximillian de Winter."

"Excuse me?"

"The husband in *Rebecca*. Grand house, rocky shoreline, unhappy secrets."

"No, *I'm* sorry! *Rebecca* is one of my favorite movies. Laurence Olivier, of course, exactly."

I had been thinking of Daphne du Maurier's novel instead of the Hitchcock movie, but so what?

She placed her hand over mine. "I was going to show you the delights of Edgerton anyhow, so let's see what we can turn up along the way. Together, we could accomplish more than you could on your own." Her dead-level glance might almost have been a plea. "You'd be helping me, too. I need something to think about besides my stupid situation." A moment of self-recognition silenced her, and she glanced away, then back at me. "Look, Ned, if I'm being pushy, or intrusive, or anything like that . . . or sort of crazy . . ."

And Sylvan told my daddy, Howard, don't trust anyone but your kin and don't trust them all that much, because you'll be

*lucky if some night I don't come along and split your head open
with an axe. I always thought it was likely that my daddy shot
Sylvan with that revolver he was supposed to be cleaning at the
time of his death.*

I told her she didn't sound even faintly crazy, compared to
some people in my family.

"All I mean is that helping you would . . ."

Would give her something to do besides brood about Stewart
Hatch. "All right. Let's help each other."

"I'm free all day tomorrow. Stewart gets Cobbie on Saturdays. Which means that a hired flunkey pushes our son on the
swings in Merchants Park until Stewart walks out of his office
long enough to stuff Cobbie full of hamburgers and candy before delivering him to my house at eight P.M."

We tried to work out where to meet. The park across the street
turned out to be the place where the flunkey pushed Cobbie on
the swings. Laurie suggested the front of the main library, four
blocks up from the hotel and two blocks south, on the corner of
Grace and Grenville.

"Grenville?"

"Half the streets in Edgerton are named after the families of
people still walking around. Like Cobden Avenue? Stewart's father was named Cobden Hatch, which is how Cobbie got his
name, of course. When should we meet? Nine-thirty? A friend of
mine, Hugh Coventry, who works at the library, volunteers at
City Hall on the weekends. Everything's closed, but he has access to all the offices, and he gets in around nine."

I asked why she wanted to go to City Hall.

"Edward Rinehart should be in the records. And you might
want to look at copies of your mother's marriage license and
your birth certificate. Nothing like hard data."

"Nothing like a brilliant dinner companion," I said.

Most of the people in the restaurant looked up as we moved
toward the podium. Vincent's smile barely concealed a leer.

In an alcove off the lobby, I went into a booth and placed two
calls. Laurie Hatch was doing her best to look inconspicuous
alongside a potted palm when I came out, and I hurried across
the lobby and followed her through the revolving door. The
doorman handed her yellow ticket to an eager kid in a black vest,
and the kid raced down into the garage.

"Adventure beckons." Laurie lifted her eyebrows in a comic, slyly conspiratorial glance.

The boy in the black vest jumped out of a dark blue Mercury Mountaineer and held the door. Laurie winked at me and drove away, and I walked across Commercial Avenue, going toward Lanyard Street and Toby Kraft's pawnshop. According to Toby, long ago the street had been called Whore's Alley, but these days all the best hookers were married to money and lived in Ellendale.

■ 33

■ I began moving down Ferryman's Road at the top end of triangular Merchants Park. Three-story brick buildings set back on postcard lawns lined both of the streets fanning out from the apex of the triangle. At the top of the steps before the first building in the row, a heavyset man in a tan uniform was flipping through a ball of keys. Wondering what sort of business required the services of a security guard on a Friday night in Edgerton, I looked for a sign, which did not exist. Then I noticed the legend carved on a stone headpiece over the front door: THE COBDEN BUILDING. I laughed out loud—here was where Stewart Hatch did whatever he did with his father's money.

Set deep within a ravaged face the color and texture of oatmeal laced with maple syrup, the guard's eyes fell on me. He looked too old for his job.

"A lot of keys," I said.

"A lot of doors." The guard continued to stare at me, not with the suspicion that would have been inevitable in Manhattan, but with an odd, expectant attentiveness. "No matter how many times I tell myself to put a piece of tape on that first one, I always forget. Here's the little sucker." He held up a key, and his belly strained the fabric of the uniform shirt.

"Do you work for Mr. Hatch?"

"Fifteen years." His smile widened without getting any warmer. "You new in town?"

I told him I was there for a couple of days.

"You should take a walk around Hatchtown, see the real Edgerton."

Ferryman's Road reminded me of certain places I'd seen in the South, parts of Charleston and Savannah. A sense of purpose having to do with my investigations into the life of Edward Rinehart buoyed me up. In time, Joy's irreconcilable story would fade.

My daddy had so much Otherness inside him, he didn't care how he acted. Cruelty was his middle name. It's nothing but a curse, that's all. Nettie, she's got her own views, and whatever's Dunstan can't be bad to her. But Nettie doesn't know. What was in our daddy mostly came down to me, and it spoiled everything.

At the wide end of the park, I turned right on Chester Street and walked through a neighborhood of rooming houses and apartment buildings. Loud music poured from open windows. Mothers and grandmothers perched on the stoops. Outside the tavern on the next corner, men and women in bright clothes were dipping and moving to Ray Charles on the jukebox. Brother Ray was pining for Georgia, and the neighborhood people were celebrating the arrival of the weekend. I turned the corner and walked past an alley where two guys were hauling crates out of a panel truck.

On Lanyard Street the old fancy-houses had been replaced by a shoe-repair shop, an appliance store, a mom-and-pop grocery. The three brass balls of a pawnshop hung above an empty sidewalk.

I looked through the metal grate over the window lettered in gold with KRAFT TRU-VALUE PAWNBROKER. Two small lights burned at the back of the shop. I pushed the bell and heard a noise like an electric drill. A rear door opened in a sudden wash of light, and Toby Kraft came into view.

He unlocked the grate and swung it outward. "Get in here, will you? What a lousy deal, makes you think there's no justice in the world anymore, if there ever was." Toby closed the door and shoved a police bar into place. He closed his hand around mine. "Kid, your mother was a champ."

Toby pulled me into an embrace. "It happened this morning, did it? Were you there?"

"We were still at Aunt Nettie's," I said.

He smoothed his hair and wiped his hands on his trousers. "How are you doing?"

"I couldn't tell you," I said.

"How about a schnocker?"

"No, I just. . . . Yeah, why not?"

"I'm still busy, but it won't take long." When I looked at the counter, he said, "Your momma sure brightened up the place when she stood back there. Who's getting your business, Spaulding?"

It took me a moment to understand what he meant. "Nettie thinks I spent too much money."

At the back of the shop, Toby waved me into a small, hot room with fluorescent lights. A metal desk heaped with papers faced out from the back wall, and a low bookcase jammed with green ledgers and a metal safe stood against a half partition dividing the office from a darker space containing rows of industrial shelving. Old calendars with pictures of naked, lushly upholstered women plastered the walls. The men I had seen in the alley were carrying boxes into the area beyond the partition. "Kraft?" one of them said.

"It's just my grandson." Toby turned back to me. "Don't let those girls poor-mouth you. They have enough to get by on. When's the funeral?"

"Wednesday morning." I sat down on the folding chair.

Toby sighed. "One second." He went around the gap in the partition and talked to the men. I heard the truck drive away.

"I'm glad Nettie and May have enough to get by on."

He rubbed two fingers together and winked. "I promised you a drink." He took a liter of Johnnie Walker Black and two smudgy glasses from a bottom drawer of his desk. "Sorry about the no ice, but I never got around to putting in a fridge." A pack of unfiltered Camels and a gold lighter came out of his shirt pocket. He poured three inches of whiskey into our glasses. "I wish it was a happier occasion. Here's to Star."

We clinked glasses.

"You getting on okay?"

"Pretty well," I said. "I saw Joy today."

"Been a long time since I did." We drank. When he thrust the bottle toward me, I shook my head. "She and Clarence doing okay, or is that too much to ask?"

"Clarence has Alzheimer's," I said. "She keeps him strapped in a wheelchair and feeds him baby food."

"I don't suppose Clarence is much of a conversationalist anymore."

"Joy did a lot of talking, though," I said.

He tilted back in his chair and smiled. "You're a smart kid, I don't have to tell you which end is up. Joy is a very unhappy person."

I took another swallow of whiskey and thought about what to say. "I don't suppose a lot of Dunstan babies were born with wings and claws, but there must have been something funny about a couple of Howard's brothers and sisters, because Clark mentioned it, too."

Toby propped his head on the back of his chair and stared up at the fluorescent light. A plume of smoke floated toward the ceiling. "First of all . . ." He grabbed the bottle and leaned forward. "Have some more goddamn Scotch. You're making me do all the work." I offered my glass, surprised that it was almost empty. He added more to his own, set down the bottle, and considered me for a moment. This was going to be good.

"First of all, think about Nettie's husband. I say that because being Nettie's husband is Clark Rutledge's full-time job. He's the vice president of Dunstan, Incorporated, and one thing about Clark, the man loves his work. What's the main thing about work?"

"The salary?"

"Nope. Work gives you a place in the world. Clark is Somebody because he's a Dunstan, and he'll milk that cow until it drops. On top of that, Clark is not on your normal wavelength. One day he's telling you why the Jewish people, one of which is me, brought on Hitler by hoarding all the gold in Germany. The next day, the Jews are a great people because they're the people of the Book."

I smiled at him.

"Okay, that's Clark, first of all. Joy, now, Joy always felt left out. You notice how she talks about her daddy all the time?"

I nodded.

"Howard was a strange guy, but him and Queenie always got along. Joy had a problem with that. Joy was one of those kids, whine, whine, whine. Gimme more, gimme more, and it's never enough, right? Women built like that, they always want more than what they got, because what they got is never enough. It can't be, on account of they got it."

Toby's description seemed surprisingly acute.

"Queenie knew how to handle the old man, but Joy only knew how to get sore. Take what she says with all the salt in the grocery store, and then some."

"Joy weighs about ninety pounds. Clarence is maybe one fifty, pure deadweight. She gives him a bath every night."

"Good trick."

"Joy says she inherited psychic powers from her father, and all that's left of them is enough to pick Clarence out of his wheelchair, lower him into the tub, clean him up, dry him off, and move him back into the chair."

"I'll give her this, her stories are getting better."

"She moved his wheelchair back and forth just by pointing at it. Then lifted her finger and made it float off the ground and swing around in midair. Clarence liked it so much, he drooled like a baby."

Behind the thick glasses, Toby's eyelids rattled down and up twice, like window shades. I reached for the bottle.

"That stupid fuckin' Joy." He heaved himself off his chair and went around the partition. I heard him check the lock on the alley door. The Camels came out of his pocket. He took out a cigarette and examined it for flaws. After he got the cigarette going, he tilted back in his chair and looked at me some more.

■ 34

■ "This is what you came here to talk about?"

"It's one of the things I came here to talk about."

He ran a pudgy hand over his face. "I don't even know that much to begin with."

"You know more than I do. And everyone else refuses to say anything at all."

"Star didn't want you to know about this business."

"What business is that?"

"What passed down through your family, starting with Omar and Sylvan. You heard about Omar and Sylvan?"

"Oh, yes," I said. "Particularly from Joy."

Joy's frail voice told me, *My grandfathers, they were the surviving remnants of pagan gods and could have ruled over earthly Dominions but cared for nothing but wealth and pleasure. To build that house on New Providence Road, Sylvan had the ancestral house in England taken apart stone by stone and brick by brick, and he shipped all those stones and bricks across the sea and put them back together again exactly the way they were in the old days. He might as well have flushed his money down the toilet. My daddy was the same way. C'est dommage.*

"She could of had the decency to keep her mouth shut."

"Because my mother didn't want me in on the family secret. Whatever it is."

Toby took another slug of whiskey and pressed the glass against the silver fur spilling out of his shirt. "Your mother wanted to protect you. I'd say she did a pretty good job."

I stared at him without speaking.

Toby raised his left hand and held it palm up, so the smoke curled around his fingers. The gesture said: it's no biggie. "You were normal. There was stuff you were better off not knowing."

"I was normal."

"When Joy was a baby, I guess, if she didn't get fed on time, shit went flying all over the place, windows broke. . . . Where with you, all that happened was, you had those fits. Which ain't that unusual for a person. Hey, does that still happen?"

Recognitions, thoughts of a kind, began to take shape in my mind.

"I always hoped you were gonna grow out of that."

"Toby, you just said, 'All that happened was you had those fits.'"

"You did! Right there on your third birthday."

"But everybody thought something *else* might happen to me. You were waiting to see if I was going to make things fly around the room."

His face sagged into a trapped, gloomy frown.

"We're talking about what passed down through the Dunstans. When it got to me, it looked ordinary enough to look normal."

"You never should of went to college," he said. "You listen too good."

"How much did Howard pass down to Queenie?"

"My wife had a lot of Dunstan in her, I'll say that much." He pulled at his whiskey and smiled to himself. "Sometimes she'd rise up a couple feet off the bed and hang there. Sound asleep. Take the covers with her. Damndest thing you ever saw in your life. And she *knew* things." A memory made him laugh. "The first year we were married, two different pairs of idiots walked into the shop to score some easy money. They were thinking, old lady like that, show her a gun, she'll give it up fast. What you call a basic error in judgment."

Toby chuckled. "Second they come in, Queenie hauls the shotgun up from behind the counter. Scares the shit out of the little bastards. 'Lady,' they say, 'you're making a mistake, put down the gun before something bad happens.' Queenie says, 'If you don't get your asses out the door before I count three, you bet something bad is gonna happen, only you won't know about it.' Never had any more problems with stickups."

"Good for her," I said.

"Queenie had talent to burn. She wasn't queen of the magpies only because of her fast hands."

"Ah," I said.

Toby showed his discolored teeth. "Say you're in the kitchen, talking about this and that, and Queenie's next to the table. You go to the fridge, get some ice. When you look back, she fell through a trap door. You go out of the kitchen and yell, 'Queenie?' The bedroom door opens up, and out she comes, holding a feather duster. 'What the hell?' you say. She says, 'There's a spiderweb over the kitchen window and, for your information, we keep the duster in the bedroom closet.' You get in the mood for a new TV set and figure you shouldn't have to pay for it, a thing like that is one hell of an advantage."

"The girls inherited their father's talents."

Toby refilled both glasses. "Queenie most of all, then Joy and Nettie. But May got her share." His eyes drifted over the collage of naked women. "When May was about thirteen, she was going down Wagon Road—that's Cordwainer Avenue now—in Howard's rumble seat. What Queenie told me, May saw two girls pointing at her from another car. You know, laughing at her. I always had the feeling it took more than that, because Howard's family couldn't go anywhere without attracting notice. Once I asked May straight out, but she went into her vague act. Anyhow, *whatever* the hell she saw made her so mad she put on a fireworks display. Smashed windshields all up and down Wagon Road, blew out tires. Snapped the telephone lines. Everything went crazy."

Joy's papery voice rustled in my ear:

And my sister May created havoc on Wagon Road by setting off thunderations, even though to hear my daddy talk she was hardly a Dunstan at all, which was a nasty, untrue insult to my sister.

Because when we were young women, a gentleman came along who showed a liking for May. Unfortunately, the gentleman did not like her in the proper way and attempted to force her to his will. Rape is what that man had in mind. May took care of that fellow through what the French would call force majeure. She came home in great agitation and told me, Joy, my young gentleman attempted to take advantage of me. I was so frightened, I found in me the power to rise up and demolish my young gentleman. After I demolished him, my young gentleman was only a stinky little green puddle I cannot bear to remember.

I don't know how you can be more Dunstan than that.

"There was some business about a boy who tried to rape her," I said.

"Good old Joy," Toby said. "Leave no rock without first you roll it over."

I asked if he knew anything about Star's father.

"Queenie said Star's father was a jazz drummer, but she didn't tell me his name. That's where Star's musical ability came from, she said. I had the idea he might have been sort of like a Dunstan himself, the drummer. Truth is, I always thought Ethel Bridges, the New Orleans woman who married Sylvan after Omar got killed, was another one like that." He grinned at me. "Didn't you get pretty good on the guitar, up there in Naperville?"

Star had boasted about my guitar playing to Toby.

"I tried," I said.

"A couple of times, customers came in with big band photographs, like Duke Ellington or Benny Goodman, where the musicians signed their names. I used to look at the drummers in those pictures and think, If you're the one, you had a daughter you never knew about, but you would have been proud of her."

"That's lovely," I said, struck by his tenderness. "I guess people have the wrong idea about pawnbrokers."

"You know what we are? Protection for people who need protection. Or we used to be, before the banks started handing out credit cards right and left."

I felt the clarity of a long-overdue understanding. "Oh, boy." My skin was tingling. "I just *got* it. My mother had me put into foster care to protect me from her family."

"Well, yeah," Toby said, as if I had said that having a lot of money and living in a mansion was more agreeable than scraping by on food stamps in a tenement.

"When I did come home, she must have ordered everyone to watch what they said. I wasn't supposed to know about the Dunstans."

"She wanted you to have a regular life."

"And her aunts didn't like that. They didn't see the point."

Toby rested his forearms on the cluttered desk. The egglike eyes were perfectly clear. "All the time you were a little kid, my wife and her sisters hoped you were going to show you had some Dunstan in you. When you got older, and Star put her foot down, it set up like a barrier."

"That's why I never came back to Edgerton after I was twelve. She didn't trust Nettie and May."

Toby poured out the last of the Johnnie Walker Black, mostly into his own glass. "About time we wrapped this up. Before you go to bed, maybe take a couple aspirins." He smiled at me. "Was there anything else you wanted to talk about?"

"Just one more thing," I said.

"Shoot."

"Right before we left the hospital, Star managed to get out a few words. They were about my father."

Toby's head drifted up.

"She said his name was Edward Rinehart."

The window shades went down and up again behind the thick lenses.

"Your in-laws want me to forget the whole thing. They know something, but they're not talking."

"What makes you so sure?"

"Star lived with the guy before she married him. Nettie would know his name."

"You'd think," he said.

"You know it, too, Toby."

He smiled. "I deal with hundreds of people, day in, day out. Names go in and out of my mind."

"You can do better than that," I said.

He pushed himself back and walked around the desk to stand in front of a picture of a black-haired woman proffering breasts like slightly deflated beachballs on the palms of her hands. "I am not a schlub who spent his whole life behind a counter. In 1946, the year after I got out of the army, I had a white Cadillac convertible and seven thousand bucks in the bank. Important people invited me to their houses, treated me like family. I killed a man once when he didn't give me a choice, and I did six months at Greenhaven for a deal where basically I stood up for someone else. Toby Kraft is not Clark Rutledge."

"And somewhere along the line, you met Edward Rinehart."

He peered at me through the thick lenses. "Star gave you that name?"

"Definally." I tried again. "Def-in-at-ly." I discovered that my glass contained only half an inch of whiskey.

"I maybe remember something." We experienced a meaningful pause. "After the funeral, suppose you work here for a week or so. Hundred bucks a day, cash."

"What's this, a trade-off?"

"An offer."

"It's still a trade-off, but all right," I said.

Toby pretended to search his memory. "I never met this Rinehart, but he got around, was my impression. From the little bit that sticks in my mind, he got into different places. A certain guy might be able to help you." He marched behind his desk, sat down, and searched through the rubble for a pen and a pad of notepaper. He leveled an index finger at me. "I didn't give you this name."

"Right," I said.

He scribbled, tore the top sheet off the pad, folded it in half, and passed it to me. "Put it in your pocket. Look at it tomorrow and decide what to do. You want to let bygones be bygones, that's okay, too."

The office swayed like the deck of a ship.

"Hasta la vista," Toby said, shrinking again as he stood up.

■ I was okay until I heard the blare of the jukebox. The more I walked, the better I got at it. Then I moved, not too unsteadily, into the noise of Whitney Houston howling about everlasting love, and the combination of alcohol and night air struck my nervous system. As I drifted across the sidewalk, a lamp post swung toward me, and I grabbed it with both arms before it could get away.

I held on until the sidewalk stopped moving and passed through the crowd outside the bar, assisted by a gentleman who seized my arm and propelled me southward. Women young and old regarded me in great solemnity from their stoops. At last I reached Merchants Park and stumbled to a bench. I dropped into its embrace and fell asleep.

I awakened with a pounding head and an ache in my gut. Lamplight illuminated the words carved into the slab over the entrance of the first building in the terrace across the street. THE CORDWAINER BUILDING. I gathered my feet under me, and the pain in my belly took solid form and flew upward. I expelled a quart of watery, red-brown stew onto the asphalt.

It was 11:35. I had been passed out on the bench for at least an hour and a half. Nettie and Clark were not yet so soundly asleep that I could get to my room unheard, and I was nothing like presentable enough to pass inspection. I needed to rinse my mouth and drink a lot of water. At the far end of the park stood a good-sized drinking fountain.

A granite basin flowed into a tall, octagonal pedestal. I located a brass button on the side of the basin and rinsed my mouth, gulped water, splashed my face, and gulped more water. I looked down and noticed the inscription on the base of the pedestal.

DONATED THROUGH THE GENEROSITY OF STEWART HATCH. "BY THE WATERS OF BABYLON SHALL YOU LIE DOWN AND REST." 1990.

Before me lay an hour of free time, waiting to be filled. I straightened my necktie, buttoned the jacket of my best blue suit, and walked not all that unsteadily out of the park in search of the night-blooming Edgerton.

■ **36**

■ Two streets vivid with neon signs and theater marquees extended eastward from Chester. A fat crimson arrow flashed like a neon finger. The darker red, vertical stripe of HOTE PARIS hung over a smoked glass door. People in groups of three and four, most of them men, meandered down the streets.

Low Street to my left, Word Street to the right. I picked Word because it was closer, and before I had taken two steps noticed a bronze plate designed to look like a curling sheet of parchment. At the top of the scroll were the words OLD TOWN. I moved up to peer at the legend.

Site of the Original Town Center of Edgerton, Illinois, an Important Commercial and Recreational Destination for All Who Journeyed on the Mississippi River. Restorations in Progress Supported Through the Generosity of Mr. Stewart Hatch.

The only signs of restoration I could see on Word Street were the lamp posts, two per block, which had the white glass globes of old Art Deco gas fixtures. The buildings, bars, movie theaters, liquor stores, transient hotels, and tenements had a hangdog look, as if they expected to be ordered off by a policeman. Splashes of neon light lay across dirty brick and flaking timbers. Men in worn-out clothes ducked in and out of the bars. Here and there, better-dressed people cruised up and down the sidewalks. A few residents sat out in lawn chairs, enjoying the night air.

A little way ahead, a couple straight from an advertisement for organically produced soap-free soap detoured around a drunk propped against the front of a bar. A familiar-looking rodent in a goatee and a black leather jacket slid past them and darted across the street.

I watched him slip out of sight into a neon-flickering passage and realized that I had entered what remained of the raffish village Uncle Clark had described. Here was the survival of the Edgerton where crews and passengers from the steamers had disembarked to gamble, visit bordellos, gape at the dancing bears and two-headed goats at the fairground, have their palms read and their purses cut. The town had remained essentially the same, at least if you stood in my great-great-grandfathers' Edgerton late on a Friday night.

I moved across the street in the direction of the lane and the rodent in the leather jacket.

■ 37

■ Seconds after entering Dove Lane, I learned that there were two Old Towns, the one comprised of Low and Word streets, and the other, separate Old Town hidden behind them. A maze of twisting lanes sprouted smaller, darker passages as they meandered into postage-stamp squares on their journeys toward dead ends or one of the wider streets. Stewart Hatch's philanthropy had not extended to the hidden Old Town, and the lamps on byways like Dove were glassed-in bulbs on top of iron columns at least seventy years old. Every third or fourth bulb had been broken, but the district's neon signs and illuminated windows washed the narrow lanes in light.

At the next corner, Dove continued past dark storefronts and abandoned buildings. I turned right into Leather, where the brightness had lead me to expect strip clubs and massage parlors. Light spilled from a glass-fronted laundromat, where a half dozen tired-looking women idled on benches in front of churning dryers.

From Leather I turned into Fish, then Lavender, Raspberry, Button, Treacle, and Wax. About the time I left Button, I became aware of footsteps behind me. The quiet footsteps continued to follow mine through Treacle and Wax, though I saw no one when I looked back. Wax led into Veal Yard, where light shone upon a dry fountain from the windows of the Brazen Head hotel. I circled into Turnip, walked past a bar called The Nowhere Near and again heard footsteps sounding behind me. I looked over my shoulder and glimpsed a dark, moving shape. My heart missed a beat, and the shape melted away.

I hurried over the slippery cobbles and emerged once again into the bustle of Word Street. What I saw on its other side told me exactly where I was.

Outside the glass doors of a two-story bar, the furtive character I had followed into Old Town's lanes jittered in a hipster shuffle as he explained something to a chunky blond woman wearing a half-unbuttoned denim jacket. She was Cassie Little, Clark Rutledge's beloved, and the rodent was named Frenchy La Chapelle. I had seen both of them in St. Ann's ICU. SPEEDWAY LOUNGE blared in pink neon above the doors.

A hand closed on my left elbow, and a well-rubbed voice whispered, "Buddy, I don't know about brains, but you do got balls."

The disheveled old man beside me grinned up at my surprise. Dingy gray curls escaping from a flat cap; concave cheeks shiny with gray stubble; layers of unclean clothes; a clear, pervasive smell of alcohol. "Piney Woods," he said. "Remember me?"

■ **38**

■ "I wasn't here on Thursday night," I said. "But I heard about you from my Uncle Clark."

"Unless you don't happen to be here now, either, you better slide back into Turnip." He pointed at four men with rocky faces and shirts open over T-shirted guts who were assembling in front of the Speedway. They had the look of small-town roughnecks who had changed in no essential way since the age of sixteen. Cassie Little had disappeared inside the bar, and the rodent had exercised his talent for evaporation. Three of the men carried baseball bats. I let Piney pull me back into the lane.

"My old poker buddies, I suppose," I said.

"Staggers and them." Piney moved to block me from view. "They got some ornery mothers over in Mountry."

I looked over his shoulder. "Which one is Staggers?"

"Him in the fatigue pants."

Him in the fatigue pants had the spoiled, seamed face of a man who had never recovered from the disappointment of learning that he did not rule the world, after all. He was smacking his hands together and growling orders and, despite his belly, looked as though he spent his work day pulverizing boulders with a sledgehammer.

"Seems like the boys are getting ready to break up again, take one last look around."

"I heard someone following me," I told him.

"Like I said, you're lucky. You want to stay that way, you should get out of Hatchtown, pronto."

I hurried back into Veal Yard. On its other side and to the left of Wax, Pitch Lane wound deeper into Hatchtown. I ran down it, hoping that it would lead me to the vicinity of Lanyard Street and Toby Kraft's pawnshop.

Pitch joined Treacle for the length of a listing ruin exhaling the odors of ammonia and rotting apples. I heard again the click of approaching footsteps. On the other side of the ruin, I dodged into the continuation of Pitch and jogged down dark twists and turns. The pursuing footsteps rang with a deliberation more frightening than haste. Midden intersected Pitch, but . . . forget Midden. Use your imagination. When I came to Lavender, I looked to my left. Two ragged boys who appeared to have sprung unaltered from a slum photograph of New York in the 1890s regarded me from the door of an abandoned building. To my right, high-pitched female laughter came through the window of a shoebox called No Regrets. From beyond it, heavy footsteps plodded forward. Whoever the first man might be, this was one of Joe Staggers's friends.

My two would-be assailants drew nearer, one approaching from behind, the other from my right on Lavender. One of the boys jerked his thumb toward his shoulder and stepped back, and I jumped through the opening into lavender-scented darkness.

Broken bands of light streamed through chinks in the front of the building. Against the rear wall a huddle of boys slept beneath tangled blankets. I prowled down the wall, looking for a gap wide enough to see through. My savior followed me.

"After ya?"

"Thanks for your help."

"Wheere's a bit o' money, den?"

I pulled a bill from my pocket, held it before a glimmering quarter-inch crack to expose George Washington's secretive face, and gave the dollar to the boy.

"Wanna hurt ya?"

I squatted on my heels and put my eye to the crack.

"You kin speer anudder dollar."

I gave him a second bill.

From the back of the warehouse, someone whispered, *"Shove 'im in the Knacker, Nolly."*

The lane before me was still empty, but I could hear the approach of heavy footfalls. From further away came a lighter *tap tap tap*. The boy lay down and pressed his eye to another crack.

"The Knacker for 'im."

A T-shirted paunch and a thick arm holding a baseball bat heaved into view. The man came to a halt and looked behind him, at the building across the lane, then at the old lavender warehouse. He ticked the bat against a cobble.

"See a guy come down this way?"

The boy in the doorway said, "Seen a couple."

"A tourist."

"Ran down there," the boy said. "Puffin' hard."

The gut swung around. "How long ago?"

"Just passed by."

The man with the bat moved away, and soon my rescuer and I slipped back through the door. I asked if they lived in the old building.

"We sleeps here when it's hot."

"Sometimes we gets fetchin' money," said the smaller boy.

"For instance," Nolly said, "if you needed a certain thing, we maybe could find that thing for you."

"Can you help me find my way out of here?"

They glanced at each other.

"For a buck," I said.

Nolly extended a grubby hand, and I surrendered another

dollar. So quickly that I scarcely saw him go, he set off down Lavender in the direction opposite to that taken by my pursuer. I followed him through passages called Shoelace, Musk, and Pineapple.

"Where do we come out?"

I would see when we got there.

We turned off Pineapple into Honey, a six-foot passage with a lamp burning at its far end. Plodding footsteps reached us from an adjoining lane. Nolly hesitated. A second later came the overlapping sound of leather soles ticking against stone cobbles. Nolly darted down the length of Honey. I ran after him, all too aware that the men could hear me as well as I heard them. We came out into a pocket court called White Mouse Yard, and Nolly pointed across to a dim opening. "Take Silk," he said. "Go Silk, Glass, Beer, and you're out." He raced into an adjacent lane.

The approaching footsteps grew louder.

I ran into Silk. The heavy steps came toward me, and I stopped and looked back. The sound swung around through the narrow lane and appeared to come from before me. I moved ahead and heard the lighter, ticking footfalls from somewhere on either side. At the bottom of the lane I turned blindly into what I hoped was Glass, jogged toward the lamp at the next crossing of the lanes, and realized that the only steps I heard were my own. Cursing, I wrenched off my loafers.

In front of me, a broad figure shifted around the corner and filled the center of the lane beneath the lamp. The figure raised a baseball bat and charged.

At that moment, someone grabbed my collar, spun me aside, and pushed me onto the cobbles. When I raised my head, I saw him *pounce*—stride forward and leap like a tiger upon the man in front of me. I groped for my shoes. The baseball bat scraped against the side of the passage, flashed upward, and swung down. I heard a squashy, battered-watermelon noise. The bat landed with a heavier, softer impact. I moved back from the carnage, and the bat skittered toward me over the cobbles.

Overhead, a man leaned through a bright square of window. In the faint light, a ponderous corpse sprawled over the cobblestones. A slim figure in a blue suit sauntered to the far end of Glass and paused. A dreamlike terror made half of anticipation arose in me.

The man at the crossing of the lanes took an unhurried step into the light and turned to face me. What he was going to say made him smile. No longer dreamlike but imported in every particular from an actual dream, terror glued me to the cobbles. The thought of what he would say filled me with horror.

"Ned, never turn down a lady's invitation." His voice was mine and not mine.

My obscene double glimmered at me in affectionate, mocking contempt. For a fragment of a second, I caught in his face an echo of the sense of recognition that had vaulted me out of my nightmare. At the moment he vanished down the gauzy lane, I realized that Star had given me his name.

I felt like fainting, like falling down and weeping for a grief lodged at the center of my heart, like ascending two feet off the ground and detonating into bloody scraps. Robert had shown himself to me. Helplessly, as if to follow, I stepped forward, then turned and ran.

39 ▪ Mr. X

▪ What *comes over* me? What demon undoes me with visitations of the river-bankish state?

I bow my head in disgrace, that I questioned my Master and his Works. Who am I? Who was my true father? *Those Whateleys meant to let them in, and the worst of all is left!*

(While transcribing these lovely words, I was gripped by a tide of laughter from which I only now begin to recover. I wipe away joyous tears and continue.)

I here record my Breakthroughs in the order they were granted.

The depression evident in the previous entry had discouraged me from night-time rambles. As a result, I collapsed into bed before midnight and arose at wretched sunrise. Seated before the unsullied section of my dining table, I was searching through the rubble for a half-eaten cruller deposited there no more than a week ago, when my hand closed around the stony cruller, and a great light shone upon me from the dark, dark heavens, and an invisible orchestra released a giant chord, complete with kettle-drums. The arrival of this radiant, light-filled (darkness-filled) harmony spoke of one thing only. That instant, Star Dunstan had ceased to be and given up the ghost, farewell, goombye, ta ta, amen.

Apart from the sense of revenge given me by the Star-sow's passing, my instantaneous knowledge of the event whisked the doomy clouds from the internal skies. Here, here, was proof that all was not illusion, that my Mission endured. My ferocious fathers smiled down, to the extent that such Beings can be said to smile. I tossed the fossilized cruller in the direction of the garbage pail, anyhow toward the glistening mound where the pail used to be, and leaped up to pace the open bits of floor until sufficient time had passed for the body to be discovered. After perhaps ten minutes, I dialed Edgerton's second-best hospital and experienced an uneasy moment in which my call was transferred to the intensive care unit. Even worse, one Nurse Zwick announced that although ICU patients could not receive telephone calls directly, my message would be passed on to the patient in question. I identified the patient in question. The admirable Zwick hesitated no more than a half second before telling me in businesslike tones that Ms. Valerie Dunstan had but moments ago expired.

Even when anticipated, an event such as this blows away the cobwebs.

◼ Revived, I spent the day perusing the Providence Master's Sacred Texts, in the process noting a hundred speaking touches in tales I had once discounted, for instance, to give but one instance, although I had read "Pickman's Model" countless times, until this very day I had not taken in the relevance of these lines:

At a guess I'll guarantee to lead you to thirty or forty alleys and networks of alleys . . . that aren't suspected by ten living beings outside of the foreigners that swarm them. . . . These ancient places are . . . overflowing with wonder and terror and escapes from the commonplace. . . .

The Providence Master was describing Hatchtown!

I once again propose—*envision*—a Valhalla-like Museum of the Elder Gods. The Record of my adventures, opened to this

very page of the Boorum & Pease journal, lies installed upon
a likeness of my table alongside a replica of my Mont Blanc
(medium-point) pen in a diorama-like affair a few steps or
slithers beyond a representation of the Master's own desk and
writing implements. An animated representation of myself rises
from the desk and paces to the sink, there to stand in a speaking
pose, perhaps even actually to speak some poignant lines from
this Record. It would be fitting, after all . . .

The sympathetic reader will understand my tears.

The Sage had turned his flat, almond-shaped eye upon me and
winked. My tears were those of long-withheld, healing resolution. The word *ecstasy* would not be out of place.

So it was that later I seized the opportunity of a thirty-minute
"break" or surcease in that humble occupation which enables me
to pay the rent and keep body and soul together to slip out and
partake of the night air. I was ready for anything, and with the
Master's confirming periods ringing in my inner ear I went ad-
venturing through Hatchtown's byways and hidden courts.

40 ■ Mr. X

■ I faded through the bands of tourists, sticking to the shadows
out of habit, even though most of those idiots would have had
trouble seeing me if I stood under a lamp post and played "Lady
of Spain" on an accordion.

In my progress up Word Street, I noticed four middle-aged
ruffians skulking out of Purse Lane. Three of the four carried
baseball bats, and their glances up and down the street, their investigations through the open doors of taverns, declared them
hounds sniffing for a coon. Mountry's rough, backwoods atmosphere enveloped them like a fog. All hills and vales strung together with muddy roads disfigured by shacks whose weedy
front yards sprouted old cars, broken appliances, and now and
then a few pigs, Mountry had provided an unending supply of
brutal dumbbells back in my days of art and crime. I did not suppose it had changed much over the years. I wandered unseen

toward the bully-boys, and the ripest of plums dropped straight into my astonished hand.

The plum's descent began with the sight of Frenchy La Chapelle bopping on the balls of his feet as he kept a wary eye on the hound pack. He *knew* about them; they made him nervous. Although alike in breaking every law they could at every opportunity, Frenchy and the Mountry boys were of different species and as instinctively natural enemies as the cobra and the mongoose. Their antithetical physical types increased the instinctive hostility, the Frenchys tending toward a rodentlike sleekness and the rednecks sharing an inclination to potato-sack bellies and beefsteak faces.

I sauntered invisible alongside the bully-boys. Their commander muttered this heavenly imprecation: "Dunstan's around somewhere. Check out the alleys and meet me back at the Speedway."

My heart, that old warhorse, foamed at the bit.

I hastened across the street and materialized beside Frenchy. In years past, I now and again had summoned him to my service, invariably with the sense of mysteriously accommodating myself within a range of visibilities rather than anything as decisive as making myself visible. As far as Frenchy is concerned, one minute I'm not there and the next minute I am, and the process dismays him far more than he wants to let on.

When he became aware of my presence, he flinched, then twitched his narrow shoulders and pretended he was doing loosening-up exercises. People like Frenchy never loosen up, and their only exercise is running from the police. "How come I never see you sneakin' up on me?"

"You don't look in the right places," I said.

He gave a rim-shot laugh, *rat! tat!,* bounced up and down, and glanced across Word Street.

"Do you know those hillbillies?"

He shot me a wary look, then thrust his hands into the pockets of the leather jacket. "Might have seen 'em in the Speedway."

I raised my head to expose, beneath the brim of my hat, my left eye.

"One of 'em's called Joe Staggers," he said. "I'm kind of busy right now."

"No, you're not," I said. "Two nights ago, you were busy behind Lanyard Street with Clyde Prentiss. Tonight you have nothing to do but listen to me."

Frenchy jittered himself back into a semblance of confidence. "Clyde's only a friend of mine, all right?"

"The old Grueber warehouse," I said. "Microwaves. How many did you get before Clyde's mishap, a dozen?"

Frenchy breathed through his mouth while admiring the lighted upper windows of a tenement across the street. "Around ten. I dumped 'em in the river."

He was telling me what he should have done. All twelve of the stolen microwaves were stacked against a wall of his tiny apartment.

"Clyde Prentiss represents a threat to your freedom," I said. "If he should happen to recover, he'll turn you in for a reduced sentence. Some would say Clyde should have done his friends the favor of dying."

Frenchy tried to look unconcerned. "The poor guy could go at any moment. Bad heart. Fifty-fifty chance."

"I am going to improve those odds, Frenchy," I said. He stopped twitching. "After tonight, you won't have to worry about Prentiss. In return, you will perform a number of errands for me. You will be remunerated. This is your first installment." A fifty-dollar bill passed from my hand into Frenchy's pallid hand, thence into a zippered pocket.

He ventured a sidelong glance. "Uh, are you saying . . ."

"You know perfectly well what I'm saying. Who are those meatheads after?" I wanted to learn how much he knew.

"A guy named Dunstan took some bread off 'em in a card game. They're sore."

"Would you recognize Dunstan if you saw him?"

"Yeah."

"I want you to work through the lanes. If you see Dunstan, tell him that someone wants to meet him in Veal Yard. Show him the way. If you run into Staggers or his pals, send them in the opposite direction."

He moved away, and I said, "Unload those microwaves in Chicago."

Frenchy took off as though jet-propelled. I slipped back across Word Street and into the nearest lane. My long-delayed encounter with Master Dunstan would not occur until the brat's birthday, but in the meantime it was my ironic duty to protect him from harm. I went gliding up Horsehair with every anticipation of spilling a quantity of Mountry blood.

Though I could wish for half a dozen Horsehairs, one will do. Swelling and contracting in width, a back alley's back alley, it snakes back and forth through Hatchtown, and from within its walls the experienced listener can discern a great deal of what is going on around him. In high good humor, I awaited broadcasts from Mountry.

Hatchtown residents stumbled home, lurched into taverns, wrangled, copulated. Children squalled, slept, squalled again. I was pretty sure I heard Piney Woods humming to himself as he shambled along Leather toward Word Street, but it may have been some other derelict old enough to remember "Chattanooga Choo-Choo." I ducked into Veal Yard, and the music for which I had been searching came to me from the direction of Pitch and Treacle.

The music in question was the *click-slop, click-slop* of cobblestones meeting steel-tipped boots with run-down heels, high-style footwear amongst Mountry's finest. I made my way into Wax. The yokel made pursuit all the easier by rapping his baseball bat against the bricks, producing a sharp, ringing *tock!* vivid as a flare. I was still unable to distinguish whether he was on Pitch or Treacle, but a little extra speed would bring me to the point where the two lanes flowed together into Lavender only seconds behind my quarry. Concentrating on the *click-slop, click-slop* and the occasional, radarish *tock!*, I ignored the other sounds drifting from adjacent lanes. Then two different sets of footsteps snagged my attention.

To those who can hear, footsteps are as good as fingerprints. Two men of approximately the same weight walking across wet ground in identical pairs of shoes leave virtually identical impressions, but the sounds they make will differ in a thousand ways. What made me attend to the pair of footsteps coming from Pitch or Treacle was their unreasonable similarity. (They were not identical. Even identical twins do not replicate each other's tread, they cannot.) One man, the first, moved in fearfully, with an irregularity that betrayed overindulgence in alcohol. The man behind him glided along in confident high spirits, not only unimpaired but as if the concept of impairments or obstacles did not exist for him—it was the walk of an *unearthly* being.

I must allude now to a circumstance beyond the grasp of any

mortal reader. In the stride of an unearthly being nothing even faintly like morality may be detected. A transcendent ruthlessness resounded from the tread of the second pair of footsteps drawing near the joining of Pitch and Treacle and their meeting with the more spacious Lavender.

And yet! Although the first set of footfalls contained virtually no resonance of the so-to-speak angelic or unearthly, it uncannily resembled the second.

~~It was like~~
~~I felt as though~~
~~I might have been standing before~~

You Mighty Ones, in his present euphoria Your Servant can find no better description of the emotional state induced by this impossible resemblance than the adjective most beloved of the Providence Master, *eldritch.* I had heard the footsteps of my son. Aware that the redneck was in pursuit, he possessed the capacity to mislead him with the false signal of, I don't know what you call it, an auditory hallucination. I could do many things, but this stunt was as beyond me as time travel. With the awareness that my adversary was more supple than I had supposed, I got myself once more in motion and hastened through Horsehair's convolutions only to arrive at Lavender after the fact.

From Horsehair's opening, I glimpsed lounging in the doorway of an abandoned warehouse one of the band of urchins who gather there at night. The bully-boy was swaggering off. After a moment of appalled indecision, I thought it possible that the wicked offspring had after all spoken to Frenchy. Back down Horsehair I flew to vacant Veal Yard.

Cursing, I rushed through the byway and heard, mystifyingly, the hallucinatory footsteps and those of a child moving down Lavender. Eventually I came near enough to recognize the child as Nolly Wheadle, whom I had betimes dispatched on harmless errands. When I realized that our journey was taking us toward Hatchtown's southern border, the exercise suddenly became clear: though my only-begotten son might have occult powers denied his father, he didn't know beans about geography. He had hired Nolly to lead him out!

Complete understanding did not arrive until after the pair in front of me reached a patch of cobbles named White Mouse Yard, where both they and I, a cautious distance behind, heard the *click-slop, click-slop* of the bully trudging down a nearby lane. The next sound to reach us, the tread of unearthly footsteps, blasted all my conjectures into powder. Nolly fled, yelling directions to the tourist. My son and adversary approached, but in the destruction of every certainty I could not tell from where—I concealed myself within Horsehair. The tourist pounded into Silk, and I sped to the next lane. At the opening onto Glass, I wedged myself against the bricks, looked out at a lamplit corner, and was given the third and greatest revelation of the day.

A man in a dark suit ran forward, took off his shoes, and trotted toward my niche. Before he had come close enough to the light to expose his face, the bully-boy lumbered around the corner of an intersecting lane. The bully-boy raised his bat and attacked. I crept out to put an end to the lout. Then, bafflingly, a second form, in every way similar to the first, sprinted down the lane. One of them was my son, but which?

I drew back. A promissory music filled my ears.

The new arrival pushed the tourist aside and leaped upon the roughneck. Surely, this was my son. In seconds, he had claimed the baseball bat and was bringing it down on the roughneck's skull.

Taking in the careless beauty of his features, the darkness of his lustrous eyes, the abrupt angle of his cheekbones, I watched my scion saunter toward the lamplight. The commission of a violent homicide had ruffled him no more than it would his old man. The Adversary's radiant monstrosity utterly belied the terror, the quailing dismay of his shadow-appearances. I supposed that the little shit had grown into this self-assurance around the time I erased from the earth, as Commanded, the last of the Dunstans no longer resident in Edgerton, those barrel scrapings through whom I had moved like a plague.

But what in the world was he up to, and who or what was the replica whose life he had saved? I hugged the wall and watched the blood-soaked center of the stage.

My foe strolled glittering into the spotlight. With the self-awareness of deliberate art, he appeared to hesitate. That devil knew exactly what he was doing. He was *posing*. Slowly, negligently, he turned his back to me and faced the man in first row center. After a beautifully timed delay, he spoke.

Unfortunately, he uttered only an anticlimactic sentence concerning the hypothetical male obligation to honor the sexual overtures of females. Evidently he had bedded someone the other fellow had rejected. My inner receptors continued to hum in expectation of more essential info. My formidable son and adversary vanished down the intersecting lane. As if linked by an elastic band, the other stumbled into the circumference of the lamplight.

The recognition of how close to understanding I had come while failing completely nearly made me burst into laughter. I was looking at the same face, more or less, considerably more than less. They were brothers.

Star had given birth to two boys, and while I had vainly sought the first, it was the second son, apparently named Ned, whose shadow-self had floated behind me on their mutual birthday. Star's death had summoned them both to Edgerton, and until a moment before, the dope now hovering at the edge of the light had been as clueless about his brother's existence as I. *Star had not wanted him to know. Star had protected him.* Stunned, the lad moved forward to pursue his brother, shuddered back, and skedaddled.

I have been given what I needed all along.

4

HOW I FOUND MY SHADOW AT LAST, AND WHAT IT DID

■ "Under the bed is not a new concept," said Lieutenant Rowley. "But you pushed that sucker way *back* there. Were you afraid someone would steal your winnings?"

Lieutenant Rowley raised his rust-colored eyebrows toward his crinkly, rust-colored hair. The wrinkles in his forehead deepened, and his mouth stretched into a narrow line. Creases like hatchet marks appeared on his leathery cheeks. He was smiling. It was 4:56 A.M., and Rowley had been having a wonderful time since 3:30, when he and Officer Treuhaft, a human totem pole swathed in blue, had awakened Nettie and Clark, charged into my room, read my Miranda rights, and arrested me for the murder of a man named Minor Keyes. Rowley was just getting into his stride.

"I didn't win that money. I brought it with me from New York."

"Do you always take along five or six hundred dollars when you go out of town?"

For the fourth or fifth time, I said, "I didn't know if my ATM card would work here. I didn't withdraw it all at once, it accumulated over the past week or so."

"Funny how it matches what Staggers and the others say you took off them. Even worse, they identified you." Some of the savagery left his face. "It's tough, Ned, but it isn't as bad as you think."

A young policeman cracked open the door, came up to Rowley, and whispered in his ear. Rowley planted a finger on his shoulder and pushed him back. "Blanks? No ridges? Will you please get the hell out of here?"

Rowley was about forty-five, roughly the same age as Stewart Hatch, but his skin looked borrowed from someone a decade older and recently deceased. "I mean that." He willed some life into his face. "Know what? Right now, I'm the best friend you have."

He hitched his chair closer to the table. "Forget the money. Joe Staggers and his friends *know* you took money off them at the Speedway, and they *know* you were in Hatchtown tonight. Keep saying you weren't involved, you're looking at life in prison."

"I wasn't in town on the night of the card game," I said.

Rowley fixed my eyes with his. "I'm on your side, Ned. I know how it went." He thumped his hand on the table. "All of a sudden, a guy was coming at you with a baseball bat. The whole thing went down in a couple of seconds. To me, you were a Marine in there. Probably you didn't even know he was dead, am I right?"

Rowley spread his arms. "In the twenty-two years I been on this force, I never heard a better defense. Come in telling the truth, chances are you walk out free and clear. Why don't we take your statement and put you on your way back home?"

"I didn't win any money in a card game at the Speedway," I said. "On Wednesday night, a truck driver for Nationwide Paper named Bob Mims picked me up in Ohio and dropped me off at the Motel Comfort. In the bar, I met an assistant D.A. from Louisville who told me she could give me a ride here the next day. Her name is Ashleigh Ashton, and she's staying at Merchants Hotel. Thursday morning, she dropped me off at St. Ann's Hospital. Last night, I ran into Mrs. Ashton and Mrs. Hatch at Le Madrigal, and they invited me to their table for dinner. After that, I went to see Toby Kraft. I drank too much. On the way home, I got as far as Merchants Park and passed out on a bench. I got back to my aunt's house around twelve-fifteen, twelve-thirty."

"Maybe twenty minutes later? A witness puts the time at twelve twenty-six."

"Why don't you call Mrs. Ashton and ask her where I was on Wednesday night?"

"We will," Rowley said. "We'll talk to Mrs. Ashton, and we'll hear what she has to say about Wednesday. It won't have any bearing on what happened at twelve twenty-six last night, but we'll check it anyhow. In the meantime, I want you to think about what I said."

"I can't confess to a murder I didn't commit," I said.

Rowley took me downstairs to a cell. I stretched out on the cot and surprised myself by going to sleep.

The clanging of the door woke me up. A gray-haired man with a pink, weary face that had a lot of miles on it walked into the cell. His belly pushed out the front of his white shirt, his sleeves were rolled up, and his tie was yanked down over his open collar. Behind him, Rowley loomed like a ferocious statue. "On your feet, Mr. Dunstan," said the gray-haired man. "We're releasing you."

I rubbed my hands over my face.

"I'm Captain Mullan," he said. "For the present, no charges will be brought against you. You can pick up your things and go back to your aunt's house. I'd like to request that you remain in Edgerton for the next forty-eight hours and inform us of any changes of address. I want to talk to that truck driver, Bob Mims, before we give you a clean bill of health."

"My mother's funeral is on Wednesday," I said. "I won't leave before that."

Mullan shoved his hands into his pockets. "You must be an old-fashioned gentleman, Mr. Dunstan." From over Mullan's shoulder, Rowley was giving me a smoky glare which suggested that he was no longer my best friend.

"Why is that?"

"Mrs. Ashton confirmed that she met you at the Motel Comfort on Wednesday night and drove you here the following day. She also tells us that you could not have been involved in an encounter with Mr. Keyes at twelve twenty-six this morning, because you came to her hotel room at approximately eleven o'clock and did not leave until exactly twelve twenty-five. The doorman and the desk clerk verify her statement." Mullan smiled at me. He looked as though he should have been pulling pints of Guinness in a Third Avenue Irish Pub.

Rowley said that I could pick up most of my property on the way out. "I'll hold the money until we talk to Mims." His face looked like a paving stone.

An arcade of fluted stone columns stood before the entrance to the big stone facade of the building alongside Police Headquarters. I thought it must have been City Hall. Down at the bottom of the long flight of steps, uniformed policemen smoked and talked in front of half a dozen angled-in patrol cars. Across the street, a fountain at the center of a grassy square sent up a glittering spray.

The policemen moved closer together. One flicked a half inch of cigarette at the bottom of the steps. I came down onto the sidewalk and saw that I was on Grace Street. Two blocks away, a pillared entrance that must have been the front of the library curved out from a row of storefronts and office buildings. The cops separated without quite spreading out.

■ **42**

■ Clark opened the door and called back into the house, "The boys didn't rough him up too bad."

"They didn't rough me up at all," I said.

Nettie surged up from the sofa, grabbed my biceps, and stared into my eyes. "I don't know when I have been so upside-down upset in all my life."

"I'm sorry," I said. "There's nothing to worry about anymore, but for your sake, I ought to go somewhere else."

Nettie re-formed into a thunderhead.

"Joe Staggers is likely to come looking for me. I don't want to put you and Clark in any danger."

"Any Mountry knotheads turn up around here, they'll be sorry they did. I'll call May, and we'll get breakfast ready."

Nettie and May attended to my edited version of the night's events as they mopped up the contents of their plates. Clark shoveled in his one true meal of the day and agreed that I should take up Toby Kraft's offer. "Mountry boys are stupider than mud, but they're persistent. Best pack your things and give Toby a call. When they come around here, we can say you took off and we don't know where."

I saw the box the UPS driver had delivered. Nettie followed my gaze. "About time you looked through your mother's few things."

■ I set the carton on the bed and folded my clothes into the duffel before looking at it again. Star's peaky handwriting glowed up from the shipping label, and sorrow, more than sorrow, heartbreak's tremendous wallop, leaked through the taped seams. When I had run out of diversions, I pulled the carton onto my lap and ripped it open.

I took out some old paperbacks and one hardback book and sorted through the thirty or forty CDs Star had shipped home—Billie and Ella, Louis and Nat and Sinatra, and a lot of records by Duke Ellington, Lester Young, Paul Desmond, and the other musicians she liked. All of these I slid into my bag. I set aside brooches, bracelets, a couple of gold necklaces, and three silk scarves for my aunts.

At the bottom of the box lay a wallet-sized photograph and an envelope on which Star had written *For Ned*. I picked up the photograph, at first saw only an image of a small boy in a striped shirt, then realized that the small boy was myself and the photograph had been taken on the morning of my third birthday. I gave an involuntary shudder, put the photograph in my billfold, and opened the envelope. It contained what looked like a safety-deposit key taped to an index card above the words *Illinois State Provident Bank, Grace Street.*

The idea that Star wanted me to have something she had secreted in a safety-deposit box gave me an uneasy tingle, but I tucked the key into my shirt pocket and turned to the little collection of books. I propped the paperbacks—*Anna Karenina, Madame Bovary, Invisible Man, Their Eyes Were Watching God, Native Son*—on an empty shelf and picked up the hardback.

The dark green boards of its cover seemed more crude than ordinary bindings. The title, *From Beyond,* had been stamped in gold on the spine and front cover. I opened the book and turned to the title page:

FROM BEYOND TALES OF THE UNKNOWN
by
EDWARD RINEHART

I looked across the room to the closet without really seeing it. I heard myself say, "Edward Rinehart?" When I looked down again, the name was still there. I turned the page and saw:

©1957 Edward Rinehart

On the facing page was the dedication:

For the Providence Master & My Great Fathers

The table of contents listed ten or twelve stories. Words like "Abandoned," "Crypt," and "Hideous" swam up at me, disconnected from whatever preceded or followed them. My numb eye took in "Blue," and I concentrated on it long enough to see that the word formed half of a title called "Blue Fire." I said something like *Oh, no*. The book slammed shut, and for a while I just looked at the binding. Hoping for a paragraph about the author, I opened it from the back, but Edward Rinehart had chosen to keep mum about his past. I crammed the book into my knapsack and went down the hall to stand under a cascade of hot water.

Clean-shaven, wearing a white button-down shirt, blue blazer, and jeans, I came downstairs and overheard Clark discoursing about the differences between murder and manslaughter. I put my bags near the door and spread the jewelry and scarves on the coffee table. "Ladies," I said, "Star would have wanted you to share the things she sent, but you'll have to come in here to do it."

While Nettie and May exclaimed over the treasures, I faded into the kitchen and called Toby Kraft. He told me to go a rooming house on Chester Street. "The landlady's an old acquaintance of mine, woman named Helen Janette. I'll set it up in five minutes, get you a cheap rate."

■ **43**

■ The cab deposited me in front of a building like a cardboard box mounted with a peaked hat. Its original pale brown had faded to the sandy yellow of old chinos. Two courses of the cement-block foundation, interrupted by basement windows, protruded above the ground, and a pitted walk led to the unceremonious front door. I went up the steps and read the names beside a vertical row of buzzers. JANETTE, TITE, CARPENTER & BURGESS, FELDMAN, a blank I supposed was for my room, BREMEN, REDMAN & CHALLIS, and ROWLES & MCKENNA. I pushed the button beside JANETTE, and a metallic buzz came through the window to my left. An interior door opened; footsteps rapped toward me. An economical white-haired woman in a short-sleeved safari shirt-jacket bored gimlet eyes into me from a face that made Lieutenant Rowley's seem like a powder puff.

"I suppose you're the one from Toby Kraft."

"That's me," I said.

Helen Janette backed up and watched me come in. Whatever she saw did not improve her frame of mind. "This is the deal. I'm giving you a nice, comfortable room on the second floor. You and Mr. Bremen are supposed to have exclusive access to the bathroom at your end of the hall, but the girls at the back go in there, too."

A door behind me clicked open. I glanced over my shoulder. A gaunt old man with a Neanderthal jaw, a mesh T-shirt, and a brown fedora was leaning against the opening to a darkened room. His shades had been pulled down, and a cartoon jittered across the television screen in the murk behind him.

"This is Mr. Tite," she said.

I turned around and held out my hand. He ignored it.

"The room is thirty dollars per night, a hundred eighty by the week. You get basic cable if you bring your own TV. For an extra ten dollars a week, clean linen every other day and vacuuming on Thursdays. No cooking in the rooms, no meals supplied, and no loud noises. If you can't behave yourself, out you go, I don't need the aggravation."

I said I'd be happy to pay for a week in advance, plus cleaning, if she took plastic. Helen Janette thrust out a hand and waggled her fingers. I dug out my Visa card, placed it on her palm, and followed her into her apartment. Mr. Tite lounged against the doorframe and eyed me from beneath the brim of his hat. After I signed the slip, she said, "I'll show the gentleman to his room now, Mr. Tite."

Tite straightened up, gave me a hard look, and backed out.

"There are two more rooms at the other end of the house," she said. "Miss Carpenter and Miss Burgess share the big one, and Mrs. Feldman has the other. Miss Carpenter and Miss Burgess have been with me fifteen years. I've never had a speck of trouble with Mrs. Feldman."

We began going up the stairs. "Your room is at the front, above Mr. Tite." She turned halfway around and lowered her voice. "Mr. Bremen is across from you. He's a crossing guard, and you know what *they're* like." She put her finger to her lips, then pointed upward with the same finger. "Drunkards."

At the top of the stairs, she marched to a white door on the far side of the corridor. An elderly guy with a ponderous belly and a flaring white mustache who was seated in front of his TV looked through his doorway and raised a hand the size of a stop sign. A broad yellow banner hung across the back of his room. "Hi there," he called. "This our new inmate?"

"I'm busy, Mr. Bremen." She slammed the key into the lock.

I followed Helen Janette inside. "Bed. Closet. Desk. Dresser. Your sink. I change the towels and washcloth every other day. If you want to move the phone to the table, there's a jack behind it. You pay all your utilities. I don't want to see any hot plates in here, but coffeemakers are okay. Mrs. Frahm left behind her radio–alarm clock, so that comes free of charge."

I looked at the digital numerals displayed on the black box next to the telephone. It was 8:31.

"At the back on this side are Miss Redman and Miss Challis. They're cute little things, but if you're a gentleman, you'll keep your distance. Mr. Rowles and Mr. McKenna are in the room across from them. Mr. Rowles and Mr. McKenna are pianists, and they're out of town most of the time. Do you expect to be here longer than a week?"

I put to rest the concern that I might form an unholy alliance with Miss Redman and Miss Challis.

She slid the key on top of the dresser. "Try to keep reasonable hours. Comings and goings after midnight wake me up."

I hung up my clothes, shoved things into the dresser drawers, and called Suki Teeter. After three rings, an answering machine picked up, and Suki's voice informed me that if I were to leave my name and telephone number she would probably call me back, unless I were looking for money. Suki was still in bed. I called Merchants Hotel and asked for Mrs. Ashton.

"My God, are you all right?" Ashleigh said.

"Thanks to you."

"I couldn't *believe* those guys. Especially that creepy Lieutenant Rowley. I hardly believe you, either. Why didn't you tell them you were here?" She giggled. "Lieutenant Rowley has a filthy mind. I said we gabbed away like old buddies until you sobered up enough to go back to your aunt's, but I could tell he knew exactly what we were doing. You know what? You were like the way you were in Chicago, sort of dangerous. Not drunk dangerous, that would have been awful, unpredictable dangerous."

My insides folded into origami. "Sometimes I surprise myself."

"They let you go, anyhow."

"About six-thirty this morning." I told her that I had moved out of my aunt's house and gave her my new telephone number.

"Am I going to see you today?"

"I don't know. Someone is going to help me track down some information. I'll call you if I can."

"This is exactly what I deserve," Ashleigh said. "I know, all right, it's okay."

"What are you talking about?"

"Would your research assistant be Laurie Hatch?"

"She knows a guy at City Hall who can do me a lot of good," I said. "It's a long story, but I'm trying to find my father, and she volunteered to help."

"No kidding." She hesitated. "I didn't mean that the way it sounded. I want to see you again, though. All right?"

When we were done, I dialed Police Headquarters and asked a desk sergeant to give Captain Mullan my new address and telephone number.

I went into the hallway. Mr. Bremen caught my eye and beamed so widely that his handsome mustache nearly touched his ears. He jabbed a thick forefinger at his chest. In one of those spread-out Western voices evocative of endless plains and starlit camp-fires, he said, "Otto Bremen."

My life appeared to be turning into a movie in which I had to invent my lines as I went along. I pointed at myself and said, "Ned Dunstan."

"Drop in any time, Ned," he told me. "Door's always open."

Two blocks west of Merchants Hotel, I turned into Grace Street and walked south toward the library. A congress of sparrows huddled on the sidewalk ascended in a flutter of wing-beats and sculpted an uptilted curve in the clean morning air. Shop windows bounced back slanting sunlight. I was present and not present, still in a movie. A boy with gilded eyes and sleek, shoulder-length hair stared down from the second-story window of a hairdressing salon. Directly across Grenville Street from the library was the foursquare brick structure of the Illinois State Provident.

A bank officer who looked about eighteen years old checked that I, along with Star Dunstan, was one of the box holders, led me downstairs, and asked me to sign a book and record the time. He let me into a chamber lined with numbered panels and indicated the panel that matched my key. I opened the panel, pulled out a wide steel container, placed it on the polished table, and worked the catch. A package wrapped in butcher paper had been wedged inside the box. From its weight and dimensions, I thought it was a photo album, and I would have opened it on the spot if I hadn't been about to meet Laurie Hatch. I signed a form and carried the package upstairs and out through the front door.

Laurie was standing in front of the colonnade on the other side of Grenville Street. She was wearing a dark green silk blouse and fawn trousers, and her perfection transformed the sunlit street and the curving row of pillars into a backdrop. For a fraction of a second, the scene before me seemed as frozen in time as an advertisement in a magazine. Laurie broke into an incandescent smile, and I was no longer in a movie.

■ 44

■ "I'm glad you're early," she said. "Stewart did his usual number and screwed up my plans. He has to bring Cobbie back around three o'clock. What's in that package? Did you rob the bank?"

I told her about the key in the envelope and the safety-deposit box.

"It's like a Russian doll. Inside the box is an envelope. Inside the envelope is a key that opens a box with another box inside it, and inside that box there's a package wrapped in brown paper. Maybe it's stuffed with hundred-dollar bills." She took it from me and weighed it in her hands. "However, it feels more like a photo album."

"If it turns out to be a fortune in hundred-dollar bills, I'll split it with you."

"I'd settle for a good lunch. Let's put your fortune in my car. I'm parked right across the street."

She slid the package under the Mountaineer's backseat. "Nice car," I said. "You ought to be ferrying lion hunters across the veldt."

"My *father* did things like that, but I don't. Stewart thought this was the proper vehicle for a suburban mother, so this is what I have." Laurie linked her arm through mine. "Let's see Hugh. He'll be thrilled."

"So who is this Hugh Coventry character?"

"Well, hmmm. Let me give you his short-form bio." She cocked her head. "Hugh Coventry broke from his ancestral New England after getting his history degree from Yale by entering graduate school at Northwestern. When he discovered that a lot of history Ph.D.s were driving cabs, he transferred into library science."

She waited for the straight line. "Weird move," I said.

"You think?" We glided on ahead. "Hugh is in love with libraries. His M.A. thesis came out of a summer spent rollicking amongst the parish records of his family's church in Marblehead, Massachusetts. He's a computer genius, he likes to work nights and weekends, and he never gets mad at anyone. Ever since he took over, the Edgerton library ticks like a Swiss clock. Hugh Coventry is practically a saint!"

One day, Coventry had wandered out of the library, down Grove Street to City Hall, and into the Records Office to inquire about volunteering. The Records Office spread wide its official arms and said, Come right in, Mr. Coventry. Within a year, the managers of every department in the building were seeking Hugh Coventry's assistance. In his second year as a volunteer, consultations with the mayor's staff had resulted in instant access on the part of His Honor to block-by-block voting records, numbers of arrests and convictions on specific charges, welfare statistics, and other matters essential to governance. Thereafter, Coventry had been given the run of the building.

Two years before, when Edgerton's upcoming 150th birthday had presented itself as an occasion for celebration, the new co-chairmen of the Sesquicentennial Committee, Stewart Hatch and Grenville Milton, asked for Coventry's aid in assembling a visual record of the city's past. The job spoke to his interest in local history, it called upon his organizational talents, it gave him yet another means of embedding himself within his adopted city. Laurie had met him when Rachel Milton had installed her on the committee, to which Rachel gave three afternoons a week. The arrangement had endured until Laurie's defection from her marriage.

"I couldn't have stayed anyhow, with Rachel scorching me with crucifixes and pelting me with garlic cloves whenever I walked in. Have you seen Town Square yet? It's kind of nice, I think."

Arm in arm, we crossed the street alongside Police Headquarters. The square and the fountain lay to our left. A bum with long red-gold hair lay wrapped in a ragged overcoat next to a guitar case on one of the benches. Half a dozen cops stood smoking and talking on the sidewalk. "I saw it this morning," I said. "While I was coming down those steps."

The cops stopped talking and stared at us in that way only cops can stare.

"You were in the police station?" Laurie asked. "Why?"

My description of having been arrested for murder made it sound like a grade-school excursion with Officer Friendly. Laurie said, "How long were you there?"

"A couple of hours."

When we had come within a few yards of the policemen, Laurie took in their stony expressions. She glared back, and the cops shuffled apart and looked away. After we had covered another six feet of pavement, she muttered, "Assholes."

"They don't like seeing someone like you with someone like me."

"Screw 'em. They don't even know you." She shook her head. "So the whole thing was a case of mistaken identity?"

"Exactly."

"Do those other guys know that, or do they still want to find you?"

I said I would have no trouble avoiding Staggers and his friends, told her about moving from Nettie's, and gave her my new address.

"Your life is shot full of adventure," she said, dropped my arm, and glided up the stairs like a ballerina.

We went through the columns. Laurie pulled open an immense, iron-clad glass door and led me into a dim lobby with a marble floor the size of a skating rink. An empty reception desk stood half of the way toward the center of the lobby. No lights burned behind the pebbled-glass windows labeled COUNTY CLERK and BUILDING INSPECTOR. At the lobby's far end, two marble staircases curved upward. "I'm surprised the doors weren't locked," I said.

"On Saturdays, they leave the place open for a skeleton staff. The question is, Where do we find the helpful Mr. Coventry? Let's go upstairs."

My footsteps ticked as though I were wearing tap shoes. A sudden sense-memory of running through Hatchtown's narrow lanes returned the phantom smell of lavender. We came to the end of a corridor on the second floor, and a single office door glowed yellow.

"Bingo!" Laurie said.

The light snapped off. The door bumped open. A tall, fair-haired man in a white shirt with rolled-up sleeves backed into the corridor holding an armful of manila folders.

"Work, work, work," Laurie said.

He jumped, clamped one arm over the tilting pile, and gaped at Laurie. What happened to his face was almost embarrassing. He seemed about to levitate from sheer joy. "What are you *doing* here?"

"I was hoping you could help my friend dig up some information about his father. He'd like to see his mother's marriage license and his birth certificate, things like that. Ned, this is the legendary Hugh Coventry. Hugh, my friend Ned Dunstan."

Coventry was glowing like a fireplace. "Let me, uh . . ." He deposited the stack of folders on the floor and stepped forward to shake my hand. "Hugh Coventry. At your service. Sir."

I said, "I hope we're not interrupting you."

He waved at the folders. "That stuff isn't important. You're a friend of Laurie's?"

"Mrs. Hatch and I met a few days ago. She's being nice to me."

"Your name is Dunstan? You're one of the Edgerton Dunstans?"

"Don't hold it against me," I said.

Coventry's eyes lit up, and he reared back in a transport of scholarly pleasure. "Are you kidding? You're from one of the most fascinating families in this city."

I thought I could see the entire pattern of his life. Hugh Coventry was a decent guy who would always live alone in a couple of upstairs rooms lined floor to ceiling with books. His emotions were generous without being personal.

"Your ancestors, two brothers named Omar and Sylvan Dunstan, founded the Edgerton Bank and Trust, now the Illinois State Provident. At one time, they owned most of downtown Edgerton. Howard Dunstan built Merchants Hotel. I wish I knew more of their story."

"Me, too," I said.

"You must be related to Annette Rutledge. Mrs. Rutledge sent over a wonderful collection of Dunstan family photographs. I hate to say this, but they seem to be misplaced for the time being. I'm sure we'll find them in the next day or two."

Mrs. Rutledge was my mother's aunt, I said, she would be overjoyed to have her pictures on display, and I hoped he might be willing to help me.

"Of course." He looked at the stack of files. "Would you, um . . ."

I picked up half of the folders and followed him into a darkened office. On a long desk, two computers sat opposite each other, like chess players. Laurie said, "You can find marriage licenses in here?"

"Birth certificates, too. It took me *months* to get this place into reasonable shape, and I'm still not done." He flipped on the overhead lights. "Next is the county clerk's office. That's going to be a nightmare."

"The county clerk's office is going to be heaven, and you know it," Laurie said. "Now, what about Ned?"

Coventry looked at me as though I had descended from a cloud. He had forgotten I was there. "You were interested in your mother's marriage license? Is there some confusion?" His eyes flickered. "I don't mean to pry, you understand."

"Confusion is probably the right word," I said. "My mother was Valerie Dunstan. She gave me her family name, although she was married. Before she died, she told me that my father was named Edward Rinehart. I'd be grateful for whatever you could tell me."

Coventry went to the computer on the far side of the desk and punched a button on the tower case. He gazed at the monitor with the fascination of a small boy watching the progress of an electric train. Laurie positioned herself behind his shoulder while he shifted the mouse and tapped keys. "Once you get here, you can access information from all these different areas."

"No wonder everyone loves you."

Flushing, Coventry looked across at me. "Do you know the year your mother was married?"

"Nineteen fifty-seven."

He pulled the mouse down the pad and double-clicked. "V-A-L-E-R-I-E?" I nodded. Laurie moved a step closer and rested her hand on his shoulder. Coventry clicked the mouse and bent forward.

Laurie frowned at the screen. "That can't be right."

Coventry looked at me. "Have you ever heard of a man named Donald Messmer?"

"Why?"

"According to this, Donald Messmer married Valerie Dunstan on the twenty-fifth of November, 1957. Peter Bontly, justice of the peace, performed the ceremony; witnesses, Lorelei Bontly and Kenneth Schermerhorn."

"Something's wrong," Laurie said. "His father was named Edward Rinehart."

Coventry did a lot of things with the mouse. "The birth certificate ought to tell us something. What was your date of birth?"

"June twenty-fifth," I said, "1958."

"Right around the corner." He beamed at me. "Happy birthday, in case I don't see you before that."

I thanked him.

"Full name?"

"Ned Dunstan."

Coventry blinked. "Isn't Ned generally a nickname for Edward? You have no middle name?"

"Just Ned Dunstan," I said.

"That's so sensible," he said. "However, if you feel deprived, take one of my middle names, will you? Your choices are Jellicoe, York, and St. George. I recommend Jellicoe. It has a nice nineteenth-century ring."

Laurie took her hands from his shoulders. "Your actual name is Hugh Jellicoe York St. George Coventry?"

"It was the only way to stay on good terms with the relatives."

"My father was like that," she said. "His name went on and on, like a list, but he never called himself anything but Yves D'Lency."

Hugh Jellicoe York St. George Coventry folded his hands over his belt buckle and smiled up.

"Weren't you looking for Ned's birth certificate?"

"Oh! Excuse me! I'm sorry, Ned."

"I'll take St. George," I said. "It has a nice twelfth-century ring."

He struck a key and leaned back again. "This shouldn't take more than a couple of seconds." We waited. "Here it comes." Coventry shifted in his chair, bent forward, and propped his chin on his hand.

Laurie said, "I don't get it."

"Don't keep me in suspense," I said.

Coventry cleared his throat. "Name of infant, Ned Dunstan. Date of birth, June twenty-fifth, 1958. Time of birth, three-twenty A.M. Place of birth, St. Ann's Community Hospital. Weight, seven pounds, twelve ounces. Length, ten inches. Mother's name, Valerie Dunstan. Father's name, Donald Messmer. Attending physician, none. Attending midwife, Hazel Jansky." He looked back at me. "All through the fifties, midwives attended nearly half of the births at St. Ann's Community. Hazel Jansky's name turns up over and over."

"Who fills out these certificates?" Laurie asked.

"People at the hospital, but they would have obtained the father's name from your mother."

His essential decency made him hesitate, and I said, "Whatever you're thinking isn't going to hurt my feelings, Hugh."

"Marriage requires proof of identification. Even a justice of the peace wouldn't marry a couple unless they showed him driver's licenses and birth certificates. However, I don't know what you'll think of this idea, but it's certainly possible for a pregnant woman to marry another man. After delivery, she'd have every reason to name the husband as the child's father. Do you see what I mean?"

"Maybe you're right," I said.

"I feel uneasy suggesting something like that, but if she gave you your father's name and another name turns up in the records . . ."

"It makes sense," I said. "We have to go now, but could I see you again? I'd like to look up a few other things."

"Want to come back tomorrow morning? The doors will be locked, but if you bang hard enough I'll hear you."

Laurie kissed the top of his head. "You're wonderful."

"Laurie?"

"Hugh?"

"Dinner tonight? Or a movie? How about dinner and a movie?"

"Not tonight," she said. "But you're a darling."

■ **45**

■ "That's ridiculous. Your father can't be a man named Donald *Messmer.*"

"Hugh had a good idea," I said. "She was pregnant when she got married. My mother was free-spirited when it came to official documents."

"We have to get in touch with this Messmer." She turned the key in the ignition and nudged the accelerator. "Posy Fairbrother, Cobbie's nanny, has a CD-ROM with addresses and telephone numbers from a million different cities. Now, where are we going?"

I showed her the slip of paper. Toby's slash-and-burn handwriting spelled out the name *Max Edison* and *V.A. Hospital, Mount Vernon.* "That's a long way away, isn't it?"

"It's a hike, but the expressway goes right to it. We have plenty of time, if we don't stay long. There's a nice place to have lunch on the other side of Marion."

We moved out into the traffic and headed toward the expressway.

"How did you get this name? Did Max Edison know your father?"

I said that I had heard about him from Toby Kraft, a pawnbroker on Lanyard Street who had been married to my grandmother, Queenie Dunstan. "After we left Le Madrigal, Toby's the person I went to see."

"Ah," Laurie said.

"He wants to keep out of the picture. Toby only gave me this

much on the condition that we never had the conversation, and
the name didn't come from him."

Laurie swung into the northbound on-ramp.

"Your father's name was Yves D'Lency, and he drove across
the African veldt to shoot lions?"

"Not really. It's a long story. You don't want to hear it."

"Try me," I said.

Yves D'Lency had been a glamorous daredevil born to an
aristocratic family in possession of a Gascony estate and a noble
art collection. At eighteen, he had escaped to immerse himself in
the literary and artistic worlds of postwar Paris, where he supported himself by literary journalism and private art dealing. He
learned to fly; he drove racing cars. At the end of the fifties, he
moved to Los Angeles, where he already had several clients who
trusted his taste in paintings. He married Laurie's mother and
bought a house in Beverly Hills. Laurie was born, and for seven
years all went well. Then he died. Laurie still had two paintings
from his private collection.

"How did he die?"

Her glance was almost ferocious. "He was flying from an air-
field in the San Fernando Valley to see a friend in Carmel. He
had a little Cessna. The engine crapped out north of Santa Barbara. Down they fell, all the king's horses and all the king's
men." Her right hand lifted from the wheel and fluttered down.

"You were seven."

"Ever since, the sight of a Cessna always makes me feel like
puking." I got another burning flash from her eyes. She straightened her arms and pushed herself back into the seat.

"Tell me how you met Stewart Hatch."

Five years earlier, a reasonably attractive man of about forty
had stationed himself beside Laurie D'Lency near midpoint of
a party spilling upstairs, downstairs, and into the garden of a
townhouse owned by an executive at the NBC affiliate in San
Francisco. Stewart Hatch was an acquaintance of a KRON executive several rungs above the owner of the townhouse; he was
neither charmless nor anything like too old; yet he did not interest her, especially when he confessed to being a businessman
from an obscure city in Illinois. After three years of doing background for the news staff, Laurie knew she had a chance of
beating out her competition, two other young women circulat-
ing like benevolent hurricanes through the townhouse, for an

opening as an on-camera reporter. The Illinois tycoon might as well have been a black hole in a distant galaxy.

Stewart Hatch had rematerialized at the end of the party and offered a ride home in his limousine. The friends who had driven her to the party had disappeared, and the alternative to the limousine was a cab service. She accepted.

Thereafter, Hatch had laid siege, sending flowers, calling two or three times a day from the limousine, between meetings, from his suite at the Fairmont. He had sweaters and blouses delivered from Neiman Marcus and on his last night in San Francisco took Laurie to Il Postrio. During dinner, Stewart Hatch had astonished her with a proposal of marriage.

"Boy, what a con job that guy did on me."

"You didn't agree to marry him over dinner at Il Postrio," I said. "Unless it was the most amazing meal you'd ever had in your life, and Stewart ordered a couple bottles of great champagne."

"Roederer Cristal. Which, as Stewart took pains to instruct me, is akin to the Holy Grail. Children in third-world countries fling themselves into bottomless chasms for a glimpse of a single bottle. We had two. And the food was spectacular. But I turned him down. Was Stewart discouraged? Stewart doesn't know the meaning of the word."

■ 46

■ At the restaurant on the other side of Marion, an elderly waiter gave us menus taller than those at Le Madrigal and asked what we wanted to drink. "A glass of that nice Bordeaux," Laurie said. I said I'd have the same.

The waiter left, and I said, "I don't usually drink at lunch. It makes me sleepy."

"One glass of wine isn't really *drinking*," she said. "So tell me, why was Toby Kraft so secretive about Max Edison? Were they bad boys together? Did they convey tommy guns in violin cases?"

"Toby implied that he used to be mixed up in something, years ago."

"These days, there are criminals everywhere I look." She gave me a brief, rueful smile.

"How did Stewart persuade you to marry him?"

"The old-fashioned way," she said. "The rat chased me until I fell in love with him." She described an aggressive long-distance courtship made up of telephone calls, deliveries of orchids and expensive clothes, and frequent visits. Hatch had promised her a busy, interesting life: trips to New York and Europe, civic involvement at home.

"I thought I'd be able to join these commissions and boards and panels he was talking about. It sounded like a great life, keeping busy and doing good works."

"What went wrong?"

"None of it happened. Stewart went out of town by himself. I couldn't get on committees because I didn't know enough about Edgerton. Besides that, Stewart wanted a son right away. Not just a baby, a son. His grandfather, Carpenter, set up this complicated family trust that keeps passing the money to a firstborn male child, like something out of the Middle Ages. Eventually, I realized that he married me to give him an heir and impress his friends, and that was that."

The details of the extraordinary trust were so complicated that I forgot most of them as soon as they were out of her mouth. What I retained was that Cobden Hatch, Stewart's father, had modified its conditions so that evidence of criminal behavior eliminated the possibility of inheritance. Apparently his black-sheep brother had embarrassed the family.

The waiter lowered our plates to the table.

"In other words," Laurie said, "if Stewart is convicted of embezzlement and tax fraud and whatever, Cobbie gets it all. And as if that weren't reason enough for my darling husband to refuse me a divorce, or to demand custody if I manage to get one, his grandfather released control of the trust to whoever is the heir on January first of next year."

"You have no doubts that Stewart is guilty?"

"None."

"I don't get it. He was risking everything."

"You don't know Stewart. Whatever he did, he did out of state, through phony companies with bank accounts in the West Indies. He's *still* sure he'll walk away free and clear."

"But why would he do it in the first place?"

"He's greedy and impatient, and he wants everything now. And I bet he loved the idea of rubbing his grandfather's nose in the dirt. Stewart's into revenge in a big way."

Laurie concentrated on the other side of her fish and lifted the entire fillet off the small, white armature of bone. "I wish I were like your friend Ashleigh. In ten years, she'll be running her own law practice. As far as a career is concerned, my life is over. The only real purpose I have in life is raising Cobbie, and Stewart is going to do his damndest to take him away from me."

"The truth is, Ashleigh undoubtedly wishes she were more like you. When most men look at her, they think about carrying her back to the cave. When they look at you, they feel like groveling at your feet."

"Imagine how wonderful that must be." Laurie grinned across the table. "Tell me about Cherry Street. Tell me about your mother."

■ During the rest of our drive, Laurie indulged me by recounting the miseries following her father's death. Her mother married a movie producer in Bel Air, an acquaintance of D'Lency's, and what she had hoped would represent security became an incarceration. Pathologically jealous, the producer refused to let her leave his house unless she was accompanied by one of his female assistants. Because he did not trust his domestic help, he fired them, then fired their replacements until he was left with a single housekeeper too old and embittered to be anything but his watchdog. Laurie's mother began to drink during the day. The producer sent his stepdaughter to a Catholic girls' school notorious for its discipline, and one day, while searching through her dresser drawers, discovered a film canister packed with marijuana.

He dispatched her to a private residential facility. For six months, Laurie shared a room with a sixteen-year-old actress and was visited by tutors, counselors, psychiatrists, and the actress's drug dealers. When she returned home, she found her mother ramming clothes into suitcases. The producer had begun divorce proceedings and rented them a small house on the edge of Hancock Park.

They scraped along on the producer's support payments. Laurie went to John Burroughs High and did her best to care for her mother, who slid pints of vodka behind the toilet, under seat cushions, and anywhere else she thought they might go undiscovered. She died the summer after Laurie's high school graduation. Laurie put herself through Berkeley with the help of scholarships and student jobs.

"And now my tale is done, because coming up on our left is the V.A. Hospital."

■ 47

■ The drive curved toward a distant hill, where a structure the size of a federal office building rose above oaks and beech trees. In the middle distance, men in shirtsleeves or bathrobes sat at picnic tables and strolled across the lawn, some of them accompanied by nurses. The stone-colored beeches sent tall shadows across the parking lot.

Inside, the scale of the building shrank to a narrow hallway leading to an open counter, a couple of pebble-glass doors, and a set of elevators. Everything had been painted government green, and the memory of disinfectant hung in the air.

"Where is Goya when you need him?" Laurie said.

A clerk too old for his smear of a goatee and ponytail leaned on the counter. "You wanted?"

I told him which patient we wanted to see.

He thought it over. "E-D-I-S-O-N, as in light bulb?"

"M-A-X," I said. "As in 'to the.' "

On the fourth floor, a lanky attendant in green trousers and tunic had tilted his chair against the wall, knit his hands behind his head, and closed his eyes outside a darkened room where a dozen men were slouched in front of a television set. When Laurie Hatch and I came up to him, he dropped his hands and shot out of the chair. He was at least six-seven and skinny, almost gaunt, like many very tall men. In a backcountry accent, he said,

"You lookin' for someone, Miss, or can I he'p you in some othuh way?"

Laurie told him we wanted to talk to Mr. Edison.

"Max? He's in the TEE-vee rahm heah. I'll tell him he has comp'ny."

The attendant moved into the flickering darkness. Laurie whispered, *"TEE-vee rahm."*

"Like CD-ROM," I said.

A few seconds later, a small, compact man of about seventy with close-cropped white hair, a neat white beard, steel-rimmed spectacles, and an air of perfect composure emerged to take us in with a curious, lively attentiveness that admitted a flicker of surprise when he looked at me. He had that flawless, dark-chocolate skin that goes unwrinkled, apart from a few crow's-feet and some lines across the forehead, until it weathers into a well-seasoned ninety. Max Edison could have been a retired doctor or a distinguished elderly jazz musician. He also could have been a great many other things. The Jolly Green Giant followed him out.

"Mr. Edison?" I said.

He stepped forward, examining us with the same wide-awake curiosity, then swiveled on the balls of his feet to look up at the Giant. "Jervis, I'm going to escort my visitors down the hall."

Edison brought us to a tiny room with a single desk and bookshelves crowded with files. "You people know who I am, but I don't believe I've had the pleasure."

I introduced Laurie and myself, and he shook our hands without any sign of having recognized our names. His jeans had a sharp crease, his shirt was freshly pressed, and his boots gleamed. I wondered what it took to maintain standards like that in the V.A. Hospital. "I hope you came to tell me I won the lottery."

"No such luck," I said. "I want to ask you about someone you might have known a long time ago."

"Why would that be?"

"Let's say it's a family matter," I said.

His face relaxed, and he seemed to smile without quite smiling, as if I had confirmed whatever had been going through his mind.

"Does the name Dunstan mean anything to you?"

He crossed his arms over his chest, still smiling without smiling. "How did you learn I was out here?"

"From someone who doesn't want to be named," I said. "When I asked him about this person you might have known, he wrote your name on a piece of paper."

"Water's getting deeper and deeper," Edison said. "I used to know a man who married a woman named Dunstan."

"That could be," I said.

"Will you stop beating around the bush?" Laurie said. "He obviously knows it was Toby Kraft."

Edison and I both looked at her, then at each other. We burst out laughing.

"What?"

"So much for that," I said.

"But you knew it was him."

"Man didn't want to be named," Edison said.

"I spoiled your fun. I apologize. But I bet Mr. Edison could already tell us who we came here to talk about, and I only have about an hour before I have to drive back to town."

"Could you?" I asked Edison. "Do you already know?"

"Why don't you tell me, so I won't have to guess?"

"Edward Rinehart."

Edison looked at the door, then, with less than his usual composure, back at me. "We should grab some fresh air. It's so pretty under those trees, you can almost forget where you are."

■ "Toby Kraft. I called him 'Mr. Inside,' because that's what he was."

Max Edison faced the tall beeches and the long green lawn from the end of the bench across our picnic table. He had slipped dark glasses over his eyes, and his legs in their knife-creased jeans extended out to the side, crossed at the ankle. One elbow was propped on the surface of the table. He looked as though he had joined us for a moment before moving on.

"When I got back from the war, I had a leg injury that kept me from doing heavy work, so instead of one big job I had a bunch of little ones. Swept floors and washed windows. Ran numbers. Driving jobs. After a while, some people decided I was reliable."

Edison turned to me. "Know what I mean?"

"You did what you were supposed to do, and you kept your mouth shut."

"Toby Kraft asked me to help out in the pawnshop three days a week. I knew he was doing more business out back than up front. I'm not accusing him of anything, understand, but when Toby gave you my name he knew I'd have to say some of this. If I'm going to talk about Mr. Edward Rinehart, he's in there, too."

I nodded.

Edison turned the dark glasses to Laurie. "You don't have to hear any more than you want to, Mrs. Hatch."

She said, "At this point, Max, you'd have to drive me away with a whip."

He smiled, uncrossed his legs, and swung in to face us. He put his arms on the table and folded his hands together. "Every town the size of Edgerton has a Mr. Inside. He can tell you where to go if you want something, and the name of the guy who can help you get it and who to see afterward."

"Valuable guy," I said.

"Mr. Inside is like the post office. His lines go *out*. Back and forth down those lines moves *information*. Take on that role, you better keep the wheels greased. Outside you and your circle, other people are taking a steady interest."

"The police?"

He shook his head. "The force gets taken care of way down the line. They don't want you in jail, they want you out on the street where you can do some good."

"Then who are these other people?" Laurie said.

Edison flattened his hands on the table and tilted his head to look up at the great beeches. "About a year after I started part-timing for Toby, a fool named Clothard Spelvin came through from the office. They called him Clothhead because his brain-power could just about hold its own against a dishtowel. Light-skinned black man, but an ugly son of a bitch. Excuse me, Mrs. Hatch."

"No problem."

"Thank you. Clothhead said, 'Max, you don't work here no more. A man wants to see you.' I went in and asked Toby, 'Who does that dumbbell work for? I'm supposed to go with him.' Toby said, 'You'll be all right, it's all set up.' He took us through the storage room and slid open the back door. A big Cadillac was out in the alley. Dark blue. Enough wax on the chassis to shine at the stroke of midnight during an eclipse of the moon. Clothhead gave me the keys and told me, Drive north on old Highway 4.

Just past the town line, he pointed at a roadhouse. The place was empty except for a goon up front at the bar and one man sitting way at the back. That man was my new boss, Mr. Edward Rinehart. For the next seven years, all hours of the day and night, I drove Mr. Rinehart wherever he wanted to go."

"Honest to God," I said. Laurie put her hands in her lap and looked back and forth between us like a spectator at a tennis match. When my astonishment let me speak again, I uttered, no less idiotically, "Really."

Edison could not entirely conceal his pleasure in my reaction to his story. "Why did you think Toby gave you my name?"

Unable to contain herself any longer, Laurie burst out with, "Well, what was he *like*?"

Max Edison waited for me to clear my head.

"He was a gangster?" I said at last.

"Maybe there is no organized crime. Maybe the newspapers made the whole thing up. But if it exists, does it seem like you can join up unless you're Italian? Even better, Sicilian? Mr. Rinehart was a man who worked by himself."

"So what did he do?" I asked.

"Where you find a Mr. Inside, eventually you will learn there is also a Mr. Outside. Mr. Outside is more important than Mr. Inside, but not many know about him. If you happen to be a professional criminal, one night you are invited to a hotel room. Shrimp, roast beef, chicken, whatever food you like, is laid out. All kinds of bottles and plenty of ice. The lights are turned down. Three, four guys similar to you are already there. Way back in the room where you can't see his face, Mr. Outside is sitting in a big, comfortable chair. At least one or two of the other guys seem to know him.

"When everybody's relaxed, Mr. Outside explains from now on, you won't do anything unless he tells you so. One-third of all your profits go straight to him. You want to walk out, but he starts to explain the benefits. He's covering all the expenses. There will be enough work to cover the missing third a couple times over. Then he lays out a couple jobs so nice and neat, you could only mess up by having a heart attack when you saw the money. There's more work on the come. Besides, you'll never go to the trouble of breaking into a place and discover it was already stripped clean. What do you say?"

" 'Show me the dotted line,' " I said.

"Edward Rinehart was Mr. Outside?" Laurie asked.

Edison pulled down his sunglasses and leaned forward. His eyes were surprisingly light, an unusual sandy brown flecked with green. The whites were the immaculate white of fresh bedsheets. "Did you hear me say that?" He turned his disingenuous gaze upon me. "Did you hear me say that?"

"You allowed us to form our own conclusions," I said.

He pushed the sunglasses up over his eyes.

"Mr. Rinehart doesn't sound like the sort of man who would write a book," I said.

Edison lowered his chin and peered at me. I thought he was going to do the sunglasses trick again.

"What book?" Laurie asked. "You didn't say anything about a book."

"It was in the box my mother sent to herself, the one with the envelope and the key."

"Did you read that book?" Edison asked.

"Not yet. Did you?"

"Mr. Rinehart gave me a copy, but it got lost along the way. You're right, he didn't seem like a man who would sit down to write a book. But Mr. Rinehart didn't do anything *ordinary*. For one thing, around the time he came out with his book, he retired. Every now and then he had me drive him somewhere, but basically, the man walked away. He told me he had a mission. What Mr. Rinehart used to say was, he wanted his stories to show people the real truth about the world."

"He talked to you in the car?" Laurie said.

Edison grinned. "I spent seven years driving Mr. Rinehart all over Hell's Half-Acre in the dead of night, him in the back of that Cadillac talking a blue streak. If Mr. Rinehart had been a preacher, his sermons would have rolled on for two days and nights."

Edison's laughter sounded as though he still disbelieved what he had heard coming from the backseat of the Cadillac.

"What did he talk about?" I asked.

"The true nature of the universe. And his book. If every book writer goes through the kind of misery Mr. Rinehart did, I'm glad I was a driver."

■ After rejection from a well-known New York house, Rinehart had decided to publish the book himself. Regent Press &

Bindery, a Chicago print shop with a subsidiary specializing in rebinding library books, shipped two hundred copies to Edgerton, where Rinehart stored them in a Hatchtown warehouse. For six weeks, Max Edison had loaded cartons into the Cadillac's trunk and ferried his employer to bookstores as far north as Springfield. Most of the stores had taken two or three copies of *From Beyond*. Rinehart never invoiced them or requested sales figures. He had no interest in making money from his book; he wanted these copies available for purchase upon publication of the dazzled reviews it was certain to receive. When praise flooded in, he would once again submit the book to the firm in New York.

Out went the review copies. A three-page letter accompanied the first twenty, sent to the newspapers and magazines Rinehart judged most crucial to literary success. Fifty publications occupying the second rung received a single-page statement. A simple card went out with the copies sent to pulp magazines.

Three months passed without acknowledgment from the significant and semisignificant publications. The pulps, from which Rinehart anticipated cries of rapture, were silent. Two months later, the irate author sent out letters reminding seventy editors of their obligations to literature. None responded.

Nine months later, *Weird Tales* propped *From Beyond* against a brick wall and dispatched it in a public execution. Eight parallel columns spread over four pages condemned Rinehart's book for being formulaic, cliché-ridden, and self-parodying. A corrosive laughter washed through the review.

Weird Tales sent Rinehart into orbit.

"He carried that review with him all the time. When we were alone in the car, he used to read it out loud. I must have heard different parts a hundred times over. Mr. Rinehart thought that magazine was going to *love* him. Whole weeks went by when he tried to talk himself into believing they really did love him, and what they said looked bad only if you didn't understand it. Then he'd give up on that and go back to telling me how the man who wrote the piece was so stupid, anybody who knew anything would see the book had to be great. I don't think he ever got that review out of his mind. It wasn't long after that he retired."

"Did you see him after he retired?"

"He wasn't the kind of man to keep in touch. Anyhow, I got sent up to do a little stretch in Greenhaven."

Edison took off his sunglasses and folded them on the table. "Then what happened, that Clothhead Spelvin I mentioned got busted for some dumb-ass thing, excuse me, Mrs. Hatch, a thing never would have happened earlier, and as soon as Clothhead started looking at jail time, he rolled over on Mr. Rinehart, and *he* got arrested."

"Edward Rinehart went to jail?" Laurie asked.

"On a minimum ten-year sentence, yes, ma'am. I was present when he came in. Mr. Rinehart acted like he was on a first-class trip to Paris. He knew the only problem he'd have in prison was the problem of being in prison, which if you have connections like Mr. Rinehart's is like being outside, except you're in prison. At Greenhaven, he was free to do just about everything he wanted—except get out of prison. He got me a good job in the library and sent over a nice Italian dinner almost every week. Once Mr. Rinehart came into the population, I had cigarettes and pints of whiskey whenever I wanted them, though I didn't abuse the privilege."

"You got whiskey and Italian dinners in jail?" Laurie asked.

"It's still prison, Mrs. Hatch. I was released in November 1958. A little over two years later, they had a big riot up there. When the troopers moved in, twelve men were lying dead in the yard, and one of them was Mr. Rinehart. He's up there in the Greenhaven cemetery. That's not a bad place for him."

"What?" Laurie said. "Oh. You were afraid of him."

Edison gave us a slow smile. "Sometimes I think I'm *still* afraid of him."

Laurie and I said nothing.

A distant amusement shone in Edison's sandy eyes. "Believe this or don't, it's all the same to me. A couple of nights, I was driving all alone in the car to where Mr. Rinehart told me to pick him up, and I hear a lighter snap open behind me and see a flare in the mirror. There's Mr. Rinehart, lighting up. 'Sorry, Max,' he says. 'Didn't you hear me get in?' Those back doors never opened or closed. Is there any way I could miss *that* sound?

"One time, three, four o'clock in the morning, I took him to Mountry to meet a man named Ted Bright in a building back of a garage. We pulled up, and he said, 'Duck down and keep down until I get back.' I looked over my shoulder, and I guess either I went blind or the seat could talk, because Mr. Rinehart wasn't there. I ducked under the wheel so you'd have to walk right up to the window to see me. Footsteps came around from in front—two guys, moving slow and careful. One of them said, 'That's his car.' The other one said, 'Let's do the deed.' I can't swear what I heard next was shotguns being primed, but I'd put a hundred dollars on it. I said to myself, *Max, you better cover Mr. Rinehart's backside.* I was reaching for the door handle when I realized he told me to keep out of sight because he knew Homer and Jethro were on the way."

Laurie asked, "Did you have a gun?"

He nodded. "When I drove for Mr. Rinehart, I carried a weapon. Never fired it. Never even drew it from the holster, though I came close that night. With Mr. Rinehart, the smartest course was to follow orders, but I couldn't be sure he knew what was going down. I waited maybe a minute. Didn't hear a thing. I decided to crack the passenger door and sneak out and keep low, just in case. All of a sudden there was enough noise out there to wake up a graveyard. I grabbed the door handle with one hand, grabbed my gun with the other. Right in front of me, Ted Bright slams against the hood, covered neck to belly in blood. Bright rolls off and hits the ground. I look at the front of the building. A body's lying facedown in the dirt, holding the door open. There's another body halfway in, halfway out. Another one's down on the floor inside. Place looks like a slaughterhouse. Right behind me, someone clears his throat, and I almost jump out of my clothes. Mr. Rinehart's sitting in the backseat. 'Let's get back to civilization,' he says."

"Did you ask him what happened?" Laurie asked.

"Mrs. Hatch." Edison replaced his sunglasses. "Even if he felt like talking, I didn't want to listen. When I got home, I put away a pint of bourbon without benefit of ice or water. Next day on the radio, they said a businessman named Mr. Theodore Bright got killed attempting to escape from a kidnapping. As good as any other story, far as I was concerned. Mr. Theodore Bright brought it down *on* himself *by* himself."

"That was the real story," I said.

"I was *there*, and I don't know if there was any real story. What I'm telling you is, Mr. Edward Rinehart could be a one-man *Halloween*."

"You're right," I said. "The Greenhaven cemetery is a good place for him."

"We were talking about Clothhead Spelvin, who rolled over on Mr. Rinehart? He was in a holding cell when Mr. Rinehart was arrested. They put Mr. Rinehart two cells down, and that night Clothhead got cut to pieces. No one saw anyone go in or out of his cell."

Edison moved first one leg, then the other, from under the table. It cost him some effort. "Folks, sorry to break up the party, but I want to get back to my room." He wavered to his feet. "Maybe Toby didn't tell you, but I came down with cancer of the pancreas. They give me two more months, but I hope to push it to six."

He did his best to conceal his pain as he sauntered across the parking lot.

■ **48**

■ "What kind of danger?"

Every time we reached the top of a hill, through the windshield I could see the low, sensible skyline of the city where I had been born. Such places were not supposed to contain people like Edward Rinehart. Families like mine, if there were other families like the Dunstans, did not belong in them, either.

"You and Cobbie shouldn't have anything to do with this Rinehart stuff. It's too risky. I'd rather be Donald Messmer's son."

"Cobbie and I can't be in danger from a dead man. And tonight, we are going to find this Donald Messmer."

"I thought Stewart was dropping Cobbie off."

"Afterwards. Posy will be back just after five o'clock, and I could pick you up around six. My son would love to see you again. He keeps saying, 'Is Ned coming to our house?' So come to our house, why don't you? Posy and I will give you dinner, and you can show me Edward Rinehart's book."

It sounded more interesting than dinner in Hatchtown and a return to the rooming house. My fears of endangering Laurie and her son no longer seemed rational; Max Edison had spooked me.

"I warn you, Cobbie is going to make you listen to his favorite music, so be prepared."

"What kind of music does he like?"

"I am baffled," Laurie said. "Cobbie is *fixated* on the last section of *Estampes*, a Debussy piano thing, a Monteverdi madrigal called 'Confitebor tibi' sung by an English soprano, and Frank Sinatra doing 'Something's Gotta Give.' He can't really be only four years old. I think he's a thirty-five-year-old midget."

"Is the English soprano Emma Kirkby?"

"You know her?"

I laughed at the unlikeliness of the coincidence. "I brought that CD with me when I came here."

"That settles it. I'm picking you up at six."

A sign twenty yards down the road marked the boundary of Edgerton, the City with a Heart of Gold. The sign floated nearer, increasing in size. We came to within a foot, to within six inches, to a distance measurable only by a caliper, to nothing. The sign flew past the hood of the car and flattened into a two-dimensional vertical stripe parallel with my head. The air wavered, thickened, and seemed to shimmer up from the highway like a mirage.

■ 49

■ Helen Janette darted out before I reached the stairs. If the manila envelope in her hand was responsible for the expression on her face, I didn't want to know what was in it.

Like a matching automaton on a Swiss clock, Mr. Tite opened his door and stepped into the frame. The fedora shaded his nose, and the lumpy jaw looked hard as granite.

"A policeman was looking for you this morning." She crossed her arms over the envelope. "I didn't like the idea of plunking a thing with *police department* stamped all over it on my mail table."

"Did he give his name?"

Mr. Tite cleared his throat. "It was a gink named Rowley."

"Lieutenant Rowley was returning this to you." She surrendered the envelope.

Otto Bremen boomed out my name before I could get the key into my lock. He was waving at me from the chair in front of his television set, and he looked a lot friendlier than my landlady and her guard dog. I went into his room.

Bremen stuck out a big, splayed hand. "Ned Dunstan, right? Otto Bremen, in case you forgot." His handsome mustache bristled above his smile. "Grab a chair."

Bremen's room overflowed with chairs, dressers, little tables, and other things from wherever he had lived before moving to Mrs. Janette's. A cheerful jumble of photographs, framed documents, and tacked-up drawings by children covered the walls. The yellow banner I had noticed that morning hung across the top of the back wall. WE LOVE YOU OTTO had been printed three times in bright blue letters along its length.

"I guess they love you."

"Isn't that the cutest damn thing?" He looked over his shoulder. " 'We love you Otto, we love you Otto, we love you Otto.' From the graduating sixth-grade class at Carl Sandburg Elementary School, 1989." He lit a cigarette. "Mrs. Rice, the principal, called me up onstage during the ceremony. Most of those kids, I'd known since you had to take 'em by the hand and sing 'The Teddy Bears' Picnic' to get 'em across the street. I was so proud, I almost burst out of my suspenders."

It was the luxuriant, gravel-bottomed Western voice I remembered from that morning. If Otto Bremen had sung "The Teddy Bears' Picnic," I would have followed him across the street, too.

He knitted his hands over his belly and exhaled. "First time any graduating class honored a crossing guard that way. Nine months of the year, I'm the crossing guard at Carl Sandburg." Bremen tapped the cigarette, and ashes drifted toward the floor. "If I had it to do all over again, I swear, I'd get a degree in elementary education and teach first or second grade. Hell, if I wasn't seventy years old, I'd do it now. Say, care for a drink? I'm about ready."

A few minutes later, I managed to get across the hall.

EDGERTON POLICE DEPARTMENT was printed on the front and the sealed flap of the manila envelope Lieutenant Rowley had entrusted to Helen Janette. Inside it was a plastic bag, also sealed, with four white identification bands. A case number and my name had been scrawled on the top two bands. Lieutenant George Rowley and someone in the Property Department had signed the other two. The plastic bag contained a wad of bills. I dumped out the money and counted it. Four hundred and eighty-one dollars. I laughed out loud and called Suki Teeter.

■ **50**

■ The bus dropped me off in College Park two blocks south of the Albertus campus. I walked down Archer Street until I saw the weathered wooden signboard, RIVERRUN ARTS & CRAFTS, over the porch of Suki Teeter's three-story clapboard building.

The room to the right of the entrance surrounded racks of posters and greeting cards with paintings, graphics, woven tapestries, and shelves of pottery and blown glass; the smaller room to the left doubled as an art-supply business and framing shop. Although she exhibited work by local artists, Suki supported herself mostly through poster sales and picture framing.

"This is the only place for decent brushes and paints in a hundred miles, but I can't afford the inventory I should have," she said. "Everything costs so much money! The roof needs fixing. I could use a new oil burner. Twenty grand would solve all my problems, but I can hardly pay my two part-time assistants. They stay on because I cook them dinner and act like Mom."

In her living room, abstract and representational paintings hung alongside shelves of clay pots and blown glass. "All this work is by artists I show in the gallery, except for that painting on your left."

A dirgelike complication of muddy, red-spattered browns occupied a fourth of the wall.

"What do you think?"

"I'd have to look at it for a while," I said.

"It's hopeless, and you know it. Rachel Milton gave me that

painting years ago, and I never had the heart to get rid of it. Can I give you some tea?"

Suki came back with two cups of herbal tea and sat next to me on the yielding cushions. "I shouldn't be bitchy about Rachel. At least she kept in touch with Star, or vice versa. She might even come to the funeral."

Suki's glowing corona glided forward, and she wrapped her arms around my shoulders. I leaned into her aura of mint and sandalwood. She kissed my cheek. The golden haze of her face swam two or three inches back from mine. Her eyes shimmered, intensifying their deep jade green and shining turquoise. "Tell me. You know what I mean, just *tell* me."

I swallowed ginseng-flavored tea and described my mother's last day and night. At the mention of Rinehart's name, Suki gave me a glance of uncomplicated acknowledgment. Without saying anything more, I told her about Donald Messmer's appearance on the marriage license and my birth certificate.

"It's like I'm walking through a fog. My aunts and uncles act as though they're guarding atomic secrets." A tide of feeling surged through me, and everything else shrank before its necessity.

"I have to get *out of the fog*. I want to know who Rinehart was, and how this Messmer came into the picture."

She patted my hand and released it.

"He was my father, wasn't he?"

"You look so much like him, it's eerie."

I remembered Max Edison's subtle relaxation when I said that I had come on a family matter. He had known instantly whose son I was. "Tell me," I said, echoing her words. "Please, just *tell* me."

Suki Teeter leaned back into her cushions.

■ In the autumn of 1957, the more adventurous students of arts and literature at Albertus noted the frequent late-night presence at a rear table in the Blue Onion Coffeehouse of a man whose strikingly compelling face, at once pallid and dark, was framed by his black hair as he bent in concentration, one hand holding a *papier maïs* Gitane cigarette and the other a hovering pencil, over what appeared to be a typewritten manuscript. This was Edward Rinehart. An awed fascination gathered about him.

Slowly, Rinehart's barriers relaxed. Yes, he was a writer; he had come to College Park to enjoy good bookstores and congenial companionship; if he wished for anything more, it was access to the Albertus Library, of course superior to its civic counterparts. Erwin Leake, a young English instructor among the earliest to establish a beachhead of acquaintanceship, soon found a mechanism, an only slightly dubious mechanism, granting Rinehart entry to the college library. Thereafter, Rinehart could often be discovered laboring over his art at one of the desks beneath the rotunda of the Reading Room. He was perhaps thirty-five, perhaps slightly older; his physical attractiveness was magnified, though it needed no magnification, by a kind of lawlessness. The Rinehart era had begun.

He became the intellectual and social focus of a select cadre of students, available for consultation at all hours. At the end of Buxton Place, an obscure cul-de-sac otherwise owned by the college, Rinehart had purchased two adjacent cottages as studio and living quarters. The elect, the chosen, the most passionate and promising of the Albertus population, congregated within his residence—the studio, being sacred, was off-limits. In Rinehart's house, someone was always talking, generally Rinehart. A perpetual sound track, usually jazz, drifted from the speakers. An unending supply of wine, beer, and other beverages magically replenished itself. Rinehart provided marijuana, uppers, and downers, the drugs of the period. His parties went on for two or three days in which the favorites wandered in and out, talked and drank until they could talk and drink no more, listened to readings, mostly by the host, and had frequent sex, mostly with the host.

Suki, Star, Rachel Newborn, and the other young women had fallen under Rinehart's spell. He was a charismatic, unpredictable man who encouraged their aspirations while seeming to embody them: unlike the boys who claimed to be writers, Rinehart had actually published a book, one they had no difficulty accepting as too fine and daring for the blockheads in charge of the publishing world. *Of course* the book was dangerous—Rinehart exuded danger. He had secrets past and present, and there were days when without explanation the house on Buxton Place stood locked and empty. At times, one or another of his harem glimpsed Rinehart getting into or out of a Cadillac parked at a Hatchtown curb. An overexcitable dual major in fine arts and philosophy named Polly Heffer discovered a loaded revolver in a bedside drawer and screeched loudly enough to bring Suki in from the living room at the moment a naked Rinehart entered disgusted from the bathroom. Rinehart silenced Polly with a growl, said that he kept the revolver for self-protection, and invited Suki to make up a threesome.

■ Did she join in?
"You think I turned him *down*?"

■ Now and then, Rinehart's devotees would come upon him in conference with men clearly unconnected to Albertus. These men drew him whispering into a corner, Rinehart sometimes laying an arm across a burly shoulder. The younger, more presentable of these outsiders surfaced during the whirlpools of long parties, and the students included them in their circle. One of these men was Donald Messmer, who lived in the Hotel Paris on Word Street and did whatever came to hand.

■ "Don Messmer wasn't a criminal," Suki said. "Basically, Don was this very easygoing guy who just sort of hung out. To us, he was like Dean Moriarty in *On the Road*, but more laid-back. And he was crazy about your mother. The guy probably never read a book in his life, and all of a sudden he's walking around with novels sticking out of his back pocket because he wants to impress Star Dunstan. I used to hear her talking to him about, you know, Cézanne and Kerouac and Jackson Pollock and Charlie Parker—*Don Messmer!*—but he didn't have a chance, she was in love with Edward Rinehart, along with the rest of us."

"How did his name wind up on her marriage license?"

"Hold on," Suki said, "let me tell you what I know."

■ At the end of the semester, Suki transferred to Wheeler College in Wheeler, Ohio, ostensibly to continue training under a lithographer who had spent the previous year at Albertus. She had lost faith in Edward Rinehart and wanted to escape his sphere of influence. Erwin Leake, once a worthwhile English teacher, had become a drunken phantom; some of the boys Rinehart had declared artists of great promise were turning into drug addicts interested only in another handful of pills; her female friends thought of nothing but Rinehart and his satisfactions. Suki wanted out.

Late in the winter of the following year, Star Dunstan appeared in Wheeler, pregnant, exhausted, and in need of a safe place to stay. Suki relinquished half of her bed. For the next few days, Star said only that she had to *hide*, to *conceal herself*. Suki let her sleep and smuggled in food from her waitressing job. Star told her that she had married a man, but that the marriage had been a mistake. She trembled at the ringing of the telephone. When someone knocked at the door, she disappeared into the bedroom. After two weeks, Star recovered sufficiently to get a job at Suki's restaurant. After another month, she began auditing arts courses at Wheeler. Eventually, she told Suki that her husband had abandoned her when a doctor told her that she might be carrying twins. At the next appointment, the doctor informed her that she might be carrying only one child after all, but this news could not bring back the vanished husband.

An obstetrician in Wheeler pronounced Star fit and healthy and predicted that she would deliver twins, although the evidence was not as conclusive as he would like. She packed her things and left for Cherry Street.

At the end of the school term, Suki drove to Edgerton, found a new apartment, and moved in hours before the descent of a powerful storm. She called Nettie, without response. Perhaps the Cherry Street telephone lines were out. She called Toby Kraft and got through. Toby told her that Star had been admitted to St. Ann's Community Hospital and was about to give birth. He was beside himself with worry. The river had overflowed its banks, and cables had blown down everywhere. Suki belted herself into her rain slicker, snatched up her umbrella, and went outside. Instantly, the umbrella flipped inside out and tore out of her hands.

■ 52

■ Floodwater sluicing around the low wall of sandbags rose over her ankles. Under the slicker, her clothing was soaked. Suki climbed over the barricade and waded toward the hospital's entrance. The lobby looked like Calcutta. In the confusion, she managed to buttonhole a nurse, who focused on her long enough to tell her that only two expectant mothers, a Mrs. Landon and a Mrs. Dunstan, were up on the fourth floor in obstetrics. She advised Suki to take the stairs instead of the elevator.

Suki ran up to the cacophony of the obstetrics department. Babies shrieked from bassinets in the nursery. A nurse frowned at her muddy boots and said that her friend was in delivery room B, attended by Midwife Hazel Jansky. Suki grabbed her arm and demanded details.

Mrs. Dunstan had been in labor five hours. There were no complications. Since this was a first delivery, the process was expected to go on for hours more. Midwife Jansky was assisting at both of the night's deliveries. The nurse peeled Suki's hand from her arm and moved on.

Suki retreated into the waiting room. Behind the blurred reflection of her pale face suspended above a bright yellow slicker, the long windows revealed only a vertical black wall pierced by the lamp posts in the parking lot. Suki put her face against the glass, shielded her eyes, and looked out upon another black wall, this one stretched over the landscape and streaked with incandescent ripples. A dark, linear form she hoped was a tree trunk bobbed along in the wake of an automobile.

Some time later, a younger nurse ducked in to tell her that

Mrs. Dunstan was making progress, but if her baby had any sense it would pull the emergency brake and stay where it was for another twelve hours. The next time Suki cupped her face to look out the window, the lamps in the parking lot had died, and objects too small to identify were swirling downstream, like toys. She lowered herself onto the sofa and fell asleep.

A muffled explosion, followed by women's screams, woke her up. The lights failed, and the screams lengthened into bright flags of sound. Suki groped toward the hallway and saw flashlight beams cutting through the darkness. She took off in search of Star.

Her hands discovered a wide seam in the wall. Suki felt her way sideways, pushed open a door, and charged into a dead-black chamber where an invisible woman wept and moaned.

"Star?"

A strange voice cursed at her.

Suki backed out. Further down, she came to the door of the second delivery room, which knocked her backward as it burst open. A figure put a hand on her shoulder and pushed her to the side. Suki groped forward and caught the door on its backswing. She stumbled in. Whoever was in the room whimpered. Suki bumped against a metal rail and reached down. She touched a wet, bare leg.

Star gasped and pulled her into an embrace. "Suki, they took my babies away."

As abruptly as it had failed, the electricity jumped back into life. Star shielded her eyes. Thick brush strokes and random spatters of blood smeared her thighs. Suki cradled Star's head and stroked her hair.

The midwife bustled in and placed in Star's hands a doll-like infant tightly wrapped in a blue blanket. Star protested—she had delivered two children, one that felt like giving birth to a watermelon, and another who had his bags packed and his passport ready. The midwife told her that what she had mistaken for a second child was the placenta.

Hours later, a harried doctor came in to reassure Star that she had delivered a single healthy child. When asked about Mrs. Landon, Midwife Jansky's other patient, the doctor said that Mrs. Landon's infant had been stillborn.

∎ Suki had stayed with Star until early the following evening, by which time the Fire Department had pumped the floodwater from the basement and ground floor of the hospital. Crews labored to clean away the sticky, foul-smelling layer of mud deposited by the Mississippi. While Star finished a lily-white dinner of chicken, mashed potatoes, and cauliflower, Nettie, Clark, and May swept in. The aunts pelted her with questions. Was it a normal baby? Could she be sure the hospital was not concealing something from her?

Nettie collared a hapless nurse and demanded that Infant Dunstan be removed from the nursery. Blissfully asleep within the confines of a bassinet, Infant Dunstan was wheeled in, snatched up, momentarily cuddled, unwrapped, and subjected to a brisk examination. Nettie passed the wailing child to its mother for rewrapping. Some abnormalities did not show themselves immediately, was Star aware of that?

Suki's indignation boiled over: what kind of late-blooming abnormality did Nettie have in mind, exactly?

Nettie turned and smiled. *I suppose her boy could wind up with different-colored eyes.*

Suki fled as if pursued by Gorgons.

Thereafter, Star maintained a resolute silence about her pregnancy and marriage. Suki had seen the child develop into a four-year-old, a five-year-old, a six-year-old, and ideas of his paternity had come to her, but she never spoke of them. The boy's face declared it for her. Around the time Star began placing her son into foster care, Suki experimentally married a harpsichord player in the Albertus Music Department and moved to Popham, Ohio, where her husband had been appointed artist in residence at an obscure liberal arts college.

The Albertus circle had exploded into disconnected fragments, some to teaching positions, some to nine-to-five jobs, to mental hospitals, Europe, communes, death in Vietnam, law practices, jail terms, other fates. Edward Rinehart had been killed in a prison riot. Rachel Newborn had redesigned herself in a manner that dismissed Suki Teeter. Of her old friends, only Star Dunstan could still be seen, and Star returned to Edgerton only infrequently.

■ Suki took me in the golden haze of her embrace and apologized for talking so much.

"I'm glad you did," I said.

Suki patted my cheek and said that maybe we could have lunch together after my mother's funeral. "I'd like that," I said, and a question came to me. "Suki, it was obvious to you that Rinehart was my father, but what about my aunts? Did Nettie and May ever meet him?"

"Huh," she said. "Not when I was around, anyhow."

■ 53

■ Otto Bremen swiveled his chair in my direction. One hand held a glass of bourbon, a cigarette burned in the other, and he was grinning like a Halloween pumpkin. "Come in and watch the Braves get the tar beat out of 'em. It's a beautiful sight."

I might have gone across the hall and spent the next ninety minutes helping Otto Bremen trounce the Atlanta Braves by drinking them to death, but Edward Rinehart's book tempted me more. After I took *From Beyond* out of my knapsack, I flopped on the bed to read until Laurie Hatch showed up.

Torn between turning immediately to "Blue Fire" and avoiding it altogether, I took the easy way out and started at the beginning.

In "Professor Pendant's Inheritance," a retired professor of Middle Eastern studies moves to an eighteenth-century fishing village where a former colleague had unexpectedly bequeathed him an old house and a vast, legendary library. The retired professor plans to complete his study of Arabic folklore with the aid of this great resource. Forced into a pub during a downpour, the professor overhears a rumor oddly similar to a tale in one of his benefactor's rarest volumes; soon after, he discovers a twelfth-century manuscript of dire incantations. . . . At the story's end, Professor Pendant is devoured by the ancient god, one-third octopus, one-third snake, and one-third indescribable but hideous all the same, summoned by the manuscript.

"Recent Events in Rural Massachusetts" described the visit to a bleak hamlet of a young scholar who falls prey to a race of stunted beings produced by sexual congress between primitive hominids and a ravenous deity from beyond the membrane of our universe.

"Darkness over Ephraim's Landing" ended with this sentence: *As the bells of St. Arnulf's chimed, I burst into the sacrosanct chamber and by the flickering light of my upraised candle glimpsed the frothing monstrosity which once had been Fulton Chambers crawl, with hideous alacrity, into the drain!*

All of this, even the exclamation point, reminded me of something I had read at thirteen or fourteen, but could not place.

As prepared as I would ever be, I began reading "Blue Fire." Half an hour later, I carried the book to the window and went on reading. "Blue Fire" was a novella about the life of one Godfrey Demmiman, whose experiences sometimes resembled nightmare versions of my own, and for all my fascination I had to struggle against the impulse to set the book on fire and toss it into the sink.

The child Demmiman receives a summons from an "ancient wood" at the edge of town. After he enters the woods, an inhuman voice informs him that he is the son of an Elder God, a new Jesus who shall bring about the Apocalypse by giving entry to his unearthly fathers. Through the agency of a sacred blue fire, he is granted unnatural powers. He displays these powers to local girls and kills them. Exiled to a military school, he drifts into madness under the influence of a sacred text.

In his early thirties, Demmiman moves to the city beloved of the text's author and is drawn to a forbidding manse. He imagines himself stalked by furtive beings connected to both himself and the house, breaks in and discovers the crypt of eighteenth-century Demmimans—it is his ancestral home. Returning night after night, he senses a presence, an Other, which searches for him but flees at his approach. Once, carrying a candle through the dusty ballroom, he glances into a mirror and catches sight of a dark figure behind him—he whirls around—the figure has vanished. Two nights later, a darkening of the atmosphere suggests that the Other will at last permit himself to be seen. The sound of footsteps padding through distant rooms brings him to the library at the top of the house.

At the sound of a car pulling up in front of the rooming house, I looked up and saw the Mountaineer backing into a parking space. I jammed the book in my pocket, opened my door, and extended a foot through the frame. I could go no further. Like an X-ray, a sharp pain pierced my head from back to front.

Instead of Helen Janette's hallway and Otto Bremen beckoning from his easy chair, before me lay the room I had seen as a child and in the midst of my breakdown at Middlemount. A dying fern, a stuffed fox under a glass bell, and a brass clock occupied a mantelpiece. Somewhere out of sight, a man muttered an indistinct stream of words. All of this had existed long before my own time on earth. I lurched backward, and the scene dissolved.

The old man across the hall was looking at me. "Kid, you okay?"

"Dizzy spell." I ran downstairs toward Laurie Hatch.

54 ■ Mr. X

■ O Great Ones, O cruel Masters, Your long-suffering but faithful Servant bends once again to the pages of his Journal. I wish to make a confession.

■ Of late, my tales have much occupied my mind, one in particular. It was my longest, my best and most regretted. While writing it, I felt *godlike and fearful*. My pen flew across the page, and for the first and only time in my life I wrote what I knew not that I knew until it was written—I knocked at the door of the Temple and *was admitted*—my life became a *dark wood*, a *maze*, a *mystery*—it was then first I entered the *river-bankish* state—

Would that tale had never laid its hand upon my breast and whispered—take me in—

■ I need a moment to collect myself.

■ The inspiration descended during a weary, late-night return from Mountry Township in the summer of my last year as a Lord of Crime. A fool named Theodore Bright had attempted to eliminate me from my position in the criminal hierarchy. The necessary payback had been devoid of pleasure. I wanted out. My thoughts turned to the consolations of art, and a pleasing notion came to me, that of adumbrating the plight of Godfrey Demmiman, a half-human creature granted the freedom of a god. My alter ego was to re-enact my struggles toward the Sacred Purpose. But as I wrote, my intentions surrendered to what rose up within me.

I PROTEST!

Every other tale went where it was supposed to go. Why should only *this* seem inhabited by art? Let me say this, let me spell it out loud and clear—

I HATE ART. ART NEVER DID ANYONE A BIT OF GOOD. IT NEVER WON A WAR, PUT FOOD ON THE TABLE, SWEPT THE FLOOR, TOOK OUT THE GARBAGE, OR SLIPPED YOU A TWENTY WHEN YOU WERE DOWN AND OUT. ART DOESN'T ACT THAT WAY.

The beginning went as anticipated. Through the medium of Godfrey Demmiman's childhood and youth, I revisited my own. We had mystical experiences in a deep wood and the descent of godlike gifts. My tears brimmed over at the discovery of the Sacred Book. Then hoodlum Imagination brushed aside intention and destroyed my peace. In place of conviction—doubt; in place of clarity—confusion; of design—chaos; in place of triumph— who knows, but certainly not triumph.

Demmiman moves to Markham, the New England village beloved of his Master, and through its winding lanes and passages imagines himself led by misshapen beings to a long-abandoned house of evil repute. He breaks in and finds it to have been the residence of his ancestors. Within, a Presence stalks him—he stalks the Presence—they confront each other—horribly—of the blasphemous ending I decline to speak. For the sake of Coming Generations, I enter the following into the Record:

I Hereby Recant the concluding passages of the story entitled "Blue Fire," those beginning with the words, *"Slowly, with dragging step, an indistinct figure emerged from the shadows,"* and place these conditions upon their distribution. They are to be banned from the Reading Lists of Your Secondary Schools and Institutes of Higher Education. Where available, access must be restricted to Historians and Other Scholars, and this Statement is to be printed in its entirety upon the facing page.

* * *

■ What follows is an account of recent actions on Behalf of the Stupendous Cause.

■ I had nearly forgotten my vow to protect Frenchy La Chapelle from the cowardice of his partner in crime, but when it came back to me, I repaired to the intensive care unit of St. Ann's Community Hospital.

At the center of a network of wires and tubes, a Hatchtown weasel I knew of old sipped the steady doses of oxygen provided by a mechanical ventilator. Like all Hatchtown weasels, including Frenchy La Chapelle, Clyde Prentiss had dared speak of me only in whispers during his urchin-hood. (None of them have ever known my name—any of my names—and for decades have referred to me by a delightfully sinister sobriquet.) On a balmy evening twenty-five years in the past, happening to overhear the prepubescent Clyde Prentiss amusing his peers by a show of irreverence, I exploded into their clubhouse, grasped the little fellow by his ankles, carried the gibbering boy down the lanes to a little-noted structure, and suspended him head-down over the Knacker.

At a time when popular opinion dismisses every sort of nastiness as unacceptable, this eternal source of Hatchtown nightmares has not only been forgotten, its very existence has been denied. Accidentally or no, the Knacker's location has slipped from public record, conveniently assisting its ascent into mythical status.

I held the wriggling boy above the pit until a fragrant evacuation stained his dungarees. Having made my point, I lowered him to the floor. From that day forth, neither the boy nor his fellows offered ought but obedience. The comatose husk of that child's adult self lay before me.

I drew my knife to slice through the accordion folds of the ventilator tube. His spindly chest elevated and deflated. I threw back the sheet, punched the blade into his navel, and dragged it to his throat, which I laid open with a single lateral stroke. The guardian machines trilled, and Prentiss flopped up and down in lively consternation. I wiped the blade on the bottom of the coverlet and swept unseen around the nurse who had appeared at the front of the compartment.

I once again put the fear of God into Frenchy La Chapelle by seeming to materialize out of the refuse of a Word Street corner.

"Good morning, Frenchy," I said. He levitated an inch or two off the pavement. "Time for your marching orders."

Frenchy emitted a moan, about what I had expected. "I tried to find Dunstan, but if he ain't here, it ain't my fault."

"I want to know where he's staying."

"How'm I supposed to do *that*?" Frenchy whined.

"Look for him. When you see him, follow him home. After that, return to this corner and wait for me."

"Wait for you?"

"Pretend it's a train station, and I'm the train."

His mouth curved downward in a Frenchy-smile. "Lots of guys tryin' to find Dunstan."

He risked a peek beneath the brim of my hat. "The cops brought him in after that friend of Joe Staggers got his head bashed open, only they let him go. Staggers and his pals aren't too happy."

"You'd better find him before they do," I said.

He rocked back and forth, gathering his courage. "Didn't you say something about a favor?"

"You could always call the hospital."

Frenchy stopped jittering, and a pulse beat in his temples.

"Step into Horsehair. I'll explain what you are going to do Monday night."

He held his breath as I moved in and blocked the opening. Frenchy had been one of the boys who had seen little Clyde's brush with the Knacker.

■ 55

■ Laurie, who had listened with only half an ear as I described Rinehart's book and my conversation with Suki Teeter, came to life as we neared the expressway. "You solved everything in one day! Yesterday you didn't know anything, and now you know more than you want to! You're done! We have to celebrate."

I asked if Cobbie had come home all right.

"Yes." Her tone was dry and ironic. "Stewart brought him

home and then favored us with his company for several hours. That's why I was late." She swerved onto the westbound ramp. "He helped himself to gallons of Scotch and repeated the same things over and over." Laurie glanced over her left shoulder and flattened the accelerator. We hit sixty before we shot out onto the expressway, and when we settled into the fast lane, the speedometer was climbing past seventy. "Most of them were about you."

I blurted, "Me?"

Grenville Milton had called Le Madrigal to complain about a man of my description who had insulted him outside the restaurant, then gone in—on Milton's recommendation! Vincent, the headwaiter, had identified me and informed Milton that I had joined Mrs. Hatch and Mrs. Ashton. Milton had reported to Stewart, who already knew, because his private detective had told him.

Laurie said, "This morning, some guy tailed me into town and watched us go to City Hall. After that, he followed us to the V.A. Hospital. When I got home, he hightailed it around the corner for a little chat with Stewart. Who of course shoved Cobbie into his car and burned rubber all the way to my house."

I looked through the Mountaineer's big rear window. "If Stewart thinks I'm working for Ashleigh, he must be going batty trying to figure out what we were doing at the V.A. Hospital."

"Everything's driving Stewart batty. Stewart is especially batty when it comes to you." Her eyes flashed at me. "Going places with a Dunstan is like associating with Charles Manson. After destroying the Hanging Gardens of Babylon and introducing the Black Death to Europe, your family got *really* awful. They settled in Edgerton, where they practiced voodoo and cheated at cards. They made the Kennedys look like the Reagans!"

Gleaming with mockery, Laurie's eyes slid to meet mine. "He actually said that. *They made the Kennedys look like the Reagans.* It was very impressive."

"We always were a little peculiar," I said.

■ The tiles on the roof of the big house on Blueberry Lane were made of rubberized plastic, and its design mismatched a Tudor manor with a Georgian townhouse. Stewart Hatch had probably fallen in love with the place the moment he had seen it.

"Who built this house?" I asked Laurie.

She grimaced. "It's one of Grennie Milton's masterpieces. To feel at home in it, you have to wear a pink blazer and green pants."

We went into a vast space in which islands of furniture seemed to float a few inches off a pale carpet. Footsteps clattered on a staircase. Cobbie hurtled around a corner, charged toward us, and wrapped his arms around his mother's legs. A dark-haired young woman in blue jeans and a loose cotton sweater appeared in his wake.

"Ned, Posy Fairbrother, my savior."

Posy gave me a crisp handshake and a smile that would have warmed a corpse. "The famous Ned Dunstan." From the mass of hair gathered behind her ears, wisps and tendrils escaped to fall about her face. She was about twenty-four or twenty-five and the sort of woman who wore lipstick only under duress. "Cobbie's been talking about you all afternoon." Posy turned to Laurie. "Feed him in about half an hour?"

Cobbie let go of his mother and tried to drag me away.

"After we get him in bed, how about helping me in the kitchen?"

Posy looked down at Cobbie doing tug-of-war on my hand and smiled at me. "The price of adoration." She knelt in front of him. "Give Ned some time to talk to your mother before asking him to listen to your music."

"Ned and I can both listen to the music." Laurie bent toward her son. "Cobbie, Ned likes that same Monteverdi piece."

Cobbie stepped into the space Posy Fairbrother had vacated. "You do?" His eyes held no trace of humor.

" 'Confitebor tibi,' " I said. "Emma Kirkby. I love it."

His mouth fell open. I might as well have said that Santa Claus lived on one side of me and the Easter Bunny on the other. He wheeled around and raced toward one of the floating islands.

Laurie and I sat on an oatmeal-colored sofa as Cobbie loaded a CD into a rank of sound equipment beneath a big, soulful self-portrait by Frida Kahlo. I couldn't take my eyes from it. I looked for the other painting she had inherited from her father, and above the fireplace to our left saw a slightly smaller Tamara de Lempicka of a blond woman at the wheel of a sports car.

"What astounding paintings," I said to Laurie.

Cobbie was exploding with impatience. "Sorry," she said. "We're ready now." He pushed the PLAY button.

Emma Kirkby's shining voice sailed out of invisible speakers, translating the flowing, regular meter into silvery grace. Cobbie sat cross-legged on the carpet, his head lifted, drinking in the music while keeping one eye on me. His whole body went still. The meter slowed down, then surged forward at *"Sanctum et terrible nomen eius,"* and he braced himself. We reached the "Gloria patri," where Emma Kirkby soars into a series of impassioned, out-of-time inventions that always reminds me of an inspired jazz solo. Cobbie fastened his eyes on mine. When the piece came to an end, he said, "You *do* like it."

"You do, too," I said.

Cobbie picked himself up from the carpet. "Now hear the piano one."

Laurie said, "I'll mess around in the kitchen for a while," and disappeared around the corner. Cobbie inserted another CD and pushed buttons until he reached Zoltán Kocsis playing "Jardins sous la pluie," the last section of Debussy's *Estampes*.

He closed his eyes and cocked his head in unconscious imitation of almost every musician I have ever met—even I do that when I'm listening hard. I could see the harmonies shiver along his nervous system. "Jardins sous la pluie" ends with a dramatic little flourish and a high, percussive E. When it had sounded, Cobbie opened his eyes and said "That's on our piano." He pointed across the room to a white baby grand angling out from a far wall, raced across the carpet, raised the fallboard, and struck the high E. I don't know what I felt most like doing, giggling in delight or applauding, but I think I did both.

"See?" He struck it again, percussively, and lifted his finger to cut off the note.

"Do you remember the big note before that?"

He spun back to the keyboard and hit the high B. "It's five down and five up, it's *funny*."

The B was a five-step down from the E, so after all the previous harmonic movement, the E came as an almost comic resolution. It was no wonder Cobbie could imitate voices perfectly. He had perfect pitch, or what we call perfect pitch, anyhow—the ability to hear precise relationships between sounds.

"How did you know where they were?"

He walked up to me, laid his forearms across my knees, and

stared into my eyes, asking himself if I were really that dumb or just pretending. "Because," he said, "one is very, very, very *red*. And the big one is very, very, very *blue*."

"Naturally," I said.

"*Very, very* blue. Now can we have the funny Frank Sinatra song?"

"Just what we need," I said.

He charged back to the player, inserted the CD of *Come Dance with Me*, and called up a crisp drum roll and Billy May's brass figures. Cobbie sank to the floor and crossed his legs, listening to Sinatra's perfectly timed entrance on "Something's Gotta Give" with the same concentration he had brought to Monteverdi and Debussy. He twinkled at me at the beginning of the bridge and smiled at Sinatra's stretching out of the rhythm after the instrumental break. Because I was listening partially through Cobbie's ears, what I heard gleamed with a loose, confident power. But for some reason, a part of me shrank away— Sinatra's "Something's Gotta Give" was the last thing I wanted to hear. The track ended with a swaggering downward phrase and an exultant *Come on, let's tear it up* that made Cobbie laugh out loud.

He fastened his eyes on mine. "Again?"

"Ring-a-ding-ding," I said.

The jazzy call to arms from the drummer; urgent shouts from the trumpets and trombones; the saxophone section unfurling a carpet-smooth lead-in; at the exact center of the exact center of the first beat of the first bar of the first chorus, a lean baritone voice took off in a racing start. Fear slid up my spine, and goose pimples bristled on my arms.

When the song ended, Posy Fairbrother appeared at the entrance of the room. "Let's tear up some wild, knocked-out, koo-koo spaghetti, what do you say?"

Cobbie plunged toward her. At the corner leading to the kitchen, he looked back at me. "Ned! We're having knocked-out, koo-koo spaghetti!"

"You and I are having spaghetti, Frank," Posy told him. "You can say good night to Ned afterward, and then he's going to have dinner with your mommy."

Laurie moved around them, holding a wineglass in each hand. "You and Posy go in the kitchen. I'll be there in a minute."

Cobbie put his hand into Posy's and vanished around the

corner. For what seemed an absurdly long time, Laurie and I walked toward each other. When we stood face to face, she leaned forward to kiss me. The kiss lasted longer than I had expected.

"What did you think? What *do* you think?"

"He's incredible, that's what I think. I think he should skip grade school and go straight to Juilliard."

Laurie put her forehead on my shoulder. "Now what do I do?"

"You should probably start him on piano lessons with a good teacher. Five years later, get him a great teacher and hire a lawyer whose nickname is Jaws."

She straightened up and stared at me, almost exactly as Cobbie had done while explaining that E and B were colored red and blue.

"What impresses me most is that he's such a good kid. I think he's going to need as much protection as encouragement. Apart from that, just stand back and enjoy the show. But, hell, I'm just making this stuff up, I don't know anything."

Laurie moved against me once more, put an arm around my back, and then broke apart and held out a slip of paper. "Posy found a listing for a Donald Messmer in Mountry. While I spend a little time with Cobbie, would you like to see what he has to say?"

I took the paper from her.

The fireplace came through into a kind of television room or den with track lighting aimed down at half-empty shelves. Toy trucks and children's books were scattered across the carpet. I sat on the sofa and picked up the telephone, but the first person I called was Nettie.

"Your Mountry trash came around this morning," she said. "I told that sorry excuse for a man he needed more than a big mouth and a baseball bat to scare *me*. Sent them away with their tails between their legs. You don't happen to have a piece, do you?"

I laughed. "No, I don't have a gun."

"Get one. Show iron to fools like that, they get out of your face lickety-split."

Rinehart's book dug into my side, and I took it out of my pocket before dialing the other number.

Posy's CD-ROM had located the right Donald Messmer, but it took me a couple of minutes to get him talking.

"You saw my name on the marriage license, and you got curious about me, huh? Guess I can't blame you for that."

I thanked him and called him Mr. Messmer.

"Star let you know I wasn't your dad, I hope?"

We spoke a little more. Messmer said, "I'm real sorry about your mom. If you don't mind my saying so, I was nuts about her. I would have done anything for Star Dunstan."

It was the reason he had married her. Two months after getting pregnant and moving in with Rinehart, Star's infatuation had curdled into fear. When she had confided to Messmer that she thought Rinehart intended to injure her, the child, or both of them, Messmer helped her escape from Buxton Place. They were married by a justice of the peace and fled across Ohio and into Kentucky, where Messmer had family. When his relatives proved hostile to Star, the couple went to Cleveland. They took jobs in restaurants and lived together in reasonable happiness. A month later, Star went for a medical checkup, and everything changed.

"I was this stupid kid," he said. "If something was more than five minutes ahead of me, I couldn't think about it. The idea of having a child was almost more than I could handle, so I just tried to forget it, figuring it would work itself out. When she came back from the doctor and said it was twins, it was like, Sorry, Don, you're spending the next twenty years in slavery."

"And the twins weren't yours," I said.

"I'm glad you can understand that. A week later, I was shaving in front of the mirror, and this corpse looked back at me. I packed my stuff and took off. I should have been a better guy, but I did what I did. Does that make sense to you?"

"You did her a favor by getting her away from Rinehart."

"That's a nice thing to say. The truth is, we wouldn't have stayed together anyhow."

After arriving in Mountry, he tended bar until he had saved enough money to buy his own place, which he still ran. His wife had died three years ago, and he had two daughters and six grandchildren. When Messmer looked back at the young man who had run away from Edgerton with Star Dunstan, he saw a person he could scarcely recognize.

"Do you know a man named Joe Staggers?"

"Everybody in Mountry knows Joe Staggers. Most wish they didn't. Why, you run into him somewhere?"

"It's all a mistake, but Staggers thinks he has a grudge against me."

"The asshole's whole life is a mistake." I could hear him wondering how far he wanted to go. "This grudge, was a guy named Minor Keyes involved in that?"

"So I hear," I said.

"If you're going to be around more than a couple days, you might see can you borrow a weapon from someone. Staggers is a mean son of a bitch."

■ Cobbie was polishing off his spaghetti at a table in a windowed alcove next to the kitchen door. Laurie asked, "How did it go?"

"He's a nice guy. Have you ever been to Mountry?"

She shook her head. "Why?"

"Let's promise never to go there."

Cobbie chanted, "Somewhere, somehow, someone's *gotta* be kissed."

Posy sprang from her chair. "Bedtime for the Rat Pack." She wiped the red smears from Cobbie's face. "All right. Upstairs."

"Do I have to?"

She put her hands on her hips. "Would I lie to you?"

"Have to have to?"

She looked at me. "Cobbie wondered if you could make out a list of CDs he would like."

"I'll try to hold it down to the top one hundred."

"Maybe we can get Ned to say good night to you once you're in bed."

Cobbie looked at me with a blast of anticipatory joy. I would have bet anything that Stewart never tucked him in or read to him at night.

"And I'll read you a book," I said, "but it has to be a short one."

"Goodnight Moon," he said. I felt an inexplicable chill of resistance.

"Goodnight Moon?" Posy said.

Laurie said, "Isn't that a little babyish for you?"

He shook his head. *"Goodnight Moon."*

"Sure," I said. "It's about the perfect way to go to sleep." The same part of me that had resisted "Something's Gotta Give" was saying *no no no* to Cobbie's chosen book. I knew it came from the same place, wherever that was.

"You're a lucky kid," Posy said.

Laurie smiled at me and told Cobbie, "Just once."

He kissed her and flew out of the kitchen, Posy behind him.

Laurie drank the last of the wine in her glass without taking her eyes from my face. "I don't suppose you have three or four children you play with every afternoon and read to every night, one after the other."

"Six," I said. "Plus the twins in Boulder."

My mouth went dry. I had intended to say "San Diego," but *Boulder* had come out as if a wizard had put a spell on my tongue. For the third time, a powerful and irrational unease spread its wings. Boulder?

Laurie stood up to get the bottle. "You know, Stewart never read to Cobbie at bedtime, not once. What happened to your glass?"

"I left it in the other room," I said. "Hold on, I'll find the dog sled." When I returned, I sat down next to her and put *From Beyond* on the table.

Laurie flipped through random pages. Something made her snicker, and I said, "What?"

She grinned. " *'Mr. Waterstone,' creaked the old librarian from the musty darkness of his sinister lair, 'the means by which you acquired that ancient text are of no interest to me.'* In books, I don't think people should *creak* or anything else like that. They should just say things."

"Edward Rinehart may not be the author for you, he surmised."

She closed the book. "Tell me about Donald Messmer."

I condensed Messmer's tale without mentioning what he had said about Joe Staggers. "It's funny. I thought there'd be more. I'm almost disappointed there isn't."

"It's amazing, how much you got done in one day. Now you can think about the rest of your life."

Posy Fairbrother swung around the entrance to the kitchen and came as far as the central island. "Your admirer awaits you. He hasn't looked at *Goodnight Moon* for so long it took me ages to find it, but he promised to go to sleep after one reading. Laurie, what can I do while Ned is being wonderful?"

"Help me with the hollandaise for the artichokes, and if you put a salad together, I'll handle the rest."

"Do you want me to clean up afterwards?"

"One of us will." Laurie pushed her chair back and stood up in a single gesture. The glowing shield of her face revolved toward me. "Ready to be wonderful all over again?"

■ **56**

■ Separated by expanses of ocher wall, doors stained to look like rosewood marched toward a floor-to-ceiling window with an arched fanlight. The second door on the right stood partially open.

Sending out waves that would set off a Geiger counter, the book lay on the chair beside Cobbie's bed. Already yawning, he was hugging the teddy bear. A stuffed black cat and a stuffed white rabbit stood guard at the foot of his bed, and a foot-high *Tyrannosaurus rex* reared on the headboard.

Margaret Wise Brown's hymn to bedtime seemed almost poisonous. To distract myself, I asked Cobbie how my namesake was getting along. Ned the bear and *Tyrannosaurus rex* had become excellent friends. Was Cobbie ready for his book? Yes, emphatically. Hoping that I was as ready as he, I opened the book, turned sideways and held it out so he could see the pictures, and began to read.

Instantly, my phobia disappeared, and all sense of danger went away. Cobbie's eyelids reached bottom when I was five pages from the end. I closed the covers and, in the spirit of *Goodnight Moon*, whispered good night to all and sundry. The phobia reasserted itself when I placed the book on the headboard. I turned off the lamp, realizing that I had learned something as mysterious as the original phobia: I was afraid of the jacket, not the book.

In my inner ear, Frank Sinatra belted out a fragment of "Something's Gotta Give": *Fight . . . fight . . . fight it with . . . aaaall of your might . . .*

Halfway down the stairs, I met Posy Fairbrother coming up. She was in a rush; she had to do at least four hours of work that night. All the more beautiful for being attuned to the task ahead, Posy's face seemed nearly kittenish as she wished me a wonderful evening.

■ 57

■ Laurie Hatch and I were borne along on a tide of conversation that seemed infinitely expandable into realms more and more intimate by grace of a shared understanding. I had not had an evening like it in at least ten years, and none of those soulful interchanges of my twenties had felt so much like real contact.

The conviction that one's own experience has been *mirrored* by the other's, that whatever is said will be understood, soon begins to confirm itself out of sheer momentum, and, of course, I did not dare to be as open as I appeared. Neither did Laurie. Of my "attacks," Mr. X, the weirdness of the Dunstans, and the shadow-double who had saved my life, I said nothing. I never considered being completely honest with Laurie Hatch. She would have been alarmed, taken aback—I did not want to make her think I was crazy.

If conversations like ours did not always contain a degree of falsity, they would not be so profound.

We managed to get through a bottle and a half of wine, and the table was covered with serving dishes. "Why don't we clear this stuff up?" I said.

"Forget it." Laurie tilted back in her chair and ran a hand through her hair. "Posy will take care of that."

"She has hours of work ahead of her. Let's give her a break." I carried bowls to the sink and scraped artichoke leaves into the garbage disposal.

Laurie helped me load the dishwasher and filled its soap trays. "I feel like one of the shoemaker's elves. What were we going to do now, do you remember?"

"Did you want to hear the end of that Rinehart story?"

"The perfect farewell to Mr. Rinehart." She emptied the last of the wine into our glasses and led me back to the sofa.

* * *

■ Curled next to me with her head on an outstretched arm, Laurie said, "This is the story you were reading when I showed up?"

"I was almost done."

She took a sip of wine. "Professor Arbuthnot has discovered a book of the extremest age and rariosity. The three old men murdered in an opium den had been tattooed on their left buttocks with an ancient Arabic curse. On his way to interview a sinister dwarf, our hero catches sight of an infant with yellow eyes and a forked tongue."

"This one's a little different," I said. "The whole first half sounds almost autobiographical." I condensed Godfrey Demmiman's early life into a couple of sentences and briefly described his adventures in the village of Markham, the obsession with his ancestral house, his simultaneous flight from and pursuit of the Other, leading to the night when he was drawn to the library on the top floor.

"Carry on, she implored."

With the conviction that it was on this night that he should encounter the figure so long hidden from view, Demmiman entered the old library and eased the door shut behind him. Immediately, Demmiman became aware that his conviction was no mere fantasy. The Other's presence etched itself upon the endings of his nerves, and as he took it in, he took in also the state in which he should discover his adversary.

After preparations no less fearful, no less uncertain than his own, the Other awaited his arrival with an equal terror, which served only to chill the blood in Demmiman's veins. Nonetheless, Godfrey found it within himself to advance forward and cast his eye over the musty vacancy.

"Who are you, unholy figure?" he brought forth.

There came an irresolute, hesitating silence. "Come forth. By all that is within me, I must see you."

The pressure of the silence about him nearly sent him in flight to the door. At the last moment of his endurance, a footfall sounded from a distant region of the library.

"It's no good if the guy comes out, and he's just another monster," Laurie said.

"We'll see," I said.

* * *

Slowly, with dragging step, an indistinct figure emerged from the shadows. Demmiman found himself unable to breathe. Here was what for either release or surrender he knew he must confront at last. The intensity of his curiosity gave him the dim figure of a man decades older than himself and formed by experiences far beyond his own, experiences before which Demmiman knew his own imagination to fall short.

His dark, formal dress was that of a provincial man of business elevated to a tyrannical success. Scarcely had Demmiman taken in a white, exposed froth of beard than he saw, upon a forward step, that what had made the face indistinct was the pair of raised hands concealing it in—Demmiman felt—a gesture of shame.

He separated his feet and planted himself on the dusty floor.

The figure lifted its head and spread its fingers, seeming to sense his shift of mood. Then, as if in a sudden moment of decision, it dropped its hands and bared its face with an aggression Demmiman knew beyond his own capabilities. Horror held him fast. A thousand sins, a thousand excesses had printed themselves upon that face. It was the record of his secret life, hideous and inescapable, and yet, however coarsened and inflamed, the Other's features were hideously, inescapably Demmiman's own.

"Are you all right?"

"Why?"

"It sounded like your throat tightened up. Drink some wine, that'll help."

Had all his efforts been designed but to bring him face to face with this monstrous version of himself? Part of Demmiman's humiliation lay in the recognition that the hideous being's strength far surpassed his own. The Other stepped forward, blazing with the claim it made upon him, and he could not bear up before the demand for recognition. Godfrey Demmiman turned and ran for his life.

He thought he heard laughter behind him, but the laughter was only an echo of his shame; he thought dragging footsteps pursued him down the stairs but heard only the pounding of his heart. From half-open doors and shrouded corners, the lithe, misshapen creatures seemed to peer out, awaiting his final surrender.

He would not yield in defeat. He had been born to a great purpose, of which the encounter in the barren room was but the key that opened the lock. His destiny, Demmiman took in, held a majesty he had only begun to comprehend.

Demmiman advanced upon the door to the gallery, thrust it open, and found in his pocket the book of matches he had used to light the tapers in the crypt. The bright flame trembled as he knelt before the first of the long curtains. A small, quivering flame sprang to life and inched upward. Demmiman moved to the next and struck another match. When the second curtain was alight, he ran to the mouldering draperies across the gallery. Then, in the dancing, irregular light, he examined his handiwork.

Rows of flame from the upright columns spread across the floorboards and the ceiling. Scouts and runners had taken another of the rotting panels, and lines of red flame crept along the surface of the wall. The walls opened to the flames as if in welcome; the floor set itself alight in a dozen places. He backed into the smoky hall and let himself out into the night.

On both sides of the narrow street, the dirty brick and blank windows of abandoned buildings took no notice of the red glare visible within their neighbor. The alarm would come long afterward, when flames rose into the dark sky. Demmiman moved into the shelter of a doorway.

The ground-floor windows shattered and released plumes so dark as to obscure the blaze within. With a great rush, the fire took the second floor. Flames surged out and vanished within a massive column of smoke.

The third floor went, and the fourth followed. Above the roar of the conflagration, Demmiman fancied that he heard the high-pitched screams of the creatures trapped at the top of the house, and the thought of their panic caused a savage rejoicing in his breast.

The dark blanket swarming over the front of the building hid from view the topmost windows, and Demmiman sped across the cobblestones to secrete himself in the doorway of an adjacent building, from whence he was able to observe the final progress of the blaze. No sooner had he cast his eyes upward to glimpse the fifth-floor windows than the first signs of firelight shone behind them, then deepened from yellow to red.

A silhouette moved into the frame of the window nearest and looked out with supernal calm. The entire structure offered a groan of imminent collapse. The figure in the window cast its unseen eyes upon him. In the distance, a siren, then another, came screaming toward the blaze. The eyes hidden within the black silhouette maintained their hold.

The window frame ignited around the dark shape, illuminating the ruined visage so like and unlike his own. The Other again issued his implacable claim. His hair burst into flame. Behind him, the fire darkened from red to the deep blue once witnessed at the heart of an ancient forest. Demmiman moved from the doorway and into the cobbled street. In the Other's demand, it came to him with the weight of a majestic paradox, lay an unforeseen fate to which Demmiman's suddenly exalted spirit gave its full assent.

He sprinted from cover and plunged into the burning building. An instant later, what remained of the interior gave way, and with a yielding sigh of capitulation the great structure folded in upon itself and shuddered downward upon Godfrey Demmiman's ecstatic release.

"He had to rid the world of himself? Not to mention his family house and the little crawly things?"

"Poor old Godfrey."

"We could manage a happier ending than that. Are you interested? Aha. What we have here is a decided show of interest. What did Edward Rinehart know about ecstatic release?"

■ The sight of that beautiful, tawny face so close to mine made me feel blessed. Some of the women I had known may have been more passionate than Laurie, but none were more gracefully attuned to the capacity of each individual moment to spread its wings and glide into the next. She also had the gift of what some would call a dirty mind and others inventiveness. The more we explored our bodies and celebrated their abilities, the more unified we seemed to become until at last we seemed to pour into each other and become a single, profoundly interconnected thing. When we swam apart to lie side by side, I felt as though filmy trails of my self were still drifting back into me.

"Can you even begin to guess how good you make me feel?" Laurie said.

"I think I'll build a shrine to you," I said.

A few hours later I awakened with the old sense of having to get on my way before trouble found me. Besides that, I was falling in love with Laurie Hatch far too quickly. I had no business falling in love with her at all. In a few days I was going back to New York, and after that I would probably never see her again. What I chiefly represented to Laurie was danger, and I had to protect her from that. I moved her arm off my shoulder and slid out of bed.

While I was groping for my socks, I bumped into a lamp, and the noise woke her up. Fuzzily, she asked what I was doing. I told her that I had to get back to the boarding house.

"What time is it?"

I looked at the green numerals on the digital clock. "One-fifteen."

She turned on a low bedside lamp and sat up, rubbing her face. "I'd drive you, but I'm so tired I think I'd go off the road."

"I'll call a taxi," I said.

"Don't be silly. Take Stewart's car—his other car, the one he left in the garage. We'll figure out a way to get it back. Because you are definitely coming back here, Ned, there are no two ways about *that*."

I went to the bed and kissed her. The sheet lay rumpled across her waist, and her torso seemed dusky and golden in the dim light.

"Call me tomorrow." She switched off the light as soon as I finished dressing.

Stewart Hatch's "other" car was an ivory two-seater Mercedes 500SL, a fact that would have amazed me had I not been past all amazement. After I started the ignition, I looked at the controls, put the car into reverse, and nearly backed through the garage door. It took me a moment to learn how to change the headlights from bright to dim, and after I had dialed them back to bright I left the car throbbing in neutral and retrieved my mother's package from the backseat of Laurie's car.

I drove back to central Edgerton in high style, singing along with the jazz on the Albertus radio station, and passed up a spot in front of the rooming house to park around the corner on Harry Street.

■ **59**

■ As I went up the stairs I heard the unmistakable noise of a party going on at the far end of my floor. A cluster of young people filled the hallway at the rear of the house. The girls were mostly gleaming legs, the boys wore bristling haircuts and polo shirts, and all of them were holding plastic cups, waving cigarettes, and gabbing. A black-haired girl whose bangs brushed her eyebrows flapped her cigarette at me.

"Hey, new neighbor! Come to our party!"

"Thanks, but not tonight," I said. "Partied out."

I waved at her and glanced through the open door across the hall. Most of Otto's lights had been turned off, and illumination from the television screen flickered over the form slumped in the easy chair. The neck of a Jack Daniel's bottle protruded from his crotch, and about half an inch of dark brown liquid remained in the glass beside his chair. I wondered if I should turn off his television and help him get to bed. When I took a step toward him, I smelled burning fabric.

A curl of smoke arose just beyond Otto's limp hand. From the tip of a half-smoked cigarette, a circle of sparks on the arm of his chair brightened and lengthened into flames.

I ran into the room and began beating the flames with my hands. Otto's head jerked up. Two scarlet-threaded eyes looked at me without recognition.

"Otto," I said. "You—"

"Get the heck out!" he yelled. "Dang crook!"

I saw a big fist traveling across his chest. The fist walloped into my shoulder, and I thumped onto the floor. A blaze roughly the shape and color of an autumn leaf arose from the sleeve of his sweater.

"Gol-durn robber!"

Otto planted his left hand in the midst of the flames and rocketed bellowing out of the chair. The Jack Daniel's bottle bounced to the floor. He staggered forward and noticed that his sweater was on fire.

I yelled, "The sink, Otto!" and grabbed a sweatshirt from the bottom of his bed, hearing him rip off a series of six-gun curses worthy of Gabby Hayes. *Dadgum dangfool tarnation shitfire dadblasted thing is this?*

A crowd of young people filled the doorframe, stubbing cigarettes on the floor and sipping from plastic cups. Otto and I were better than television.

I flattened the sweatshirt over the arm of the chair and smacked it.

The black-haired girl with the bangs edged forward. "Mr. Bremen, he isn't a robber, he's the guy who moved into Mrs. Frahm's room."

"I know, honey."

She smiled at me. "Hey, I'm Roxy Redman, and this is Charlie and Zip and my roommate, Moonbeam Challis."

A pretty blond in what looked like a slip that showed her bra straps fluttered her fingers. "My real name's Audrey, but everybody calls me Moonbeam."

"Of course they do," I said. "My name is Ned, but everybody calls me Ned."

Moonbeam tittered, and Charlie or Zip gave me a look that was supposed to make me pee in my pants.

Otto appeared beside me, holding a glass of water. Footsteps came pounding up the stairs. "Peel her off." I pulled the sweatshirt away, and Otto emptied the glass onto the blackened mess.

Invisible behind the throng, Helen Janette announced that the party was over. Mr. Tite's fedora floated into view. "You heard the lady. Get on home."

"Sorry, kid," Otto said. "Guess the stupid old man got a little fuzzy." He picked the bottle up off the floor and dropped it in the wastebasket. "Time to eat a hundred miles of you know what."

Roxy, Moonbeam, and their friends drifted away in a cloud of muted laughter, allowing me a glimpse of Mr. Tite that explained the mirth. Beneath the fedora, Tite was wearing the mesh T-shirt I had seen that morning and striped boxer shorts stained yellow at the fly.

Cinched into a pink bathrobe over a nightgown, Helen Janette marched in and established a command post. "I demand an explanation."

Otto did his best. He had fallen asleep while smoking, I had startled him, he was sorry for all the excitement. Nothing like this had ever happened before, and it would never happen again.

Mrs. Janette intensified her air of authority. "I am *disgusted.*" Mr. Tite moved into position behind her. "This room *reeks* of alcohol. You passed out with a cigarette in your hand and almost started a fire. We can have no more of this, Mr. Bremen."

"Right," said the watchdog.

"This here was a one-time mistake. I'll take more care in the future." Otto straightened up. I thought he looked like John Wayne. "Is there anything else you care to say?"

"Open your windows and let out the stink. This is supposed to be a decent house."

"My windows are open already. If you want to run a decent house, you could get rid of Frank Tite. Just my humble advice."

Tite lurched forward, and Mrs. Janette halted him with a raised hand. She glared at me. "Mr. Dunstan, I want no further difficulties from you."

"I did you a favor," I said.

She stamped out.

Bremen looked at me and shrugged. We heard them march

downstairs and close their separate doors. "What's Tite's story?" I asked.

"Frank Tite's a bum who got thrown off the police force, that's his story." He pulled off his sweater and tossed it in the direction of the wastebasket. "There's another bottle of sour mash around here somewheres. Join me in a nightcap?"

I got out with a promise to visit him soon. Rinehart's book and the package from the safety-deposit box had been kicked into the corner near the window. I carried the package to my table and stripped off layers of brown paper until I uncovered a large, old-fashioned scrapbook in a quilted forest-green binding. Taped to its front cover was a notecard inscribed with my mother's handwriting: *For Ned*.

◼ **60**

◼ I flipped through the pages of Laurie's Russian doll, my last, secret gift from my mother, growing more and more baffled. Glued front and back to more than half of its thick pages were . . . newspaper clippings about crimes? A few of them came from the *Edgerton Echo*, but most of the articles had been clipped from out-of-town papers. Nearly all the stories reported unsolved violent deaths, none of which seemed to have any connection to Star or me. Disturbed, I began going through the scrapbook more methodically, and a name I had heard from both Hugh Coventry and Suki Teeter jumped out at me from the first few articles.

The headline above the first clipping read MIDWIFE ACCUSED OF BABY-SNATCHING, ADMITS CHARGES. Hazel Jansky, a local midwife, had come under suspicion when an administrator at St. Ann's Community Hospital noted that over the previous decade she had been present at nine stillbirths. Jansky had given plausible accounts of the incidents, but the hospital had asked nurses to monitor her performance. Two weeks later, one of the nurses learned that a patient of Jansky's had delivered a dead child moments before. A hospital maintenance man told her that he had seen the midwife rushing down the service stairs. Inspired, the nurse took the staff elevator to the basement, there to find Hazel Jansky trotting toward a flight of steps leading to a back door. She caught up with her outside the door and saw a waiting car speed off. The nurse conducted Jansky to the administrator's office, where the infant was discovered concealed inside her coat, bathed, swaddled, and unquestionably alive. At Police Headquarters, Jansky admitted participation in four transactions involving the sale of newborn infants to couples unable or unwilling to go through the normal adoption process. She denied having an accomplice or accomplices.

The story was dated March 3, 1965. Four months before my seventh birthday, my mother had opened the morning paper and discovered what she considered proof that she had delivered not a single child, but twins.

A day later, the *Echo* announced BABY-SNATCHER MIDWIFE CONFESSES, DEFENDS ACTIONS. Hazel Jansky had identified the four "black-market babies" and claimed to have acted in their interests by rescuing them from unfit mothers. Jansky had also named their purchasers, but efforts to trace the new parents had not been successful, "which," reported the *Echo*, "has led to speculations that the purchases were made under false names."

Her trial began in May and lasted three weeks. Of the four mothers whose children had been abducted and sold, one had been killed in a tavern brawl; another died in a drunken traffic accident that took two other lives; one disappeared without a trace; after hearing that her son was alive, the fourth complained that the defendant kept the money for herself instead of splitting it fifty-fifty.

The jury found Jansky guilty and recommended mercy. A week later, the judge spoke. Although the illegality of the defendant's actions could not be overlooked, neither should it be forgotten that Midwife Jansky had chosen infants whose mothers' conduct put them at risk. The judge wished also to take into account her record of service to the community. Therefore, he accepted the recommendations of the jury and sentenced the defendant to three years at Greenhaven Penitentiary, with possibility of parole after eighteen months.

She stole four children and told their mothers they were dead, this Hazel Jansky. Because a judge and jury found that she had acted in the interests of the stolen children, she spent only eighteen months in jail. Hazel Jansky's photographs did not depict a person to whom one would entrust social policy. A compact blond in her mid-thirties, she glowered from the pages of the *Echo* with the irascibility of one who had learned that unrelenting crabbiness served her far better than cheerfulness and was not about to forget it.

I thought the court had shared her contempt for her victims. If Hazel Jansky had sold the babies of middle-class mothers, she would still be in jail. And I wondered if the murdered woman and the one killed while driving drunk would have turned out differently had they not been told that their babies were stillborn.

The next clipping, from the *Milwaukee Journal* and headed DOUBLE MURDER IN SUBURBIA, introduced the unsolved homicides. Milwaukee County pathologists had discovered that Mr. and Mrs. William McClure, previously thought to be victims of the fire that had destroyed their house on Salisbury Road in the suburb of Elm Grove, had died as a result of multiple stab wounds. Their three-year-old daughter, Lisa McClure, had not, as originally supposed, perished from asphyxiation but from traumatic injury to the neck. Resident in Elm Grove for only six months, the couple had remained largely unknown to their neighbors, one of whom told the *Journal* reporter that Mr. McClure claimed to have moved from St. Louis for business reasons. Missing from the scene was eight-year-old Robert McClure, Mr. McClure's nephew, who had been enrolled in the coming term's third-grade class at Elm Grove Elementary School. While not ruling out the possibility that the boy had been abducted by the assailants, police held out hope that he had escaped before his presence was noted. Efforts to reach the boy's parents had not been successful, but Elm Grove's chief of police, Thorston Lund, expressed confidence that they would soon be heard from.

The next clipping was headed MYSTERY OF SLAIN COUPLE.

The investigation into Wednesday's brutal triple murder and arson in Elm Grove took a surprising turn this morning with the announcement that two of the victims, William and Sally McClure, may have been living under assumed names. According to a confidential source in the Elm Grove Police Department, a routine background check has revealed that on at least two previous occasions the couple had given fictitious addresses.

When purchasing the Salisbury Road property and again when enrolling eight-year-old Robert McClure, Mr. McClure's missing nephew, in Elm Grove Elementary School, the McClures listed their previous residence as 1650 Miraflores, San Juan, Puerto Rico, a nonexistent address. On Robert McClure's enrollment form, his previous school was given as St. Louis Country Day School, which has no record of his attendance.

A high-ranking officer in the Elm Grove Police Department reports that the McClures purchased the Salisbury Road residence through the Statler Real Estate Agency by means of a cash payment. Thomas Statler, the president of the agency, says that a cash sale is unusual but not unprecedented in the Elm Grove area.

One local resident described Mr. McClure as "swarthy," but with no trace of a Puerto Rican accent. Sally McClure is said to speak with a "New York" accent. "Mr. McClure wasn't like the normal person from around here. He tried to be polite, but you wouldn't call him a friendly man."

In a statement issued today, Elm Grove's chief of police, Thorston Lund, speculated that the murders could be connected to Mr. McClure's past.

The child claimed to be the couple's nephew, eight-year-old Robert McClure, remains missing.

On the next page, the *Journal* announced SLAIN ELM GROVE COUPLE HAD CRIMINAL BACKGROUND.

At a press conference yesterday evening, police departments of Milwaukee and Elm Grove announced that the Federal Bureau of Investigation identified William and Sally McClure, slain last Wednesday in their exclusive Salisbury Road residence, as Sylvan Booker and his common-law wife, Marilyn Felt, fugitives from criminal justice. Their two-year-old daughter, Lisa Booker, was identified as the third victim.

Agent Charles Twomey of the FBI's Milwaukee office

announced that Booker and Felt had been under intensive investigation in the Philadelphia, Pennsylvania, area. "Arrests were expected imminently," said Agent Twomey. "It is our speculation that they were tipped off. They tried to run, but the wrong people caught up with them."

Agent Twomey could not account for the presence of eight-year-old "Robert McClure" in the household, and said, "We continue to see the boy as a valuable source of information."

In the next story, the *Minneapolis Star-Tribune* reported the murders in their Hennepin Avenue apartment of Philip and Leonida Dunbar, a retired couple described as "private" by their neighbors. Police expressed confidence that the guilty party would swiftly be apprehended.

POLICE STATION ENIGMA, from Ottumwa, Iowa, described another sort of mystery. A police officer named Boyd Burns had noticed a boy of eleven or twelve loitering on the local fairgrounds and suspected him of being a runaway. When approached, the boy refused to give his name or home address. "He didn't act like the normal runaway," Burns said. "If anything, he acted cocky. I took him to the station house, sat him down, and told him his parents had to be worried half to death about him."

When asked to turn out his pockets, the boy proved to be carrying more than four hundred dollars. Suspicious, Burns fingerprinted him, only to discover that the tips of his fingers were devoid of the ridges and whorls that make up individual prints. Questioned about this anomaly, the boy replied that he had no need of fingerprints.

"It was like he was making fun of me," Burns said. "I asked him to give me his first name, anyhow, and he told me I could call him 'Ottumwa Red.' I have to say, that made me smile. I asked if he wanted anything to eat, and he said he wouldn't mind a hamburger. So I sat him down in the Duty Office and told the half dozen guys there to keep an eye on him until I got back." Burns walked to Burger Whopper, a block away. "Before I went in, I heard this big whooshing sound. I turned around and saw the whole station go dark for a couple of seconds." He ran back.

The desk sergeant and the officers in the reception area lay groaning on the floor. Prisoners groaned in the holding cells. "My friends in the Duty Office, they were gone, vanished—the place looked like the *Marie-Céleste*. And the kid was gone, too."

Asked for his opinion about what had happened, Burns said he believed the boy had been an alien being. "Like from another galaxy. One thing about earth people, they do have fingerprints. All I can say is, I'm glad the kid isn't in Ottumwa anymore."

A building had imploded in Lansing, Michigan, killing thirteen people. Three other couples had been slaughtered in their houses. On the next page was a clipping about the murder of two young women who had been hiking in Vermont. I turned off the light and fell into bed without bothering to take off my clothes.

■ **61**

■ Dream-ropes and dream-weights held me to the bed. Held captive in the mind of Mr. X, I saw a door mist into haze; I saw a knife blade, a dark-complected man rise frowning from a chair. When he opened the door, Mr. X flowed in and said, "Mr. Booker, you have something that belongs to me."

Was that something me? No: the something was gone, it had already escaped.

Booker sank to his knees, and Mr. X glided behind him and slashed his throat.

No, I thought, *that was Anscombe . . .*

No, there was Frank Sinatra singing *"Fight . . . fight . . . fight it with . . . aaaaall of your might . . ."*

It was not the spectacle of Mr. X savaging a man named Sylvan Booker that whirled me away, it was what happened when Frank Sinatra was singing and the air smelled like pine needles and the people were named . . .

A stuffed black cat and white rabbit lay tumbled on the floor. Into the mirror before me swam a misshapen figure shaking with malicious laughter. Horrified, I burst my ropes, threw off the weights, and woke up standing beside the bed with my hands flattened over my eyes.

■ The Russian doll gave me the detail that explained everything I was ready to understand. Nearly all the entries were dated within a day or two of June 25th. I had visited the murdered couples with Mr. X—I had *seen* them murdered. Star had collected these stories because she feared . . . that Robert was behind them? That Rinehart was? She thought that Robert had obliterated half a dozen policemen in Ottumwa, Iowa, and killed two young women hiking in Vermont. The newspapers had told her that her second son was loose in the world, wandering from one tragedy to another like a furious ghost.

Robert had sent Ashleigh Ashton to the Motel Comfort because he had known I would be there. The next day, he had rescued me from life in prison by going to bed with her.

I felt as though I, too, were a kind of Russian doll, hiding secrets inside secrets that led to an unknowable mystery. Robert; Edward Rinehart. It was too much, I could not work it out. Neither could I continue to endanger Laurie Hatch. I decided to go out and walk the streets until weariness forced me back to bed.

When I stepped outside, a white sliver of my landlady's face disappeared behind the fold of a curtain. I closed the door with a loud, satisfying bang. I wanted a drink. Maybe three drinks.

Sounds of a commotion grew louder as I walked down Chester Street. All the troublemakers in Hatchtown had not yet found their beds. *I did not want to be Robert's toy.* I hated the idea that he had been maneuvering me, directing me, shaping my life. Well, why? I stopped walking, struck by the most obvious question imaginable.

The answer came when I remembered: *"Mr. Booker, you have something that belongs to me."*

Once a year, Mr. X had gone in search of Robert, my shadow. A connection of which I had known nothing had pulled me, the shadow's shadow, into the search. Star and Robert had met at least twice, in front of Biegelman's department store and outside

Nettie's house; surely, there had been other meetings. Maybe she had somehow kept Mr. X at bay. Our birthday arrived on the day after her funeral, and Robert could not face the annual challenge alone. He had saved my life because he needed me.

I didn't need him. Robert could go to hell. It was fine with me if Mr. X erased him.

Brimming with rage, I took another step forward and realized that what I had missed all my life was the being I had just consigned to destruction. A tide of emotion I can only describe as *yearning* nearly brought me to my knees. Every cell in my body called out for reunion with its other, split-off self. All over again, more painfully for being an adult, I felt like an amputated half, bleeding for the want of what would make it whole. *This is crazy,* I said to myself. *You felt like that when you were three years old.*

The enormous ache of yearning slipped back beneath its scar tissue, and Chester Street once again stretched out through the lamplight, peaceful and empty in the night air. It was past 3:00 on a Sunday morning in Edgerton. If Robert needed me to defeat Mr. X, I would help him or not, depending on how I felt at the time. But I was here because he was: Robert had set me on the path that led from Ashleigh Ashton to Laurie Hatch.

I was still worrying about Laurie when I reached Merchants Park, decided to get a drink from her husband's self-aggrandizing fountain, and finally noticed the flashing lights of the squad cars and ambulance in front of the Cobden Building. The voices I had heard came from the crowd at the top of the park and the smaller groups scattered beneath the trees.

■ **63**

■ A little man with a halo of curls fanning out beneath his cap waved a brown bag at me from a bench.

I sat down next to him. "Hello, Piney. What's going on?"

"Hell if I know. Looks like trouble in the Cobden Building."

Two more patrol cars came screaming into Ferryman's Road. At the top of the stairs, the ambulance attendants were talking to a gray-haired man whose tired face shone pink and red in the flashing lights. His stomach protruded like a shelf over the waistline of his suit. "Captain Mullan," I said.

"Your buddy. Have a taste."

Whatever was in the bottle tasted like cigar smoke.

"Just a naive little domestic burgundy, but I thought you'd be amused by its pretensions." Cackling, Piney raised the bottle. "A saying of my old friend Erwin Pipey Leake's. Pipey used to be a professor at Albertus, came out with the damndest shit." He stiffened with emotion. "*Follow a shadow, it still flies you;/Seem to fly it, it will pursue.* You know who wrote that?"

I shook my head.

"Ben Jonson. *Darkling I listen; and for many a time/I have been half in love with easeful Death,/Called him soft names in many a mused rhyme,/To take into the air my quiet breath.* John Keats."

My scalp tingled.

"People took Pipey for a bum. Nobody gave a damn when Black Death come along and took him out." Piney wiped his eyes and jerked himself off the bench.

He shambled forward, and I followed him through the crowd at the narrow end of the park. A man in a black leather jacket glanced at me, glanced away. Frenchy La Chapelle had been drawn out of his hole.

Across Ferryman's Road, bands of colored light flew across the front of the Cobden Building. Captain Mullan stood in front of the half-opened door in conversation with a man in a blue suit who looked as though he were hoping he might wake up to find himself back in bed.

"Who's that with Mullan?"

A burly guy with slicked-back dark hair said it was Hatch's chief of security, Frank Holland.

"My boy, Bruce McMicken," Piney said.

"I'm not your boy," Bruce said.

"Somebody broke into the Cobden Building?"

Bruce McMicken gave me a sidelong glance. His slablike face made him look like either a bartender or a patrolman. "According to one of the cops, whoever got in trashed the place. Screwed up the computers. Roughed up the guard, too. That's why the ambulance."

"An older man? I saw him going in the other day."

"Yeah, Earl."

"I got no use for Earl Sawyer," Piney said. "Standoffish."

"Earl's just unfriendly," said Bruce. "At least he doesn't sleep in alleys, like you."

Piney uttered a phlegmy chuckle, as if he had been complimented.

"Here's the boss."

A thickset man in a blue button-down shirt, khaki shorts, and loafers without socks burst through the door and took charge. He had the broad, executive face and beveled haircut of an untrustworthy senator.

"Stewart Hatch?"

"Of the Hatchtown Hatches," Piney said.

The paramedics carried the stretcher through the door, and the three men on the steps went down onto the lawn. Earl Sawyer's battered face protruded from one end of the blanket. His eyes were closed, and a stripe of blood crossed his cheek like a banner. Lieutenant Rowley followed the paramedics down the steps and joined Captain Mullan on the short front lawn. Stewart Hatch climbed into the ambulance after the paramedics.

Bruce, Piney, and I moved onto the sidewalk. The paramedics were shifting the unconscious guard onto a gurney. Frank Holland wandered up to the rear of the ambulance.

"Shitting in his pants," Bruce said. "They got a top-of-the-line security system in there. A fly lands on a lampshade, sirens are supposed to go off."

Holland turned away from the ambulance, and Hatch and one of the paramedics jumped down. The paramedic shut the doors and trotted up to the driver's seat.

"By the way," Piney whispered, "it wasn't you, was it?"

"Me?" I thought he was talking about Earl Sawyer and the Cobden Building. "I just got here."

"That deal Friday night."

"No," I said. "It wasn't me."

Piney patted my arm. The ambulance pulled out into Commercial Avenue. Stewart Hatch began jabbing his index finger into Frank Holland's chest.

Bruce McMicken said, "Adios, amigos," and vanished through the diminishing crowd.

I saw Lieutenant Rowley take in my presence. He bent toward Mullan. None too happily, Mullan looked at me. I nodded.

Stewart Hatch gave a dismissive glance at the onlookers. "Go home," he called out. "The show's over." His eyes stopped when they came to me.

Stopped is not quite the word. When Stewart Hatch's eyes met mine, they widened with a kind of shock of recognition that immediately gave way to what looked like loathing.

He had us followed, I thought. *He saw pictures of Laurie and me.*

"Don't expect no Christmas cards," Piney said.

Hatch's thick, already suntanned legs propelled him before Rowley and Mullan. Looking as though some portion of him were continuing to churn forward, he rammed his fists into the pockets of his shorts and tilted his head to Rowley's ear.

Rowley found me with his dead face and dead eyes. Hatch churned into the Cobden Building with his security director scuttling behind him.

Rowley looked as happy as someone like Rowley can get. He no longer had to pretend to be my best friend. Piney had disappeared. The few people near me melted away as Rowley moved up onto my side of the street, planted himself in front of me, and exhaled recycled cigarette smoke.

"Nice seeing you again, Lieutenant," I said.

Rowley looked from side to side. His corpse's face swung back to me, and the creases dividing his cheeks filled with shadows. "You're even dumber than I thought. What is your problem, Dunstan?"

"I couldn't sleep," I said. "I went out for a walk and saw all the excitement."

He stepped forward, forcing me back. "The bus station is on Grace Street, three blocks down from Town Square. That's one choice. Or, stick around and have us drop in tomorrow morning."

"Did Hatch tell you to say that, Lieutenant?"

Rowley hit me in the stomach, hard. All the air went out of me, and I staggered backward. He clipped the side of my head with a jab that spun me onto the grass. I rolled away, fighting for breath. Rowley skipped up and kicked me under my ribs. He squatted and thumped my head. "Help me out here. You were saying something?"

I managed to drag in a breath. "I'm beginning to get your point."

The cops on the other side of the street had turned their backs. Rowley stood up and took a step back.

"One thing," I said.

He placed his hands on his knees and bent toward me. His face was a black, featureless pane.

I took another breath. "When I opened that package, I thought we had an arrangement."

"An arrangement."

"I thought a hundred bucks would keep me from getting kicked in the side."

Rowley snapped to his feet and walked away.

■ When I put my key in the front door the back of my neck tingled, and I glanced over my shoulder, expecting to find Rowley summoning me into the back of a patrol car. All I saw was Frenchy La Chapelle twitching up Chester Street. Frenchy checked the number on an apartment building, then glanced at me. He shoved his hands into the pockets of his leather jacket, wandered to the curb, and looked down the street as if waiting for a ride. After another glance in my direction, he shifted into his usual sidewalk boogaloo and slid around a corner into Hatchtown.

■ 64

■ At 10:00 A.M. on Sunday morning, there was a rap on my door while I was trying to persuade Laurie Hatch to drive Posy Fairbrother into town to retrieve the Mercedes. "I have a visitor," I said.

"Get rid of her and come to my house. I'll give you a tremendous brunch."

The knock came again, in triplicate. "I think it's a cop who doesn't like me very much."

"Put down the phone and let him in, so I can hear what happens. Then let him know you're talking to me."

Helen Janette's voice came through the door. "Mr. Dunstan, if you don't open up, I'll do it myself."

Clustered behind my landlady were Captain Mullan, Lieutenant Rowley, Officer Treuhaft, the human totem pole who had come with Rowley to Nettie's house, and, so close to Rowley that they could have held hands, Stewart Hatch. Stewart was wearing white trousers and a blue double-breasted blazer over a polo shirt with an upturned collar. All he needed was a yachting cap.

"This is the last straw, Mr. Dunstan," said Helen Janette, and barged away.

Captain Mullan said, "May we come in?"

"Be my guest. I'm on the phone."

The four men pushed past me. Hatch started walking around and smirking at my surroundings, and the other three watched me sit on the bed and pick up the telephone.

"I have to hang up. Captain Mullan, Lieutenant Rowley, Officer Treuhaft, and a gentleman who appears to be Mr. Stewart Hatch just came in."

"Stewart's there?"

Hatch turned around when he heard his name. "Who are you talking to?"

"My attorney," I said.

Hatch looked at Mullan. "I take that as an admission of guilt."

"The great Roy Cohn," I said. "A little dead, a little moldy, but still vicious as all get-out."

Mullan smiled, and Hatch spun around and opened my closet. "Step back, Mr. Hatch," Mullan said.

"Should I talk to him?" Laurie asked.

"Probably not a good idea," I said, and put down the telephone.

"I want this man arrested for auto theft, Mullan," Hatch said. "This time, keep him in a cell while we work on the other charges."

"Sit down, please, Mr. Hatch," Mullan said, giving a disgusted look at Rowley. "You're an interested party, not a police officer."

"Mr. Hatch is the victim here, Captain," said Rowley.

Mullan stared at Hatch until he dropped into the chair near the window. "Mr. Dunstan," Mullan said, "do we have your permission to search your room?"

"Please do," I said. "But if this is about Mr. Hatch's Mercedes, you're wasting your time. It's not here."

Treuhaft unzipped my knapsack and turned it upside down

over the bed. Rowley pulled out dresser drawers and rummaged through my socks and underwear.

"Mr. Dunstan," Mullan said, "did you remove a Mercedes 500SL from a garage at the residence at 4825 Blueberry Lane in Ellendale between the hours of midnight and two A.M. this morning and transport it to Harry Street, around the corner from this building?"

"Of course he did," Hatch said.

"Of course I did," I said. "At the request of Mrs. Hatch."

"Ask him what he was doing there in the first place."

Mullan looked back at me. I said, "Mrs. Hatch invited me to dinner. I don't have a car, so she came in and picked me up. During and after dinner, we had several glasses of wine. At the end of the evening, she asked if I would mind driving myself back in a car her husband had left in her garage."

I looked over at Hatch. "It's a beautiful car, Mr. Hatch." His eyes went flat. To Mullan, I said, "This morning, I suggested to Mrs. Hatch that she and Posy, the nanny, come in together, so that Posy could drive the Mercedes back to Ellendale."

"Posy," Hatch said. He made it sound like the name of a poisonous insect.

"This guy always gets his alibis from women, have you noticed?" Rowley came over to the bed. "Why did you conceal the car?"

"I didn't conceal it. I parked around the corner so my landlady wouldn't see me getting out of a Mercedes."

Rowley picked up the scrapbook and dropped it back on the table. "You have the keys?"

I took them out of my pocket and offered them to Mullan, who looked at Stewart Hatch. "Do you want us to call your wife? Frankly, I don't think there's any point."

"Okay," Hatch said. "Let's stop farting around and get to the point." He stood up and came forward, extending his left hand. I held out the car keys. Hatch stepped closer than I had expected and grasped my wrist. He snatched the keys with his right hand, rammed them into a pocket, and bent down to inspect my fingertips.

"Let go of him," Mullan said. "Now."

Hatch dropped my wrist and wiped his hands on his white trousers.

"Mr. Dunstan has been fingerprinted," Captain Mullan said.

"And if I see any more initiative out of you, Mr. Hatch, I'll have Officer Treuhaft escort you out."

I remembered what Officer Boyd Burns had told a reporter about "Ottumwa Red," and Rowley saying to a young cop, *"Blanks? No ridges?"*

The knowledge of who had broken into the Cobden Building and beaten an elderly guard made me feel sick to my stomach. Stewart Hatch pointed at me. "This man is in league with my wife, that's obvious. Who drove him into town? Who has he been seen with, for God's sake?"

"You must be desperate," I said.

"How much are they giving you?" he asked me. "Or are you in it for something besides money?"

"Shut up, the two of you," Mullan said, and turned to me. "Do you have any interest in Mr. Hatch's legal affairs?"

"None at all."

"Your relationships with Assistant D.A. Ashton and Mrs. Hatch are purely social and grew out of accidental encounters?"

"That's right," I said.

"From our viewpoint, you understand, that's a little hard to accept. If you bear no animosity against Mr. Hatch, why did you go out of your way to insult his friend and associate Mr. Milton, on Friday night?"

"Mr. Milton insulted me first. Ask the doorman."

"And you had nothing to do with the break-in at the Cobden Building early this morning?"

"I'll tell you what interests me about that," I said. "I wonder why Mr. Hatch told Lieutenant Rowley to order me out of town and rough me up if it looked like I wasn't going to obey."

Hatch's voice was low and measured. "I don't give Rowley orders, because Rowley doesn't *take* orders from me."

"The lieutenant is a hard man when it comes to orders." Mullan sounded more than ever like an Irish bartender. "Did you have words with Mr. Dunstan, Lieutenant?"

Rowley's dead eyes met mine. "I made sure he knew he was supposed to stick around."

"Do we need to listen to more of this crap?" Hatch said.

Mullan had been eyeing Rowley in a speculative manner, and Rowley had been pretending not to notice. "Mr. Dunstan, are you willing to accompany us to St. Ann's? Mr. Sawyer, the security guard who was injured during the break-in, is being held in the ICU. If you refuse, you will be taken to the station, go through the procedures all over again, and then be escorted to the hospital. If you come with us now, Mr. Sawyer will either identify you or put you in the clear."

"I'll come," I said, hoping that the guard had not had anything like a good look at Robert. "But you should know that Mr. Sawyer and I had a short conversation while he was letting himself into the building on Friday evening."

Rowley and Hatch erupted. They erupted all over again after I explained how I had happened to talk to Earl Sawyer. I had been casing the Cobden Building, I was laying the groundwork for the case that any identification now was mistaken.

"Let's see what our victim has to say." Mullan opened the door.

"*I'm* the victim here," Hatch said. He marched out like a general at the head of his troops.

■ **65**

■ Treuhaft opened a rear door of the patrol car, and Mullan gestured me in. Stewart Hatch moved up beside him. "You want to get your Mercedes out of this neighborhood, Mr. Hatch," Mullan told him. Hatch grunted and spun away. Mullan followed me into the backseat. Rowley got in beside Treuhaft, shifted sideways on the front passenger seat, and grinned at me. "What were you supposed to find? Did your friend the lady D.A. give you a list of files?"

"It wasn't me, Lieutenant," I said.

"You're a computer geek, aren't you?"

"I know how to write programs. Whatever it would take to convict Stewart Hatch is a mystery to me, and he can't be dumb enough to leave it on a hard disk."

"I was hoping for peace and quiet," Mullan said. "Let's all get together and make a great big effort."

■ Rowley pushed the button for the elevator, and a few couples gathered in the familiar corridor. I felt as though I had gone back in time—everything, even the visitors in their shorts and T-shirts, looked exactly the same. The people with us recognized Stewart Hatch. Like a movie star, he was used to being recognized. Following Hatch's aristocratic example, we sailed through the swinging doors. Nurse Zwick goggled at Hatch and blinked when she saw me, but instead of sending us out to wash our hands, she darted around the desk and led us toward the far side of the unit.

Yellow tape sealed off the compartment where the despised Clyde Prentiss had languished. Beneath the curtain, loops of dried blood covered the floor. I asked what had happened.

"It was terrible," said Nurse Zwick. "Mr. Dunstan, I'm so sorry about your mother."

June Cook strode toward us. "You want Mr. Sawyer, I gather? I'd like to ask why."

"We want him to look at Mr. Dunstan," Mullan said.

The head nurse gave him a doubtful nod. "Mr. Sawyer's condition is stable, but he is still seeing double as a result of concussion. I'd strongly advise waiting another twenty-four hours."

"My doctor says he's healthy enough to make an identification," Hatch said. "I imagine you know who I am. And I'm sure you're acquainted with Dr. Dearborn's reputation."

June Cook was as valiant as I remembered her. "I imagine everyone on this floor recognizes you, Mr. Hatch. And I have the greatest respect for Dr. Dearborn, but his evaluation was made on the basis of a telephone conversation."

"Which led him to conclude that Sawyer is fit enough to make an identification."

June Cook's eyes flicked at me, then back at Hatch. "You can spend ten minutes with my patient. But if he makes an identification in his present state, I will have something to say about it in court."

Hatch smiled.

I asked her what had happened to Clyde Prentiss.

"Mr. Prentiss suffered fatal knife wounds," she said. "Nobody saw anything. Mr. Hatch's friends on the police force seem to be as baffled as we are."

"Imagine, a thing like that in this well-run hospital," Hatch said.

June Cook went through the curtain. Treuhaft obeyed a silent command from Mullan and stayed outside when she returned to wave us in.

The old man in the bed glared at our invasion through glittering eyes surrounded by an interlocking network of bruises. A cone-shaped structure had been taped over his nose, and his mouth described a downturned U. He glanced back and forth as Mullan and I went up one side of the bed, Hatch and Rowley the other. I wondered how many people he saw.

"Nice of you to drop by, Mr. Hatch."

Hatch tried to pat his hand.

Sawyer pulled his hand away. "I talked to your doctor a couple hours ago. He wants me to go to Lawndale, but the only place I'm going is home. You know how much it costs to rent space in an ICU?"

"Earl, your costs are taken care of," Hatch said. "Don't worry about anything. We'll work something out."

"I got no health insurance and no pension plan," Sawyer said. "You want to talk about working something out, let's work it out now, in front of witnesses. How do I know I'll ever see you again?"

"Earl, this is not the time to discuss business." Hatch grinned at the two cops. "We'd like you to look at the man in the blue shirt on the other side of the bed and tell us if you recognize him."

"You used the word 'business,' " Sawyer said. "Considering I got injured on the job, what are we talking about? You agreed to cover the medical expenses. Health insurance would have been a better deal, but I'm not complaining. In fact, I'm grateful."

"Thank you," Hatch said. "Can we get down to the present business, Earl?"

"Present business is what I'm talking about. I put in fifteen years with you, and some guy comes along and pounds the bejesus out of me. I'm sixty-five years old. You know what would be right? A lifetime pension at seventy-five percent of my salary."

"Earl, we can't—"

"Here's another option. A one-time settlement of twenty-five thousand dollars. You'd probably come out ahead that way."

Hatch stared up at the dim ceiling of the ICU. "Well, Earl, I hadn't really expected to get into a negotiation here." He sighed. Mullan and Rowley were both eyeing him. "If you think a settlement like that would suit you, you got it. It's the least I can do to express my gratitude for your years of service."

Sawyer nodded at him. "I'm glad we're in agreement, Mr. Hatch. You'll cover my medical bills, and the check for twenty-five grand will be waiting for me at your front desk by . . . what day is this? Sunday? By Wednesday morning."

Hatch raised his arms in defeat. "Earl, I could use you on my team. All right, Wednesday morning."

"You had me on your team, Mr. Hatch. That's what you're paying for. Who am I supposed to identify? Him?"

Hatch moved away from the bedside, shaking his head. Mullan said, "You've already had an opportunity to take a look at him, Earl, but I want you to look again and tell us if he resembles the man who assaulted you in the Cobden Building."

Earl Sawyer squinted at me. "Come closer."

In their nests of bruises, the old man's eyes were shiny with malice. "Bend down."

I leaned toward him.

"Didn't I talk to you a couple of days ago? When I was letting myself in?"

"Friday evening," I said.

"You heard Mr. Hatch agree to my deal, didn't you?"

"I did."

"You got the wrong guy," Earl said. "You have to remember, I hardly saw the guy. But this isn't him."

"Are you seeing double?" Rowley asked.

"So I see two of the wrong guy. I see two of you, but I still know you're a son of a bitch named Rowley."

"This is a travesty," Hatch said. "Earl can't see straight. He had us come in here to work out a pension deal."

"He can see well enough to clear Mr. Dunstan," Mullan said.

"Send the nurse in here, will you? Mr. Hatch, I want you to sign a written agreement."

Outside the cubicle, June Cook gave me a small, triumphant smile and said, "I heard the patient's request." She leaned over the counter for a sheet of paper and drew a pen from the pocket of her green tunic.

While Hatch signed away $25,000, the four of us drifted toward the top of the unit. I looked again at the bloody floor inside Prentiss's sealed cubicle. It reminded me of something I had heard in the past few days, but could not quite remember. Mullan was looking at the bloodstains, too, and I asked him how soon his men would be done with their work. "In there?" he said. "Rowley, we're finished with this scene, aren't we?"

"I'll send a man over," Rowley grumbled.

"Clothhead Spelvin," I said. "I knew this reminded me of something."

Captain Mullan slowly turned his head to regard me in ill-concealed amazement.

"What's that supposed to mean?" Rowley asked.

"An oldie but goodie," Mullan said, still marveling at me. "That's very interesting. Would you care to say more?"

"Wasn't Spelvin knifed to death in a cell? Whoever killed him got past the guards and the other prisoners without being seen."

"Pretty good trick, wasn't it?" Mullan said.

"Funny thing, nobody ever sees squat when jungle justice goes down. You close it as a suicide, right?"

"That's how it was closed," Mullan said, still looking at me.

Stewart Hatch thrust the curtain aside and stamped out. His face was tight with anger. No one spoke during the wait for the elevator, and the arctic silence continued as we descended, elbow to elbow with strangers, to the ground floor.

Instead of ramming his way through the people before him, Hatch let them depart and nodded at me to get off. I thought he was going to go back to the ICU and rip up the agreement he had signed, but when the elevator had emptied, he moved out into the corridor. For a moment, he pressed his hands to his face and held them there, as if concealing his anger or reining it in.

Hatch lowered his hands. He took a deep breath. "I didn't know the old bastard had it in him." His face split into a grin, and he chuckled. The chuckles built into outright laughter. I would not have been more surprised if he had started passing out hundred-dollar bills. All of us started laughing. Treuhaft boomed out huge bass cannonballs, and Rowley contributed a toneless noise that sounded like a child's first assault on a violin.

"Old Earl," Hatch said through gasps of laughter. "He *snook-ered* me. He flat *bushwhacked* me." He tilted back his head and roared.

I confess, this performance disarmed me. In spite of everything I knew or thought I knew about Stewart Hatch, at that moment I could not help liking him. His ability to laugh at himself put him in a different category from self-important toads like Grenville Milton.

He wiped his eyes with the back of a hand, still chuckling. "All right. Live and learn. I can take Mr. Dunstan home. You guys have things to do, and it's on my way."

When we had all spun through the revolving door, Mullan questioned me with a look, and I said, "Sure, why not?"

Stewart Hatch opened the passenger door of his Mercedes and beckoned me in with a flourish.

■ 66

■ We drove out of the hospital grounds like a couple of old friends. Hatch was smiling, and his eyes were filled with a comfortable, humorous light. Top down, the car flowed up the street with the weighty ease I remembered. "You liked this little sweetheart, didn't you?" Hatch asked me. "I keep forgetting how much I enjoy driving it."

"If you're going to Ferryman's Road, I'll get out there. There's no reason for you to take me back to my place."

"Let's drive around a while. It'll give us a chance to get to know each other. Wouldn't you agree we should talk?"

"If you think so." I braced myself.

"Oh, I do, definitely." He smiled at me again, his eyes dancing. "There's something I'd like to show you. We can get there in about twenty minutes."

"What is it?"

"I don't want to spoil the surprise. Can you spare the time?"

"As long as you're not going to march me into a field and show me a gun."

Five green lights and a nearly empty road had appeared before us. Hatch twinkled at me. "Watch this." He touched the accelerator, and the car concentrated upon itself for a tenth of a second before rocketing ahead. I watched the speedometer glide past sixty before we sped through the first light. It kept climbing as we blasted toward the second. The breeze whipping past our heads shifted the line of Hatch's hair about an eighth of an inch backward. He kept the car at a steady eighty miles per hour through the fourth light, and brought it smoothly down to thirty only in time to make it past the fifth and swerve right onto Commercial Avenue. His hair sprang perfectly back into place. "You can get this baby up to a hundred and ten before you actually feel like you're speeding."

"Now that we're together like this, Stewart," I said, "can I ask you a couple of questions?"

"Anything."

"Between you and me, is Rowley your inside guy at Police Headquarters?"

"Lieutenant Rowley works for the city of Edgerton. The man is a dedicated public servant. His passion for justice may sometimes get the better of him, but that comes with the job."

"And you didn't tell him to order me out of town."

"Of course not."

"And you realize I had nothing to do with what happened at your building."

"I'm relieved, as a matter of fact. Now I don't have to figure out how you broke in. We have the most sophisticated security system you can imagine. Nobody not on the inside could get around the pressure sensors and the electronic beams and disarm the contact points, so it must have been an employee of the security company. We'll get him, but that still leaves me with the computer damage." Hatch gave me an inquiring look. "Aren't you an expert in that area?"

"I wouldn't go that far," I said.

"Would you like to make ten thousand dollars a week? It looks like about half the files are missing from our hard disks, and I need to recover them. All I'd ask is that you sign a confidentiality agreement. The work might not even take as long as a week. You get me set up and running in a day or two, the money's the same. Sound interesting?"

"It sounds great," I said, "but the answer is no."

"Can I ask why?"

"No offense intended, but I'd rather not be on the Hatch payroll."

"Too bad. It was a long shot, but too bad."

We cut through the southern end of the business district, turned west, and drove into a part of town I had never seen before. Uptilting blocks lined with peeling frame houses dropped away toward an overgrown baseball diamond and rotting bleachers. Beyond the next rise, a few women trudged along dusty paths in a trailer park. A bare-chested kid aimed a BB gun at us from beneath a limp Confederate flag.

"You liked this car, didn't you?" Hatch asked.

"It handles beautifully."

"And what about my wife?" He grinned. This time, the light in his eyes was still humorous, but not at all comfortable. "Would you say she handles beautifully? Accelerates smoothly? Did you find her well engineered?"

"Forget it, Stewart," I said. "Your marriage has nothing to do with me."

"You would admit, wouldn't you, that my wife is an extremely good-looking woman? Even a beautiful woman? What you might call an attractive bit of horseflesh?"

"She's attractive, yes," I said. "But if you're having someone follow her around with a camera, I feel sorry for you."

"Bear with me," he said. "I bet you wondered why a woman like that would marry me. After all, I'm rich, but not superrich, I'm twelve years older than she is, and I live in a nowhere Midwestern town. Am I right?"

"I wondered about some of that," I said.

"Sure you did. If you hadn't, she would have done it for you. Now, between us, she isn't so great in bed, is she? When it comes to performance, this car is a lot more satisfying. My wife is too selfish to be a good lay."

"Stop it. You're embarrassing yourself."

"You ought to know who you're dealing with. Laurie is nothing like what you think she is. For her, you're only a convenient way to make more trouble for me. She's a soulless bitch."

"If she's that terrible, divorce her."

"Jesus, I don't care about her personality." He laughed at me. "This isn't the fucking Boy Scouts. I just want her to do what I say."

"You should be wearing a loincloth and carrying a club."

"Good Lord," he said. "A feminist. Did my dear wife tell you anything about the trust?"

"What trust?"

"Let's find out what she said about herself. Did she tell you about her background, her family, anything like that?"

"A little," I said.

"Wonderful story, isn't it? I'm crazy about it."

An empty, brown hillside sloped down to the right side of the road. Far away on our left, little ranch houses stood on quarter-acre lots. Every other one looked unoccupied. Stewart pulled to the side of the road and switched off the engine. He drew up one knee and twisted on his seat to face me.

"I take it you heard about Yves D'Lency, the poet and art dealer who ran away from his noble family and palled around with artists and so forth before he came to America. The poor guy's plane went down outside Santa Barbara, right?"

"What's your point?" I said.

"Laurie's father's real name was Evan Delancy, a product of Trenton, New Jersey. He was a part-time bricklayer with a big appetite for booze. When he couldn't get work in Trenton anymore, he packed up the family and drove to Los Angeles, where he branched out into the stickup business. One day a tough old bird who owned a liquor store blew him away. Bye-bye, Dad. Mom traded her ass for favors from her boyfriends until she married a cameraman at Warner Brothers. This is the guy my wife refers to as a movie producer."

"You want me to believe this," I said.

"Believe it, don't believe it, but this information cost me more money than I just gave Earl Sawyer. Mom married the cameraman. Guess what? He's another drunk. After the studio fired him, he took out his frustrations by beating up his wife and stepdaughter. Laurie dropped out of high school and did so many drugs she wound up in a mental hospital. When she was straight enough to figure out how to act, she got acquainted with a nice old doctor named Deering. Deering thought she was a poor, misguided orphan who deserved a break. He and his wife took her in. They bought her good clothes and sent her to private school, which is where she learned about table manners and grammar. After she graduated from the private school, she ran away to San Francisco. Pretty soon, she was living with Teddy Wainwright. Remember him?"

I knew that Teddy Wainwright had played the leading man's best friend in a lot of romantic comedies made in the fifties. Later on, he had starred in two television series.

What I had not known was that in the early seventies, no

longer able to find roles in Hollywood but grown rich from real estate investments, Wainwright had decked himself in beads and Nehru jackets and moved to San Francisco to enjoy a second youth. Laurie Delancy had moved in with him when he was seventy-one, she twenty-one. Through multiple infidelities and other tempests on her part, including the refusal to marry him, they stayed together until his death four years later. Wainwright had rewritten his will to give her two paintings from his extensive art collection, a Frida Kahlo and a Tamara de Lempicka, plus $250,000 and the use of his apartment until she married, when the apartment reverted to his only child, a daughter. The daughter inherited the majority of his estate, including the rest of his collection, at the time appraised at $5 million.

"Turns out, back in the twenties old Teddy bought two Picassos, a Cézanne, and a Miró, and sometime in the fifties, he squirreled them away in a vault. His collection wound up being worth seventy, eighty million. You can bet Laurie's still kicking herself for not marrying the old guy. She landed a job at KRON, where she wanted to end up doing the local news, but oops, no experience. No journalism background, no degree, nothing. She was a production assistant—a gofer. A year later, when I met her, she was a PR girl. Laurie acted like she fell in love with me, and I do mean acted. It could have worked out, except she was a phony."

"How soon after you were married did you hire the private detective?"

"I hired a detective as soon as I got interested in her. I didn't tell her until we were on our honeymoon. A bungalow at a great resort in the Caribbean. Champagne on the balcony. Moonlight on the water. 'Listen to this,' I said. 'You won't believe it.' She cried real tears. An amazing woman."

"And she gave you a son and heir."

Hatch smiled. "Cobbie's going to be a fine young man after I knock that music crap out of him and get him involved in sports."

"And your son is the reason you can't divorce Laurie."

His smile shrank. "It seems she mentioned my family's financial arrangements after all. What kind of spin did she put on it?"

I described what I could remember.

"Not bad, as far as it goes," Hatch said. "At thirty-five, Cobbie will come into a great deal of money. I want to make sure he knows how to handle it." His eyes charged with amusement. "Do you know why my father wrote in the condition about criminal charges?"

"Laurie said something about his brother."

"It had nothing to do with that." The amusement came back into his eyes. He was trying to charm me, I realized, and he was doing a good job. "When were you born?"

"In 1958."

"You were too young for the sixties. I turned eighteen in 1968." He laughed. "My senior year at Edgerton Academy, my hair came down to my shoulders. I used to lock my door and crank up the stereo until I couldn't hear the old man bitching at me. The Stones, the Doors, Iron Butterfly. Cream. Paul Butterfield. I played rhythm guitar with this band, Delta Mud. You can imagine how terrible we were."

"White-boy blues," I said.

"White *preppy* blues. White *Midwestern* preppy blues." He biffed my upper arm, jock-style. "God, we were crazy. Toke up on the way to school. Get wasted from Thursday night to Monday morning. We had one honest-to-God musician in our band, the guy played the *shit* out of the blues. Amazing player, *amazing*. We'd show up in front of these Albertus frat boys who didn't care about anything except a steady beat, and . . . it was like hearing God play guitar. You probably heard of him. Goat Gridwell?"

Gridwell's power-guitar blues jams had sold millions of records through the seventies and into the next decade. Whenever someone had made me listen to a Goat Gridwell record, what struck me was how much better he was than most guitarists who played that kind of music. I remembered noticing his yellow-gold hair and green eyes on the cover of *Rolling Stone* and thinking that I had never before seen a face that looked cherubic and dissipated at the same time.

"Our senior year, he got kicked out of the academy and took off for San Francisco. I asked Laurie if she'd ever heard him play, and she had no idea. To her, all music sounds the same. Anyhow, Goat got too rich and too famous. The old story. Fried his brain, the poor bastard. He's back in Edgerton now. There's nothing left. I slip him a couple of bucks now and then, but the guy stares right through me."

If I were Goat Gridwell, I'd ignore you, too, I thought.

"So one night after dinner, I forgot to lock my door. I'm sitting on the floor with 'Jumpin' Jack Flash' blasting through my speakers and smoking dope. Wham! In comes my father. Cobden goes nuts. He let me stay in school, but I had to cut my hair, and he let me know that if I ever got into trouble with the law, I wouldn't get a penny from the trust."

"Are you worried about the case in Kentucky?"

"It's nothing but dust and hot air. Be gone in a week. But this might interest you. Yesterday afternoon my wife called the attorney for the trust, Parker Gillespie. He's the son of Charles Gillespie, who set it up. Seventy-three years old, loyal as a pit bull. Laurie never showed the slightest interest in him before, and all of a sudden, she's looking for an education. You tell me, what did she ask Gillespie?"

"No idea," I said.

"She's concerned about the clause my father added to the agreement. If I'm convicted of these crimes I of course did not commit, am I really disinherited? Unfortunately, Gillespie said, that would be the case, Mrs. Hatch. Then she asked, What's my son's position? Well, in the absence of any other male heir the child would inherit the whole of the trust. Who would look after the trust? she asks. That is the role of the administrator, Gillespie said. Laurie asked him, If the worst happens, will you continue to administer the trust, Mr. Gillespie? Gillespie told her he would be pleased to give her all the assistance she desired. Beginning to see the picture? She wants the money."

"She wants to protect it for Cobbie."

Hatch's sneer was worthy of Uncle Clark. "Cobbie wouldn't inherit until thirty-five. In the meantime, the administrator has discretion over the money. Laurie would appoint herself administrator and grab whatever she wanted. That's what she is about."

"Thanks for the explanation," I said. "Take me back to town."

"I want you to see something, remember? You'll be astonished. History is going to rise up and speak." He smiled in spurious camaraderie. "I'd never forgive myself if I didn't show it to you." He switched on the engine and dropped the car into gear.

■ Sixty years ago, the overgrown field had been a meadow, the stark remains at the edge of the wood a tall stone house with dormers and a portico. I was trying to control the disquiet brought on by the feeling that if I walked into the woods about thirty feet to the right of the ruined house, I would find a lightning-blasted oak.

"Has anyone ever told you about the old Dunstan place?"

"After his brother was killed, Sylvan imported the stones from England and had it rebuilt."

Hatch raised his eyebrows. "*England?* It was Providence, Rhode Island. That's why this street is named New Providence Road. I know more about your family than you do."

"That wouldn't be hard to do," I said, thinking that there were things about the Dunstans Stewart Hatch would never know or guess.

"Do you know who originally built the place?"

"Who was Frank Lloyd Wright?" I said. "Sorry, Alex, I hit the buzzer by accident." My ears were ringing, and my stomach was queasy.

"A man named Omar Dunstan. He turned up in Providence in the 1750s with a bunch of West Indian servants and a lot of money. Dunstan called himself an importer and shipowner, but none of his ships ever docked in Providence. He made frequent trips to South Carolina, Virginia, and New Orleans. What do you think he was importing?"

"What are the blues?"

"Human beings. His men bought or captured slaves in West Africa and the Caribbean and sold them in the Southern colonies. Dunstan wasn't married, but he produced three or four children who almost never left the house. The neighbors heard strange noises and saw peculiar lights in the windows. There were rumors about witchcraft and black magic. Finally, a party of citizens raided the house with the intention of driving the family out of town. They were too late. The place was empty."

I had to sit down, and I parked myself on the hood of the Mercedes.

"The place stood empty for decades. Its reputation was so bad that the city couldn't find anyone willing to tear it down. People called it 'the Shunned House.' In the end, they built a fence around it and let it crumble for the next hundred years."

The Shunned House? It rang a bell too distant to be identified. Stewart Hatch's voice wavered like a bad radio signal before the emanations coming from the ruin.

"During the Civil War, two brothers named Dunstan escaped from the stockade, where they were being held for corpse robbing. In 1874, Omar and Sylvan Dunstan turned up in Edgerton and moved into the Brazen Head. Before long, they had enough money to set up in business, Omar as a pawnbroker and Sylvan as a moneylender. These were Reconstruction days, remember. Ten years later, they had taken over the bank and were living out in the boonies on Cherry Street. When floods bankrupted people, they foreclosed and Sylvan bought their properties for next to nothing. I always thought it was kind of strange that Omar was the one who got killed, because people here really hated Sylvan. Like to hear my father's theory?"

"Life wouldn't be complete without it."

"No one but Sylvan ever saw the so-called gunman who shot his brother and rode off down the street. My father thought Sylvan made him up because he killed Omar. By then, Omar was turning into a respectable citizen. He owned half the properties on Commercial Avenue. My father said Sylvan didn't give a damn about respectability. And he was tired of sharing Omar's wife."

"I heard about their arrangement," I said.

"Sylvan shipped these stones from Rhode Island and brought out a crew of Portuguese workmen he put up out here in shacks. He said he wanted the house restored to its original condition, and the local guys didn't know enough about the detail work. People in town thought he didn't want them to know what his house was like."

"There were rumors," I said.

"Chains attached to beds in the attic. Concealed hideaways. Weird stuff. You know what small towns are like. Sylvan could have let people in, showed them around, but instead he holed up and fended people off. When he came into town, he carried a gun. His kids grew up like animals. Some of them ran off, no one knows where. A couple got killed swimming in the river and fighting in taverns. Howard, your grandfather, stayed on the plantation, even though he hated his old man. Supposedly, Sylvan shot himself cleaning a gun, but some said your grandfather did it for him. Sounds like poetic justice to me." Hatch's voice came from a long way away.

"People who talk about poetic justice don't know anything about poetry."

"Cute. I'll have to remember that. Anyhow, Howard buried his father behind the house. Then he had Omar's coffin moved from Little Ridge and buried next to it. Then he went the same way as Sylvan and screwed every woman he could get his hands on. If his wife didn't run off, he killed her, too. Ran the bank into the ground, threw away his money. You know what people used to say about him when I was a kid?"

"That he could be in two places at once," I said. "Go through doors without opening them. Read your mind and predict the future. Float off the ground and hang in the air."

Hatch gave me a surprised disgruntled look—I was not supposed to know about Howard Dunstan. "It's a good thing his daughters moved back to Cherry Street, because one night the house burned up around him."

"How did that happen?"

"This part's extremely interesting," Hatch said. I could scarcely hear him over the tumult from where I least wanted to go. "My father told me that on the night of the fire his father, Carpenter Hatch, locked himself in the library with Sylvester Milton, Grennie's father, and a little guy named Pee Wee La Chapelle, who used to do odd jobs for them. He saw them go out, and late that night he heard them come back. Do you suppose *they* burned the place down?"

"Stewart," I said, "I don't care who burned it down."

"These bones turned up. Not human, but not from any known animal, either. We're talking 1935, remember, practically the Dark Ages. Who knows what they were? Howard's daughters got the insurance money, and that was that."

I barely felt him putting his hand on my shoulder.

"No matter what my wife says, Stewart Hatch is not a bad guy." He patted my cheek. "Out of the kindness of my heart, I am presenting you with certain facts."

"Mighty white of you," I said.

"You turned down my offer. Fine. It's time to go back where you belong."

"I can't believe you were in a band with Goat Gridwell," I said.

He laughed. His teeth were marvels of dentistry, his eyes shone with a companionable gleam, the blazer clung to the back of his neck like a tape.

"Stewart, you can be completely charming, but you belong in jail. It would be a tragedy if you got custody of your son."

He jerked his hands out of his pockets. "If you want a lift back to town, try the pay phone down the road."

I turned my back on him, stepped across the dusty verge and moved like a sleepwalker into the dense growth covering the field. An engine whirred into life, and gravel flew like buckshot from beneath squealing tires.

■ 68

■ Darkness and nightmare boomed from the ruined house and the trees behind it. My dream-shadow had told me, *All your life, you have felt the loss of something extraordinarily important. If you found it, could you live with the consequences?* I had answered *Yes*, and in spite of my fear and nausea, in spite of my desire *not to know*, now my response was the same.

Something brushed my mind and instantly faded. I almost turned back. Whatever had touched me was what I did not want to know.

The two remaining stone walls supported what was left of the roof. Two blackened chimneys reared upward. The right half of the house had collapsed into a soft depression. The old entrance yawned over a mat of vines. I walked up to an empty casement and looked in at a filthy cement floor gradually disappearing beneath the green carpet rolling in from the back of the house.

I moved to the rear of the house. It was like looking at a photo-

graph from a bombed city—blackened walls and empty space. I
stepped back, and my feet met a flat stone surface. When I bent
down and parted the grasses, I saw a gray marble slab carved
with the legend OMAR DUNSTAN D. 1887. My heart jumped
into my throat. Its companion was three feet away. SYLVAN DUN-
STAN D. 1900.

"How about you, Howard?" I said.

About six feet from Sylvan's marker was: HOWARD DUNSTAN,
OUR DEAR FATHER. 1882–1935. "Better than you deserved," I
said, and noticed an area where the grasses bent over the ground.
Before the first of the trees, a flat granite slab lay over the gray-
brown mulch. I read the eroded, still legible words:

ANGELS NOT OF THIS EARTH.

Altogether, eight other markers lay hidden in the grass. Some
of the names had worn away, and none were the kind of names
parents give their children. I remember FISHY, SCREAMER, GOS-
SAMER, SPLITHEAD, BRIGHTNESS, and TONK. *Dogs and cats,* I
told myself, shuddered back as from a terrible recognition, and
snagged my foot in a tangle of weeds. I spun around to keep
from falling and saw a green carpet rolling into a dim, two-sided
room. My foot tore free of the snag, and I went forward over the
cushiony pad of the carpet.

Pigeon feathers stirred in the sun-shot air. Remembered pain
pierced my forehead, and I dropped through an empty shaft like
a stone.

■ 69

■ *I'm not in my time,* I thought. Then, *Oh, I'm here again.*

On all sides, the scene solidified. A tired fern and a stuffed fox
in a glass bell flanked a brass clock on a mantelpiece. Tobacco
smoke fouled the air. Across the room, a white-haired man in a
dark blue, once-elegant velvet smoking jacket faced the window.
He held a cigar in one hand and a glass half-filled with amber
liquid in the other. The world was dark. I realized that I knew the

man's name. The hands of the brass clock said the time was
11:40.

The man facing the window had been expecting me; he was
going to speak. These facts declared themselves in the weariness
of his posture and the theatrical, even stagy unhappiness in the
slouch of his back. Impatient irritation replaced my nausea and
pain: Here I was, what did he want? The man at the window
raised his glass. He sipped. His shoulders slumped. Finally, he
spoke.

*You're here again, but I don't care what happens to you. Things
fall apart. The center cannot hold. Do you know who said that?*

"William Butler Yeats," I said. "Fuck you, too, Howard."

*The golden bowl is broken, it bears an unseen crack. I hear
the roar of cannons everywhere.*

"What are you trying to tell me?"

*Once your father had been created, I decided to amuse myself
by driving him mad. He was to be the tool of our destruction. Yet
since you have found your way to me over and over, perhaps
after all you will destroy him instead. The outcome of the game
no longer matters to me.*

I called him a wicked, malicious old man—it was the main
thing I understood. He chuckled.

*We flew from the crack in the golden bowl. We were stolen from
the corpse on the battlefield. We are the smoke from the cannon's
mouth. I drove my son mad to hasten our end. Their faith in us died.
Everything happens over and over, and each time it means less.*

"You say things, but they don't make sense. Whose faith?
Why am I here?"

*In my great-grandfather's time, the god Pan was a composer
of remarkable accomplishment. In my grandfather's, he was a
pianist who excited the females in his audiences to incomprehensible ecstasies. In mine, he is a drunken poet who writes of
nothing but descents to hell and similar degradations. By your
time, he will become a mindless addict of alcohol and opiates. If
you see him, tell yourself, Here is what remains of Pan and
understand why we should be gone from the earth.*

"Pan never existed," I said. "Not in the real world."

*What you call the real world never existed, either. It was cre-
ated over and over by belief. Belief is subject to change. Human
beings need stories to make sense of their accident-ridden lives,*

and their stories refused to let us go. I'm sick of it. They're always telling one small fragment of the same huge story, and they'll never get it right.

Torchlights wobbling toward us appeared in the window. Overhead, I heard a scurry of wings and claws.

You were to come here with another. Perhaps you and he are here, but elsewhere. We shall see, you and I. My toy, my game, is ending. Mistake upon mistake. What wretched lives we were given.

My eyes darkened. My joints sang with pain, and someone banged me on the head with a mallet. When my vision cleared I was on my knees, drooling vomit into the tall grass behind the ruin.

■ 70

■ Helen Janette was stationed in front of her door. "I hope you're prepared for what I have to say, Mr. Dunstan."

The door behind me clicked open. Mr. Tite had joined the party.

"This morning, two detectives and an officer in uniform came knocking at my door."

"Plus Stewart Hatch," I said. "Didn't you feel honored?"

"Stewart Hatch should hang himself from the nearest tree." She crossed her arms over her chest. "You have half an hour to pack your things. No refund on your charges."

I stamped upstairs. Resonant snores came through Otto's door. When I came back down, they were posted on opposite sides of the entry like Swiss guards. "I wish I knew why you're so afraid of cops."

Helen Janette held out her hand. "My key."

The bitter satisfaction I saw in her face as I surrendered the key gave me my answer. "Excuse me, Mrs. Janette."

"We have nothing to say to each other."

"Did your name used to be Hazel Jansky?"

I heard Mr. Tite breathing through his mouth.

"You went to prison," I said. "That's why you don't like cops."

"Get out of here." Mr. Tite jabbed my shoulder with an index finger that felt like a lead pipe.

I moved out of range and kept my eyes on her.

"My name is Helen Janette."

"You were the midwife at my birth—the twenty-fifth of June, 1958. St. Ann's was struck by lightning. The power went out."

Her face filled with grim pleasure. "Mr. Tite, assist the gentleman outside."

Tite gripped my shoulders with both hands. His sick breath enveloped me. I twisted to one side and knocked him off balance with the duffel bag. He stumbled a half step away and cocked his right fist.

I lifted my hands. "I'm going. It's all over."

They watched me wrestle the duffel through the door.

I turned into Word Street and found my way to Veal Yard and the Brazen Head Hotel. A clerk with purple bags under his eyes informed me that I could have a second-floor room with a bath for sixty-five dollars a night or one with a bathroom down the hall on the fourth floor for fifty. I took the second-floor room. He pointed to the stairs. "Elevator tends to be slow," he said. "Tends to stall, too."

Room 215 at the Brazen Head, directly across from the staircase, was twice the size of my accommodations at Helen Janette's. The bed jutted out into the room, pointing toward a desk and two wooden chairs in front of a dusty window looking out onto Veal Yard. A sign taped to the mirror advised guests to use the bottled water in the minibar instead of drinking the tap water. The bottled water was free of charge.

For a while, I drank Poland Spring water and tried to make sense of what had happened to me. Had I traveled back to 1935 and called on Howard Dunstan?

I wasn't that crazy. On the other hand, neither did I believe that I had been hallucinating. The Dunstans were not an average American family, though we could match dysfunctions with the best of them. Maybe I was a late bloomer, and time-travel had come down to me from an eighteenth-century slave trader resident in Rhode Island. Maybe I was having another breakdown and would spend the next few weeks in a padded room.

But this did not feel like a breakdown. If I was sane, then I had traveled back to 1935 and met my great-grandfather.

The god Pan lived on as an Edgerton derelict? We were stories whose time had ended? I put this stuff out of my mind and considered Helen Janette–Hazel Jansky. Almost certainly, they were the same person, but I doubted that I could get her to admit to abducting the infant Robert, if she *had* abducted him. Then I began wondering about the coincidence of my having taken a room in Hazel Jansky's rooming house and remembered that Toby Kraft had sent me there. Toby and Helen-Hazel had a relationship. Of what kind? Toby's predilection for women with pretty faces and beachball breasts eliminated the obvious answer. It was another brick wall.

I gulped Poland Spring and wondered why the Brazen Head did not trust Hatchtown's water. Then I recapped the bottle and set off for City Hall.

■ 71

■ No lights burned in the vast lobby, and I rapped on the monumental door with a sense of comic hopelessness. Upstairs in a closed office, Coventry might as well have been in another building. I pounded the glass again, felt even sillier, and walked back through the row of columns. When I reached the top of the stairs, the door clanked open and Coventry called out, "Ned, hold on!"

Smiling, he held the door and beckoned me in. "I had to run down all those stairs!" His rolled-up sleeves, bow tie, and khakis made him look like an aged schoolboy. "I'm glad to see you!" Coventry glanced past me, then to both sides.

"She's not here," I said. "It's nice to see you, too." I went in and waited while he locked the door. "How did you hear me?"

"I was kind of waiting for you. How goes the research?"

"I'm making progress," I said. "Do you have time to look up some property records?"

"No problem." He smiled at me again, almost apologetically.

"Too bad Laurie couldn't join you. She really brightens up the day, don't you think?"

"You're fond of her," I said.

"Whenever I see Laurie, I feel better about everything. She has a sort of gift."

"I suppose Laurie has all kinds of gifts," I said.

"Odd you should say that. I have the same feeling. Extraordinary, I must say." He tilted his head and smiled at the ceiling, remote and all but invisible in the darkness. "That you should sense it, too, I mean. You're a sensitive man." Coventry's chin snapped down. "I'm sorry. Did that sound condescending?"

"Maybe a little," I said.

"Dear me. I meant, you must be more perceptive than most men. You know what I mean, don't you? Of course you do." He pressed his fingertips to his forehead. "Do I seem to be making sense?"

"Indirectly."

Coventry guffawed and ducked his head. He was a nice, sweet guy. "When most men look at Laurie, all they see is . . . well, the obvious. You and I see someone with a brilliant mind, a wonderful soul, and a whole range of abilities she's only begun to tap."

"She must value your friendship," I said.

He gave me a quick glance. "The two of you are fast friends, and all that?"

"I enjoy her company," I said. "But I'm not going to be in Edgerton very long."

Coventry bounded up the stairs. I had lightened his spirits. When he reached the landing, he turned around and propped a hand on a marble upright. His eyes were glowing. "Did she tell you about her background?"

"She said a lot about her father."

Coventry restrained himself to keep pace with me. He wanted to take the stairs three at a time. "He had a tremendous influence on her, *tremendous.*"

On the second floor, he snapped on the fluorescent lights over a counter in front of two cluttered desks and rows of filing cabinets. "I confess I still haven't turned up Mrs. Rutledge's photographs, but I promise you, they will be found." He went behind the counter. "What properties were you interested in?"

"The first one is a tract of land near the woods on New Providence Road."

Coventry disappeared into the rows of cabinets and came back with a thick file.

In 1883, Sylvan Dunstan had purchased from Joseph Johnson ten thousand acres that included Johnson's Woods. Howard Dunstan had inherited the property, and in 1936 Carpenter Hatch bought it from his daughters for a surprising sum. I thought that my aunts must have invested the money and lived on it ever since.

"What else?"

"Have you heard the term 'the Shunned House'? Someone mentioned it today, and I can't figure out why it sounds familiar."

"Isn't that from H. P. Lovecraft? I read a lot of Lovecraft when I was a kid. I think he based the Shunned House on a building in Providence. He spent most of his life there."

Lovecraft was the writer of whom Edward Rinehart's stories had reminded me.

"Weren't you interested in some other properties?"

"Yes," I said. "One was a little street in College Park. I can't remember the name, damn it."

"It'll come to you in a second. Fascinating area, College Park. Do you know it was the site of the old Hatch Brothers Fairground?"

"The Hatches owned the fairground?"

Hugh Coventry's smile contained more than a hint of complicity. "You'd never guess, would you? Mr. Hatch doesn't want you to, either. He made it clear that we were to underplay his family's earlier endeavors, but the fairground was a money-spinner for years. That was how they were able to buy up the area that came to be known as Hatchtown."

"What happened?" I asked. "Did they sell it to Albertus?"

"An unbelievable bit of luck. The Hatches moved up in the world, and by the 1890s they were just leasing the land. It was pretty seedy. Strippers and freak shows, bootleggers and prostitutes thrown in. The houses for the fairground workers were put up higgledy-piggledy. There were a couple of shady doctors, too. A Dr. Hightower peddled drugs to his patients, and the other one, Dr. Drears, was, I'm afraid, the archetypal backstreet abortionist. Infected or killed half of his patients."

"So Hatch wants to sweep this part of the family history under the rug?"

"I can't blame him," Coventry said. "After all, they just owned the property. By the mid-twenties, it was nothing but vacant land and empty houses. Then the Albertus people came along and bought the whole shebang. Before long, enrollment went up, merchants moved in, and the area took off. What street did you want to check?"

"Buxton Place," I said, naming Edward Rinehart's old address as if I had remembered it from the start.

Coventry disappeared into the files again and returned with a bound journal about two feet high and a yard wide. "This is a curiosity." He thumped the journal onto the counter, turned it sideways so that we could both see the pages, and opened it. A hand-drawn map of four or five streets divided along property lines took up the right-hand page. The page on the left recorded the sales of the buildings and lots, with a numbered key referring to the map. "What a gorgeous artifact," Coventry said. "You hate to replace a thing like this with entries in a data base."

I asked him how to find Buxton Place in the gorgeous artifact.

"With luck, there'll be an index." He turned to the last pages. "Oh, these people were great. So, Buxton Place . . ." He ran his finger down a handwritten column and flipped back through the pages. "Here we are." Coventry squinted down and tapped his finger on a tiny lane. "It's a cul-de-sac. What was on it? What used to be stables, mostly. And two houses, probably for the grooms and stable hands. Let's see the ownership records for lots 60448 and 60449."

We went down the list of numbers on the facing page.

"Here, 60448," Coventry said. "Owned originally by Hatch Brothers Fairground, as of 1882, anyhow. What do you know?" He started to laugh. "In 1902, sold to Prosper Hightower, M.D."

I looked at him.

"Hightower. The drug doctor, remember? Then what? Acquired by Edgerton Township, 1922. Sold to Charles Dexter Ward, 1950. So what about its next-door neighbor? Lot 60449. Hatch Brothers Fairground. Purchased in 1903, Coleman Drears, M.D. Incredible! Here is our abortionist. They lived next door to each other! And I bet I know why—Buxton Place was more a back alley than a street. No neighbors watching their patients come and go. What happened when Drears took off?

Acquired by the township in 1924, sold to a Wilbur Whately in 1950." His head jerked up. "Weren't we just talking about H. P. Lovecraft?"

I nodded.

Coventry giggled and shook his head in a transport of disbelief. "What?"

"Lovecraft wrote a novel called *The Case of Charles Dexter Ward*, and Wilbur Whately is a character in 'The Dunwich Horror,' one of his stories. I am truly happy. I'll have to mark the day on my calendar. Never before have I come across a literary allusion in City Hall."

"Would you mind looking up one more?"

"After that? Of course not."

I gave him the address of the rooming house on Chester Street. In less than a minute Coventry was back at the counter with a manila folder. "How far do you want to go with this one?"

"Who's the present owner?"

Coventry took the last page from the folder and slid it toward me. Helen Janette's building had been purchased by a company on Lanyard Street in August of 1967. "T.K. Holding Company. Does that tell you what you want to know?"

"It tells me something I should have known," I said.

Toby had bought the rooming house one month before Hazel Jansky was due for release. By present standards, $27,000 wasn't much of a down payment, but after twenty-six years it still represented an impressive gift.

The great door closed behind me. I went down the long steps and looked across Grace Street to the square. An old woman was scattering bread crumbs before lots of bustling pigeons. The golden-haired derelict I had seen before rocked back and forth over his guitar. Beyond the fountain, a graceful male figure was leaning against the trunk of a maple. The arm dropping in a straight line between the tree and the angle of his body ended in the rectangular outline of a briefcase.

The breath stopped in my throat. The man across the square was Robert. Although the shadow of the maple hid his face, I knew he was smiling at me. Robert pushed himself off the tree and walked into the sunlight, the case swinging lightly at his side.

72

■ I trotted down the steps, across the sidewalk, and into the street, only barely registering the traffic. Horns blared, brakes squealed. I got to the median unscathed and dodged through the southbound traffic, then jumped onto the pavement and ran up the long path to the fountain. Pigeons feuding over bread crumbs scattered at my footsteps. The golden-haired tramp on the other side of the path hunched over his guitar. I looked past an elderly couple at the opposite end of the square and glimpsed Robert's head and shoulders in a group waiting for the light to change at the end of the next block.

When the group moved ahead, Robert was a few paces behind the others. His blazer and jeans were identical to mine. The tramp played a sequence that gave me the title of the song he was playing, "Keys to the Highway," one of Goat Gridwell's signature tunes. He was bending notes and stretching out his phrases, and when I came to within about six feet of him I took my eyes off Robert and glanced down. From a beaten, hardscrabble face, bright green eyes met mine. It felt like slamming into a force-field, and I stumbled forward. The green eyes charged with playful knowledge.

Goat Gridwell held my eyes with his until I trotted past him. For all I know, he watched me pick up speed and run out of the square.

Robert had reached the middle of the next block when I came around the fountain and started down the path to the east end of Town Square. He was moving with an easy stride that ate a lot of ground. I got to the end of the path and saw him turn right at the corner. I plunged ahead. Robert had deliberately invited me to follow him, but I had no faith in his patience.

I ran two blocks and wheeled right. The tail of a blue blazer and a portion of a caramel-colored satchel swung past the building on the next corner and vanished.

Robert seemed to be working toward Commercial Avenue. I

could beat him to it by running straight down to the right from where I stood, but he might have been directing me to some other location along the way. I took a few deep breaths, ran down the block, flew across the next intersection, and spun into Grenville Street. The blazer and the elegant satchel were slipping left onto Commercial Avenue.

"Damn you," I said, and took off down Grenville. Through the plate-glass window of a pizzeria I took in Helen Janette leaning over a table and waving a peremptory finger at Toby Kraft. I picked up speed and raced out onto Commercial Avenue.

Thirty yards down the sidewalk and a short distance from the entrance to Merchants Hotel, Robert was leaning on one hip, swinging the satchel in his hand, and looking right at me. Then he was gone. I moved along the sidewalk. When I reached the spot where he had been, the revolving door of Merchants Hotel released a chalk-faced old party under the care of the doorman who had witnessed my encounter with Grenville Milton. The doorman assisted his charge into the backseat of a waiting car, nodded at me, and swept his arm toward the entrance. Having been told what to do, I walked into the lobby. A good-looking clerk smiled at me from behind the desk. I smiled back at her. Thanks to Robert, I was a familiar visitor. At the top of the stairs to the right of the lobby, Vincent's unoccupied podium stood guard over the darkened reaches of Le Madrigal. I turned to the marble stairs on the other side of the lobby. From the mezzanine, Robert looked down at me and disappeared again.

I mounted the marble stairs and went into the men's room. Robert was leaning against one of the sinks, both of his hands on the grip of the leather satchel. The mirror behind him reflected only the row of urinals and the tiled wall.

Robert was grinning. "So here we are, at last."

5

HOW I LEARNED TO EAT TIME

73

■ Afterward, I changed my mind about the similarities between Robert and myself almost every time I was with him, but what struck me then was the magnitude of the differences between us. I didn't see how anyone could mistake him for me: despite a structural likeness, the ruthlessness stamped into Robert's features obliterated any resemblance. That he should not be reflected in mirrors seemed absolutely right. Then my eyes moved to the mirror and saw there the reflection of the back of his head. It was as though he had increased in substance at the expense of my own. When I looked again at his face, it was identical to mine in every particular.

"What the hell are you?" I asked.

"You know what I am." Robert held out the satchel. "Go up to 554 and give this to Ashleigh. She'll be so grateful, she'll rip off your clothes."

"What's in here?" As soon as I asked, I thought I knew.

"Don't be stupid." He thrust it into my hands. "This morning, someone who refused to give his name called the Brazen Head and said he heard you had dinner with Ashleigh and Laurie Hatch last Friday. He assumed that you would be willing to assist the case against Stewart Hatch. These documents will give Ashleigh everything she needs to mount a successful prosecution. Hatch has no idea they're gone."

"So you did break into that building." He shrugged. "Hatch must have checked to see if this stuff was still there. How can he not know it's missing?"

"Because it wasn't missing after the break-in. I went back to the Cobden Building last night. By the time Stewart takes another look, everything will be back in place. Tell Ashleigh to make copies and return the originals."

"How did this anonymous guy get them?"

"He broke into the building, how else? The guy has an old grudge against Hatch. In the process of smashing up the offices, he stumbled on these papers. He told you to go to a bench in Town Square, you went, you found the bag, you're bringing it to her. End of story." Robert left the sinks and moved to the door. "Good thing you were thrown out of that rooming house."

He stepped back and passed through the door. I mean that in the most literal sense possible. Robert did not open the men's room door, he *passed through* it, smiling at me as his body melted into the white wood and, like the Cheshire cat, disappeared from view.

■ **74**

■ I locked myself into a stall and unbuckled the satchel. It was filled with fat manila folders: statements from a bank in the Virgin Islands; incorporation papers for companies named Glittermax Inc., Eagle Properties, and Delta Mud Holdings; deeds to buildings in Louisville and Cincinnati; letters from law firms. I thumbed through partnership agreements signed by Hatch and Grenville Milton. Two bundles of computer disks were tucked into side pockets.

Ashleigh put her arms around me and gave me a resounding kiss. "The unpredictable Ned Dunstan. What's in that beautiful bag?"

I put it on the table and sat facing her. "You tell me."

Ashleigh tucked her lower lip under her front teeth. "That's an interesting answer." A couple of seconds went by. "Are you interested in lunch?"

"That's an interesting question," I said.

"I'll have room service send up a couple of club sandwiches. How about that Pinot Grigio you liked so much?"

"Good old Pinot Grigio," I said.

She called room service, then sat down, opened the leather bag, and peered in. She glanced at me. I shrugged. Ashleigh took out one of the files and leafed through the papers. Her frown of concentration melted into blank surprise. She sampled another file. "Where did you *get* this stuff?"

I told her the fairy tale about the man who left a bag in Town Square. "He wants you to make copies. I guess he's going to put the originals back."

"Did you see him?"

"No. If this guy can break into the Cobden Building, he's a tricky customer."

"This guy did more than break in." Ashleigh sorted through another set of papers. "He found Stewart's top-secret stash. Can you imagine how well this was hidden?"

"Can you use it?"

"Use it? This is like striking oil. He set up paper companies out of state, took over a bunch of nightclubs, and skimmed every penny he could. He sent the cash to banks in the Virgin Islands and laundered it through phony companies in the form of loans." She reached into the bag and brought out the disks. "Every transaction he made is probably on these things. Every crook has a fatal flaw, and Stewart is a control freak. Do you know what this means?"

"Tell me."

"There is no way on earth I can lose this case. It'd be nice if I could use this stuff in court, but I won't have to. Once we scare the shit out of the secondary parties, Stewart's going to be hung out to dry, and so is Milton." Her eyes changed. "Did Laurie Hatch arrange to get you these papers?"

"No. She did not."

Ashleigh leaned back in her chair. "I was about to come home empty-handed. My boss would have been patronizing and sympathetic. My colleagues would have disguised their glee at how badly I fucked up, and I'd be handling dipshit cases for the next two years. Now my boss is going to pin a gold medal on my chest, and the other assistant D.A.s are going to have to pretend they're overjoyed."

"You'll be able to explain . . . ?"

"How I got this material? Enter our old friend, the anonymous informant."

Ashleigh talked about her case until the room-service waiter showed up, and when he had uncorked the wine bottle and departed, she bit into her sandwich like a stevedore. "God, the way everything happened, it's like it was all set up in advance."

"I know what you mean," I said.

"And I have to say, Ned, when you're in that mood you were in Friday night, you're God's gift to women."

I slumped in my chair, and her face turned red. "Let's go down to the business center and copy this stuff."

■ **75**

■ When Ashleigh and I came back to her room, we looked at each other and undressed without saying a word. Later on, Ashleigh told me about her childhood in Lexington, Kentucky, and her marriage to Michael Ashton, who on their honeymoon had seduced the cocktail hostess at their hotel. I told her some things about Star, Phil and Laura Grant, and what I had done since leaving Naperville.

"Why did you leave Middlemount?"

"I couldn't handle the math and science courses."

"Wasn't it harder to learn programming than freshman calculus, or whatever it was?"

"Yeah," I said. "Come to think of it."

"Do you like your job?"

"It's the best job I ever had," I said. "Every time I get my paycheck, I'm astonished."

"Is money important to you?"

"No," I said. "That's why I'm astonished."

"Do you have close friends?"

"Medium close," I said. "Also semiclose, semidistant, and completely distant, except for insincere camaraderie. We're guys, we like it that way."

"How about girlfriends?"

"Off and on," I said.

"What about Laurie Hatch?"

"What about her?"

"You're enormously attracted to Laurie. And vice versa."

"There is some truth in that," I said.

"What are you going to do about it?"

"What do you think I should do?"

Ashleigh gripped my arm and shook it like a sapling. "Why are you asking me? If I had Laurie on the witness stand, I'd feel like I was questioning the Sphinx. But considering the way you feel about her, you should give yourself a break. I can't believe I'm saying this."

"You don't like her," I said. "Or you don't trust her."

The ends of her mouth curled up. "Have you slept with her yet?"

I wondered if I could get away with refusing to answer on the grounds of self-incrimination. I did not want to lie to Ashleigh, and she would have seen through any attempt to evade the question. By the time I had worked this out, the answer was already obvious. "Yes," I said.

"I knew it!"

"Then why did you ask?"

"I knew it was going to happen, I just didn't know how *soon*. Why do you think she let you do that? Laurie Hatch isn't some bimbo on the make, she's. . . . Let's forget about Laurie Hatch. I want to concentrate on Ned Dunstan for a while."

■ 76

■ I woke up about 1:30 A.M., too late to visit Toby Kraft or look at the houses on Buxton Place. I felt my way around the room-service cart and took a shower. After I got dressed, I sat next to Ashleigh and stroked her back until she woke up.

"Who was that masked man?" she said. "Call me tomorrow morning, okay?"

I left the satchel in her room. It was safer than the Brazen Head, and the records of Stewart Hatch's peccadillos had to be stashed somewhere until Robert collected them. The ideal hiding place suggested itself as I watched the panel above the elevator door count down to L.

A solitary car moved past the front of Merchants Park. I stepped down into the empty avenue and saw a red glow above the townhouses along Ferryman's Road. When I got near the center of the park, I caught the unmistakable odor of smoke.

At Chester Street, I looked north. Arcs of water turned from silver to red as they fell glittering onto a burning building. A small crowd stood behind a rank of fire engines. Then I realized that the fire was in the same block as Helen Janette's rooming house, and I sprinted toward it.

Flames poured through the front windows on both floors of the rooming house. A column of charcoal-colored smoke billowed from the roof. Helen Janette hugged her pink bathrobe over her chest, and Mr. Tite's fedora-topped head jutted behind her like an Easter Island statue. Beneath the cuffs of his pajamas, his bare feet glared angry white.

Miss Redman and Miss Challis had claimed the arms of an enchanted young firefighter. Roxy and Moonbeam wore gleaming satin slips no different from their party attire, and, like Frank Tite, were barefoot, but seemed to be having a much better time. Policemen and firefighters moved through the fire engines and squad cars. A clutch of onlookers, many of them in bathrobes, occupied the middle of the street.

A sheet of flame burst upward and tinted the smoke blood-red. The roof fell in with a barely audible crash. I had never before seen a serious fire, never heard how a fire celebrates destruction in a rushing, inhuman voice. Helen Janette screamed, "That's him! He burned down my house!"

Frank Tite plodded toward me, wincing. Roxy and Moonbeam fluttered forward. Two men in bathrobes appeared on either side of me. One of them twisted my arm behind my back.

"If you don't let go of my arm, I'll take your head off your shoulders."

Helen Janette screeched, "It was him!"

The man holding my arm was about forty pounds overweight. Prominent keloids dotted his face, and sweat cascaded from his every pore.

"I apologize to you," I said. "I got mad, so I said something stupid. How well do you get on with Helen Janette?"

He let go of my arm. "Mrs. Janette would sooner lick spit off the sidewalk than give me the time of day."

Mr. Tite minced up. "Get hold of him again."

"You hold him. I got no reason to believe your girlfriend or you either, Frank."

Followed by a bearlike man with CAPTAIN stenciled in yellow across the front of his rubber coat, Helen Janette bustled beside Mr. Tite. "That's him. I want him put in jail."

The men around me retreated.

"Sir, what do you have to say?"

"I was walking back to my place from Merchants Hotel," I said. "When I noticed the flames I ran up, hoping it wasn't Mrs. Janette's house."

"He's lying," said Helen Janette.

"Do you really think I'd burn down your house because you kicked me out?"

"No!" she yelled. "You know why you did it."

"Helen," I asked, "did Otto get out in time?"

She closed her mouth.

The fire captain asked my name and said, "We were unable to rescue the tenant who did not exit with the others." He looked into my eyes. "Was the victim a friend of yours?"

"Otto was a nice man," I said. "Sometimes he fell asleep when he was smoking."

"Why are you just *standing* here?" Helen Janette shouted.

A police car came flashing around the corner of Ferryman's Road. "Here's what's going to happen," the captain said. "I will ask Mr. Dunstan to sit in the police car and sort things out with the officer. Mrs. Janette will be allowed to speak her piece, and she will do so in an orderly fashion. You, sir, will go back over there on the sidewalk, where you belong."

Helen Janette nodded at Tite. He stalked away, and she tightened her bathrobe around herself, ready for battle.

Treuhaft and Captain Mullan got out of the car. Helen Janette said, "I want you to arrest this man on charges of arson and murder."

Mullan followed the direction of her extended finger. "Not you."

"Believe it or not," I said.

"Mr. Dunstan, you spread joy wherever you go."

"I was at Merchants Hotel until about one-thirty this morning. The desk clerk saw me leave, but you could confirm my story by talking to Assistant District Attorney Ashton."

"I love these familiar old songs." Mullan went back to Helen Janette. "You are accusing this man of setting the fire?"

She wrenched her robe tight as a sausage casing. "Maybe you

remember the trouble I got into when my name was Hazel
Jansky. I was punished for trying to do good for a few helpless
babies."

Mullan was completely unhurried. "I remember that name."

"Mr. Dunstan heard a filthy lie from Toby Kraft. I call it a
filthy lie because that's what it was, and Toby Kraft knows it."
She shivered. "The way people carried on, you'd think I was a
criminal, instead of someone who helped little babies find good
homes."

Mullan gave me a weary look. "Can you help me out here?"

"My mother thought Hazel Jansky abducted one of her children. Even if I thought she was right, I wouldn't have done this."

Mullan closed his eyes, opened the rear door, and waved me
in. He and Treuhaft got in the front seat. "Merchants Hotel,"
Mullan said. "Dunstan, why don't you save yourself travel time
and move into the place?"

"I like the Brazen Head."

"You should know a few things about the night clerk," Mullan
said. Treuhaft gave an evil chuckle.

When we pulled up in front of the hotel, Mullan told Treuhaft
to ask the desk clerk if he had seen a man of my description
leaving the hotel at any time past 1:00 A.M., and if so, to give an
approximate time. "I'm sick of waking up Assistant District Attorney Ashton with inquiries about Mr. Dunstan's whereabouts.
If the clerk didn't see him leave, we'll take it from there."

Mullan rested the back of his head on the seat. "I don't suppose you started that fire after all?"

"It was going before I left Ashleigh's room," I said. "The man
who lived across the hall from me used to fall asleep smoking in
his chair. Last night, he almost burned the place down."

"This fire was no accident," Mullan said. "Our first call said
there was a broken basement window in back of the house.
Someone crawled in and poured an inflammatory over everything in sight. Then he crawled back out and torched the place.
We have to wait for the investigators' report, but that's what it's
going to say."

"Joe Staggers?"

"I'll check on him, but Staggers wants to deal with you in
person. Have you seen any other characters hanging around the
building?"

"Well," I said, "after the break-in at the Cobden Building,

Frenchy La Chapelle looked like he was following me back to the house."

Treuhaft let himself into the driver's seat, and the car sagged under his weight. "The desk man says Mr. Dunstan left the hotel around one forty-five."

Mullan nodded. "How does a recent visitor to our city become acquainted with Frenchy La Chapelle?"

Treuhaft swung his head toward Captain Mullan.

"My Uncle Clark pointed him out when he and Cassie Little visited Clyde Prentiss at St. Ann's. All I'm saying is that he watched me go up Chester Street to the rooming house."

"Frenchy followed you home from Merchants Park?"

"It looked like it," I said.

"Can you think of any reason why one of our favorite dirtbags should take an interest in you, Mr. Dunstan?"

"None at all."

Mullan's face stretched into a yawn. "Officer Treuhaft, Mr. Dunstan and I are going to step out for a private word."

Mullan strolled past the hotel's entrance and wagged his head toward the polished stone, and I leaned back against the facade. A thick smell of smoke drifted toward us. Mullan sighed and buttoned his suit jacket. He thrust his hands into his pockets and looked down at his shoes. He sighed again.

"You have something on your mind," I said.

Mullan turned halfway around and looked across Commercial Avenue. A solid column of smoke darkened the air above Chester Street. "I have been very good to you, Mr. Dunstan. You keep popping up at crime scenes, you are accused of one thing after another, but I have not let the system run over you."

"I know," I said. "And I'm grateful."

"Do you have any kind of professional relationship with Assistant District Attorney Ashton?"

"I do not."

"Are you an employee of any federal agency?"

"No."

"Do you have a professional association with any law enforcement body?"

"Of course not," I said.

"Do you work as a private detective?"

"I write software programs for a company called Vision, Inc.

I'm not in the CIA, the FBI, the Treasury Department, or any other outfit that might be interested in Stewart Hatch."

"I assume you'd have no objections to my checking you for a wire."

I told him to go ahead. He patted my chest and back and knelt to run his hands down my legs. "Open your jacket." I held my jacket away from my sides, and Mullan felt under my arms and around the back of my collar.

"All right," he said. "Maybe you are a civilian who happened to meet an assistant D.A. from Kentucky on the way to Edgerton. And maybe you stumbled into a friendship with Hatch's wife. I guess that's almost possible. But no matter what the hell you are, I want to say a few things, and I want you to listen to them. I don't like Lieutenant Rowley. Cops like Rowley give us all a bad name. What did he do, hit you?"

"He caught me off guard and punched me in the stomach," I said. "Then he knocked me down and kicked me. He wanted me to get a bus out of town, and I didn't cooperate. After that, he stole a hundred bucks from the money I turned in at headquarters."

"You didn't file a complaint."

"I didn't think a complaint would turn out too well."

"You could have come to me, Mr. Dunstan. But so be it. This morning, you implied that Lieutenant Rowley has an arrangement with Stewart Hatch. Most likely, he does. When I was a patrolman, the captain of detectives and the chief of police lived in houses Cobden Hatch paid for. I bought my own house, Mr. Dunstan. The only money I get comes in salary checks from the City of Edgerton, but I do live here, and if you're not what you claim to be, you'll crawl on your hands and knees over a mile of broken glass before you squirm your way into another job."

"My mother's funeral is on Wednesday," I said. "The day after that is my birthday. On Friday, I'll go back to New York. You'll never see me again."

Mullan spun away and went back to the police car.

77

■ The remaining firefighters aimed their hoses at the smoldering mound beneath the rows of concrete blocks. A corner post jutted up into the smoke like a used kitchen match. Somewhere down there, whatever was left of Otto Bremen waited to be unearthed. A photographer set off a heartless flash of light that exposed the remains of a shattered wall, a picture frame, a twisted metal lamp. Side by side in front of a fire engine, Helen Janette and Mr. Tite numbly watched flames poke out of the wreckage.

At the sight of me, Helen Janette quivered and stepped back. Mr. Tite moved between us. "What are we supposed to do now? Got an answer for that?"

"Someone will find you a place to stay," I said. "You're not the first people to be burned out of their house."

Enraged, Helen Janette moved beside him. "You should be in jail, you lunatic! Burn me out of house and home."

"I'm not the person who burned you out of house and home, Mrs. Janette." She muttered something I could not hear. "Can you tell me what happened?"

"If you think you have to know. I woke up and smelled smoke. I went out of my room. There was fire all over the floor and fire running up the stairs. You could hardly see for the smoke. I banged on Mr. Tite's door, and we ran down the hall to help Miss Carpenter, Miss Burgess, and Mrs. Feldman out the back door. Mrs. Feldman almost got me killed looking for her fur coat, which is the last time I do a favor for that woman. The girls climbed out through their window, and we all came around and tried to wake up Mr. Bremen. One of the neighbors must have called the Fire Department, because the trucks came about two minutes later. By then the whole house was burning."

"It started in the basement," I said.

"You know where it started," she said. "What I want to know

is, where am I going to stay? All my cash is down in that hole, along with my credit cards and my checkbook."

"Some money recently came to me," I said. "Four hundred and eighty dollars. I'll split it with you. You and Mr. Tite can get a room for the night and buy some clothes in the morning."

"You're joking."

I reached for my wallet and counted out $240.

"We don't take blood money," said Mr. Tite.

"Speak for yourself, Frank." She held out her hand, and I put the bills onto her palm. "I'm not too proud to accept charity."

"I'm glad I can help," I said. "And I'd be grateful for whatever you can tell me about the night I was born."

She thought about it for a couple of seconds. "For an even three hundred. Clothes cost money."

I counted out another three twenties. "You were supposed to bring out a baby that night. But everything went crazy during the storm, and the baby died."

"That baby was born dead."

"I know. But then my mother unexpectedly delivered twins, and the second one came out so easily it might as well have been the placenta."

"Came out *with* the placenta. It was so dark, I didn't know what was going on until I caught it in my hands. I'm going to give you a good home, I said to myself."

"Through Toby Kraft. Who set you up in the rooming-house business after you served your time."

"What the hell are you people talking about?" Mr. Tite said. "There was no other baby, the night of the storm."

"You don't know," she said. "I never told you, but now I can say what I like. I served my time." She looked back at me, her eyes dark with anger. "We had a *system*. Our system rescued innocent babies from terrible homes. The judge admitted that."

"It was for the good of the children," said Mr. Tite. I almost laughed out loud.

"You took the second baby from the delivery room in the middle of the storm. Where did you put him?"

"Same place I put you. Down the hall, in the nursery."

"Only that didn't happen," said Mr. Tite.

Helen Janette whirled on him. "What jail did they put you in, Frank? I forget the name." She turned back to me. "I cleaned him up in the dark, same as you. In the nursery, there was a cradle marked Dunstan, and I found it with my flashlight, and I picked you up and put him in it. Then I brought you back to your mother. 'I had twins,' she said, 'where's the other one?' I told her it was only the placenta, and then the lights went back on. I made my report to the doctor. I told him what your mother said, so he wouldn't be surprised later. Then I went back to the nursery. Nearly died of a heart attack. The Dunstan cradle was empty. I thought I put it in the wrong cradle by mistake, but the ones on either side were empty, too."

"Someone else grabbed the kid?" said Mr. Tite.

"It didn't get up and walk out by itself. I think it was that Mrs. Landon, the one who had the stillbirth. I think she snuck out to the nursery, picked up the baby, and hid it in her bedclothes. She checked out of the hospital as soon as the storm was over. I didn't realize it was probably her until the next day. Her records said her address was the Hotel Paris, but she checked out of there the same morning she left the hospital."

"You tried to find her," I said.

"I was thinking about the health of that baby."

She had been thinking about the health of her wallet. And then I thought: *Maybe Robert did get out of the cradle and leave by himself.*

"If you burned down my house to get back at me, it was all for nothing."

She tugged at the sleeve of Mr. Tite's robe and led him to a policeman seated at the wheel of a squad car. After a few words, the officer let them in, turned on his lights, and drove down the street toward me. Helen Janette was looking straight ahead. I followed their tail lights as far as Word Street.

■ A minute or two after entering the first of the lanes, I got the same prickly feeling I'd had before seeing Frenchy La Chapelle's imitation of an innocent pedestrian. I glanced over my shoulder at an empty lane and shuttered buildings. I began walking faster as I turned into Leather. Either one of Captain Mullan's dirtbags had taken an interest in me, or recent events had made me unreasonably jumpy. The latter sounded closer to reality.

On the other hand, Frenchy had trailed me to the rooming house. Maybe he had set the fire and discovered that he had killed the wrong person. Where Fish crossed Mutton, I came to a halt beside a burned-out street lamp and looked back at a dark,

dimensionless well that could have hidden a dozen men. A few
cars swished along Word Street. In a nearby lane, a man hawked
up sputum. I heard no other sounds, but the back of my neck still
prickled.

Fish Lane intersected Raspberry and Button before meeting
the fifty feet of Wax leading to Veal Yard. On an ordinary night,
this distance would have been no more than a short, not uninter-
esting walk; with the specter of Frenchy La Chapelle lurking behind me, it felt like a wasteland. I quickened my step and moved
into the next length of the narrow lane.

A nearly inaudible sound like a footfall came from behind me.
If I had been walking along Commercial Avenue in daylight, I
don't think I would have heard it. In the confines of Fish Lane,
the little sound made me spin around. I could see only empty
buildings and the dull reflection of starlight on the cobbles. Joe
Staggers had not stopped looking for me, I remembered.

I ran the rest of the way to Raspberry, darted across the intersection of the lanes, and raced toward the hovering gray haze
marking the crossing of Fish and Button. Although I could not
hear footsteps at my back, I *felt* the approach of a pursuing
figure. I shot across Button and heard another delicate footfall.
My heart nearly burst. I raced up the lane and glanced over my
shoulder a second before I swung into Wax.

I don't know what I saw. The image vanished too quickly for
me to be certain I had seen anything at all. I thought I saw the tails
of a dark overcoat whisking into an unseen passage. At the time, I
could think only that the old adversary I called Mr. X had just
slipped out of sight. My blood turned to glue. When I could move
again, I sprinted down the fifty feet of Wax Lane, clattered into
Veal Yard, and burst through the front door of the Brazen Head. A
bald night clerk with a hatchet tattooed above his right ear looked
up from a paperback.

I tried to imitate a person in a normal state of mind as I walked
across the lobby. The night man kept his eyes on me until I
started up the stairs. I came to the second floor, pulled out my
key, and opened the door to room 215. A lamp I had not switched
on shed a yellow nimbus over the end of the bed and the worn
green carpet. Seated beside the round table with his ankles
crossed before him, Robert closed the covers of *From Beyond*
and smiled at me.

78

■ "Old Dad was a pretty lousy writer, wasn't he? Don't you get the feeling he *believed* all this stuff?"

"I hope you didn't set that fire."

"Why would I?" Robert said. "Any fatalities?"

"One. An old man named Otto Bremen."

"I don't suppose anyone is going to miss him very much."

"I was supposed to die in that fire, and you know it."

Robert cocked an ankle on his knee, dropped his chin into his hand, and gazed at me with an expression of absolute innocence.

"You knew the building was going to burn down. You said it was a good thing I moved out."

"Wasn't it?"

"Couldn't you have told me what was going to happen? You let a man die."

"I wish I had twenty-twenty foresight, but it isn't that specific. I knew you'd be better off out of there, and that's as far as it went."

I sat on the other side of the table. Irritatingly, Robert adjusted his chair and resumed the chin-on-hand, elbow-on-table posture. "You set me up to meet Ashleigh."

"The sweetie must have been thrilled by those documents."

"Yes," I said. "When you want to put them back, they'll be in Toby Kraft's office safe."

"You don't want me to call on our little friend?" Robert was grinning. "Hatch won't check his hiding place for a couple of days. He's too secure to get worried."

"Why should you give a damn if Stewart Hatch goes to jail?"

"Brother dear," he said, "do you suspect me of manipulation?"

Because right and left had not been reversed, the face across from me was as strange as it was familiar, and the strangeness contained a kind of rawness I thought other people had always seen in me.

"I suspect you of manipulation, yes," I said. "And I resent it. Enormously."

Robert took his hand from his chin and uncrossed his legs in an elaborate display of concern that suggested that I had missed the point. He placed his forearms on the table, knitted his hands together, and sent me a glance agleam with irony, as if to say that he and I had no need for such games.

"Can you honestly say you're not *enormously* attracted to Laurie Hatch? Haven't you had fantasies about marrying her?"

"You make me sick."

"Even someone like me would appreciate occasional access to a fortune."

"Laurie doesn't get any money if her husband goes to jail. You should have done your homework."

Robert straightened up and took his arms off the table. "Let's examine what happens if Stewart is convicted. Approximately twenty million dollars fall into the hands of little Cobden Carpenter Hatch. His mother has discretion over the entire sum. I know this goes against your puritanical instincts, but if you follow your own desires and marry Laurie, the rest of your life will be extraordinary."

"Unfortunately, it already is," I said.

"Doesn't perfect freedom appeal to you?"

"Marrying for money doesn't sound like freedom to me. Just the opposite, in fact."

"Then forget the money and marry for love. You even like her son. In fact, you love him, too. It's perfect."

"How do you come into this arrangement?"

"You would agree to one condition."

"Which is?"

Robert leaned back and spread his arms. "To share it with me. Once every couple of months, you go out on an errand, and I come back in your place. Eight hours later, twelve hours later, we do the same thing in reverse. No one would ever know, Laurie and Cobbie least of all."

"No thanks," I said.

"Let it sink in. Your wife would have no idea she was sleeping with two men instead of one. The time will come, as it does in all marriages, when you'll find it convenient to leave the house undetected. And we'd be carrying on a family tradition. Our great-great-grandfathers did it all the time."

"Right up to the time when Sylvan killed Omar," I said.

"You're kidding. I never heard that."

"So it would be in the family tradition for you to kill me and get everything for yourself."

"I don't *want* it!" Robert said. "Ned, remember who I am. I am not domestic. The idea of living with one woman, tied to a schedule. . . . I'm not really a human being, after all. I'm pure *Dunstan*. We weren't supposed to be like this, we were supposed to be one person, but we were separated in the womb, or on the night we were born, I don't know, it happened anyhow, and I couldn't harm you in any way, I *can't*. I need you. Besides that, ordinary human life makes me want to puke. How could I want to settle down with Laurie Hatch?"

"You haven't needed me so far," I said, though Robert's assertion had moved me.

"Why do you think I came to Star in Naperville and told her you should leave college? When you insisted on going back, why did I make sure someone would look out for you? Or meet Star in front of Nettie's house and tell her you were in danger?"

"Maybe you do need me," I said. "I need you, too, Robert. But I am not going to marry Laurie Hatch so you can buy Armani suits and gold Rolexes. Even if she would agree to marry me, I have no idea who she really is."

"Are you going to let a small-town Daddy Warbucks like Stewart Hatch poison your mind? You don't give a shit about her background. Look at ours! It only means you have more in common with her than you thought."

This notion had already occurred to me.

Robert leaned toward me again. "Ned, you're already half in love with Laurie Hatch. It's karma."

"If I don't know what to think about Laurie, I really don't know what to make of you."

"Imagine how I feel about you. Yet in some way we are the same person, after all. And you might stop to consider that my life has been much more difficult than yours."

"How would you know anything about my difficulties?"

"That's a fair question, but you are more or less human, and I'm scarcely human at all. Do you think that's been easy for me?"

"I have no idea," I said.

"But aren't you grateful for what you've learned in the past two days? And that we came together like this?"

I wanted to say, *No, all of this sickens me,* but the truth spoke itself. "Yes."

Robert smiled. "At the right moment, you always say 'Yes.'"

This unexpected allusion to my recurring dream gave me the beginning of an idea. "You must have paid a visit to New Providence Road."

I had taken him unawares. "Where?"

"Howard Dunstan's old house. The one Sylvan reconstructed with the original stones from Providence."

"That place is bad luck. It's like black magic, it'll eat you alive."

"It's where you always wanted me to go," I said.

Robert gathered himself before once more regarding me with what appeared to be absolute sincerity. "You're talking about the dreams you used to have. They were *dreams*. I wasn't in charge. You were. That's how dreams work—you're saying something to *yourself*."

"How do you know what my dreams were about?"

"We were supposed to be the same person," he said. "It's not surprising that we should have the same dreams now and then."

I wondered what would have happened if Robert and I had been born into the same body and felt a disorienting rush of emotions, a kind of swoon made equally of attraction and repulsion. I heard Howard Dunstan say, *We flew from the crack in the golden bowl. We are smoke from the cannon's mouth.* We had flown through the flaw in the bowl and been ripped from the pockets of fallen soldiers—it was as good as any other explanation for the joy, equal to but more powerful than the fear that accompanied it, flooding through me.

"Whatever you are, you're my brother," I said. "It's even more than that. You're half of me."

"I fought this." Robert shivered in his chair. "You have no idea." He turned his head away before looking back with a quantity of feeling that equaled mine. "I despised you. You can't imagine my resentment. I hardly *knew* our mother. You got to *live* with her, at least off and on, and when you couldn't, she visited you. She sent you birthday cards. I didn't have any of that. Robert was stuck away in the shadows. Star had to protect her little Ned. We only met once."

A recognition with the force of a locomotive moved into me.

"Yes?" Robert said.

"It was our ninth birthday. Something happened. I got sick the day before."

"No kidding," Robert said.

"I didn't get there in time. Wherever it was."

"You almost got me killed," Robert said.

"I had a fever, and I couldn't get out of bed. Star came into our room. I thought I was safe, because my seizures usually hit me in the middle of the afternoon. She was standing next to my cot. . . . Where were you? Where did I go?"

"That year, it was the Anscombes," Robert said. "Or so they called themselves. They took me in because their own kid died."

"Oh, my God," I said. "You were in Boulder."

"Until then, I could always feel him sniffing me out in time to get away. That year, you picked the wrong day to get sick, and I didn't feel anything."

Inside my head, Frank Sinatra sang the word *Fight* at the top of a beat and hung back for a long, stretched-out moment before coming in with:

> *fight,*
> > *fight it with aaall of your might . . .*

and on the downward curve of the phrase, everything I had chosen to forget came flooding back to me.

"I was you," I said.

■ **79**

■ *By 10:00 P.M. of their mutual birthday in 1967, Ned Dunstan and the boy known as "Bobby Anscombe" imagined themselves safe from the annual trial. Ned had spent the previous day and most of this one in a fever that spun him between dehydrated exhaustion and episodes of cinematic delirium. The fever had peaked before sundown, leaving him soaked in sweat, thirsty, and rational enough to think that he had deflected his annual seizure. "Bobby Anscombe" had received none of the signals—a sense of electricity in the air, an intermittent tingle running along both of his arms, sudden glimpses of a scatter of bright blue dots floating at the corners of his vision—that came to him two or three days before his birthday and announced that it was time to surrender again, until his next release into the human world and the care of a couple who would take him in because they would recognize him as family, to the formless void in which most of his ravenous childhood had been spent. "Bobby" was kneeling on the attic floor, wondering how much money would not be missed if he removed it from the leather trunk he had discovered behind an unfinished wall. Another cache of bills was secreted in the kitchen, but "Michael Anscombe" kept his eye on that one. Ned Dunstan lay on Star's bed, the sweaty sheet thrust aside, while his mother stroked his forehead.*

■ In the bedroom on Cherry Street, Ned felt a great pressure settling down upon his body, as if the air had doubled in weight. A buzzing sensation he knew too well moved into his chest and traveled along his nerves. When his mother leaned over him, the deep green of her blouse and the black at the center of her eyes blazed and shimmered.

■ Something had happened within the house, Robert could not tell what. An unexpected noise, a shift in the air currents, an opened door, a footstep on the attic stairs? If "Mike Anscombe" had checked his bedroom, he would have to invent an excuse for his disobedience, fast. "Mike Anscombe" had no tolerance for disobedience. Robert scuttled toward the attic door, and blue flames shot through the gaps in the floorboards.

■ Ned's body stiffened, twitched upward, and slammed back down on the mattress. Before he plummeted away, he saw Star's stricken face glide toward him.

Through walls of blue fire, he was rushing behind Mr. X up an asphalt driveway to a suburban house with a conspicuous new addition on its left side. A bicycle leaned on its kickstand. A flat-faced moon glared down from above a row of mountain peaks unreal as a backdrop. Fir trees scented the chill night air.

Theatrically, Mr. X pressed the bell. When the door opened, he rammed a knife into the belly of the man before him and walked him backward. The invisible pressure that had blown Ned up the asphalt drive pushed him into the room. From speakers on either side of the fireplace, the voice of Frank Sinatra unrolled a long phrase about an immovable object and an old, irresistible force.

■ Robert stood listening at the attic door.

■ "Mr. Anscombe, I presume," said Mr. X.

The man gaped at the purple ropes sliding out of his body. In an unexpected atmospheric shift that returned to him the odd memory of a stuffed fox lifting its paw within a glass bell, Ned took advantage of Mr. X's pleasure in his task and stepped backward until he struck the door. Veils of blue fire drifted over the walls, and Frank Sinatra insisted that someone had to be kissed.

Gleeful Mr. X opened "Michael Anscombe's" throat.

Ned glanced to his left and through an intervening wall caught a snapshot-like vision of a heavy woman with tangled blond hair lying in bed reading *Goodnight Moon*. With the vision came certain unhappy information: the woman on the bed had given birth to a dead child who had been horribly, appallingly *wrong*.

Ned raced into a brief hallway ending at a closed door. Before him, uncarpeted stairs led to another, narrower doorway.

■ Robert pressed his hands against the wood and focused on what was going on beneath him. Transparent blue flames licked in past his feet and traveled in bright, ambitious lines across the attic floor. The faint sounds from below told Robert that "Michael Anscombe" had been slit open by a joyous being finally within reach of its quarry. Robert's life depended upon his capacity to evade this predatory being's annual descents into this strange, transitory existence.

Footsteps of an unearthly softness, lighter than a child's and completely inexplicable, glided toward him from the bottom of the staircase.

■ Ned moved half of the way up the stairs and froze where he stood. With the ease of a figure in a dream, a boy identical to himself was emerging through the unopened door.

* * *

■ Robert looked down in amazed relief at the goggling figure of his overprivileged, sheltered brother and understood that here before him was the means of his survival. He pressed a finger to his lips and pointed down. His brother retreated, and Robert floated noiselessly to the ground floor.

■ Ned moved away from the bottom of the stairs. His astonishing double pointed to the end of the hallway. Ned went to the door and attempted to open it. His hand melted through the doorknob and closed upon itself.

He glanced over his shoulder and, past the figure of his enraged double, looked through a transparent wall to see Mr. X striding away from the triangular hump of "Michael Anscombe's" body to invade a room stacked with cardboard boxes. The woman with tangled hair shuffled forward, holding *Goodnight Moon* to her chest like a talisman.

■ Robert saw the double's fingers pass through the knob of his bedroom door and knew that he was not *real*. The *real* Ned Dunstan dreamed on in Edgerton, and what had been sent to Boulder was an illusory replica. For the first time in his peculiar life, Robert found himself capable of setting resentment aside long enough to grasp that although his mother's darling was not physically present, some aspect of Ned Dunstan had been delivered to him, and that this *figment*, this *duplicate*, was what he needed to get out of this house.

Robert spun on his heel to observe exactly what his brother had seen a moment before.

■ A second after Robert took off down the hall, Ned followed, expecting his double to dash into the living room and melt through the front door. Robert reached the end of the hallway and disappeared. Baffled, Ned moved a few steps forward and saw the woman still plodding across the bedroom. Mr. X plunged on into the new addition. "Michael Anscombe's" corpse bent over its knees in a widening pool of blood. Frank Sinatra was making clear his intention to kiss those lips that he adored. Ned looked across the living room and, on the other side of the half partition that separated it from the kitchen, saw Robert glaring at him. He raced out of the hallway.

* * *

■ Robert couldn't believe it. His brother—his brother's *replica*—was gawking like a tourist at the Grand Canyon. Just when Robert had begun to think he would have to throw the toaster at the kid to get his attention, Ned looked into the kitchen and saw him. *Come on,* Robert urged, and his brother started to move at last. Robert went to the sink, squatted down, pushed aside bottles of cleaning supplies, and opened a secret compartment some previous owner had installed to hide his wife's jewelry. His hand closed around the edges of a metal box.

■ Ned couldn't believe what he was seeing. With his back to the opening in the wall, his double was kneeling in front of the sink and rooting around in the washing supplies. In about a second and a half, either the woman or Mr. X, or both of them, would come into the living room.

"Stop messing around," he whispered.

"Shhh," the double whispered back.

Ned moved into an alcove for a washer and dryer next to the back door and watched Robert emerge from the sink cabinet holding a flat metal box. He opened the lid and took out two stacks of bills. He reached into the box again, and his body tensed. His head snapped to the side.

They were going to die. That was it. The double's greed had killed them.

■ Robert watched "Alice Anscombe" stumble into view and swing her head toward the kitchen. Her eyes went flat with shock. "Shit on a shingle," she said.

"Alice" dreamily turned her head to the hallway, smiled, and said, "Who the hell are you, Bob Hope?"

■ Robert and Ned felt the atmosphere about them intensify and mysteriously seem to brighten. The only other living being in the house had heard "Alice Anscombe's" words.

■ A voice in Ned's mind said, *I can't be killed, I'm not here, but he can,* and he stepped out of the alcove. The instant he did so, Ned at last understood his baffling double to be precisely that which he had missed and yearned for all his life. He was looking at his brother.

* * *

■ Robert jumped to his feet, thrusting wads of bills into his pockets. "Alice" waded into the lake of blood, came bemused to a halt, and looked down. Robert thought he saw the corners of her mouth lift when she took in her husband's body, but the smile, if it was a smile, faded. The book fell from her hands, and blood splashed over the tops of her feet. "Alice" turned her head to the empty hallway.

■ Frank Sinatra sang:

> *Fight . . .*
>> *fight . . .*
>>> *fight it with aaall of your might . . .*

and Ned felt himself begin to fade out of existence with the abruptness of a raindrop on a hot sidewalk. He held out his hands and through their hazy, lightly tinted fabric saw the tiles of the kitchen floor.

■ The madwoman in the living room shouted, "Why are you doing this? Don't you understand I'm already in hell?"

A dry male voice said, "Don't worry, Mrs. Anscombe. You will be taken care of soon enough."

■ Robert and Ned stared into their identical faces and seemed to glide toward each other without any sort of conscious movement. Ned's being trembled with the awareness that his brother's survival, and in some sense his own, depended upon an extraordinary act of surrender.

■ They heard the woman shout, *Shit, I really am in hell, only the son of a bitch isn't RED, it's BLUE!*

■ Gliding toward Robert, Ned experienced a new sort of terror, which was focused on the awareness that he was on the threshold of a change that he could neither control nor foresee. The terror became exquisite when he realized that part of his being was already stretching out its arms in yearning.

* * *

■ A rational, self-protective portion of Robert also welcomed the coming mystery, for it recognized a chance of survival. The part of Robert that was chaotic and irrational resisted in a terror greater than Ned's. He felt despair and revulsion at having been swindled into a destructive bargain.

■ Irresistibly, Robert and Ned sailed toward each other, met, and melted together, each with his own fears, doubts, and resentments, and for a moment their psyches tangled and rebelled, one aghast at the other's depth of rage and violence, the other repelled by what seemed the unbearable narrowness and smallness of his confinement, therefore burning to *mutiny,* to *lay waste—*

■ No sooner than registered, this ambivalence dissolved into a resolution and harmony, a wholeness shot through with the perception of an even greater, more roomy wholeness, equal to the possession of a kind of magnificence, withheld from them only by the fact of Ned's actual *absence.* Such depth of personal surrender accompanied this sense of possibility that both instantly drew back, but in one mind and body they soared together through the kitchen wall with what their Ned-half experienced from his inextricable other self as an acknowledgment of a compounding sweetness and satisfaction equal to his own.

■ Together they fled into the fir-scented night, and their Robert-half seized control and sped them away. Ned felt as though pedaling uphill on a leaden bicycle, then as though swimming underwater against a strong current. His muscles ached, his lungs strained for oxygen. Mile after blurry mile slipped by. With no transition, they came to rest in a vacant lot where Queen Anne's lace trembled about them. Robert peeled him off like a dirty shirt. Millions of stars gleamed down from the night sky. *It's too much,* Ned thought, *way too much.*

"Where are we?"

"I'm somewhere in Wisconsin," Robert said. "You're in Edgerton, with Mom."

Ned pulled his knees to his chest as a spike drove into his head.

■ "And I was you," said Robert. "Long enough to get us out of Boulder, anyhow."

"I can't believe I forgot what we did," I said. "I saved your life."

"I've saved yours a couple of times," Robert said. "Can you stay alive until our birthday? I can't protect you every minute of the day."

"We have more to talk about," I said, but he was gone.

81 ■ Mr. X

■ O You Hoverers, You Smoke Ravening from the Cannon, Your Son is wondering if in Your Triumphant Millennium what used to be called "the servant problem" still exists. Do You, in Your Exalted Realms, employ the services of humbler beings, no doubt enslaved, no doubt from Conquered Territories? If so, You know what I'm talking about. A slave is no different from a servant, except for being an even greater responsibility. The patron saint of servants is Judas. My earthly parents suffered the depredations of disloyal maids and housekeepers, and I, too, have had my Judases, the first of them one Clothhead Spelvin, whose betrayal I answered with a summary visit to his jail cell. And now, that twitchy collection of street-sweepings, Frenchy La Chapelle, has failed me.

This morning I snatched sans payment a copy of the *Edgerton Echo* from the newsstand and nipped up Chester Street, scanning the front page. The editors had been allowed time enough only to insert a paragraph reporting the destruction by fire of a "modest rooming house." A single fatality was considered a possibility. Tomorrow's rag would supply photographs and complete details.

I strolled to the scene of the happy event in the guise of an ordinary mortal. My visible, daytime self possesses the dignity of a retired statesman or diplomat, with perhaps a hint of a general's authority. In a weathered manner, I am still handsome, if I say so myself. (To complete these details of my mundane existence, I employ a false or assumed name, which contains a revelatory joke no one is likely to perceive, and I have recently retired from an executive position.)

One matter niggled as I neared the site. I should have *known* of my son's death, as I had *known* of his mother's. Yet this was the weakling offspring, whose share of my legacy may have been too insignificant to permit telepathic transmission.

The "modest rooming house" had been reduced to a heap of rubble. Within a network of red tape declaring DO NOT CROSS HAZARDOUS AREA DO NOT CROSS HAZARDOUS AREA, investigators in orange space suits prowled through the mess. A collection of dimwits and ghouls had assembled across the street.

I circulated through them and picked up what I could. Several blamed the fire on faulty wiring. Many considered Helen Janette, the landlady, an ill-tempered harridan. I nearly went mad with impatience: *What about the fatality?*

At last I buttonholed a wheezing wreck. *Didn't one of the tenants perish?*

"Say what?"

Some guy died.

"Oh, yeah. Otto. Damn shame. Did you know him?"

Not to speak to.

The wreck nodded. "It shakes you up more than you want to let on."

Oh, it does shake me up.

I hastened back to the sty and fastened onto the news broadcasts. An unidentified body had been removed from the scene. An hour later, identity was suspected but unconfirmed. Identity had been confirmed but withheld. Not until noon was the victim named as Otto Bremen, a seventy-year-old crossing guard at Carl Sandburg Elementary School.

By evening, the broadcasters were exercising their internally amplified voices to announce that investigators and fire specialists in the pay of Edgerton's Departments of Fire and Police had concluded that the fire was of suspicious origin.

You understand my complaints about the servant problem.

■ Truth be told, Frenchys are hard to come by. I have decided to give the snake a second chance. Frenchy is not so stupid as to boast of his crime. (Except to Cassie Little.)

Frenchy's life shall be spared, as long as he can repair the damage and look up some old acquaintances to discover if they have been unwise. Star would never have divulged the name "Edward Rinehart": she was good at secrets. Clearly, she never told the weakling that he had a brother. Blast him. Blast his brother, too. *I thought there was only one of them—*

Years back, I nearly *had* the boy—the atmosphere electric— my excitement profound—I sensed the *presence*—yet the quivering shadow slipped from me—the singularity of the occasion troubled & intrigued—now I understand.

I believe the two *connected—joined together.* The Dangerous Son was close to hand—*Resolution* nigh. My failures had a single cause—*Ignorance.* I thought there was but One—not Two—I believed the *Shadow* the image of my Prey—not the helpless *Shadow* of his brother.

I object! You People got things wrong!

But no more complaint. During her lifetime, the cow apparently exerted a protective influence. Understanding strengthens me, as does blessed Recognition—success in maturity—in what some may call old age—is sweeter than in youth.

82 ■ Mr. X

■ Six hours later. I require sleep. Unpleasant dreams beset my brief doze, and I tossed and turned for yet another hour. However.

The morning's edition of the *Edgerton Echo* informs all and sundry that the Chester Street fire resulted from an act of arson. Below the fold, two elegiac columns accompany a photographic representation of Crossing Guard Bremen's bloated visage. PLUS!—the mind reels—in devotion to the memory of Mr. My Mustache Is Bigger Than Yours, Carl Sandburg Elementary School has announced a $10,000 reward for information leading to the arrest and conviction of the arsonist.

I am on the verge of palpitations. If I were found incinerated, would anyone fork out $10,000 for the name of the incinerator? Besides that, Cassie Little would slit her mother's throat for a handful of nickels, much less $10,000.

Before the sun travels another five feet of sky, Frenchy receives his marching orders.

■ 83

■ Before Ashleigh's flight the next morning, I walked over to Merchants Hotel to pick up the satchel and tell her about the fire and Captain Mullan while we had breakfast.

"Laurie called earlier. I told her I managed to get some useful information. I didn't say how, and she didn't ask."

"Good."

Ashleigh jabbed her spoon into her granola. "Mullan checked you for a wire? It sounds like he's being investigated. Or is afraid he will be. I bet he's worried about what's going to come out if Hatch is indicted. About two days from now, these guys will be sweating bullets."

"Not Mullan," I said.

"You've been here no longer than I have, and you know that. You're an interesting man, Ned."

"You don't know the half of it."

"Ned?" She put down her spoon. "Why are you laughing?"

■ Toby Kraft came from behind his counter and wrapped his arms around me. "Heard the news this morning, couldn't believe my ears! You okay? What happened?"

I said that I had moved to the Brazen Head after his friend had evicted me. "I guess you knew her when her name was Hazel Jansky."

"We did some business together about a million years ago. The lady got in trouble, and I helped her out. I do favors for my friends." Toby was not even faintly uneasy. "What did she do, tell you her life story?"

"Part of it. I hope you had that building insured."

"Bet your ass. Do your aunts know you're all right?"

"I didn't tell them where I was, but I should call them anyhow," I said.

Toby looked at the satchel, and I asked him if he would keep it in his safe for a while. He caressed the soft leather. "Touch an item like that, you feel like J. P. Morgan."

He shoved the bag on top of the jumble of files and loose papers in his safe and grunted back onto his feet. "Helen chewed me out for telling you her old name. But you didn't get that here."

"I saw some old articles from the *Echo*," I said. "Toby, was that why you went to Greenhaven?"

"Sit down."

The same piles of papers flowed across the top of his desk; the same women in the same sad, blunt poses covered the walls. Toby folded his hands on his belly. "Want to know the truth of that deal? Certain people have problems with the adoption process. Other people, they don't want the babies God gave them. I can't defend the legality of what I did, but I do defend its morality."

"The morality of selling babies," I said.

"Adoption agencies don't take fees?"

"They don't abduct babies and tell their mothers they died."

"A child deserves a good home." Toby spread his arms. "Me, I am a guy who takes care of people. I took care of your grandmother, I took care of your mother, and I'm going to take care of you. The day I am dragged kicking and screaming from the face of the earth, and I hope at the time I am in the sack with a good-looking dame, you are going to hear from the greatest lawyer ever lived, Mr. C. Clayton Creech, and it will be your duty to get your ass back to Edgerton. No fooling around." His magnified eyes made sure I got the message. "Understood?"

"Understood," I said.

"I should give you his particulars." Toby snapped a business card out of his wallet.

> C. Clayton Creech, LLP
> Attorney at Law
> 7 Paddlewheel Road
> Edgerton, Illinois

A telephone number was printed on the lower left corner, and on the lower right, *Available at All Times*.

"Get into any kind of trouble around here, you call this guy first. Promise me?"

"Greatest lawyer that ever lived."

"You have no idea."

"On the day you die, he's going to read your will? What's the rush?"

"You let things slide, funny shit can happen. Know the basic principle?"

I shook my head.

"Take 'em by surprise," he said. I laughed out loud. "Listen, why not start working for me now? You got nothing else to do, and I can explain the whole job in fifteen minutes. The hours are eight A.M. to five-thirty P.M. A little time off for lunch. Ready?"

"Take 'em by surprise," I said. "I guess so, sure, but it can only be for a couple of days. Let me call Nettie first."

"Be my guest," Toby said.

Nettie wasted no time on an exchange of greetings. "I thought we were going to be seeing you, but all you do is call on the telephone."

"How did you know it was me?"

"I heard your ring. Come over for dinner around six. And if you still don't have a piece, the best thing is, get one from old Toby Kraft. You want a piece with no registration on it. The time comes when you have to use it, wipe it off, drop it, and walk away. You'll be cleaner than the Board of Health. May will be here, too, so show up on time."

Toby tilted back in his chair and clasped his hands behind his head. "The old warhorse had some words of advice?"

"You know what she's like," I said. "How about giving me a lesson in pawnbroking?"

"You're gonna be great at this. It's in your blood." He pushed himself away from the desk.

■ He explained the procedure for writing out the tickets and storing the goods. Cameras went on one set of shelves, watches on another, musical instruments in a display case, arranged in the order of the numbers on the ticket stubs. He put flatware in wrapped bundles lined up in drawers, stemware and china in cabinets, paintings against the wall, rugs and furniture at the side of the back room. Pledges were charged at 3 percent interest, weekly. I asked him about the money given for the pledges.

"Generally, you know by looking at the customer. It's in their eyes. You'll see. When you know what they hope they're gonna get, offer half, and they go away happy. Anything suspicious, like a guy with a shopping cart full of computer monitors, pick up the phone and tell him you're calling the cops. That shit catches up with you."

"What about guns?"

"Paperwork up the keester. The firearms are in a locked cabinet on the other side of the shelves. A guy wants a handgun, go to the cabinet, slide out a tray, put it in front of him. Prices are all tagged. When he makes his choice, he signs the forms here in the drawer. We send copies to the State Police, and he comes back in five days. Rifles, shotguns, no problem, he gets it that day. No assault weapons, on account of I'm not running an armory."

"Nettie thinks I should carry an unregistered gun," I said.

"She wants you to get into the stickup business?"

After I had explained my history with Joe Staggers and his friends, he gave me a long, careful look. "I got a couple pieces here for use in emergencies. Don't let anyone see it unless you have to, and never say where you got it."

Toby disappeared into the rear of the shop and came back with a small, black pistol and a holster that looked like a glove. "This here's a twenty-five-caliber Beretta automatic. I put a clip in for you. To chamber a round, pull back this slide. This is the safety—see the red dot? That means the safety is on, and you can't pull the trigger. Push it down with your thumb, you're ready to fire." He put the pistol in the holster. "Clip it to your belt in the small of your back, no one'll know it's there. Give it back the day you leave."

"This probably won't happen, but what if I have to use it?"

"Throw it in the river. A gun with no paper on it, you only use once." He watched me clip the holster to my belt and asked me to turn around. "Now forget you're carrying it. Don't keep on reaching around to fiddle with the thing."

We went into his office. "Your job is to stick behind the counter. If I'm out or in here by myself, bring in copies of the slips every couple of hours and record the transactions in the journal on my desk. You'll see how—put down the number, the customer's name, a description, and the amount. When you get to the amount, record it at half value. Then take the other journal out of my bottom left-hand drawer and write down everything all over again, but with the right numbers. At the end of the day, that one goes in the safe."

I laughed.

"You want to keep your head above water, you need an edge. Is this concept new to you?"

"Toby," I said, "I'm a Dunstan."

He stuck out his furry paw, and in the light of a sudden recognition I surrendered my hand to be tenderized. Toby Kraft's loyalty to my aunts, by extension to me, would forever overlook the petty cruelties they wished upon him, because Nettie and May represented his only surviving connection to the wife whose extraordinary talents had delighted him beyond measure.

■ **84**

■ I spent the rest of the day in the doze of the pawnshop. Separately, two men who looked as though they had never pawned anything in their lives came in and proceeded to the office. On his way to lunch, Toby introduced me to the second of these visitors, "Mr. Profitt," who brushed his manicured hand against mine and said, all in one word, "Goodameetchakiddonledimdownawright?"

"I hear you," I said.

Toby came back alone and handed me a brown bag containing

a tuna-fish sandwich, a packet of potato chips, and a Coca-Cola. He apologized for not giving me a lunch break and said I was doing a great job. To my surprise, the customers I dealt with during the day bore out his promise that I would know how much to offer for a pledge: by a flick of the eyes, a hesitation of speech, a wayward gesture, each had communicated the hoped-for amount. When I named half of the sum, they accepted on the spot.

At 5:00 P.M., Toby patted me on the back and told me I could get "spruced up" for the aunts. He gave me a set of keys. "Let yourself in a half hour early tomorrow, okay? We're going to rearrange the storage room. When you leave, lock up in front and show the CLOSED sign. I don't want no more customers today."

After I locked the gates, I went to an agency on Commercial Avenue, checked the boxes for all the insurance I could get, and rented a Ford Taurus painted the saturated green of a Spanish olive.

◼ 85

◼ The map in Hugh Coventry's old journal put the entrance to Buxton Place, where Edward Rinehart had occupied two cottages purchased under the names of characters from H. P. Lovecraft, near the top of Fairground Road, not far from the campus. I pulled into a parking space in front of a coffee shop. Two blocks ahead, Fairground Road came to an end at a deep swath of green intersected by paths leading to red brick, neo-Georgian buildings. I glanced backward and saw the bus stop where I had gotten off to visit Suki Teeter. Buxton Place lay ahead and on the other side of Fairground Road. I walked past the gilded window of an Irish bar called Brennan's, then stepped between the parked cars and jogged across the street.

Storefronts lined the sidewalk all the way to the intersection. Buxton Place had to be in the last block before the university. I went past an unbroken row of comic-book stores, clothing outlets, student restaurants, and candy shops. My memory had tricked me, and the cul-de-sac came into Fairground Road further south, maybe a block past Suki's corner.

I walked past the same storefronts I had seen on the way up. When I came parallel to Brennan's, I glanced through the window at an aproned bartender aiming a remote control at a television set I could not see. I glanced to my right and between a Canadian pancake house and a Middle Eastern restaurant saw a cobbled alley no wider than my rented car. If the alley had a name, the City of Edgerton had seen no reason to put up a sign. I stepped down onto the cobbles and peered into the gloom. Past the rear of the shops on either side, the alley widened out. I made out the double doors of old stables and, at the far end, two small cottages.

Thick padlocks hung from the doors of the old stables. Beneath their dusty windows, stenciled letters spelled out AL-BERTUS UNIVERSITY STORAGE FACILITY. Edward Rinehart's houses stood side by side, separated by a common wall. Each had two windows up and down and a fanlight over an arched doorway. Narrow chimneys pierced the slanting tiled roofs, and iron crestings ran along the gutters. They looked distorted, diminished, as if squeezed down from some larger, original size. The windows reflected my cupped hands and the dark, indistinct oval of my face. I hurried back into the sunlight.

With eight minutes in which to accomplish a fifteen-minute drive, I whirled into an illegal U-turn and sped south on Fairground Road. A traffic light flashed yellow, and I bumped the accelerator and shot through the intersection a moment before it turned red. Robert, who had abruptly appeared next to me in the passenger seat, applauded. "Dash! Verve!"

I almost drove into a parked car.

"Did I startle you? Please accept my apologies. I trust that our documents are now in Toby Kraft's safe."

"Go to hell. Yes, they're in Toby's safe."

"Do we have plans for the evening?"

"I'm having dinner with Nettie and May."

"Do you know, I have never enjoyed a meal in the company of our great-aunts?"

"You wouldn't like it," I said. "Their conversation tends to be repetitious."

"Let me relieve you of the tedium. I'll take your place."

"No."

"After the tedious dinner, were you thinking of driving to Ellendale?"

"Stay away from Laurie Hatch," I said.

"If you insist. For the time being, anyhow."

"Robert," I said, but I was talking to an empty seat.

■ 86

■ From her station in the window, Aunt Joy pointed at Nettie's house, then herself, telling me that I was to come over after dinner. I nodded. Joy and I had a lot to talk about.

The aunts smiled up from the sofa as I came into the living room. Clark granted me the indulgent sneer of a man fresh from an appearance at the Speedway Lounge. He was arrayed in pearl-gray trousers, the jacket of a purple suit, and a wide necktie with yellow polka dots on a red background. "I guess you got a vehicle now."

"Just a rental," I said. I kissed my aunts, and May handed me a brown paper bag.

"I hope I got the sizes right."

In the bag were two three-packs of Calvin Klein briefs, size 34, and six pairs of black over-the-calf wool socks, size 10–12. After the aunts had divided up the loot from the ICU, I had jokingly asked May to get me underwear and socks, and she had taken me at my word. "The sizes are perfect," I said. "I don't really approve of this, but thanks, Aunt May. I can use them."

"Is that blazer your only coat, Neddie? I can get you a new one from Lyall's. They have some beautiful coats in their men's department."

"No, no," I said hurriedly, "I have all the jackets I need."

"Have any this color?" Clark asked, almost belligerently.

"No, but it's very pretty."

"What would you call this particular color?"

"Purple?"

"I hate to see a young man make a fool of himself."

"Midnight purple?"

"The true name for this shade is aubergine. Now you don't have to walk around in ignorance."

"Good," I said. "I've been walking around in ignorance most of my life."

Nettie said, "I think we had better get into the kitchen. Do you still like fried chicken, Ned?"

"Do I ever."

The table had been set with bowls of mashed potatoes and string beans and a pitcher of iced tea. Nettie peeled aluminum foil off the top of a platter of fried chicken. May hobbled up to distribute the chicken onto our plates. Uncle Clark lowered himself into a chair, and I poured him a glass of iced tea. "How's your friend Cassie?"

He took in just enough liquid to extinguish a match. "The girl didn't show up for work today. Bruce McMicken was rough around the edges."

May settled into the chair across from me while Nettie brought out gravy and biscuits. I poured iced tea into the other three glasses. Nettie thanked me, formally. In silence, we helped ourselves to the potatoes and beans.

"This is a wonderful dinner, Aunt Nettie," I said.

"When you were a child, you were fond of fried chicken."

"Nobody makes it better than you," I said.

Silence descended again. My remark about being raised in ignorance had spoiled the fun.

Nettie, for whom even a pointed silence was an unendurable challenge, said, "What have you been doing all this time? Touring the town in your new car?"

"Or playing cards?" May asked. "Mountry trash is on the lookout for you. And one of them is dead. That is no great loss to the world."

Nettie sent me one of her thousand-pound glances. "I guess the police didn't give you much trouble." She paused. "Unless you're not saying."

"They let me go right away," I said. "It's a strange thing, but there's a man in town who looks a lot like me."

"So that's your story," Clark said, maneuvering a tiny portion of mashed potato into the gravy.

"It's not a story," I said. "Yesterday, when I was coming out of

City Hall, he was standing at the far end of Town Square. I tried to follow him, but he got away."

Clark fixed me with a disapproving glare. "City Hall gets locked up on Sundays. What business would you have there, anyhow?"

"A friend of Laurie Hatch's volunteers at City Hall on the weekends. He's been giving me some help."

"Mrs. Hatch introduces you to her friends?" Nettie asked.

I explained about meeting Laurie at Le Madrigal. "I wanted to get some information about Edward Rinehart, and she introduced me to Hugh Coventry, her friend who helps out at City Hall."

"Hugh Coventry?" Nettie asked. "He's the man who lost our pictures. If Mrs. Hatch is such a good friend of yours, she could help us get them back."

"There's no need to trouble Mrs. Hatch with our affairs."

"You already involved Mrs. Hatch in our personal affairs," Nettie said.

"In mine, yes," I said. "If it makes you feel better, I didn't learn much about Rinehart at City Hall. He bought two little alleyway houses in College Park. And he was a criminal. Supposedly, he died in prison."

"Then stop rooting in the dirt," Nettie said.

Rooting in the dirt. I saw myself kneeling on the carpet of grass behind Howard Dunstan's ruined house—I remembered falling through a trap door and hearing a theatrical phantom say, *Once your father had been created, I decided to amuse myself by driving him mad. . . . Perhaps you will destroy him instead. The outcome of the game no longer matters to me.*

Sudden, stupendous understanding took my breath away.

All three of them were looking at me as if they had seen my understanding come into being, but they really had seen no more than the expression on my face at the moment of comprehension. Howard had told me what I most needed to know. Telling me what I needed to know helped to keep him amused.

"But Edward Rinehart didn't die at Greenhaven," I said. "He's living in Edgerton. From what I hear, he sounds a lot like a Dunstan."

Nettie's chin sank to her chest, and May found a need to gaze at the stove. Clark dissected a string bean.

"Never in all my life," Nettie finally said.

"A lot of things about our family were hidden from me."

Nettie glared. "You've been listening to gossip."

"If you wanted me to think that the Dunstans were a normal family, you should have kept me away from Aunt Joy," I said.

"Joy lives in a world of her own," Nettie said. "Put it out of your mind."

"You want me to forget the way she waggled a finger at Uncle Clarence and floated him through the air?"

"Joy was never a happy person like you and me, Nettie," May said. "She blamed Daddy for her troubles."

"We're not talking about her troubles," Nettie growled. "We're talking about what she *did*."

"We're talking about the Dunstans," I said. "Aunt Nettie, you're not all that different from Joy, are you?"

She cast me another thunder-and-lightning glare. "I'm a *Dunstan*, if that's what you mean. Would you like to see proof of that?"

Before I could answer, Nettie tucked her hands into her armpits and frowned at the table. The pitcher of tea rose up and wafted down the table to refill my glass. It coasted to May, who said, "No, thank you, I've had enough." The pitcher landed with a tinkling of ice cubes.

Nettie turned her head to Clark. An alarmed look crossed his face. "No! I don't—"

He ascended three feet above his chair and sailed toward the stove like a man on a magic carpet. "Put me down, Nettie!"

She spun him around and brought him back to his chair. Clark put his hands on his chest and took a couple of noisy breaths. "You know I don't like it when you do that."

"You married me," Nettie said.

"*I* like it," May chirped. "I *always* liked it."

Nettie wiped her forehead and stared at her sister. Giggling, May shot out of her chair, made a circuit of the table, and came to rest.

Nettie looked angrily at me. "You want some, too?"

What came out of my mouth was "Yes."

She beetled her brows, gazing not so much at me as at my position in the room. A drop of sweat rolled out of her hairline. The tingle that predicted my "attacks" bloomed in my chest. I felt my being grasped up and held within a firmly accommodating restraint precisely like Mr. X's confinement. With the same sense of powerlessness before an irresistible pressure, I lifted off my chair. A great wall of wind pushed me into the living room. The wind shifted on its axis, hurtled me back into the kitchen, and tumbled me head over heels a moment before I struck the wall. A shout of glee burst from my throat. I floated to the table and saw **Nettie gazing at nothing, her eyebrows contracted and her face damp with sweat. I moved over my chair, swayed right-left, then left-right, and, like a helicopter, settled back on earth.**

"You like that more than I do," Clark said.

"Ned's a *Dunstan*." Nettie wiped her face with a napkin. "You get old, your batteries run down."

"Nettie," I said, "I drove out to your old house yesterday. Something happened to me there. I can't explain it, but I can tell you what it was. I got dizzy, and pretty soon I was standing in a room with a stuffed fox next to a brass clock on the mantelpiece."

My eyes on Nettie, I only dimly saw May lean forward and clasp her hands before her chest. Nettie touched the napkin to her temple.

"Your father was in that room," I said. "He was wearing a velvet smoking jacket, and he had a cigar in one hand."

"How did our father look?" May asked me.

"Tired. But like he was acting, too."

"I don't recognize that description," May said. "My father was all too energetic."

"I recognize it," Nettie said. "Joy would, too."

"He spoke to me," I said.

"Joy used to say Daddy talked to her, out at our old house." May looked warmly at me. "It seems your Dunstan share came out strong late in life, to make up for lost time."

"What did he say when he spoke to you?" Nettie demanded.

"That he created my father. I think his son called himself Edward Rinehart when he came back to Edgerton from wherever he was in the meantime. What I'm wondering is, who was his mother?"

"You're looking for a woman who might have fooled around with Howard?" Clark said. "There is no shortage of candidates."

"Our mother used to say, some of those fine ladies are not what they pretend to be," May said. "Daddy told her, None of them are."

"Fine ladies," I said.

"Those people sent their sons to boarding schools," Nettie said. "To make the right connections. And you know, May, we seldom got into town when we were little girls. Out tutors came to us."

"There were many things our daddy did not wish us to encounter."

I said, "He didn't protect you from whatever made you blow out windshields and power lines up and down Wagon Road."

May stiffened in her chair. "I got mad. That's all that happened. Our father was very angry, but I couldn't help what I did, I just *did* it."

"You saw two girls making fun of you?"

"Mainly, I remember Daddy shouting at me in his big, loud voice. I cried all the way home."

"Let's talk about something pleasant, for a change," Nettie said. "Our grandnephew's birthday is the day after our niece's funeral. Would you like to have a party on your birthday, Ned? I could make a sweet-potato pie."

"That's very generous," I said. "But you know what happens on my birthdays. I wouldn't want to spoil all the fun."

"Your fits?" May asked. "We've seen *that* before."

Nettie said, "We'll have the party early in the day. If you feel your trouble coming on, go to your mother's old room until it passes. You know how to handle it after all this time, don't you?"

"I guess I do," I said. "Sure, let's celebrate everything we can."

■ I escorted May down the steps. "Is that your car, Neddie? Did it cost a lot of money?"

"It's a rental," I said.

"Little thing like that wouldn't be hard to appropriate." Sudden inspiration brought her to a halt. She turned to me with a brilliant smile. "Would you like a new car for your birthday?"

"No, thank you, Aunt May. It's too hard to find a parking space in New York."

"A parking space is something that cannot be stolen," she said. "I'll get you something else. But seeing that car . . ." She shook her head. "You mentioned Wagon Road? Daddy was *so* mad at me, that day. I knew why, too. He was mad because I was mad. At *him*."

Joy raised a silhouetted hand, and I waved back. May saw

nothing but Wagon Road. "You mentioned those girls—you know, I remember them! They were *laughing* at us. I wanted to die. So I turned my head, pretending I was too proud to notice, and . . ." She shook her head. "The upshot was, I did something I didn't know I *could* do! I had as much Dunstan in me as my sisters, no matter what they thought. You never saw such a hubbub! Glass exploding all over everywhere, wires falling, the poor horses so frightened. And that was *me*! Scared me worse than Daddy's yelling."

We reached the other side of the street and moved toward her house. "The girls were laughing at you, and you turned away. That was when you got angry. It wasn't the girls, was it? You saw something else."

"A little girl has eyes, too, that's all I can say." She tightened her grip on my arm, and we went up the steps to her porch.

"What was it? What did you see?"

May released my arm and opened her door. "Oh, Neddie, you don't know anything at all."

■ **87**

■ Joy's hunched figure toiled down a lightless tunnel and through the entrance to a cave. As the living room took shape around me, the stench increased. Clarence had been teleported elsewhere.

"I want to talk to you! Would you like a glass of sherry?"

"Thank you. Where is Clarence?"

"He's sleeping in the closet." Joy moved back and regarded me, her eyes gleaming. "You saw Daddy, didn't you? He told me you would. I bet my sisters are so jealous they could spit. *They* could never see him. Nettie and May think they know everything, but they don't, not by a long shot." She put the tips of her fingers to her mouth, almost dancing in her glee. She waved me toward a chair. "I'll be back in a second."

Faint rustles and thuds came from another region of the house. Clarence had awakened, I thought, and he objected to the closet. Joy returned with two glasses the size of thimbles. I took one of them and said, "Maybe Clarence wants to be let out."

"He's sound asleep. That noise is the wind in the attic." She perched on the other chair and tilted the contents of the thimble into her mouth. I did the same. The sherry, which was not sherry, burned down my throat like kerosene.

"Homemade," Joy said. "According to my bad, mad daddy's recipe. I don't have but a little bit left, but I wanted you to have some."

"The ambrosia of the Dunstans," I said. "I guess you've seen him, too."

"So what did my sisters say? That I made it all up? I didn't, though. My daddy, Howard Dunstan, stood right in front of me, same as he did with you. Wasn't he *funny*? Wasn't he all *impressive* and *unhappy*?"

"He didn't seem to think he had any reason to go on living," I said.

"According to Daddy, we were washed up a long time ago. He appeared to me because I was a true Dunstan, like him, but he didn't enjoy the condition. He wanted us all to go away."

"He told you I would see him, too?"

"Because you were a *vrai* Dunstan, like me. He didn't like you, though. Daddy didn't like anybody, especially Dunstans. He didn't even like his daughters, because they reminded him of his futility. That is the conclusion I have come to."

"Aunt Joy," I said, "how could you and I talk to your father? It wasn't like seeing a ghost, it was like being there with him."

"My daddy couldn't be a *ghost*," Joy said, amused. "Someone like that could never be an ordinary old *fantôme*. Time made that happen."

"Time?"

"It's all around us. You can use time, if you're able. I don't see why you're so *stupide* about it. According to my daddy, you keep on bothering him over and over. That's what he *said*."

"I don't understand," I said. "What do you mean, use it?"

"You saw my daddy, didn't you? You were in his study, and he was alive, he had to be alive, because he could talk to you."

I realized what she meant. "Oh."

"You went into his time, that's all," Joy said. *"C'est simple."*

I stared at her for a moment, trying to reconcile the memory of what I had experienced with my instinct to deny Joy's version of the simple.

"I had this feeling of . . ."

"Of what?" Her voice had an impatient edge.

"Falling."

"Well, of course. *C'est normal.* I don't know why I should have to *explain* it to you. When you go *backwards*, it feels like you're *falling.* How else could it feel? I hope you know how lucky you are. Hardly anybody can ever do that. Some can do it once but never again. Queenie couldn't, and Nettie can't do it, and for sure *May* never could. There was Daddy, and then me, when I had the strength, and now there's you. You know what Daddy used to say?"

I shook my head.

"He used to say he *ate* time. He didn't like it, but he ate it anyhow, because an ability like that has a reason behind it, and if you have the ability, you have to find the reason. He said once he saw Omar and Sylvan Dunstan robbing dead soldiers on a battlefield, and he thought maybe that was the reason he had the ability."

"What's the reason you had it?"

"Maybe so Howard Dunstan could make me unhappy. Maybe so I could talk to you. I hope your reason is better than mine."

"Howard made your mother unhappy," I said.

"Yes." Joy nodded. "In a great many ways."

"He had other women."

"Didn't he, though! Up and down, and hither and yon, and there's the car, I'll be going, don't wait up."

"Did he have children by any of his other women?"

She looked at me with a show of interest. "Would you care to hear a funny story?"

I nodded.

"One day, I finished my lesson with our French tutor, which I had alone because I was gifted in French, and Queenie and Nettie, who were not, came in for their lesson. May was sick in bed. She wouldn't *eat,* you see, my sister May hardly ate a speck all through her childhood. I was all alone with nothing to do. Well, I got up the courage to slip into my father's study, which was a room I loved but was not supposed to enter *sans permission.* Can you guess what especially fascinated me in that room?"

"The fox," I said.

Joy clapped her hands. "I loved that fox! I thought if I looked at him long enough, old Reynard would forget I was there and finish that step he was taking. I wanted to see him move *une fois seulement.* I was kneeling in front of the fireplace, and the telephone rang. Oh! I nearly fainted. Daddy came walking to the study door, boom, boom, boom. I ran around the back of his couch. In he marched, boom, boom. Slammed the door. I saw the bottom of his legs going toward his desk. He picked up the receiver and did not speak for quite a while. Then it was 'Ellie. Please calm down.' I *knew* he was talking to *une autre femme.* He said, 'All will be well. He will think it's his.' When he hung up, he said, 'An excess of cannon smoke.' Then he walked out, not stamping at all."

"You never knew who Ellie was?"

"We never met any Ellies," Joy said. "We never met anybody." She peered at the dark hallway. "I should be attending to my duties." Joy showed me out with more dispatch than I would have thought her capable.

■ **88**

■ A metal brick pushed into the small of my back when I got behind the wheel. I unclipped the holster and put Toby's pistol on the passenger seat. It was about 9:30 on a Monday night in June. The lamps cast yellow circles like spotlights on the sidewalk. Cherry Street looked improbably beautiful, and the world seemed motionless. All I had to do was get to the Brazen Head and catch up on my sleep. This schedule felt almost sinfully luxurious. I decided to drive along the streets I had walked after my first visit with Joy, to erase the impressions made when I had seen them through a veil of grief and rage.

I turned left at the end of the block, and a pair of headlights sped toward me from down the street. The cab of a pickup flew past in a gray blur. I looked in my rearview mirror and saw the truck swerve into Cherry Street.

I took the next right and saw green light shining above the intersection of Pine Street and Cordwainer Avenue, three blocks ahead. I didn't care if I got there before it changed; I was enjoying the journey. Frame houses like Nettie's rolled past my windows. As I coasted down another block, the light stayed green, and I nudged the foot pedal. A white dazzle of light burst in my mirror. I looked up and saw, half a block away, the gray pickup speeding toward me with its beams on high.

My stomach jumped into my throat. Mountry had come again to Cherry Street. I flattened the accelerator. The pickup's lights doubled in size while my little car swam forward. With a clank that shook the chassis like a wet dog, it dropped into a lower gear and shot ahead.

The light changed to yellow when I was about thirty feet from the intersection. It was still on yellow as I blasted my horn and barreled out into Cordwainer Avenue. In my rearview mirror, the headlights of the pickup kept coming.

On the far side of the median, two cars jolted to a halt a moment before I flew past them. In the mirror, I saw the pickup run the red light. It slammed into an oncoming car and sent it skidding across the road. The dazzle in my mirror wobbled and swung back.

Ahead lay the chain-link fences and one-story brick buildings of Pine Street. I glanced into the mirror and saw the pickup fly out of the intersection.

Looking for a way out, I bent toward the windshield. A massive figure was standing under a street lamp. The warrior in the red and green dashiki whom I had encountered on the day my mother died turned his head to watch me flash by.

The dazzle filled the rearview mirror. I slammed the brake pedal. The Taurus's back end spun to the right, and I cranked the wheel the same way. The landscape revolved around me. The pistol sailed off the passenger seat. When the car stopped moving, I was looking into the lights of the pickup. I released the brake and stamped on the accelerator. The car jolted forward, shuddered, stalled. I smelled burning rubber and frying circuits. The dashboard lights went off.

The doors of the pickup opened on a burst of hoarse laughter. Joe Staggers jumped out of the cab. A heavyset man lumbered toward me from the other side of the truck. He was carrying a baseball bat. Staggers hitched up his belt. "Looks like Mr. Dunstan's car quit on him. Isn't that a damn shame?"

His friend laughed, *yuk, yuk, yuk.*

I turned the key, and the Taurus muttered. Joe Staggers slapped its hood. "Hey, don't you want to talk to us?"

Yuk, yuk, yuk.

I groped under the dash without touching anything but the floor mat.

Joe Staggers's face filled the window like a Halloween pumpkin. "Coming out to play?" He reached for the door handle.

I was going to have to fight two men. No matter how well I fought, they were going to kill me. I was minutes from a miserable, painful death. Suddenly, Aunt Joy's voice spoke to me with absolute clarity. *He used to say he* ate *time.*

You can use time, if you're able.

My stomach knotted. I closed my eyes and dropped into darkness.

When I opened my eyes again, I knew that I had eaten time. I was still in the car. Staggers had disappeared. The lights of his pickup were gone. Nothing around me resembled the Pine Street I had left. Tar-paper shacks grew from a muddy field ending at a wooden fence with a NO TRESPASSING sign. Far back from the road, flames from a trash barrel in front of a ramshackle wooden structure illuminated a dozen men in clothing like layers of dried mud. It could have been a photograph from the Depression. My head cleared enough for me to realize that it *was* the Depression. I had fallen through nearly sixty years.

At first cautiously, then with a kind of surly boldness, the men moved toward me. Suspicion and hostility came from them like an odor.

I turned the key. The ignition growled.

One of them shouted, "You spyin' on us, Fancy Dan? What's that you're drivin'?"

Uncertain, intimidated, they gathered at the side of the road. The man who had shouted drew a knife from his pocket and stepped forward. The others shuffled along behind him.

I tried to remember what I had done a moment before. Footsteps plodded toward me. I thought of Joe Staggers; I remembered walking over a grass carpet into the wreckage on New Providence Road. For the first time, I grasped the means I had used twice before. I wish I could describe it, but it would be like trying to explain a color. The bolt once more passed through my forehead. I ate time, although it felt as though I were the one being eaten.

Headlights streamed through the darkness, and someone yelped. I swallowed vomit.

Staggers was beside his pickup, his brutal face turned to look over his shoulder. Four feet away, Yuk Yuk stared at me in utter terror.

"Get in the truck, Shorty," Staggers ordered. Yuk Yuk let go of the bat and blundered around the front of the truck.

I twisted the key. The dash lights glowed, and the engine came to life.

■ 89

■ Numbly, I went through the usual night-time rituals and got into bed. I would never understand what was happening to me. All the familiar definitions had disappeared. I would never be able to go back to writing computer programs, because I was no longer the person who had done that. I lost myself in a mystery novel until I turned off the light.

At 6:00 A.M., I woke damp with sweat and forced myself out of bed, showered, and pulled on a blue polo shirt and my last pair of fresh jeans. I picked up the Beretta. Six-thirty A.M. was a ridiculous hour to wear a pistol. I put it down again. Joe Staggers had been humiliated, and he was going to come after me again, but not in the daytime. I stashed the gun behind the minibar and went to a diner for scrambled eggs and coffee.

On my way to the pawnshop, I bought a copy of the *Echo* at a newsstand. The mayor of Edgerton had introduced his good friend Stewart Hatch to a gathering of the local press. The mayor's good friend had announced the construction of an arts center and convention facility on the banks of the Mississippi immediately north of St. Ann's Community Hospital, at the cost of no more than half of the hospital's extensive parking space.

A smaller headline at the bottom of the front page reported MURDER IN OLD TOWN. Cassandra Little, thirty-two, a bartender at the Speedway Lounge, had been brutally slain in her Low Street apartment. When she failed to come to work, the Speedway's manager, Bruce McMicken, had gone to Little's residence and discovered her body. A Police Department source speculated that Ms. Little had surprised a burglar.

On Chester Street, charred beams and incinerated wreckage had settled into the basement of the rooming house. The walls on either side looked like burnt toast.

I turned into Lanyard Street. Toby was probably still in bed. I let myself in and spent about twenty minutes straightening the shelves and sweeping the floor. Then I arranged the papers on the counter and discovered two slips tucked under a paperweight. I took them toward the office and saw light shining through the crack at the bottom of the door.

"I wondered where you were," I said, and went in. Toby Kraft looked at me moodily from behind his desk. "Didn't you . . ." My question vaporized.

From the neck down, a sheet of blood painted his chest. The white filaments drifting across the top of his head made his hair look like a wig. His eyes were colored stones, and his cottage-cheese face looked grumpy. For a moment, I thought Toby was going to jump up and laugh at my shock. I took a step forward and saw the gash in his neck. Abruptly, the smell of blood bloomed in the air.

Robert?

I wanted to walk out and keep traveling until I got somewhere only the waiters and street vendors spoke English. Then I went back into the shop and called the police.

The moment I hung up, I remembered the lawyer with the funny name and dug his card out of my wallet.

C. Clayton Creech said, "Murdered? How?"

"Someone cut his throat."

"Is the safe closed?"

"Yes."

"Have you called the police?"

"Yes."

"Do two things right now. Take the ledger out of his bottom desk drawer and hide it in the storeroom. When you're done, I'll tell you the second."

His dry, unemphatic voice was without any resonance. I thought this was not the first time C. Clayton Creech had been told of the murder of a client. I tried not to look at Toby's body when I took the ledger out of the drawer, and after I wedged it between two boxes in the storeroom, I returned to the telephone.

"We are entering into an agreement, Mr. Dunstan. For the sum of one dollar, I have been hired as your legal representative. I'll be there in ten minutes."

"I don't need a legal representative," I said.

"You will. In accordance with Mr. Kraft's wishes, I want to meet you and the other surviving members of his late wife's family at two o'clock this afternoon. At that time, you will understand why I prefer not to speak of this matter in the presence of the police. Keep your trap shut until I get there."

I put down the receiver and waited for Lieutenant Rowley.

■ **90**

■ A police car followed by a dark blue sedan came whooping down Lanyard Street and pulled up in front of the shop. Two men in uniforms left the squad car and watched Rowley climb out of the sedan. He charged up to the door, saw me coming, and banged his fist against the glass. Rowley kept on banging until I opened up.

"What the hell are you doing here, Dunstan?"

"I was helping out in the shop. This is my second day."

"You found the body?"

"You know I did. I gave my name when I called headquarters."

Rowley pointed at one of the cops. "Nelson, get the preliminaries from Mr. Dunstan and take him to headquarters. Where's the body?"

"Back there," I said.

Rowley stormed into the office. Toby seemed to be looking at me, and I had the crazy impulse to go in and straighten out his hair. Two more police cars swung in front of the shop. Captain

Mullan and a detective I had not seen before got out of the second one.

Mullan gave me an arctic glance before going into the office. The detective followed him. I heard Mullan say, "You know, I don't think I really believe this shit."

Two more squad cars and an ambulance screeched up in front of the building. Suddenly, the shop was filled with policemen. Officer Nelson flipped to a clean page of his notebook.

Mullan emerged from the office with Rowley treading on his heels. When Rowley saw the other detective, his jaw snapped shut.

"I thought this was me," said the detective.

"What's Oster doing here?"

Mullan's expression was completely disingenuous. "Don't you have the Little case?"

"You know I do."

"Then go back to headquarters, Lieutenant. Detective Oster's getting this one."

All the policemen in the shop were staring at Rowley. "Fine," he said. A trace of red came into his cheeks. "But Dunstan's already—"

"Already what, Lieutenant?"

Every head in the room turned to a gaunt, pale man in a gray suit who seemed to have appeared at my side through some magical agency, as if from a burst of smoke. He had thin, colorless hair, a narrow, deeply lined face, wire-rimmed spectacles, and a mouth like a mail slot. I recognized his flat, dry voice. "Please, Lieutenant, go on."

"Just what we need," Rowley said. "C. Clayton Creech."

Creech was impervious to Rowley's contempt. He would be impervious to most things. Far past shock or surprise, Creech existed in a state of neutral readiness for whatever might come his way. You could not show him anything he had not already witnessed so often that it was incapable of provoking anything but ironic recognition. He was so far beyond conventional human responses that he might as well have been from another planet. Under the circumstances, his presence made me feel more relaxed than I would have thought possible.

"This is your lawyer?" Mullan asked.

"He is."

Rowley made a disgusted noise and pushed his way through

the crowd of uniformed policemen. Officer Nelson looked un-
certainly at Oster and said, "I was about to question him."

"Do that," Oster said.

As if inquiring about the score of a minor-league baseball
game in a distant city, Creech asked, "Is my client to be taken to
headquarters?"

"Your client will be invited to assist us in our investigation."
Mullan turned wearily to me. "Would you be willing to make out
a statement at Police Headquarters?"

Without moving a muscle, Creech encouraged assent.

"Of course," I said.

"I shall be present during the questioning," Creech said. "If
my client wishes."

"I'd like Mr. Creech to be present," I said.

A tired-looking man with mushroom-colored skin came in
and pronounced Toby dead. The ambulance attendants carried
out what looked like a giant loaf of bread hidden under a sheet.

Mullan said, "The counselor won't mind if I tell you we found
out who was responsible for last night's fire."

Creech's motionless figure somehow displayed mild curiosity.

"Carl Sandburg Elementary put up a ten-thousand-dollar reward for information leading to an arrest."

"Handsome gesture," Creech said.

Mullan smiled. "Late yesterday afternoon, your old friend
Frenchy La Chapelle and a miscreant called To Me From Me Blunt
decided to unwind over a bottle of bourbon and a crack pipe."

"Toomey Frommey?" I asked.

"*To* Me, *From* Me," Mullan said. "Six years ago, this genius
went to the post office to pick up a suitcase full of grass from
Humboldt County, California. He used his own name and return
address on the shipping label. Luckily for him, he was one of Mr.
Creech's clients, and he walked."

"Lamentable negligence on the part of the arresting officers,"
Creech said.

"After they got high, Frenchy started bragging about the
money he got for torching a building on Chester Street. To Me
From Me decided that his obligations as a citizen outweighed his
loyalty to a friend. We brought Frenchy in and charged him, and
he was put in a cell. Just before four o'clock this morning, a
strange thing happened to Mr. La Chapelle."

My scalp tingled.

"Frenchy had nothing on him sharper than his fingernails, but he figured out a way to cut his throat. He looked a lot like Toby back there."

"Oh," I said.

"You mentioned Clothhead Spelvin the other day," Mullan said. "Might you be able to shed a little light here?"

C. Clayton Creech's indifferent gaze at the pawnshop counter recommended silence.

"I wish I could," I said.

Mullan rocked on his heels. "Nelson, take Mr. Dunstan to headquarters. You can give Mr. Creech a ride, too."

"Thank you, Captain, but I believe I will take the opportunity to enjoy the fresh air." Creech interrogated me with a glance directed at the ceiling. I looked over his shoulder in the direction of the storeroom and the hidden ledger.

Twenty minutes later, C. Clayton Creech padded into the interrogation room and communicated by his usual mysterious means that all was well. The stolid Nelson opened his notebook and began asking questions. Creech folded into the chair to my left and stayed there for the next three hours. Now and then he uttered a gentle reproof to whoever was grilling me at the moment. He seemed about as involved in the procedure as a lizard stretched out on a warm rock. Just before 12:30 P.M., the Edgerton Police Department released me with instructions to keep in touch.

Creech and I went past the desk sergeant, who conspicuously ignored him. "All is copacetic," Creech said. When we came to the top of the steps down to Grace Street and Town Square, Creech said, "My office at two o'clock?"

"I'll be there," I said, and Creech was gone.

■ 91

■ In an anteroom lined with hunting prints, a woman with the face of a hanging judge looked at me from behind a desk the size of a coffin. "We are Mr. Dunstan?"

"We are," I said.

She picked up a stenographer's notebook and a pen and opened the door to the inner office.

Seated in wooden chairs with high, narrow backs, Clark, Nettie, and May turned their heads when I entered. Hats trimmed with black lace perched on top of the aunts' white hair. A scuffed leather couch stood in front of a wall of law books, and brown threads showed here and there through the pattern of the faded Oriental rug. The high windows looking onto the bright park at Creech's back admitted a weak light that died as soon as it entered. In the tenebrous gloom, the lawyer was a faceless outline.

Creech took a paper from a folder on his desk and positioned it in front of him. He placed a fountain pen on top of the paper. "Before you get seated, Mr. Dunstan, please sign this agreement formalizing our relationship in the terms we discussed this morning and give me the sum of one dollar in fulfillment of its terms." To the others, he said, "Mr. Dunstan is merely signing an authorization engaging me in the capacity of legal counsel. This authorization is necessitated by his discovery of the deceased's body and has no bearing on the matter before us now."

I signed the one-paragraph statement and unfolded a dollar bill onto the paper. The dollar disappeared before he put the paper in a drawer, but I never saw him touch it. I went past the chairs and sat on the near end of the leather couch. The secretary perched at the other end. Creech said, "Miss Wick will be taking notes during this conference."

She opened the notebook and held the nib of her pen over an empty page.

"Mr. Dunstan, I have informed your great-aunts and great-uncle of this morning's events on Lanyard Street. I offer my heartfelt condolences. I knew Mr. Kraft only in my capacity as his legal adviser, but I filled that capacity for many years, and Mr. Kraft's personality made a great impression on me."

"Scoundrels will do that," Nettie said. "But I can't say that Toby didn't have his good points. He visited our niece on her deathbed."

"My client had a great fondness for his stepdaughter," Creech said. "However, now that Mr. Dunstan has joined us, we may turn to the business at hand. It was my client's instruction that the contents of his last will and testament be made known in timely fashion upon the occasion of his death, if possible within twenty-four hours of that event, and be it noted that we have assembled in observation of that instruction."

"So noted," said Miss Wick.

"Be it further noted that the parties desired by my client to be present at the reading of said last will and testament are assembled, with the exceptions of Mrs. Joy Dunstan Crothers, who is absent of her own volition, and Mr. Clarence Aaron Crothers, who is absent by reason of ill health."

"So noted," said Miss Wick.

Creech looked up from the folder before him. "My client also instructed that his mortal remains be given a swift burial. Of course, Mr. Kraft did not anticipate that his demise should be the result of homicide. The procedures of the County Coroner's Office and our Police Department may render it impossible to observe the letter of his instructions. Therefore, let it be noted that the spirit of the instructions shall be honored and the aforesaid remains given burial within twenty-four hours of release to the Spaulding Heavenly Rest Funeral Home."

"So noted."

Mr. Creech appeared almost to smile at his audience, although the dim light and the character of his face made it difficult to tell. "I am instructed to inform those present of several matters. My client provided for all arrangements necessary to the disposition of his remains, including the purchases of coffin, headstone with inscription, and burial plot adjacent to that of his late wife. Furthermore, he desired no memorial or funerary service in a house of worship, whether Protestant, Catholic, Jewish, or any other faith or creed. Said burial is to be conducted without benefit of clergy, and may be attended by any persons who wish to be present. My client stipulated that any mourners in attendance shall be free to speak in a spontaneous fashion. Let it be noted that these instructions have been read and understood."

"So noted," said Miss Wick.

"Did I hear the word 'inscription'?" Clark asked.

"Let me find the exact wording." Creech turned a few pages. "The inscription on my client's headstone is to read as follows: first line, TOBIAS KRAFT, in capital letters; second line, the dates of his birth and death; third line, TRUST IN THE UNEXPECTED, in smaller capital letters, followed by an italicized attribution to Emily Dickinson."

" 'Trust in the unexpected'?" Clark said. "What the devil is that supposed to mean?"

"I gather that my client found it a helpful sentiment." Creech turned the page and looked back up. "We have now reached the reading of Mr. Kraft's last will and testament. May I assume that the parties assembled here are willing to forgo a reading of the introductory paragraphs and move directly to section C, his bequests?"

Nettie leaned over to whisper to May, and Creech said, "I assure you that nothing relevant to your concerns shall be neglected by moving to section C. In any case, copies of the entire document will be distributed at the conclusion of this meeting."

"Skip the mumbo jumbo," Nettie said.

"Be it noted that it has been agreed to begin the reading of the will at section C, Bequests."

Miss Wick uttered her echo.

Creech began reading in his flat, emotionless voice. "I, Tobias Kraft, therefore direct that upon the occasion of my death the entire contents of my estate be distributed in the following manner. (1) The sum of five thousand dollars is to be given anonymously to the Red Cross. (2) The sum of five thousand dollars is to be given anonymously to the United States Holocaust Memorial Museum, located in Washington, D.C. (3) All clothing in my possession at the time of my demise is to be donated to Goodwill Industries. (4) The remainder of my estate, including all funds in checking accounts, money market accounts, stocks and bonds, mutual funds, and real estate held either by me personally or by the legal entity T.K. Holding Corporation, I hereby bequeath to Valerie Dunstan, known as Star Dunstan. Should Valerie Dunstan predecease me, the bequest shall be made to her son, Ned Dunstan."

He looked up from the will. "Let it be noted that Mr. Tobias Kraft's bequests have been read and understood."

Nettie drowned out Miss Wick's response. "Either you left something out, or I didn't hear you right."

"Let me explain it clearly, then, so that there will no misunderstandings. The terms of my client's last will and testament donate ten thousand dollars to charitable causes. His clothing goes to Goodwill. The majority of his estate has been inherited by the young man seated on the couch behind you."

In varying degrees of shock, they swiveled their heads and gaped at me.

Clark looked back at Creech. "What kind of estate are we talking about here?"

"If you will give me a moment . . ." He took another bundle of papers from the folder, scanned the top page, put it aside, and glanced at the second. "In liquid funds, the estate consists of five hundred and twenty-five thousand, four hundred and twenty dollars, not counting interest earned since the last statements. Mr. Kraft also owned the building in which he resided and conducted his business, as well as one multiresidential unit on Chester Street and two commercial properties in downtown Edgerton. Their accumulated value would be approximately eight hundred thousand dollars, taking into account the insurance settlement due on the property recently destroyed by arson."

Nettie and May sat rooted to their chairs.

"In addition," Creech said, turning to another page, "my client held two insurance policies on his life. His wife was the original beneficiary of both policies. Upon her death, he named Valerie Dunstan as his beneficiary or, in the case of her demise, her son, Ned Dunstan. Each policy provides a three-hundred-thousand-dollar death benefit, so the total death benefit is six hundred thousand dollars. I have spoken to Mr. Kraft's insurance agent, and he and I will be handling the forms. With luck and the cooperation of the authorities, the checks from the insurance companies should arrive within three to four weeks."

He may have smiled again, but I could not tell. "Mr. Dunstan, soon you will be a rather well-off young man. If you do not already enjoy the services of a good accountant, I suggest that you find one."

"I didn't hear my name yet," May said.

"You aren't going to," Nettie said. "How much are you getting out of this deal, Creech?"

"I will overlook that remark, Mrs. Rutledge." Creech straightened the papers and closed the folder. "Under stress, people often speak rashly."

"You haven't begun to hear rash," Nettie said. "How much was it?"

"Well, let me think," Creech said. "For the preparation of Mr. Kraft's will, I was compensated at my usual hourly rate. The total fee probably came to something like five thousand dollars, what with the various changes made over time. Mr. Dunstan and I have entered into no prior arrangement, apart from the one executed in front of you, for which I received one dollar. Mr. Dunstan will be invoiced for the time I spent on his behalf earlier today, which had no connection to this matter. Far from colluding with me to change the terms of Mr. Kraft's bequests, I believe it is clear that Mr. Dunstan had no prior knowledge of those terms. I would go so far as to say that Mr. Dunstan is flabbergasted."

Nettie whirled in her chair and sent out storm signals. "I want to hear the truth. Did you know what was going to happen when you came in here?"

"I had no idea," I said. Miss Wick's pen flew across her pad. "I'm flabbergasted, all right. Toby told me he was going to take care of me, but I thought he was talking about a job in the pawnshop."

"Now I see it," Nettie said. "Now I know why you told the old scoundrel he should come to the hospital. I bet you've been paying him social calls."

Creech's emotionless voice was like a splash of cold water. "Mr. Kraft's will was last amended two weeks after the death of his wife. The date was April seventeenth, 1965. At the time, I believe Mr. Dunstan was a few months short of his seventh birthday. I also believe it is clear that Mr. Kraft's intention was to bequest the bulk of his estate to Mr. Dunstan's mother, and that he has inherited by default."

"Nettie," May said, "did the old swindler leave everything to *Star*?"

"He sure did," said Nettie. "And because she was taken from us, the whole wad comes down to her little boy."

May craned her neck to look at me. "Neddie, you're not going to keep it all, are you? Maybe you haven't gotten very far in life, but you're a good-hearted boy all the same."

Without deigning to turn his head, Clark said, "For a factory hand, you're getting a whole lot of money, boy. I hope you can stay on the straight and narrow."

"Mr. Dunstan," Creech said, "have you any intention of assuming my client's pawnbroker business?"

"No."

"In that case, we can arrange to liquidate the shop and sell the property. If you wish, we can also put the other properties on the market. My client's will must be probated, a process that customarily takes at least a year to conclude, but it would be advisable to take care of these details now."

"Thank you, yes," I said. "Arrange to sell Toby's properties." I watched Miss Wick's pen dance over her notebook.

"Fast cars," Clark said. "A big house. French champagne and buxom girlfriends. You know what they say about a fool and newfound wealth. If you were to let me handle that money, you might have a chance of coming out of this with a few cents in your pocket."

"Uncle Clark," I said, "I have to think about what I'm going to do, and I wish you'd all shut up for a second."

"I have to speak from my heart," Nettie said, not to me but to the air in front of her, like Clark. "I have to say one little, tiny thing, or it will magnify itself into a great burden and weigh on me forever. Mr. Toby Kraft married our beloved sister. Although he took Queenie from us, we never failed to welcome him into our homes. When our sister passed away, Mr. Toby Kraft remained a member of our family circle. You could say, he even became a pest. Toby Kraft was in the habit of dropping in uninvited and staying for dinner, and for the sake of my dear sister's memory I prepared a whole lot more meals for that man than I ever felt like cooking, and the same is true of my sister May. If you were to add up the costs of all the times Toby had the pleasure of a home-cooked dinner, it would come into the thousands of dollars, all out of Christian charity. That old crook never gave any signs of having a fortune squirreled away, did he, May?"

"He did not," May said.

"To look at the man, he barely had two nickels to rub together. Wore the ugliest clothes you ever saw in your life. He was a drinker, as we knew, and a scoundrel, on top of all that whiskey. But we gave him our love, because we knew no other way. That is the kind of people we are."

C. Clayton Creech looked at her in undisguised admiration.

"Neddie," May said, "think what your mother would do."

"I am thinking of what my mother would have done," I said. "Mr. Creech, I'd like you to draw up an agreement dividing Mr. Kraft's estate into four equal parts. One for Aunt Nettie, one for Aunt May, another for my Aunt Joy, and the last for me."

"Do you want to sleep on it for a night?" he asked.

"No," I said.

"Are the death benefits from the insurance policies to be included in the division of the estate?"

"Yes," I said. "How much would each share come to?"

Creech took a notebook from a desk drawer and lit a Lucky Strike from the pack on his desk. "Are we keeping up with these developments, Miss Wick?"

Miss Wick assured him that the developments were being entered into the record.

Creech bent over the notebook and exhaled a substantial plume of smoke. "We have five hundred and twenty-five thousand dollars in cash on hand. Add to that the probable value of the real estate holdings and the insurance benefits, and we have one million, nine hundred and twenty-five thousand dollars. A one-quarter share of Mr. Dunstan's inheritance comes to four hundred and eighty-one thousand dollars, more or less."

"Draw up the papers," I said. "Toby left the money to my mother, and I know she would have shared it with her aunts."

"Your decision is final," Creech said.

"You heard the boy, Creech," Clark said. "Get hopping."

May looked at me again. "You know, Joy doesn't need all that money. And Neddie, four hundred and eighty-one thousand dollars sounds like an awful lot to give to a young fellow who has his whole life in front of him."

I smiled at her. "You're right. Mr. Creech, I want to donate twenty thousand dollars from my share of the insurance benefits to a woman named Suki Teeter."

"Could you spell that name for me?" Miss Wick asked.

I spelled Suki's name. "She's at the Riverrun gallery on Archer Street, in College Park."

"That's all I require," Creech said. "Would you like me to inform Ms. Teeter of her good fortune?"

"Please."

Nettie glared. "You're giving money to that *Suki*?"

"Star would have," I said. "I saw Suki Teeter the other day, and she needs the money. If you think I shouldn't do things like that, I could always keep everything for myself. Which would be . . . ?" I glanced at C. Clayton Creech.

"One million, nine hundred twenty-five thousand dollars." His delivery made it sound like what you would spend to get into a movie and pick up a medium-sized container of popcorn.

"Suki was a dear friend to Star," Nettie said. "Your mother would be proud of you. I knew you had a good heart."

Creech suggested attaching to my gifts the condition that all funds remaining be returned to me upon the death of the recipients, and Nettie said, "I don't plan on leaving any money to the Red Cross or museums about Nazis. Draw it up and get probate cracking. I want a gas range with two ovens and a griddle, the kind they have in restaurants, and I'd like to get it before they plant me in the ground." When we all stood up, Creech asked me to come back at 5:30 to sign the papers.

Downstairs, I opened the front door of the townhouse onto a burst of sunlight and a shimmer of green.

Clark wobbled down the steps with the hint of a strut. Nettie and May filed out into the brightness of Paddlewheel Road, and I came down behind them. The Buick gleamed from a parking meter two spaces from Commercial Avenue. A feeling of unreality clung to me. I had given away about a million and a half dollars.

Clark inspected the sleeves of his jacket. "Seems to me I'm in danger of falling a little bit behind the current styles. How much are we supposed to get from Toby?"

"Four hundred and eighty thousand," Nettie said.

"It isn't that much, considered in the cold light of day. You couldn't say that a man with four hundred and eighty thousand dollars in the bank is a man of wealth, so don't start putting us in that category."

"I want a big gas range with a griddle," Nettie said. "And I'm going to get one, no matter what category we're in."

"Do you know what I'd like?" May said. "A home entertainment center and a satellite dish, instead of my no-good little TV that only gets three stations."

"We can both have one," Nettie said. "But I can't get over the idea it's wrong to pay for a frivolity like that."

"We don't have to *pay* for our home entertainment centers," May said. "I'd just like one, that's all."

"New clothes," Clark said. "The day we get that first check, I'm going into Lyall's and coming out *clean*. Then I'll stroll over to the Speedway and buy Cassie a double Johnnie Walker Black in honor of old Toby, God rest his soul."

"Clark," I said. "There's something you should know."

"Toby Kraft will rest easier now," May said. "I have always said that in spite of his faults, Toby was a very loyal man."

I said, "Clark, this morning—"

Nettie broke in. "Since he did not wish us to aggravate our grief, we should honor his wishes and let him have the dignified burial he requested. Reverend Swing is officiating at Star's burial, Neddie. Reverend Swing is famous for his funerals."

"I'm sure I'll love Reverend Swing," I said. "But I have to tell Clark—"

"You don't want to go against the last wishes of a dying man," Clark broke in.

"*Clark,*" I said, too loudly. "You won't be buying any drinks for Cassie Little."

Irritated, he said, "And why is that, pray tell?"

"She's dead."

"You're mistaken. She had a little cold the other day, but otherwise that girl's in the pink."

"I'm sorry, Uncle Clark." It was too late to go back and do this the right way. Ashen shock was already moving into his face. "Cassie was killed in her apartment last night. Her boyfriend, Frenchy, was killed too, in a cell at Police Headquarters."

May said, "They were in that Clyde Prentiss gang. Killed to keep them quiet, that's what they were."

Clark's eyes looked glazed.

"Bruce McMicken found her body. It was in the paper this morning."

Clark closed his mouth, opened it, closed it again. "That's cold, boy. Cold. You should have broken the news a little easier."

"I tried," I said, "but everybody kept interrupting."

"You should have more respect for a man's grief." He sneered ferociously at the sidewalk. "That Frenchy murdered her to keep her away from other men, and then he killed himself in remorse. I hope I can get my new clothes in time for her funeral rites."

"Here we are, baking on the sidewalk," Nettie said. "Time to get home."

I said, "I'll see you at Little Ridge, ten o'clock tomorrow morning."

"They can't put her in the ground all that fast," Clark wailed.

"It's Star's funeral tomorrow, not your girlfriend's. Open up that car, so it airs out." Nettie brought a slip of paper from her bag. "You had calls this morning, Ned, from Mrs. Rachel Milton and your friend Mrs. Hatch. We had a nice conversation. I wrote down their numbers." She thrust the slip at me.

■ **92**

■ I felt as though I were no longer quite anchored in reality, or in what I had assumed to be reality. In Merchants Park the grass flared brilliant green. Hard, white-gold light shattered across the tops of the cars. I alternated between gliding above the pavement and slogging against a heavy current. Toby Kraft's blood-soaked body and disgruntled face kept swimming into view.

Glittering darkness beckoned from the entrances to the lanes along Word Street. Bruce McMicken barreled head-down across the sidewalk and yanked open the door of the Speedway. The ghost of Frenchy La Chapelle jittered along behind him. A blue neon sign above a narrow window said PEEP INN, and when I peeped in I saw a man stroking the bare arm of the young woman whose head blocked his face. She lifted her profile and exposed a slender neck. The man leaned forward to say something that made her laugh. My heart stuttered and turned cold.

Robert put a cigarette to his lips. His mouth tightened as he inhaled, and hot, acrid smoke poured into my lungs. I turned from the window and stumbled ahead, coughing. I raised my hand to wipe my forehead and found I could see through it, as if through a smeary, hand-shaped piece of glass, to the buildings along Word Street.

I held the other beside it, my fingers spread. Indistinctly, the pavement was visible through both of them. I rushed to a shop window to see if my entire body was disappearing. The window reflected a thoroughly visible face. Normal, nontransparent hands emerged from my sleeves. I started to breathe again. When I looked back at the shop window, the reflection of the giant in the dashiki who had spoken to me on Pine Street was disapprovingly regarding me from three feet away.

"What's wrong with you now?" he asked.

I laughed. "I hardly know where to begin."

"Give it a try."

"This morning, I found a dead man covered in blood. This afternoon, I discovered that the dead man had left me about two million dollars in his will. I gave three-fourths of the money away. And about five seconds ago, I started to disappear."

The giant threw back his head and boomed out spacious laughter. I couldn't help responding any more than I had been able to do with Stewart Hatch, and I laughed along with the giant until I had to wipe my eyes.

"Well," said the giant, still emitting subterranean rumbles, "if you can laugh at your own foolishness, at least you're not crazy. But you're a study, Ned Dunstan, I have to say that."

"How do you know my name?"

"There could be a lot of reasons why a man might start to disappear. People disappear all the time, for reasons good and bad. But getting a boatload of money is the worst one I ever heard." He shook his head, grinning.

"How do you know my name?" I asked again.

"Ned." He looked down at me with an expression critical only to the extent that it remarked what I had failed to notice. "How do you think I know your name?"

I moved back to take in all of him. He was about six foot eight and 275 pounds, with a chiseled face, gleaming eyes, and teeth white enough for toothpaste commercials. A woven African cap covered his scalp from hairline to the inch of gray above his ears. He wore black, sharply creased silk trousers and black, polished loafers no smaller than size 13. The dashiki, darker and subtler than the one I had seen Friday on Pine Street, combined deep greens and blues with widely spaced crimson stripes. His skin shone like burnished mahogany. He looked like the culmination of an ancient line of African royalty. His dazzling grin widened.

No, I thought, *he doesn't look like a king, he looks like a—*

A wave of compacted light and warmth rolled out from the center of his being, and my thoughts died before the recognition that, whatever this man might have been, he was mysteriously of my own kind, not a Dunstan but *akin* to the Dunstans. A sense of protectiveness and security accompanied the surge of warmth, and I wanted to clasp his hand and ask for his help.

I heard myself say, "What's your name?"

"Walter," the giant said. "Pay attention. Walter, not Wally. If there's one thing I can't stand, it's being called Wally."

"Do you have a last name, Walter?"

"Bernstein. If I happened to be a little guy, I suppose I'd have to put up with some snickering, but I never hear anyone laugh."

"Was your father . . . ?"

"My father was a shade or two lighter than me. I don't see any reason to be so all-fired curious."

"But I am curious," I said. "I feel so *baffled.* Every time I think I finally understand something, I have to start all over again at the beginning." I stopped talking. I did not want to whine in front of Walter Bernstein.

"You're still taking baby steps," he said. "On top of that, you're a goddamned Dunstan. Dunstans never focus on the big picture, they run around stirring up trouble and leaving their messes behind them. The same things happen over and over again, understand? You can make a difference, if you watch your back and do your best."

"At what?"

"There's more to you than you know. Keep that in mind, not how *baffled* you are. Why shouldn't you be baffled? Did you think life was supposed to be simple?"

"Why do you care? What makes you *pop up*?"

"Maybe I'm sick of watching the Dunstans screw up over and over. You're not the only ones who got left behind, you know. Ever listen to Wagner? Read any Norse mythology, Icelandic mythology? Celtic? The Mediterranean isn't the whole damn world. I look at Goat Gridwell, I want to puke. You want to talk about disappearing, there it is. Makes me sick."

"But what can—"

"Take care of business, that's what you can do." Walter Bernstein moved around me and strode on. Then, as at our first encounter, he stopped and looked back. "You got a chance, if you use your *head*." He gave me a searching look and marched off down Word Street through the blazing sunlight. No one saw him but me.

■ Rachel Milton picked up a moment after her maid put me on hold. "Ned, I'm so relieved you got back to me. Suki told me about your mother. How are you doing?"

"I seem to be a little disconnected," I said.

"I could kick myself for not putting everything else aside and running down to the hospital. Did you get my flowers?"

"Thank you. That was very thoughtful." I stretched out on my bed and watched two heavyweight flies circling between the ceiling and the window. Every second or third time, one of them flew into the glass, dropped under the table, and buzzed back up two or three seconds later.

"I hear you and Laurie Hatch have gotten to know each other."

"A little bit."

"She and I used to be good friends until a silly misunderstanding came between us. The next time you talk to Laurie, would you tell her that I would like to repair our friendship?"

"I'll mention it," I said.

Rachel Milton asked about the funeral, and I gave her the details.

"I have to say goodbye to Star, and I want to see you. I remember when you were born!" She paused for a purposeful beat. "And I knew your father. We were all so jealous when he decided that your mother was the one for him." Another meaningful pause. "Suki told me you were interested in Edward Rinehart."

"I'd like to hear anything you could tell me," I said.

"After the funeral, we'll go somewhere for lunch."

A fly struck the window with the sound of a tennis ball hitting a concrete wall and dropped to the floor. I wondered what was buzzing around in Rachel Milton's brain and decided to postpone speculation until after the funeral. Then I succumbed and called Laurie Hatch.

"Where are you?" Her voice sounded like music. "I was so, I

don't know what I was, but I didn't know where to find you, and I called your aunt. Did she tell you?"

"It took her a while," I said. "I'm at the Brazen Head."

"The Brazen Head? Where's that?"

I gave her my number. "All this stuff has been going on, I hardly know where to begin."

"Start with the fire."

I told her about the fire and Toby Kraft. "In another part of the forest, these goons who mistook me for someone else nearly jammed me up, but I got away. Compared to Edgerton, Manhattan is like a tropical island."

"So come to my tropical island."

"I have to go to a lawyer's office and sign some papers. After that I should probably just crash here."

She paused for a second. "I gather that you and Stewart had a long conversation."

"Nothing he said made any difference to me, Laurie."

"Did Ashleigh call you? An amazing thing happened."

"I seem to be out of the Ashleigh loop," I said. "Good news?"

"I don't know how, but she found exactly what she needed. Did you have anything to do with that?"

"How could I?" I asked.

"Ashleigh wouldn't tell me how she got the papers, so I was wondering. . . . Forget it. The best part is, Stewart still thinks he's in the clear. He's sickeningly pleased with himself, especially since he's certain that you'll never talk to me again."

I said that I had understood Stewart's motives.

"But I told you those dumb stories I made up fifteen years ago because the real one was so ugly. I appalled myself." I thought I heard ice ringing in a glass. "He must have had a field day when he came to Teddy Wainwright."

"I didn't pay attention. Oh! I almost forgot. Rachel Milton tried to get in touch with me, and when I called her back, she asked me to tell you that she wants to be friends again. Anyway, she's eager to talk to you."

"While we're on the subject of astonishing tales . . ." Laurie's voice had fallen into its old, easy amusement. "Grennie has a thirty-five-year-old girlfriend from Hong Kong who's a financial genius. He met her when she came to his office to set up a charitable foundation, and he's been seeing her on the sly for months.

She's extraordinarily pretty—Ming-Hwa Sullivan. She got married to a guy from Edgerton named Bill Sullivan when they were at Harvard Business School. They came back here because he got a job at First Illinois. She went into business for herself and became a huge success, and they split up. Grennie wants to marry her."

"And Rachel wants to cry on your shoulder," I said.

Her voice changed again. "I told you a stupid lie, and Stewart poisoned your mind. I have to explain what really happened."

"The real story," I said.

"Should I pick you up?"

I told her that I'd rented a car.

"Get inside the thing and drive it to my house."

"I'll be there around six," I said.

■ **94**

■ Laurie and I carried our glasses and the remainder of the bottle into the living room and sat on the sofa near the fireplace and the big Tamara de Lempicka. She set the bottle on the carpet and leaned back into the cushions, cupping the glass in her hands. "I'm so embarrassed, I can hardly speak."

"You don't have to," I said.

"This enormous lie is right in front of us. This stupid habit! I thought no one could accept me if they knew my real story. I could hardly accept myself. It was so *shameful*." Tears rose to the surface of her eyes. "We were so *poor*. My father was killed holding up a *liquor store*. Is this the kind of person you want to have dinner with?"

"It's no disgrace to have a tough start," I said.

Laurie fixed me with a burning glance. "I grew up with the idea that the world . . . Okay. There was no safety *anywhere*. You didn't know if there was going to be food for dinner, and we were always getting evicted because my mother couldn't pay the rent. Every time we moved, I went to a different school, so I never had any friends. Not that I would have had friends anyhow. My clothes were from secondhand stores, not the cool ones, the ratty places. I was a laughingstock. Every day, I thought a big hole was going to open up in front of me, and I'd fall in and just keep on falling. I thought we were going to wind up on the street. Or that I'd be taken away to some kind of *prison*, and my mother would *die*."

She wiped her eyes. "Anyhow, when she got married to this cameraman at Warner Brothers, Morry Burger, it was like being rescued from drowning. He had a job and a house in Studio City. For a while, everything was okay. But good old Morry drank a bottle of gin a day, and he started beating up my mother when he came home from work. I hid in my room, and I listened to him hitting her, and her crying, and him yelling at her to stop crying, and it was like . . . the hole opened up, and I fell in. I stopped feeling anything at all, I was like a zombie. Which was just as well, as it turned out. Here we get to the first of the good parts."

Laurie sank back again, holding her glass in front of her face. "When I was eleven, Morry started climbing into my bed at night. My mother was passed out. She would have killed me if she knew. Well, maybe she did know, but she never admitted it.

"Then Morry got fired from Warners. He managed to find some work, but the jobs never lasted more than a couple of weeks. I ran away from home about a dozen times, but the cops always brought me back. We lost the house in Studio City, which Morry found really depressing, I might add. For about six months, we moved from one dump to another, mainly on the edges of Hancock Park. And then, one night my mother went out and someone killed her in back of a drugstore. They never found the guy.

"I was already smoking a lot of grass. After my mother got killed, I met this girl named Esther Gold. Esther Gold was a rich screwup who gave me amphetamines and 'ludes, and we got tight. One night, Morry grabbed my bag and found some pills, which gave him the brilliant idea that I was so depraved he might as well make money and influence people by selling me to his friends. Which he did, once or twice a month. But even though having to get into bed with Morry's friends as well as Morry was vile, disgusting, hideous, Esther Gold started scoring Percodans and Dilaudids, and whenever one of Morry's pals came over, I zoned out."

She wiped tears off her cheeks and smiled at the other side of the room. "We have gone through childhood, such as it was, which means we come to the next really good part, adolescence. Esther went to Fairfax, and I went to L.A. High, so I never saw her again, but L.A. High was full of dopers, you could get anything you wanted. One day in English class, I said to the teacher, 'I'm the Queen of Heaven, and you're a pimple on the ass of God.' My exact words. She threw me out of class. I started walking home. But home wasn't *home*, it was just the dump where I lived with Morry. I stood right where I was for about four hours. When a cop drove up and asked me my name, I told him I was the Queen of Heaven."

Laurie started giggling, and more tears spilled from her eyes. I brushed them off with the tips of my fingers. "Thank you. I wound up in the hospital. At least I told the cops about Morry, and Morry went to the slammer, three cheers for the L.A. child-welfare system.

"There isn't much to say about the hospital except I started getting a little more clarity. A wonderful man named Dr. Deering, a psychiatrist who was about sixty years old, told me I had a placement in a halfway house, but he and his wife would take me in, if I liked the idea. Dr. Deering was the only man in the world I trusted, and I only trusted him a little bit, but I said I'd give it a try. And after that, everything was different. No matter how paranoid and suspicious I got, they were always patient. I understood the deal, you know? I said to myself, *These are nice people, and they're probably your last chance to have a decent life. Don't mess up.*"

Laurie drank some wine, and her face filled with resentment. "To Stewart Hatch, of course, this means I was some kind of parasite. But I loved the Deerings. I was this person I can hardly remember anymore, and they took care of me. They hired tutors. They suffered through dinners when I screamed at them. They *talked* to me. When I learned how to act like a normal person, they put me in a private school and helped with my homework. College seemed completely remote, so when I graduated, they found me a job as a receptionist at a medical center in San Francisco. David and Patsy Deering. God bless them."

We clinked glasses.

"Did Stewart tell you I ran away? He did, didn't he?"

I said I didn't remember.

"Dr. Deering drove me to San Francisco. We found an apartment. I called them at least once a week for the next year, when I guess God decided to drop me into the hole again. David and Patsy were killed in an automobile accident, driving home from a party. It was terrible. When I came back from their funeral, I was so depressed I hardly got out of bed for a month. No more job, of course. So there I was, feeling like something the cat threw up, but I stumbled into a job in an art gallery, and one night at an opening I happened to meet Teddy Wainwright.

"Stewart undoubtedly implied that I took advantage of Teddy. There's no point in going over the whole thing, but I realized later, *of course* I fell in love with an older man, I couldn't have fallen in love with anything *but* an older man. Teddy was a father figure, so what? He loved me. Oh, God, Teddy did, he did love me. I think . . . Teddy helped me put myself together just by being such a great guy. I wish he was still alive, so I could introduce you to him. You would have liked each other."

"Back when you first met Stewart, did he remind you of Teddy Wainwright?"

Laurie slid closer and collapsed against my shoulder. "Wasn't that dumb? Hmm. On second thought, I don't like this. You're too perceptive."

"You don't dislike it that much."

She put her hand on my thigh. "The guy was from this town in the middle of nowhere. He seemed sort of square, but I thought that was almost charming, in a way. Little did I know how sick he was. He is sick, he likes hurting people." Laurie swung her arm across my chest and pressed her face against mine. Her body felt as hot as a feverish child's.

∎ 95

∎ After midnight, I rolled over and noticed a shape beside the bed. *Stewart,* I thought, and shot upright. Stewart Hatch moved toward me and bent down to reveal Robert's grinning face.

"Want to change places?" he whispered.

"Get out. No, don't. I have to talk to you."

Laurie mumbled, "Whuzz?"

"I'm going downstairs for a glass of milk," I said, and she lapsed back into sleep.

I slipped into my shirt and pants. The gun, which I had hidden beneath my trousers, went into one of the blazer's pockets. Robert kept grinning at me. My limitations amused him.

We padded past Posy's and Cobbie's bedrooms and down the stairs. I switched on the light over the butcher-block counter and took a glass to the liquor cabinet, where I found a half-empty liter of Johnnie Walker Black.

Robert eased into one of the chairs in the alcove. "Does our Laurie have a tendency to hit the bottle? You're putting away more than usual, too."

"Maybe a little. It's been a hell of a week." I lifted the glass. "Anyhow, to Toby Kraft. I guess he was a crook, but he sure did his best for Star. And me, come to think of it."

"Certainly looks that way," Robert said.

A little belligerently, I took the chair opposite his. "That's interesting. I want to explore what you mean by that remark, but first you have to keep your mouth shut and listen to me. Last night, you were waiting for me in my room, looking at Rinehart's book. You said something like, 'Old Dad was a lousy writer, wasn't he?' How did you know Rinehart was our father? I didn't tell you."

"Am I allowed to talk now? How did I learn about Rinehart? The same way you did, I suppose. From Star. You're not her only son, after all."

"You're lying."

"Don't forget, you had dinner up in the lounge with Nettie and May."

"And you came to the hospital?"

"How do you think the poker money wound up in your pocket? Maybe I shouldn't have done that, but I couldn't resist. Then I went in and said goodbye to Star, and she told me about Rinehart. Obviously, she was going to tell you the same thing. I was sure I could count on you to take it from there. For all your flaws, you're a dependable lad."

I could only stare at him. "You knew you could count on me."

"To take the next step. I'll shut up again, and you can fill me in."

"Oh, I'll fill you in," I said. "Edward Rinehart was Howard

Dunstan's son. I'm pretty sure he was illegitimate. He's been looking for us most of our lives." I described what Howard Dunstan had said to me by pretending that I had heard it from Joy. I told him about meeting Max Edison at the V.A. Hospital with Laurie. "Edison was still afraid of Rinehart, and so was Toby. Toby didn't want me to mention his name. I'll never say this to Laurie, but I think we got him killed. She said his name."

Robert absorbed it all. "You don't know that Rinehart killed Toby Kraft, and you shouldn't blame yourself. You thought Rinehart was dead. Besides, Toby was in a dangerous profession, and I don't mean pawnbroking. Concentrate on being grateful for the money he left you."

"How do you know about that, I wonder?"

"I went into his safe, remember? When I took out Hatch's papers, I came across Toby's will and his insurance policies. With the real estate, it must come to about two million. Think of it as your dowry."

"Too bad I gave most of it away," I said.

Robert looked at me in genuine dismay. Then his eyes narrowed and his mouth lifted in a smile. "You're joking."

I told him about asking Creech to divide the money.

"What possessed you to do a ridiculous thing like that?"

I explained and said, "After all, Star should have inherited the money, not me."

"I wish I didn't believe it. Did the lawyer suggest that the money revert to you when the old girls kick the bucket?"

"C. Clayton Creech doesn't miss a trick."

"Could be another twenty years."

"The aunts don't spend money," I said. "They use a one-way barter system."

"Once they get their hands on a few hundred thousand, they might turn into model citizens. I can see Clark buying the biggest car in sight. Joy will put Clarence in a nursing home. Eventually, all three are going to wind up in nursing homes."

"Good," I said. "If they need nursing homes, they'll be able to afford decent ones. That's what the money is for."

"It was supposed to be yours. Ours."

"I hope you're not thinking of killing them for it," I said. What I thought was a joke earned me a sizzling glance of disgust. Robert shook his head and looked away.

"Robert, you didn't kill Toby, did you?"

He sighed and shook his head again. "I should give up on you."

"Tell me you didn't murder him because you knew I would inherit his money."

"It would get you off the hook, wouldn't it? You wouldn't have any reason to wallow in guilt, or to blame Laurie."

I thought about the timing of Toby's death, and the world seemed to stop moving.

"But to answer your question, no. I did not murder Toby Kraft. Sorry, you'll have to live with your guilt."

"When I found him, he was sitting at his desk. Which means that he was killed before he went upstairs to his apartment. He was already dead by the time you got there."

"Not a pretty sight. But then, Toby never was much to look at. I wish you hadn't given away three-fourths of his estate."

"A shadow doesn't need money," I said.

"How would you know? I'm getting tired of being on the edges. I'd like more stability, more continuity. You're my retirement plan. My pension fund."

"You could go into any bank in the world and walk out with a fortune. Why bother setting me up with Ashleigh Ashton and Laurie Hatch?"

"I promised Star I'd look out for you. She didn't warn you about *me*, did she? Once we get past our birthday, we can carry on, apart and together, together and apart, for the rest of our lives."

I did not *believe* Robert. "This afternoon, I walked past a bar called the Peep Inn and saw you talking to a girl. Something happened to me. I started to disappear."

"I disappear all the time. How far did it get?"

"I could see through my **hands**."

"No one ever prepared you for certain aspects of Dunstan life. Probably means you're getting a little stronger."

"Did it have anything to do with seeing you?"

"You're seeing me now. More to the point, I can also see you."

"The day I came here, you were in bed with a woman, and I felt everything you did. I was making love to a woman who wasn't there."

Robert's eyebrows shot up. "Really?" He was not unhappy to have this information.

"You didn't know you were doing it."

"No." He smiled. "That's an interesting phenomenon." The whites of his eyes seemed whiter, and his teeth shone as if they came to points. When he noticed my unease, he moved out of the chair. "Don't plan on seeing me at the funeral, but I'll be there. Tomorrow night we'll discuss our birthday. In the meantime, please try to stay alive."

"Don't underestimate me, Robert," I said.

"I'm not sure I could." He gave me an ironic smile and faded through the door like a phantom.

I regarded the back door. It consisted of a tall wooden panel separated into two equal portions by a recessed horizontal division. I stood up, walked around the table, and aimed my index finger at the center of the upper panel. My finger met solid wood. Telling myself I was a Dunstan, I tried to will my finger through the surface of the door. My fingertip flattened and bent upward.

■ **96**

■ I sat at Laurie's table, staring at my glass and thinking about my brother, my shadow, whose absence had shaped the entire course of my life. He had known what would happen to me at Middlemount and saved me from death by starvation or exposure—it was Robert who had flirted with Horst while I was drinking myself into a stupor. He had set up my encounter with Ashleigh because he knew it would lead to dinner with Laurie Hatch at Le Madrigal. Yet he had not known that I would give away three-quarters of what had come to me from Toby Kraft, and he had been surprised to hear of my visit to New Providence Road. Robert wanted me to think that he knew everything about me, but he had not known about my semidisappearance on Word Street or my new ability to eat time.

Robert seemed blind to the moments when I acted in accordance with my Dunstan legacy, especially what had come directly from Star. Virtually everything I had learned since arriving in Edgerton distanced me from his unseen claim on my being. The parts of myself least familiar to me were out of his range.

But Robert had been delighted to hear that I'd participated in his sexual adventures and had watched my hands disappear on Word Street—maybe he wanted me to disappear altogether. For thirty-five years, Robert had lived on the fringes of human existence like a starving wolf: what could be more natural than that he demand more? Did I think he intended to marry Laurie Hatch, get his hands on Stewart's family trust, and then dispose of both Laurie and Cobbie? A final sip of whiskey made this farfetched idea almost entirely implausible. Yet enough of it lingered so that I could not spend the night in Laurie's bed.

■ 97

■ I put on the rest of my clothes in the dark. In a sleepy voice, Laurie said, "You're always going somewhere."

"I have to be ready for the funeral."

She raised her head for a kiss.

"I'll call you tomorrow."

"That's what the guy last night said."

I drove on past dark houses to the highway. Eighteen-wheelers loomed up from behind like yellow-eyed monsters and swung out to wash by before sailing ahead to become red dots poised at the edge of infinity. A handful of cars ghosted along the streets of Edgerton. I found a parking place in front of the Speedway, crossed the street, and entered Turnip Lane.

In my haste, I nearly stumbled over a figure like a heap of discarded clothes. I bent down, thinking that if he was Piney Woods, I would give him the price of a bed at the Hotel Paris. The odors of unwashed flesh and alcohol floated up from a stranger with matted hair and scabs on his cheeks. His eyelids twitched, as if he sensed me looking at him. Somewhere near, a man snored in bursts like the starting and stopping of a chain saw.

On Leather Lane, a man reeled out of a doorway and collapsed facedown on the cobbles. A woman's voice rose from a basement room, saying, *It's always the same, always the same. It is always the same, exact story, and I'm sick of it.* Somewhere a toilet flushed. Under the feeble illumination of an iron street lamp, I turned into Fish.

I had gone about thirty feet between the huddled buildings when, in a signal as old as childhood, someone whistled two notes, the second an octave down from the first. I turned around and saw an empty lane. I turned back. About twenty feet away, Joe Staggers was lurching into Fish out of Lavender Lane. He laughed, steadied himself, and planted his feet.

"Well. Well, now. Looks like party time." With the fluidity of practice, Staggers drew a knife from his back pocket and snapped his wrist. The blade locked into place with a heavy metallic *clunk*.

I looked over my shoulder. Yuk Yuk—Shorty—stood beneath the light at the other end.

"Are you ready, Dunstan? Are you, little pal?" Staggers said. "No fancy bullshit tonight." He stepped forward.

I yanked the pistol out of the holster, pushed down the safety, and aimed at Staggers. "Stop right there." I looked at Shorty, who had not moved, and chambered the first bullet. "Drop the knife."

"Whoa, boy. Are you gonna shoot me?"

"If I have to." I swung the pistol across the front of my body and pointed it at Shorty. "Get out of here. Now."

"He won't shoot," Staggers said. "That's Gospel."

"He busted in Minor's head," Shorty said.

"This guy never fired a gun in his life. But he cheated us out of our money, in case you forgot."

"Not enough money to get killed for."

I swung the barrel back to Staggers. He had advanced a couple of feet.

"Forget the money, think about being a man for a change," Staggers said. "If he shoots anybody, it'll be me."

I looked at Shorty without taking the gun off Staggers. When I glanced back at Staggers, he was in a crouch, his arms at his sides, smiling at me. "Shorty," I said, "take off while you can."

Staggers said, "Fancy boy ain't gonna hit anything. Come ahead."

I heard Shorty take a hesitant step forward, rotated, and aimed at his chest. Then I sighted an inch to the left and pulled the trigger. A red flare came from the barrel, and the explosion kicked the pistol upward. The bullet smacked into a brick wall, ricocheted across the lane, and struck a boarded window. Shorty lumbered off. I chambered another round and heard the shell case ping off a cobble.

Still crouching, Joe Staggers was within four yards of me, the knife edge-up in his lightly extended hand. "Missed him on purpose, you dipshit."

"I won't miss you," I said.

"Suppose I drop the knife and you drop the gun. Suppose we take it from there."

"Suppose you get out of here before I put a bullet in your head," I said.

A crablike step brought him closer.

I aimed the pistol at his forehead. "Put it down."

"Guess I'll do that."

Staggers lowered his knife hand, glanced up at me, and vaulted forward, like a frog. I aimed at the big plaid shape speeding over the cobbles. There was a flash of red, an explosion, the sound of a bullet pinging off a stone. Staggers rammed into my legs and knocked me onto my back.

Now, I thought, *do it now!*

My stomach cramped. Pain blossomed in my head. The fabric of the world melted into yielding softness, and I fell through sixty years, more or less, with Joe Staggers clinging to my legs.

There came the familiar sense of *wrongness,* of *dislocation.* In a miasma of horse dung, beer, and sewage, Fish Lane tilted up and down like a seesaw. When my vision cleared, I was lying on my back a few yards beyond the entrance to a tavern. About twice the usual number of stars blanketed the night sky. I lifted my head and saw Joe Staggers struggling onto his hands and knees. I knew what I was going to do to him even before the tavern door opened upon a grim knot of men in worn jackets and thick caps. An amazed and sinister chuckle spread through them. One of the men came toward us, and two or three others followed. Staggers sank onto his heels and raised his knife.

It would never have occurred to him that his clean shirt, his sturdy yellow Timberlands, his fresh haircut denied him sympathy from the men before us. He did not look rich, but he looked richer than they were. Waving his knife made it worse. He swiveled his head to look at me, and the pain and confusion in his eyes nearly made me pity him. "Where the hell are we?"

Most of the men standing at the entrance to the bar pulled out knives of their own.

One of the men moved away from the others. The ripped pockets of his jacket flopped like rabbit ears. A rough voice said, *You got that one, Bumpy.*

I threw the pistol down the lane and heard it skittering over the cobbles. Bumpy took another step, and I did what I had to do.

Darkness stretched out on either side. My head pounded, and sweat ran down my face. Abandoned buildings and boarded windows looked down in calm silence. I pushed myself upright and smelled cordite. Down at the crossing of the lanes, two drunks goggled at me from beneath a street lamp. A siren wailed on Word Street. "He ran down there," I shouted, pointing to the far end of Fish Lane. The drunks turned unsteadily around, and I raced into the darkness.

■ 98

■ Mr. Spaulding's hearse preceded Clark's gleaming Buick on the way to Little Ridge, and I followed both, headlights on. Through the gates we went and over the crunching gravel to a narrow drive that ribboned past orderly headstones. The hearse glided to a stop beside a little rise, and Clark and I swung in behind it. We all got out of our vehicles. It was a fine, sunny morning without too much humidity. In their dark print dresses and lace collars, Nettie and May could have been a pair of deacons' wives. In his eggplant-colored suit, white shirt with a Mr. B collar, black necktie, and a chocolate brown, wide-brimmed fedora, Clark looked more elegant than I had ever seen him. A carpet of artificial grass the bright green of AstroTurf lay over the mound of earth soon to be muscled back into the ground by the yellow bulldozer parked further along the asphalt ribbon. On the other side of the open grave stood a device like a forklift with metal uprights and protruding braces. Two cemetery employees squatted in the shade of the bulldozer.

Clark adjusted the angle of his fedora. "I've been thinking

about your mother day and night, son. I'm happy I lived long enough to pay her my respects."

"Uncle Clark," I said, "it wouldn't be the same without you."

Mr. Spaulding and three black-suited assistants slid the coffin out of the hearse and carried it up the hill. In the sunlight, the coffin gleamed an odd yellow-bronze. The smooth contours and rounded edges made it look like an object meant to be shot into outer space.

"Those brass handles will last forever," Clark said.

I helped May uphill as she muttered about the heat. Spaulding's assistants eased the coffin onto the armature over the rectangular space in the ground. A stocky man in a black robe and gold-rimmed glasses unfolded his hands from the leather-bound Bible on his belly and introduced himself as the Reverend Gerald Swing.

"Are other mourners expected?" he asked.

"Here's one now," I said. A dented old Volvo wagon was pulling up behind my car. Reverend Swing strolled to the head of the open grave and went into a contemplative trance.

May said, "I told Joy about that money Toby left us. It seems she feels that Clarence should be placed in a nursing home."

"I'll try to find a place for him before I leave, but if I can't, you and Aunt Nettie will have to do it."

"Son," May said, "when are we supposed to get those checks?"

"Maybe three weeks," I said.

"This outfit looks pretty smart, if I say so myself," Clark said. His voice trembled. "Your mother held the opinion that I was a handsome man." I peered under the brim of his hat and saw tears leaking from his eyes.

Suki Teeter came swinging uphill in a voluminous black pants suit, sunglasses, and a black hat the size of a sombrero.

"There's that girl who came to the hospital," May said.

"Ned gave her a fortune, but I will never understand why," Nettie said.

"It was a lot less than I gave you and May," I said.

"Neddie," May asked, "what in the world did you give *us*?"

Suki silenced whatever I might have said by wrapping her arms around me and bringing the golden haze of her face to mine. "Thank you, thank you, *thank* you. I'm stunned!"

I kissed her cheek. "I'm glad I could help," I said.

"Let's get together afterward."

Clark raised the brim of his hat a quarter of an inch and lowered it again. "Nice of you to pay your respects, Miss. I compliment you on your appearance, which is most attractive."

"I could say the same for yours, kind sir."

Clark displayed a magnificent sneer and crowned his glory by removing from his breast pocket a pair of oversized, black-framed sunglasses I thought I had seen on Mr. Spaulding's desk that morning, snapping out the temples with the same wrist-flick the late Joseph Staggers had used to open his knife, then mounting them on his nose. He looked a bit like an ancient Tonton Macoute.

In a close-fitting black suit that made the most of her legs, Rachel Milton emerged from a white BMW. Her sunglasses surpassed even Clark's or, as I suspected, Mr. Spaulding's. Rachel moved gracefully up the rise and embraced me. "Dear Ned, I'm so sorry. We'll get together later?"

I introduced her to the aunts and to Clark, who tipped his hat with a lady-killer's polished charm.

Nettie scowled at me. "I don't know how we can get your Uncle Clarence into a decent nursing home. We're two old ladies almost in need of one ourselves."

Rachel took the hint and moved away. I said something reassuring to Nettie, watching Rachel Milton's uncertain approach to Suki. After a moment of suspicion, Suki swept forward, and the two women fell into each other's arms.

Lurking at the head of the grave, Reverend Swing questioned me with a glance. I nodded. The reverend coughed forcefully into his fist and opened his Bible to gaze at the text as if for spiritual refreshment. Then he slammed it shut.

"We gather here today to mark the passing from this earthly realm of Valerie Dunstan, known to her beloved family and friends as Star, and to commend her soul to the Lord." It was as though he had flipped a switch and brought into play a bass-baritone richer, more vibrant, and louder than his normal speaking voice.

I looked along the rise to a grove of maple trees, then behind us, but did not see Robert.

Although Reverend Swing had been denied the honor of personal acquaintanceship with Valerie Dunstan, these few minutes with the bereaved family had proved to him that Star Dunstan—

to use that sweet sobriquet—had been a loving mother, a loving daughter to her mother, and a devoted niece to her aunts and uncles. Reverend Swing knew that Star Dunstan had packed thousands of nourishing peanut-butter-and-jelly, tuna-fish, and egg salad sandwiches into the lunch box her son Ned carried to school. Reverend Swing knew that she had spent many nights by little Ned's bedside while he ran temperatures and suffered childhood's illnesses. She spent hours washing and ironing his school clothes. Star had assisted her son's struggles with multiplication and long division; she had aided his research into historical periods for his little papers; he could not help but wonder if together they had investigated the glories of Jerusalem and the Holy Lands, which the Reverend Swing had been privileged to visit in the company of his wife and helpmeet, Mrs. Violetta Puce Swing.

Nettie and May were nodding away like robots, and I managed to keep from laughing. I wondered if Star had ever seen a lunch box. She had never made a peanut-butter-and-jelly sandwich in her life, and the only clothes she ever ironed were the dresses she wore onstage. I looked down the ridge and saw Robert, in a blue suit identical to mine, leaning against a maple in the grove. The white-hot memory of our encounter in the Anscombe house and our union into one being shivered through me. Tears burned in my eyes.

Reverend Swing intoned, "This young man's mother, the niece of the noble women I see before me, sought daily inspiration in the pages of a book that had a special place in her good and simple heart."

In spite of the absurdity of Swing's portrait of Star, somehow also because of that absurdity, the emotions evoked by Robert's appearance flowed into my grief for my mother, ripping in half a thick wall of matter extending from breastbone to spine in the middle of my chest. I began to sob. Everyone present, including the reverend, stared at me, but instead of embarrassment, I felt the deep, two-sided current of human life at work in me again; I felt more than ever like my mother's son.

The next time I looked at the maple grove, Robert was gone.

Reverend Swing commended Valerie "Star" Dunstan to the earth from whence she had come and invited us to rejoice in the ascent of her soul. I liked the first half of that sentence. I liked it a lot. Let us commend Star Dunstan to the earth, if that was from whence she had come. It was certainly where she was going, so let us commend her to it anyway, adorned in her best black dress and her good pearl earrings, unless the aunts had twinkled them away on the grounds that pearls served the living better than the dead. Let us hope that the earth might treat her with its customary kindly regard, let us trust that whatever was not to be buried within Mr. Spaulding's gleaming space capsule would find the peace it deserved, whether in the paradise recommended by Reverend Swing or in realms unknown to him.

Swing crooned a beautiful bass-baritone prayer. One of Mr. Spaulding's assistants pulled cosmetic sheets of AstroTurf from the grave, and another glided to the machine and pushed a button. Star's coffin sank into the trench and almost soundlessly came to rest.

Clark said, "Gerry Swing tells the people what they want to hear."

He and the aunts moved a short way down the slope. The atmosphere had loosened and relaxed as it widened out to include the rest of the landscape. The concentrated group of mourners separated again into individuals. The bulldozer cleared its throat. I started walking toward Suki Teeter and Rachel Milton, and a large figure in gold-rimmed spectacles and a black robe appeared beside me.

In his vibrant sermon voice, Reverend Swing said, "I felt I knew your dear mother as well as if she had been a member of my congregation."

"Thank you, Reverend." I gave him a fifty-dollar bill, which sailed beneath his robe.

"You were moved by my evocation of your mother's spirit."

"Reverend, my mother would have laughed her head off at the part about the sandwiches, but it was lovely anyhow."

Still pressing on the organ pedals, Swing said, "I know your mother was a good Christian."

"She loved Billie Holiday and Ella Fitzgerald, and she sang in clubs," I said. "Does that count? In her own way, she was a fantastic mother."

Swing clapped his hand on my back and laughed. In his real voice, he said, "Know the trouble with gigs like this? They never give you enough information. If Will Spaulding had told me your mother was a singer, I could have done five minutes on

Billie and Ella to make the people bawl their eyes out. Would have been a memorable funeral."

"It was probably just as memorable this way," I said.

He wandered down the slope, uttering benedictions. Nettie instantly sailed in front of me, May at her side. "The reverend has a beautiful speaking voice," said Nettie, "but I would not choose to listen to it night and day. And he did not know beans about Star, although he was very complimentary to May and me."

"I expect the reverend brought Violetta Puce to the Holy Land in hopes of losing her over there," said May. "Are you coming home with us, Neddie?"

"I'll drop in later," I said.

"Going off with the ladies, I expect," said Clark, sauntering up. "The reverend did us proud, but Star would have wanted him to mention her devotion to me, too. The apple of her eye, I was."

■ **99**

■ Suki glowed at me from beside the BMW, and Rachel said, "Star and I used to get together at our old place, Brennan's. Grennie *Milton* certainly wasn't going to walk in. I know it's a little early for lunch, but all I've had today was a cup of yogurt at seven-thirty."

"I never had breakfast at all," I said.

"I just got up," Suki said. "Brennan's is right around the corner from me, and I haven't been there in centuries. It'll be like going back in time."

"They still have that picture," Rachel said.

"Ned, you have no idea what you're in for. Do you know how to find it? Doesn't matter, just follow us."

"I know Brennan's," I said. "But I'll follow you anyhow."

Suki wafted up to her car. Rachel said, "Is one of Star's aunts worried about placing someone in a nursing home?"

"Aunt Joy's husband, Clarence Crothers," I said. "He's in an advanced stage of Alzheimer's."

"Grenville put me on the board of Mount Baldwin, the best

elder-care facility in southern Illinois. I could call Liz Fanteen, the director, this afternoon and settle the whole thing in five minutes. Is Clarence ready to be admitted?"

"He has ripened on the vine, if that's what you mean."

"I'll take care of it after lunch. That's a promise."

■ 100

■ Rachel parked in front of the Irish bar on Fairground Road, and Suki and I found spaces around the corner. When I got out of my car, she was standing on the sidewalk, looking at me a little shyly. "I haven't thanked you enough for your generosity. It's amazing, Ned. You don't even really know me."

"It was supposed to be Star's money. She would have done exactly the same."

Suki put her arm through mine. "That's the only thing that makes me feel right about accepting the money, even though I can't afford to turn it down. I just want you to know how grateful I am."

We filed into a long, dark interior with a polished mahogany bar on one side and wooden booths on the other, which opened into a dining room. A big man with graying temples smiled at us from behind the bar.

"Mrs. Milton," he said. "Haven't seen you in a long time." His eyes met mine for a moment before he glanced at Suki and returned to Rachel. "Would you and your friends like a table in the back?" He gave Suki another glance, and his eyes softened. His entire face opened into a smile. "What do you know, Suki Teeter has come back to Brennan's. As beautiful as ever, too."

"Bob Brennan, you're just like your father," she said.

"You were a great crowd. Will Star Dunstan be joining you?"

A needle traveling at the speed of light went through my heart.

Rachel said, "We just came from her funeral. This is her son, Ned."

"No," Brennan said, shocked. "That's terrible. I'm sorry for your loss, Ned." He reached across the bar and engulfed my hand. "My dad always liked having your mother in the place, and I did, too. Let's set you up in back, and we'll get you anything you like."

He seated us and handed out menus. "The first drink is on the house."

"I'll have a Manhattan, please, and thank you, Bob."

"Same here," said Suki.

"Is that what she used to drink here?" I asked.

"One Manhattan, light on the vermouth, straight up," Brennan said. I ordered one, and he went back into the bar.

Suki examined the walls. "This is spooky. Bob looks just like his father."

"We have to show Ned the picture," Rachel said.

"If you can stand it, I can," Suki said. "Come on. Time for your history lesson." She led me to the back wall.

Rachel said, "God, would you *look* at us?"

Just above eye level hung a picture of ten young women and two young men ranged along the bar in summery clothing. Unforced happiness shone from their faces. Radiantly beautiful, Star smiled out from between a stunning young Suki Teeter and an equally stunning young Rachel Newborn.

"Wow," I said. *Wow* pretty much summed up my response. "This was your group?"

"Most of us." Rachel named the girls in the photograph: "Sarah Birch, Nanette Bridge, Tammy Wackford, Avis Albright, Zelda Davis. Mei-Liu Chang, next to Sammie Schwartz. And that girl who got high on Benzedrine inhalers and talked in rhymes."

"Georgy-Porgy," Suki said. "She just published her second novel, she's got two kids, no husband, and she's the most satisfied person you ever saw in your life. I hate her guts."

I asked what had happened to some of the others. Zelda Davis won a fellowship to Harvard and worked for the State Department. Sammie Schwartz had run off with a Hell's Angel and now taught third grade in Arizona. Nanette Bridge was a partner in a Wall Street law firm. Moongirl Thompson had disappeared, literally, after telling her boyfriend she was going to take a walk up the beach.

Brennan brought in the drinks and took our orders: a salad for Rachel, hamburgers and fries for Suki and me.

"Remember Sujit? Remember the Big Indian?"

"Could I forget them?" Suki said. "When Sujit went back to

Bombay, she created a huge national scandal. Two or three cabinet members had to resign. The Big Indian makes avant-garde films. Her real name is Bertha Snowbird."

"I've seen some of Bertha Snowbird's films," I said. "She's really good. Which one is she?"

We returned to the back wall, where Suki pointed out a fierce young woman with straight, center-parted black hair, athletic shoulders, and lioness eyes. A man of twenty-five or twenty-six with matinee-idol cheekbones and close-cut blond hair had his arm draped around her neck.

"Who's the guy?" I asked.

"Don Messmer," Suki said.

Messmer smiled at the camera with the self-consciousness of a man who knows that he is simultaneously out of his depth and onto a good thing. At the other end of the group, a dark-haired man with a cigarette in his mouth leaned against Sammie Schwartz. "Who's the other guy?"

"He taught English at Albertus," Rachel said. She raised her half-empty glass to her mouth and drained it. "His name was Erwin Leake."

I saw Piney Woods sitting on a bench in Merchants Park. *Follow a shadow, it still flies you; / Seem to fly it, it will pursue.*

■ "Why isn't Edward Rinehart in that picture?"

Rachel said, "Edward hated having his picture taken. Suki, remember that time—"

Around a mouthful of hamburger, Suki said, "Sure do." She held up a finger and swallowed. "The other time, too."

"Why were we so *stupid*? Someone takes his picture, and he smashes the camera. Three months later, Sujit takes his picture on the street, and he grabs her camera and rips out the film. Shouldn't we have been suspicious?"

"We thought suspicion was bourgeois," Suki said. "How are you doing, Rachel?"

Rachel Milton finished her second Manhattan. "Not all that well, actually. It's *rotten* that Star died. And my husband decided that he needed something new in his life, namely a thirty-five-year-old iceberg who is a whiz at estate planning. He has his heart set on marrying this iceberg."

"How old is the guy?" Suki asked.

"Seventy-two, but that doesn't bother him. He's in love. If

Grennie hadn't fallen in love, he'd be selfish, but of course this way everything's all right. Have you ever been married?"

"Officially, once," Suki said. "Unofficially, two and a half times. Rachel, you forgot I married Roger Lathrop!"

"The harpsichordist who wiggled his fanny when he played. I remembered as soon as you told me. I want another drink, but not a Manhattan. A glass of white wine."

"I'll have another Manhattan."

I waved at Bob Brennan.

Suki turned to me. "I told you about Roger. We went to Popham College, and six years later the University of Michigan at Ann Arbor made him artist in residence. Both of us were happy to get out of Popham, believe me. And then."

"Fatal words," Rachel said.

"*And then,* Roger told me I was inhibiting his artistic progress, although I was not to take it personally."

"What was the bitch's name?" Rachel asked. "I bet she was a student."

"His prize pupil, Sonia Skeffington. She went to Michigan instead of me, and I came back here. I'd rather not talk about the unofficial husbands. One of them was really great, but he died while he was out on his daily five-mile run, and the other two turned out to be human fortune cookies."

■ Twenty minutes later, Suki said, "When I saw Star in the hospital, I thought my heart was going to break in half."

"Me, too," Rachel said.

"You didn't go to the hospital, Rachel."

"Oh! You're right. I was horrible that day. I was nasty to everyone." She did her best to focus on me. "I was nasty to you, too, wasn't I?"

"Semi-nasty," I said.

"Grennie had just reminded me that my services would no longer be required. Suki, I have a tremendous idea. We should both get married to Ned."

"That would be adventurous," I said.

"He maybe looks too much like Edward," said Suki. "He's much nicer, though."

"Edward wasn't nice at all. That's what we liked about him."

"Edward didn't care about anybody. Not even Star. But you know who did? Don Messmer."

"Forget *him*," Rachel said. "You know how some men are too handsome for their own good? Because all they have to do is coast along? Don Messmer."

"I wonder what Don is doing now," Suki said.

"He owns a bar in Mountry," I said.

They burst into laughter.

"Rachel, that means . . ." Suki dissolved again. "That means he has to steal from *himself*."

"We should probably get going," I said.

"You have to forgive us," Rachel said. "Suki and I haven't seen each other in a long time. We're in a funny state of mind."

"You were right," Suki said. "Let's marry Ned."

"Before we get married, let me take the two of you home," I said.

"In a minute," Rachel said. "Two questions. The first one is . . . do you still want your uncle to get into Mount Baldwin?"

"Yes," I said.

"I'll take care of it. Write down his name for me, or I'll forget." She fumbled in her bag and came out with a notebook and a pen. I wrote Clarence's name and *Star's uncle, placement in Mount Baldwin* and added Nettie's telephone number.

Rachel squinted at the page and put the notebook and pen back in her bag. "Question number two. No, it isn't a question. Was I going to tell you something?"

"Take your time," I said.

"I have to go home," Suki said. "Ned, will you drive me?"

"I'll drive both of you," I said.

"If I decide to tell you anything," Rachel said, "I didn't. Understood?"

"Understood."

Rachel put on her sunglasses. I had the feeling she thought she was disguising herself. "My husband is ditching me for a thirty-five-year-old Hong Kong vampire, have I made that clear?"

"A *female* Hong Kong vampire," said Suki. "Question for our studio audience: Does she blow, or does she suck?"

"Grennie thinks he can get away with anything. So does his best friend. Who is that, do you know? Don't say his name, just his initials."

"S.H."

"Good. Suki, guess what this best friend used to do when he followed me into the kitchen in the middle of a party?"

"Grab your boobs and rub your hand on his dick," Suki said. "That was easy."

"What a pig. Grenville and his friend do business together, right?"

"So I gather," I said.

"And all of a sudden this best friend gets accused of this and that."

"Okay," I said.

"And the best friend's friend is *undoubtedly* in trouble if Stewart gets into trouble. We're not using any names here, are we?"

"I heard two so far," Suki said.

"I'm not talking to you. Now suppose the wife of the friend's friend decided that both of them deserved whatever they got. Suppose she managed to protect herself financially while her husband still cared enough about her to put her on the *operating table* for her birthday."

"Attaway," Suki said.

"Now we get to Mr. Edward Rinehart."

"How?" Suki asked. "Oh, I forgot. You're not talking to me."

"Do you think that was his real name?"

"No," I said.

"Huh?" Suki said.

"I'm co–vice chairperson of the Sesquicentennial Committee. Laurie was the other one before Stewart kicked her off. Listen to me. You have to see the pictures."

"What pictures?" I asked.

"The *photographs*."

"They lost some photographs of my family," I said, and realized what she was telling me. "Photographs of Edward Rinehart. You saw them at the library, and you recognized him."

"I never never said that. Did I, Suki?"

"I have to go home now," Suki said. "Really."

I asked Rachel if her maid was working that day.

"Lulu's working today, yes. If you can call that work."

"I'll drive you home in your car, and Lulu can ride back with me while I take care of Suki."

"You think I'm not going to remember what I said about your uncle," Rachel said. "But I made a promise."

I helped Suki get up from her chair. On our way out, I grabbed a matchbook off the bar, thinking I would call Bob Brennan later that afternoon.

101

■ Rachel's housekeeper, Lulu White, helped me coax Suki out of the BMW and into the Riverrun gallery, where one of her young assistants promised to get her to bed. I walked back to my car and drove to Grace Street.

A woman behind the checkout desk indicated a door at the back of the reading room. In a gray, institutional hallway I found the words ASSISTANT HEAD LIBRARIAN on a gray, institutional door. I knocked, and Hugh Coventry told me to come in.

Metal shelves crammed with books and folders filled the walls of an office the size of a dormitory room. Half-visible behind the heaps of files and papers on his desk, his eyes squeezed shut and his back to a window, Coventry pressed a telephone to his ear. "I know, I know. I understand that." He opened his eyes to see who had walked in, and his nice, descendant-of-the-*Mayflower* complexion pinkened. Hugh waved a greeting and pointed to a chair. Then he made a loose, twirling gesture with his hand, communicating helplessness in the face of unexpected difficulty.

"I wish I *could* explain it." He squeezed his eyes shut again. "With all respect, the problem is *not* my organization. After all, I did get this library into. . . . No, sir, we *are* talking about the library. All of that material is here now."

I sat down and tried to look as though I were not listening.

"Mr. Hatch, I have a visitor. . . . Yes, I am responsible for the actions of my staff. . . . Well, there has been one other instance. . . . I think one of the volunteers misplaced a couple of files."

Coventry craned his neck and placed his free hand over his eyes. "Yes. Mrs. Hatch was here yesterday morning. . . . No, only for a minute. . . . Yes, if need be. . . . All right."

He put down the receiver, lowered his head, and flattened his hands on his temples. "This is crazy." He groaned. Then he raised his head, stood up, and extended his hand over the desk.

"Hello, Ned. Nice of you to drop in. It's been like Dunstan Central around here."

"You met my aunts," I said.

"Charming women. They came here with Laurie, though I didn't see any point in saying that to Mr. Hatch. Mrs. Rutledge and Mrs. Huggins seemed impressed with our systems, but they would have been more impressed had I located their photographs. We're losing family heirlooms right and left."

"Tell me about your selection process," I said.

Administrative details made him feel more comfortable. "Your aunts submitted exactly what the committee was looking for. A few studio portraits of each generation, snapshots, a marvelous photograph of Merchants Hotel under construction. What I did not intend to use I returned, and the rest went into a labeled box file for final selection. We were flooded with submissions around that time, and I wanted to guarantee everything could be accounted for. This was when we were still working in City Hall."

"Who makes the final selections?"

"Then, the co–vice chairmen, or chairpersons, I should say, Laurie and Mrs. Milton. Twice a week, I sent my choices down the hall to their office. They approved my choice of the Dunstan photographs, and Mrs. Rutledge's pictures were replaced in the box file. Late in September, we ran out of space, and I had everything moved out of City Hall and into the basement here. When I wanted to check the Dunstan file, I found the box, but not the file. And now, as you must have gathered, the same thing has happened to the Hatch file."

"How long has it been missing?"

"I don't know! Mr. Hatch sent in his submissions last February. Yesterday morning, he called to say that he wanted to make some changes in his family's portion of the exhibition, and I made a note to send the file back to him. He called again around noon today, asking for his file. *Immediately.* I went downstairs, and . . . you know what happened. He was furious. Stewart Hatch doesn't have any trouble getting in touch with his anger, let me put it that way."

"Of all the files to lose," I said.

"Precisely. Of course, it can't really be lost. One of the volunteers must have put it in the wrong box during the move. I'll find it, and I'll find your family's material, too, but it's going to be a tedious job." He uttered a nearly inaudible sigh. Then his natural courtesy erased the wrinkles from his forehead and brought him upright in his chair. "Why don't I show you our operation?"

He led me down a metal staircase to what had been a staff cafeteria. Gray tracks on the cement floor marked the locations of the old counters and display cases. The former dining tables had been arranged into a giant U in the middle of the room. Two white-haired women, one in a Greenpeace T-shirt, the other a light blue running suit, and a boy of sixteen or seventeen with pink hair, a nose ring, and black eyeliner were sorting through stacks of manila envelopes.

"Hello, people," Coventry said. "Let me introduce you to Ned, a friend of Mrs. Hatch's. Ned, this is Leona Burton, Marjorie Rattazzi, and Spike Lundgren. I have to say that Mr. Hatch is not happy with us."

"It'll take a while," said Spike. He looked at me indignantly and waved a skinny arm at three walls lined with files in boxes. "See all that stuff?"

"I know it won't be easy, Spike," said Coventry. "Ned, let me show you where they should have been."

From a shelf on the inner wall, Coventry pulled down a black archival box. *D–E* had been typed on the white card in its metal bracket. Beneath the letters, the card read, *Dunstan (Mrs. Annette Rutledge), Dorman (Mr. Donald Dorman, Mrs. George Dorman), Eames (Miss Alice Eames, Miss Violet Eames).*

He set the box on the table and removed the top. Handwritten letters and computer-printed pages half-filled the box. "This is Mrs. Rutledge's initial letter to us, along with my reply. Then comes a list of the photographs we retained, and a separate sheet coding the photographs to the time-line chart."

Coventry gestured at a blackboard ruled into sections, some headed by the names of years, others with slogans like "Steamboat Traffic," "Urban Growth," and "Increasing Prosperity." Lists of names and numbers filled three-fourths of most sections. "The Dunstan photographic file should be beneath this material. Unfortunately, it isn't, so we have to find it."

He replaced the box on the shelf. "The Hatch material was over here." We moved down the wall, and Coventry drew out a box labeled *H—Hatch Family (Mr. Stewart Hatch).* "This is even harder to understand than the Dunstan misfiling. We had two separate folders in here, one with photographs and advertisements related to the fairgrounds and other early business interests of the Hatch family. The second folder contained photographs and studio portraits, plus some class photographs from Edgerton Academy. Worth their weight in gold."

"That's what he's looking for, right?" Spike asked.

Leona Burton and Marjorie Rattazzi stared at him. Spike threw out his arms and leaned toward them. "Ladies, you weren't even here when that stuff came in. It was just Hughiebaby, me, and Florence Flutter."

"Fluther," said Marjorie Rattazzi, the woman in the running suit. *"Floo-ther."*

"Whenever Florence *Floo-ther* wanted to remember if R came before S she had to recite the whole alphabet. I had to check her work about six times a day. If something got balled up, you don't need a detective to figure it out. One more thing about Florence. She used to hold her breath whenever I came into the room, but *she* was the one who smelled."

Coventry looked at me with a mixture of apology and chagrin. "Mrs. Fluther volunteered here at the library for years, and we all appreciated her contribution."

"Okay," Spike said, "but he wants the Hatch stuff, doesn't he? You and Marjorie went through the Dunstan submissions, but I . . ." Spike swiveled his pink head and gave me a lengthy scrutiny. An all-encompassing blush rose into his face.

"You thought I was interested in the Hatch photographs?"

"Hugh-baby, you got something else I could do? My eyes aren't focusing."

Coventry told him to go upstairs and reshelve books, and he scooted out of the room.

"That boy isn't nearly as terrible as I thought when I first laid eyes on him," said Marjorie Rattazzi, "but I don't think I understand half the things that come out of his mouth." She smiled at me. "I was here when Mr. Coventry came down with Mrs. Hatch and your aunts. Women like that are so strong, aren't they?"

"Never lost a match," I said.

102

■ Side by side on the davenport, hands clasped over their stomachs, their white-crowned heads bent in ferocious concentration, the aunts drank in the soap opera booming from the television set. Clark slumbered in the rocking chair. "Good thing I'm not a burglar," I said.

"Well, hello, stranger," Nettie said.

Clark smacked his lips and took in my presence with a yellow eye. "Happen to pick up a six-pack on the way?"

"Sorry," I said.

"We still have a few in the fridge. I'd appreciate one. If you're in the mood, help yourself."

"There's tuna casserole on the table," Nettie said. "Fix yourself a plate."

"I want to talk to you two ladies."

"Oh, we heard all about it!" May said.

I took two bottles from the refrigerator, twisted off the caps, and came back into the living room. Clark accepted his beer in the way royalty accepts a chair, without looking at it. "What did you hear?" I asked the aunts.

"Took care of the whole shebang two seconds before you walked in," Nettie said. "My sisters and I know we are doing the right thing."

Clark detached the beer bottle from his mouth. "Maybe I should tag along behind Clarence and settle in beside him. A tragedy has the power to make a man think."

I looked back at Nettie. "You already heard from Mount Baldwin?"

"I spoke to a Mrs. Elizabeth Fanteen," she said. "Mrs. Fanteen is the executive director at Mount Baldwin. She asked for you, but in your absence Mrs. Fanteen was grateful to speak to me instead. You may be surprised, but that gracious Mrs. Milton called Mount Baldwin and found a place for Clarence. Mrs. Fanteen tells us that Clarence is welcome any time."

"Wonderful," I said.

"When Mrs. Fanteen asked me about Clarence's financial setup, I assured her that my sister and her husband are destitute."

"I'd better talk to Creech," I said.

"I spoke to Mr. C. Clayton Creech the minute I got off the phone with Mrs. Fanteen," Nettie said. "His manners may be peculiar, but Mr. Creech is a man who knows what's what. If you can stir yourself, Mr. Creech wants you to sign a few papers in his office at nine o'clock tomorrow morning."

"Which will give you plenty of time to pay our respects to old Toby," Clark said.

I looked back at Nettie.

"Mr. Creech informed me that the burial will take place at ten A.M. tomorrow. We would like you to represent our family."

"I'll be there," I said.

"I'd like some of that tuna casserole," Nettie said. "Keep you company."

"I could manage a few bites," May said.

"Count me in," Clark said. "Food takes your mind off your sorrows."

I brought in plates and forks and watched them eat. "Did you tell me you called Laurie Hatch?"

"I believe so," said Nettie. "A lovely young woman. My heart goes out to her, with her husband under suspicion of wrongdoing."

"You said you were thinking about calling her. You didn't mention that you went to the library, too."

Nettie rebuked me with a glance. "Mrs. Hatch merely helped my sister and myself try to recover the photographs mislaid by Mr. Coverly, a man who couldn't point out the sky if he was lying flat on his back in an open field."

"Coverdale," said May. "You Coverdale. He can't be from around here. People around here don't name their babies *You*."

"Hugh," I said. "Hugh Coventry."

"An exceptionally nervous man," said May. "It's a pity when a man has a nervous disposition."

"In my opinion, it was Mrs. Hatch who made him nervous," said Nettie.

The faint, almost playful suggestion of an idea came to me, and I said, virtually without thinking, "I don't suppose Mrs. Hatch mentioned any other photographs."

"I don't remember anything like that," Nettie said. "We were thinking of having your birthday celebration at eleven A.M. to-morrow, if it suits your crowded schedule."

"You're changing the subject."

"Mrs. Hatch asked us to give her regards to Neddie. Didn't I tell you that, Neddie? Your friend asked us to convey her regards."

I smiled at May. "You're telling me you walked out of the library empty-handed?"

"Goodness, only a fool would pass up an opportunity like that. I found all kinds of useful things in there. A whole box of rubber bands, *two* boxes of those nice big paper clips, jumbo they call them, and a date stamp where you can change the numbers. We can stamp our own books!"

"May," I said, "you don't have any books."

She smiled at me like a cat.

"Oh, dear," I said. "Would you mind if I called Rachel Milton?"

"If you think it necessary," Nettie said.

When Rachel got on the phone, I said, "I can't believe you acted so fast. Thank you."

"I took a nap as soon as I got home and had two cups of coffee afterward. Liz Fanteen told me she would work out the details and get everything set up. Liz is a genius at the numbers game. By the way, Grennie raced in about an hour ago, fit to be tied. He locked himself in his study and made a million phone calls. Then he ran out again, shouting about having to see Stewart. For once, I don't think he was lying. If you hear anything from Laurie, will you let me know? It'd be easier to be supportive if I knew he was going to jail."

A few minutes later I went across the street, where Joy hovered in her doorway as I told her about Mount Baldwin. To my relief, Joy was delighted by the news. And did I know? Another wonderful thing had just happened—Toby Kraft dropped dead and left everyone a fortune!

103

■ It was a few minutes past 3:00 P.M. when I walked past the shop windows on Fairground Road and turned into Buxton Place. The sunlight abruptly died. Beneath their Gothic rooftops, the cottages looked like malignant dwarfs. I was beginning to feel as though I had been strapped to a treadmill, and for a moment I thought about going back to my room for a nap.

The windows of 1 Buxton Place showed me no more than my own reflection. The same was true next door. I was wasting my time. The answers I needed were to be found in the present, not the past, and the nap was the best idea I'd had since telling the Reverend Swing about my mother's taste in music. Something Star said to me long ago, a description of an alto saxophone solo on "These Foolish Things" she had heard at a concert before I was born, came back to me, evoking her with painful clarity. I turned away, took a step toward the brilliant shaft of light at the end of the lane, and a man in a black Kangol cap and a short-sleeved blue shirt turned the corner and walked into the darkness. Moving over the cobbles with the trace of a limp, he began fingering through a crowded key ring. His dark skin had the dead pallor of flesh too long deprived of sunlight.

"Mr. Sawyer," I said. "How are you doing?"

Startled, Earl Sawyer looked up from his keys.

"I'm Ned Dunstan. I saw you in the ICU at St. Ann's."

"I remember." He took a slow step forward, then another.

"How do you feel?"

Sawyer found the key he wanted. "Fine. Got out of the hospital that night. After a few hours, all I had was a headache. Even the bruises went away. I don't keep bruises long, never have. What brings you up here?"

"My mother knew the man who owned these houses."

Sawyer tilted his head and waited for more.

"She died five days ago. I was hoping I might be able to talk to him."

His eyes seemed to change shape. "They were close?"

"Once upon a time," I said.

"What was his name, this friend of your mother's?"

"Edward Rinehart."

"You got the wrong address, sorry to say. I've been coming here twice a week for ten, fifteen years, and I never heard of him."

"This is the right place," I said. "Mr. Sawyer, who hired you? The owner?"

"Could be."

"Was his name Wilbur Whateley? Or Charles Dexter Ward?"

All expression drained from Sawyer's face, and his eyes momentarily retreated. A shy smile flickered over his mouth. He surveyed the stable doors on either side. "You surprised me with that one, my friend."

"So I noticed," I said.

He chuckled. "I was thinking, this guy got the address all wrong, and you come up with Charles Dexter Ward."

"Do you know Mr. Ward?"

"Never met him." Sawyer came up beside me and faced the bottom of the lane, as if to ensure that no one would overhear. "I answered an ad in the *Echo*. Thirty dollars a week for checking in on these properties, Wednesdays and Saturdays. Now it's up to fifty a week. I think I'll stay on. You know? Fifty dollars a week, quick trip on the bus, in and out."

His nod said it was better than stealing and twice as easy.

"How do you report to Mr. Ward?"

"He calls every Saturday, six P.M. sharp. 'Any problems?' he says. 'No problems, sir,' I say. Monday afternoon, a kid from Lavender Lane hands me an envelope with five ten-dollar bills. Nolly Wheadle." Sawyer chuckled at the image of the boy who had led me out of Hatchtown on the night Robert had first shown himself. "One time, years back, I had a rotten cold and missed a Wednesday. Mr. Ward called on the Saturday, and I said, 'No problem,' same as always. Mr. Ward—let's say I learned not to lie to Mr. Ward. My next envelope had only ten dollars in it."

"How did he know?"

"You got me. He comes here two or three times a month, though. There'll be glasses in the sink at Number One. A different stack of books on the table in Number Two."

"Mr. Sawyer," I said, "I know I'm asking an enormous favor, but would you let me look inside?"

He pursed his lips and jiggled his keys. "Your mother was a friend of Mr. Ward's?"

"Yes," I said.

"What was her name?"

I told him. He bounced the keys in his hand and debated with himself. "Just keep your hands off Mr. Ward's belongings."

Sawyer opened the door of number 1 onto a musty, charcoal-colored space shining with ghostly shapes. He slipped away to the left, and I heard the clicking of a switch. An overhead fixture shed reluctant light over the contents of Edward Rinehart's living room. Empty bookshelves covered the wall to my right. A Fisher amplifier, a Wollensak reel-to-reel tape recorder, and an A.R. turntable, stereo components that would have knocked your eyes out in 1957, lined a shelf on the near side of the fireplace. A Spanish bullfight poster and a reproduction of Picasso's *Three Musicians* hung over the sound equipment. A shelf lined with LP records bracketed the fireplace on its far side, and past the records was a narrow door. A sofa and three chairs draped in languorous-looking sheets accounted for the ghostly shapes I had seen from the entrance.

"The door goes into Number Two," Sawyer told me.

Here, Rinehart had conducted his parties and unofficial seminars. He had posed in front of the fireplace and read passages of his work. He had draped himself across the sofa and murmured provocations. Albertus students, poor damned Erwin "Pipey" Leake, and people like Donald Messmer had streamed up Buxton Place and brought their various passions through the front door.

Earl Sawyer walked to the far end of the room and into the kitchen, where garbage overflowed from a metal washtub. We went upstairs and looked into a room with a bare double bed, an oak dresser and table. "Any of this interest you?" Sawyer asked.

"All of it interests me," I said. I had probably been conceived on that bed. Robert seemed to flicker into being alongside me— I felt his demanding presence—and disappeared without having been any more than an illusion.

"What?"

"I thought I heard something."

"These places make noises by themselves," Sawyer said.

Downstairs, he opened the door beside the record shelf. The room beyond gaped like the mouth of an abandoned mine. "Wait a second. I'll get the lights."

Sawyer walked into the darkness and became a thick shadow. I heard a thump and the sound of wood sliding over wood, then another thump, like the opening and closing of a drawer. "I always hit that damn table."

He turned on a lamp atop a side table. A book-lined wall came into view. Sawyer moved to a larger table in the middle of the room and switched on a lamp surrounded by mounds of yellowed newspapers and empty food containers. Tall bookshelves took shape on all sides. "Come on in."

Rinehart had turned the cottage into a library. The shelves extended upward to the roof and all the way to the back of the house. An iron ladder curved up to a railed catwalk. There were thousands of books in that room. I looked at the spines: H. P. Lovecraft, H. P. Lovecraft, H. P. Lovecraft. I moved to the ladder and went up a couple of rungs. Multiple copies of every edition of each of Lovecraft's books lined the shelves, followed by their translations into what looked like every possible foreign language. First editions, paperbacks, trade paperbacks, collections, library editions. Some of the books looked almost new, others as though they had been picked up in paperback exchange stores. Rinehart had spent time and money buying rare copies, but he had also purchased almost every Lovecraft volume he had seen, whether or not he already owned it. "I think I know the name of his favorite writer," I said.

"Mr. Ward thinks H. P. Lovecraft was the greatest writer who ever lived." Sawyer scanned the shelves with mute, secondhand pride. "Years back, I started reading a couple stories when I finished my job. Mr. Lovecraft put a lot in them, but not everything he knew. I've had a lot of time to think about this subject."

This was the source of his pride—his theories about Lovecraft.

"You know what a parable is, I hope."

"I went to Sunday school," I said.

His smile vanished before the significance of what he had to say. "A parable is a story with a concealed meaning. You might not see it, but it's there."

"Some parables seem to have lots of meanings," I said. "The

more you think about them, the less you can be sure what they say."

"No, you're reading them all wrong, they wouldn't be any *good* that way. A parable has only one meaning, but the trick is, you have to look for it. Mr. Lovecraft's stories are the same. They can teach you a lot, if you're strong enough to accept the truth."

I had seen the same kind of pleasure in the faces of men devoted to theoretical, Hydra-headed conspiracies that connected the Kennedy assassinations, the FBI, organized crime, the military-industrial complex, and Satanic cabals. The stink of craziness always enveloped these people.

"Look there." Sawyer pointed at a shelf filled with copies of *From Beyond.* "A friend of his wrote that book. Mr. Ward said it ought to be famous, and he's right. It's a great book. Maybe my favorite."

His eyes met mine. "So were you telling me that Mr. Ward and Edward Rinehart are the same? Rinehart is what they call a pseudonym?"

He wanted to display his knowledge of the word.

"So is Charles Ward."

Sawyer's unhealthy face turned sullen.

I moved down rows of books and saw lodged at the end of a shelf what looked like a first edition of *The Dunwich Horror.* I pulled it out and saw penciled on the flyleaf *W. Wilson Fletcher, Fortress Military Academy, Owlsburg, Pennsylvania, 1941.*

Earl Sawyer materialized at my side like an angry djinn and snatched the book from my hands. "I'm sorry, I should have said." He nudged the book back into place. "Mr. Ward told me not to touch that particular book. It's sacred, you could say."

Sawyer cut off my apology. "You have to leave. I made a mistake."

■ 104

■ A tingling like the piercing by needles too small to be seen came over my hands when I drove through the southern fringe of

College Park. I looked down and saw the steering wheel waver beneath two hand-shaped blurs.

A voice from the backseat said, "How do you do that?"

"You do it!" I yelled.

"Don't be paranoid," Robert said. "It's over. Look."

My utterly visible hands gripped the wheel.

"I could explain it, but you wouldn't understand." He patted my shoulder. "What were you up to in College Park? And what's the latest on the Joe Staggers front?"

"You don't know?"

"I can't keep up with *everything*." Robert folded his arms on top of the passenger seat. "Talk to me."

"You can forget about Joe Staggers," I said, and described going through the Buxton Place cottages with Earl Sawyer.

"That gives me an idea. In the meantime, point us toward Ellendale. I think Stewart Hatch is hiding something we want."

The mystery of Robert's limitations faded before the suggestion that Hatch himself had walked off with his family photographs.

"He isn't at home," Robert said. "Stewart had troubling news today. He and Grenville Milton are deep in conference with their lawyer."

"I'm not going to break into his house."

"You won't have to. I'll go in and open the door."

"You don't need me to ransack Hatch's house," I said.

"Who knows? You might learn something about Laurie. In the meantime, explain why I should forget about Joe Staggers."

I told him that he wouldn't understand.

■ 105

■ One leg planted on the driveway, a knee bent into the Mountaineer, Posy Fairbrother was leaning through the rear door to strap Cobbie into his seat. She looked like an idealized figure on a frieze.

Robert sighed. "Pity that Posy's too straitlaced to mess around with her employer's lover. Turn left, here's Bayberry."

Stewart's angular, contemporary house stood on two treeless acres at the end of the first street off Blueberry. I drove past it and parked around the corner on Loganberry.

In a hot, green emptiness, Robert and I cut across the lawn and climbed the steps to the gray wooden deck. *"Momentito,"* Robert said. He glided through the back door and, after a pause longer than I had expected, opened it. "Stewart didn't install an alarm system. I guess there's nothing worth stealing."

I looked around at the kitchen. "Not unless you have a fork-lift." A gas range faced a twelve-foot marble counter that extended past a double-doored refrigerator and a glass-fronted wine vault. On the shelves beside the wine vault were ranked a half dozen bottles of single-malt Scotch and a couple bottles of Belvedere vodka, undoubtedly awaiting their turn in the freezer.

A partition separated the dining room from what people like Stewart Hatch called a "great room." The furniture marooned in the vast space had been picked up at a Scandinavian furniture outlet in the local mall.

Upstairs in the master bedroom, a monumental television set faced the bottom of an unmade king-sized bed. Polo shirts and khaki trousers were strewn across a sofa. Robert opened the closet doors. I went through a rolltop desk and found boxes of canceled checks, flyers from Caribbean resorts, and two videotapes, labeled *Kinky Bondage, USA* and *Love in Chains.*

A book titled *Management Secrets of the Ancient Chinese Warlords* lay on the bedside table; in the drawer underneath was a box of steel-tipped cartridges and a nine-millimeter pistol. The next drawer down contained a jumble of handcuffs, leather thongs and straps, lengths of rope, metal-studded wristbands, and a couple of things I neither recognized nor wanted to think about.

I looked under the bed, saw only the carpet, and joined Robert in a space about the size of Star's old room at Nettie's house. Something like fifty suits and jackets, at least a hundred neckties, and dozens of belts and suspenders hung beneath yards of open shelves with sweaters and shirts sorted by color and shade. Robert reached up to a stack of Brooks Brothers boxes, chose one, and opened it to reveal a striped, button-down shirt in a plastic wrapper. I thought of Gatsby.

"Let's look at the office downstairs," I said.

Robert roamed through a file cabinet. The closet was empty, except for an unopened case of Belvedere. Just above eye level, a carton from Bear, Stearns tilted at an almost unnoticeable angle on the narrow shelf. I pushed back the carton and uncovered a legal-sized manila envelope. I pulled it off the shelf. "The green light at the end of the dock."

Robert came up beside me. "I don't even want to know what that means. Open it."

I took a folder crammed with photographs out of the manila envelope and silently apologized to Laurie and my aunts before I even realized that I had suspected them of walking off with Hatch's pictures.

"Three cheers for the home team," Robert said.

The two men in the double portrait on top of the pile could only have been Omar and Sylvan Dunstan. Both my heart and my stomach seemed to drop six or seven inches within me, and I went to the desk and dumped out the rest of the photographs. Attired in wing collar, dark, linear suit, and high-buttoned waist-coat, the twenty- or twenty-one-year-old Howard Dunstan stared up at me. As his daughters endlessly reiterated, Howard had been a handsome man. He looked intelligent, charming, reckless, willful, and, I thought, half mad: cruelty and despair had already begun to tug at the features of a face uncomfortably similar to Robert's and mine.

Stewart had stolen our folder, not his, from Coventry's files.

A car, then another, pulled into the driveway. Two doors slammed. I looked at Robert. He shrugged.

"You asshole," I said.

"Everybody makes mistakes."

I scooped up the photographs and shoved the folder back into the envelope. Through the window behind Robert, I saw Stewart Hatch entering the garage with Grenville Milton towering beside him. They moved out of the frame of the window, and their footsteps sounded on the cement floor.

"What do we do now?" I heard them enter the kitchen.

Signaling for quiet, Robert eased the door shut. "After the old guy leaves, Hatch will go upstairs."

Grennie Milton's voice thundered from the kitchen.

"If they come here, I'll take care of it," Robert said.

The refrigerator door opened. Ice clinked into glasses.

I put my hands on the window's sash and saw the screen blocking my way. "Wait," Robert whispered.

Like a blip traveling across a radar screen, Milton's aggrieved voice marked their progress through the dining room and into the main part of the house, where his words became audible. "These people have *something*, Stewart. They want financial records back to 1983. Does that sound like a coincidence to you?"

"Give me a break," Hatch said.

The footsteps advanced to the front of the big room. The two men dropped into chairs.

"My Louisville attorney wants me to separate our cases."

"These people don't know anything. They can't. It's as simple as that."

"I am not interested in going to jail. Jail is not in the program. Are you listening to me, Stewart?"

"Am I ever," Hatch said. "I've been listening to your hysterics all afternoon."

"Then hear this. If you go down, you go down by yourself."

"That's nice. Grennie, nobody is going down. It's all smoke. If you separate our cases, you make both of us look guilty. That's not exactly the perception we want to put out there."

"They're preparing indictments, how does that make us look?"

"You want to know why they're preparing indictments? Ashton went around taking statements from everyone under the sun. In the process, she rented cars, she flew in airplanes, she stayed in nice hotels and paid for expensive meals. Where does she come from? Kentucky. These people had no *idea* of the expenses she was running up. So she goes back home empty-handed."

"But—"

"Ashton gets back to bluegrass country and says, Sorry guys, no dice. I *know* that. Her boss says, Ashton, this is my job on the line here, we can't afford to give up now. So what do they do? They make up the indictments, Grennie, that's what they do, because the indictments justify her expenses. If nothing new turns up, hey, maybe they can cut a deal. It's about saving face, that's all."

"You can't argue away the break-in," Milton said.

"My system failed. A guy got into the building and trashed the computers. But, Grennie, our records, they were never touched. I guarantee it."

"I hope you're right," Milton said. "I'm too old for prison."

"So am I. Not to mention getting screwed eight ways to Sunday on the home front. I should never have put Laurie on the damn committee. Yet another example that trying to be good to people is generally a terrible idea. What about Rachel?"

"Rachel put a death lock on my wallet about a month before I gave her the best cosmetic surgery money can buy," Milton said. "I can't see her turning vindictive. Well, okay. We're just going around and around. I have to get home and change before I meet Ming-Hwa."

"You want something to worry about, pick her," Hatch said. "But what do I know?"

"You wish it was you instead of me," said Milton. They drifted to the front door and repeated half of what they had already said before Milton's size 13 wingtips clumped down the driveway.

Hatch closed the front door, walked to the staircase, and went up a few steps. He hesitated and began coming back down. When he reached the bottom of the stairs, he turned toward the office. Robert winked at me and disappeared, leaving behind a vacant Robert-sized space.

The knob revolved, and the door began to swing open. I did the only thing I could, short of assault—at the moment Stewart Hatch walked into the room, I bit into time.

■ When my eyes cleared, I was standing in an open field, experiencing the pains of my previous journeys, but to a lesser degree. Empty grassland rolled over the hills, and birds soared on outstretched wings through the flawless sky. I walked in what I hoped was the direction of the future Bayberry Lane, trying to remember the distance to the corner. When I thought I was getting close to the car, I did my trick and returned to the tiled border of a backyard swimming pool. Another foot to the right, and I would have been underwater.

My head felt fine, and my gut reported no more than a mild twinge. However, the woman wearing the bottom half of a bikini who was tilted back in the chaise ten feet in front of me seemed about to go into shock. She propelled herself forward and snatched up a towel. "Where did *you* come from?"

"Miss, I'm as embarrassed as you are," I said. "I was hoping to find someone who could give me directions. I'm supposed to deliver this envelope to an address on Bayberry Lane, but I can't seem to find it. I hope you'll forgive me."

She tucked the ends of the towel under her arms and smiled. "Whose house are you looking for?"

"Mr. Hatch's," I said.

"Stewart?" She pointed without raising her arm. "That's his place." Fifty yards away, the gray deck jutted out over a smooth, vibrantly green lawn. I had come nowhere near the car. "Go down Elderberry, turn right on Loganberry and right again at the next corner."

When I turned the corner into Loganberry Street, Robert was leaning against the Taurus, grinning at me. "To hell with you," I said.

"I knew you didn't really need my help," Robert said. "But I hope you're going to tell me how you got away."

"Magic carpet," I said.

"Mysteriouser and mysteriouser. What do we do now?"

"I'm going to Laurie's, and you're not. Come to the Brazen Head tonight."

"You won't give me a ride back to town?"

"Robert," I said, "I don't think you'll have any trouble getting back to town by yourself."

He touched his forehead in a mocking salute and was gone. I went to the door of my car and heard someone say, "Mister?"

A woman in shorts and a halter top was staring at me from across the street. "I have to ask. How did you *do* that?"

"My brother's been pulling that stunt ever since we were kids," I said. "It used to drive our mother crazy."

■ 106

■ When Laurie opened her front door, I saw sheer, unalloyed pleasure radiating through all the complications of her beautiful face. "Ned! I'm so glad. Come in."

She moved into my arms. "Tell me about the funeral."

"It was all right. An old friend of my mother's named Suki

Teeter came, and so did Rachel Milton. The three of us had lunch afterward. Rachel isn't so bad, after all."

"I should phone her. Would you like to hear some good news? Ashleigh called to say they're working on the indictments. Grennie may not have long to enjoy true love."

"Even shitheads get the blues," I said.

"Let's celebrate with a really good bottle of wine." She went into the kitchen and returned with a bottle of Heitz Private Reserve cabernet and two glasses.

After I poured, she said, "I have to make sure this won't be too hard on Cobbie. I don't know how you explain to a kid that his father is going to jail, but I want to protect him. He's out with Posy, by the way. She took him to see *Aladdin*."

"It's nice to see you alone."

"I've been thinking." She leaned back into the sofa. "Columbia accepted Posy into their Ph.D. program. Cobbie's going to need more training than he could ever get here. New York might make a lot of sense for us."

"Would Posy stay on with you?"

"She'd jump at the chance, and having her with us would give Cobbie some continuity. Besides, I'm crazy about Posy Fairbrother—I don't want to lose her, either. If I bought a big apartment or a brownstone, we'd all have enough privacy."

"The kind of place you're talking about costs a fortune," I said. "Private schools would be another ten or fifteen thousand a year. Plus the music lessons. Can you afford all that?"

"The trust can," she said. "I'm not going to let Parker Gillespie run my life."

It was the reason she had called Gillespie: Laurie had been thinking about moving to New York before she had ever met me. I said, "It sounds like a great idea. I want to be around the first time Cobbie hears Bach. Or Charlie Parker."

"You should be around. Cobbie needs more than music." Laurie smiled to herself, as if realizing that she had said too much. "Let me back up. Would you like it if I moved to New York?" She moved an inch away and, in a kind of compensation, put her hand on my knee. "I don't want to put you in an awkward position."

"Of course I would," I said. "Think of all the nice places we could go." I heard myself say the word "nice" and knew that I was talking about a fantasy. I wanted the fantasy to be true.

"What places?"

"The Metropolitan Opera. The Frick museum. The corner of Bedford and Barrow in the Village. Second Avenue on a Sunday morning in August, when all the lights turn green at once and you hardly see a car for miles. The Great Lawn in Central Park. The Esplanade in Brooklyn Heights. The Gotham Book Mart. About a hundred great restaurants."

"Let's find our favorite one and go there once a month, religiously."

"Laurie," I said, "when you met my aunts at the library, did you ask them to take some photographs?"

"Take snapshots? They didn't bring a camera."

A more innocent answer could not be imagined. I laughed. "I meant, take as in walk out with."

She looked puzzled. "Why would I do that?"

"Forget I asked. Hugh told me that Stewart's family photos had disappeared. He discovered they were missing after you visited the library with my aunts, who could stuff the Empire State Building into a couple of shopping bags without anyone noticing. I don't know, maybe you wanted to shake him up a little. It was a bad idea. Sorry." It was worse than a bad idea—it was ridiculous. Laurie could not have known that Stewart was going to demand the return of his archive.

"Now two sets of pictures are missing? Yours and Stewart's?"

"Awfully strange coincidence, isn't it?"

"So strange that you thought I must have had something to do with it. And then didn't tell you. Which makes it sound like, instead of trying to annoy Stewart, I was concealing something from you."

She was right: it did sound like that. I remembered what Rachel Milton had said to me about the Hatch photographs, but Laurie's talent for perception had already pushed this conversation past anything intended by my thoughtless question. "Whoa," I said. "Too far, too fast. Around you, I have to watch what I say."

"Who drove you to the V.A. Hospital?"

"I know," I said.

A car rolled into the driveway and stopped in front of the garage.

Laurie kissed my cheek. "Remember who your friends are."

* * *

■ Cobbie burst in and squealed with pleasure. "Ned, Ned, I have a *trick*!"

Posy smiled at me, put down the stroller, and set two shopping bags on the counter. "After the movie, I bought some books and a couple of the CDs Ned recommended."

"I have a *trick*!" Cobbie's eyes were dancing. He smelled like popcorn.

"Let me know how much you paid, and I'll add it to your check." Laurie hugged Cobbie. "Hello, squirt. Did you like the movie?"

"Uh-huh. And I—"

"You want to show us a trick."

"Uh-huh." He paused for dramatic effect and sang an odd series of notes. Then he went limp with laughter.

"It's beyond me," Posy said. "He's been singing it over and over, and it cracks him up every time."

Cobbie began singing the peculiar melody again, and this time he found it so funny he could not get to the end.

"Do it all the way through," I said.

Cobbie stationed himself before me, looked directly into my eyes, and sang the entire sequence of notes.

I thought I knew why it sounded so odd. "Um, backwards something singing you are, Cobbie?" It took me longer to work out the order of the six words than Cobbie had taken to reverse eight bars of melody.

"Huh?" Laurie said.

Chortling, Cobbie trotted to the piano and plunked out the notes.

"Now play it the right way," I said.

He hit the same notes in the opposite order and grinned at Posy.

"Oh, my God," she said. "It's from the movie."

"Wholewide Worl," Cobbie said.

"That settles it," I said to Laurie. "He's going to be Spike Jones when he grows up."

"Is Ned staying for dinner?" Cobbie asked.

"Is he?" Laurie asked me.

"As long as Cobbie and I can listen to one of those new CDs," I said, thinking that after dinner, I would go back to Buxton Place to see what Earl Sawyer had hidden in a drawer. Earl Sawyer was a troubling man. He cherished the notion that

H. P. Lovecraft's stories described a literal reality, and he had nearly fainted when I had touched the first edition with the owner's inscription on the flyleaf. I tried to remember the name: Fleckner? Flecker? Fletcher. W. Wilson Fletcher, of the Fortress Military Academy in Owlsburg, Pennsylvania.

■ For about half an hour, Cobbie sat entranced through most of Haydn's *Theresienmesse*, occasionally turning to see if I had heard some particular sonic miracle. Now and then, he said "Huh" to himself. During the "Credo" movement, he looked at me with an expression of puzzled delight. "That's called a fugue," I said. He turned back to the music and muttered, "Foog." When the movement came to an end, he announced that it was time for cartoons and sped into the room on the other side of the fireplace.

In the kitchen, Laurie and Posy were gliding back and forth between the counter and the stove. Posy asked if I had seen the books she bought for Cobbie, and I went back into the living room. Posy had found short biographies, written for children, of Beethoven and Mozart. The last book in the bag was *The Best of H. P. Lovecraft's Bloodcurdling Tales of Horror and the Macabre*.

I brought it into the kitchen and said, "You didn't get this for Cobbie, did you?"

"Oh, sure," Posy said. "Laurie and I were talking about the book you brought over the other day. Somebody Rinehart? Lovecraft's name came up, and I was curious. A guy in my neurobiology seminar is a big Lovecraft fan. I've never read anything by him, so I thought I'd take a look. One instance is chance, two are design."

"Huh," I said, and realized that I sounded like Cobbie.

"You're not allowed to ogle the staff," Laurie said. She handed me the wine bottle. "We'll be ready in about twenty minutes."

I poured out the last of the wine, went to the sofa, and began reading "The Dunwich Horror."

The story began with an evocation of a sinister area in northern Massachusetts. Cramped between looming hills, the town of Dunwich exuded decay. Generations of inbreeding had warped its native population into degeneracy. The story moved into particulars with the introduction of Lavinia Whateley, cursed by ugliness and albinism, who at thirty-five had given birth to goatish, dark-skinned Wilbur. The child began walking at seven months and learned to speak before his first birthday. Well in advance of his teens, he developed thick lips, yellow skin, wire-brush hair, and the ability to throw dogs into savage fits.

In the way a particle of food sticks between the teeth, an otherwise unnoticed detail seemed to have lodged in my mind, and I leafed back and found this sentence: *"The only persons who saw Wilbur during the first month of his life were old Zechariah Whateley, of the undecayed Whateleys, and Earl Sawyer's common-law wife, Mamie Bishop."*

I flipped through a couple of pages and saw, *"Earl Sawyer went out to the Whateley place with both sets of reporters and camera men."*

Goose pimples rose on my arms. Once was chance, twice was design. The Buxton Place houses had been bought under names taken from Lovecraft characters, and their caretaker went by the name of another. Earl Sawyer adored Edward Rinehart because he was Edward Rinehart.

"Laurie," I said before I knew what I was going to do, "I think I left something upstairs yesterday."

"What?" she called.

"I'll be right back." As though driven by a malign compulsion, I double-jumped the stairs and went into Laurie's bedroom. While a part of me stood by in horror, I pulled open her dresser drawers and searched through her clothing. I went to her closet and compounded my crime.

Laurie's voice came from the bottom of the staircase. "What are you looking for, Ned?"

"A pair of sunglasses. I just realized they're gone."

"I don't think they're here. Dinner in five minutes."

I looked under her bed and into her bedside table. I searched the bathroom. When I came out into the hallway, I glanced at Cobbie's door and moved to Posy's. I considered taking a look inside, rejected the idea, and turned toward the stairs. Posy Fairbrother was regarding me from the end of the hallway.

"Thank you for not going into my room," she said. "Am I to gather you thought I might have taken your sunglasses?"

"No, Posy, please," I said. "I was just trying to figure out where the blasted things could be."

"I don't think I've ever seen you wear sunglasses," she said. "Anyhow, we're ready to eat."

I got through dinner by steering the conversation toward cartoons, a subject on which Cobbie had a great many observations, and Haydn's *Theresienmesse*, to which I had listened just often enough to fake an expertise. Posy sent me suspicious glances, and Cobbie, for whom dinner with the grown-ups was a special treat, threw in a couple of four-year-old aperçus. ("That music was like very, very, very good food," and "It's nice when a bunch of singers don't make the notes *smeary*.") Both women seemed put out with me, and my apologies for fussing over a lost pair of sunglasses and having to leave after dinner did nothing to warm the atmosphere. A puzzled Laurie walked me to the door. I said that I expected to be busy all the next day, but would call if I could. Cobbie rocketed out of the kitchen, and I gathered him up and kissed his cheek. He reared back and said, emphasizing every word, "I—want—to—hear—another—FOOG!"

■ 107

■ I parked a block south of Brennan's and hurried into narrow Buxton Place. Twilight had begun to sink into real darkness, and moonlight glinted from the windows in the old stables. As I had expected, the doors and windows of the cottages refused to budge. I kicked at cobbles until one dislodged. I wrapped it in my jacket, carried it back to number 2, and stepped up to the window.

A hand closed on my shoulder. I thought my heart would explode.

An inch from my ear, Robert's voice, my voice, said, "Have you lost your mind?"

I wanted to club him with the stone.

"You can't still be angry. I did you a favor."

"You ran out on me."

"Didn't you disappear a second after I did?"

"Did I?"

He chuckled. "Brother dear, the more you can discover in yourself, the better off we'll be tomorrow."

"Where have you been?"

"Speaking of favors," he said. "Blueberry Lane."

His smirk was unbearable. "Someone had to repair the damage. I apologized for my moodiness. I hadn't even thanked Laurie and Posy for their lovely dinner, and I hoped they would understand that my mother's funeral was having a terrible effect on my manners. I found the sunglasses in the car, sorry for letting them become the focus of my anxieties. Blah blah blah. There are things about human beings I don't understand, I know, but your fondness for that little boy really baffles me. I had to keep peeling him off my leg. If you don't watch out, you're going to spoil that child."

"You followed me?"

"No. I had the pleasure of an early supper at Le Madrigal. Julian flirted with me so sweetly that I'm joining him for a drink around one-thirty this morning. The boy is all aquiver."

"You're going to have sex with Julian?"

"I don't make pointless distinctions. Now that the ladies of Blueberry Lane have been pacified, tell me why we're breaking into this hovel."

"After we get inside," I said.

Robert filtered through the front door of number 2. As always, it looked like a special effect in a movie. The door swung open, and I dropped the cobblestone and walked in.

"Make sure the curtains are drawn," Robert said.

I tugged the curtains until they overlapped. "Can you see?"

"Not much better than you." He felt his way to the central table and fumbled with the lamp. "If Earl Sawyer already gave you the tour, why are we here?"

"His name isn't Earl Sawyer," I said, and told him what I knew.

For once, Robert seemed dumbfounded. "How can that ugly old man be Edward Rinehart? He doesn't look anything like us, and he's supposed to be our father?"

"Thirty years ago, he probably looked exactly like us. He's had a lousy life, he's about fifty pounds overweight, and he eats terrible food. On top of that, he's as crazy as a shithouse rat, which tends to distort the way you look."

"I could have killed him in the blasted Cobden Building."

"He didn't know who you were, either. He never really saw

you. But he sure knew who I was when he let me in here this afternoon. He had to."

"Why didn't he try to kill you then?"

I gave him the only reason that made sense to me. "Because killing only one of us is no good."

"You're wrong, wrong, wrong," Robert said. "He doesn't know there are two of us. That's the reason I'm still alive."

"He has to know it now, Robert," I said. "Maybe he saw us on that night in Hatchtown. He's waiting until tomorrow, when he's counting on getting us together. But whatever he tries to do, we have one advantage over him."

Robert grasped the point. "He doesn't know *we* know."

"I hope that's an advantage. Anyhow, it's the only one we have."

He moved frowning across the floor and switched on the other lights. "Don't make assumptions about what I'll be willing to do."

"Robert," I said, "we will do what we have to do."

Two parallel lines cut through the dust on top of the table where Earl Sawyer had been standing when he summoned me into the room. One of the lines was about eight inches long, the other no more than two. A picture frame, I thought, propped on its cardboard leg. I pulled out the drawer and found nothing but mouse droppings. Sawyer had taken with him whatever he had hidden from me.

"Let's rattle his cage." Robert was virtually shimmering with excitement. "Let's make Edward Rinehart so angry he won't be able to think."

"How?"

Robert looked across to the thirty or forty copies of *From Beyond*. "I suppose he is amazingly attached to those books."

"You have an evil mind," I said.

"I have some matches with me, but we'll need more."

"I believe I can help you there," I said.

"Then all we need is a metal container thingie about half the size of a bathtub. I want to do this outside, so we don't set the house on fire."

"Hold on." I went through to number 1, groped into the kitchen, switched on the overhead light, and overturned the washtub I had seen earlier. Garbage showered onto the messy floor. I carried the tub back and found Robert standing outside in a small, bricked-in yard beneath the steadily darkening sky.

Robert wheeled around, and I put down the tub and followed him to the shelf filled with copies of *From Beyond*. It took us three trips to carry them outside. I brought the matches out of my pocket and picked up one of the books.

"Not yet." Robert folded back its covers and wrenched the glued pages away from the spine. He separated the wad of pages into halves, then into smaller and smaller sections. I began dismembering another copy. Loose pages fluttered to the cement floor.

When nearly half of the books had been destroyed, Robert knelt alongside the wreckage. "Now we get to the fun." He lit a match and held it to the bottom of a quire of pages. Yellow flame traveled up the first of them and spread to the second. Robert turned them over. The flame shrank and lost strength, then crept around the edges and took hold. Robert lowered the burning papers into the tub and held another section of pages over the fire.

"This is as close as you can get to feeling right about burning books," I said.

"Don't be an asshole," Robert said. Laughter bubbled in his voice.

I ripped books apart while Robert fed pages into the fire, laying in each new section like wood on a hearth and spreading the fire across the whole of the washtub. Scraps lifted burning into the air and floated toward the walls. In flight, some pages consumed themselves entirely, leaving behind not even ash. Some shrank to traveling dots of light, to fireflies; others blazed into flaming birds. A few burned on as they ascended, whirling far up into the night sky on the wind of their own destruction. Flames sent abrupt shadows capering along the walls.

As Robert bent over the washtub, erratic flickers of red and orange illuminated his face. It seemed almost ideal, no more like my own than mine was like Michelangelo's David. Robert's crisp eyebrows were streaks of black paint, the same smooth thickness all along their length. His eyes were clear and lustrous, his nose so perfect it might have been shaped by a godlike chisel. Deep shadows emphasized the cut of his cheekbones and the broad, well-defined mouth. The entire face spoke of quickness, assurance, grace, vitality—also, as he watched the fireflies and blazing birds dance upward, of the pure hunger that made him rejoice in destruction.

"Your turn." Robert jumped up to chase a soaring yellow wing.

I squatted beside the washtub and eased in pages, snatching back my hand from sudden flares. Beneath the body of the fire, lines of type seethed and coiled. Robert danced after his skittering yellow wing until it shrank to a glowing constellation of red sparks, then whirled to chase another flaming bird toward the back wall. He looked like the follower of some ancient god, his hair tied with ropes of golden grasshoppers, ecstatic in the performance of a sacrifice. Then I thought Robert looked not like a follower, but like a god himself, a god rejoicing in conflagration and disorder.

He danced back to hold a binding over the flames until a yellow tongue unfurled across the green board. My sense of the incomprehensible depth of his experience disappeared into, was *erased by,* the awareness that his insatiability, the intensity of his deprivations, had forever trapped him within childhood. Suddenly, Robert seemed stunted by the weight of all he needed, and for the first time I understood that he was imprisoned in a half-life from which only I could rescue him. Robert needed me more crucially, more centrally, than I had always needed him. Within whatever jealous, smoke-filled chamber that passed for his soul, Robert knew this, too, and pretended he did not.

His beautiful face darkened when he noticed me looking at him.

"I was thinking how we look exactly alike in one way, and not at all in another," I said, and received another edgy glance.

We went back to business until every copy of Edward Rinehart's book had turned into ashes and a few, half-burned bindings at the bottom of a washtub. The yard smelled like the remains of Helen Janette's rooming house. Black, charred black leaves littered the ground. Robert kicked one into fragments. "Let's trash some of his Lovecraft, too."

"I'm not burning any *good* books," I said, "but that gives me an idea." I went inside and saw that my hands were smeared with ashes. I supposed the same was true of my face. Already distant, Robert stood in the doorway. Unlike me, he was immaculate. I used my handkerchief to slide *The Dunwich Horror* from its shelf. "I think this is the first Lovecraft he ever read. I bet it's his bible."

Robert displayed a trace of interest.

"He'll do anything to get it back."

"In that case, we'll make him jump through hoops." He looked at his watch. "Clean yourself up. You're a mess."

"What about tomorrow?"

"Our adventures usually begin around three or four in the afternoon. I'll see you before that, wherever you are. In the meantime, don't do anything stupid."

"You, too."

Robert smiled at me. "Ned has a trick up his sleeve. Ned is not laying all his cards on the table. Let me ask this. *He* doesn't know that *we* know that *he* knows there are two of us. Would you spell out how we're going to use that against him?"

"The way we did in Boulder," I said. I had no intention of telling him the rest.

"I refuse."

"You won't have any choice. It's all we have."

Robert glared at me, trapped between what he knew to be true and what he did not want to admit. "I'm not agreeing to anything."

I walked to the table from which I thought Earl Sawyer had removed a framed photograph of his younger self. "Come here." Robert moved unwillingly across the room. "Hold your hand under the light."

"If you must." He thrust his right hand, palm up and fingers extended, beneath the lamp. No creases divided his palm, and there were no ridges on his fingertips. His hand could have been made of a remarkably lifelike plastic.

"There weren't enough fingerprints to go around," Robert said. "I can't say I miss them."

Missing them causes you more pain than you can afford to admit, I thought.

He pulled his hand from the pool of light. "You have a lot to learn."

"At least I learned that much," I said. Robert was already gone.

■ A ragged boy squatted in front of the warehouse on Lavender Lane, his hands between his knees, a cigarette drooping from the fingers. His shoulders twitched, the cigarette rose, his mouth captured it. He had memorized every gesture ever made by Frenchy La Chapelle. When I came toward him, the boy shot to his feet and slithered around the door. A bolt slammed home.

I put my hands on the door and whispered. "I want to see Nolly Wheadle."

The words passed into silence.

"Nolly? You helped me out of Hatchtown last Friday night. I want to talk to you." These words, too, met a waiting silence. "There's five bucks in it for you."

I heard a scuffle of feet. A wised-up little voice said, "Ten."

"You got it," I said.

"Push it under the door," the voice said.

"Let me hear you slide the bolt."

"First the money."

I pushed a bill under the door. The bolt moved out of its clip, and the door rattled a foot sideways. I slipped inside. At my back, the door closed on utter blackness. Not to me, Nolly whispered, "Get away." Small, bare feet retreated over the earthen floor. My eyes began to adjust, and I saw dim outlines arranging themselves against the wall, like birds settling in for the night.

Nolly's vague figure moved toward the side of the warehouse. "Keep your voice down."

"You remember me."

"Aye," Nolly said.

"Two men were following us."

"People say you took care of one of them." His voice sounded like air leaking from a punctured tire.

"Somebody did," I said. Nolly made a hissing sound that I realized was a chuckle. "I think another person was there, too.

Someone who saw us but was never seen. Someone you know. A man who pays you to do favors for him."

"We does favors," Nolly said. "It don't *mean* nothing."

"I met him today. He said his name was Earl Sawyer." Whispers came from the rear of the old warehouse. "I think he sometimes wears a black coat and hat."

Nolly's shadowy form went rigid.

A voice from the back of the warehouse said, *Black Death.*

Nolly hissed, "Shut yer traps!"

"You call him Black Death?" I whispered.

A small voice said, *Into the Knacker with 'im, Nolly, into the Knacker.*

He leaned toward me. "You're not supposed to have heard of him, someone like you, and besides, you're mixed up in the head. You're putting together two different fellows who aren't the same."

"The Knacker?" I asked Nolly.

"Where they go when they go permanent," Nolly whispered. "Not only horses, neither."

He backed away, and I grabbed the tail of his shirt and pulled him deeper into the corner. Nolly submitted with a glum, heartbreaking passivity. I knelt down and put another five-dollar bill in his hand. "I know you're scared. I am, too. This is important to me."

"Life-or-death important?"

"Life-or-death important."

So softly that I could barely hear him, Nolly whispered, "There's a name you can't say, because he can hear through walls. Those that see him when he doesn't want to be seen are taught to be sorry. That is B.D. You know what I mean by that name?"

"Yes," I whispered back.

"He lives at night, and he has always been here. B.D. is not a true human being. Most of those back there, they see him as a vampire. I say, he's not a vampire but a demon from hell."

"He's always been here?"

"He was made when *Hatchtown* was made. B.D. *is* Hatchtown, as I think. That's why things are this way."

"Which way?" I asked.

Nolly made a contemptuous noise. "Water's bad, sewers don't work. Every time the river floods, we're underwater and covered in mud. This is Hatchtown. B.D., he's like *us*, except he's a demon. If there is a Mr. Hatch, I reckon he made B.D. but I wish he hadn't."

I leaned back against the wall and put my hands over my face.

Nolly bent closer. "Earl Sawyer will be another five dollars." I gave him the bill.

"Mr. Sawyer is a sour old creature," Nolly said. "He'd sooner kick you than say a kind word, which he never does."

"Where does he live?"

"I usually see him in the vicinity of Leather Lane. But when he goes to ground, he goes to ground like a fox."

"All right," I said, and stood up. Nolly urged me toward the door and slid it open. I stepped into the lane, and, to my surprise, he slipped outside behind me. What I could see of his face looked like a catcher's mitt. He glanced from side to side and whispered something so quietly I merely saw his lips move.

I bent down, and he put his mouth close to my ear. "From what I heard, it was you seen two nights ago in Fish Lane with Joe Staggers from the town of Mountry."

"It might have been," I whispered, realizing that these kids heard everything.

"Joe Staggers has not been seen again. Which has caused no tears to fall. Not in Hatchtown. Nor in Mountry, either, I figure."

"The gentleman was called away," I said.

"It must have been a powerful call."

What was Nolly doing, what was he looking for? "Too powerful for him, anyhow."

"A gun was fired, but no one was hit," Nolly said. "That's not your way, is it?"

"Nolly," I whispered, "do you **want** to tell me something?"

He hitched up one shoulder and tugged at the waistband of his trousers. He shifted his feet and jerked his head back and forth. In an imitation of Frenchy La Chapelle even better than the lookout's, he pulled at his sleeves and squinted as if trying to see around the curve in the lane. Frenchy had been one of these children, I realized, he had spent his nights in the old lavender warehouse and performed occasional services for B.D., the Hatchtown vampire. I thought Frenchy had continued to perform these services for the remainder of his wretched life.

Nolly was still trying to peer around the corner. "Do you know Horsehair?"

I shook my head.

"Horsehair is *small,* and it is *dark.* Horsehair winds *back* and *forth.* In Horsehair, you can get to where you are going without no one knowing you are already gone. The general public never sees it, on account of its being the kind of thing it is." Nolly again tilted his mouth to my ear. "*He* uses Horsehair. So if you wanted to find him, which I never did, you could maybe find him there."

"Where is it?"

"Everywhere," Nolly whispered. "For one example, right *there.*" He pointed a grubby hand at a barely visible gap between two buildings and vanished back into the warehouse.

■ **109**

■ I stepped inside the space Nolly had shown me. Ahead, a dark, narrow artery stretched out for twenty feet or more before curving leftward. I felt as though Nolly Wheadle had shown me the secret within the secret, the key to Hatchtown's true interior. Horsehair brought me to Raspberry, then into desolate little Barrel Lane, and from there on a winding trail leading, I hoped, in the direction of Veal Yard. Sounds from other lanes reverberated off the narrow walls. A stench like that of Joy's house came to me, then sank back into the bricks. From somewhere near, I heard a man humming "Chattanooga Choo-Choo" and thought it was Piney Woods, staggering down Leather Lane. When at last I emerged into Veal Yard, I saw Horsehair opening like a paper cut beyond the dry fountain and knew how Edward Rinehart had witnessed Robert's first appearance before me.

6

HOW I SPENT MY BIRTHDAY

■ The next morning I wished myself a happy thirty-fifth birthday and hoped I would live to see thirty-six. When it came to birthday presents, you couldn't beat survival. After I dressed for Toby's funeral in a clean white shirt, gray trousers, a rep tie, and my blazer, I picked up the telephone and got the number for the Fortress Military Academy in Owlsburg, Pennsylvania. Who was W. Wilson Fletcher, I wondered, and how did Rinehart get his book? If Fletcher had made it through World War II, he was probably still alive, and he might remember giving the book to a fellow student.

I told Captain Lighthouse in the Alumni Office that I was doing background for an arts-page feature in the *Edgerton Echo* concerning the world's most extensive H. P. Lovecraft collection. For a sidebar tracing the history of the cornerstone of the great collection, a first edition of *The Dunwich Horror*, I wished to speak to its original owner, W. Wilson Fletcher, who had inscribed the book with his name, the name of the academy, and the year 1941.

"Sir, did Fletcher inscribe his name without indication of rank?"

"Just his name."

"Then he was a pledge. Let me check the Alumni Directory." He put me on hold. "W. Wilson Fletcher is not listed in the Directory, which means one of two things. Either he is deceased, or he fell through the cracks, which is something we don't like to happen. 1941, you said?"

"Right." I resisted the temptation to say "Affirmative."

"I'll look up the class lists for 1941 and the years on either side."

I asked Lighthouse if he was an academy graduate.

"Affirmative," he said. "Class of 1970. Did my twenty years and came back to help out my old school. I love this place, I really do. Let's see, now. 1941, no, not there. Maybe he was Artillery that year, which would put him in the class of '42. Yep, there he is, Wilbur Wilson Fletcher, class of 1942. No wonder he used the W. I take it that you will be mentioning the academy in your article?"

"Of course," I said.

"If you don't mind being put on hold again, I want to check a few other sources. The Fortress Academy Roll of Honor will tell us if Fletcher was killed in action during his military service. If that fails, I'll try Major Audrey Arndt, the Academy's executive secretary. The major has been here since 1938, and she remembers everything and everybody. This place could hardly run without her. Do you mind waiting?"

"Not at all. I'm surprised you're still on the campus."

"My job goes year-round, and the major doesn't believe in vacations. Hold on, sir."

Captain Lighthouse kept me on hold for ten minutes. It seemed like enough time to wallpaper my room. I gathered that Wilbur had not helped raise the flag at Iwo Jima or won the Congressional Medal of Honor. I carried the telephone to the table and for the first time noticed that someone had carved, with a careful, almost witty precision, his initials and a date into its surface. *P.D. 10/17/58.* P.D. had done an elegant job. The almost calligraphically incised letters and numbers ran in an arc along the table's edge, so small as to go unnoticed unless you were looking directly at them. P.D., I gathered, had been excruciatingly bored. I wondered if he had been a musician waiting for the start of a concert.

The line clicked, and a muted Captain Lighthouse told me, "Major Arndt is on the line." Another click.

An authoritative female voice said, "Major Arndt here, Mr. Dunstan. Please explain your interest in Pledge Fletcher."

I repeated my story. "I was hoping to talk to Mr. Fletcher, and I thought the academy could give me his telephone number."

"Mr. Dunstan, the Fortress Military Academy is pleased to cooperate with the press, but cooperation works both ways. I want your assurance that what I am about to tell you will be handled discreetly and tastefully. And you will agree to fax me a draft of your article previous to publication."

My skin prickled. "Agreed."

"Unwittingly, I assume, Mr. Dunstan, you refer to the single unhappiest incident in the history of the Fortress Academy. Artillery Pledge Fletcher died as the result of an assault by an intruder shortly before the Christmas break of 1941. His assailant was never identified. As a result, this fine institution was subjected to a great deal of unwelcome publicity."

"You don't say."

"I would prefer that you make no mention of Artillery Pledge Fletcher's death in your article. More realistically, I ask you to describe it as an unfortunate tragedy, and leave it at that."

"Major Arndt," I said, "nothing in my piece requires me to dig up a fifty-year-old scandal. There is one more favor I'd like to ask, and I promise you, the same conditions will apply."

"Proceed," she said.

"Pledge Fletcher can't tell me how he acquired or disposed of the book, but some of his classmates may be able to fill in the gaps. If you would consent to fax me the 1939 to 1941 class lists from the Alumni Directory, I can take it from there. Nothing I might hear about the circumstances of Fletcher's demise will appear in the article. I'm only interested in the fate of the book."

"You are going to squander a great deal of time, Mr. Dunstan."

"Here at the *Echo*, Major, we practically eat time," I said.

■ **111**

■ A Ford identical to mine drifted toward the long line of cars on the shimmering drive. Attired in a charcoal-gray wool suit and a gray felt hat, C. Clayton Creech took in the assembled gathering with his customary matchless cool. I glanced at the headstone next to Toby's grave. HENRIETTA "QUEENIE" DUNSTAN KRAFT, 1914–1964, A VIRTUOSO NEVER TO BE SURPASSED.

"Between you and me," I said to Creech, "how much of a crook was Toby, actually?"

"Indicted only once," Creech drawled. "Bum rap."

Down the slope, my Taurus's doppelgänger parked at the end of the row of cars. Mr. Tite emerged from the driver's seat and opened the door for Helen Janette.

"Had nothing to do with the adoption business," I said.

"Hazel kept her mouth shut." Creech had not so much as glanced down the slope.

"What was it, then?"

"Jive bullshit."

Helen Janette and her guard dog reached the top of the slope. Frank Tite pretended not to notice that Helen was walking toward me.

The lawyer tipped his hat. "Good day, Mrs. Janette."

"Mr. Creech, I have something to say to your friend." She motioned me aside. "I want to apologize for the way I behaved the night of the fire. I was a miserable old woman, and I couldn't think straight."

"It must have been terrible for you," I said.

"Lose everything you own, you'll learn the meaning of terrible. I don't understand why that La Chapelle boy went so crazy."

"You knew him?"

"Frenchy grew up right around the corner. Him and Clyde Prentiss, knee-deep in trouble from day one."

The last of the mourners joined the throng behind Toby's grave. All but two or three of them were black, and everyone had dressed for the occasion.

"It starts with *Hatchtown*," said Helen Janette. "Who needs a convention center? Stewart Hatch should tear down the whole place, rebuild it from the ground up. Or at least fix those properties. Your family would be happy to see some work done on Cherry Street, too, wouldn't they?"

"With them, you never know," I said. "But why would Hatch have anything to do with it?"

She said, "Okay, never mind," and left me.

Mr. Spaulding stationed himself beside the open grave. The quiet hum of conversation from the mourners ceased.

"Dear friends and neighbors, Mr. Kraft declined the services of a clergyman at his last rites, but he welcomed spontaneous reflections from those who have assembled here. If you care to express your feelings, step up and speak from the heart."

A little stir came from the crowd, and an elderly woman came forward. She raised her head, and sunlight sparkled off her glasses.

"Toby Kraft was not what I could call a close, personal friend, but I appreciated the man. He was honest with his customers. He treated a person with respect. He had a generous heart, too. Toby had a rough side, but I know there were times he offered a helping hand to lots of us here today." The crowd murmured affirmation. "In my opinion, Toby Kraft was a man who made a contribution. That's all I have to say."

One after another, seven other people moved up beside the grave and spoke about Toby. A white-haired man said, "Toby never appeared to be a romantic or a sentimental man, but no one could say he did not have a deep love for his wife."

I asked Creech if he had known Queenie.

"Toby was completely smitten," he said. "She could make his jaw drop open and his eyes spin around in his head. They had me to dinner many times, and Queenie's sweet-potato pie was like nothing I have tasted before or since." Creech smiled, more to himself than at me. "Hers was the only pie I ever observed rise an inch or two above the table, as if begging to be eaten."

The last speaker said, "Mr. Kraft acted like he ate hubcaps and razor blades for breakfast, but he was on our side. He once told me, 'Georgia, I may be a son of a bitch,' excuse my French, 'but watching out for you is part of my job.' He helped pay for my husband's funeral. When my daughter went to Morehouse, he sent her money every week and never asked for anything in return. I say, Toby Kraft was a good, good man."

Mr. Spaulding sifted through the crowd to shake hands with his future customers. People moved down toward their cars.

"Toby was an excellent fellow, all in all," said C. Clayton Creech. He gave me a lizardlike glance. "I trust you do not regret your decisions of the other day?"

"Toby would have approved," I said.

"I always enjoyed that whimsical streak of his. Most of my clients resist whimsy. As the years go by, I more and more appreciate evidence of the imaginative faculty."

We moved down the slope. "What was the reason he went to jail?" I asked.

Creech's car keys twinkled in his milk-white hand. "I suppose he possessed enough imagination to recognize he had no other choice."

■ The aunts were bustling back and forth in front of the stove. Splendid in a canary-yellow sports jacket, Clark looked up from the table. "Look here, boy, I got a new coat to celebrate your birthday!"

Nettie sang out, "Happy Birthday!" and bussed my cheek. May said, "Stay right there, I'll get your present."

"Old Toby's funeral was a lonely business, I reckon," said Clark.

"No, a lot of people turned up," I said. "Some of them spoke about how much he loved Queenie."

"You can't take that away from him," said Nettie. "From the moment Toby Kraft laid eyes on my sister, he was a man under a spell."

"And I wanted to ask you something," I said.

May returned with a plastic bag bearing the logo of a local grocery store. She looked almost coquettish. "When I gave you those socks and undergarments, Ned, I was keeping a secret for your birthday."

"You're giving me a secret for my birthday?"

"It won't be a secret any longer." She pulled from the bag a pink sports jacket randomly imprinted with golf bags, golf clubs, and greens with flags jutting from the cups. Grenville Milton would have drooled.

I shrugged off my blazer and got into May's pink extravaganza. It was exactly my size.

"Damn, boy," Clark said. "Now you look like you know how to have a good time."

"And there's another treat," said Nettie. "Sweet-potato pie. Mine is as good as Queenie's, you wait and see."

"What else do we have in the works?" I asked.

"Dry-rubbed pork ribs and my black-eyed peas. May brought over homemade bread. There's the marshmallow salad from *The Ladies of Galilee Cook Book*, and we still have plenty of that tuna casserole from yesterday. There is no need to worry about *food*."

"We deserve a feast, after all our sorrows," Clark said. "Now that he has passed away, I miss old Toby more than I expected I would. Is there any progress on bringing his murderer to justice?"

"I don't think so."

"Jack the Ripper is running around Edgerton, but the police won't admit it. Tell you why. The news would alarm the populace."

"It isn't only Jack the Ripper," Nettie said, sounding ominous.

"No, sir. Take the events in College Park last night."

I felt as though I had been stung by a bee. "What events?"

"Around one A.M., people up there heard a god-awful noise. A good many windows blew out of their frames. They say a light filled the sky, and that the light was *blue*."

"It is undoubtedly a sign," May said.

"A fellow on the radio this morning said the ruckus was brought on by an alien spacecraft. That idea deserves consideration."

Through the kitchen window, I looked out at the paper tablecloth and jugs of Kool-Aid and iced tea on the old picnic table. "Too bad Joy can't be here."

"Joy wouldn't talk to me this morning," May said. "I wouldn't be surprised if she has had second thoughts about putting Clarence in that home."

A premonitory tingle coursed through my chest, in its mildness suggesting that I had three or four hours before onset of the seizure. "Mr. Creech was at the funeral," I said. "I asked him why Toby went to jail, but he wouldn't talk."

"Today," Clark said, "we should remember the good things about the man, not his misdeeds."

"Which were legion," said Nettie.

"Numbered like the grains of sand on a beach," said May. "Are we ready to start the festivities?"

■ On the other side of the picnic table, Clark made the most of a single black-eyed pea. Substantial piles of bones had accumulated on the aunts' paper plates. My warning signals hummed quietly in the background. All of us felt the warm, expansive sensation that follows a satisfying meal. At the moment when I was thinking about bringing up Toby Kraft's incarceration again, May did it for me.

"Nettie, do you remember? When Toby was sent away, Queenie still had that little icebox, and she was upset because she wouldn't have the time to pick out a new one for six whole months? When Toby came back, I remember, he told Queenie to get a new icebox right away."

"If he served only six months, his crime wasn't very serious," I said.

"Not only was his offense not serious," May said, "he didn't do it. Why would Toby Kraft break into another man's house? If that was what he wanted, he would have had some fool do it for him."

"He was home with Queenie the whole time." Nettie glanced at me. "She testified to that effect, but the jury chose not to believe her, which was the same as saying that she told a pack of lies. Our sister was the picture of honesty. Honest as sunshine."

"At times," May said, "our sister's honesty was of a sort to make you check and see where you were bleeding. I'd like more ribs, please, Ned, and some of the marshmallow salad from the Ladies of Galilee."

"Toby didn't say anything to save himself?" I asked.

"Didn't, couldn't, wouldn't." Nettie took the bowl of marshmallow salad from May and spooned half of it onto her plate. Disgust won out over her reservations. "Toby hardly talked to his own lawyer. They convicted him of stealing a silver picture frame, all because a Hatchtown no-good claimed he saw Toby hanging around outside the house."

A familiar sensation, that of steady electrical pulsations, flowed into my arms, and the colors around me blazed. I could not be sure how much time was left me. Robert lingered somewhere close by, burning with jealousy. I said, "This is a wonderful birthday party, but I should go inside and lie down for a while."

"That's all right," Nettie said. "If you were to fall to the ground and foam at the mouth, I'd feel like a miserable old woman."

The buzzing pulse quieted in my veins; the yellow flare around Clark's chest and shoulders receded back into his jacket. "At Toby's funeral, someone made a comment that made me think Stewart Hatch owned these houses. I always thought they belonged to you."

May frowned. Clark sneered thoughtfully at a flake sectioned from a pork rib. Nettie patted my hand. "Son, you don't have to worry about us."

"Which means, I suppose, that he does own your houses."

"Over the years, our family has done a lot of business with the Hatches. At a time when money was running low, Mr. Hatch became aware of our difficulties, and he stepped in to do us some good."

"What kind of good?"

"Mr. Hatch plans to develop this area. In the meantime, we can stay here for the rest of our lives."

"What if Hatch goes to jail?"

"No matter what happens, we'll be fine."

"We are protected, and we did it all ourselves," said May. "Toby's money is what I call the icing on the cake."

Clark said, "Speaking of dessert, where's that sweet-potato pie?"

"You'll wait until the boy's had his fit," said Nettie. "It isn't your birthday."

■ **113**

■ I walked through the kitchen, feeling his hovering presence with every step, and said, "Show yourself, Robert."

I came into the living room. "Did you know Stewart owned their houses? What's going on? He can't develop one block on Cherry Street." I imagined my silent double standing before me, grinning at my perplexity.

Trudging up the stairs, I thought: *Four hundred and eighty thousand dollars is just the icing on the cake?*

I moved over the landing and shuddered to a halt. Howard Dunstan regarded me with dispassionate curiosity from the end of the hallway. I resisted the impulse to run downstairs. A faint smile played over Howard's mouth. He was enjoying my birthday. Robert and I had eased the boredom of eternity by providing him a drama more entertaining than he had expected.

"Go outside, give your daughters a thrill," I said. "I'm sick of the sight of you."

The expression on his face said, *You don't get it, you are missing the point.* He turned aside, inclined his head to the window behind him, and faded from view.

I went to the window and looked down. Four people in festive spirits sat at the picnic table. Imbuing his duplicate of the pink extravaganza with an elegant raffishness, Robert spoke to Nettie and made her dimple with pleasure. He looked astonishingly handsome, even as I took in the roaring deprivation I had seen while he cavorted among fireflies and flaming birds.

I moved from the window and saw the door to Nettie and Clark's bedroom. It was half open. Scarcely believing what I was doing, I went into their room. Two freestanding wooden cabinets stood against the back wall, and two upholstered chairs faced me from beyond a double bed with white pillows and a faded yellow coverlet. I felt like a rapist. A tall chest of drawers faced the bed. The room's only closet took up the wall to my right.

The sweet, musty odor of a lavender sachet filtered toward me. Clark's outfits took up half of the rail, Nettie's long, loose dresses the other. Tidy stacks of sweaters and sweatshirts covered most of the shelf above the rail. A manila folder lay an inch back from the edge of the shelf beyond the sweatshirts.

The folder contained a lot of black-and-white photographs. They could have been of Nettie and her sisters arranged tallest to smallest in front of the house on New Providence Road; of Clark Rutledge striking a pose in high-draped pants; of Star Dunstan beside a nightclub piano, singing "They Can't Take That Away from Me." Looking at them was the only way to clear the aunts of my suspicions. I took out three of the photographs and knew that whoever these people might have been, they were not Dunstans.

A young man in a straw boater propped one foot on the running board of what I thought was a Marmon. In a studio portrait, a girl of perhaps eighteen with straight, dark bangs and wearing pearls, a white, midcalf dress, and gleaming silk stockings smiled at a rolled diploma. Older versions of the same people, he in a three-piece suit, she in a cloche hat, posed behind two boys in sailor suits, one of them not long out of infancy. I slipped the photos back into the folder and took out another. My symptoms surged back into life, promising me a merry ride.

Dressed for the occasion in a doll-like jacket and bow tie, a small boy with bangs like his mother's perched on a photographer's stool in front of a backdrop depicting an Italian hill town. His face was nearly identical to that of the three-year-old Ned Dunstan in the photograph my mother had given me.

I pulled out one of the Edgerton Academy class photos pink-haired Spike had assumed I wished to find. Twenty boys in their early teens stood in three rows on the steps in front of a school. Glowering at the camera from the end of the last row, apart and unhappy, as dark as Caliban, was the image of myself at thirteen.

I walked out of the bedroom to find Robert leaning against the wall, smiling at me. He said, "Nettie and May are a perfect pair of rogues. And I can't say enough about Clark. The man belongs in the Senate. You don't mind my taking advantage of your absence to get acquainted with the family, do you?"

"Would it make a difference?"

Robert looked at the folder and narrowed his eyes. "Is that what I think it is?"

I pushed it toward him. "Take this to the car. I have to get back to the Brazen Head before my attack."

"Can you hold it off that long?"

"I have more control than I used to," I said.

"We're developing all sorts of new skills." Robert took the folder and disappeared.

When I came back out into the backyard, Clark and the aunts looked at me with gratified surprise. "Bounce back faster than a rubber ball, that's what you do," Nettie said.

"It's still on the way," I said. "I should get back to my hotel. But thank you for my birthday party. And I love my new jacket, Aunt May." An unanswered question came to me. "We were talking about Toby. Did they say he broke into a house in Hatchtown?"

"Do they have silver picture frames in Hatchtown?" Clark sneered.

"Nettie said a Hatchtown character saw him outside the place."

"A lowlife named Spelvin claimed to see Toby out in Ellendale. People like him didn't go wandering through Ellendale in those days, not without getting rousted."

"Where in Ellendale?" Electrical current sparkled through my veins.

"Manor Street," Clark said. "Where the mansions went up in the twenties."

"Whose mansion in particular?" I already knew.

"Carpenter Hatch's place," Clark said. "I don't know how a jury decided Toby Kraft could get so down and out stupid."

I faded from the backyard with none of Robert's impressive immediacy.

■ **114**

■ Sprawled across the backseat, Robert said, "What do you make of these pictures?"

"You first."

He put on a mock-professorial voice. "These photographs represent approximately fifteen years in the life of an increasingly well-off Midwestern family. We begin with a clever roughneck and the little beauty who had the misfortune of marrying him. In time, the roughneck transforms himself into a stiff-necked dictator, and the bride dwindles into a cringing phantom. They have two sons, seven or eight years apart, who are sent to a horrible school established to reinforce the fantasy that they are landed aristocracy."

"Anything else?"

"The first son looks like us."

"He also looks a lot like Howard Dunstan."

Robert waited.

"The roughneck was Carpenter Hatch. The girl who turned into a phantom was called Ellie, short for Ellen, as in Ellendale. Their first son wound up in jail, disappeared, and supposedly died. The second son, Cobden, went to work for his father, got married, and had a son. All his life, Cobden Hatch was afraid his son, Stewart, might turn out like his brother."

"Who happened to resemble Howard Dunstan. And when he

was supposed to be dead, this cuckoo in the nest came back to Edgerton, calling himself Edward Rinehart."

"He came back a second time as Earl Sawyer. A lot of people have done their best to keep me from finding out that he was my father. Our father."

"That would mean . . ."

"Tell me," I said. "I'd like to know."

"It means Edward Rinehart was a Dunstan, and you and I are Hatches. Good old Dad ties the two families together, and what's the physical proof? Ned Dunstan. No wonder Stewart grabbed our photographs and wanted you run out of town. You could ruin his family's reputation." He laughed. "It's delicious. Rinehart worked for his nephew for fifteen years, and he was so blown out Stewart never recognized him. The only way Stewart knew him was in these pictures."

What about Nettie and May? I wondered. Nettie would instantly have recognized "Edward Rinehart" as her father's illegitimate son. But "Edward Rinehart" had avoided the Dunstans as he must have avoided the Hatches; he had never even allowed himself to be photographed. If the aunts had not known the identity of Star's lover, they could not have blackmailed Stewart Hatch, and there was no way they could have known it.

I swerved into a parking place on Word Street, where the facade of the Hotel Paris shimmered like lava. A hot electrical tingle moved across my scalp, down my spine, and into my arms. The more I learned, the more confusing it became. Every new bit of information led into another blind alley.

"Go to my room," I said. "I'll be right there."

"I'm not making any promises." Robert disappeared from the backseat.

I sped through the bursting sounds and blooming colors in the lanes and charged across Veal Yard. The grain of the wood on the Brazen Head's reception desk swam up through layers of lacquer. "Yes, we have a fax for you, Mr. Dunstan," the day clerk said. With a thunderous explosion of summery blue from his shirt, the clerk produced a bundle of ivory-gray fax paper.

I went to the stairs reading the brilliant black lines of the fax. Major Audrey Arndt was pleased to supply, so on and so forth, with the understanding that I had agreed, so on and so forth. Her signature boomed from the page like a cannonball. I read down names listed under the years from 1938 to 1942. The fifth name down in the class of 1941 was Cordwainer C. Hatch.

Robert was standing near the window when I came in. From the edge of the table, the jewel-like arc of *P.D. 10/17/58* floated out into the room. "You got a fax?"

"Cordwainer Hatch," I said. "Cobden's brother. I think he killed a student at a military school to get his hands on the book I stole from Buxton Place." Blue light flashed at the periphery of my vision, and the immense pressure in the atmosphere concentrated into a steady urgency. "You know what we have to do, Robert."

He held up his hands. "You don't understand. It would be harder on you than on me. I don't know if you could take it."

I moved toward him. An ivory-colored haze I would not have seen at any other time floated through his skin and hung like tobacco smoke. In the second before I reached for him, I took the copy of *The Dunwich Horror* from the table and rammed it into a pocket of the pink jacket. Everything crashed and boomed. I fastened my hand on Robert's, knowing exactly what we were about to see.

115 ■ Mr. X

■ O You Swarming ~~Majesties~~ Cruelties, Who Giveth with one hand and Taketh Away with the other—I begin to see—

■ First I must address a ~~more~~ crucial point. ~~I only now~~
It is bitter, bitter, with a bitterness I only now begin to comprehend.

* * *

■ As the decades passed—I grew accustomed to the consolation of a Fancy—that a Godlike & Ironic Amusement—abstract—beyond the ken of the Providence Master—had ~~Blessed~~ Lumbered me with the Task—Mighty—of Killing the Antagonist—or—as I have discover'd—Antagonists.—I ~~can only~~ here inscribe that the Horrors—perpetrated by these Same—have ~~led me to believe~~ taught me that I misunderstood Your True Nature. Gifts and Revelations encouraged this Servant's Illusion of a Favored Election—~~foolish,~~ IMBECILE me.

■ Last night—in Darkness—my Madness Soared—before the evidence of a Great Destruction. The Sacred Flame ~~boiled~~ tortured the Heavens—I stood in Ashes—below—

And—in Horror & Despair—Receiv'd the Gift.

I stood, as if You ~~didn't know~~ knew not, a'midst the Ashes—as Smoke from the Cannon's Mouth—sent Rage streaming forth—& then—Devour'd—the Substance Molten—Which is Time—& Travel'd Back—Godly & Engorg'd—to Where I shall once again slay Ferdy Dunstan, called Michael Anscombe, and Moira Hightower Dunstan, called Sally Anscombe—and Then—in Triumph—Destroy the Twin Antagonists—

■ Humor—has no Place in Your Realm—Irony—as foreign as Pity. I lash myself, that I so fell short—that I could not see my Gethsemane—my Golgotha—

■ The River-bank—has its Purpose & its Purpose—Terrifying. Pain equal to Pain—Rage equal to Rage—no Triumph without a Testing. Here are my wrists and ankles Pierced—here the Centurion's Sword is Thrust—

Crucifixion is no picnic, let me say that. Let me add that a half-human Wretch and Outcast can only take so much! I scream—my Scream shall reach the Heavens—they have Destroyed my Work!

Yet—in the midst of Annihilation—I get the point—You Creeping Obscenities—& Bless my Wounds & Sword Slits—My Great Loss—& Torment—is foreshadowing of the Great Fire to come—For my Identity cannot be Gainsaid—the Great Fire Follows the Smoke from the Mouth of the Cannon—

Half-mad with rage—with insult—Since discovery of the

Crime, sleep has not been mine—I tremble & sweat, soak my clothing through & cannot eat—These Blessings are given in earnest of the End—when I shall Perish—to gain Eternity—

My foes Torment me—I call to them—as of old—the Advantage Mine—my Army Mightier—in Intelligence—a New Ability given me by Need—& the Foe ignorant of my Earthly Name—Even more—I known them Two—a Grand Superiority—They do not Suspect—And will Show One—whilst I conquer Time—

In the midst of Rage—I Laugh—to regard such Play—

I set down the Pen—& close the Book—the *Triumph* hastens—My Heartless Fathers—

■ 116

■ A half second before we were to be delivered to Boulder, Colorado, I was united with my shadow again.

As in childhood, I recoiled from trespass and invasion; this time, I felt Robert's revulsion as well as my own. We were thirty-five, not nine, and the shock was far greater. But I had become more like Robert than I knew: the powers I had discovered and those he had known all his life shared a common root. There came again a breathtaking expansion into unguessed-at wholeness and resolution that in no way erased our separate individuality. We knew what the other knew, felt what the other felt, but within this symbiosis remained a Robert and a Ned. Surprisingly to both, it seemed that Ned was in charge of the decisions.

In the year 1967, we stood, adorned in a pink sports jacket flecked with golf bags and putting greens, on the Anscombes' front lawn. The moon hung like a monstrous button over a ridge of mountains, and the air smelled of fir trees. Blue fire shone from a window in a new addition at the far left of the house. The Mr. X of 1967 was prowling in search of his son. A shaft of blue light, sent as a flag of ironic welcome by *our* Mr. X, Cordwainer Hatch, flared through a crack in the living room curtains. On the steps to the attic, our nine-year-old selves were meeting for the first time. Neither we nor the demon in the living room were to be seen, because we had not been seen *then*.

A well-known pressure moved us through the front door. In a shapeless garment that fell to the tops of her feet, *Goodnight Moon* in one hand, her hair a matted tangle, Mrs. Anscombe stared down at her husband's corpse. Our Mr. X loomed behind her, displaying an enraged, grotesque smile beneath the brim of his hat. Mrs. Anscombe padded into her husband's blood. Frank Sinatra sang of the encounter on a lovely night between a force not to be resisted and an object not to be moved.

Mrs. Anscombe said, "Shit on a shingle." She turned her face to us. "Who the hell are you, Bob Hope?"

Unable to see the thirty-five-year-old man who had materialized near the front door, nine-year-old Robert was watching her from the kitchen. As if following the direction of my thoughts, Mrs. Anscombe looked toward him and walked deeper into the red pool. A dim recognition moved across her face, and the book slapped into the blood. Her eyes swung back. "Why are you doing this?" she shouted. "Don't you understand I'm already in hell?"

"Don't worry, Mrs. Anscombe," said Cordwainer Hatch. "You will be taken care of soon enough."

She took another dazed step toward the kitchen. "Shit, I really am in hell," she shouted, "only the son of a bitch isn't RED, it's BLUE!"

The Black Death of the Hatchtown lanes drifted toward us. A sickening wave of almost limitless rage poisoned by an insanity deeper than Alice Anscombe's streamed from him as his mind reached out to engulf mine and Robert's. For the first time, I knew I could resist his strength. Robert yelled, *Do something!* and I told him, *Wait.* Cordwainer's mind battered on mine like a wind flattening against an oaken door.

That means nothing. Move!

The air gathered into a solid substance, pushed us back through yielding walls, and deposited us in a small room stacked with cardboard boxes. Cordwainer was only inches away. He stank of riverbottom. Blue light filtered in from the living room, where the Mr. X of 1967 berated Mrs. Anscombe. Our Mr. X blasted a roar of outrage into our minds: *You destructive, destructive, destructive little vandal! You monster!* He drew a knife from his coat.

A furious bellow and a series of muffled noises reported the demise of Mrs. Anscombe. Mr. X's younger self uttered a screech of frustration, thundered into the kitchen, and transported himself outside in pursuit of a small boy he knew had escaped him yet again.

"I guess you're angry about the books," I said.

Cordwainer grabbed our shoulder, spun us around, and clamped us to his chest. He dug his knife into our neck.

Is this what you had in mind? Robert asked me. *Sorry, but I'm not hanging around to get killed.* I told him to calm down.

"You could say that, yes. I am angry about the books." He nudged the blade another eighth of an inch into our neck. "Satisfy my curiosity. Where did you learn the name Edward Rinehart? Was it your mother? That old fool Toby Kraft?"

"Lots of people told me about Edward Rinehart," I said. "Where are we?"

He sniggered. "Don't you remember the Anscombes? Does Boulder, Colorado, ring a bell? We have journeyed back through time, the Substance Molten, a matter undoubtedly beyond your comprehension, that I might inquire how you managed to get away from me that time. Speak, please. I am deeply interested, I assure you."

Why aren't you DOING anything? Robert yelled. *Are we just going to TALK to a guy who's sticking a knife in our neck?*

Shut up and let me handle this, I said to Robert. *We have to talk to him.*

To Cordwainer, I said, "I can tell you who you really are. You'll find that tremendously interesting, I promise. It surprised me, too."

"Enough of this charade. Let's see if any other book burner wants to join the fun."

A great wind whipped into the room, flattening the pink jacket against our chest. Furniture slid across the living room floor. It sounded as though every dish and glass in the kitchen blew off the shelves and smashed against the walls. The window behind me exploded. I told Robert part of what I had in mind and heard him chuckle.

Did you think you actually had me fooled?

Everything in the house flew before the heightening wind. The living room window bulged and detonated. A kind of ecstasy flowed from Robert.

"Are you looking for someone?" I asked.

You destroyed my books! That is an OUTRAGE! Where is he?

"I want to show you something, Mr. Sawyer," I said. "People are going to be able to see us. If you have any sense, you'll take the knife out of my neck."

His arm tightened over our chest. "I'll humor you," he said. The knife came out of our neck and jabbed into our lower back.

Robert asked, *What the hell are you doing now?* I told him to hope for the best, and all three of us dropped through the floor into suddenly malleable time.

■ **117**

■ I was aiming for something I wasn't sure I could find. Even if I could find it, I had no certainty of what we would see.

The world ceased to swim. We were standing on a beaten footpath beside a two-lane macadam road. Horse-drawn wagons and old-fashioned automobiles rolled past in both directions. Robert was shouting that he did not understand what was happening, and Cordwainer was jabbing a knife into our back. Immediately, proof that we had arrived at the right place appeared before us.

To our left, Howard Dunstan's mad, bearded face scowled through the windscreen of a high-topped car chugging toward us down Wagon Road. His wife languished beside him. As they pulled nearer, two pretty young women who must have been Queenie and Nettie became visible behind them. Just entering their teens, May and Joy peeped out from the rumble seat.

This means nothing, Cordwainer said. *Nothing. An illusion, a sideshow. Where is the other, you wicked boy?*

On the far side of Wagon Road and in the wake of a horse-drawn cart heaped with burlap sacks, a vehicle sleeker and more expensive than Howard Dunstan's floated into view. Carpenter Hatch, already frozen into eternally disapproving vigilance, muttered a remark that made the already wilting Ellie sink away. Through the rear passenger window of their automobile peered a sulky replica of myself and Robert at the age of five. Putting along behind the Hatches and moving inexorably toward the Dunstans was a third vehicle, grander than Howard's but less impressive than the Hatch swan boat. The little girls in its rear seat pointed at the Dunstans, now nearly parallel to the swan boat. May Dunstan fixed her eyes upon the sullen childish face in the passing car. Howard stared straight ahead. Ellie Hatch, visible for a final second, shifted in her seat and regarded an empty field. A moment after the two cars separated, Wagon Road turned into chaos.

Every windscreen and headlight within fifty yards exploded into flying glass. Tires flew from their axles and spun over the macadam. Panicked horses reared, bolted forward, and rammed their carts against whatever was in their way. Burlap sacks spilled potatoes across the road. I saw a horse go down and vanish beneath wreckage, its toothpick legs sawing the air. The pressure of Cordwainer's arm lessened, and the knife fell away.

Over the sounds of collisions came the screaming of horses and the shouts of men. As the swan boat swerved off the road to veer around the damage, Ellie Hatch's weeping sounded in my ear from two feet away: it was not the voice of the woman now speeding into the distance, but her voice as remembered by the child in the seat behind her. Robert and I had colonized Cordwainer's mind and memory.

A bluebird tumbled to the floor of the ruin on New Providence Road; a naked girl of eleven or twelve pressed her hand to the wound in her bleeding chest and reeled over the filthy cement; the young Max Edison nodded from behind the wheel of a limousine; *The Dunwich Horror* leaped from the extended hand of a uniformed boy; a uniformed man said *disease*; in a doorway on Chester Street, a knife entered a whore's belly; cartoon monsters descended from a cartoon sky; a fountain pen glided across a lined page; something lost, something irrevocably damaged, flew through the Hatchtown lanes, and that something was Cordwainer Hatch.

Robert shouted, *Kill him, kill him! What's wrong with you?*

I tasted Cordwainer's egotism and the illusion of a sacred cause and thought: *I know how this ends.*

The screams of terrified horses, the noises of collisions billowed from Wagon Road. I took the knife from Cordwainer's hand. *Release me!*

"Okay, I'll release you," I said, and set him free. Robert shrieked in protest.

Cordwainer stumbled back, laughing. "You're too weak, you couldn't hold me." He looked at his empty hand. "Do you think I need a knife? Without your brother, you're nothing."

"What did you see?" I asked. "Did you see yourself?"

He surged over the grass. When Cordwainer slammed into me, I twisted sideways to absorb the shock and wrapped my arms around him. The three of us fell through a sudden trapdoor at the side of the beaten path.

▪ **118**

▪ Still in the momentum of his assault, Cordwainer Hatch rolled from my grip and struck the table in my room at the Brazen Head. He groaned and pressed his hands over his eyes.

"Take your time," I said.

Cordwainer lowered his hands, examined his surroundings, and swept the hat from his head. The ghost of Edward Rinehart shone in his ruined face. "Even the weakling has a little fight in him." He glanced over his shoulder and backed against the wall, weighing his options.

Kill him! Robert urged. *He's confused, he doesn't understand what happened.*

It's going to get a lot worse for him, I told Robert. *Just wait.* To Cordwainer, I said, "Do you remember that day? Do you know what happened on Wagon Road?"

I could see him decide to sound me out. He lowered his hat to the table in a parody of a diplomatic gesture—he was hooked, and his next words proved it. "Let's declare a temporary truce. This is about the last thing I anticipated, but now we have this interesting opportunity to hear what the other has to say. I want you to describe your fantasies. When you have finished, I will explain reality. Reality is going to *astound* you. Considering what you did to me, my offer is extraordinarily generous. But you will pay for your obscene crime, I assure you."

Robert said, *Let's put his eyes out. Let's make him squeal.*

He's going to squeal, all right, I said back. *The worst moments of his entire life are about to happen.*

"Looks like I guessed wrong," I said to Cordwainer. "You were supposed to get so angry you wouldn't be able to function."

"Oh, you *angered* me. And I'll grant you this, you're stronger than I imagined. But there's no sense continuing this discussion without your brother. You've lost whatever surprise factor you were counting on, so bring him in."

"I eliminated my brother this morning. He was a useless impediment. Since you're willing to listen to my fantasy, as you call it, I want to show you a few things."

Cordwainer gave me a wary scrutiny. Whatever he saw must have persuaded him that I was telling the truth. "Congratulations. Why don't you begin by telling me what you find significant about a few ancient collisions on Wagon Road?"

At that moment, I felt very much like Robert. "Instead, why don't you begin by telling me about the house on the edge of Johnson's Woods?"

Cordwainer's face twisted into a smug, ghastly smile. "You wouldn't understand. You couldn't."

"Then I'll give you some information you probably don't know. Carpenter Hatch bought that property from Howard Dunstan's daughters. It was where Howard spent his whole life, and when it burned down, he died in the fire."

He moved alongside the table, settled his hand on the back of a chair, and gazed at the ceiling. Cordwainer had decided to humor me. "Really, this is completely absurd. The man I thought of as my father bought that land to build houses for what he called the rising scum. The Dunstans never had any connection to the property. They swarmed into Cherry Street like roaches, and they never left."

The same crazy triumph with which he had told me about secret messages in H. P. Lovecraft irradiated him. "That house was the residence of a god."

"Howard Dunstan was a sort of Elder God," I said. "That's what is so interesting about what he did to you."

Cordwainer's mouth opened in soundless hilarity.

"You're amused," I said.

"I'm in awe. Your mother filled you with the most amazing nonsense."

I took the photograph of Howard in his wing collar and high-buttoned waistcoat from the folder and slid it toward him. He smiled at it in negligent disdain. "You're looking at Howard Dunstan," I said. "Your real father."

"Did you make this up all by yourself, or was Star crazy, too?"

I moved a photograph of Carpenter Hatch alongside the first. "Which one of these men would you say was your biological father?"

Cordwainer barely glanced at the photographs. "I don't expect you to understand this, but my true fathers were not of this earth."

"Let me tell you about your half-sister Queenie," I said. "The first of Howard's four daughters. Queenie could read people's minds and go from one place to another in an eye-blink. She didn't walk, she didn't bother to open doors or climb stairs, she just *went*. It's a Dunstan talent, like walking through walls, and she got it from Howard. When May Dunstan, her sister, was a young woman, a boyfriend tried to rape her. She turned him into a green puddle."

Cordwainer's face twitched. His eyes rose to meet ours.

"May caused that scene on Wagon Road. The instant she saw you, she knew you were Howard's son. You looked too much like him to be anything else. Look at his picture, Cordwainer. Whatever abilities you and I have, we inherited from Howard Dunstan."

"She reduced a man to a green puddle?" Cordwainer was staring from the far edge of the table. "You know that for a fact?"

"I hardly know what a fact is anymore," I said. "Neither one of us ever had much contact with facts. Only instead of H. P. Lovecraft, I had you."

His mouth tucked in at the corners, and his eyes shifted. Once again, I saw a remnant of Edward Rinehart momentarily surface in his face. "What was my mistake? Calling myself Earl Sawyer? I didn't think anyone would catch that."

"I almost missed it," I said.

Cordwainer moved the photographs closer to him. "You want me to talk about Wagon Road? I remember that girl staring at me from the rumble seat. I had no idea who she was. Then our windshield blew up, and everything went crazy. My father—my legal father—drove home as if nothing had happened."

"How did your father treat you?" I sorted through the pictures until I found a seven- or eight-year-old Howard posed in front of a seated, blazing-eyed Sylvan.

Cordwainer put it alongside the others. "When he wasn't lecturing me, he tuned me out. I depressed him. Of course, he had Cobden, the apple of his eye. Cobden could do no wrong, the little prig."

"And Cobden looked like him."

"This is so interesting." Cordwainer was still staring down at the photographs. "I'm not saying you're right, but it would explain a great deal about my childhood. Neither of my parents ever showed me much warmth, but they doted on my brother."

"Carpenter probably never really admitted the truth to himself. It would have been too disgraceful."

"I could almost believe it." He smiled down at the photographs. "You know, I think I do believe it. My mother must have been more adventurous than I ever imagined." He looked up. "And it would explain where my looks came from. I was always a handsome devil, like you. But the identity of my earthly parents . . . really, that's all the same to me."

"Howard Dunstan manipulated you. He led you into the woods and brought you to what was left of his house. He *showed* you things. He made sure you came across a certain book and primed you with fantasies about H. P. Lovecraft. All along, he was just amusing himself. It was a game."

Cordwainer glanced at the photographs again, then turned his poached eyes and lifeless face back to us. "All nature spoke. The Old Ones spoke."

"Haven't you ever had doubts? Weren't there times when you realized that everything you believed came from short stories written by a man who never pretended they were anything but fiction?"

"I have had my doubts." Cordwainer spoke with undeniable dignity, and, unlike Robert, I felt a spasm of pity. "I have known the Dark Night of the Soul."

"Now and then, even false Messiahs probably have their bad days."

"I am not *false*!" Cordwainer thundered.

"No, you're not," I said. "You're a real Dunstan. Everything your father made you believe was half true. Howard settled in to watch you try to eliminate me. He doesn't care how the game turns out."

"Evidently, my fathers have toyed with you," Cordwainer said. "They are merciless, I can testify to that."

"What happened to a Fortress Academy pledge named W. Wilson Fletcher?"

Cordwainer eyed us. "Busy little bee, aren't you?"

"You were startled that May Dunstan turned a man into a puddle of bile," I said.

I had guessed right: his face turned to lard.

"Maybe Fletcher showed you a certain book. Or maybe you saw him reading it one day. But something happened to you. You needed that book, didn't you?"

I pulled *The Dunwich Horror* from my pocket. Cordwainer's eyes fastened on the cover. (*Got him,* Robert said. *Landed. Flopping on the deck.*)

A bolt of feeling ran through his stolid face. "You stole that book from me, and I demand its return. You have no idea of its meaning."

"I'll give it back after we visit Howard Dunstan. He's been waiting for us." I set the book down. When Cordwainer lunged across the table, I wrapped my fingers around his wrist.

◼ **119**

◼ Resistlessly, we fell into the dense, darkly teeming world, half Hansel and Gretel and half unknowable mystery, of a forest at night. I hoped it was late evening, June 25, 1935.

Cordwainer seized our arm and yanked us to his side. "I don't recognize this. Where are we?"

"Johnson's Woods, about sixty years ago," I said. "On this night, you're a little boy asleep in a house on Manor Street."

"I rarely slept in those days," Cordwainer said. "Human life was a torment, and I preferred to bellow. I also wet the bed, deliberately. Compared to mine, your childhood was straight out of Mother Goose." In the darkness, his cannonball head loomed over his black coat, as if hanging in midair. "All right, make a fool of yourself. Where's the house?"

"Not far away," I said, without any idea of where in Johnson's Woods we were.

Cordwainer jerked us off balance, clamped an arm around our neck, and held us against his body. He was much stronger than I had expected. His arm tightened on our windpipe, and the twin stenches of mania and river-bottom invaded our nostrils. His mind probed at the perimeters of mine, like Aunt Nettie's before she had lifted me off her kitchen chair. I slammed my mental gates, and Cordwainer chuckled. His arm closed in and cut off our air. "Funny, I don't see a house. I don't see any lights."

As my eyes adjusted, the trees separated from the darkness and became a series of stationary columns daubed by moonlight. Before us stood a big maple I had seen before, though not in my waking life. I made a croaking sound, and Cordwainer eased the pressure on our neck. "You had something to say, little Robert?"

"The house is up ahead, about thirty yards to the right."

"I could almost believe you." A wave of river-bottom vapor floated from his pores, his bald head, his mouth. "How much longer are you going to keep up this pretense?"

Robert was seething. Robert had had enough, and he was ready to explode. My mouth opened, and Robert spoke through me: *"Is the fucking truce over, then?"*

"Oh, no," Cordwainer said. "I haven't explained Reality yet. Are you admitting that you were lying? Are you ready to listen to the truth?"

"Let me ask you something in return," I said. "Are you afraid of what you might see?"

"That's ridiculous."

"All right, humor me. Take your arm off my neck and give me five more minutes." To which Robert added, *"And if you don't, I'll finish what I started in the Cobden Building."*

"I owe you for that, too," Cordwainer said. "Five minutes, that's what you get. Go on, continue the charade."

We crossed the open ground and entered the scattering of maples I remembered from my dream. Ahead, the massive oak reared through the canopy. Robert knew this terrain as well I did, although he, too, had never seen it while awake. It occurred to me that after a thousand repetitions we had changed places: now I was the shadow moving toward our destination.

"I reject the idea that you are capable of moving through

time," Cordwainer said. "It was I who took us back to Wagon Road."

"Then who brought us here?" I asked.

"I have no doubt of your ability to move through space," Cordwainer said. "That, you inherited from me."

"Look to your right. In about ten seconds, you'll see a lighted window." We moved through the last of the oaks. Cordwainer chuckled at my attempts to hoodwink him. Two steps later, a yellow glow shone through the trees.

Cordwainer stopped moving. The triangular outline of a dormer rose above the cloudy heads of the trees. "Think I'll fall for that?" Cordwainer strode into the meadow. I heard the hissing of his breath. Cordwainer was staring at the portico, the facade slanting across the edge of the forest, the chimneys rearing against the sky.

"What house is this?"

"Move closer," I said. "He can't hear us, and he can't see anything but his own reflection."

Cordwainer took a couple of paces along the back of the meadow and came to a halt. "I know those walls." Unwelcome recognition had begun to blossom in his face. "That front window is like the very one I crawled through as an ignorant boy." He spun to glare at me. "Oh, you are a treacherous, treacherous fiend, but I see your shabby plan. You have brought me to its likeness."

"Wait until you see who's inside," I said.

"This is *unbearable*. It is *blasphemy*. Within walls like those, my Great Fathers spoke to me. That building was my *school*."

"And your teacher was Howard Dunstan. He's in the big room on this side. Go on, look in the window. Think of it as a test of your faith."

"My faith has been tested my whole life long," Cordwainer muttered. "And so has my patience, but never as sorely as this."

We came to within ten feet of the shining window. Across the shabby room, an expiring Boston fern and a fox strutting to the edge of a glass bell occupied a white mantel. Shiny weights whirled left-right, right-left beneath a brass clock that reported the hour as 11:31 P.M.

"If anyone is there," Cordwainer said, "let him show his face."

On cue, Howard Dunstan strolled into sight, his face ravaged, his hair and beard white, but still recognizable as the subject of his studio portraits and the man who had driven his family down Wagon Road. He was speaking with the slow, unstoppable rhythm of a hypnotist. I knew who stood just out of sight. Howard's weary despair concealed a witty, calculating expectancy that had eluded me until this moment. His face was that of a being who had never spoken a straightforward word, committed a spontaneous deed, or revealed more than what was necessary—it was a face poisoned by isolation.

As if drawn by magnetic attraction, Cordwainer Hatch unwillingly moved forward.

I saw myself walk into the shining frame and the year 1935 from an afternoon on which Stewart Hatch had gestured across an overgrown field and more than hinted that his grandfather and Sylvester Milton had destroyed the building in front of us. Now I knew that Stewart had it all wrong: Cordwainer had already given me the real story. I also knew that two earlier versions of Ned Dunstan, aged three and eighteen, had minutes or seconds before momentarily flickered into view and disappeared again because they had come too early, and they had come alone. I looked dazed but irate enough to take care of myself. When I said something to Howard, he kept talking, and I tried to interrupt his flow by asking, *What are we?*

Howard shook his head and mouthed, *We are what flew from the crack in the golden bowl,* then something I could not lipread. Beside me, Cordwainer gasped. All the air seemed to leave his body. Howard moved down the room and out of sight. I thought: *He knows we are out here, he's playing to both of his audiences, every last lousy flourish is in place—*

Cordwainer took a quick backward step, stumbled around, and dove into the woods with surprising speed. I went after the bulky form dodging through the trees. He stopped running when he reached the maple grove. His face was an unreadable blur.

"Still think it's some kind of trick?" I asked.

"Did he say, *We are the smoke from the cannon's mouth?*" He might have been talking in his sleep.

"I think so, yes. I remember that."

Cordwainer made the phlegmy, guttural sound of someone attempting to expel a foreign substance from his lungs. "I was watching his lips. He said something about a golden bowl. Then he said, *We are the smoke from the cannon's mouth.*"

"Have you heard that before?"

"Oh, yes. I have, yes. I have heard it on a number of occasions." His voice was wet. "During my boyhood."

Heavy footsteps came toward us from the center of the woods. Cordwainer turned around with a stiff, grave immobility, as though his neck had fused to his spinal column. A dancing glimmer of light bobbed toward us out of the darkness. "Men from town," I said. "They're coming to burn him out. About a hundred and fifty years before this, the same thing happened in Providence."

"Howard Dunstan never lived in Providence."

"One of his ancestors built a place people called the Shunned House. Sylvan Dunstan moved it here brick by brick."

The light separated into three torches advancing through the trees. Cordwainer yanked me behind the shelter of a pair of maples.

■ **120**

■ Torchlight surrounded them with a uniform glow traveling through the forest like a spotlight. Occasionally, a cluster of leaves popped into brief flame. Cordwainer plunged deeper into the woods. He paid no attention to me—he no longer cared if I existed.

The man in the lead was Carpenter Hatch, older and heavier than when seen on Wagon Road. Apart from the torch in his hand and the vindictive expression on his face, he looked precisely like the affluent small-town stuffed shirt he had always intended to become. Three feet behind him and side by side marched a pair of men separated as much by mutual distaste as by social standing. The grim, balding man at least ten years older and nearly a foot taller than Carpenter Hatch had to be Sylvester Milton. Ferrety Pee Wee La Chapelle hustled along beside him.

Cordwainer and I moved behind an oak twenty feet in front of them. Breathing hard, he watched the man he had thought was his father march toward us, his torch upright and his face blazing with hatred. Milton's torch ignited another low-hanging cluster of leaves.

"Watch that, Mr. Milton," said La Chapelle.

"Shut up, Pee Wee," Milton said.

Cordwainer jumped into their path. The three men halted, confronted by what must have looked for at least a couple of seconds like the sudden appearance of a severed head.

Carpenter Hatch recovered from his shock and said, "Clear off. This business does not concern you."

"He's seen us," Milton said.

"Stop quaking, Sylvester, and take a good look at that old man," Hatch said. "He's a degenerate half-wit." In a ringing voice, he said, "Listen to me, old fellow. You no longer work for Mr. Dunstan. He is a wicked man and must be punished. I have fifty dollars in my pocket. That's a lot of money, I know, but it will be yours if you take off now and keep your mouth shut afterwards."

Cordwainer let out a howl and charged them. Milton and La Chapelle dropped their torches and ran. Carpenter Hatch glanced over his shoulder, jumped back, and hurled his torch at Cordwainer. Before Cordwainer snatched it out of the air, Carpenter was already in flight. I sprinted from cover, picked up the fallen torches, and stamped out the advancing flames. Cordwainer held his torch over his head, listening to the panicky sounds of their retreat. His shoulders rose and fell like pistons. I couldn't tell if he was sobbing or just breathing hard.

He spun around and hurtled toward the house. Over his head, leaves sputtered into flame.

When I ran out of the woods, Cordwainer was plunging up and down the side of the house, keening. Tears shone on his face. I came to within six feet of him, and his face went slack with shock, then flared in a kind of recognition. An anguished bellow erupted from the flap of his mouth. *"Do you know what he did to me?"*

"He lied," I said.

Gripping the torch like a lance, Cordwainer ran to the edge of the meadow and circled away, circled back. Because I did not understand that he was looking for something, I thought he had passed into pure animal craziness. On his second circuit, he fell to his knees and unearthed a long, flat, dirt-encrusted rock. He picked up the torch with his left hand and plunged back to the building. The rock sailed like a discus toward the window and smashed through it in a glittering shower of broken glass. With another wide swing, he lobbed the torch through the broken window.

Cordwainer whirled around, uttering squeals of excitement and agony. All he saw of me were the torches he ripped from my hands before he took off for the front of the house.

The portico light switched on. A bolt slid into its catch with a tremendous metallic clank, and the front door swung open on an empty hallway leading to a room where flames mounted between piles of books.

Cordwainer screamed, *"Where is he?"*

Through the lighted front windows, I saw Howard's white-haired figure slipping into a doorway at the far end of the room in which Cordwainer had received his tutorials in lunacy. From the back of the house, feeble light appeared in the window above the portico. I heard, or imagined I heard, batlike squeals. Streamers of fire moved across the floor of the study, fattened on the night air, and billowed into the hallway. "He's going to the attic," I said.

Cordwainer turned a furious glare upon me.

"Where the others are. You must have heard Carpenter and Ellie whispering about them."

Cordwainer's strangled voice said, *"A octopus, centipede, spider kind o' thing."*

We stepped back and looked upward. The attic windows turned soft yellow.

What Cordwainer did next, when I was expecting him to fulfill his own prophecy and run into the burning house, astounded me—he uttered a scarcely human sound that expressed condescension and mirth by wrapping them in lunacy. I needed a second to realize that he was giggling.

"Robert! It's a shame you didn't have the wit, the courtesy to read my stories before destroying them. Had you done so, you would comprehend our position. All is written! We brought each other to this place."

I tried to find Robert, but Robert had departed. "Written?" I said, now really playing for time. "How?"

"By grace . . ." An ecstatic smile widened across his face. "By grace, I am delighted to say, of my genius. What a fool I was. I rejected my masterpiece." Cordwainer started laughing in high-pitched, ecstatic scoops of sound.

This evidence that his humiliation had ascended nearly without transition into euphoria scared me more than anything that had happened earlier, and I moved away, furious with Robert for having abandoned me again. "Are you saying you wrote about Howard Dunstan?"

"I wrote of an Other, whose name I knew not. He betrayed me, Robert—you were absolutely, wonderfully right!"

"So join him," I said. "If that's what you wrote, get in there before it's too late."

"How is it possible you don't comprehend?" Cordwainer shouted. "Both of us are meant to join him."

In a repetition of the worst moments from my childhood, a force like a giant hand lifted me off my feet and muscled me in the direction of the open door. Exalted, his feet inches above the ground, Cordwainer sped toward me. I flew back at least ten feet, the fire seeming to stretch out its arms behind me, before I summoned the strength to resist him. It was as though—looking back, I remember, it seemed as though—I managed to draw upon some lingering portion of Robert's being. When I slammed to a halt at the edge of the portico, the heat curled against my back like a huge animal and threatened to ignite my clothes through sheer proximity. Cordwainer stopped, too. From a couple of yards away, he blasted out the same dictatorial energy that once had held me helplessly in thrall, and I found I could stand fast. Hairs crisped in my nose. I didn't move.

Cordwainer howled in frustration.

We faced each other, locked in a stalemate that would endure until one of us weakened. Without Robert, I felt handicapped, doomed. Then a secret door opened in my mind, and from the great, dark, unknown space beyond it Star Dunstan said, *Like hearing the whole world open up in front of me.* With a sense of yielding to that which all my life I had most feared and distrusted, I passed through the door—I can't put it any other way. In terrified, necessary surrender, I moved into an elemental darkness, I *passed through.* Forces and powers I had never known I possessed and never wanted to command streamed out from the center of my being and went prowling through Cordwainer's psychic hurricane.

"You must go inside!" Cordwainer bellowed. "Don't you understand? Move!"

"It was your story, not mine," I said, took a step away from the portico, and wrapped him in the terrible glamours I had inherited from Howard Dunstan. My old enemy, Edward Rinehart, Mr. X, Cordwainer Hatch, opened his mouth and screamed like a rabbit that had just felt the trap bite into its leg. I felt like screaming, too. Instead, I propelled him howling past me and into our blazing ancestral house.

Somewhere within, timbers crashed down. The attic windows flickered red, then an incandescent blue. I moved back from the conflagration and softly, stupidly, spoke Robert's name. The fire drowned my voice. Another beam thundered toward the basement. Flames erupting through the roof vanished into the sheet of darkness welling behind them, and I sent myself back to the Brazen Head.

■ 121

■ My body shook from the inside out, and the smell of smoke clung to my clothes. I flattened my hands on the table. When they stopped trembling, I tugged Cordwainer Hatch's bible out of my pocket. Like my clothes, it stank of destruction. I opened it at random and read the first sentence to meet my eye:

". . . It was a octopus, centipede, spider kind o' thing, but they was a haff-shaped man's face on top of it, and . . ."

I threw the book on the table.

Feeble lamplight shone on the fountain in Veal Yard. Perhaps two hours of my time had brought me into the ordinary world's night. I scrubbed my hands and face, shoved the photographs into their folders, and went down to the lobby.

The night clerk pretended not to smirk at my jacket. "Message for you, Mr. Dunstan. I was about to send it up this very second."

"Read it to me," I said.

Raising his eyebrows, he reached under the desk and unfolded a slip of paper. " 'Happy Birthday. I called Nettie to see if you were there, and she spilled the beans. Want a nice present? Come to my house. Laurie.' " The clerk managed to make every word sound obscene. He refolded the paper and offered it to me with elaborately ironic courtesy. "Would you care to keep this lovely memento, sir?"

■ Stewart Hatch's 500SL slanted over the edge of Laurie's driveway with its front wheels on the lawn. I swung around it, trotted to the front door, and let myself in.

Posy Fairbrother was holding Cobbie in her arms at the bottom of the staircase. He looked as rigid as a flagpole. Stewart shouted in the kitchen, but I could not make out his words. Cobbie reached for me, and I pulled him to my chest. I could feel his heart beating.

"Should I call 911?" Posy whispered.

A plate smashed against the kitchen wall. Stewart let out a drunken bellow. Another plate exploded. Cobbie began to cry. "I'll take care of it," I said. "Cobbie, can you go back to Posy?" His head nodded against my neck. "Here we go." Posy folded him into an embrace and moved up the stairs.

I walked into the kitchen. Standing at the counter next to the alcove, Laurie looked at me and communicated that she was frightened but in charge of herself. Fragments of broken plates covered the floor between her and Stewart Hatch, who was beside the gaping china cabinets, his feet planted wide to keep himself steady. He had perspired through the back of a nice small-check Italian shirt. "Don't you ever get sick of lying?" Stewart yelled. He grabbed another plate and fired it against the wall five feet to her left. Laurie glanced at me again, and Stewart turned to look over his shoulder. Sweat glued his executive hair to his forehead, and the whites of his eyes were blotched with red.

"Get the hell out of my house." Then he brought his legs together and put his back against the counter, smiling. "Jesus, Dunstan, even you ought to know better than to wear a jacket like that."

"Cobbie's frightened," I said. "Why don't you go back to your place?"

"This isn't about Cobbie! This bitch ruined my life." He

wagged a finger at me. "But you know all about that, don't you?" Stewart took an insinuating step forward. "Screw my wife, send me to jail, is that the deal?"

"Are you going to jail, Stewart?"

"I hate to say it, I *really* hate to say it, but I may be given that delightful honor. Ashton did the impossible, and we know how, don't we? I'm a reasonable guy, I'd just like to hear the truth for a change." Boozy rage darkened his flush.

He was getting close to losing control again, and he liked the idea. Losing control would make him feel better than he did now.

"This is what puzzles me," Stewart said. "That Kentucky nobody tied me into deals she couldn't have known about unless some underhanded piece of *shit* turned over the documentation. Which nobody knew I had, except Grennie, and he sure as hell didn't do it."

He grinned at me, looked down at half of a perfectly bisected plate, and kicked it aside with one of his tasseled, basket-weave loafers. He gave a demented Huckleberry Finn chuckle. "We have been requested to appear at Police Headquarters at nine o'clock tomorrow morning to undergo"—he raised his head and searched for the word—"the *formalities* before questioning on a number of criminal charges. Fraud, for example. Tax evasion. Embezzlement. Getting down and dirty with that glorious institution, the U.S. Post Office. Grennie is shitting porcupines. My guess is, he'll eat a bullet. Won't that make me look good?"

"I like your compassion," I said.

"Yeah. I like yours, too." Stewart wiped his hands over his face. "Be a stand-up guy, tell me how you did it. I'm in the dark here. Help me out."

"Stewart," I said, "I don't know what you're talking about."

He flattened a hand over his heart. "Did you break into my building after all? The rules of evidence say that's a no-no."

"You were a lousy criminal," I said. "You didn't even know enough to hire C. Clayton Creech."

Stewart wheeled sideways and raised his arms. "*Creech!* My father would rather have crossed the street than say good morning to C. Clayton Creech."

"Your father wasn't a criminal," I said. "Cordwainer took care of that for him."

Stewart's face took another incremental step toward purple. He looked at Laurie, who shook her head. "No? Well, no. I suppose not." He swung back to me, ticking toward eruption. "Now, little buddy, did I happen to tell you about my departed Uncle Cordwainer? Refresh my memory."

"You told me about him," I said.

"Did I happen to mention his name? I think not."

"Cordwainer's name is plastered all over town. But I understand why you'd prefer to keep quiet about him."

He reared back. "Who have you been talking to?"

"All secrets come out in the end," I said. "Even yours. Go home, Stewart."

"You know? I think the Sesquicentennial was a really crummy idea." He laughed, making a sound like a crow, dry, self-important, completely without humor. "Maybe this bitch with a cash register for a soul, and I speak of my dear wife, maybe she didn't sell me out after all."

"Don't think I wouldn't have," Laurie said.

"And she's *married* to me," Hatch said. He laughed his ugly laugh, *caw caw caw.* "Does that tell you anything?" He was on the edge of the explosion he had wanted all along. "Tell me about secrets, Dunstan. I'm getting a better picture here, I'm getting, what's the word, some perspective."

"If you don't get out, I'll put you out."

"Do you think I have anything to lose?" He stepped toward me. There was a tight grin on his face. "I don't. But you do." He threw a lazy punch at my head.

I dodged to the left and hit him in the stomach.

Laurie yelled, "Stop it!" Stewart staggered back. "Cute," he said. "Know my golden rule?"

I shook my head.

"Never fight when you're shitfaced." Stewart dropped his hands and took a step toward the back door. When I moved closer, he pivoted on his heel and fired off a fast, hard left that would have broken my jaw if I hadn't ducked. His fist rammed into my skull. My head rang. I saw Stewart move in to follow up with a right and punched him in the gut again, harder than the first time. He shuffled into the counter and said, "Uh-huh." His eyes were almost entirely red. He reached behind his back, fumbled in a drawer, and came out with a paring knife.

"I was looking for something a little more imposing," he said.

Laurie started to move toward the living room. Stewart pointed the knife at her and yelled, "You stay put!" She glanced at me.

"I'm sick of Hatches coming at me with knives," I said. Too angry for common sense, I went straight at him. "Stick me, you white-bread, chicken-shit, overprivileged future convict."

To keep me in my place, Stewart jabbed at nothing. He shifted to the side, went a hair off-balance, and tried to correct himself by leaning forward and taking another poke at me. I grabbed his wrist, yanked him forward, and kicked him in the ankle. He toppled facedown onto the kitchen tiles and the broken plates. In tribute to Lieutenant Rowley, I kicked Stewart in the ribs.

"*Stop!*" Laurie shrieked.

I straddled him and dropped to my knees. He grunted. I took the paring knife out of his hand.

"Don't kill him!" Laurie said.

"Be quiet, please, Laurie," I muttered, and twisted Stewart's right arm behind his back. Then I hauled on his arm and pulled him to his knees. Another pull got him upright. "Damn, Stewart," I said. "You need a keeper." I biffed him in the ear with my left hand. "Should we call the police, tell them how you tried to knife me?"

"Fuck you if you can't take a joke," Stewart said. "I'm under a little stress right now."

I wrested his arm another two inches up his spine, and he cried out in pain. "I know you're troubled, Stewart. But you pulled a knife on me, and I can't say I dislike the idea of hurting you."

Stewart kicked the heel of a tasseled loafer into my right shin and tried to break away. I rammed his arm toward the back of his neck and heard the tearing of ligaments and the loud pop of the ball detaching from his scapula.

Stewart groaned and staggered forward.

"You broke his arm!"

"Actually, what I did was, I pulled his shoulder out of joint," I said. "After good old Stewart drives to Lawndale and checks into emergency, a nice doctor will pop it back into place right away. You can drive with your left arm, can't you, Stewart?"

"They wouldn't let you in the door at Lawndale," Stewart said.

I whapped him in the shoulder. Stewart yelped, and his knees wandered.

"I can drive."

I pushed him down the counter and told him to open the door. We went out to his Mercedes. "Where are your car keys?"

"Right pocket."

I dipped into his pocket for the keys. Stewart collapsed onto the leather seat and dragged his legs under the wheel. I put the keys in his left hand. Sweating and grimacing, he managed to start the car. He twisted sideways to get his left hand on the shift lever. Whimpering, he put the car into reverse and backed into the driveway. The sound of crumpling metal and breaking glass told me he had also backed into the Taurus. The Mercedes shot down the driveway and rocketed into Blueberry Lane. One of its tail lights swung from a tangle of wires. The right rear panel of the Taurus looked like a used tissue. I took the folders off my passenger seat and looked over the top of the car to see Laurie gazing speculatively at me from the living room window.

■ **122**

■ She stepped outside and hugged me. "Thank you, thank you, thank you for coming. I don't know what he would have done, he was so out of his mind." I smelled a faint, not unpleasant trace of whiskey.

"Is Cobbie all right?"

"I told him you helped calm his father down." She moved through the doorway, sighed, and rested her head on my shoulder. "The poor kid should fall asleep in about a minute and a half."

"I hope so," I said. "Cobbie didn't need that." I kissed the top of her head, and she clung to me a moment longer.

"I really *am* grateful, Ned." She looked up at me and smiled. "Did you get my message?"

"Yes. Thanks."

"You didn't tell me it was your birthday! I had to find out from Nettie."

"I didn't want you to go to any trouble," I said.

She raised her mouth for a kiss. "Until you got here, was it a nice birthday?"

I laughed. "You could say that."

"What did you do?"

"My aunts had a party for me. I've kind of been on the run ever since."

"They must have had a barbecue. Your jacket smells like smoke." She leaned back with her arms still around me and smiled beautifully up. "It's a very *suburban* sort of jacket."

"May magpied it for me," I said. "Do you like it?"

"Of course. After the way you handled Stewart, I want to keep you in a good mood. You look gorgeous in pink. You should always wear pink pants, pink shirts, and pink suits with little sailboats and nautical flags."

Her ability to reduce the ugly scene into a shared joke pulled me into her private aura. I felt the deep tug of having whatever troubled me being met with this same teasing, dissolving irony. Then the thought came to me that seeing it in this way meant that I had already separated myself from it.

"I'm sorry if I frightened you."

"*Stewart* frightened me. You impressed me."

"You knew you were going to take care of things, in the end. Maybe I made it worse."

"Hardly." She kissed me again. "After demolishing my china cabinet, I think he was going to move on to the glasses. Will you help me clean up the wreckage?" She glanced at the folders under my arm. "What's that?"

"I'll show you later." I put the folders on the coffee table, and we went into the kitchen and started sweeping up broken plates. Shards and sections of china lay in archipelagos down the floor and made irregular islands on the counters. Shaken, Posy came in and began picking up the mess beside the butcher block. "Cobbie finally went to sleep, but I practically had to read every book he owns. Is everything all right?"

"Ned was heroic," Laurie said. "You should have seen him. Stewart pulled a knife."

"A paring knife," I said. "Even he was embarrassed."

When we had bagged all the broken china, Posy asked if she could do anything else.

"No, we're fine," Laurie said.

"I'm glad Ned came along to drive out the wild beast."

I bowed, and she blew me a kiss and left the kitchen. Her soft footsteps went up the stairs.

"Wouldn't you say we deserve a drink?" Laurie asked.

"I don't think we can catch up with Stewart," I said, "but I'm willing to give it a try. I'm going to have a whopper of a bruise on the side of my head, and my hand hurts. No wonder boxers wear gloves."

Laurie took a glass from the shelf and another from beside the sink, pressed them against the ice lever in the refrigerator door, and brought out a liter of the late Tobias Kraft's favorite liquor. She poured whiskey over the ice until the glasses were three-fourths full.

"You were having a drink when Stewart showed up," I said.

"Was I?" I could not tell if she had forgotten, or was pretending to have forgotten. Then I saw that she was presenting me with a mild challenge. "Oh, yes. I gave you a clean glass, but I took this one from the counter. Ah, I see. Whilst enumerating my flaws, Stewart included heavy drinking."

"He skipped that one. People who drink as much as Stewart don't think it's a flaw."

"Good point," Laurie said. "God, let's sit down." She put an arm around me, and we moved into the living room.

We settled on the long sofa in front of the coffee table. The big room seemed as vibrantly empty as an abandoned airline terminal.

"I'm sorry about yelling," Laurie said. "Vastly to my surprise, I discovered that I felt sorry for Stewart."

I took a slug of Scotch.

She let her head roll back on the cushion. "What do you think is going to happen to him? Is he going to be all right?"

"You want to know what's going to happen to good old Stewart?" I said. "Let me tell you. After a year in prison, Stewart will have a personal encounter with Jesus and become a born-again Christian. For the rest of his sentence, he'll lead prayer groups and Bible study classes. When he gets out, he'll get ordained by some third-rate Bible college and devote a few years to a prison ministry. He'll send out press releases, and a lot of articles will be written about him. Let's face it, it's a great story—civic leader and heir to private fortune falls into crime, finds salvation in jail, devotes himself to good works. The guy can't miss. In three years, he'll have his own church and a good-sized staff. When he describes his past, Ellendale will sound like Sodom and Gomorrah. Rare steaks, fancy cars, expensive suits, chains, leather, and whips. His congregation will quadruple, and he'll buy a new building with a television facility. Then he'll write a book and get on talk shows."

The bit about chains and leather popped out while I was rolling along. That so much anger still boiled away within me came as a surprise.

She was clear-eyed and amused. "I bet you're right. Where did you get the stuff about chains and whips? He's too normal for S and M."

"I threw it in for the sake of a better conversion story. Once Stewart's locked up, I should write him that fiction is way more effective than reality."

Laurie looked at me with the same contemplative speculation I had seen from over the roof of my car. "You said you were sick of Hatches coming at you with knives."

"Heat of the moment."

"You threw that in, too? How many Hatches are there, after all?"

Oh, no, I thought.

Her eyes underwent a subtle change. "What? I don't get it."

I swallowed another mouthful of whiskey, preparing myself. I did not want to prepare myself.

"Ned?"

"You're right," I said. "I have to explore something with you."

"You were going to show me those folders." Her crisp voice rose wonderfully to the challenge. Laurie sounded like an army poised at the top of a hill, pennants flying and weapons at the ready. I felt nothing but admiration.

"First you have to hear about the past two days. I owe that to you. You introduced me to Hugh Coventry, and you helped me learn about Edward Rinehart."

"That's what you want to explore?" The pennants rippled beautifully in the wind.

"That's what we have to explore," I said.

■ I began with Buxton Place and Earl Sawyer. After leaving the cottages, I said, I had come to Blueberry Lane and seen the care-taker's name in Posy's Lovecraft collection.

"That's why you got so strange?" Laurie said. "Posy and I couldn't understand what happened to you."

"I know, I'm sorry. I had to get away and think."

"Well, thank God, you came back. What then?"

"At Toby's funeral, someone implied that Stewart owned my aunts' block on Cherry Street. It didn't make sense. All along, I never understood why they pretended not to know anything about my father."

"Me, neither," she said. "But I don't see the connection."

"I did something I shouldn't have. I looked through Nettie's closet. That's where I found one of those folders. The other one came from Stewart's house."

"You broke into *Stewart's* house?"

"I didn't have to break in. I took the folder, but he stole it first. I was reclaiming it."

"He had your aunts' pictures?"

"He wanted to keep them out of the exhibition."

"The other ones were at Nettie's? Well, at least you got that settled. They were holding them for ransom. Nettie and May, they're not stupid."

"Nettie and May know how to get what they want." I grinned. "The question is, what did they want?"

Laurie gazed imperturbably back. "They must cherish those photos."

"Let me show you some of them."

"I can hardly wait." She set down her glass and leaned toward the coffee table.

I slid the photograph of Omar and Sylvan out of the folder. "Remember these faces." Next came the photograph of Howard Dunstan I had put before Cordwainer.

"He looks like you." She turned to me with a shining smile and looked back down at the picture. "In a way. You don't have those heebie-jeebie eyes."

"That's Howard Dunstan. Nettie and May were his daughters."

"Complicated so and so, wasn't he? What's this?" She took another photograph from the pile. Under the eye of a squat foreman in a derby hat, two men pushed wheelbarrows toward a lattice of scaffolding and girders rising from a muddy lot. From the right side of the frame, two others carried an armload of two-by-fours across Commercial Avenue. A Model T Ford and a slat-sided truck were parked a little way down from the site. A well-upholstered onlooker in a seersucker suit and a boater like the one worn by the young Carpenter Hatch took in the excitement from a few feet behind the supervisor in the derby. The angles of their hats and their postures matched with the neatness of a rhyme.

"That's Merchants Hotel, under construction in 1929. Hugh Coventry liked this picture."

"It's good, isn't it? There's a lot of movement in it, and the two guys in hats are like a joke."

"Here we have baby me." I put down the photograph from my third birthday.

"God, what a beautiful child." Pleasure and humor shone from her eyes. "I mean, of course you were a great-looking kid, but you were a *really* great-looking kid. You should have been on billboards."

"My mother would have agreed with you. Now, here are some from the Hatch folder." I showed her the photographs of Carpenter showing off his new car and Ellen's graduation.

"Who are these people? Stewart's grandparents?"

"Right."

"She was a nice-looking girl, wasn't she? On the other hand, he looks like an excellent source of ham steaks. Look at those soon-to-be ponderous thighs."

I pulled out the image of bow-tied Cordwainer Hatch peering from beneath his bangs.

Laurie bent forward. She took a swallow from her nearly empty glass and looked back at me. "Is that you? It can't be. You weren't even born when this was taken."

"This is the black sheep of the Hatch family," I said. "Stewart's Uncle Cordwainer."

"He looked like you."

"I look like him. Laurie, back when the first submissions were coming in, did you see any of these pictures?"

Her lower lip tucked under her front teeth. "I honestly don't remember."

"Rachel Milton did. She told me to look for them."

"I don't understand." Her eyes showed nothing but innocent confusion. "Did Rachel say that I had seen them?"

"No. Just that you could have."

"Maybe I did. I wouldn't have paid much attention. I didn't even know you then."

"Stewart knew who I was the second he saw me. Cordwainer was supposed to have died before Stewart was born, and I don't imagine he ever saw any pictures of his disgraced uncle while he was growing up, so he didn't even know what Cordwainer looked like until he collected the family pictures for the exhibition. He couldn't have missed the resemblance between his uncle and Howard Dunstan."

Laurie shook her head. Her hair sifted over her cheek, and she brushed it back. "I have to say . . ." She shook her head again. "I think I need another drink. How about you?"

I propped my head against the cushion. I felt completely uncertain. A voice in my mind said: *I want to be uncertain.*

Laurie circled back into the room and moved around the table rather than sliding in over my legs. She sat down about a yard away and took a swallow from her amber, ice-filled glass. "I'm trying to figure out what's going on with all these pictures. Your aunts took Stewart's pictures as ransom, but why would Stewart hide theirs?" She moved Cordwainer in his bangs and bow tie next to me in my striped T-shirt. "Oh. Because the black sheep uncle was your father?"

I picked up the studio portrait of Howard Dunstan and placed it beside the other two. "Does anything else occur to you?"

She leaned forward, looked at Howard, then at me.

"If you want, I can show you some other pictures of Cordwainer."

She pushed herself back into the sofa and smiled at the nice white emptiness in front of us. "I don't have to see any more. I guess I understand why Stewart wanted to squirrel these away."

"I think he gave my aunts a lot of money," I said.

She laughed. "Stewart isn't exactly an egalitarian, you know.

He would not be overjoyed by a blood connection between his family and the Dunstans. In fact, he'd do everything he could to hide it." An idea moved into her eyes, and she edged toward me, radiating conviction. "Your aunts knew it right from the beginning!"

"I guess so, but they claim they never met Edward Rinehart. Even if they did, how would they know who he was?"

"It doesn't matter how! They knew! Of course they could never tell Star—it was their secret. And Stewart tried to have you run out of town before you could even begin to learn anything."

"But why would he give my aunts a fortune for three old houses? I can't believe he cares that much about his grandmother's reputation."

"Stewart's a snob. He likes being a high and mighty Hatch. He'd spend a fortune to protect that."

"I feel like I came to the end of something, only it didn't *end*."

Laurie twisted sideways, drew up a leg, and slid her elbow over the back of the sofa. She propped her head on her hand and waited for more.

"I don't know what to say," I told her, having left everything crucial unsaid.

"Say something about Hatches coming at you with knives."

I swallowed watery whiskey and slivers of ice. "In all honesty, Laurie, if I told you everything, you'd think I was either lying or crazy."

One of her knees floated above the cushion, and her calf slanted down over the edge of the sofa. She was leaning sideways, her chin on her hand. Evenly suspended, compassionate determination shone from her face.

"You met your father, this Edward Rinehart. Cordwainer Hatch. Am I right? And he attacked you with a knife. Was it in Buxton Place?"

"Boy, you're smart," I said.

"I pay attention. Where did it happen?"

"A couple of places." I smiled at her.

"You went to a couple of places with your father. And, for reasons yet to be explained, the gentleman tried to do away with you."

"Laurie," I said. "I'm really sorry, but you're not going to get anywhere."

"Since you are here, he did not manage to do away with you. Should I assume that you did away with him?"

I said as much as I could. "He did away with himself when he found out that he was Howard Dunstan's son. That's all I can tell you."

She did not move. "Somewhere in or around Edgerton is the dead body of Cordwainer Hatch. Eventually, this body will be discovered. Not long afterward, it'll be identified."

"That won't happen," I said. "Believe me."

Her hand sank away from her chin; her forearm slipped down the back of the sofa; her knee moved to the edge of the cushion. In a paradoxical form of rejection, Laurie's face came nearer to mine. "Everything you say is so *vague*. You want me to believe you, but you get less and less believable. Trust me enough to tell me where you went, at least."

Hostility I barely knew I felt made me reckless. Laurie Hatch hung before me like an untrustworthy angel, and at that moment, more than I wished to open to her the secret parts of my life, I wanted to repay her for being untrustworthy.

"I'll do better than that," I said. "I'll show you."

"Show me? I don't want to go anywhere now, Ned."

I held out my hand, unable to stop myself from making an irrevocable mistake. "Put down the glass and take my hand."

Slowly, without taking her eyes from mine, Laurie placed her glass on the table. I thought that she had not been so unable to read a man's intentions since the days with Morry Burger. By the time she moved in with Dr. and Mrs. Deering, Laurie's peripheral vision had taken in everything on both sides and behind her, too. Ever since, she had been able to see around corners and the corners beyond those corners.

If you want to know about me, I thought, *you'd better know about this.*

Laurie Hatch grasped my hand, and with the usual sense of dropping through a sudden hole in the earth I pulled her into what I already knew she would never be able to accept. We came to rest on the corner of Commercial Avenue and Paddlewheel Road, a short distance from the future offices of C. Clayton Creech. The brownstones were still single-family houses with private access to the park, which was enclosed within a tall iron gate. Directly across the avenue, a Model T Ford and a truck with slat sidewalls stood at the curb beside a construction site.

Scaffolding encrusted the first two floors of a structure ascending into a skeleton of girders. Men crawled along the scaffolding and disappeared into the regions behind it. At the front of the unfinished building, a man in a derby hat yelled at two workmen next to a vat of cement; directly across the gated tip of the park on our side of the avenue, two men unloaded timber from a horse-drawn wagon. A man in a boater and a seersucker suit that did not disguise his resemblance to either President Garfield or Luciano Pavarotti, depending on your frame of reference, strutted toward the frame from behind the parked vehicles. It was a mild, slightly overcast afternoon in what felt like mid-September.

About ten feet from Laurie and me, the photographer who would freeze this moment watched his composition move into being from behind a tripod and a bellows camera the size of an orange crate. One arm held his flash and the other the black veil attached to his camera. He looked like a magician.

Laurie sank to the sidewalk, pressing her free hand to her forehead. I pulled her to her feet. *You wanted answers?* I thought. *Look around.* Her face had an unhealthy shine, and her eyes were dazed. "Try not to throw up," I said.

"I never throw up." She lifted her head. "Where *are* we?"

"Paddlewheel Road and Commercial Avenue," I said. "In 1929. Take a look."

The elements of the scene moved toward their defining moment. Garfield-Pavarotti rounded the corner and came to a halt behind the foreman, whose bellow at the men just now trundling their wheelbarrows away from the vat could barely be heard over the din from the building. The photographer ducked beneath the black veil. The sawmill hands finished unloading the wagon, got their arms under the ends of a dozen two-by-fours, and began their journey across the avenue. The cement workers bent like pit ponies to their task. The foreman crossed his arms, pushed out his chest, and spread his legs in a posture of command. The heavyweight in the seersucker suit crossed his arms, pushed out his chest, and spread his legs to keep his balance. Under the black veil, the photographer spread his legs and leaned into his viewfinder. The workmen advanced into the frame and turned their eyes to the girders. A row of flashbulbs exploded with a yellow flare and a sharp, percussive *pop!*

Laurie jumped. The wheelbarrows rolled up a plank runway

to the scaffold; the two-by-fours passed over the curb. The spectator in the boater navigated around the foreman, and the foreman bawled at the pit ponies. The photographer emerged from
his veil and arched his back.

"Ned, I don't want . . . Ned, *please,*" Laurie whispered.

The enormous room on Blueberry Lane took shape around
us. Laurie reeled around the coffee table and sank to her knees a
foot from the sofa. She doubled over and rested her head on the
carpet, like Mr. Michael Anscombe in his last moments. I knelt
beside her and stroked her back. She waved me away.

"Can I help you?" I asked.

"No." She crept forward, levered herself onto the sofa, and
went limp. After about a minute, she sat up and flopped against
the cushion. "I almost broke my golden rule and puked all over
the carpet."

"How does your head feel?"

"Attached." She tilted forward, picked up her glass, then sank
back and held the glass to her forehead. Her eyes closed. She
stretched out the parallel lines of her legs. The glass descended
to her mouth. "I want to see that picture again."

Laurie hitched forward and fumbled through the photographs.
Her eyelids looked swollen. "Two minutes ago, we were standing right there."

"Any closer, we would have been in it," I said.

"I don't understand this, and for sure I don't like it."

"I don't like it much, either," I said.

Laurie pushed herself back and straightened up. "But you *did*
it. You *took* me there. That isn't *right.*"

"It isn't right or wrong," I said. "But you sure could say it's irregular. Unexpected."

"Unexpected!" Her face blazed a smooth, bright red. "Why
didn't you tell me what you were going to do?"

"Would you have believed me?"

Observant insightful intelligence moved back into her eyes.
She was fully present again. That she felt as though she had the
flu meant nothing. She saw it all, even the anger to which I had
been blind. "Do you do that a lot?"

"I do that as seldom as possible. I'll probably never have to do
it again."

"Is this something you inherited from Cordwainer Hatch?"

"From his father," I said.

"I can't deal with any more of this tonight."

"Whatever you say." I began pushing the photographs into their folders. My mind felt as though it had been clamped in a vise and beaten with a hammer. Laurie drew her knees under her chin and watched me leave. After I made it through her door and into the Taurus, I looked at my watch. My thirty-fifth birthday had disappeared into history. On the way back to town, I had to pull off the highway and pass out for an hour.

■ **124**

■ Officer Treuhaft monitored my progress around the dead fountain as though waiting for me to bolt.

"Looks like I have guests," I said.

"Captain Mullan and Lieutenant Rowley are waiting for you, sir."

"What do they want to talk about?"

Treuhaft blinked. "I believe it's related to your visit to Headquarters this evening, sir."

"Makes sense to me. Have you been here long?"

"Maybe two minutes."

Inside, the night clerk waved me toward the desk. He leaned on his counter and spoke almost without moving his lips. "Two cops went up to your room. If you want to split, the back door's that way." He extended his little finger and pointed past the desk to stairs descending to a narrow hallway.

I gave him a five-dollar bill and put the Lovecraft book and the folders on the counter. "Would you hold these things for me?"

The clerk shrugged, and the counter was clear.

When I walked into my room, Lieutenant Rowley uncoiled from the side of the bed. Captain Mullan gave me a weary nod from the chair at the near end of the table. "Please be seated, Mr. Dunstan." He gestured at the chair across from him.

My fingers met the little calligraphic arc of *P.D. 10/17/58,* and

I heard my mother telling me *If I could sing the way that man played alto, Neddie, I'd stop time forever . . .*

"Describe your actions before your visit to Headquarters."

Robert had been busy.

"I drove around."

"Drove around." Rowley thrust his hip against the table. "Did our travels take us to Ellendale?"

I heard Star say, *At first, I wasn't even sure I liked that group. It was a quartet from the West Coast, and I was never all that crazy about West Coast jazz. Then this alto player who looked like a stork pushed himself off the curve of the piano and stuck his horn in his mouth and started playing "These Foolish Things." And oh, Neddie, it was like . . .*

"I believe they did," I said.

"About ten-thirty P.M., Stewart Hatch turned up in the emergency room at Lawndale Hospital," Mullan said. "He claims that he surprised you in an intimate situation with Mrs. Hatch, and you attacked him with a knife."

"Are you carrying a knife?" Rowley asked.

"Mr. Hatch further claims that during the ensuing struggle, you dislocated his shoulder and otherwise assaulted him. He wishes to bring charges."

. . . going to some new place you'd never heard about, but where you felt at home right away. He just touched that melody for a second before he lifted off and began climbing and climbing, and everything he played linked up, one step after another, like a story . . .

"I don't care what Stewart Hatch does," I said. "It won't work. He's telling his story backwards."

"Mr. Hatch dislocated *your* shoulder?"

"Let's see the knife, Dunstan," Rowley said.

"I don't have one." I told them about going to Ellendale and tussling with a drunken Stewart Hatch. "Finally, he reached into the knife drawer and came out with a paring knife. He said something like, 'I was looking for something a little more impressive.' Then he rushed me, and I yanked him off his feet and dislocated his shoulder. I kicked him in the side, too, because by that point I was not in a good mood. After that, I threw him out of the house. He rammed into my rental and took off for Lawndale at about a hundred miles an hour. I'm surprised he's so stupid. His wife saw the whole thing."

"His alcohol level was four times over the limit," Mullan said. "By the way, according to the officer who took Mrs. Hatch's statement, the word her husband used when he saw the paring knife was 'imposing,' not 'impressive.' 'I was looking for something a little more imposing.' That's a nice touch."

"Captain," Rowley said, "they cooked this story up between them. Mr. Hatch caught them in bed, and Dunstan pulled a knife."

"The officer who questioned Mrs. Hatch was shown a garbage bag loaded with broken plates. I think we can dismiss Mr. Hatch's accusations."

"You went out there already?"

"We can move pretty quick, when we want to."

Neddie! I heard my mother say. *It was like hearing the whole world open up in front of me. It was like going to heaven.*

A chain-saw noise came from Rowley's throat. "This guy is all over the place. Wherever we go, there he is. Nobody's seen Joe Staggers in two days, and we *know* Staggers was after him. What do you think happened to Staggers?"

"So far, no one's filed a Missing Persons."

"Dunstan hands out alibis, and women back him up. Mr. Hatch's troubles are going to blow away, and before long, Dunstan's going to blow away, too. Then it'll be business as usual. Who do you want in your corner, Captain?"

Mullan clasped his hands on his belly and regarded the ceiling of my room. "All in all, Lieutenant, I think you can go home for the night. Tell Officer Treuhaft he can leave, too."

"Think it over, Captain."

"Thank you for your assistance, Lieutenant. We shall see each other tomorrow."

Rowley's dead eyes moved from Mullan to me and back to Mullan. "Up to you, Captain." He slammed the door behind him.

Mullan regarded me with the same opaque, detached gaze he had trained on my ceiling. "You're a strange man, Mr. Dunstan."

"So I've heard," I said.

Mullan's bleak smile told me only that Robert had been unimaginably reckless. "I assumed you would be waiting to hear from me."

"I am."

Mullan did not move so much as a centimeter. Even the wintry smile stayed in place. "Do you remember my mentioning an anonymous telephone call from someone accusing Earl Sawyer of a number of homicides?"

"Sure," I said.

"That's what makes you a strange fellow. I didn't mention it."

"I'm sorry," I said. "There's too much going on."

"You wouldn't be the fellow who placed that call, would you?"

"I would not," I said.

"But the subject is of interest to you."

"I can't deny that," I said, feeling my way through the mine-field Robert had laid.

"At approximately nine o'clock P.M., you visited my office for the purpose of informing me that you suspected Earl Sawyer of being the man once known as Edward Rinehart." He raised his eyebrows, as if for corroboration. I nodded. "That would make two people who wanted to talk to me about Earl Sawyer. I don't believe in coincidence, Mr. Dunstan."

"I thought the police got anonymous tips all the time."

"Be nice if we did. This old man wouldn't have to work so hard. All right, forget the call. Correct me if I'm wrong here. When we went to St. Ann's, didn't you refer to Clothard Spelvin? Clothhead?"

"There's nothing wrong with your memory," I said. "I don't suppose there ever has been."

"At Headquarters, you said your mother had given you Rine-hart's name."

His smile still looked like a map of the tundra, but he did not seem hostile. In a series of careful steps, Mullan was working up to something, and he had sent away Rowley and Treuhaft because it had to be kept between us. I had no idea what Robert had said to Mullan, and I could not afford to make a mistake. Nor did I have a hint of where Mullan was going.

"Not long before she died," I said.

Mullan stretched out his legs and put his hands behind his head. "Let's see if I have this straight. You got word that your mother had returned to Edgerton in ill health. How did that happen? Did one of her aunts call you in New York?"

"Yes, but I was already on my way," I said. "I had some vacation time, so I thought I'd hitchhike across the country. I know that sounds crazy, but the idea appealed to me. I was going to work my way to Illinois, visit my aunts, and fly back. Two days before my mother died, while the truck driver you talked to, Bob Mims, was taking me across Ohio, I. . . . I don't know how this is going to sound to you."

Mullan said, "Give it a try."

"I had a strong feeling that she was having serious health problems, and that I had to get here in a hurry."

"Although your mother was not a resident of Edgerton."

"I knew she'd come home if she thought she was dying."

"You were driving across Ohio with Bob Mims. You got the strong feeling that your mother had come home because she thought she was dying."

"It sounds funny, but that's what happened."

"Then what?"

"Mims went off his route to drop me in front of the Motel Comfort, where I met Ashleigh Ashton, and she agreed to give me a ride here the next morning."

"When you reached Edgerton the following morning, you requested Assistant District Attorney Ashton to drop you at St. Ann's Community. Not on Cherry Street. You must have had another strong feeling."

"You could put it that way. Captain Mullan, why are we talking about this?"

"For a couple of reasons. Okay. You go to the ICU. You learn that your mother had a stroke. Her heart's in bad shape. Deep down, you know she's dying, but at least you got there in time to see her, talk to her. Communication isn't easy. Every word costs her tremendous effort, and you have to strain to make them out. All these factors make everything she says extremely significant. Am I right?"

Mullan was still gazing across the room with his legs out before him and his hands laced behind his head.

"It sounds like you were there."

"I have been there," Mullan said. He took another step toward his mysterious destination. "Under these conditions, your mother does something unexpected. She grabs your hand and says, 'Edward Rinehart.' And she manages to give you some information about this unknown gentleman."

Captain Mullan had fed me precisely enough to let me off the hook. Anything affirmative I said would be right. Mullan wanted to see if I knew that Rinehart was my father. *He* knew, and at a mere agreement that Star had indeed given me information about the unknown gentleman, he would tell me in a way that implied I had known, too. Mullan was leading me through a maze. He had pulled the rug from under my feet, but even more, I thought, he had yanked it from beneath Robert's. For reasons of his own, he wanted to find out how deeply into the maze I had already penetrated.

"She said Rinehart was my father."

"You must have wanted to see what you could learn about the man. You thought Toby Kraft might be able to help you."

"Toby was the first person I asked," I said.

"Did he help you? Indirectly, I mean? For example, did you and Mrs. Hatch go to the V.A. Hospital in Mount Vernon on Toby's recommendation?"

Mullan had been doing his homework. "He suggested I talk to a man named Max Edison, and Mrs. Hatch offered to take me there."

Mullan turned his head to me without altering his posture in any other way. "I don't suppose you know about Edison. It never made the papers."

I could already see the corpse lying across the bloody bed, the severed throat.

"It was a lot like Toby Kraft, except there was a knife next to him. Same night. Suicide, is the general opinion. Which is fine with me. The guy has maybe three, four months to live, and he decides to get out while he can still make decisions for himself. But here's an interesting thing. A clerk out there says a private detective named Leroy Pratchett turned up to see Edison the day before. A scrawny guy in a black leather jacket. He had a goatee."

"Frenchy," I said.

"You have a suspicious mind," Mullan said. "How did you connect Rinehart with Earl Sawyer?"

I told him about Buxton Place and Hugh Coventry's recognizing the owners' names. I described meeting Earl Sawyer, being let into the cottages, seeing the books by Rinehart and Lovecraft and finding Sawyer's name in "The Dunwich Horror."

Mullan tugged his chair closer to the table and did his best to look as though he believed what I was saying. "Did you pay a second visit to Buxton Place at a time when Sawyer was not present?"

I shook my head.

"You were not responsible for the destruction of those books?"

I realized what he was telling me. "You went to Buxton Place."

"Mr. Dunstan, I have spent the evening going wherever I thought I might find Earl Sawyer." He stretched his arms and yawned. "Excuse me. I'm too old for this crap. Fairly soon, or so I hope, Edward Rinehart's coffin at Greenhaven penitentiary will be disinterred. Maybe we'll find out who is buried in the damn thing. It sure as hell isn't Rinehart."

"I don't suppose it can be," I said.

"What do you call that, understatement?" Mullan asked me. "On your feet, Mr. Dunstan. You and I are going for a walk."

■ 125

■ Mullan gestured to the far end of the reception desk and the steps down to the back door. "This way." The clerk came through the office door and spun around to inspect the junk mail on a shelf behind him.

I followed Mullan down the stairs and over the concrete floor to the exit. Moving faster than I had expected, the captain banged the door open and marched out. I caught the door on the backswing and went into a narrow brick trench that had to be Horsehair. The gray blur of Mullan's suit and a smudge of white hair were vanishing into the obscurity to my left.

I thought I recognized Lavender's double doors and listing buildings as we rushed across into the continuation of Horsehair. Mullan stopped moving, and the pale blur of his Irish face revolved toward me. "Let's talk about your suspicious mind. This so-called Pratchett turns up at the V.A. Hospital. Suppose he was Frenchy. What does that mean? Prentiss, he's already dead. The next night, bang, like ducks, all in a row, Edison, Toby Kraft, Cassandra Little, and La Chapelle. Between you and me, is it possible that you have some hypothetical sort of explanation?"

"Speaking hypothetically, I guess I do," I said. "Helen Janette told me Frenchy grew up in these lanes. Maybe Rinehart—Earl Sawyer—had scared him, one way or another, since he was a kid." I told him Sawyer's story about "Charles Ward" having a boy named Nolly Wheadle deliver his weekly salary and Nolly's account of a figure he called Black Death.

"Maybe Rinehart, Sawyer, whatever you want to call him, sent Frenchy to the V.A. Hospital to find out if I had been there asking questions. Some of the staff told him that two people had been talking to Max Edison, and maybe Edison said these two people got his name from Toby."

"In all our many conversations, Mr. Dunstan, you never said a word about Edison or Edward Rinehart."

"Captain, as entertaining as our get-togethers were, they didn't seem to have anything to do with my father."

"Was Edison the person who told you about Clothhead Spelvin?"

"Yes," I said. "I liked Max Edison. He deserved better than being slaughtered in his bed." I remembered that we were supposed to be speaking hypothetically. "If that's what happened."

"*If* that's what happened, tell me the rest."

"Sawyer took care of Max and Toby, and after that he had to get rid of Frenchy. He thought Frenchy probably said more than he should have to his girlfriend, so he killed her, too. Clyde Prentiss, I don't know." I remembered seeing Frenchy and Cassie Little in the ICU. "You know, maybe it was a kind of down payment. Prentiss could have saved himself some jail time by naming Frenchy."

Mullan bristled. "Earl Sawyer killed four people because he didn't want you to know he was your father, is that what you're saying?"

"He felt betrayed," I said.

"Do you want to add anything to that?"

"Do you want to tell me what you're doing? Why did you think I might be working for the Louisville D.A.'s office or some federal agency?"

"Let's say I feel betrayed." Another glacial smile appeared and disappeared on what I could make out of his face. "You may be able to do your bit for civic order, Mr. Dunstan." Mullan plunged ahead.

The odor I associated with Joy's house again filtered out from the bricks; after another twenty paces, Mullan wheeled into Raspberry. In the darkness, the cobbles descended into a sunken vale where two policemen leaned against the walls on either side of a door sealed with yellow tape. They pushed themselves upright when they saw Mullan.

"This should interest you."

By the time we reached the door, the two cops looked like sentries guarding Buckingham Palace. "Take off," Mullan said.

They gave me that indifferent cop scrutiny and sauntered up the lane.

Mullan pulled away strands of tape. "Earl's phone is still listed under Annie Engstad, the person who lived here before him, but Hatch's security chief had the address on file. I had to bust the lock to get in. If you're worried about Mr. Sawyer's rights, Judge Gram, one of the guys I play golf with every Saturday, signed a search warrant."

He opened the door, and the river-bottom stench moved out at us like an invisible wall. Mullan went inside and switched on a light. I heard rats scrambling for cover.

I said, "Good God."

The door opened into a low-ceilinged room about twelve feet square that looked as though a bomb had gone off inside it. It was the ultimate residence of Cordwainer Hatch. Heaps of refuse, some waist-high, undulated over the floor. Newspapers crisped against the walls like dried sea foam. Against the wall to the left, a jumble of filthy shirts, socks, sweatshirts, and sweatpants lay over a narrow bed; against the opposite wall, geological deposits of junk flowed over the edge of a table to meet junk rising in layers from the floor. The enormity of the disorder made me feel dizzy. Rags, pizza boxes, glasses, crumpled magazines, paperback books without covers, plastic cups: the frieze of rubble lapped beneath and around a chair and washed into the room beyond, here and there parting to allow for passage.

"Earl's living room and bedroom," Mullan said. "This is going to sound funny, but don't touch anything unless I give you permission. Some of this material is going to be used as evidence." He pointed at the back room. "That was his kitchen and work room, I guess you'd call it. It's even worse. Before we go in there, look at the closet."

He waded through debris and tugged open a door. The shirt and trousers of Sawyer's uniform hung beside a tan windbreaker and a pair of khaki pants. One wire hanger was empty. The uniform cap faced visor-out from the shelf alongside his Kangol cap, a long, black flashlight, a billy club, and the rounded ends of objects I could not immediately identify. The yellow eyes of a scrappy-looking rat stared up from a jumble of shoes on the closet's floor.

Mullan yelled, "Scram!" and stamped a foot on the rubble. The rat whisked through an opening in the wall about as wide as a dime. "Look next to the baton."

I stepped over spongy detritus, went up onto the balls of my feet, and saw a row of knives—kitchen knives, knives with stag handles and wooden handles, knives that folded into black metal handgrips, and knives with blades that flicked out of molded steel cases.

"Look closer," Mullan said.

I leaned forward and saw rusty stains and dried palm prints.

"Earl liked knives," Mullan said. "But he didn't care about cleaning his tools any more than he did about cleaning anything else, as long as he kept his uniform and a few other things presentable enough to wear outside."

I slogged behind him to a fan-shaped stain in the far right corner of the room, where he unearthed a half-buried cardboard box. "Fortunately, Earl kept souvenirs." Mullan picked up a bent metal rod that had once been part of an umbrella and pried open the flaps on top of the carton.

I peered in at a jumble of wristwatches, bracelets, mismatched earrings, a couple of key rings, and old wallets scattered with small, white bones and the curving fragment of a human skull to which adhered a nugget of gristle.

Mullan tapped the fragment with the umbrella rod. "I wouldn't be astonished if this used to be part of a gentleman named Minor Keyes. Remember him?"

"How could I forget?" I said. "It was the first time I was ever accused of murder."

"See these little bones? My guess is, they're what's left of the hands cut off a newborn baby we found on top of a Dumpster about four years ago. We brought in the mother the next day. Sixteen years old. Charleen Toomey, a nice Irish girl. She confessed that she had placed her infant daughter on top of the Dumpster, but swore it was breathing at the time. According to Charleen, she hoped some good Samaritan would come along and give her baby a home."

"And according to you?"

"According to me, she was going to toss it in, but she chickened out at the last minute." He poked one of the wallets. "Property of a drunk named Pipey Leake, who was beaten to death in the service alley alongside Merchants Hotel in 1975. This one came from a kid named Phil Doria, hung around the Buffalo Hill area at night and mugged older guys. In 1979, someone stabbed him to death. This bracelet probably belonged to a runaway smack addict who peddled her tail along Chester Street under the name Sidewalk Molly."

"Shouldn't this stuff be taken to Headquarters?"

"It will be," Mullan said. "Shortly after that, Earl Sawyer–Edward Rinehart is going to become public property. And you are, too, Mr. Dunstan. Right now, we still have a chance to decide what kind of story it's going to be, and how much attention you come in for."

"What are you saying?"

Mullan tossed the rod onto a mound of refuse. He no longer looked anything at all like a bartender. "Certain aspects of the way your friend Stewart Hatch likes to operate are probably bringing my department under investigation. I'd like to keep the scandal down to a dull roar. It'll be bad enough without dragging in Jack the Ripper."

"You want to cover this up?" I was—only one word will do—aghast.

"Even if I was stupid enough to want to, I couldn't. You can't cover up a story like this. Even Rowley can see that he might pocket some more of Hatch's money by pushing you into the spotlight. It wouldn't do that much good, but it sure as hell would draw attention away from Stewart."

"Pushing me into the spotlight," I said.

"About two hours ago, Grenville Milton packed a bag and drove across the river to a motel outside Cape Girardeau. He booked two first-class tickets to Mexico City on a seven-thirty A.M. flight tomorrow from St. Louis. He had a hundred and thirty thousand dollars and a Ruger .45 with him. I don't know what it is about Rugers. Guys like Milton, they want a weapon, that's what they buy."

"Two tickets," I said. "First class."

"Then he called a woman named Ming-Hwa Sullivan. Ming-Hwa is a piece of work. She refused to come to the motel, and she laughed at the idea of meeting him at the airport. He said he'd kill himself, and she said, 'Grenville, if you were a grown-up, you'd understand how little I have to do with that decision.' Her words. When she got off the phone, she called us, and we talked to Cape Girardeau. They had two units out on a gunfire report. Fifteen minutes later, the captain there called back. Milton fired the Ruger four times. He killed the telephone in his room. He killed his TV set. He opened his window and killed the neon sign in front of the motel. Then he sat down on the floor, stuck the barrel in his mouth, and blew off the top of his head."

"Does Hatch know about this?"

"Not yet."

"I don't understand what you're doing," I said.

Mullan stepped carefully around me. "Come into the kitchen."

■ 126

■ More rats, along with several cockroach nations, scuttled into hiding when he switched on the overhead bulb. In the back half of the room, ecstatic flies congregated over coalesced, shining foothills of green jelly divided by trails leading to the bathroom, the sink, and the back door. The bathroom door stood open far enough to let me know that I never wanted to see it when the light was on.

Like a clearing in a forest, a rectangular section of the table at the left of the kitchen stood apart from the mess rising up around it. At the center of the clearing, a black, gold-trimmed fountain pen lay parallel to the edge of a bound journal similar to those in which Toby Kraft had entered his fictional accounts. Above the rubble at the far end of the table hung a photograph in a silver frame. Crayons and a golden marker had overlaid the image within the frame: the photograph had been taken out and deliberately altered before being replaced. I moved up through the chaos surrounding Captain Mullan and myself; I stood in front of the table and took in what my father had done to a formal portrait of the Hatches.

Hand-drawn knives and arrows bristled like quills from Carpenter and Ellen Hatch. Their eyes had been inked out, and vampire smiles erased their mouths. Swirls of black crayon eradicated small Cobden Hatch. A golden crown broadcast vibrating rays from the head of young Cordwainer, and a golden heart flamed at the center of his chest.

"You noticed that picture," Mullan said.

It was what Earl Sawyer had shoved into a drawer on Buxton Place; it was what Edward Rinehart had ordered Toby Kraft to steal from his family's house on Mansion Row.

"Tell me the name of the kid wearing the crown."

"Earl Sawyer," I said. "Edward Rinehart."

"Congratulations, Mr. Dunstan. Your father and Stewart's father were brothers, which makes you and Stewart first cousins."

"I guess Earl wasn't too fond of his family," I said.

"Pull that chair out," Mullan said. "Swing it around and sit down."

I pulled out the chair in front of the table and sat down.

"Here we are, Mr. Dunstan," Mullan said. "You and me. Lieutenant Rowley is working the phone, shoring up his walls, doing his best to bribe or threaten himself above flood level, but Rowley can't touch what we do in this room. Do you understand that?"

"What does Rowley know about Earl Sawyer?"

Another wintry smile. "He knows that Earl has been going around murdering people for the past thirty years. The exciting little twist that Earl Sawyer happens to be long-lost Cordwainer Hatch has not yet come to his attention."

"And are we supposed to hide that?"

"We can't keep that from coming out. I don't give a damn if it *does*. All I want to do is hold the publicity to a minimum and walk away with my reputation and my pension intact. Reporters are going to pile in from all over the country. I'll have to dodge microphones every time I walk out of Headquarters. I can handle that."

"So why are we here?" I asked him.

"If you're willing to help me see what's going on, maybe we can salvage something out of this mess. Do you trust me, Mr. Dunstan?"

"I can't answer that," I said.

"All right. Nothing you say to me is on the record. That is a promise. Do you want to keep talking?"

"Let's see how it goes," I said.

"There may be hope after all." Mullan gazed at the mutilated photograph behind me. "You weren't surprised to hear that the boy in that picture was Cordwainer Hatch."

"I learned that Cordwainer Hatch was my father about twelve hours ago." I told him I had dropped into Hugh Coventry's office and heard about the disappearance of the Hatch photographs. I gave him a vague reason for suspecting Nettie and described finding the file in her bedroom. "As soon as I looked at them, I knew Cordwainer was my father."

"I take it that Cordwainer is dead."

I did not answer.

"What I want to do is going to be a lot easier if I don't have to set up a manhunt for Cordwainer Hatch while his nephew is on trial. I think something happened today—a showdown—and because you're still here, he probably isn't. Say something to me."

I said nothing.

"This is between you and me, Mr. Dunstan. If you tell me you killed him with your own hands, I wouldn't consider bringing charges against you."

"Cordwainer Hatch is dead."

"You could do us both some good by telling me where to find his body."

"Nobody is ever going to find his body."

Mullan regarded me utterly without judgment. "Two years from now, some guy on a backhoe, or a kid out walking in the woods, is not going to come upon his remains. The next time the river floods, his body is not going to wash up on a sandbar."

"Nothing like that will ever happen. It's your turn to trust me."

"Did you kill him?"

"Are you wearing a wire?"

He smiled.

"You'd have to say he killed himself."

"Let me ask you a question completely from left field. Did any of these missing photographs, including the ones of your family, have anything to do with that?"

"Is there something you're not telling me, Captain?"

"I'll be a little more explicit. When Stewart Hatch accused you of attacking him with a knife, he also said that he suspected you of having broken into his house for the purpose of retrieving some photographs he had mistakenly removed from the library. I don't give a damn if you went into Stewart's house and took back something that belonged to your family. I want to know if you showed those pictures to Cordwainer Hatch."

The alarms ringing throughout my nervous system were getting louder. "Why would I?"

Mullan took a moment to answer, and when he did, it took me another moment to understand what he was telling me. "When I was a boy, my mother once pointed out Howard Dunstan to me on the street. He was an old man, but he didn't look tame, like most old guys. In fact, he scared me. My mother said, 'When I was a girl, Howard Dunstan could make you feel like the first day of spring just by smiling at you.' I gather that he had the same effect on a lot of women."

I stared at Mullan in forthright awe complicated only by my shock. He knew everything—he knew everything he *could* know. Ever since we had been left alone in my room at the Brazen Head, Mullan had been leading me toward the point I had been trying to conceal. "You're too good for this town," I said.

"They don't have stories like this in Cape Girardeau. The minute Stewart Hatch laid eyes on you, he tried to get you arrested or run out of town. But he never had any idea who *Earl* was, did he?"

"He thought Cordwainer was dead."

"And Cordwainer didn't know, either. But I have an idea of what he thought he was. Turn around and open that journal, or whatever you call it. He had beautiful penmanship, I'll say that for him."

I swung around and put my hands on the journal. My fingers turned a thick wad of pages, and I read *I, too, have had my Judases, the first of them one Clothhead Spelvin, whose betrayal I answered with a summary visit to his jail cell.*

Further down the page, Cordwainer Hatch's calligraphic hand-writing declared, *In a weathered manner, I am still handsome, if I say so myself.*

On an earlier page, in irate black capitals: *I HATE ART. ART NEVER DID ANYONE A BIT OF GOOD.*

And on an earlier still: *Great Ones, You with whom this Drudge shares a common Ancestry, should You exist at all, I humbly request a degree of recognition commensurate to my Service.*

Then I turned to the last words he had written. *I set down the Pen—& close the Book—the* Triumph *hastens—My Heartless Fathers—*

Behind me, Mullan asked, "Did you show him a picture of Howard Dunstan?"

I closed the journal. "What are you going to do with this?"

"That's an excellent question. While the officers you saw posted at the door were looking through the front room, I came in here, opened that book, and read a couple of paragraphs. I ordered the officers outside and skimmed through the rest. Cordwainer Hatch thought he came from a race of alien monsters who put him here to set up their takeover. He claimed he could transport himself through space, enter locked rooms, and make himself invisible. What happens if that goes public? A thousand reporters start digging into these murders. The whole town turns into the *National Enquirer.* The chief is out, and I'm out, spending the rest of my life running from people who want to write books about the Edgerton monster."

"Won't you need this as evidence?"

"That cardboard box has all the evidence I'll ever need." He looked down at a glistening garbage-undulation four feet away. A well-fed rat had poked half of its body through the surface and was staring back at him. "Get away from me," Mullan said.

Sleek, prosperous, and unafraid, the rat twitched its nose and emerged from the garbage. Mullan stamped on the floor. The rat inched forward, its black eyes fixed on him.

He unbuttoned his jacket and reached for his revolver. "Sometimes self-respect makes you do things you know you shouldn't." Mullan cocked the revolver and aimed it at the rat.

Baring its teeth, the animal elongated over the floor. Mullan jumped back and fired. A second before it reached Mullan's feet, the rat turned into a bloody lump of hair and an open pink mouth. My ears rang. A tinny echo of Mullan's voice said, "At least I can claim I fired in self-defense." He kicked the corpse into the garbage and reholstered the pistol.

"Good shot." I sounded as though I were speaking through a towel.

"I must be losing my mind." His mouth moved, but all I could hear was the tinny echo. "I think this guy could do everything he says. I don't know any other way to explain how Prentiss and Frenchy were killed."

My muffled voice said, "Good point."

"Do you have a twin brother, Mr. Dunstan? *He* says you do. He claims this brother of yours killed Minor Keyes."

"I have a brother. He isn't really a human being." Mullan was looking at me, hard, as though seeing more than he wanted to. "I didn't know he existed until he showed himself in that lane."

"That's as far as I want to go, Mr. Dunstan." I thought he wished he had an excuse to plug another ambitious rat. "The position of the Edgerton Police Department is that your father, Cordwainer Hatch, committed his crimes out of rage at his family's rejection. Prints from this hovel are going to match those taken at the time of Cordwainer's first arrest. The FBI will have Rinehart's prints on file, and the body buried at Greenhaven will be an administrative error. Frenchy La Chapelle and Clyde Prentiss were suicides. The murders of Toby Kraft and Cassandra Little have been linked to organized crime. A witness currently under police protection has established to our satisfaction that Cordwainer Hatch, alias Edward Rinehart, alias Earl Sawyer, died in the course of a struggle and that his body can never be recovered."

"Unless you plan to hang me out to dry, I'll have to be a lot more precise about the body." Both of our voices might as well have come from the realm of my father's Cruel Gods.

"Shut up and listen," Mullan said. "Remember what I say, because you'll have to repeat it about a hundred times."

127

■ I will never know, but I'd give three-to-one odds that Captain Mullan was one of those people gifted with the capacity to dream in long, coherent narrative structures. Maybe years of detective work, or of homicide investigations especially, develop the ability to create fiction, in the way working out at a gym develops other muscles.

What I do know is that Mullan reached into his imagination and instantly, without hesitation, unfurled the story that rescued us both. Here and there, I gave him some help. He prompted me to get some details clear in my mind. This is what he told me:

■ After my mother had given me Edward Rinehart's name, I learned of his arrest in 1958 and death in the Greenhaven riot. Suki Teeter told me more. Still curious, I asked Hugh Coventry to check the Buxton Place property records and noticed that they had been purchased in the names of characters from the works of Rinehart's favorite author. I visited the properties and encountered Earl Sawyer, who admitted me inside them. Sawyer learned that I was staying at the Brazen Head, remarked that he lived nearby, and gave me his address. The following night, an anonymous man called me from the lobby of the Brazen Head and said that he was in possession of certain missing Dunstan family photographs. He refused to say how he had obtained the photographs, but wondered what they were worth to me. We settled on one hundred dollars. I came downstairs, glimpsed a man going outside, and followed him into Veal Yard.

■ "What did he look like?" I asked.

■ In the darkness, he had appeared to be a Caucasian male of five-ten or five-eleven and approximately 160 pounds. He had been wearing a dark blue or black zippered jacket, dark trousers, and gloves. I brought the photographs to my room and noticed the resemblance between Howard Dunstan and myself. After my mother's funeral, Rachel Milton advised me to look at some photographs in the care of Hugh Coventry, not the Dunstan photographs I had already obtained. I went to the library and found that the Hatch file had been discovered missing shortly after Mrs. Hatch had accompanied my aunts to the archive.

It occurred to me that my aunts may have taken the Hatch file to hold in ransom for their own, and I later discovered it concealed in my Aunt Nettie's house. The resemblance of a young man I assumed was Cordwainer Hatch to both Howard Dunstan and myself suggested that I had learned Edward Rinehart's true identity.

I visited Mrs. Hatch; I tangled with drunken Stewart. When I returned to the hotel, I thought about calling Earl Sawyer to ask if he would be willing to examine some old photographs. Earl might let slip some small detail that could lead me to his employer. He was not listed in the telephone directory, so I spent half an hour wandering through the lanes in search of his address, then found myself before a derelict building. I realized that I'd had nothing to drink since midafternoon and was extremely thirsty. Yet, there I was, in front of Sawyer's residence. I knocked. Sawyer recoiled at the sight of me, but after I explained why I had come, readily let me in.

I pretended not to notice the condition of his rooms. Sawyer said he knew his place was a mess, but if he could live that way full-time, I could stand it for a couple of minutes.

■ "Got that?" Mullan said. " 'If I can live this way full-time, you can stand it for a couple of minutes.' "

"Why is that important?" I asked.

"Because it's specific enough to sound real."

I repeated the phrase, and Mullan went on with my story.

■ Sawyer took me into the squalor of the front room. My presence evoked an odd, amused courtliness that seemed edged with hysteria. He asked to see the photographs. I gave him the Dunstan folder, and told him to look at the image of the young Howard Dunstan. He did so without any apparent recognition.

I put the Hatch folder in his hands. Sawyer stared at certain individual photographs with unmistakable interest. He looked again at the photograph of Howard Dunstan and placed it beside a picture of Cordwainer Hatch. He seemed a bit dazed. I asked him if he had any bottled water, and he thrust both of the folders at me and went into the kitchen. I followed, to be certain that whatever I drank came from a bottle and was poured into a clean glass.

Unaware that I had followed him, Sawyer kicked away rubble from in front of his icebox. I noticed the photograph above the table and went up for a closer look. As soon as I had seen what Earl had done to the photograph, I understood that he was Cordwainer Hatch.

He whirled around and asked what I was doing. I pointed at the boy wearing the crown and flaming heart and said, *This is you.*

What if it is? he asked me. *I stopped being Cordwainer Hatch a long time ago.*

◼ "Repeat that," Mullan ordered.

" 'I stopped being Cordwainer Hatch a long time ago.' "

"Then you said, 'You came back to Edgerton as Edward Rinehart, and whether you know it or not, I'm your son.' Repeat that, too."

◼ Earl Sawyer had not been surprised by my announcement. He nodded, regarding me with the faintly hysterical excitement I had seen on Buxton Place. He said, *For what it's worth, I guess you are. I never wanted any part of you.* I began to back out of the kitchen, wanting only to return to my room and drink sanitary water from a sanitary glass. Sawyer came toward me, saying, *I want to show you something.* He opened the back door. *I owe you that much.* I followed him out into a close, winding passage.

◼ Mullan opened the back door and said, "Come along, Mr. Dunstan."

128

■ He plunged up the tiny lane, swerving with its abrupt shifts of direction, charging with the ease of long familiarity across unexpected corners and through boxlike courts.

"Do you know what this thing is called?"

"Horsehair," I said.

"Do you know why?"

"Because it's so narrow, I suppose."

"Good guess," Mullan said, leaving me to wonder if it had been no more than that, and turned into a lane twice the width of Horsehair. His dim figure moved aside and waited. The wider lane extended twenty feet to the right and met a brick wall. This was where Horsehair came to an end: not, as I had thought, into one of the streets bordering Hatchtown, but at a bluntly abbreviated lane between a brick wall and the slanting facade of a long-forgotten foundry. I looked at the wall and saw the word *Knacker.*

"Do you know what knackers used to do?"

I did not.

He waved to the building I thought was a foundry. Its wide double doors were inset with windows, like the old stable doors on Buxton Place. Mullan lowered his shoulder and pushed one of them sideways, and the entire structure trembled. We went into a long, wide space where hooks glinted from listing walls. In the center of the hard-packed earthen floor was a sunken circle about six feet in diameter. A cold, biting vapor scraped into my sinuses, and I sneezed.

Mullan moved toward the pit. "A hundred years ago, they led old horses through that lane and brought them here. The double doors were supposed to remind them of their stables."

"Tell me what knackers used to do," I said.

"Most places, knackers slaughtered worn-out horses and rendered their hooves into glue. Some stripped the hides and shipped them to tanneries. Here in Edgerton, they sheared the tails and manes and sold them to wig makers and mattress companies. When a horse came inside, the boomer—that's what they called him—hit it in the forehead with a sledgehammer. The horse dropped, and the guy they called the hoist picked it up with that thing." He pointed to a long, half-rotted sling suspended from the ceiling. "The shearers harvested the hair, and the hoist lowered the carcass onto a hook. When the time came, he raised it up again, swung it over the pit, and lowered it in. The pit . . . the pit disposed of the carcass."

"How deep is it?" I looked down at the still, black pool six or eight inches below the top of the pit.

"Deep enough. On busy days, the knackers dropped ten, twelve horses down there, and none of them ever came back up. Nothing has ever come up since, either. If all the bodies supposedly dumped into the Knacker are really there, they make quite a crowd."

"What's in there, acid?"

Mullan walked over to the side of the long room and scuffed in the earth. He bent down and picked up what looked like a small loaf of bread. When he brought it back, he was holding a broken cobblestone. "Watch this." Mullan gave the stone an underhanded toss toward the pit. When the cobble fell to within two or three inches of the surface, I thought I saw the liquid ripple upward to engulf it. A sizzling jet from beneath the surface twirled the stone like a cork, and a twist of smoke drifted away to cut into my nasal passages. My eyes watered. Whipping end over end, the cobble surged across the face of the pit, already half its previous size. It looked as though a tribe of piranhas kept it afloat. In seconds, the cobble had become a spinning wafer, a crust, a speck.

"That's what acid wants to be when it grows up," Mullan said. "For a couple of months back in the early thirties, the city had the bright idea of using it as a supplementary garbage disposal for this part of Hatchtown. When the word got out, they stopped and issued the usual official denials. Anyhow, this is where Earl Sawyer wound up. He took you here, he pushed open the door, you went in behind him, and he pulled a knife. You dropped your folders right about here." He brushed the sole of a shoe over the earth. "You struggled. Without knowing what was going to happen, you pushed him into the Knacker. Goodbye, Earl. Without a body, that's the best we can do. It'll work. No one's going to waste any time looking for his corpse. And you'd have to be brought here by someone who knew where it was, because you'd never find it by yourself. Most people in Edgerton have never even heard of the Knacker, and three-fourths of those who have think it's a fable. Let's get the rest of this night over with."

He led me back to Sawyer's house and told me to take the journal. "I never saw it. From here on, it never existed."

I moved through the rubble and lifted the book from the clearing on the table. "What now?"

"We're going back to the Brazen Head for the pictures. Then I'm taking you to Headquarters, where you will be questioned until dawn, probably. Can you remember your lines?"

"I think so," I said.

"We'll have time to go over your story again. Anything else you want to do beforehand?"

"I'd better call C. Clayton Creech."

"You and Stewart Hatch." Mullan locked the back door and turned off the lights in what felt like a parody of domesticity.

■ 129

■ In the interrogation room where Lieutenant Rowley had told me he was my best friend, I recounted Captain Mullan's dream to audiences numbering from a pair to half a dozen at a time, over and over, like a jukebox, like a Scheherazade who knew but a single story and would tell it as long as it worked. Before me, displaying curiosity, suspicion, indifference, or weariness, passed male and female police officers of my age dressed in business suits; uniformed men two generations older who smoked cigarette after cigarette, heroically, and instead of looking at me regarded the table in exhausted cynicism; an aide from the mayor's office; the Police Department's press liaison, who patted her hair and blinked at the one-way mirror; Edgerton's chief of police, who advised me to get an unlisted number; and two un-explained, parchment-faced men with the look of Kremlin func-tionaries destined soon to be erased from state photographs. To all of these people, I sang Captain Mullan's song, and most of the time, Captain Mullan observed my performance from a corner of the room.

Shortly before sunrise, I was declared a "protected informant," or something like that, and led to a cell. The clanging of the door woke me up at 7:30 A.M. With his customary air of having enjoyed a refreshing stroll through a graveyard, C. Clayton Creech glided in, splendidly attired in his old gray suit and old gray felt hat and carrying a black, well-worn briefcase. Creech perched at the foot of my cot and regarded me in a manner that almost suggested a degree of affection.

"Thank you for recommending my services to Mr. Hatch," Creech said. "Stewart comes to me late in the day, but I'll do what I can. On a happier note, you'll be sprung from this shithole pronto." He settled into a comfortable position without visibly moving. "The official viewpoint has it that you have rid Hatchtown of a verminous character and demonstrated the utmost cooperation in your dealings with the constabulary."

"I'm glad to hear it," I said. "What's the unofficial viewpoint?"

"Some of the local bluebottles harbor reservations concerning the anonymous fellow who swapped those photographs for five portraits of Andrew Jackson. It pains me to tell you this."

"I can see that," I said.

"We may take a primitive comfort in two developments. The first is the inability of these gentlemen, due to the support given you by our chief of police, to do anything about their reservations. The second is that Mr. Stewart Hatch does not dispute your claim to be the illegitimate son of his Uncle Cordwainer. Apparently, the photographs you supplied to our law enforcement officers offer striking corroboration to the claim."

"Stewart knew it all along," I said.

"Whatever Mr. Hatch knew or did not know is irrelevant to the present conversation."

I swung my legs out and put my back against the wall. "What is relevant, then?"

"Mr. Hatch's admission of prior knowledge. In the light of Mrs. Hatch's failure to support him in his time of trial, Stewart no longer wishes to impede your claim to the inheritance of his family's trust."

"*My* claim? I don't have any claim to his money. I never said I did."

"We are speaking now of 'claim' in the sense of 'right or title to,' not in the sense of 'demand' or 'assertion.' "

Stewart was up to something: he thought he could use me to keep the trust money for himself. I was the extra pass of the hand that misled the eye. Creech had undoubtedly designed this scheme with the impartial, nerveless skill he brought to everything else.

"Mr. Creech," I said, "if Stewart is convicted of a crime, the trust goes to Cobbie. I'm not going to let him swindle his son."

Creech's patience was sublime. "Mr. Hatch has been eliminated from the food chain. I may be able to help him in a number of ways, but I cannot save him from conviction. The state of affairs is this: If *you* were out of the way—if, for example, you were to remain ignorant of your parentage—Cobden Carpenter Hatch would inherit his family's trust, that is correct. As things stand, however, it must rightfully go to you."

I absolved Creech of complicity. Stewart had made an elementary mistake. "Stewart forgot that the same condition that cuts him out also eliminates me. Cordwainer Hatch was arrested and convicted twice. He's out, so I'm out."

"The condition to which you allude does not apply to Cordwainer. His brother, Cobden Hatch, altered the terms of the trust in May of 1968. The amendment is not retroactive."

"What do you mean?" I asked.

"The clause has no application to actions performed previous to May 1968."

"You're kidding."

"I seldom 'kid,' Mr. Dunstan. It doesn't suit me." Creech folded his left leg over his right, crossed his arms, and drew himself into a tight, self-contained package. A lizardy smile appeared on his face. He was in a state of Creech-bliss.

"Before coming to this delightful facility, I enjoyed a lengthy telephone conversation with Mr. Parker Gillespie, the attorney for the Hatch estate. Mr. Gillespie is a gentleman of choleric disposition. He did not enjoy our little confab, but neither did he fudge. Cobden Hatch wished to drive his son into the path of righteousness by that tried-and-true method, carrot and stick. In 1968, his errant brother was believed safely dead. It never occurred to Cobden Hatch that the trust might wind up in the hands of anyone but his own son. However, we may assume that Stewart Hatch got the picture the second he had you in his peepers.

Cordwainer was the first child of his generation; you were his son; the trust was yours. Illegitimacy has no bearing on the conditions as written. Cordwainer Hatch was born to Carpenter and Ellen Hatch. Carpenter's name appears on his birth certificate. Legally, he was Carpenter's son."

"According to my birth certificate, Donald Messmer was my father."

"Meaningless in the face of Stewart's admission of prior knowledge. Face it, Mr. Dunstan. The Hatch trust will be made over to you."

"I don't believe it," I said.

"You didn't the first time, either."

The lizard-smile widened before my incomprehension.

"Now and then, Mr. Dunstan, it is my task to inform you of a substantial inheritance. My role in your life appears to be that of a kind of celestial messenger."

"Sorry," I said. "That first time."

"Due to Carpenter Hatch's desire to stay the dead hand of the past from restricting the financial options available to his heirs, the entire contents of the trust comes to you unencumbered. On a personal note, the spectacle of the Hatch family being so royally harpooned affords me nothing but pleasure."

"How much money are we talking about?"

"Mr. Gillespie estimates the current value at twenty to twenty-five million, conservatively. Mr. Gillespie will be in touch with you today, and I am certain that he will advise you to retain his services. I would anticipate a spine-quivering description of the sorry state awaiting you, should you decline."

"I guess I have to talk to him," I said, which amused Creech.

"In the meantime, I'll prepare the documents necessary to sever Gillespie's relationship to the trust and FedEx them to you in New York. If you wish, I could also do some background work to discover if my colleague has given you an accurate accounting."

"How would you charge me for that?"

"You would be billed at my usual rate of two hundred dollars an hour. If that is acceptable, fax Mr. Gillespie the day you return to New York, instructing him to copy me on everything he sends you. My esteemed colleague will probably defile the seat of his trousers. I suspect that your two hundred dollars an hour should net you an extra two or three million."

"Mr. Creech," I said, "you're my hero."

"Your money is going to be rigorously accounted for. And since I have more experience of your temperament than Mr. Gillespie, let me ask how much of the windfall you intend to give away."

I smiled at him, but he did not smile back. Creech sat on the edge of my prison cot, folded into himself, gaunt, ageless, and impersonal in his gray suit and hat, waiting for whatever I would say.

"I want to take care of Cobbie Hatch," I said.

"Is it your wish to care for the boy by supplying the funds for his education and allowing his mother a reasonable annual stipend sufficient to allow them a comfortable life, or do you intend to make him wealthy?"

"He gets half of the money," I said.

"You are consistent in your methods," Creech said. "I expected you to divide the pot into equal shares. May I make a suggestion?"

I nodded.

"I recommend that you establish a trust similar to the Hatches', which would grant the boy a certain sum each year, along with a separate sum for his mother's living expenses. At twenty-one, twenty-five, thirty, whatever age you specify, the boy would be given the principal. By the time he is twenty-one, it should be equal to the present value of the original trust."

"How long would it take you to set that up?"

"It's about a week's worth of paperwork."

"Let's do it." I thought about the details. "Have Cobbie come into a quarter of the principal at twenty-one, another quarter at twenty-five, and the remainder at thirty. Give Mrs. Hatch two hundred fifty thousand dollars a year in expenses."

He nodded. "Mrs. Hatch's payments will be made from the trust set up for her son. This arrangement, which is extremely generous, will require my involvement on an ongoing basis, you understand. I have the feeling that you would prefer that my services be billed to you rather than to Mrs. Hatch and her son."

"Would you please send Mrs. Hatch a letter outlining the terms we've discussed?"

"Of course." Creech unfolded his legs and placed his hands between his knees in what I thought was preparation for departure. Instead, he took a clutch of papers from his briefcase and placed them in my hands with a feathery glance of rebuke. "These are the documents concerning Mr. and Mrs. Clarence Crothers's financial obligations in regard to Mount Baldwin Elder Care Facility. We agreed that you would sign them in my office the other day, but never mind, I brought them along. Mrs. Crothers will not be beggared."

Apologizing, I signed the papers and watched them disappear into the briefcase. Creech leaned back without bringing his spine into contact with the wall. "Previous to last night, had you heard of the Knacker?" His voice made the question seem weightless.

"I heard some kids in Hatchtown talking about it, but I didn't know what it was."

"Are you aware that the city once used it for garbage disposal?" I said that Captain Mullan had mentioned it.

"A week after the city put the policy into effect, Hatchtown residents began falling ill at an unprecedented rate. Flu, intestinal disorders. In the first month, six people died of undiagnosed infections. By the end of the second month, birth defects increased noticeably. At the end of the third month, public opinion brought an end to the practice. When I was a boy growing up on Leather Lane, Mr. Dunstan, I knew children younger than I who had been born blind, deaf, severely retarded, with deformed or missing limbs, or with combinations of all the above. The original business had folded long before. The owners opened a fairground."

I said nothing.

"I suppose the Hatches knew that whatever was in that pit, whether they put it there themselves or not, was eventually going to seep into Hatchtown's water supply. To this day, Hatchtown people never drink anything but bottled water."

"So I noticed," I said.

"If Cordwainer Hatch died in the Knacker, he had the honor of meeting several of my former clients." Creech grasped the handle of his briefcase and stood up, uttering a raspy sound I understood was a Creech-chuckle only after he had gone across the cell and called for the guard.

■ A quarter of an hour later, an officer escorted us to the lobby. A few cops turned away when they saw Creech. We emerged into an overcast morning twenty degrees cooler than the day before. Wisps of fog meandered across Town Square. The tips of fingers lightly tapped my elbow, I thought in acknowledgment of my new freedom. On a bench near the fountain, Goat Gridwell's golden hair tumbled out from beneath a mound of blankets. "Thank you, Mr. Creech," I said, and discovered that he was gone.

■ 130

■ Through coiling fog I went up the lanes, Dove, Leather, Mutton, Treacle, Wax, with each step anticipating the footfall, the low smear of laughter that would announce Robert's presence behind me. I knew what he had done, and I knew why he had done it. And Robert knew what *I* had done—there could be no more pretense between us. The threat posed by the being I had known as Mr. X had been forever eradicated. I had *done* that, I had *carried it off.* Robert and I had come into equilibrium, I thought, and I wanted to tell him that I had given away half of the fortune he had schemed to get. Each of us had saved the other's life. We were finished. It was *over.*

I crossed Veal Yard and turned around to scan the narrow buildings and shadowy openings beyond the fountain. Robert was hovering; he was awaiting his moment. I went into the lobby and saw Laurie Hatch floating out of a leather armchair.

She wrapped me in her arms and pressed her smooth cheek against my unshaven cheek. "Thank goodness." She tilted her head and looked into my eyes. "How are you?"

"Reports are still coming in," I said.

"I feel so. . . . I don't how I feel. I had to see you. Last night, the world turned upside down, and everything went flying. I felt numb. Then the police barged in and asked all these questions. They even asked about the pictures. Did they talk to you?"

"They talked to me all night long," I said.

"And let you go. You're not in trouble."

"I'm fine."

Laurie put her head on my chest. I glared over the top of her head at the bug-eyed day clerk, and he scuttled down the counter.

"I'm sorry about what I did to you," I said. "It was a mistake."

"No, Ned, please." She placed her hand on my cheek. "You didn't make a mistake, I did. *God,* I've been worried. I didn't know if I'd ruined everything, I just kept rolling over and over, wanting you next to me."

I held her hand as we went up the stairs.

When I pushed the door shut behind us, Laurie brought her entire body into contact with mine.

"How long have you known?" I asked.

"Known what?" Her smile widened along my shoulder.

"Did you know who I was the first time you saw me?"

The top of her head nearly struck my chin. She moved a few inches away. "How could I?"

"Stewart pushed you off the committee because he didn't want you to see the pictures I showed you last night."

"Never mind Stewart. Do you think I recognized you?"

"I'm trying to figure that out."

She took another exasperated step away. "Stewart is about a hundred times more interested in his family than I ever was. I don't remember how much attention I paid to the Hatch stuff. I looked through it, if that's what you mean. Maybe your face looked familiar when you came up to me in the hospital, but I wouldn't have known why."

"Didn't you call Parker Gillespie two days later?"

"Of course I did!" She raised her arms and held out her hands, palms up. "Ashleigh was in town, remember? I was worried about what would happen to Cobbie if Stewart went to jail. The natural person to talk to was the lawyer for the estate. Ned, don't make both of us unhappy."

I took her hand in mine and kissed it. "I don't want to make anyone unhappy. I'm just looking for explanations. Tell me about this. A day after you did everything you could to help me find Edward Rinehart, you wanted me to forget the whole thing."

Laurie settled her hand on my hip. "Honey, you told *me* you thought you might be putting Cobbie and me in danger."

"You probably haven't heard about Grenville Milton."

Her eyes deepened.

"Last night, Grennie charged two first-class tickets to Mexico City and took off for a motel in Cape Girardeau. He was carrying a hundred and thirty thousand dollars and a gun, and he begged his girlfriend to come with him. When she refused, he killed himself."

The shadow of a thought as precise as a Euclidean theorem moved across Laurie's eyes. She moved toward the table, tapping her lips with an index finger. "Does Stewart know yet?"

"That's probably why he called C. Clayton Creech."

"Stewart's going to ruin as many people as he can. He'll try to bring down everyone who ever had anything to do with him." Laurie slid out the chair from which Captain Mullan had begun our progress toward a believable fiction and sat down almost heavily. "He's going to smash up everything he can."

"Like the Hatch trust," I said.

The sketchy smile brought to her face by the thought of her husband's destructive passions disappeared. She crossed her legs and waited for what I was going to say. Her face looked as transparent as a mountain stream.

"He called Parker Gillespie," I said. "He couldn't have known that I was talking to a cop named Mullan about Cordwainer Hatch. He just wanted to smash things up."

"He wanted to smash me up," Laurie said.

"He said he was relinquishing his claim to the trust. He told Gillespie that he had discovered the existence of the rightful heir, Ned Dunstan, who was the illegitimate son of his father's older brother. Too bad for Cobden Carpenter Hatch, but he could not suppress the truth. It would have gone something like that."

Laurie shifted sideways in the chair and noticed the tidy graffiti on the edge of the table. She lifted a hand and glided her fingers along it, as Mullan had done. In the inner ear of my inner ear, Star said, *He kept moving deeper and deeper into that melody until it opened up like a flower and spilled out a hundred other melodies that got richer and richer . . .*

"I never heard very much about Cordwainer," Laurie said. "Wasn't he arrested for something, ages and ages ago?"

. . . and there I was, with you growing inside me, and I thought it was like one beautiful birth after another.

"The part about arrests and convictions doesn't apply to Cordwainer. Cobden Hatch added it in the late sixties."

"I hardly know what to say."

"You don't sound too surprised."

"You gave me a big, fat hint about thirty seconds ago," Laurie said. "That doesn't mean I'm not surprised. Mr. Creech talked this over with Gillespie? There isn't any doubt?"

"Stewart knew what he was doing," I said. "Was any of this on your mind when we talked about you moving to New York?"

Her composure saw her through a long moment of silence. "That was nasty."

"I couldn't blame you for wanting Cobbie to get what he was always supposed to have."

"He should get it." She faced me with a direct appeal. "Ned, I'm still adjusting to your news, and I haven't had time to think about how it will affect you and me, but you must see that this isn't right. Don't you agree? Twenty-four hours ago, you had no idea that Stewart's uncle was your biological father. *He* didn't want to inherit the trust. He wasn't even a real Hatch!"

"Legally, he was," I said.

"But you—*you,* Ned Dunstan—you're not that kind of person. You're not like Stewart. I want us to have a life together in New York. You'd be a better father to Cobbie than Stewart ever was or could have been. That's *true.* And I love you. There's no reason for the two of us not to have a wonderful life together. But Cobbie's right to the trust is more valid than yours. You see that, don't you?"

"What I see doesn't make any difference," I said. "According to the law, Cobbie has no right to it at all. Before we can start talking about the rest of our lives, you have to deal with the real situation, not what you want it to be."

She continued to focus her utter transparency upon me. "What would have happened if Grennie hadn't killed himself? If Stewart hadn't called Parker Gillespie?"

"You know the answer to that," I said. "I would have gone back to New York and waited for you. I thought that sounded great."

"It still sounds great to me," she said.

"But if Stewart hadn't called him, Parker Gillespie would be about to find himself in a terrible dilemma. This afternoon, everyone in Edgerton is going to learn that Sawyer was Cordwainer Hatch, and that I was his son. What do you think Gillespie would have done?"

"Spoken up," she said. "Obviously. I don't know if he would have done it right away, but it wouldn't have taken him more than a couple of hours. And then we would have celebrated at Le Madrigal."

"Like a happy family."

"Isn't that what you want most of all?"

"Even Stewart had me figured out better than I did," I said. "You saw through me right away."

"I saw the most interesting man I had met in years," Laurie said. "I started falling for you when we had dinner with Ashleigh. You know what you did? You told Grennie he was a jerk, you understood my sense of humor, and you were *all there*, Ned, you looked at me with those incredible brown eyes and you were *there*. You weren't judging me, you were looking at my face instead of my breasts, and you weren't trying to figure out how fast you could talk me into bed. The last thing I wanted to do was get interested in some new guy, but I couldn't help it. Ashleigh knew what was happening in about ten seconds. If you don't believe what I'm saying, you're a fool."

"I started falling for you in the hospital gift shop," I said. "After Creech told me about the trust, he asked how much I wanted to give away. He could see through me, too, but C. Clayton Creech sees through everybody." I told her about the division of the money and the new trust to be set up for her son. "In the meantime, you'll have two hundred and fifty thousand dollars a year, paid from his share."

Nothing had changed in the bright shield of her face. "You don't think we should have talked about these arrangements?"

"I was in a cell at Police Headquarters, Laurie. Creech came in for about fifteen minutes before they let me out. I did what I thought was right."

"Creech convinced you of what he thought was right. It isn't too late to change things." Shining with the utter, straightforward sanity of twenty-twenty foresight, she opened her hand before her as if the world lay in her palm.

"Creech doesn't know about us. And he doesn't understand New York. How could he? The kind of apartment I'm going to need costs about two million. I'll have to have dinner parties, meet the right people, and do the right things. We'll need teachers and tutors and lessons in Europe. How much do you need to be set for life? Three million? Five? The rest could be made over to Cobbie, with a provision that I have something between five and eight hundred thousand a year. We would be together. If we got married, it would be as though you never gave anything up."

"Would you want a prenuptial agreement?"

Laurie leaned back and regarded me in a steady, unflinching manner that seemed less measuring than conducted in the light of previous measurements and considerations held up for revision. None of this was even close to being cold or calculating. The quality of her steady regard spoke for her—it declared the terms of her immense attraction. What I saw in her face was sadness suffused with irony, and it struck me that until then I had never so much as imagined the existence of ironic sadness. I felt the pull of a future open to nuances beyond my own reach: at that moment I could not have denied what seemed the central principle of her life, that in the realm of adult emotion range meant more than depth. Like great, cool wings, Laurie's range extended for miles on both sides. I had taken this capacity for a shield, but it did not fend off or deflect, it took in, and all that it took in increased it. She sat before me, blazing with consciousness.

"I hate the whole idea of prenups," she said. "What a way to begin a marriage. You might as well buy a Coca-Cola franchise." Her face settled into a smile of unreadable privacy. "Philadelphia might be good for us. It's less expensive than Manhattan, and the Curtis Institute is a great music school. Lennie Bernstein went there."

Like C. Clayton Creech, Laurie reassembled herself without altering her posture or moving any part of her body, then smiled at me and stood up.

Her next words clarified whom she had included in "us." "You'd visit Philadelphia, wouldn't you?"

"Better tell Posy to apply to Temple or U. Penn," I said.

"I can always find another Posy." Laurie knew that she had shocked me. The administration of the shock was a deliberate acknowledgment of our new relationship. "Especially in Philadelphia. The hard part was finding one in Edgerton." She kissed my cheek. "Call me before you leave. I need your address and phone number."

I watched her saunter across the hallway to the staircase.

■ Wisps of fog drifted across Veal Yard. A film of condensation gleamed on the cobbles. In the gray light, the buildings around the square seemed on the verge of departure. On the far side of the fountain, a woman's black pump stood with its heel lodged between two stones, as if abandoned only minutes before. A woman leaving, a woman walking away with such finality that she had left her shoe in token. . . . I remembered the eloquence with which Laurie had passed through my doorway and the undiminished clarity of Star's voice, describing an alto solo in a concert she had seen while pregnant with me.

All at once, grief spoke from every gleaming cobble and wisp of fog, and the world seemed to deepen and enlarge. *Grief,* I thought, *it's everywhere, how could I have supposed I would ever get away from loss—*

Robert's face vanished backward into a lane.

"Robert!" I called. "I have to—"

On the way to Cherry Street, I kept glancing over my shoulder to find him sprawled across the backseat and opening his mouth to say something funny and cruel, but I was still the only person in the car when I pulled up in front of Nettie's house. It was a little past 9:00 A.M. All three of my favorite relatives would be in the kitchen. I got out of the car and looked at Joy's front windows. The net curtains hung straight and undisturbed. It was too early in the morning for Joy to take up her post.

Nettie and May bustled around the stove, preparing scrambled eggs, bacon, and what smelled like chicken livers. Clark Rutledge sneered up at me from his bowl of pebbles and sugar.

"Good to see you wearing that pretty jacket, boy."

Nettie asked if I wanted to join them for breakfast, and I said that I was hungry enough to eat anything they put in front of me. I sat down next to Clark.

"They say on the radio Grenville Milton killed himself last night. Care to hear my opinion?"

"Fill me in," I said.

"It's a setup, pure and simple. Stewart Hatch has enemies who would stop at nothing to put him in a bad light."

"Mrs. Hatch must be going through the torments of hell," Nettie said. "And such a lovely woman. Isn't she, Ned?"

"One of a kind."

May ladled eggs and chicken livers onto the plates, and Nettie took a foil-wrapped package of bacon from the oven. Clark pushed his empty bowl to the center of the table. "Left Mr. Hatch holding the bag. That was the point of the exercise."

"And him with a wife and child," May said.

"His wife and child are going to get ten or twelve million from a family trust," I said.

"They will have a roof over their heads," May said. "I am comforted."

"I'm comforted to know you'll have a roof over yours," I said. "When Stewart Hatch heard about Milton's suicide, he told his family's lawyer, Parker Gillespie, all about his Uncle Cord-wainer, so you won't have to worry about that anymore."

Nettie and May applied themselves to the chicken livers.

"By tomorrow, everyone is going to know he was Edward Rinehart," I said.

May sank back in her chair and gazed heavenward. "That is a great relief. I may not be an eater, but I am a talker, and silence comes hard to me."

"What the devil are you gabbing about?" Clark asked.

"Mr. Hatch has released us from our vow of silence," Nettie said. "It seems we have the boy to thank for that. You've done well by us, son, and we are grateful for your efforts on our behalf."

"I second the motion," Clark said. "Although I regret that Mr. Hatch is bound for the clink. He was generous to a fault."

"Stewart Hatch laid out a lot of money to keep you from talking about his uncle. Which is why you couldn't tell me about Edward Rinehart."

"Well, son," said Nettie, "we couldn't help but know a lot more about Mr. Edward Rinehart than your mother ever did."

"Because he looked like your father."

"You could not miss the resemblance," said May. "And we couldn't tell her the facts. You can't talk about a thing like that to an innocent young girl."

I laughed. "I guess it would have been hard to suggest that her boyfriend was your father's illegitimate son without actually coming out and saying it, but how in the world did you know he was Cordwainer Hatch?"

"Why, that was Joy," said May. "You know how she sits in that window day after day. One evening, she called up and said, 'May, I just saw that scalawag Cordwainer Hatch waltz into our sister's house with Star hanging on his arm.' That was the one and only time Star had him over to meet her family. I put on my best coat and hat and hurried across the street quick as a bug. Right after they left, I called Joy and said, 'Joy, that young man must have fallen off our family tree, but his name was not Cordwainer Hatch.' And Joy said to me, 'Honey, you're wrong as you can be. He must be passing under an assumed name by reason of his scandalous reputation.' "

"How did Joy know he was Cordwainer?" I asked.

"Joy spent three whole months working in that house," Nettie said. "She was eighteen years old. It was the Depression, you know, and while we were still comfortable from the sale of our land out of town, it was all you could do to get a job. Carpenter Hatch advertised for a girl of good character willing to do household work, and Joy interviewed for the position. She said she wanted to get out of the house, can you imagine? To think of her now, you can hardly believe it."

"Carpenter Hatch hired her?" I asked. "Didn't he know who she was?"

"If you ask me, he liked the idea of a Dunstan girl changing his sheets and cleaning his bathroom. Joy started at the end of October. Cordwainer was in boarding school at the time. His parents were forced to send him away, you know." Nettie nodded in a beautiful imitation of sympathetic sorrow. "One day while rearranging the contents of Mrs. Hatch's dresser drawers, Joy came across some photographs the lady had hidden from view. She noticed the resemblance between the boy and our late father. It was not long after that she was let go."

"Hatch fired her because of something she said?" Then I understood what Nettie had told me. "No, Joy wasn't rearranging Mrs. Hatch's dresser drawers, she was redistributing their contents. She was a magpie, like Queenie and May."

"Though not up to our standard," May said. "All the same, Mr.

Hatch could never prove anything, but his suspicions settled on her, and then it was farewell, job."

"She told you what she had seen, and you saved it up. When did you have these helpful discussions with Stewart Hatch?"

"When was that, Clark?" Nettie asked.

"Around 1984 or '85. Mr. Reagan was in the Oval Office. Like the man said, it was morning in America."

"I suppose you had gone through the money Carpenter Hatch paid for the property on New Providence Road."

Nettie said, "Clark put a large sum into cranberries."

Clark informed me that the cranberry was a fruit of remarkable versatility. Its juice, health-giving and enjoyable by itself, appeared in several popular cocktails. Rendered into sauce, the cranberry appeared on every table in the country, come Thanksgiving. A note of regret accompanied this recital of the cranberry's virtues.

"Unfortunately," Nettie said, "the cranberry did not render us into millionaires."

"The man I dealt with could be called a common criminal," Clark said. "Though he was as smooth as silk."

"So you had a talk with Stewart Hatch."

"For the purpose of presenting him with a real estate opportunity," Clark said.

"And one of the terms of your agreement was never to divulge what you knew about Edward Rinehart."

"Which is what makes us so happy to be frank and open now," Nettie said. "You came along and hit us with that name Rinehart, that was a *shock*. We had no choice, son, we gave you the best advice we could."

"I am completely impressed. You blackmailed Stewart Hatch into giving you a fortune."

" 'Blackmail' is not a pretty word," Nettie said. "We reached a business agreement. All of us walked away happy, including Mr. Hatch."

"How much did you squeeze out of that crook?"

For once, Clark's smile bore no resemblance to a sneer. "A handsome sum."

"I bet it was." In spite of everything, I was delighted with these three old hoodlums. "You've been living off Hatch money for years and years, haven't you? First you sold the land, and then you sold them a secret. I'm proud of you. The Dunstans have never exactly been law-abiding citizens, but the Hatches were a lot worse."

"Neddie?" May set down her knife and fork on a plate that looked as though it had been steam-cleaned. "Now that we can be frank and open, I want to ask you a question. Mr. Rinehart, as he was called then, perished while in prison. I can't quite see how you came upon his real name."

"Now it's my turn to make a confession," I said. "I had to borrow those photographs Aunt Nettie was storing in her closet."

"Isn't that interesting?" May said. "I have to say, I never did understand why Mrs. Hatch asked me to magpie them out of the library. It was a piece of cake, though. Those people wouldn't notice if you took the clothes right off their backs, especially Mr. Covington."

"You remember, May," Nettie said. "Mrs. Hatch told us that Ned had remarked upon your talents, and deep in her heart she had the feeling that those pictures would help us to get back our own precious photographs."

"Why, that's right," May said. "She did. We never did get them back, though. Maybe we should visit the library again."

"Both sets of pictures are in my car," I said. "I'll give them to you in a minute. If you send them back to Hugh Coventry, they'll be perfectly safe."

"Isn't that nice?" Nettie said. "Mrs. Hatch is a very *attractive* person. She reminds me of those girls on the news who look straight into the camera and say, 'Earlier today, three children were ripped to pieces by tigers during an excursion to the county zoo. Details after these messages.' And I liked her little boy."

"Me, too," I said.

Nettie turned to May. "I met Mrs. Hatch's son when we were comforting Star at St. Ann's. He was so comical! That little boy leaned over the front of his stroller and told me, 'I ain't jumped to any conclusions, Mrs. Rutledge.' I could hardly believe my ears."

"You could put a boy like that on television, along with his momma," Clark said.

"He said to me, 'I ain't jumped to . . .' No, it was, 'I ain't concluded, and . . .' What was it, Neddie?"

" 'I ain't concluded, and so far I ain't jumped,' " I said. "I'll go out and get the photographs, and then I want to drop in on Joy. I'm going back to New York later today."

"So soon?" May said. "Goodness, it seems like you only got here five minutes ago."

Clark gave me a roguish sneer and pushed himself away from the table. "I'll walk out with you."

■ **132**

■ On our way down the steps, Clark gave me a worldly glance Maurice Chevalier could not have surpassed. The fog had coalesced into a thin gray veil that made everything seem further away than it was. When I handed Clark the folders, he cocked his head in a show of confidentiality that implied the presence of unseen eyes and ears. "I guess you had something going with Mrs. Hatch."

"Only a little something," I said.

Fatherly pride warmed his red-rimmed eyes. "I believe you could be a real Dunstan, after all."

"I believe you're right." Then I remembered the unseen eyes and ears and looked across the street. "Do you know if Joy called Mount Baldwin?"

"Hasn't been a peep out of Joy in two days. Since we got this far, let's check in on her."

Joy did not respond to a knock on her door. I knocked again. Clark's forehead divided into what looked like hundreds of parallel creases. "She puts out a key in case of emergencies and the like. Hold on. I'll remember where it is."

I lifted the edge of the mat and picked up a house key.

"Second you bent down, I remembered. Give that to me."

Clark opened the door and flapped his hand in front of his face. "I don't know how people can live with a stink like that. JOY! IT'S ME AND NEDDIE, STAR'S BOY! HOW YOU BEEN?"

I heard a high-pitched humming sound.

"YOU HEAR ME?"

Silence, except for the humming sound, which Clark could not hear.

"We better go in." We moved over the threshold, and the stench enfolded us. "JOY! YOU IN THE CAN?"

"Let's try the living room," I said, hoping that Joy had not died of a stroke while lowering Clarence into the bath. The humming sound grew louder. When we entered the living room, Clarence goggled at us with a mixture of relief and terror and threw himself against the strap. *Hmmmmm! Hmmmm!*

"Clark, call Mount Baldwin and have them send an ambulance right now."

"Will do," Clark said. "You scout around for Joy. I don't like the look of this."

Clarence's Morse code followed me into the dining room and kitchen. Joy had been taking lessons in housekeeping from Earl Sawyer. She had a long way to go, but she was making progress toward the glistening-jelly stage. The bathroom fell even further below Earl's standards.

I flipped the light switch at the bottom of the stairs and heard Clark summoning the ambulance from Mount Baldwin. Above me, a bulb stuttered on, and viscous yellow light flattened against a narrow, partially opened door. Clark Rutledge ranted on in the living room. A dull thump I had heard before came from the attic. Some heavy object had been brought into contact with the side of a wooden crate. What came to mind was a softball the size of a pumpkin.

Clark said, "I'll wait, but I won't wait long. You may take that as a warning." By the time I got to the top of the stairs, he was repeating everything he had said earlier to someone else. On the other side of the attic door, the big softball again thumped the side of the crate. I opened the door the rest of the way and saw a pair of black running shoes with their toes on the pine boards and the soles slanting upward at a right-to-left angle. Extending from the tops of the shoes, two thin legs disappeared beneath a black hem. I said, "Oh, no," and moved up beside Joy's body.

A tray, a spoon, an inverted bowl, and the dried remains of chicken noodle soup lay beyond her outstretched arms. Her skin was cold. A few minutes after I had last seen Joy, she had warmed up a can of soup, poured it into a bowl, taken the tray to the attic, and died.

A small bed enclosed within a boxlike wooden frame butted against the wall at the far side of the attic. Flat plywood sections three feet high had been nailed to two-by-fours at the bed's corners. A cot covered with an army surplus blanket stood along the wall at a right angle to the enclosed bed. Whatever was inside the bed struck the side of the frame.

I remembered the names on the stone slabs behind the ruins on New Providence Road. What had held Joy prisoner had not been a phobia. She and Clarence had been captive to a merciless responsibility. I didn't want to know about it. I wanted to walk out of the attic, go down the stairs, and drive away. The being—the *thing*—that was my mother's cousin struck the frame around its bed hard enough to shake the plywood.

I walked past Joy's outstretched arms and the spray of noodles. When I came up to the foot of the bed, a nearly solid cloud of river-bottom stench soaked into me, and I forced myself to look down. Lying on the mattress at the bottom of the wooden frame was a being made up of a filmy, insubstantial body glowing with light and the face of a man with a graying bush of hair and Confucian white tendrils of beard. His ecstatic brown eyes were already widening in shock. The layers of color sifting through the limbless rectangle of his body darkened from robin's-egg blue and ripe peach to a violent purple in which swirls of black bloomed like ink. The creature fixed me with a monstrous demand, shuddered sideways, and slammed its head against the side of the pen.

Without the intervention of anything that could have been described as thought, I went to the cot, pulled the pillow from beneath the army blanket, and pressed it down upon the terrible face. The thing struggled and surged against the pillow. Its jaw opened and closed as its teeth sought my hands. Bands of brilliant red rose to the surface of its body. Then the jaw stopped working, and the color faded. A pure, depthless black swam up over the filmy surface of the little body and faded to a lifeless gray.

My arms and legs were shaking, but I could not have said if the source of my horror was the thing whose teeth I could still feel beneath the pillow, what I had done to it, or myself. An inarticulate sob flew from my mouth. I released my grip on the pillow and hung on to a length of plywood. The floor seemed to waver, and I thought of Joy's body sliding toward me over the stiff, snaky shapes of the noodles.

An unconvincing voice weaker than mine said, "I had to."

A wave of crazy hilarity went through me. The same unsteady voice said, "He didn't have much of a future, did he?"

No, I thought, *he didn't have much of a future. He didn't even have his last bowl of chicken noodle soup.* I had said that aloud, too.

I watched my hands tear the pillow out of the pillowcase and fling it onto the cot. My right hand dipped into the pen, closed on a wispy rope of beard, and lifted the thing I had murdered. A limp, ragged substance like old spiderwebs drooped from beneath the beard. I rammed it into the pillowcase and stumbled down the stairs.

Clark was standing in the hallway. "The ambulance should be here pretty soon." He glanced at the pillowcase. "Did you locate Joy?"

"I think she had a heart attack," I said. "She's dead. I'm sorry, Clark. We have to call the police, but before you do that, I need a little time."

Clark's eyes moved again to the pillowcase. "I guess little Mousie starved to death."

"You knew about him." I came down the hall with the pillowcase swinging horribly at my side.

"Speaking personally," Clark said, "I *heard* about him, but I never saw the boy. Queenie and my wife assisted at the birth. Clarence and Joy, that child took over their lives. From the time it was born, they never knew a moment's peace."

"They couldn't have named it Mousie," I said, and remembered the names on the flat granite stones on New Providence Road.

"Never really named it at all," Clark said. "Joy took pride in her command of the French language, you know. The way I heard it, Queenie burst into tears when the baby came out. Joy said, 'I want to see it.' And when Nettie held that baby up, Joy said, *'Moi aussi.'* That means 'Me, too,' in the French language. She blamed Howard for the way her baby came out, and she never forgave him. So we called the baby *Moi Aussi,* which pretty soon it turned into Mousie."

"Would you care to say farewell to Mousie?"

"The shovel's out behind the kitchen," Clark said.

■ The shortest and grimmest of the three funerals I attended during my stay in Edgerton took place in Joy's back yard, and the single mourner performed the functions of undertaker and clergyman. In the tangle of weeds against the rotting wooden fence, I dug a hole two feet wide and four feet deep. While I was digging, I heard Clark haranguing the ambulance attendants from Mount Baldwin. I lowered the pillowcase into the hole and scooped earth on top of it. Then I covered the raw earth with severed weeds and yanked living weeds over the dead ones.

"Mousie," I said. "Not that it matters to you, but I'm sorry. Your mother wasn't able to take care of you anymore. Even when she could, you had a terrible life. You never got anything but the short end of the stick. I hope you can forgive me. If you happen to come around again, things almost have to be better, but if you want my advice, stay where you are."

I pitched the shovel into the weeds and came back into the house. Clark called 911. We went into the hallway. Ten minutes later, two baby cops piled out of a squad car and jogged to the door. I said that I had found the deceased, Mrs. Joy Crothers, my mother's aunt. The family had been worried because no one had seen her in two days. My Uncle Clark and I had let ourselves in. Mr. Crothers was in an advanced stage of Alzheimer's disease, and when we discovered his wife's body, we telephoned the nursing home to which he had been accepted and had him removed there. "It looks to me like she had a heart attack while bringing lunch up to her husband."

On the way upstairs, one of the cops finally mentioned the smell. "Mr. Crothers lost control of his bodily functions years ago," I said. "And my aunt was an old woman. She didn't have the strength to clean him properly."

"No offense, sir, but this smells worse than that," one of the cops said.

In the lead, Clark intoned, "You fellows may be ignorant of

what can happen to the human body when it is left to its own devices. Be grateful you still have your health."

"Why did she put him in the attic?"

"I guess she thought he'd be safe there," I said. "She had a special bed made for him. You'll see."

Clark opened the door, and we trooped in. The cops walked around the body and wrote in their notebooks.

"She died in the commission of an act of human kindness," Clark said. "That was her way."

"Chicken noodle soup," said one of the cops. "This isn't any homicide, but we'll have to wait for the M.E. to make it official. Is that the bed you were talking about, sir?"

"She put up the plywood to keep him in," I said.

They stared down into Mousie's crib and looked at Clark. He saw an occasion to which he did not doubt his ability to rise.

"The woman stayed by his side night and day, ministering to his needs as best she could. The tragedy is, the day before yesterday we found a placement for Clarence at Mount Baldwin. I believe the shock of his imminent departure was a factor in Joy's demise. Clarence was her life. Boys, always remember to display affection and regard for your wives. A woman needs that kind of thing."

"If I come down with Alzheimer's, I hope my wife won't dump me into a plywood crib," said one of the cops.

"An act of the purest tenderness and love," Clark said. "You may get an idea of the man's stature when you hear that it was Mrs. Rachel Milton who arranged for his placement at Mount Baldwin."

The cops glanced at each other. "Let's wait downstairs," one said.

■ Clark excused himself to tell his wife what had happened. They came out onto their porch before the medical examiner drove up in front of Joy's house, and they crossed the street in time to hurry up the walk behind him. It was the same weary man with mushroom-colored skin who had released Toby Kraft's body to the police. I was standing outside, and the two cops loomed in the doorway. Nettie caught up to the medical examiner and squared off in front of him. She looked like a mountain with a reputation for rockslides. "Have you come to examine my sister's body?"

"That's my job," he said.

"I trust that you will conduct your business in a respectful manner and allow us to deal with my sister's departure as she would have wished."

"Mrs. Rutledge, you will probably get what you want. I'm here to pronounce your sister dead and rule out the possibility of foul play. But to do that, I have to go into the house."

"Am I in your way?" Nettie asked.

One of the cops told the M.E. that the body was upstairs. He turned to Nettie. "How do you account for the odor in this house?"

"Clarence, mainly," she said. "Once his mind faded, his personal hygiene was a matter my poor sister addressed as best she could. The rest of it comes from the refuse my sister accumulated in her kitchen, which is in a sorry state."

"That's not a garbage smell. Did your sister have problems with groundwater in her basement?"

"Doctor," Nettie said, "these two handsome young officers are waiting to assist you."

The M.E. stepped backward, nearly bumped into me, and murmured an apology. The smirking cops led him up the stairs.

Nettie sidled up to me. "You did the right thing, son."

"I hope so."

"My sister's child claimed her energies from the moment the poor thing first drew breath. Joy sends you blessings for giving Mousie a decent burial. I hope you'll be coming back to see us on a regular basis."

"Aunt Nettie," I said, "don't pay too much attention to anything you read about me in the papers. The stories will die down when Stewart Hatch goes on trial."

Footsteps descended, and the M.E. came toward us. Nettie took my arm and lifted her chin to stare him down. "Later today, Mrs. Rutledge, I will make out the death certificate, naming heart attack as cause of death. You are free to make any arrangements you wish."

"Thank you," Nettie said, glacially.

"Was Mr. Crothers an unusually small man? A 'little person'?"

"Not at the height of his powers," Nettie magnificently said. "Illness robbed Clarence of his physical stature in a manner cruel to behold."

The M.E. dodged around her and left the house. Nettie directed her commanding gaze upon the policemen. "You young men have been a great help to us in our time of sorrow. It is a comfort to me that gentlemen like yourselves have devoted your lives to public service."

A minute later, one of them was on the phone to Mr. Spaulding while the other stood guard at the door.

"Should I stick around for another day or two?" I asked.

"I'm thankful you could spend so much time with us," she said. "And you rescued our pictures! That takes a great weight off my mind, Neddie. Make your travel arrangements, and be sure to keep in touch."

"Take care," Clark said. "There's not but a few of us left, now Mousie's in his grave."

■ **134**

■ The sky had disappeared above Cherry Street. A wet, silvery mist coated my windshield. I sent the wipers back and forth and cleared two transparent semicircles onto a street visible enough for driving.

Back in my room, I charged a seat on a 6:00 P.M. flight from St. Louis to New York, giving me more than enough time to lose my way and find it again. After that, I called the rental agency to say that I would be returning their car to the airport in St. Louis with a damaged rear end. A supervisor with the manners of a prison guard put me on hold while he wrangled with the office in St. Louis, then came back on the line and said, "You'll get away with it this time, Mr. Dunstan. When you drop off the keys, leave the details of the accident, the name, address, and telephone number of the other party and the name of his or her insurance carrier."

"You can get that information from Stewart Hatch," I said. "He got drunk and backed his Mercedes into the rear end of your Taurus."

"The surcharge for nonlocal return will be fifty dollars," he said, and hung up.

I called the airline and upgraded my reservation to first class. According to C. Clayton Creech, I had at least ten million dollars, and what was good enough for Grennie Milton was good enough for me. My companions in first class were going to love my pink jacket, and they give you an extra bag of pretzels up there at the front of the plane.

■ **135**

■ A few ghostlike relics wandered through the fog thickening on Word Street. The neon stripe of HOTE PARIS tinted the cobbles a soft, slippery red. I threw my bags onto the backseat and got behind the wheel. At Chester Street I turned north, thinking that eventually I would see a sign to a bridge across the Mississippi and the highway to St. Louis. Before I reached College Park, the buildings on either side had retreated into vague backdrops, and the headlights of oncoming cars were like cats' eyes. I remembered Mousie's teeth rising into the pillow, and I saw inky flak bursting within the bands of deep red glowing across his abbreviated body. The dirty spiderweb that body had become, the bowling-ball weight of his head in the pillowcase. The empty expanse of the Albertus campus slid past my car on what seemed the wrong side. I kept driving. I had not turned, therefore I was still going north and following the river as it wound toward St. Louis.

Then I remembered that Chester Street became Fairground Road when it crossed into College Park, and Fairground Road did not go past Albertus, it came to an end at the southern boundary of the campus. Somehow, I had managed to circle around and drive south on an unknown street. Albertus had not shifted its geography, I had shifted mine. Fortunately, I still had hours to get to St. Louis. All I had to do was turn around.

Mousie's pillowcase landed softly, although not softly enough, at the bottom of the hole in Joy's neglected garden. I heard it hit the ground, and thought about the words I had spoken over Mousie's grave. They had not been the right words. Mousie deserved better from his murderer. Mousie had been one of the real

Dunstans—Clark had told me that I was turning into a real Dunstan, but I was nothing compared to Mousie. Mousie was up there with Brightness and Screamer. What leaked from the cannon's mouth and the crack in the golden bowl was a being like Mousie. Howard had known it, and the knowledge had poisoned him.

I could not see where I was, and I could not tell where I was going. Looking for a familiar name, I bent over the wheel and peered through the windshield. Ten feet beyond the front of my car, the green banner of a road sign materialized out of the opacity and advanced toward me. A runic scrawl slipped behind me a moment before it would have become decipherable. No matter, I thought: I was still going south when I wanted to go north, so all I had to do was turn right, or west, on the next street, then right, or north, at the one after that.

Two more indecipherable road signs floated past, and I was headed north, moving parallel to the river. In my mind, I could see a map of the Mississippi and the towns in Missouri and Illinois on either side. I was looking for Jonesboro, Murphysboro, and Crystal City. North of Crystal City lay Belleville, only a little way from East St. Louis. The fog would lift; even if it did not, eventually I would drive into clear air. As long as I kept moving, I was making progress.

At ten miles an hour, at five, I followed my headlights through a yielding gray wall. When I could see nothing but the headlights, I stopped, put on the emergency lights, and waited for the boundaries of the road to reform before continuing. If headlights came toward me, as they sometimes did, I pulled over and slowed to a pace that would have let a jogger swing past. An hour crawled by. The fog parted and thinned, and I saw two-dimensional houses set close together on narrow lawns. I had come to Jonesboro, I thought. The fog drew in to erase the houses. Half an hour later, I drove into a gleaming mist widening out over open fields on both sides of the road. It gathered itself into a melting darkness and forced me back down to five miles an hour.

Then I slammed my foot on the brake pedal. The blue plastic of the steering wheel seemed to be rising through my hands as they faded from view. I felt a tingle at the back of my neck and became aware of a presence behind me. I shouted Robert's name and twisted my head to look at the empty backseat. I spoke his name again. Hostility swept toward me like a winter wind.

"Robert, I have to . . ." His invisible presence had left, and I was alone in the car.

"Where are you?" My voice bounced off the fog and died. I held up my hands and saw them restored and solid.

I have to talk to you? I have to know what you want from me?

I remembered the face burning from the end of a lane across Veal Yard. *He wants everything,* I thought.

Beyond the window, a regal figure in a dashiki of gold, ink-black, and bloodred emerged from the swirling fog. I cranked down the window, and chill, damp fog seeped into the car. Walter Bernstein nodded like a king granting a benediction.

"Walter, where is he?" I asked. "Where did he go?"

"Can't no one tell you that, but you're on the right road. As right as you can make it, anyhow." He faded back into the purple fog.

I wrapped my fingers around the door handle, opened a nimbus of hazy light deep enough to enter, and pushed myself off the seat. At the front of the car, the headlights picked out the shadowy pole of a road sign. Robert hovered beside me, behind, I could not tell which.

"Show yourself," I said. "You owe me that much."

Robert thought he owed me nothing. Robert was like Mousie, he had leaked from the crack in the golden bowl, he had trickled from the mouth of the cannon. *Moi aussi.* I went up to the shadowy road sign, stood on tiptoe, peered at the white marks on the green metal, and laughed out loud. I had come back to New Providence Road.

I walked past the sign. Because my life depended upon movement, I kept moving. Quiet footsteps ticked from behind, and I whirled around to see no more than two blurry yellow eyes and the glow spilling from the open door. Profound silence rang in the gray air. "This is where we are, Robert," I said. "Do your best."

A hesitant footfall, then another, sounded from behind me. I did what I had to do and went forward. The ground rose to meet my step, and I felt the release of a crazy sense of joy. *Where we were* was the place we all along had been fighting to reach. Footsteps ticked through the shining fog. I did the one thing my furious double could not and slid thirty-five years down my gullet.

■ On the seventeenth day of October in the year 1958, I was standing at the rear of a densely crowded Albertus University auditorium. Sweatered girls, still innocently "co-eds," and boys in sports jackets filled the pitched rows of seats facing the stage, on which a drummer with thick glasses and close-cropped blond hair, a smiling bassist who could have been Walter Bernstein's cousin, and an intense-looking piano player were hammering their way toward the end of what sounded like "Take the A Train." Hands folded over the body of his alto saxophone, a storklike man with retreating hair, black glasses, and a wide, expressive mouth leaned into the curve of the piano and attended to the sounds coming from his fellow musicians. His mingled detachment and involvement reminded me of Laurie Hatch.

Looking down over the audience, I went toward the top of the wide central aisle. Crew cuts; ponytails; daffodil flips; French twists; sleek, short hair with definitive partings. A few measures before the conclusion of "A Train," I caught sight of my mother's dark, unmistakable head. There she was, the eighteen-year-old Star Dunstan, seated ten or twelve rows back from the stage, one seat in from the aisle. The angle of her neck said that she had heard enough of this concert. I moved across the aisle until I had a good view of her companion. The piano player nailed down a chord, the drummer announced a conclusion. The man sitting next to my mother raised his hands and applauded. His profile looked too much like mine.

The piano player turned to the audience and said, "We'd like to do a ballad . . . called 'These Foolish Things.'" He looked up at the saxophonist and sketched a few bars of the melody. The saxophonist pushed himself off the piano, approached a microphone at the front of the stage, and settled his fingers on the keys. He closed his eyes, already in a trance of concentration. When the introduction came to an end, he fastened his mouth to his horn and repeated the fragment of melody just played as if it were newly minted. Then he floated above the line of the song and blew a liquid phrase that said, *You know the song, but do you know this story?*

Star's head snapped up. Listening without hearing, Edward Rinehart lounged in his seat and concealed his disdain.

At the start of his second chorus, the alto player said, *That was just the beginning.* An ascending arc of melody streamed from the bell of his horn and printed itself upon the air. The melody expanded, and the alto player said, *We are on a journey.* As he settled into his story, it opened into interior stories, and variations led to other, completely unexpected, variations. The alto player climbed to passionate resolutions, let them subside, and ascended further.

Star shifted in her seat, opened her mouth, and leaned forward. I felt tears slide down my cheeks.

It was like hearing the whole world open up in front of me. . . . He kept moving deeper and deeper into that melody until it opened up like a flower and spilled out a hundred other melodies that got richer and richer . . .

That alto player never moved anything but his fingers. He stood with his feet pointed out, his eyes closed, his shoulders in a negligent slouch. In its grip on the reed of his horn, his mouth looked like a flexible sea creature. Note after note, the tremendous story and all of its details soared into the reaches of the auditorium, building on the structure it distilled from its own meaning. The drummer tilted his head and plied his brushes over the crisp drumheads; the smiling bass player set in place the familiar harmonies; the piano player breathed a soft "Yeah, Paul." It seemed effortless, natural, inevitable, like the long unfolding of a landscape seen from the top of a mountain, and it went on and on for what might as well have been a thousand choruses.

In another time, my own, fog swarmed across a road where two sets of footsteps advanced toward whatever was to come. I put my shoulders against the wall and listened for as long as I could—the whole world opened up in front of me.

■ 136

■ What? Ah, you want to know what happened to Robert? I'm sorry, that has already been answered—answered as well as it can be, anyhow. Step after step, through the long transitional passages of airports, down the corridors between the glowing lobbies and welcoming bars of resplendent hotels, along the pavements of every city I inhabit for a week or two in my endless flight, the ticking of Robert's footsteps sounds in my awaiting ear.

But since you have put a question to me, I can ask one in return. Are you sure—really sure—you know who told you this story?

Author's Note

■ The dedicated Lovecraftian will have noted the liberties I have taken with the publication history of "The Dunwich Horror." The story's first appearance between hard covers was in the collection *The Outsider and Others*, edited by August Derleth and Donald Wandrei and published by Arkham House in 1939, some years prior to Mr. X's enthralled discovery at the Fortress Military Academy of the tale within a fictitious book bearing its name. The collection entitled *The Dunwich Horror and Others*, edited by Derleth for Arkham House, was not published until 1963.

S. T. Joshi's definitive biography, *H. P. Lovecraft: A Life,* makes brief mention of "a very strange individual from Buffalo, New York," named William Lumley, who took Lovecraft's mythology of Elder Gods and Great Old Ones, now commonly referred to as "the Cthulhu Mythos," as literal fact and clung to this belief in the face of all denials by the writer and his circle of colleagues and friends. Joshi quotes Lovecraft's ironic summary of Lumley's position from a letter written to Clark Ashton Smith in 1933: "We may *think* we're writing fiction, and may even (absurd thought!) disbelieve what we write, but at bottom we are telling the truth in spite of ourselves—serving unwittingly as mouthpieces of Tsathoggua, Crom, Cthulhu, and other pleasant Outside gentry."

I wish to thank Bradford Morrow, Warren Vaché, Ralph Vicinanza, David Gernert, Dr. Lila Kalinich, Sheldon Jaffrey, Hap Beasely, my editor, Deb Futter, and my wife, Susan Straub, for their suggestions, support, and assistance during the writing of *Mr. X.*

Peter Straub

MR. CLUBB AND MR. CUFF

■ I never intended to go astray, nor did I know what that meant. My journey began in an isolated hamlet notable for the piety of its inhabitants, and when I vowed to escape New Covenant I assumed that the values instilled within me there would forever be my guide. And so, with a depth of paradox I still only begin to comprehend, they have been. My journey, so triumphant, also so excruciating, is both *from* my native village and *of* it. For all its splendor, my life has been that of a child of New Covenant.

When in my limousine I scanned the *Wall Street Journal*, when in the private elevator I ascended to the rosewood-paneled office with harbor views, when in the partners' dining room I ordered squab on a mesclun bed from a prison-rescued waiter known to me alone as Charlie-Charlie, also when I navigated for my clients the complex waters of financial planning, above all when before her seduction by my enemy Graham Leeson I returned homeward to luxuriate in the attentions of my stunning Marguerite, when transported within the embraces of my wife, even then I carried within the frame houses dropped like afterthoughts down the streets of New Covenant, the stiff faces and suspicious eyes, the stony cordialities before and after services in the grim great Temple—the blank storefronts along Harmony Street—tattooed within me was the ugly, enigmatic beauty of my birthplace. Therefore I believe that when I strayed, and stray I did, make no mistake, it was but to come home, for I claim that the two strange gentlemen who beckoned me into error were the night of its night, the dust of its dust. In the period of my life's greatest turmoil—the month of my exposure to Mr. Clubb and Mr. Cuff, "Private Detectives Extraordinaire," as their business card described them—in the midst of the uproar I felt that I saw *the contradictory dimensions of* . . . .

of . . . .

I felt I saw . . . had seen, had at least glimpsed . . . what a wiser man might call . . . try to imagine the sheer difficulty of actually writing these words . . . the Meaning of Tragedy. You smirk, I don't blame you, in your place I'd do the same, but I assure you I saw *something*.

I must sketch in the few details necessary to understand my story. A day's walk from New York state's Canadian border, New Covenant was (and still is, still is) a town of just under a thousand inhabitants united by the puritanical Protestantism of the Church of the New Covenant, whose founders had broken away from the even more puritanical Saints of the Covenant. (The Saints had proscribed sexual congress in the hope of hastening The Second Coming.) The village flourished during the end of the nineteenth century, and settled into its permanent form around 1920.

To wit: Temple Square, where the Temple of the New Covenant and its bell tower, flanked left and right by the Youth Bible Study Center and the Combined Boys and Girls Elementary and Middle School, dominate a modest greensward. Southerly stand the shop fronts of Harmony Street, the bank, also the modest placards indicating the locations of New Covenant's doctor, lawyer, and dentist; south of Harmony Street lie the two streets of frame houses sheltering the town's clerks and artisans, beyond these the farms of the rural faithful, beyond the farmland deep forest. North of Temple Square is Scripture Street, two blocks lined with the residences of the Reverend and his Board of Brethren, the aforementioned doctor, dentist and lawyer, the President and Vice-President of the bank, also the families of some few wealthy converts devoted to Temple affairs. North of Scripture Street are more farms, then the resumption of the great forest in which our village described a sort of clearing.

My father was New Covenant's lawyer, and to Scripture Street was I born. Sunday I spent in the Youth Bible Study Center, weekdays in the Combined Boys and Girls Elementary and Middle School. New Covenant was my world, its people all I knew of the world. Three-fourths of all mankind consisted of gaunt, bony, blond-haired individuals with chiseled features and blazing blue eyes, the men six feet or taller in height, the women some inches shorter—the remaining fourth being the Racketts, Mudges, and Blunts, our farm families, who after generations of intermarriage had coalesced into a tribe of squat, black-haired, gap-toothed, moon-faced males and females seldom taller than five feet, four or five inches. Until I went to college I thought that all people were divided into the races of town and barn, fair and dark, the spotless and the mud-spattered, the reverential and the sly.

Though Racketts, Mudges and Blunts attended our school and worshipped in our Temple, though they were at least as prosperous as we in town save the converts in their mansions, we knew them tainted with an essential inferiority. Rather than intelligent they seemed *crafty*, rather than spiritual, *animal*. Both in classrooms and Temple, they sat together, watchful as dogs compelled for the nonce to be "good," now and again tilting their heads to pass a whispered comment. Despite Sunday baths and Sunday clothes, they bore an uneraseable odor redolent of the barnyard. Their public self-effacement seemed to mask a peasant amusement, and when they separated into their wagons and other vehicles, they could be heard to share a peasant laughter.

I found this mysterious race unsettling, in fact profoundly annoying. At some level they frightened me—I found them compelling. Oppressed from my earliest days by life in New Covenant, I felt an inadmissible fascination for this secretive brood. Despite their inferiority, I wished to know what they knew. Locked deep within their shabbiness and shame I sensed the presence of a freedom I did not understand but found *thrilling*.

Because town never socialized with barn, our contacts were restricted to places of education, worship, and commerce. It would have been as unthinkable for me to take a seat beside Delbert Mudge or Charlie-Charlie Rackett in our fourth-grade classroom as for Delbert or Charlie-Charlie to invite me for an overnight in their farmhouse bedrooms. Did Delbert and Charlie-Charlie actually have bedrooms, where they slept alone in their own beds? I recall mornings when the atmosphere about Delbert and Charlie-Charlie suggested nights spent in close proximity to the pig pen, others when their worn dungarees exuded a freshness redolent of sunshine, wildflowers and raspberries.

During recess an inviolable border separated the townies at the northern end of our play area from the barnies at the southern. Our play, superficially similar, demonstrated our essential difference, for we could not cast off the unconscious stiffness resulting from constant adult measurement of our spiritual worthiness. In contrast, the barnies did not play at playing but actually *played*, plunging back and forth across the grass, chortling over victories, grinning as they muttered what must have been jokes. (We were not adept at jokes.) When school closed at end of day, I tracked the homebound progress of Delbert, Charlie-Charlie and clan with envious eyes and a divided heart.

Why should they have seemed in possession of a liberty I desired? After graduation from Middle School, we townies progressed to Shady Glen's Consolidated High, there to monitor ourselves and our fellows while encountering the temptations of the wider world, in some cases then advancing into colleges and universities. Having concluded their educations with the seventh grade's long division and "Hiawatha" recitations, the barnies one and all returned to their barns. Some few, some very few, of *us*, among whom I had determined early on to be numbered, left for good, thereafter to be celebrated, denounced, or mourned. One of *us*, Caleb Thurlow, violated every standard of caste and morality by marrying Munna Blunt and vanishing into barnie-world. A disgraced, disinherited pariah during my childhood, Thurlow's increasingly pronounced stoop and decreasing teeth terrifyingly mutated him into a blond, wasted barnie-parody on his furtive annual Christmas appearances at Temple. One of *them*, one only, my old classmate Charlie-Charlie Rackett, escaped his ordained destiny in our twentieth year by liberating a plow horse and Webley-Vickers pistol from the family farm to commit serial armed robbery upon Shady Glen's George Washington Inn, Town Square Feed & Grain, and Allsorts Emporium. Every witness to his crimes knew what, if not who, he was, and Charlie-Charlie was apprehended while boarding the Albany train in the next village west. During the course of my own journey from and of New Covenant, I tracked Charlie-Charlie's gloomy progress through the way stations of the penal system until at last I could secure his release at a parole hearing with the offer of a respectable job in the financial planning industry.

I had by then established myself as absolute monarch of three floors in a Wall Street monolith. With my two junior partners, I enjoyed the services of a fleet of paralegals, interns, analysts, investigators, and secretaries. I had chosen these partners carefully, for as well as the usual expertise, skill and dedication, I required other, less conventional qualities.

I had sniffed out intelligent but unimaginative men of some slight moral laziness; capable of cutting corners when they thought no one would notice; controlled drinkers and secret drug-takers: juniors with reason to be grateful for their positions. I wanted no *zealousness*. My employees were to be steadfastly incurious and able enough to handle their clients satisfactorily, at least with my paternal assistance.

My growing prominence had attracted the famous, the established, the notorious. Film stars and athletes, civic leaders, corporate pashas, and heirs to longstanding family fortunes regularly visited our offices, as did a number of conspicuously well-tailored gentlemen who had accumulated their wealth in a more colorful fashion. To these clients I suggested financial stratagems responsive to their labyrinthine needs. I had not schemed for their business. It simply *came to me*, willy-nilly, as our Temple held that salvation came to the elect. One May morning, a cryptic fellow in a pin-striped suit appeared in my office to pose a series of delicate questions. As soon as he opened his mouth, the cryptic fellow summoned irresistibly from memory a dour, squinting member of the Board of Brethren of New Covenant's Temple. I *knew* this man, and instantly I found the tone most acceptable to him. Tone is all to such people. After our interview he directed others of his kind to my office, and by December my business had tripled. Individually and universally these gentlemen pungently reminded me of the village I had long ago escaped, and I cherished my suspicious buccaneers even as I celebrated the distance between my moral life and theirs. While sheltering these self-justifying figures within elaborate trusts, while legitimizing subterranean floods of cash, I immersed myself within a familiar atmosphere of pious denial. Rebuking home, I *was* home.

Life had not yet taught me that revenge inexorably exacts its own revenge.

My researches eventually resulted in the hiring of the two junior partners known privately to me as Gilligan and Captain. The first, a short, trim fellow with a comedian's rubber face and dishevelled hair, brilliant with mutual funds but an ignoramus at estate planning, each morning worked so quietly as to become invisible. To Gilligan I had referred many of our actors and musicians, and those whose schedules permitted them to attend meetings before the lunch hour met their soft-spoken advisor in a dimly lighted office with curtained windows. After lunch, Gilligan tended toward the vibrant, the effusive, the extrovert. Red-faced and sweating, he loosened his tie, turned on a powerful sound system and ushered emaciated musicians with haystack hair into the atmosphere of a backstage party. Morning Gilligan spoke in whispers; Afternoon Gilligan batted our secretaries' shoulders as he bounced office-ward down the corridors. I snapped him up as soon as one of my competitors let him go, and he proved a perfect complement to the Captain. Tall, plump, silver-haired, this gentleman had come to me from a specialist in estates and trusts discomfited by his tendency to become pugnacious when outraged by a client's foul language, improper dress, or other offenses against good taste. Our tycoons and inheritors of family fortunes were in no danger of arousing the Captain's ire, and I myself handled the unshaven film stars' and heavy metallists' estate planning. Neither Gilligan nor the Captain had any contact with the cryptic gentlemen. Our office was an organism balanced in all its parts. Should any mutinous notions occur to my partners, my spy the devoted Charlie-Charlie Rackett, known to them as Charles the Perfect Waiter, every noon silently monitored their every utterance while replenishing Gilligan's wine glass. My marriage of two years seemed blissfully happy, my reputation and bank account flourished alike, and I anticipated perhaps another decade of labor followed by luxurious retirement. I could not have been less prepared for the disaster to come.

Mine, as disasters do, began at home. I admit my contribution to the difficulties. While immersed in the demands of my profession, I had married a beautiful woman twenty years my junior. it was my understanding that Marguerite had knowingly entered into a contract under which she enjoyed the fruits of income and social position while postponing a deeper marital communication until I cashed in and quit the game, at which point she and I could travel at will, occupying grand hotel suites and staterooms while acquiring every adornment which struck her eye. How could an arrangement so harmonious have failed to satisfy her? Even now I feel the old rancor. Marguerite had come into our office as a faded singer who wished to invest the remaining proceeds from a five- or six-year-old "hit," and after an initial consultation Morning Gilligan whispered her down the corridor for my customary lecture on estate tax, trusts, so forth and so on, in her case due to the modesty of the funds in question mere show. (Since during their preliminary discussion she had casually employed the Anglo-Saxon monosyllable for excrement, Gilligan dared not subject her to the Captain.) He escorted her into my chambers, and I glanced up with the customary show of interest. You may imagine a thick bolt of lightning slicing through a double-glazed office window, sizzling across the width of a polished teak desk, and striking me in the heart.

Already I was lost. Thirty minutes later I violated my most sacred edict by inviting a female client to a dinner date. She accepted, damn her. Six months later, Marguerite and I were married, damn us both. I had attained everything for which I had abandoned New Covenant, and for twenty-three months I inhabited the paradise of fools.

I need say only that the usual dreary signals, matters like unexplained absences, mysterious telephone calls abruptly terminated upon my appearance, and visitations of a melancholic, distracted *daemon*, forced me to set one of our investigators on Marguerite's trail, resulting in the discovery that my wife had been two-backed-beasting it with my sole professional equal, the slick, the smooth Graham Leeson, to whom I, swollen with uxorious pride a year after our wedding day, had introduced her during a function at the Waldorf-Astoria Hotel. I know what happened. I don't need a map. Exactly as I had decided to win her at our first meeting, Graham Leeson vowed to steal Marguerite from me the instant he set his handsome blue eyes on her between the fifty-thousand-dollar tables on the Starlight Roof.

My enemy enjoyed a number of natural advantages. Older than she by ten years to my twenty, at six-four three inches taller than I, this reptile had been blessed with a misleadingly winning Irish countenance and a full head of crinkly red-blond hair. (In contrast, my white tonsure accentuated the severity of the all-too Cromwellian townie face.) I assumed her immune to such obvious charms, and I was wrong. I thought Marguerite could not fail to see the meagerness of Leeson's inner life, and I was wrong again. I suppose he exploited the inevitable temporary isolation of any spouse to a man in my position. He must have played upon her grudges, spoken to her secret vanities. Cynically, I am sure, he encouraged the illusion that she was an "artist." He flattered, he very likely wheedled. By every shabby means at his disposal he had overwhelmed her, most crucially by screwing her brains out three times a week in a corporate suite at a Park Avenue hotel.

After I had examined the photographs and other records arrayed before me by the investigator, an attack of nausea brought my dizzied head to the edge of my desk; then rage stiffened my backbone and induced a moment of hysterical blindness. My marriage was dead, my wife a repulsive stranger. Vision returned a second or two later. The checkbook floated from the desk drawer, the Waterman pen glided into position between thumb and forefinger, and while a shadow's efficient hand inscribed a check for ten thousand dollars, a disembodied voice informed the hapless investigator that the only service required of him henceforth would be eternal silence.

For perhaps an hour I sat alone in my office, postponing appointments and refusing telephone calls. In the moments when I had tried to envision my rival, what came to mind was some surly drummer or guitarist from her past, easily intimidated and readily bought off. In such a case, I should have inclined toward mercy. Had Marguerite offered a sufficiently self-abasing apology, I would have slashed her clothing allowance in half, restricted her public appearances to the two or three most crucial charity events of the year and perhaps as many dinners at my side in the restaurants where one is "seen," and insured that the resultant mood of sackcloth and ashes prohibited any reversion to bad behavior by intermittent use of another investigator.

No question of mercy, now. Staring at the photographs of my life's former partner entangled with the man I detested most in the world, I shuddered with a combination of horror, despair, loathing, and—appallingly—an urgent spasm of sexual arousal. I unbuttoned my trousers, groaned in ecstatic torment, and helplessly ejaculated over the images on my desk. When I had recovered, weak-kneed and trembling I wiped away the evidence, fell into my chair, and picked up the telephone to request Charlie-Charlie Rackett's immediate presence in my office.

The cryptic gentlemen, experts in the nuances of retribution, might seem more obvious sources of assistance, but I could not afford obligations in that direction. Nor did I wish to expose my humiliation to clients for whom the issue of respect was all-important. Devoted Charlie-Charlie's years in the jug had given him an extensive acquaintanceship among the dubious and irregular, and I had from time to time commandeered the services of one or another of his fellow yardbirds. My old companion sidled around my door and posted himself before me, all dignity on the outside, all curiosity within.

"I have been dealt a horrendous blow, Charlie-Charlie," I said, "and as soon as possible I wish to see one or two of the best."

Charlie-Charlie glanced at the folders. "You want serious people," he said, replying in the same code. "Right?"

"I must have men who can be serious when seriousness is necessary," I said, replying in the same code.

While my lone surviving link to New Covenant struggled to understand this directive, it came to me that Charlie-Charlie had now become my only true confidant, and I bit down on an upwelling of fury. I realized that I had clamped shut my eyes, and opened them upon an uneasy Charlie-Charlie.

"You're sure," he said.

"Find them," I said, and to restore some semblance of our conventional atmosphere asked, "The boys still okay?"

Telling me that the juniors remained content, he said, "Fat and happy. I'll find what you want, but it'll take a couple of days."

I nodded, and he was gone.

For the remainder of the day I turned in an inadequate impersonation of the executive who usually sat behind my desk and, after putting off the moment as long as reasonably possible, buried the awful files in a bottom drawer and returned to the townhouse I had purchased for my bride-to-be and which, I remembered with an unhappy pang, she had once in an uncharacteristic moment of cuteness called "our townhome."

Since I had been too preoccupied to telephone wife, cook, or butler with the information that I would be late at the office, when I walked into our dining room the table had been laid with our china and silver, flowers arranged in the centerpiece, and in what I took to be a new dress, Marguerite glanced mildly up from her end of the table and murmured a greeting. Scarcely able to meet her eyes, I bent to bestow the usual homecoming kiss with a mixture of feelings more painful than I previously would have imagined myself capable. Some despicable portion of my being responded to her beauty with the old husbandly appreciation even as I went cold with the loathing I could not permit myself to show. I hated Marguerite for her treachery, her beauty for its falsity, myself for my susceptibility to what I knew was treacherous and false. Clumsily, my lips brushed the edge of an azure eye, and it came to me that she may well have been with Leeson while the investigator was displaying the images of her degradation. Through me coursed an involuntary tremor of revulsion with, strange to say, at its center a molten erotic core. Part of my extraordinary pain was the sense that I too had been contaminated: a layer of illusion had been peeled away, revealing monstrous blind groping slugs and maggots.

Having heard voices, Mr. Moncrieff, the butler I had employed upon the abrupt decision of the Duke of Denbigh to cast off worldly ways and enter an order of Anglican monks, came through from the kitchen and awaited orders. His bland, courteous manner suggested as usual that he was making the best of having been shipwrecked on an island populated by illiterate savages. Marguerite said that she had been worried when I had not returned home at the customary time.

"I'm fine," I said. "No, I'm not fine. I feel unwell. Distinctly unwell. Grave difficulties at the office." With that I managed to make my way up the table to my chair, along the way signalling to Mr. Moncrieff that the Lord of the Savages wished him to bring in the pre-dinner martini and then immediately begin serving whatever the cook had prepared. I took my seat at the head of the table, and Mr. Moncrieff removed the floral centerpiece to the sideboard. Marguerite regarded me with the appearance of probing concern. This was false, false, false. Unable to meet her eyes, I raised mine to the row of Canalettos along the wall, then the intricacies of the plaster molding above the paintings, at last to the chandelier depending from the central rosette on the ceiling. More had changed than my relationship with my wife. The molding, the blossoming chandelier, even Canaletto's Venice resounded with a cold, selfish lovelessness.

Marguerite remarked that I seemed agitated.

"No, I am not," I said. The butler placed the ice-cold drink before me, and I snatched up the glass and drained half its contents. "Yes, I am agitated, terribly," I said. "The difficulties at the office are more far-reaching than I intimated." I polished off the martini and tasted only glycerine. "It is a matter of betrayal and treachery made all the more wounding by the closeness of my relationship with the traitor."

I lowered my eyes to measure the effect of this thrust to the vitals on the traitor in question. She was looking back at me with a flawless imitation of wifely concern. For a moment I doubted her unfaithfulness. Then the memory of the photographs in my bottom drawer once again brought crawling into view the slugs and maggots. "I am sickened unto rage," I said, "and my rage demands vengeance. Can you understand this?"

Mr. Moncrieff carried into the dining room the tureens or serving dishes containing whatever it was we were to eat that night, and my wife and I honored the silence which had become conventional during the presentation of our evening meal. When we were alone again, she nodded in affirmation.

I said, "I am grateful, for I value your opinions. I should like you to help me reach a difficult decision."

She thanked me in the simplest of terms.

"Consider this puzzle," I said. "Famously, vengeance is the Lord's, and therefore it is often imagined that vengeance exacted by anyone other is immoral. Yet if vengeance is the Lord's, then a mortal being who seeks it on his own behalf has engaged in a form of worship, even an alternate version of prayer. Many good Christians regularly pray for the establishment of justice, and what lies behind an act of vengeance but a desire for justice? God tells us that eternal torment awaits the wicked. He also demonstrates a pronounced affection for those who prove unwilling to let Him do all the work."

Marguerite expressed the opinion that justice was a fine thing indeed, and that a man such as myself would always labor in its behalf. She fell silent and regarded me with what on any night previous I would have seen as tender concern. Though I had not yet so informed her, she declared, the Benedict Arnold must have been one of my juniors, for no other employee could injure me so greatly. Which was the traitor?

"As yet I do not know," I said. "But once again I must be grateful for your grasp of my concerns. Soon I will put into position the bear-traps which will result in the fiend's exposure. Unfortunately, my dear, this task will demand all of my energy over at least the next several days. Until the task is accomplished, it will be necessary for me to camp out in the ------- Hotel." I named the site of her assignations with Graham Leeson.

A subtle, momentary darkening of the eyes, her first genuine response of the evening, froze my heart as I set the bear-trap into place. "I know, the -------'s vulgarity deepens with every passing week, but Gilligan's apartment is but a few doors north, the Captain's one block south. Once my investigators have installed their electronic devices, I shall be privy to every secret they possess. Might you not enjoy spending several days at Green Chimneys? The servants have the month off, but you might enjoy the solitude there more than you would being alone in town."

Green Chimneys, our country estate on a bluff above the Hudson River, lay two hours away. Marguerite's delight in the house had inspired me to construct on the grounds a fully-equipped recording studio, where she typically spent days on end, trying out new "songs."

Charmingly, she thanked me for my consideration and said that she would enjoy a few days in seclusion at Green Chimneys. After I had exposed the traitor, I was to telephone her with the summons home. Accommodating on the surface, vile beneath, these words brought an anticipatory tinge of pleasure to her face, a delicate heightening of her beauty I would have, very likely *had*, misconstrued on earlier occasions. Any appetite I might have had disappeared before a visitation of nausea, and I announced myself exhausted. Marguerite intensified my discomfort by calling me her poor darling. I staggered to my bedroom, locked the door, threw off my clothes, and dropped into bed to endure a sleepless night. I would never see my wife again.

MAGIC TERROR
by Peter Straub

Published in paperback by Ballantine Books.
Available in bookstores November 2001.

To learn more about
the life and works of

Peter Straub

visit him on the Web at
www.net-site.com/straub/

And don't forget to visit
Ballantine Books
on the Web at
www.randomhouse.com/BB/